Evangeline:

Paradise Stolen

Volume I: 1485 - 1755

Volume I of the Literary Series

Evangeline, The True Story of the Cajuns

M. M. Le Blanc

A Caeruleum Publishing Book

Pre-publication Commemorative Edition Revised, November 2011

*Commemorating the 256th anniversary of the Unlawful British
Deportation from Nova Scotia of the French Acadians,
Ancestors of the Cajuns*

EVANGELINE: *Paradise Stolen*
Pre-publication Commemorative Edition Revised, November 2011.

Edited by Jessica Kaye

Cover design by Jason Kruppa
Photographs of interior maps by Jason Kruppa
Cover Copyright © 2011 Caeruleum Publishing, L.L.C.

Photographs courtesy of Musée acadien de l'Université de Moncton :
"Evangeline" engraving by James Faed, 1863
"La Dispersion des Acadiens" painting by Henri Beau, 1900

Portrait courtesy of Warren A. Perrin and Acadian Museum of Erath:
"Evangeline" painted by Jules Dupré, ca 1840's,
Photograph courtesy Lucius Fontenot, 2005

Novae Hispaniae map (1720), courtesy The Law Library of Louisiana

ISBN#978-0-9836008-3-1
Printed in the United States of America in 2011
10 9 8 7 6 5 4 3 2 1 00

Dedication

Mesdames, messieurs et mes chers amis,

This novel is dedicated to the honor of the author's illustrious ancestors, the late Louisiana Senator Dudley J. Le Blanc, Father of the Cajun Renaissance Movement, his wife Evelyn Hébert Le Blanc and their elder daughter Kay Thérèse, for their inspiration, faith, steadfast support, and oral family histories; and for Couzan Dud's incomparable genealogical and historical research obtained over fifty years in the United States, Canada and France culminating in his non-fiction works on the Deportation, *The True Story of the Acadians*; and for his unwavering efforts to preserve, protect and promote our French and Cajun heritage, language and culture. From their experiences and revelations this literary series, *Evangeline, the True Story of the Cajuns,* was born to share the epic true saga of our French, Acadian and Cajun roots.

Vive la France. Vive l'Acadie. Vive les Cajuns. Merci St. Thérèse.

Remerciements / Acknowledgements

As no man (or woman) is an island, no writer, particularly of historical fiction, is a loner. Thus, I extend sincere thanks to the untold number of librarians, researchers and archives staff in France, Canada and the USA who answered questions, provided research, suggested sources and greatly assisted in my search over a period of years for authentic records and details about French and Acadian life, culture, politics, and history.

Additionally, special acknowledgement is given to Dr. Carl Brasseaux, University of Louisiana at Lafayette; Bernard LeBlanc, Conservateur, Museé acadien de l'Université de Moncton, Canada; Philippe Gustin, Director of the Centre International in Lafayette, Louisiana; Dr. Florent Hardy, Jr., State Archivist and Director of the Louisiana State Archives, the Office of the Secretary of State of Louisiana; Warren Perrin of the Acadian Museum of Erath, Louisiana; Michel Tauriac, Claude Théboul and Martine Esparbet of France-Louisiane and Retrouvailles of Paris; Beth Courtney and everyone at Louisiana Public Broadcasting for their support in co-producing the documentary on Dudley J. Le Blanc, *Cajun Renaissance Man*; and numerous staff at the Louisiana State Supreme Court, the Law Library of Louisiana and the Archives de Paris, France.

A warm "merci beaucoup" is given to those who took time from their (very) busy schedules to wade through and comment on earlier drafts of the story including Yvon Cyr, Marcia Groff, Dr. Florent Hardy, Jr., Jane Jackson, Kay Jarrell, Damien Larere, Sharon Metoyer, Milton Moore, Warren Perrin, Bradley Tate, Larry Thomas, Vicky Yiannoutsos and many others too numerous to mention who assisted in reading, critiquing and assisting in this long-time-in-the-making work.

My personal special thanks go to attorney June Denlinger for her sharp eyes and sharper pen that, at times, seemed mightier than a sword, and whose efforts are greatly appreciated.

Sincere thanks go to the talented and creative graphic designer, Jason Kruppa, for the beautiful cover and for his hours of research to locate the perfect 18th century French fonts, drop caps and historical style for the authenticity that the novel deserves.

Thanks to Lucius Fontenot for his lovely photograph of Evangeline from the collection at the Acadian Museum of Erath the use of which Warren A. Perrin and the Museum kindly allowed.

My deep personal gratitude goes to fervent and loyal Evangeline advocate J.R. Roberts whose long-term encouragement of this project and numerous acts of kindness and support have been much appreciated.

My thanks go out to fellow Cajun activists Warren Perrin, Mary Broussard Perrin and Sam Broussard for their appreciation and support of the author's works and for Warren's important Foreword.

A particular note of gratitude is given to Governor Robert "Bobby" Freeman and Marianne Freeman for their consistent support and resolute encouragement during many (long) years of effort.

My personal recognition is offered for the untiring efforts of the late Louisiana Senate Sergeant-at-Arms, Wilmer J. "Shorty" Baudoin, his loyalty to Senator Couzan Dud Le Blanc and his vast knowledge of family history for the Le Blanc documentary and for this novel.

Also appreciated are the efforts of other Louisiana politicians who encouraged the continuation of Louisiana Senator Dudley Le Blanc's work, particularly Lieutenant-Governor Jay Dardenne, former Senator Nick Gautreaux, former Louisiana Governors Edwin Edwards (who shared his insights in French), Kathleen Blanco and Mike Foster, and the late Secretary of State Fox McKeithen.

Merci mille fois to Xavier Larere, long-time advocate of Ma Belle Evangeline, whose spirited and knowledgeable discussions of French history and culture enriched the story, and who encouraged the incorporation of my original screenplays and television mini-series teleplays into the book, and who is my co-author on the French adaptation of this novel.

A special thank you to my editor, Jessica Kaye, for her long hours, fastidious editing, and lengthy discussions which made the novel want to be (and did become) a better book. For me, a first-time novelist, Jessica was patient in her explanations, generous in her assistance, kind in her critiques and unmatched in her encouragement throughout the process, to which I convey my most heartfelt "merci beaucoup."

To the descendents of Couzan Dud Le Blanc spread throughout the world and those in Cajun Country, including Kay, Jean, Morgan, Roland, Bertha Anne and the late Dudley Jr. and their families, especially Byron Le Blanc, your support over the years has been invaluable. Our mutual heritage is the raison d'être for this book and my literary series on our French, Acadian and Cajun roots, "Evangeline, The True Story of the Cajuns," of which this is the first volume written with warmth, love and pride.

Readers will understand the poetic license taken with certain events, persons and dates for dramatization. Any errors are inadvertent and mine.

Editor's Note

There is magic inside the covers of a good book. It is the type of magic which can transport the reader to the time and place of the story's setting. A magic book teaches. It inspires. It transforms.

Evangeline: Paradise Stolen is such a book.

This very human story, this beautifully written piece of historical fiction, instills in its reader the desire for the wellbeing of the Acadian community of the eighteenth century. It has given me knowledge about events of which, formerly, I knew nothing. I am shocked by them and informed by them and yes, inspired by them because although it appears to be a constant of human nature that some people wish to subjugate others and treat them as a lesser species, the rest of us recoil at those attempts to do so and we burn at the injustice of such acts. That is the story of the Acadians of eighteenth century North America, a gentle people who could not believe in the ill intent of others toward them and who would bear arms solely in defense of themselves or their community, never as a first strike.

But this we know: All people are created equal. We don't know this only from the United States' formative documents. We know it instinctually. One's moral compass, for those fortunate enough to own one, spins freely and of its own accord, to due north –to the imperative to treat each other squarely. It's a close relative of the Golden Rule.

I knew nothing of the ancestry of the Cajun people before delving into this masterful work by M. M. Le Blanc. With the reading of this book, the fictionalized but true story of a brave group of émigrés to North America has enlightened and entertained me.

It accomplished both of these things by interweaving a tale of historical facts with that era's human faces and hearts; it shares stories which we all can recognize as constants of societies. We witness love, hardship, family, and friendship; the panoply of emotions, both noble and otherwise. These same elements make up the fabric of modern life.

You will come away from this book with an appreciation for these brave people who fought against tyranny and, no small thing, gratitude for the good writing which brings the past alive again so that we may be a part of it and benefit from the lessons it offers to us.

Jessica Kaye, October 2011

Foreword

A Cajun's Perspective on the Acadian Deportation

In 2004, Acadians the world over celebrated the 400th anniversary of the genesis of our people and culture in North America. Our Acadian roots are in France, but it was only after 1604 that a people known as Acadians (and later as Cajuns in Louisiana) emerged. In October 2011, the pre-publication date of *Evangeline: Paradise Stolen*, there can be no better time than the 256th anniversary of the Acadian deportation to revisit the role played by Cajuns in the diaspora.

It is said that extraordinary times produce extraordinary people. That was certainly the case with Cajuns. But to say that *Le Grand Dérangement* was an extraordinary time is a gross understatement. It is one of the darkest chapters in North American history in that it represents the first -- and perhaps the only -- example of ethnic cleansing of Europeans in the history of the continent. Beginning in 1755 and ending in 1763, British and New England militia cleared Acadia of Acadians. It is impossible to capture in words the agony, pain, suffering and humiliation of the Acadians during the years of expulsion. Thousands of Acadians died of disease and malnutrition on overcrowded and under rationed British ships. Thousands more were imprisoned in England and Nova Scotia. Yet, despite insurmountable odds, the Acadians fought back with Joseph *Beausoleil* Broussard as the leader of their insurgency.

Centuries later, modernity would call the Acadians tactics guerilla warfare, but they simply called it *la guerre*. The fighters -- farmers, fishermen and trappers -- armed with agricultural implements, homemade knives, swords -- and an occasional rifle -- were no match for the British Empire. Unlike many other Acadians who chose to accept their fate, that of forcible exile by the British, Beausoleil's insurgents, who had learned much about aboriginal warfare tactics from his good friends the Mi'Kmaqs, decided to fight. We do know that the result of those efforts allowed the Acadian culture to continue developing in a new environment, Louisiana's bayou country, thus allowing those Acadians to live in peace and community once again and to maintain their cultural identity. This identity continued to evolve as a vibrant part of the American mosaic.

For two centuries, the collective consciousness of the exiles pined for a grand hero, someone of their own cultural identification with the charismatic stature of a Napoleon. In the beginning they had many heroes and knew them quite personally, but the distances of time and geography, continuous ethnic persecution by humiliation and fragmented isolation had eroded their history. There was also, apparently, a reluctance to remember. Perhaps the past was just too painful, each successive present too tense with difficulty and the only goal for the future one of simple survival. Whatever the cause, in Louisiana, where a large number of the émigrés settled, the paucity of written or oral history or even folksongs pertaining to the aftermath of the deportation was astounding.

In Louisiana, we say *"Lâche pas la patate"* ("Don't drop the potato"). Life may be a hot potato, but Cajuns feel they cannot drop it because it may turn out to be all they have to eat! Cajuns had every opportunity to learn this. They were -- and continue to be in the cultural consciousness -- an example of a man who lost a war, a homeland and much of their extended family to death. Cajuns were literally destroyed by exile in a physical way. They were forced into an environment where a disease (yellow fever) which was nonexistent in his homeland, thereby providing them no natural resistance, periodically sliced through the countryside with the sickle of death. It was a horrid death, too. Victims often vomited black, congealed blood and bled from their eyes. And yet, after all the suffering and numerous defeats, somehow through their progeny Cajuns eventually won. They were descendants of the first Europeans who had left feudalism and oppression behind to forge a newfound freedom and identity in this place called Acadie. That identity, inherited from ancestors, represented the years of struggle that they had experienced in order to give their progeny the opportunity to live in a land free of servitude to tyrannical governments where they could live in peace and practice their own religion.

Although we know these Acadians were extremely anti-British and had contentious, militant characters, one must conclude by the sheer number of Acadian descendants in Louisiana today that their life's ultimate struggle did, in the end, merit them the distinction of being the champions of the Acadian culture. They set out to accomplish one thing and ended up accomplishing something far more positive. From our vantage point in the twenty-first century, what did these Acadians actually accomplish? At what cost? In the beginning, it appears that revenge was the motivation for leading the resistance against the British. Revenge may, at times, be a natural human response to certain situations, but it is not a positive motivation. Because of their tenacity, many of their decisions resulted in the tragic loss of the lives of family members and fellow insurgents. Toward the end of those military efforts against the British, when they must have finally realized the fruitlessness of continuing the resistance -- after even France gave up the fight -- only then did they set about uniting Acadian families and preparing to depart from the beloved homeland to what they hoped would be a better life in a New Acadia.

According to Louisiana historian Dr. Shane K. Bernard in his book *The Cajuns: Americanization of a People*, the Cajun people have evolved dramatically. The Cajuns of the early twentieth century differed relatively little from their Acadian ancestors. Like the exiles, Cajuns before the mid-twentieth century worked as subsistence farmers; if not farmers, they held other folk occupations, such as trapping, fishing, moss-picking, logging and boat-building.

Around 1940, however, the Cajuns' world began to change with increasing rapidity: the engine of change was World War II. Unlike previous historical events, this global conflict and its aftermath served as major Americanizing agents in south Louisiana, resulting, for instance, in the near demise of Cajun French by the end of the century: in 1990 only about 30 percent of Cajuns spoke the dialect as their first language, and most of these were middle-aged or elderly.

The unifying thread of recent Cajun history is Americanization -- the process of becoming like the Anglo-American establishment that has traditionally dominated the nation's mainstream culture. Americanization meant embracing the work ethic, materialism and patriotism of Anglo-America, all of which were foreign to the majority of Cajuns before World War II. It also meant speaking English, despite the fact that the Cajuns and their forebears had spoken French as their primary language since coming to America three centuries earlier. Americanization thus ranks as one of the most important events in the entire Cajun experience, along with the expulsion of their ancestors from Nova Scotia, and south Louisiana's devastation during the Civil War. These events resulted in fundamental changes forever altering the nature of the ethnic group.

Beginning in the 1960s, however, the Cajuns, swept up in the national trend of ethnic pride and empowerment, mobilized to save their culture. The rise of a grassroots Cajun pride movement signaled the Cajuns' efforts to reclaim their heritage through a variety of measures: from protecting the French language in the state constitution of 1974, to demanding in the Petition of 1990 that the British Crown acknowledge its mistreatment of the Acadians during the deportation.

The Petition alleged that the Acadian expulsion had not only been illegal according to international law of the period, but the expulsion order, an overt act of "ethnic cleansing," had never been repealed. On September 14, 2004, on the occasion of the opening of the new session of the Canadian

Court of Appeal in Fredericton, New Brunswick, Justice Michel Bastarache of the Canadian Supreme Court stated: "Then came the deportation order which itself was *illegal* because it was contrary to British public law and passed without the vote of the assembly."

The event which primarily inspired the Petition was passage of the Civil Liberties Act of 1988, which apologized for America's internment of about 120,000 U.S. citizens and resident aliens of Japanese ancestry during World War II. The Petition was successfully resolved on December 9, 2003, with Queen Elizabeth II's Royal Proclamation. We look upon this act approvingly as a form of redemption. Nevertheless, after the passage of 256 years, the legacy of the Acadian deportation continues to define the Cajun people.

Warren A. Perrin

Warren A. Perrin has a Juris Doctorate degree from Louisiana State University School of Law, and is an attorney with the firm of Perrin, Landry, deLaunay, Dartez & Ouellet, President of CODOFIL (the Council for the Development of French in Louisiana), an Adjunct Professor at the University of Louisiana at Lafayette and author of Acadian Redemption: From Beausoleil Broussard to the Queen's Royal Proclamation. *He was a member of the board of directors of the Congrès Mondial Acadien - Louisiane 1999, President of the Lt. Governor's Task Force of FrancoFête '99, and the founder of the Acadian Museum of Erath, Louisiana.*

Prologue
1485 - 1528

"Et in Arcadia Ego."
- *Virgil*

I

1524, *The New World*: Discovery

artographers of the future might change the name of this place, mused the Admiral quietly. But he hoped they would not. For Giovanni da Verrazzano, there could be but one name for this land; one name that the Admiral instantly recalled because of his Italian education and passion for literature and poetry. Adjusting the plume of his great hat, he had definitively decided the name for the new land.

The year was 1524. The place, the Atlantic Ocean off the coast of a land mass far west of his adopted French home. For Giovanni da Verrazzano, his loyalties were given to France though his family origins were in Italy. Still, he always considered the sea to be his only home. It was here that he breathed most easily, though he did enjoy the many comforts generously given to him by King Francis the First.

The pox on that Spaniard imposter Cristóbal Colón thought Giovanni. He was still known in Italy twenty years after his death by his Latin name, Christophorus Columbus, not the Castilian name Helizabeth gave him. Despite outfitting his caravels and a large Nao over the years and making four major voyages to the New World from the Canary Islands, Columbus always managed to slip through Giovanni's net of French brigantines plundering Spanish galleons in those very waters.

Verrazano mused with discontent. Other than returning with native islander slaves, what did Columbus discover? And why was he still granted a hero's welcome after all of Europe learned of the vicious atrocities he had committed, decimating the indigenous populations on his last voyages? Giovanni ruminated that the man got away with everything, including murdering innocents.

Verrazzano later lamented that his birth came three decades too late. The attention garnered by the Columbus voyages had overshadowed Verrazzano's discovery of the New World. Because he found terra firma, not a handful of uninhabitable islands like Columbus, Giovanni always felt cheated of his deserved acclaim. Had he been born earlier, *his* voyage would be the one written about in historical chronicles. But now, on deck of his ship, Giovanni da Verrazzano was exactly where he wanted to be.

He raised his spyglass over the beautiful ocean before him. Jehan Hébert, a mere boy of twelve, stood quietly at attention behind the Admiral. Despite his youth, the boy had been hired as first aide to Giovanni for the voyage.

Jehan was the second son of the French King's Maritime Master Builder François Hébert. His elder brother Charles was the future heir to the family holdings which their father continued to increase. That left Jehan at a crossroads, with a choice of only two careers -- the priesthood or the sea. Jehan was far too restless to be locked up in a country monastery. He longed to see the world. So while his mother cried over the baby boy she would soon lose, François purchased a commission for his son in France's maritime service.

Just at the time Jehan reported for duty with a hundred other young nobles whose families had enough money to send them off as naval officers, the Admiral happened into navy headquarters. Other new young officers remained seated as Giovanni entered, but Jehan immediately saluted, followed by a sweeping bow. Apparently he had impressed the Admiral, Jehan thought, because only days later he received orders to report to the Admiral as his personal aide. Little did Jehan realize that Verrazzano had planned to take him on all along because of the Admiral's esteem for Jehan's father. François Hébert had built many of the seagoing vessels that Giovanni commanded including the one for the upcoming expedition.

Verrazzano hoped that Jehan possessed the diligence and intelligence of his father and would not be a disappointment. His last aide had run off with the first silly girl who had smiled at him in port after their last voyage. And Jehan never imagined he would work for one of France's greatest Admirals, and one of Spain's worst enemies: a mercenary pirate who sank untold Spanish galleons and garnered a great fortune.

As the feathers of his headdress blew over the spyglass and blocked his view, Verrazzano looked questioningly at Jehan. What was the boy thinking? But instead of a forgetful young man, he saw a reflection of himself. Jehan's arms were outstretched, his eyes closed, as he deeply breathed in the salt air. Like Verrazzano, Jehan felt at home on the sea.

"Jehan?" Verrazzano woke the boy from his reverie.

Jumping to attention, Jehan at once held back the feathers as the Admiral lifted his spyglass to admire the view once again. The land ahead vaguely appearing through the mists was then known as Terranova, the New World.

Admiral Giovanni da Verrazzano took a long slow breath. Then he turned to make the announcement to his crew. They would soon learn of his discovery of a new land and its name.

II

1485, Val di Greve, Italy: Waterbaby

iovanni da Verrazzano always sensed that the manner of his birthing was in some unique way an accident. Fortuitous, but accidental nonetheless.

When Giovanni was six, his tutor verified his intuition was correct and that his mother's physician had become quite popular ever since the birth.

Giovanni's delivery was flawlessly performed in 1485 by a Florentine midwife and overseen by Dottore Moroni, who informed everyone within earshot that he was official physician to Lorenzo de' Medici, the de facto ruler of the Florentine Republic. The doctor would always add, "But at Court we call him Lorenzo Il Magnifico." Being appointed to such a prestigious position by the sovereign during the height of the Italian Renaissance gave great stature to the little doctor from Siena.

On the day of Verrazzano's birth, crowning occurred after eight hours of painful labor by his mother, Fiammetta Capelli da Verrazzano. The doctor had ordered large bowls of warm seawater to be ready at all times during the birth. He wanted the midwife Antonia to rinse her hands in one bowl and have one ready for the infant. As a precaution Moroni would wash his hands too, although he did not participate in such "women's work" unless the birth was problematic requiring his skill or his tools.

The da Verrazzano family had been wealthy bankers since the Middle Ages, which position was augmented by their friendship with the powerful de' Medici ruling dynasty. They could afford such luxuries as barrels of water from the Mediterranean and a houseful of servants to keep the water warmed.

The doctor believed such water had superlative powers of cleanliness, which was next to godliness in his mind. And since money was no object,

Moroni's request was easily granted without question. If the doctor had requested twelve dancing girls to be present at the birth, Signor Piero Andrea di Bernardo da Verrazzano would have agreed without hesitation.

The pacing husband was oblivious to the actual content of the requests. He was too busy lighting candles and praying for a son to join him at his bank and later, much later he hoped, to inherit the family's vast holdings.

An old bull still active at his age, Piero could still show his wife a thing or two. But how many more times could he keep going like the Italian stallion he once was? He was running out of time and needed this baby to be male. So all the doctor had to do was open his mouth to make a request and Giovanni's father readily agreed, saying, "Yes, yes, anything; just deliver a son."

While the sea water was being brought, the Signora readied herself to push the infant into the cold world outside the safe womb. By her labor pains she felt it was past time for the child to make an entrance. She prayed with all her heart she would bear a son.

At that moment, Fiammetta's reverie was interrupted when the young servant girl entered the room and tripped ever so slightly while carrying the heavy bowl of water over to Antonia. She missed the bedside table and instead dropped it on the bed between the Signora's sprawling legs just as the exhausted woman made her final push. The midwife cried out, "Alleluia!"

Before anyone was aware of it, Giovanni's head had popped out and he slipped readily -- some would say eagerly -- out of the womb and into the warm water, frolicking like a tadpole in a pond. In his watery crib heavily scented with sea salt, he knew he was home. He gurgled with delight until the midwife lifted him out of the water. At that point he screamed so loudly, Moroni motioned to place the infant back in the bowl.

Fiammetta would swear for years that Giovanni cooed at her like a little dove while swimming around in the fresh seawater. She called him her waterbaby from then on.

The young maid dried Moroni's hands, after which he scribbled notes about the birth. He noted in his journal to use warm seawater for future births. Quiet babies, very efficient. When the doctor finished writing, Antonia pulled Giovanni from the water, wrapped him in fine linens and handed him to Dottore Moroni.

Signor Verrazzano entered the room smoking his huge cigar, the mark of success and pride. "Let me see my son," he said and beamed, taking the child from Moroni. He walked over to Fiammetta, kissed her chastely on her forehead and said, "Signora, you have done well. He is perfect. We shall call him Giovanni."

Fiammetta nodded weakly and smiled as her husband beamed with pride at their newborn son, followed in subsequent years by other siblings, including additional sons, much to Pietro's delight.

When Giovanni da Verrazzano became famous, wealthy Italian mothers would all demand that their babies be birthed in a bowl of seawater, hoping for famous sons. And after Giovanni's death in 1528, pregnant Italians started a tradition by laying coins or flowers, and sprinkling sea water, on Giovanni's tomb while praying for a male child.

The momentous event of Giovanni's birth occurred in the family mansion in Val di Greve, a wealthy mass of villas and castles south of Florence in the heart of the region to be called Tuscany. The estate had been built on the foundations of a Roman building that had itself been constructed on the ruins of an earlier structure. Giovanni's father used to proudly proclaim that Castella Verrazzano's origins dated back to the Etruscan period of 500 B.C.

At the beginning, Verrazzano could not have known the meaning of any of it. He only remembered smelling the ocean and floating in a watery cocoon at the moment of birth. The feeling of security made him completely independent from his first breath.

As he grew older Verrazzano felt embarrassed by his family's wealth except for the seafaring commissions it could buy him. He only knew the family's prosperous vineyards paid for seaworthy vessels, allowing him to remain longer at sea. In his opinion, that was the only good use of money.

Giovanni's only love was the sea and he was determined to live life as an adventure; one that would bring him meaning and purpose, one that smelled like the sea. And he knew he could only inhale the intoxicating scent of the salt air for the rest of his life by leaving Castella Verrazzano once and for all.

He was ready to travel the world, to be lured from his privileged life to the savage Normandy coast of Dieppe in northern France. It was there that Giovanni was to commence his long career at sea, first as a navigator, then a corsair, and finally Admiral.

But it would take Verrazzano thirty-eight years to meet his destiny, in France.

III

1523, *Palace of Fontainebleau, France:* Corsair

 iovanni da Verrazzano's exploits as a mercenary were well-known among French sailors. They called him the "Italian Pirate" though the more chivalrous term "corsair" was applied by the noblemen in Giovanni's adopted homeland.

Sailors fought to be chosen for Verrazzano's voyages hoping they, too, would reap the rewards of conquered Spanish galleons laden with gold coins that would be divided among every last member of the crew.

Giovanni had a nose for adventure. The sea was his ever-expanding cradle. He yearned to know every part of it, whether round or flat, and once learned, was never forgotten.

All of this explains why no one was surprised when King Francis I commanded the Italian sailor of the Castella da Verrazzano to a private audience at Fontainebleau Palace in 1523. The Court, however, was shocked to learn the King had granted an Admiralty commission to Giovanni plucking him directly from the ranks of the French corsairs.

This decision was a bold precedent. French naval officers had always gone through years of rigorous training, education, and testing on the high seas before reaching the highest rank. But Francis I made choices based on instinct, together with information from his spies in Italy and Spain.

One coded message from Valladolid said Queen Isabella had her eye on Verrazzano for the Spanish Armada and was considering an offering of wealth beyond a corsair's dream. The news from Tuscany was of marriage discussions between Verrazzano's wealthy banker brother Bernardo and a beautiful cousin of King Ferdinand in the Spanish Court.

The French monarch could not let Spain, much less a woman, best France in the race to rule the world. Francis choked on his anger every time he thought of the pact between Spain and Portugal which claimed to divide the rest of the world outside Europe between their two countries. How dare they, how dare *she* exclude his powerful kingdom?

Francis was determined to buy Verrazzano first, no matter the price. Verrazzano would discover new lands for France, which would make Spain drool with envy, thought Francis. No amount of gold was too great for

Francis' particular pleasure, so he planned to open the French coffers to Verrazzano.

But unbeknownst to the King, in recent times "Helizabeth," as the Queen was called by those who feared her, including many nobles in her own Court, had made Verrazzano's plunder of her galleons more difficult. She was cunning, sending decoy vessels loaded with heavy cargo of painted lead and bricks that caused them to sail slower and to give the appearance of gold on board. As soon as Verrazzano took the bait and began the chase, the galleon carrying actual Spanish gold departed a port too far away to be captured.

Verrazzano had been unable to sink any Spanish vessels since the galleon *El Oro* for months and his income had dropped dramatically. He welcomed the King's command to meet at Fontainebleau where Francis came face-to-face with the man who had instilled such a fury in his arch-enemy Isabella. The King's command that his new Admiral explore different parts of the New World and claim them for France seemed completely plausible to Giovanni. He had been finding new routes to apprehend the treasure of Ferdinand and Isabella for years.

Giovanni humbly accepted the King's appointment as an Admiral and Royal Explorer of the High Seas for the Kingdom of France. Verrazzano's mission was to find an all-water route to the Pacific Ocean through the Americas discovered by that upstart Columbus. Verrazzano had sought a new route to China for France although he looked no further once he reached the New World.

But when a Templar map was found depicting the same territories where Verrazzano voyaged, others said Giovanni's true mission had not been made public -- to locate and destroy a lost colony of Templars who had sailed from Malta across the ocean. The rumors persisted for years that the Admiral had done so and returned to France with the treasure buried by the Templars in the New World.

But whatever the mission, secret or publicly announced, Verrazzano was certain to have accomplished it for his King.

Thus began French exploration of the New World.

IV

1503, *Palace of Valladolid, Castille, Spain:* Helizabeth

 he was buried in 1504, beneath a stone chiseled with the Latin version of her name for the good Catholic she was. At her birth in 1451 in Madrigal de la Altas Torres, Spain, she was christened Ysabel. Thereafter she was known by an array of other names, including Elizabeth, Isabel and Isabella Queen of Castile and León. But in the end "Helizabeth" was chosen for her final resting place.

As was the custom of European royal families in the fifteenth century Princess Isabella was engaged at age three to the son of another royal family. The one chosen was Prince Ferdinand II, the son of John II of Aragon and of the same house as Isabella, that of Trastámara. The marriage would unite their kingdom with Castile and León, ruled by her father, King John.

When the King died in 1454, Isabella's older half-brother Henry IV ascended to the throne. Isabella and her mother and her other son were provided for in the King's will but Henry IV refused to honor it. Times became very difficult for Isabella as Henry provided little money. Their mother began to lose her wits, a trait common to the Spanish monarchy and European royal houses that married this direct line.

During this period Isabella's spirituality deepened and she befriended Beatrix de Silva, who would later become a Roman Catholic saint. Isabella aided Beatrix in founding the order of the Conceptionist nuns and devoted herself to the Catholic faith.

Eventually Henry, at the thought of losing such an asset as Isabella to the Church, proved that monarchs are fickle. He saw Isabella's marriage into a powerful family as a way to create an advantageous political alliance. He reasoned that if a more valuable potential union surfaced it was as simple matter to find an impediment to annul the prior marriage contract. In Isabella's case, a papal dispensation was required due to the co-sanguinity of the couple, their grandfathers being brothers.

Relying on the unresolved defect, Henry IV quickly voided the agreement for Isabella's hand with Prince Ferdinand II. Henry then set about negotiating at least four other politically expedient marriage contracts for his half-sister. However, none ever came to fruition.

When he moved Isabella into his Palace at Segovia, Henry could not have suspected Isabella would become a quick study of politics and eventually one of the world's most powerful sovereigns. There Isabella learned political strategy and intrigue.

Her first lesson was when Henry's wife Joan gave birth to a daughter, Joana. At Court, Isabella discovered that the girl, her niece, was not the child of Henry but of one of Joan's many lovers, Beltran. Spanish commoners and some members of Court nicknamed the child "Beltrana" stigmatizing her as her the daughter of mother's lover. Isabella locked that knowledge in her heart until it was time to further her own ambitions.

During Henry's reign, the next in line to the throne, Isabella's younger brother Alfonso, died. Many suspected poisoning by Alfonso's opponents to eliminate the male heir to the throne. After that, the noblemen who had followed and controlled Alfonso tried to manipulate Isabella into accepting the crown. The young woman realized such an act would have meant sanctioning the death of the King. Instead, she made her own decision and, rather than attempt a coup, she took the hereditary title Princess of Asturias.

To Alfonso's supporters she appeared content to wait her turn but she had secretly negotiated an agreement with Henry acknowledging her as the next legitimate heir to the throne of Castile. This placed Isabella firmly ahead of Beltrana in the line of succession. Henry did not find the decision to put his sister ahead of his wife's lover's child on the throne a difficult one. His reasoning resulted in keeping his head and the crown until his death.

Isabella showed great political cunning as she created her own destiny. Unbeknownst to the King, she met with John II of Aragon and renegotiated the original marriage contract with his son, Ferdinand. Obtaining the requisite dispensation from Pope Pius II, Isabella and Ferdinand wed in secret in 1469 in Valladolid, Castile. The process they began of unifying their kingdoms would later be finished by their grandson Charles V, the Holy Roman Emperor.

When King Henry learned of Isabella's marriage he asked the Pope to annul it. Henry knew the marriage would not benefit him as he had dishonored John II by cancelling the original agreement when Henry became King. But Pius II died and the new Pope Sixtus issued his own papal bull, granting a second dispensation to the couple. This time Henry knew he was powerless; he fought the marriage no longer. And again Isabella had accomplished her goal alone, quietly and secretly.

Despite her ability to plan for the future, not even Isabella could have foreseen how her reign would be considered one of the most powerful in Europe, then and through the centuries. She could not have foretold that she and her husband would transform their kingdoms into a dominant world power. She could not have known Spain would extend its holdings into the New World, even gaining through skillful treaty negotiation a colony that would be named for a French king, Louisiana.

Helizabeth's route towards territorial expansion began with a proposal from a brash sailor named Cristóbal Colón. Hailing from Genoa, Italy, he proposed the earth was not flat and that its circumference was much smaller than scholars predicted, taking only a matter of weeks to sail to the Indies. Although Isabella believed the earth was round, as did many others dating back to the days of Ancient Greece, the only idea she could accept was that such a voyage would take years.

The Council of advisors for Queen Isabella and King Ferdinand studied the proposal for months. They learned the King of Portugal rejected it, and they did as well. But Colón persisted and repeated his proposal four times until finally Isabella agreed to fund his voyage to the New World in 1492.

Spain's new age of colonization began upon his return as a hero with island slaves and maps of new lands discovered for Spain. The ugly rumors of his vicious native killings were quickly hushed. Thereafter, in 1494 the Spanish sovereigns divided the world outside Europe with their long-time ally, the Portuguese King.

But not even new colonies could calm Queen Isabella's anger when French pirates and privateers started looting Spain's gold and sinking their galleons. The drain on the Spanish treasury was a heavy burden that Isabella was determined to stop.

One of the most frequent threats to Spain was an Italian mercenary working off the coast of France named Giovanni da Verrazzano. Isabella and Ferdinand called a secret meeting at their Palace in Valladolid with a cadre of advisors and admirals to resolve the problem. Isabella wanted the situation handled peacefully but she was prepared for any outcome.

Ferdinand asked, "What can be done about those French pirates plundering our Armada?"

Isabella answered without hesitation, "It is not the French who are the problem but their most successful corsair. An Italian named Verrazzano."

The Admiral of the Spanish Armada nodded. "True, he is fearless and stops at nothing. He has looted every one of our vessels he finds."

The wizened Minister of War added, "Not even our cannons have deterred him."

Isabella agreed. "He is the one to take care of."

Ferdinand said, "Are you suggesting we hunt him in his own French waters? King Louis has gone to war for less."

Isabella put her hand on her husband's arm. "Shall we hear the strategies proposed by our well-paid council?"

Ferdinand understood instantly that she already knew what she was going to do. But she wanted to see their Ministers dance like puppets while dreaming of a reward for the chosen proposal, similar to the one given to Columbus. Each Court advisor was thinking to himself that the Queen would pay much more to a high-ranking Minister for protecting the Armada and the Treasury.

The Minister of State cast his eyes to the ground and said, "Majesties, this complicated situation requires much research, but...."

Isabella cut him off with a wave of her hand and looked at the Minister of International Affairs, their chief espionage expert.

The spy said, "Your Majesties, he must be taken at night. My spies have found his favorite mistress and we know how to enter her bedroom."

The Queen nodded, and turned to the Minister of War who bowed and said slowly, "He has many siblings, though only one is needed for a royal marriage, thus binding his loyalty and kinship to Your Majesties."

The Admiral of the Royal Armada waited until Isabella turned to him, then he said, "We shall set a trap with one of our largest but oldest vessels in the fleet, and cut holes in the hull. When he and his men go below and find the hold empty, the ship will sink with them in it."

Isabella and Ferdinand waited patiently as each of the myriad of advisors and ministers with long names gave solutions, some long-winded, some utterly impossible and some outright murder that could thrust Spain into a war with France immediately.

When they had all spoken, each leaned forward on the table, anxiously awaiting which solution Her Majesty would select. They imagined the riches they would get for simply taking care of a common criminal, something that was done daily in Spain.

Ferdinand and his wife looked at each other. His eyes told her he knew she had the matter taken care of. He chuckled under his breath. His father knew what he was doing when he matched him with this one. She was as shrewd as she was beautiful...and a wildcat in their private rooms. He followed her lead.

The Councilors, confused, all stood hastily, some dropping their hats and other letting papers flutter to the tile floor.

The Queen looked at them, not with anger or pride but pity. This is where so much of their money had gone, she thought. And she and her husband still had to devise all of their strategies and plans. They were useless government functionaries and were just as much a drain on the Treasury as Verrazzano. Isabella would have liked to have told them so but out of respect for Ferdinand she held her tongue. Many of the Ministers were his relatives who needed their do-nothing jobs.

She began to walk away, then turned slightly and said, "No one mentioned the most obvious solution. " She looked pointedly at the Minister of International Affairs and whispered, "And without bloodshed." Then Isabella spoke to all the Ministers. "This pirate works for a living, does he not? So pay him more than his share of the plunder to not risk his life."

She walked off, but Ferdinand remained to watch the faces of their esteemed Council of advisors. One by one, each Minister fell back into his seat as his mouth dropped. It was true. They had never thought of bribing him with more money to forego his dangerous line of work. Who would not want more money for less work and no risk?

Ferdinand walked away, immensely proud of his wife. My queen, he thought to himself, is smarter than a dozen educated men.

The Council later called it "The Italian Affair" to disguise the real mission. The Minister of the Treasury was called upon to work with the Minister of International Affairs. Then the Minister of State and the Admiral insisted it was imperative that they participate. Their decisions by committee caused endless delays without results, and Queen Isabella died the following year.

Without knowing wealth without risk was within his grasp, Verrazzano continued to plunder Spanish galleons until King Louis honored Verrazzano with an Admiralty commission.

And after Helizabeth's death the Italian Affair was never mentioned again.

V

1524, *Aboard "Le Nouveau Monde"*: Acadia

o one but Verrazzano knew his true intention once he reached land. He furrowed his brow, remembering the King's last command. "Burn this paper once you commit it to memory. This shall be between you and me only. Do not trust any minister or aide."

Verrazzano, on bended knee before his King had vowed, "I shall not fail you, Your Majesty. All that you command shall be done for the glory of your kingdom."

Of course Giovanni did as he promised, feeding the fire in the hearth with the parchment in his elegant quarters in the Palais de Fontainebleau. Then he left for the Port of Le Havre, where he had spent much of the King's gold on the most modern sailing ship in all of Europe. Giovanni christened her *Le Nouveau Monde*...The New World.

Giovanni returned his thoughts to the present and lifted his spyglass once more. This time he saw wondrous trees, sandy beaches and the entrancing scene before him. The sheer beauty of it all overwhelmed him and his sharp intake of breath nearly caused him to drop the spyglass. Fortunately Jehan was at his hand and managed to right the instrument for the Admiral.

The Admiral's silent admiration was interrupted as the watch in the crow's nest far above him cried, "Land ho!"

Verrazzano was no longer alone in his discovery. His crew shouted with jubilation at the sight of France's new territory.

As the ship edged closer to shore, Verrazzano peered at the coastline, undaunted by waves continually dashing against a rock-lined beach of fine sand. Beyond, row upon row of magnificent trees stood proud against the winds and rains, swaying in whispered chorus, "We have battled the elements and won our rightful place here amongst all things honest and true."

Verrazzano was mesmerized. Jehan too was speechless at the beautiful scene. Peering studiously towards the coast, Verrazzano murmured nearly inaudibly. "The most beautiful trees in the world."

Jehan squinted in the same direction. He saw nothing, but tentatively asked, "Land in sight, sir? Shall I give the order?"

The Admiral slowly handed the eyeglass to Jehan. "Arcadia, Jehan. That was what he called it." Verrazzano quietly mused. "It shall be His Majesty's refuge. Simply paradise."

The young aide scratched his wigged head in bewilderment. Partly to interrupt his aide's scratching, unbecoming to anyone in the French Maritime Service, Verrazzano turned to Jehan. "Surely you have read works by the Italian poet Jacopo Sannazaro. His poetry tells of an idyllic land in ancient Greece called Arcadia."

The young Jehan shook his head in shame. He should have studied his tutor's assignments more diligently. But then, who could have imagined literature would be needed at sea?

Turning back to the sea, Verrazzano whispered to himself. "The grace of the trees and greenery caused men to fall to their knees. They wept in gratitude to be in the presence of such beauty."

Had anyone asked him the source of his passion, Giovanni would have scoffed and replied it was merely a pastime. But he knew better, gazing on the mesmerizing scene before him, which brought him back to his days at the new Platonic Academy founded in 1493 by Cosimo de' Medici. Being an avaricious reader he sought out anything in print -- flyers, papers, manuscripts and the harder to come by books. He was thankful his parents provided him with an outstanding, albeit expensive, education.

Giovanni participated little in the Academy's literary and philosophical discussions, preferring the written word to the spoken one. Most published works were Greek or Latin, but one day he found, tucked away in the Academy's library, an Italian book by a relatively unknown poet, Jacopo Sannazaro, entitled *Arcadia*. The poem had been published in 1502 by the Aldine Press, a well-respected publishing house in Venice. But the publisher, Aldus Manutius, was not wealthy enough to print hundreds or even dozens of books. So *Arcadia* was only printed in small quantities. However, once the poem became known, over sixty editions were eventually published and sold to the waiting lines of noblemen and their wives.

After reading the poem in the Academy library, Giovanni was determined to own a copy of the book for himself. He sought out the publisher but Manutius refused to print a single copy. Gliding through the open canals, Giovanni scoured the book fairs and stalls of Venice. One day in the middle of winter, he came upon a bookseller with the very book he sought. The bookseller wanted far more than Giovanni had in his purse and the vendor would not wait for more funds to arrive, even for the son of a banker. A quick negotiation resulted in a mutual bargain.   Verrazzano walking away shivering but happy, without his best cloak but with the cherished book. The bookseller never looked more elegant than in Giovanni's cashmere wrap.

Verrazzano began reading in the morning and did not stop until the sun was setting. As the other academicians entered the room they found Giovanni sobbing uncontrollably for the lost Greek paradise, a land of wondrous trees and unimaginable tranquil beauty that made him weep to think about it. The mere thought of the idyllic place brought tears to his eyes again.

Jehan stared at the silently weeping Admiral, praying his ignorance would not incur Verrazzano's wrath or thwart Jehan's destiny. The Admiral remembered himself and, clearing his eyes, he slowly mused. "I have modified the name to fit our modern times as we head towards the seventeenth century."

Holding the spyglass above his head, Verrazzano shouted. "Praise God. Let everyone know we have discovered a new land for our good King Francis, which is hereby named Acadia."

Jehan jubilantly cried out to sailors on deck below. "Land ho! A mystical land of beautiful trees. Admiral Verrazzano has discovered Acadia." All hands moved up on deck. Bedlam and joy ensued as crew members cheered and danced jigs.

When the full landing party arrived on shore, the Admiral was the first to step on solid ground. He led the men to the edge of the beautiful tree grove where they planted a flag and Giovanni declared Acadia the New World territory for France.

Upon returning to the ship, Giovanni wrote a report to King Francis in his journal detailing the marvels that delighted his senses in the new land.

"Acadia's seashore is completely covered with fine sand at least fifteen feet deep, which rises in the form of small hills about fifty paces wide. After climbing farther, we found other streams and inlets from the sea which come in by several mouths, and follow the ins and outs of the shoreline. Nearby we could see a stretch of country much higher than the sandy shore, with many beautiful fields and plains full of great forests, some sparse and some dense; and the trees have so many colors, and are so beautiful and delightful that they defy description. And do not think, Your Majesty, that these forests are like the Hyrcanian Forest or the wild wastelands of Scythia and the northern countries, full of common trees; they are

adorned and clothed with palms, laurel, cypress, and other varieties of tree unknown in our Europe. And these trees emit a sweet fragrance over a large area, the nature of which we could not examine for the reason stated above, not because we found it difficult to get through the forests -- indeed, they are nowhere so dense as to be impenetrable. We think that they belong to the Orient by virtue of the surroundings, and that they are not without some kind of narcotic or aromatic liquor. There are other riches, like gold, which ground of such a color usually denotes. There is abundance of animals, stags, deer, hares; and also of lakes and pools of running water with various types of bird, perfect for all the delights and pleasures of the hunt...."

While Verrazzano had been writing in his cabin, the robust cook had rolled barrels of rum onto deck and crew members crafted makeshift musical instruments. When the letter was complete, the Admiral returned to the deck, making his way through the crowd of sailors dancing jigs and clapping to the music. As more rum was passed around, his crew lifted Verrazzano on their shoulders and raised their cups to him.

Verrazzano looked down on his crew and cried out, "To the King and his Acadia."

"Zze Kinnng Zakaddie," cried the ditty-singing, whirling dervishes trying to repeat the Admiral's words.

VI

1527, *Venice Italy*: Mapmaker

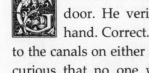iovanni da Verrazzano looked up at the rusty brass numeral on the door. He verified the number, thirty-two, with the paper in his hand. Correct. Giovanni gazed up and down the cobblestone street to the canals on either side. Empty. The lamps were still lit but he found it curious that no one was walking about this morning. The Republic of Venice was reputed to be the most active in all of Italy, even busier than its rival Genoa. Why no one was stirring was a mystery.

Suddenly he heard a shout from above. "Nightsoil!"

He looked up and scrambled to get out of the way just seconds before a large bucket of stinky slop landed next to his newly shined black leather boots. It was quickly followed by a pitcher of clear water, which drained to the low side of the cobblestone street. The mess then disappeared into adjacent ducts.

Down the street he heard several other cries of "nightsoil" and "night bucket," followed by additional large dumpings onto the street. What Giovanni found amazing was that in a matter of moments the black watery substances disappeared into drainage channels which, presumably, flowed into the Venetian Canals.

Before the streetworks project, the black mess eventually drained or was swept down into the canals, but the wives of prominent Venetian aristocrats had sullied their new shoes once too often. Their complaints were repeated to their husbands so often that the noblemen en masse reduced their payments to the Doge, whom they called the "Doxe." They called an emergency meeting, reminding him who had elected him from their midst as chief magistrate of their Republic for life; his life, that is.

The veiled threat was enough for the Doxe to propose a modern street improvement plan. With a flourish of his quill, he signed the treasury document that allocated a small fortune to pay for laying pipes and ducts into the cobblestone streets to drain the daily messes more quickly. Once the works were completed, the Doxe passed an edict requiring an advance warning cry prior to dumping anything onto the streets.

Thereafter the system seemed to work and everyone seemed content. Noblewomen wore their new shoes without fear of stepping in filth and they stopped shrieking at their husbands. The nobility showed their appreciation with compensation to the Doxe. Yes, all was well in the Venice Republic in the modern age of civilization on this cool morning in 1527.

Giovanni now understood why the streets were empty. He heard more warning cries on this street as if he were in an eerie echo chamber. Cries erupted on streets all around him. He tapped the brass knocker again. Then, as if choreographed by the director of the Venice Opera himself, doors burst open, followed by a sudden flood of people into the streets. Venice was alive once more with throngs who avoided stepping into the new drainage pipes on their way to gondolas, markets, shops, or the Academy where he once studied.

The mess had drained away so Giovanni walked to the single window of the building. Peering in, he wiped the grime as best he could from the window until his impeccable white gloves matched his black wool coat. Still he could not see anything through the glass except what appeared to be a wall on the other side of the window.

This could not possibly be right. How could the beautiful work that the famed cartographer Giacomo Gastaldi was known for come out of such a place, he wondered. He rapped on the door with the rusty brass knocker. Suddenly, a peephole cover grate slid open. A squeaky voice questioned through the hole in the door. "Who calls and what is your business here?"

Giovanni was startled. He had never been treated like this before but he swallowed his pride and announced himself. "Admiral Giovanni da Verrazzano. It was I who ordered the gift for the King."

The grating slammed shut and the door opened. A young boy standing on a stool jumped down and said, "Enter, Admiral. My father Signor Gastaldi is waiting for you. I am the young Gastaldi." He held a candle and motioned for Giovanni to follow him.

They passed through a narrow hallway and entered a huge, well-lit room. Upon entering, Giovanni saw that the front window had been blocked with black fabric, completely isolating the office inside. Dozens of candles were burning in candelabras from the ceiling. Tall tapers blazed at each of the dozen tables arranged in a circle around the master's drafting table.

The young man led Giovanni directly to the center table where Signor Gastaldi bowed and shook his hand repeatedly. "Admiral, I have long awaited your visit." Gastaldi checked Giovanni's boots. "I see you knew about the bucket dumping." He turned to his clerks and waved his hands. "He has no nightsoil on his boots." Then he turned back to him. "Remarkable. First time visitors here never have such luck."

Giovanni seemed bemused. "I am a lucky man, Signor." He glanced anxiously at the desk but did not see anything resembling his map. He looked questioningly at Gastaldi. "I came to procure my order."

Gastaldi took him by the arm and led him around the circle to the back rooms. There he saw scores of platemakers and engravers using their magnifying glasses strapped to one eye during the engraving process. The platemakers were hard at work cutting and finishing copper plates. Several young boys of about six years old picked up baskets of copper plates, then circulated throughout the engravers tables and filled their boxes with the plates while picking up the finished ones. Those plates that were finished were then carried back to the platemakers, surrounded by copper boards, expensive parchment, rolls of linen and bottles of expensive ink. Then the striking would commence.

"Your reputation precedes you, but I never expected to see such a large working shop. Most mapmakers use other publishers," complimented Giovanni.

Gastaldi, the master, was proud of his staff and was pleased that Giovanni was suitably impressed. "We do likewise, but for special personages such as yours," at which he bowed deeply. "I supervise the work myself. We Italians are honored you are a countryman, and certainly the French are pleased with the glory you provided them with this discovery," responded Gastaldi.

"All is done for my King," Verrazzano said modestly.

"As an Italian you must derive great pleasure from making that Spanish Queen Isabella squirm, eh? Each time you capture her gold and sink one of her ships?"

"Is such news commonly known here?" quizzed Giovanni.

"It is rumored you have taken a liking to Spanish conquistadors, those beautifully struck gold coins." He sighed. "If only I had engravers like that."

Finally the two men returned to the circle of tables. At the first table, two clerks worked in a team. The first held a large glass magnifier above a small drawing, while the other looked through the glass to draw particularly fine lines outlining portions of what appeared to be the country of Italy.

Gastaldi smiled. "This map is for the geography lessons of the son of Count de' Medici. So he can learn the size and location of the family land holdings."

Giovanni nodded, and followed the mapmaker to the next table. There he watched a clerk apply a brilliant shade of blue ink to the oceans on another map. Around the circle he walked in awe, watching clerks coloring large maps, small inserts to be put into books, and several unique custom style maps. Gastaldi showed him the coloring system he taught his clerks -- purple for mountains, green for trees, brown for the plains, and so on.

"The colors were a special request by the English King Henry. It seems their inks do not take to parchment as well as ours, and they have not mastered gold leafing their maps," the mapmaker explained.

Giovanni had seen similar maps on one of the galleons he overtook. He turned to Gastaldi, who had anticipated the question.

"Of course we accepted those beautiful Spanish coins for maps of the Colón exploration in ninety and two." Gastaldi braced himself for harsh words from Giovanni, who instead burst into a hearty laugh.

"I should have guessed how you knew so much about Spanish treasure. But tell me, did you use my voyage records to embellish those of that Spanish sailor Columbus?"

Gastaldi put his finger to his lips, but it was in jest. He shook his head vigorously. "We have nothing if not our reputation. Each map is created for the procurer. We cannot change lines on an explorer's map even if we believe them to be wrong based on other maps we have knowledge of…one way or another. But no, our talent lies in the design, the colors, the etchings."

Giovanni pondered his words for a moment and then nodded his head. "I would have expected no less of the master of mapmaking."

Gastaldi bowed. "You are too kind, Admiral."

Moving on, they watched a clerk melting a small gold leaf, then dipping in a thin brush and gilding the edges of a map scroll. Gastaldi took the brush and wiped half of the gold leaf back into the pot. He admonished the clerk. "The gold must be applied in thin coats, gently, like caressing a woman."

The clerk nodded his understanding and dipped the brush slowly. He tried again, this time following his master's exact instructions. "Perfect," said Gastaldi, giving his approval.

Gastaldi patted his son's head with pride. "The gilding was my son's idea. He will make a better mapmaker than his father, I believe. He is teaching me new things now."

Giovanni nodded. "The gold is a fitting touch for this special map. Excellent idea, young Gastaldi." The Admiral handed the boy a coin.

With that the boy bowed and said, "Thank you, kind sir." He ran out of the workroom and back to his post at the door.

Then they stood at the last table in the circle. The clerk bowed and moved away from the table.

"It is completed for your approval," Gastaldi told Giovanni.

Verrazzano looked carefully at the map and gasped. It was more beautiful than he had imagined, with the various painted colors and muted shades blending just perfectly. The gold leaf trim surrounding the map was a wider border than any of the others Gastaldi had shown him. Giovanni saw the map claiming his discovery of what is now the Atlantic Coast north of Virginia all the way to Acadia, now named Nova Scotia in Canada.

He looked at the title "Arcadia" and turned back to Gastaldi. "I was clear that this discovery is entitled 'Acadia'."

Gastaldi made a long sweeping bow and replied evenly, looking up at Verrazzano. "You took your inspiration from our poet Sannazaro, who named it Arcadia after being, in turn, inspired by Greece. We must be true to the origins of our art."

Verrazzano argued, "This work is to be given to the King of France, not Greece."

Gastaldi reasoned with him. "You and I are artists, each in our own way. You create a sculpture as your vessel cuts through the deep blue sea, then your art is lost forever. My art is the only way to give a visible form to yours. Each of us creates truth but as we see it."

Verrazzano nodded but was not completely pleased. Mapmakers, creative artists? Verrazzano had never thought so. They were copiers of his work, not creators of their own.

Gastaldi nodded to the clerk at the last table, who dipped a quill in a large inkpot, and handed it to his master. Gastaldi signed his name on the map with a huge flourish. The clerk pressed a small roller over the signature to fix it to the map and dry it. Then he proceeded to roll the map and seal it with melted red wax. Gastaldi pulled his ring off his finger and pressed it into the wax, sealing it. The clerk then wrapped it in protective paper and string before handing it to Gastaldi.

With a bow as flourishing as his signature, Gastaldi handed the package to Verrazzano. In return, Giovanni took from his leather purse a gold coin and placed it in Gastaldi's palm. The mapmaker smiled and led Verrazzano to the workroom door. "Good voyages to you, Admiral."

Giovanni walked straight to the front door where the young Gastaldi smiled at him. "One day your map will read as it should."

Giovanni patted him on the back. "You will become a renowned mapmaker if you follow the desires of your clients." Then he was gone.

Some time later, the elder Signor Gastaldi died. A few months after the funeral, Giovanni received a duplicate of the map that had been drawn for the King with an important distinction. This map was properly titled "Acadia."

Giovanni read the note. "May this gift merit the lesson you taught me, which was more valuable than the gold coin you put in my pocket." The card, like the map, was signed with a flourish, "Gastaldi."

Within twenty years, that flourish was on every map of major consequence throughout Europe. Indeed, the young Gastaldi had lived up to Giovanni's prophecy even though the Admiral had passed on.

VII

1528, *Caribbean Antilles Islands*: Rubies

ing Francis I was so pleased with the gold-leafed map of Acadia he received in 1527 that to show his gratitude he placed on Giovanni's finger a monstrous gold ring encrusted with thick rubies.

"Where shall we send you next to conquer more lands for us?" asked His Majesty as he clapped his hands.

It was Giovanni's turn to be grateful, though little did he realize the next voyage would be his last and the ostentatious ring would be his undoing.

He and his favorite brother, Gerolamo, set sail the following year. Due to a combination of winds, storms, and geographic miscalculations, the ship reached land months later in the Antilles Islands of the Caribbean Sea, far south of Giovanni's first discovery.

The Admiral's sibling sadly reported to the King what he observed from aboard their ship *The New World* as Giovanni led a landing party to shore. While trying to position the French flag in the ground and claim the island for France, the men were greeted by a band of natives.

Verrazzano, however, did not meet the fate of Columbus, who was welcomed with food and gifts, even if he did return home to spend his last days shunned and penniless. In fact, the surprise that awaited the Admiral was more fitting for Columbus, given that explorer's previous acts towards the indigenous peoples of territories he discovered.

With great pomp and circumstance, the natives lit bonfires on the beach to welcome Giovanni and his entire landing party. Then the roast commenced. After the cannibals had feasted on the great Admiral and his crew, all that remained were Giovanni's bones, picked clean, and his ruby ring.

The natives believed the ugly red stones were a bad omen that would bring bloodshed to their tribe. They knocked the stones out of the large gold ring, which fit perfectly on their Chieftain's little toe.

They tossed the rubies into the sea.

The New World: Acadia, New France,
the British Colonies and Spanish Territories, 1720,
cartographer: Johann Baptiste Homann

Part I
France: 1738

"Clarity of mind means clarity of passion, too…a great and clear
mind loves ardently and sees distinctly what it loves."
- *Blaise Pascal*

CHAPTER 1
Carriage

PALACE of VERSAILLES, FRANCE

he two young Royal Guards were brothers. Their family had distinguished themselves in service to the French royal family now presided over by King Louis XV. The young men stood at attention outside the ornate entry doors to the opulent Versailles Palace.

The shorter boy, Laurent, a plump fourteen year-old, sweated profusely under the collar of the woolen jacket he wore year-round. Ever since he could remember, everyone called him Laurent the Fat, which he considered disrespectful since his older brother was called by his proper name, Claude, after his father. His mother had continually reminded him that he was younger only by ten months but that did nothing to console him. She bestowed on him much more affection than the older boy, who was the apple of his father's eye. In fact, it seemed his father ignored Laurent except to beat him on occasion upon returning from a late night at the local tavern.

So used to the lack of his father's attention was Laurent that he hardly noticed when Claude was admitted to service as a palace entry guard at his father's request. A year later the second entry guard was dispatched to Marseille to bury his family, victims of the Black Death. The young man himself quickly succumbed to the plague and the Palace was short one Royal Guard. Knowing the reputation of the Arnaud family for impeccable service beginning at a young age, the King's Prime Minister, Cardinal

Hercule de Fleury, turned to Claude Arnaud, the father. Arnaud had faithfully served the King as a valet until he was lamed by a poacher on the King's lands.

Claude had tried to free a rabbit caught in the poacher's trap when the man crept up behind him and cut Claude's leg while deftly killing and removing his dinner from the trap. The thief did not take kindly to theft of his dinner, though he himself stole it from the King. The poacher was found and rightly hanged and Claude's leg was saved but his days as a valet were over. He then placed all of his hopes for advancement on his elder son and namesake. As for Laurent, well, he would have to find his own way.

When Claude was called to send his other son to Versailles, it was with reluctance that he sent Laurent. He knew the boy was intelligent and might be able to surpass his favorite son at Court. But the man was trapped and could not refuse the King's wishes. Madame Arnaud refused to agree and a violent argument had erupted in the Arnaud household, the likes of which Laurent had never seen. He tried to reassure his mother.

"I am no longer a child and must earn a wage to help the family."

She replied through her tears, "You are noble, my son. You need not earn your keep. You should live as a member of Court instead of opening their doors. I should have done better by you."

"Mother, you jest. We are not titled. Our family has worked at Versailles for three generations now and I am proud to join their ranks."

She shook her head. "You were not meant for service. Not even for the King. I must tell you...."

Before she could say another word Claude pushed her out of the way. "You shall say nothing more, wife."

Madame Arnaud wiped her tears with her apron and cried out, "Leave him be Claude. Just leave him be."

Her husband slapped her so hard she fell to the floor. Laurent tried to rescue her but Claude grabbed the boy by the collar and pushed him out of the door. "Do not show your face again until you make something of yourself. That is, if you can. And send your wages here."

After the door slammed in his face Laurent still heard his mother's tears but he gladly took to the road, away from his father's cruel temper. Soon he was sitting on the back of a vegetable wagon heading for Versailles.

Laurent's memories were interrupted at that moment by his brother, who constantly rebuked him. "And you said you could match me in this job. You should work harder, for our father's good name is at stake if you fail."

Laurent retorted, "I am no dawdler. But the uniform causes prickly heat in summer and slows me down. I should be wearing nothing underneath."

"You complain of heat now in summer and next you will curse the cold of winter. Can you never be content with your lot?"

Laurent knew not to question Claude, not out of respect but fear. Claude had a streak of meanness he kept well-hidden in public but in their shared room at the Palace, Claude taunted Laurent mercilessly.   Nonetheless, the younger boy held his tongue when he was near his elder brother.

The brothers were so unlike each other they should have come from different parents. Claude had inherited enviable physical characteristics. He was tall, thin and exceedingly handsome. Not much for book learning, he preferred the outdoors and had learned pyrotechnics by working at the fireworks extravaganza for the King's birthday the year before. His swordsmanship was second to none his age at Court and he often was called upon in his free hours to train with the nobles, who needed worthy partners to keep their skills sharp. With coal black hair and piercing blue eyes, Claude was always the one that the young maids at the Palace swooned over. Fortunately for them, he was not selective and took one and all, where he found them --- on a straw sleeping mat or in the lush green maze of the Versailles gardens or behind a curtain in a Palace hallway.

On the other hand, Laurent boasted a stout, short frame, long, thick golden hair and a round baby face. His features were marred only by a scar that ran from his right temple to cheek, the result of a childhood encounter with a female boar who did not appreciate him touching her baby. Laurent had been extricating the young boar from the underbrush and was so intent on his task he never heard the animal's huge mother approach. Fortunately, Claude chased both boars away then rebuked Laurent for his stupidity for weeks. Laurent was afraid of nothing and no one, except his brother.

Perhaps to compensate for his lack of other admirable traits, Laurent was born with the gifts of linguistics and ciphers. His kindness was innate and he offered help to all whom he saw in need. He quickly gained expert riding skills. Shy and reserved, he was a romantic waiting chastely for that one perfect woman to become his wife, lover, and best friend for life's journey. He kept these thoughts to himself as he saw a stream of kitchen hands, maidservants and even several Ladies-in-waiting to the Queen who met his brother for private trysts. Laurent could not have married any of them. But, of course, his brother did not either.

Laurent sighed quietly. He could not understand why his personal talents never attracted the attention Claude did. Especially the attentions of

Lady Véronique de Navarre. She was the youngest and, Laurent believed, the most beautiful, of all the women at Court. Laurent prayed to fall asleep quickly each night to meet her in his dreams. He stirred himself from his daydream when he spied a faint cloud of dust fast approaching the Palace. Excitedly he pointed to the south entry gates. "Carriage a-coming!"

Claude frowned. He asked himself why his brother must embarrass him like this. Their job was to wait for the carriages, not announce them. He straightened his jacket, buttons gleaming in the sunlight, and nodded to Laurent to do the same. Then, as if on cue, they simultaneously clicked their heels, standing at attention, eyes forward, feet planted firmly on the ground.

Expecting the excitement of a sumptuous royal chariot, the boys were disappointed when the dust bowl created by the horses' hooves had disappeared. What appeared was a quite ordinary carriage rolling up to the sweeping steps. A footman in a reserved but elegant uniform hopped off the back to place a set of steps beneath the carriage door. The gold ecclesiastical heraldry emblazoned on the door had become so faded over the years Laurent nearly missed it.

He realized this was the carriage of a Cardinal, but not just any Prince of the Church. This was the carriage of the King's Prime Minister. He had heard about the carriage many times before but had never witnessed the Cardinal's arrival. Court rumor had it that the Cardinal was the only one of the King's Ministers who did not spent exorbitant amounts of money on himself and his own pleasure, but instead worked honestly for the benefit of France. He was beloved not only by the King but by all who knew him.

Laurent was intrigued. He stepped as close as he dared without falling down the massive steps of the Palace entry. The coat of arms consisted of a shield topped by a scarlet galero with fifteen tassels on each side and a cross of gold above the shield. The sun shone too brightly for Laurent to read the escutcheon but he was certain, with his penchant for languages, if he could ever get close enough he would be able to read it. Perhaps the Cardinal might need someone to help him with his important works, Laurent thought. That would surely take him from under Claude's onerous thumb.

An imposing, grey-bearded man in a Cardinal's peaked scarlet silk cap pulled back the curtains of the carriage. André-Hercule de Fleury perched at the top of the steps, taking in his surroundings as if he had been asleep for a hundred years and the Palace had just appeared out of the briars. He absentmindedly descended the carriage stairs, watched unobtrusively by the royal footman in case he should slip. Clearly de Fleury was preoccupied. He reflected on the gravity of the events that brought him to Versailles. He had been working incessantly on a solution to the issues in the urgent letter from the King Louis XV. And of course he had brought the requested diary.

The time was upon him to put his plan in motion...if His Majesty approved. The Cardinal marched swiftly over the stone road and trudged up the Palace steps two at a time, his scarlet cape rustling. He mused, "The King will surely build a new cathedral when this business is done."

Taken by surprise at how quickly the large man bounded up the steps, Claude and Laurent hurried to open the doors, bowing deeply as the Cardinal stopped in the entryway. He soberly re-adjusted his birette, pressing the pleats of his robes. De Fleury cast a critical eye downward, and noticed Laurent curiously regarding the escutcheon.

The bemused Cardinal asked, "Considering a life of the cloth?"

Laurent's face turned red, as embarrassed at being spoken to by the great Cardinal as he was being caught. Stunned for a moment, he regained his composure and managed to respond, "Please excuse me, Your Holy Excellency, but no. I was merely reading the inscription 'fuisons'."

"Do you speak the old Latin then? Tell me what does it mean?"

"We were?" Laurent was sure he had translated correctly so he answered with confidence this time. "It means 'we were'."

"Well done. But do you know why?" the Cardinal queried.

Laurent hated to be ignorant of the answer but knew the Cardinal's reputation for disdaining impertinence. He calculated being honest was better than guessing. The King's Prime Minister was speaking to him...*him*, a lowly guard! He could not risk a mistake. He bowed and shook his head.

"No, I am sorry but I do not, Excellency."

For de Fleury honesty was the right answer. He nodded and patted Laurent's shoulder. "Always better to admit when you do not know rather than to pretend you do. It is because my family ancestors, the kings of Scotland, had their origins here in France. Normandy to be exact. We were originally here and still belong here. And your name, my son?"

"Laurent Arnaud, son of Claude Arnaud, former valet to His Majesty." Laurent quickly spit out the words, then bowed and returned to his post.

"I am pleased to see that Monsieur Arnaud sent an intelligent son for the post." The Cardinal looked over at Claude who was winking at the garden maid watering the flower pots on the stairway. De Fleury turned back to Laurent. "You shall hear from me again, Monsieur Laurent Arnaud. Keep up your excellent studies."

The Cardinal made a mental note to see that the boy was given more responsibility and more education in the Palace. He looked down at the dust on his cape but Laurent quickly brushed it off. The Cardinal was impressed with the boy, a difficult thing to do with a Prince of the Church and Prime Minister of the King who has seen, or heard, it all. De Fleury nodded, careful not to dislodge his birette, and breezed past the two young men.

The Arnaud brothers breathed a sigh of relief as they shut the heavy doors. Laurent cringed, waiting for the scolding he knew was coming from his older brother. Instead he was in for a surprise.

"Well done? That is a compliment as valuable as gold, coming from the Cardinal Prime Minister. I thought he was going to sweep you up and take you under his wing," Claude said, a bit awestruck.

Laurent straightened himself and adjusted his hat. He thought, "If only I had spoken to the Cardinal before now, I would not have suffered at Claude's hands. But no more. I will take charge of my life and instead of joining the Church...." He cut off his silent thought and expressed his final thought aloud. "I shall marry a Lady."

At once Claude regained his power and guffawed, "You, marry a Lady? You who are of no consequence, with no title, no resources and no prospects for the future except being a Royal Guard like me? In these times you believe you can do better than your lot with a Lady, no less?" Claude turned away, still chiding him. "Who do you think you are? If I cannot marry a Lady, surely you shall not either. Our rank and lack of fortune forbid it."

Determined not to be humiliated any longer, Laurent confronted his brother, perhaps for the first time in his life. "No matter what you say or think or do, you shall not deter me from my quest. I shall find a Lady and marry her and do great things for His Majesty."

Not to be outdone Claude challenged him. "*If* you find a Lady and *if* she agrees to marry you, and *if* she actually does so, and *if* all those uncertainties come to pass, then be sure I shall serve you as your valet until the day I die."

Laurent smiled and thought to himself, "I will have difficulty overlooking your cruelty, though I shall." Wisely, he replied instead, "The day will come that you shall make good on your promise."

Claude shrugged as he took his place on *his* side of the great Palace entry doors. Standing on the opposite side of the doors, Laurent already felt like royalty. He stood taller, felt stronger and knew that a royal Lady was waiting for him, perhaps even dreaming about him. He knew his dreams would be about the beautiful Lady Véronique as *his* Lady while Claude attended him as his servant.

CHAPTER 2
Secrets

VERSAILLES

The beautiful woman-child stared at herself in the tall gilted mirror. She had dismissed her maids and was alone in the immense bedchamber. Carefully, she untied the ribbons of her sheer silk nightdress. As if in slow motion, the diaphanous gown floated to the floor. Analyzing her body with a critical eye, she turned left, then right, then left again. Though only sixteen years of age, Lady Eugenie de Beaufort was already very much a woman.

The young noblewoman steeled herself for the upcoming ordeal. It would not do to complain in front of the Queen, even though she was her cousin. She needed to calm herself so she poured a handful of oil mixed with soothing herbs. Slowly, sensuously, she rubbed the oil on her arms and legs, then her blossoming breasts and round belly. She turned to the side and saw the protrusion she had known for months would eventually show itself.

No doubt the Queen, and perhaps others at Court, had noticed that Eugenie's gowns had become ill-fitting. Indeed, some were already too tight to squeeze into even with the corsets, which Eugenie had ordered her servants to loosen on many occasions of late. Lady de Beaufort had planned to order new dresses in Paris, as the Court seamstresses could not be trusted to hold their tongues. But before Eugenie gathered the courage to ask permission to leave, the Queen must have guessed her secret. It was she who ordered the examination which Eugenie knew would confirm her greatest fear...and a scandal at Court.

Eugenie was the first child born to Count Gilbert de Beaufort and Countess Eveline Opalińska, a Polish princess and first cousin to the French Queen. After Eugenie was born an unexpected child slipped out. They named him Guillaume. When the twins were two years old a third infant, a little boy, was stillborn. Eveline was grief-stricken but after months of prayer, she had finally recovered. A week later she was back on the de Beaufort estates helping a midwife with a difficult birth for the wife of one of their tenant farmers. For twenty hours she labored with the birth, which resulted in a scrawny little girl who died in her crib. The mother died just after the birth, relieved of all her burdens. Two nights later the Countess passed away in her sleep. The doctor said it was sheer exhaustion. Count Gilbert was inconsolable until precocious three-year-old Eugenie climbed onto his knee and put her arms around his neck.

"Papa, tell me stories of Maman." With that, the Count began the tradition of handing down their family histories. Each night Gilbert would tuck his daughter into bed and tell her their complicated family lineage, although he knew she would be too young to understand. Then he described Eveline's great beauty, her kindness to their tenants and serfs, her bravery in helping bring forth new souls into the world and her religious nature.

When Eugenie was six her father gave the young girl her mother's gold chain with a cross encrusted in precious stones. "Never lose this, my child. Your mother is with the angels and shall watch over you." Eugenie clasped the cross and kissed it. Then they knelt by the bed to say their nightly prayers.

Eugenie's brother Guillaume had been named for his illustrious ancestor who made the first expedition with Samuel Champlain to settle Acadia. The Count scowled when he thought of how the boy grew up quite the opposite of illustrious and had simply been an adventurer. Guillaume was lazy and content with wine, women and a good game of cards. He showed no interest in handling the affairs of the estate with his father, preferring to idle his time away with the scoundrels who always seemed to latch on to sons of wealthy nobility.

De Beaufort had looked the other way at his son's lifestyle until the boy disappeared one summer day with a sack of gold coins from the Count's private library. The money was part of the boy's inheritance but his father had wanted to choose the time to bestow the gift.

News reached the Count that Guillaume had been injured in a duel in Venice after cheating at cards, and he had not been seen since. Despite sending couriers and spies throughout Italy, de Beaufort had not been able to find his son, alive or dead. He feared the worst and after several years believed he was gone forever.

With his son no longer alive, the Count pinned his hopes for the future of his estate on his daughter Eugenie. Such a beauty should be at Court. Then she would attract no end of suitors, he thought, and bear an heir to the Count's fortune. He wrote to his old friend the Duc d'Orleans, who arranged a private audience with the Queen and discussed how the branches of their family trees intertwined. Within the month, Eugenie moved to Versailles and was presented at Court as the Queen's cousin. Not six months had passed when de Beaufort received the invitation to the wedding feast. He was overjoyed with the match. Surely their union would bring the requisite male heir and Gilbert could erase that concern. And he hoped his daughter would be very happy.

As a relation of Queen Marie, Eugenie had been furnished a lavish apartment and maidservants in Her Majesty's wing of the Palace. An endless stream of noble suitors sought to woo her but Eugenie rejected them all. The Queen was soon to learn why and to rue the day she brought her little cousin to Versailles. Eugenie already knew what the next meeting would bring and hoped the Queen would not attend. It would only add to Eugenie's humiliation. Her cousin could be quite cruel, although no one had seen that side of her at Court.

Eugenie had just completed the ritual of oiling her body when she heard a slight tap at the door. She quickly tied the ribbons of her dressing gown and slid into her bed, burying herself to her neck under layers of quilts and silk coverlets. The knock came again, this time, louder and more urgent. She called out nervously. "Enter."

A stern-faced heavyset man with a menacing black bag pushed open the heavy door, followed by a young woman with flaming red hair. Doctor Hébert nodded curtly to Eugenie, and he stood by the edge of the bed while he opened the bag.

"My Lady, I shall try not to take any longer than necessary." Doctor Hébert was the consummate professional but time was immaterial to him, so thorough was he with his patients. Today he had been commanded by the Queen to take all the time he required without regard to the Lady.

Eugenie nodded, a bit fearfully, as the physician nodded to one of the Court midwives, Christine de Castille. She was not yet the age of Eugenie but she was quite experienced, having assisted midwives with many births and having attended her father and brothers who were all physicians at the Hôtel Dieu, the largest hospital in Paris. Her maternal origins dated back to the nobility in Spain under the rule of Queen Isabella and King Ferdinand, where her family had produced a long line of Court midwives.

Christine pulled out a series of frightening silver instruments, each of which looked as though it could cause agonizing pain. While Christine organized the utensils, the doctor took out a large closed glass jar filled with what appeared to be pulsating herbs. The herbs parted and several leeches slid against the inside edge of the glass. Eugenie shuddered at the thought.

Christine noticed and smiled at the Lady de Beaufort. Not so large a smile that Doctor Hébert would chide her but not so small so that Eugenie would not know she had a friend. Christine had inherited two and a half centuries of familial ability to handle such delicate matters as faced her today. Doctor Hébert handed Christine a pile of linen cloths, freshly washed but rusty with blood stains nonetheless. The midwife had long considered that leeches accomplished the opposite of the intended result -- she had seen patients become weaker when their blood was let rather than stronger. She hoped that the Doctor would not have to leech Eugenie.

Eugenie became extremely apprehensive. "Doctor, the leeches. They are not necessary for a mere examination, are they?"

Doctor Hébert was agitated at a woman questioning him on his profession. "Lady de Beaufort, I shall determine in my sole discretion what treatment is needed. Rest assured it will be for the best of all parties concerned."

The door was abruptly opened. Suddenly an angry Queen Marie Lecszinka glided in, visibly with child which she would bear two months later. Christine and Hébert bowed. The Queen's Ladies-in-Waiting, Lady Louise Opalińska and the young Véronique de Navarre followed on her heels, each having done so upon her arrival at Court. Being at Court and bearing nine living children and a stillborn had aged the Queen beyond her mere thirty-four years. She continually requested Doctor Hébert to provide potions to make her look younger.

What could the Doctor do with such a condition so completely out of his control? He tried to placate the Queen with scented ointments and flavored liquids but nothing would change her appearance to the King, certainly not when women of such beauty as the Lady de Beaufort were at Court.

The Queen seated herself in the velvet chair nearest the bed. She nodded curtly to Eugenie, who bowed from her bed. The Queen signaled Doctor Hébert and Christine to continue their work.

Eugenie clenched her hands until she was white-knuckled. The Queen's hands were placed quietly in her lap and were as motionless as her eyes.

Doctor Hébert opened his mysterious bag and handed Christine a sinister apparatus. She positioned it under the quilts but on top of Eugenie's gown as was the custom. Doctors did not actually see the bodies of their female patients but groped on top of clothes, or had a female assistant perform the searches for them.

The Doctor directed Christine to move the instrument. "More to the left" and, "Now to the right."

The doctor impatiently held out his hand and Christine returned the apparatus to him. He handed her another one, this time larger and heavier. Christine took care not to hurt Eugenie as she placed it across Lady de Beaufort's belly. Christine nodded to Dr. Hébert when it was in place. The doctor started tapping on the metal piece on top of the quilt. Eugenie winced, not due to pain but in anticipation of being hurt.

"Hush, my Lady, you cannot feel anything yet," said the doctor in response to Eugenie's facial expressions. Then he pushed down on the instrument and Eugenie let out her breath, moaning but trying to be brave.

The Queen glared at Eugenie. "My poor cousin, you flinch at the touch of an instrument yet it is nothing compared to childbirth." Her Majesty continued, "You shall have much pain to bear. Be mindful of your station. We shall hear no further complaints from you."

Eugenie smiled wanly. "Yes, Your Majesty." She had always addressed her so despite their family ties. In fact, most of the European royal houses were related by intermarriage with one another. Popes issued dispensations to many royals over the years, though the present French King and Queen were an exception to the rule.

The Doctor bid Christine to remove the instrument from under the quilts and place the stethoscope on top of the belly area. Christine confirmed it was in place. Then Hébert directed Christine to move it right, left, up, down, in a circle, in a diagonal, then in a zigzag motion.

When the Doctor was satisfied, he nodded and Christine pulled the instrument from under the covers. He gave a slight bow to Eugenie, then bowed to the Queen, who stood and walked with him to the other end of the vast room. Christine repacked everything in the bag, including the jar of leeches. Eugenie gave an audible sigh of relief -- no leeches today.

Eugenie and Christine waited patiently as the Doctor and the Queen looked over at them from time to time, whispering together. Hébert nodded several times, then bowed to the Queen and walked out of the door. He expected Christine to follow with the bag, which she did, but not before she gave Eugenie another quick smile.

Eugenie cringed with more fear than before as she saw the Queen approach, her face stone cold and her voice merciless. "Doctor Hébert confirmed you have just over five months remaining. Thankfully he does not know who the father is. Nor shall anyone at Court. Your action is unforgiveable, cousin, especially after all we have done for you."

Tears streamed down Eugenie's angelic face. The Queen was taken aback by her beauty, even as she cried. The girl had been at the Palace less than six months and was nearly four months with child. So someone at Court had succumbed to the beauty of the little minx just after she arrived.

"We must keep your horrid little secret from the rest of the Court. The King has graciously arranged a marriage."

Eugenie's eyes widened. "I am to be wed? But who wants me now?

"A young nobleman of status and property, and a cousin to His Highness. Lord René Le Blanc de Verdure, our Royal Notaire.

"Lord Le Blanc de Verdure? I did not dream he ever noticed me."

The Queen stared coldly at Eugenie. "Do not flatter yourself. He knows his duty to the King's command. You shall be kept under guard and not allowed to leave this room except to meet us in the Royal Chamber for the announcement to the Court tomorrow, then for the wedding and marriage dinner once preparations have been finalized. Speak to no one about your condition. Soon you shall be out of our lives."

Eugenie tearfully reached for the Queen's hand but Marie pulled it away. Eugenie begged, "The King would not banish me? Not now?"

The Queen was irate. "Selfish girl. We stand on the brink of war and you worry about a place at Court?"

"I humbly beg Your Majesty to reconsider."

"After the wedding night you shall leave the Palace, never to return. Pack what you intend to take. All else shall be given to the villagers."

"Please grand me permission to speak with the King."

The Queen retorted coldly, "You shall not speak to His Majesty about this or anything else. He has more than his share of problems with the English across the ocean, where you shall be sent."

"The New World? Does the doctor approve such a long sea voyage?"

"He shall be going with you."

The Queen glided to the door, then turned one last time.

"Find a wedding gown that will hide your shame. We shall send down some dresses from our last confinement for your voyage. There is no time for the seamstresses." She glared at Eugenie from the doorway. "Even on a ship you must be presentable. You are, after all, our cousin."

Soon the Queen disappeared in a flurry of silks and satins, holding her belly as she waddled away. Her entourage followed closely behind.

Eugenie dabbed at her eyes with a linen handkerchief. Then she smiled, raised her eyes heavenward and prayed.

"Thank you for taking me away from a Court green with envy. And most of all, for sending a good man to protect me and my child. Lord Le Blanc shall make an excellent father. And I shall be the best wife to my savior."

CHAPTER 3
Mirrors

VERSAILLES

imple in its concept -- framed mirrored walls reflecting on marble inlaid floors -- yet the most opulent of all rooms in Versailles Palace, the Hall of Mirrors, always took his breath away. At only age twenty, René Le Blanc, Sieur de la Verdure, was already a respected aristocrat at the Court of King Louis XV.

René had studied diligently at the faculty of laws in Paris at the Sorbonne and graduated with honors and a Doctor of Laws degree at the tender age of sixteen. Then he had begun the mandatory two-year apprenticeship required for an "avocat", or attorney, to be accepted in the Paris Bar. He worked with the attorney renowned for defending the rights of property ownership in France, Maître Antoine Poirson. But in 1736, the avocat became more well-known for one legal case in which he defended men's rights to speak freely in a newspaper about government officials. The case was "Marat versus Delaunay."

Poirson's client Delaunay, the publisher of the Parisian newspaper the "People's Voice," was sued by Marat, a magistrate in Paris, for distributing "False, Seditious and Scandalous Print and Malicious Libel about the Magistrate and His Activities in Government." René had burned many candles late into the night writing legal essays and Poirson's closing argument for the case.

Maître Poirson's stirring summation of René's argument to the jury had been nothing less than brilliant. His final words to the jury of twelve freehold landowners, all men of course, were:

"How often has the abuse of power by administrators been the primary cause of the loss of liberty or property, and that such injustice and oppression by these powerful men nurtured contempt within the people? The art of such men is to introduce arbitrary rule, and to destroy a free people.

It is my fervent desire that men may, within the confines of the truth, exercise their freedom to write and speak their sentiments of the conduct of powerful men, as such conduct affects the lives and estates of those under their administration. Every man who loves his country prefers its liberty to all other considerations, well knowing that life without liberty is a misery and they are mere slaves. And yet upon the denial of such right to publish the truth, the next step may make them slaves; for what else does slavery do but oppress men by preventing the liberty of complaining, or if they do, by destroying their lives and lands.

And so we come to the decision before you today, honored Gentlemen of the Jury, which is neither a small question nor a private concern. It is not the cause of one poor printer, or even of all the printers in Paris. No! Dare I remind you it shall affect every free man that lives under the rule of France?

It is the best cause -- it is the cause of liberty, justice, domestic tranquility and general welfare of the people. Every man who prefers freedom to a life of slavery will bless and honor you as men who have thwarted the attempt of tyranny, and by an impartial verdict have laid a noble foundation for securing the blessings of liberty to ourselves and our posterity, for which God and the laws of our country have given us the absolute right to expose and oppose corrupt arbitrary power by speaking and writing truth. And truth is our liberty and our escape from slavery.

So, as you see, Gentlemen of the Jury, the truth is an absolute defense to any claim of defamation."

Maître Poirson let his final words ring in the chamber for a moment. Then he bowed deeply to the jurymen, to the court and to the gallery who had been breathlessly hanging on his every word. Now, they were on their feet, stomping, clapping and cheering loudly. Victory was his, he thought, as he took his seat.

The winning verdict for Poirson's client, Delaunay, was handed down in less than a quarter of an hour, to the profuse applause of the audience. It was the first known case in France where the truth was a successful defense to a public official's claim of defamation. Women even tossed roses to Poirson from the balconies above until they were escorted out of the building for fear they might swoon in the heat of the moment due to their admiration for the Maître.

Years after the trial, Thomas Jefferson obtained a copy of Poirson's closing argument in the case, which had been written by René Le Blanc. Jefferson incorporated the main points into a document he framed for the American colonies called the Declaration of Independence.

After completing his apprenticeship and being called to the Paris Bar, René had the opportunity as a noble to purchase a magistrate's position. Instead, he accepted a professorship lecturing new students in the intricacies of property rights, land title, boundary disputes, riparian and agrarian rights, successions and other courses of study relating to property law. Rarely did the renowned University ever grant a teaching position to a young attorney. But once it became known that René had written most of Maître Poirson's arguments the university wanted the prestige of having him as a member of their faculty of laws.

After a year as a professor of law, René was called to the Versailles Court of his cousin, King Louis XV. He still remembered walking down the Hall of Mirrors the first time, waiting in the outer chamber while nobles looked up at him then turned their noses down. Until, that is, they learned he had been appointed the King's Royal Notaire.

René, a handsome young man, had gone largely unnoticed the few times he had been at Court between his travels throughout the Kingdom for the King. He was slight of build and of medium height. He carried a tall feathered hat but preferred not to wear it. He felt such trappings were more to impress the members of the Court, other lords or ladies, rather than out of personal choice. He preferred to leave his head uncovered except when convention required a powdered wig or hat, such as meetings with the King or in a court of law.

His long black tresses, pulled back and tied neatly in the style of the day with a matching silk ribbon, were marked by a distinctive natural white shock running from crown to ends. It was the general belief at Court his white streak was a sign of great knowledge, which commanded greater respect in his position as Royal Notaire.

Sophisticated for his age, Lord Le Blanc de Verdure gazed at his infinite image in the gilded mirrored walls. The narrow white streak in his locks looked as if it had been painted for effect, but he was quite aware of the effect it had on others, particularly those who knew of his royal lineage. Even as a child, before he took his first step, René knew he was special, not by the looks of awe reflected in the eyes of his parents but, rather, by the unique shock of white locks proudly standing tall among his black tresses. That, he knew, was a mark of singularity.

He had discovered that the snow white streak in his mane ran intermittently in the family, though not in every generation. Some called it holy, the Celtic tribes called it magical, but to the bearer of this distinguishing feature, it was royalty personified. What he did not know was that many of his ancestors had experienced the same thoughts and feelings. That is, that he was unique and would be called upon to do great things, sometimes daring, at times perhaps considered foolhardy, but always successful in his endeavors for what began as the Frankish kingdom and was now the kingdom of France.

René wore a rich brocade waistcoat and breeches tied with silk ribbons over his silk stockings. A pair of perfectly polished silver buckled shoes completed the ensemble. His manner was elegant, of good breeding, but without the frivolity and expensive jewelry of wealthier nobles and aristocrats at Court, so little notice was taken of him. But much would be spoken about him in the coming weeks and years.

The King had insisted, albeit short of a royal command, that René participate in Court affairs more often. Ever obedient, he began to come to Court monthly when the great feasts were given for visiting royalty, ambassadors and the country lords. He did not forget the hat and wore it when required. Sweeping bows always made a more favorable impression when a hat with a feather was involved.

The Notaire, or Notary as it was sometimes called, was a position created generations ago by the King of France. The position and the great seal were awarded to a small number of men of royal blood who had studied at university for years and earned a Doctor of Laws degree. The title was important because it was granted in perpetuity. Once given it could not be retracted, and the title and its benefits were valuable property inherited by descendents through the centuries.

The Notaire was responsible for certifying official documents written by the King, providing writing services to those within the Court who could not write (of which there were many, to René's surprise), assisting the royal secretaries to the King, Queen and Ministers of the King's Cabinet, and providing the irrevocable seal of authenticity for important legal documents such as transfers or inheritances of land and property.

Notaires took their responsibilities very seriously and for their services were remunerated well. The notarial position was nearly the only appointment that had not been corrupted by the nobility or Court ministers in their thirst for power and wealth. As a result, documents with the notaire's seal were given absolute credibility as the symbol of unquestionable legality for real property and title in France. With the French system of obtaining ownership of seigneuries through title or royal grant, a notaire's seal was indispensible on a title in the event of boundary disputes, successions or family feuds. In this way members of the nobility were assured of clear title to their properties, which were then able to be sold or used as collateral for loans if the owner fell on hard times.

René felt honored to be a Notaire. He was in great demand at Court not only for his position but also his unwavering policy of absolute discretion. He knew Court secrets that would astonish. He knew which married nobleman had recognized an illegitimate child to inherit both title and fortune in his will. He notarized a letter signed by the mother of a certain minister to the King who had lost her own child but acquired her son from a passing troupe of gypsies, which letter would be delivered privately to the minister only after his mother's death. So many secrets. But René gladly locked them in his heart and in a strongbox with a single key always worn around his neck.

René was, as were the other nobles, a spiritual man whose convictions of honesty, service and faith were deeply rooted in his Roman Catholic religion. He often recalled the oral histories of his father and grandfather, occasionally interrupted by the older women in the family, of Clovis and Clothilde, rulers of Francia in the fourth century who became the first converts to Catholicism in their kingdom. The succession of Kings of France had followed in Clovis' footsteps. The Kingdom became staunchly Catholic and its rulers remained devoted to their religion, protecting it with their lives and their armies.

René prided himself on education, paramount above everything except God, his family and France. He was a voracious reader, particularly of French history as well as that of other European nations including Great Britain, which in 1709 had united the two separate countries of England and Scotland into one Kingdom. He studied politics, war and the law and had a special affinity for his family genealogy and heraldry dating back centuries.

René was the descendent of several lines of Le Blancs and other nobility in both his maternal and paternal lines. He was proud that his family name was one of the oldest in France, dating back at least to Hugues Le Blanc whose son, Hugues Capet, was the founder of the Capetian dynasty and had ruled France beginning in the tenth century.

The branches of the family trees of the monarchs and René continued to intertwine together through other royal relations who had led accomplished, if not adventurous, lives.

One of his ancestors had been an illegitimate child of King Henry IV, who acknowledged the son but he was far down the line of succession. Another was Claude Le Blanc, who had joined French explorer and cartographer Samuel Champlain on his expedition as one of the first colonists in Acadia in 1603. Still another Le Blanc relative had married a first cousin of King Louis IX, who was later canonized by the Catholic Church as Saint Louis. René had been told these family histories and others that he recorded in his private journal to preserve for his descendents. The book was one of his most precious possessions.

Where knowledge was power and the ability to use, misuse or twist it in one's favor was crucial, René kept to himself. He preferred being absent from Court more often than present, abhorring gossip and political games of intrigue. Instead he provided direct responses to questions and added forthright comments in discussions, which were refreshingly honest to some and quite shocking to others.

The Notaire had earned the respect of those who knew him and became a person of great interest to those who had not had the occasion to be introduced. He was considered mysterious by some but important by all who wanted to know more about a cousin of His Majesty who had only recently come to Court. The more questions the Court thought of the fewer answers they received, catapulting the King's Royal Notary René Le Blanc de Verdure to the top of the list of subjects for gossip and conjecture. Such was the life at Versailles. And it was a life that René wanted as little a part of as possible, even considering his position.

Being a new member of the Court and Royal Notary to His Majesty still seemed but a dream to René. As a relation to the King, the young aristocrat had been given an apartment befitting his position, though he rarely stepped foot inside it. He had only recently made his first appearance at Versailles to accept his notarial appointment. The mysterious young man stirred much gossip and conjecture among both women who sized him up as lover or confidant, and men who regarded him as rival and threat.

Ignorant of the intrigue at Versailles, René was courteous to all he met yet revealed little of himself. Each time he could escape the madness of Court he retreated to this Hall and immersed himself in the blonde's beauty and refinement. And except for the tension in the air, today was like his few previous visits. He found the Palace guards polite yet curt as they showed him in and bid him to await the Cardinal's arrival. He smelled mystery in the air and wondered if it had to do with the King's command for his immediate appearance.

How had Cardinal de Fleury become such a powerful force in the Royal political arena, he wondered. His rise to power was an astonishing story. He began as a local parish priest in Paris, then was sent to Acadia, France's far-flung territory in the New World, after which he was appointed tutor of Louis XV as a child king. Upon the death of his predecessor, the King named him Prime Minister and seemed to rely heavily on the Cardinal's counsel.

René hoped he would have an opportunity to learn more about His Grace during their meeting this morning. The Cardinal had sent a royal carriage to the Sorbonne with an urgent request for René. The coachman finally found him teaching riparian rights of coastal properties to students along the banks of the River Seine.

René pulled the royal parchment from his waistcoat and slowly read it again, careful not to loosen the broken red wax seal. "You are commanded by His Royal Majesty Louis Fifteen, King of France and Navarre, to present yourself at the Palace of Versailles and to meet with Prime Minister André-Hercule de Fleury, Cardinal of the Holy Roman Catholic Church and Prime Minister to His Majesty, on a matter of urgent service to the realm." It was signed with a flourish by the King.

Le Blanc rolled the parchment and replaced it inside his jacket pocket then walked down the hallway toward the painting. The closer he came, the more oblivious he became to the glittering room. He stopped suddenly and gasped audibly. He gazed at a view more entrancing than the Hall of Mirrors itself.

The large painting never ceased to attract his attention. The tableau featured a series of vignettes of couples in the courtship ritual. In it, the central female character was a blonde goddess with remarkable hazel eyes. She drew him closer to the magnificent artwork, "La Fête Champêtre," meaning, "The Country Picnic."

Transfixed by the woman-child in the painting, René was unaware of the Cardinal's footsteps that stopped behind him. The Cardinal felt the young Lord had already fallen in love with the goddess in the large painted canvas. De Fleury eagerly anticipated what René would do when he knew what was in store for him.

"Does Lord Le Blanc de Verdure admire Pater's latest painting?" asked the Cardinal softly.

Le Blanc reeled around and quickly lowered his red face to kiss the jeweled ring proffered by de Fleury, murmuring, "Excellency, I have never seen such an entrancing beauty."

"His Majesty is quite pleased with the work of his Royal Artist," the Cardinal began. Then he continued, "But we must be on our way. The King shall see us shortly. Come. Your future awaits."

The Cardinal glanced about the hall, nodding in satisfaction. The guards had kept the hallway empty, as requested. Falling into line with the Cardinal's long strides, René wondered what the day would bring. As they walked together, their reflections continuing to infinity in the mirrors, de Fleury suddenly stopped and tapped lightly at the base of one of the gilded mirror frames. A panel slid open to a secret corridor.

René had heard gossip of the Palace's secret passages but until now had not given credence to the rumors. He sighed at the thought of spies and servants watching one's movements and noting one's conversations. He had much to learn about politics as he followed the Cardinal through the opening onto an ancient stone staircase.

Water dripped and rats scurried as de Fleury grabbed a lighted torch from the wall sconce and pulled a lever which returned the wall to its original position.

CHAPTER 4
Procuration

CHÂTEAU de WISSEMBOURG, FRANCE

he young girl was not really ugly, but no one had ever considered her very pretty. Of course, because her parents were the ousted King and Queen of Poland who might regain the throne, everyone complimented their child's beauty, though their words were insincere. Marie Leszczyński was, well, adequate, nothing more.

Marie's parents, King Stanisław Leszczyński and Queen Catherine Opalińska, came to grips with their daughter's homeliness. But the time was at hand when their Royal Majesties had to take stock of their daughter and make the best match they could. They were determined to betroth her to a powerful political family in Europe. Families were united for political power and holdings, not beauty or love. Everyone knew that.

Stanislaw planned to leverage this marriage to regain his rightful seat on the throne of Poland and to punish those responsible for the coup and his overthrow. He did not believe the rumors uncovered by his spies until they had read letters indicating his days were numbered in the Palace. When his sponsor Charles XII of Sweden was conquered in Russia, he knew he had to get his family out quickly.

He thought back to those dark days, having to slip out of the Palace in the middle of the night, the shame of losing family heirlooms and the royal jewels, and he and his family being handed off from one royal family to another, first in Germany and now in France.

At the French Château Wissembourg, courtesy of the generosity of his friend the Duc de Bourbon, the ousted Polish monarch had found a home. Even his wife had stopped nagging him. So he decided the girl should be married to a member of the French royal family. He did not care which one, but he must be French. They were the only ones to support him in his great time of need…and shame.

The girl's ample bosom, even in her youth of only ten, complemented her full round figure as she danced round a maypole. The girl softly kicked up her awkward feet ensconced in pink ribboned slippers until she slipped and fell. Her mother wrung her hands as she watched the beautiful brocade dress fashioned with a pearl and ruby bodice slowly deflate around the plump figure sitting in the dust. Her governess, Louise Opalińska, cousin to the ousted Queen, tried to lift the girl who refused to budge.

"Marie Leszczyński, you must come in the house and prepare yourself. Your father will be here any moment." Catherine was about to step outside when the King appeared at the window.

"Marie?" called Stanislaw.

The girl immediately jumped to her feet, waited for her governess to brush the dust from her dress, and calmly walked up to her father. She curtseyed and waited at the door. He patted her head in forgiveness, and she entered the house without another word. Louise rushed in and grabbed Marie's hand, marching her out of the room.

"Will you make the arrangement today? Otherwise, where shall we live?" The Queen was quite worried about their status, and, most importantly, their future lodgings which determined if they maintained their status among other royalty.

"If all goes as planned, there will be a royal wedding in Marie's future. Her very near future," said Stanislaw.

"To the Duke de Bourbon? That would mean we could remain here at Wissembourg. How I would love to stay and continue to wear the latest French fashions." Catherine preened in front of her husband.

"Housing is not a concern. The Duc d'Orleans has offered in any case a generous pension of fifty thousand livres. That would pay for handsome quarters. However, we need the prestige of a royal union. That is the sole solution to regain our rightful position upon the throne."

"I should not miss Poland if we remain here. Just marry the girl quickly, before she gets any uglier. Your family does as they get older, you know," the woman said disdainfully. She added with venom, "This is your entire fault. The poor child has the same face as your grandmother and mother."

Stanislaw did not respond immediately, but then said, "You shall wish she were back in your home the moment she is gone. Give me a few minutes with the Duc, then bring the girl downstairs. Make certain Louise has cleaned her face and covered it with a large ribbon or hat. She will think of something. We must try to present her best assets."

Stanislaw waved her off and retired to his study to think on the matter. He looked bitterly out of the window. Ever since he had been deposed as King of Poland, he and his family had been like wards of lower level royals in Germany, and now France. He yearned to regain his regal status, if not with himself as King, then through his daughter. He thought her becoming a Duchess was a good solution but not as good as being Queen. And he had heard rumors that the royal advisors were quietly seeking a bride for Louis XV.

A knock was heard at the heavy front door and Ludwig, the aging butler, slowly made his way to the door. Ludwig had served Stanislaw since his days on the Polish throne from 1704 until the King was rudely overthrown in 1709. The butler knocked on the door to Stanislaw's study, bowed and offered a silver tray bearing a card. Without a word, Stanislaw took the card, read it and motioned that Ludwig show the man to the drawing room.

Stanislaw slicked back his balding curls, slapped a powdered wig on them, and straightened his waistcoat. Standing at attention at his desk, Stanislaw gave a curt bow to the Duc d'Orleans, who entered, smiling. Ludwig entered and offered wine to both Stanislaw and the Duc, who both readily accepted it. Ludwig knew his place and retreated to a corner, awaiting a signal from his employer.

First the small talk. The host, Stanislaw, began with an inquiry. "How is your family, Monsieur le Duc? All well, I trust?"

The Duc responded in kind. "Very well, Your Majesty. And may we inquire the same about your lovely wife and daughter?"

"Yes, of course. They are both quite fine."

During lapses in their conversation, both men drank their wine freely. Stanislaw gave an almost imperceptible nod to Ludwig, who disappeared quietly out of the room. Minutes later, right on cue, Madame paraded Marie in front of the Duc.

"Monsieur le Duc, my wife the Queen, whom you know."

The Duc bent to kiss Madame's hand then turned his gaze to Marie's bosom while speaking to the Queen, "Majesty. If it is possible, you become younger each time we meet."

Madame gave a slight bow and a smile, gloating at her husband. "Monsieur le Duc, you are too kind."

As predicted, Stanislaw was pleased his ruse worked. "My lovely daughter Marie, Monsieur le Duc."

The Duc regarded the young girl's face which was partly hidden by a large bow. What he could see dazzled in the light reflected by her jewels. He smiled and sighed with relief knowing he could report favorably to the Duke de Bourbon. Then he bowed and kissed Marie's hand. "Enchanté, mademoiselle, enchanté."

Marie responded to the Duc as if she conversed with royalty every day. "Monsieur le Duc, you honor me with your presence. My gracious thanks to you for traveling from Versailles Palace to meet me."

Both the Duc and Stanislaw were startled. Stanislaw frowned as tension flowed throughout his body. Like all children, especially children of royal blood, Marie should be seen and not heard. The blood drained out of Madame's face as she clasped Marie's hand tightly but subtly so as not to alarm the Duc or to upset the delicate negotiations about to take place. Just tightly enough to warn the child not to speak again.

Marie bowed her head, trying not to move a muscle, not even blink. She held her breath, waiting for the Duc or her father to dismiss her. Then the Duc threw his head back and laughed aloud. Stanislaw relaxed and thought, thank goodness she learned manners from the succession of nannies we hired for her. The Queen loosened her grip on Marie's hand and she let out her breath as quietly as possible, stifling the need to gasp for air.

Madame turned to the Duc. "Monsieur we apologize for taking our leave, but we must get our rest for the ball tonight."

Stanislaw looked on with pride as the Duc gave Marie another glance from her chest to her feet, and thankfully did not dwell on the face.

The Duc bowed. "And we shall toast to your beauty again then."

The women curtsied, then sashayed out while Ludwig filled the men's wineglasses again and disappeared behind the women. The heavy carved doors closed, leaving the two men alone.

The niceties over, now it was time to speak in earnest. This time it was the Duc's turn. He leaned forward. "She is everything you said. A pearl just waiting to be polished. Perhaps even a diamond in the rough."

Stanislaw just nodded, sipping his wine, not leaning forward. No need to show too much interest without hearing an offer.

The Duc relaxed, took a long swig of wine and crossed his legs, leaning back in the uncomfortable high-backed, narrow seated chair. "The title of Duchess de Bourbon, naturally," he offered.

"Naturally," repeated Stanislaw.

"An annual pension of course."

"Of course," he replied knowing that to ask the amount was uncivilized.

"Rooms at Court in Versailles, apartments in Paris and a château in Provence."

Stanislaw nodded understandingly. "She does bring a dowry, you know."

The Duc sipped his wine and smiled. "Certainly." Then he stumbled a bit. "Is she still a...she has not been.....?"

Stanislaw nodded reassuringly. "She is untouched."

"Such is one of the Duke's requirements, Your Majesty. You can see why condition rather than age is the major concern."

"I understand. She was too young in the Palace at Warsaw and on our extended stay in Germany. Here in your lovely château she has been under the watchful eye of both her governess and the Queen. In fact, other than myself, no man has seen as much of her as have you today."

The Duc continued, "You know, of course, it would not do if she had a mind of her own and has had dalliances here and there...."

Stanislaw replied firmly but politely. "You have my word as the King of Poland, she is unsullied and ready to be married...to the right man."

The Duc nodded his assent. "Then as a man of honor you will not mind if our physician examines her?"

"Name the day and it shall be done."

"He waits in my carriage. If that is agreeable?"

Stanislaw sputtered before regaining his composure. The Duc was always one step ahead of him. "Br...bring him in, of course."

The Duc bowed. "If the examination is acceptable I shall contact the Duke de Bourbon and arrange for him to dance with her at his ball."

Stanislaw rose and they gave each other the perfunctory royal bows, shaking hands. Ludwig appeared and led the Duc out of the study. As soon as the front door shut, Stanislaw took out a sheet of writing paper, a quill and a pot of ink and started scribbling rapidly. He signed the paper with a flourish, folded it and poured red wax, then stamped it with his royal seal. He tugged on the bell pull and Ludwig appeared. Stanislaw handed him the sealed document. "Take this to Madame de Prie immediately." Ludwig bowed and placed the letter inside his jacket. He rushed as fast as his creaking legs could take him out of the door.

Shortly thereafter, Madame entered with a breathless look on her face. Stanislaw relished the agonizing moment and then gave in because after all, he did love his wife, even if she had borne an ugly daughter.

"He made the offer on behalf of the Duc de Bourbon subject to the...test. If she passes...."

"*When* she passes, you mean to say. She has never been with a man."

"Quite. They shall meet at the ball. However, I have sent word to Madame de Prie to assure other suitors."

Madame was upset. "Other suitors? You had best not topple this apple cart. Our little Marie shall have no other hope. Besides, who could possibly be a better match than the Duc?"

Stanislaw retorted, "Who indeed? Have you not heard the King seeks a bride?"

Madame nearly fainted at the thought of it. "The King? Louis of France marrying our daughter?"

"None other, my dear."

"Of course. The King of France should marry someone who is not related within the usual incestuous bloodline. Someone to give him fine strong sons and assure his succession. An educated young lady who speaks French and is knowledgeable of French culture."

Stanislaw nodded gleefully. "And her religion. Let us not forget the religion. That is most important to the King."

She harrumphed. "Even as he no doubt shall take one mistress after another once his heir is born. But yes, our Marie is a very good Catholic. I have seen to that, you know." She turned to him suddenly. "Will this affect our arrangement with the Duc?" She looked at her palatial surroundings.

Stanislaw replied, "All in good time, dear wife. Madame de Prie is quite close to the royal family. In fact, she is most likely discussing it with the Duc this instant, if Ludwig is as efficient as usual."

Madame slumped into the chair, exhausted by the thought of it. Not simply a royal wedding, but *the* royal wedding of the century. The one everyone would be talking about. The invitation everyone would want. But what would she wear? And where would she get the funds for the wedding dress to outdo all others for Marie?

Stanislaw realized what was running through his wife's head. One cannot be married to a woman for as many years as they had without gaining insight into reading a wife's mind at crucial moments. He reassured her. "It is merely a hint of a proposal. But Madame de Prie is a brilliant schemer. Her plan will make the Duke de Bourbon a hero to the King while he gives up a homely girl in favor of a young beauty chosen by Madame de Prie."

Madame nodded slowly. "Yes, they will all come out ahead in the bargain. But please arrange for the Duc d'Orleans to allow us to remain here."

Stanislaw waved his wife's idea away. "Perhaps he can be the bridegroom by proxy, which will not only save face but make it appear as though he were part of the strategy from the start. His power increases by generously housing the parents of his Queen."

Madame said wistfully, "So we would hold two weddings and our daughter would become Queen of France and Navarre." She turned to her husband, her face gleaming with arrogance. "Those revolutionaries in Warsaw will soon realize they made a huge mistake." She clapped her hands with childlike glee. "We shall regain the throne. We would not need this castle if we had our country again."

Stanislaw nodded and finished the rest of his wine, unwilling to provoke an argument. Not now. They had to work together for this marriage. Besides, he was not certain he wanted his throne back now. He was safe and wealthy here, with everything at his fingertips. Why run a Court with all the intrigue and treachery of Poland when he would be the father of the Queen in the most prestigious and powerful Court of all Europe at Versailles?

*

The marriage by procuration between Marie and King Louis XV, represented by the Duc d'Orleans, was performed at Strasbourg Cathedral, officiated over by His Excellency Cardinal de Rohan, Grand Almoner of France.

Marie's face-to-face wedding to the King in person occurred at Fontainebleau Palace on September 5, 1725. Later written accounts would describe Marie's ceremonial dress as silver brocade embroidered with precious stones, a gift of the King.

Louise Opalińska was brought to Versailles as the Queen's Lady-in-waiting. She utilized her knowledge of the intrigues and political sabotage she had observed Marie's parents implementing during their reign. Lady Louise molded the headstrong young girl into a politically knowledgeable monarch whose marriage was to last for decades and produce many children. The former governess became the second most powerful woman at Court. But Louise was much more approachable for favors and gifts than the Queen.

The family name was changed from the difficult Polish version "Leszczyński" to the French "Lecszinka."

The deposed King and Queen never discussed the Polish throne again.

CHAPTER 5
Winterberries

VERSAILLES

he sounds of footsteps grew closer to the rodent hunting for food near the stairway. The rat slipped into a nearby pool fed by the constant drops from above. Crawling through the water to the other side, the creature scurried into a tiny crack in the stone wall. It opened into the Palace's bustling kitchen filled with just the delights the hungry rat sought.

René followed the magenta-clothed Cardinal, their torchlights dancing on the moss-covered steps until de Fleury stopped at the bottom of the underground passage. He held up his torch. They were at a crossroads where five tunnels converged at the stairs. René wondered where they all led.

De Fleury only waited to hear René's steps behind him and then turned right into a narrow passageway.

"This way," he said, knowing Le Blanc's intuitive mind would be calculating possibilities as to where they might end up. No doubt he believed they were going to the King's chambers forthwith. But of two things the Cardinal was absolutely certain -- that René had no inkling of their true destination, and that the young man would be overwhelmed with joy when they arrived there.

René followed closely behind as the Cardinal led the way through a dank winding passageway. Except for the light moving a few feet in front of them, they were surrounded by darkness. There was no sound except the steps of their boots and the interminable dripping water along the stone walls. The Cardinal walked in such long strides, spryly and quickly for a man of his advanced years, that the much younger René had difficulty keeping pace.

They came to another divergence where their tunnel opened into four directions. The Cardinal, without hesitating, took the tunnel to the left and shortly thereafter stopped, hanging his torch in one of the iron sconces imbedded into the stone wall. His bejeweled rings flashed prisms of color in the light. René followed the Cardinal's lead, placing his torch into a sconce.

A soft grating in the wall could be heard as the Cardinal opened a peephole. He gently pushed René forward to look through the opening in the wall. Le Blanc was completely unprepared for the vision in front of his eyes.

A younger version of the goddess in the painting wearing a gossamer gown walked across a room. His gasp of surprise was audible. She could not be a day over sixteen, he thought, though she had the elegance of a well-bred woman of greater age. He watched her every move until she disappeared from his view through an adjacent doorway. He craned his neck looking through the grating in all directions but she did not reappear. He wondered who the woman was. He had to meet her.

Only then did René notice her chamber, elegant, tasteful and filled with only fine, expensive things. The room was a large one, with tall glass windows covered with thick brocade drapes, some pulled back with satin ties to reveal lace undercurtains. Her bed was in the corner of the room near the windows, a large canopied platform laden with mattresses and satin coverlets, with multi-colored silk pillows scattered about. The side posts held lace curtains embroidered with pearls and tied with brocade tassels, easily released for privacy from the many maids he imagined served the Lady. He saw luxurious velvet settees punctuated with silk pillows on which lay many gowns, shoes, hats, bags and other ladieswear.

At the back of the room was a large dressing table holding crystal trays of silver brushes, combs and hair ornaments. Next to it stood a gold-leaf trimmed mirror as tall as a man. Throughout the room were marble tables and tufted chaises covered with jewelry boxes and more apparel, hand-carved wooden armoires that displayed a rainbow of clothing, many times more than on the settees. He noted large crystal decanters filled with wines and silver trays with plates of food and bowls of fruit. This was truly the room of a royal princess, or one who was treated as such.

Eugenie re-appeared and directed a train of maids to light candles in tall silver candlesticks in all corners of the room and near the bed. In the twinkling candlelight he saw the servants pile the clothing into their arms before they exited into the adjoining room twinkling in candlelight. They bowed to their mistress and closed the door behind them.

René surmised the clothes would require many large trunks. That indicated she was going on a long voyage, perhaps leaving the Palace forever. He was too late! He was determined to ask the Cardinal to arrange an immediate introduction, and more than that, to arrange a match. But he could not bring himself to turn away from her beauty. Not just yet.

The woman-child was alone in the large room, an innocent child lost in a paradise of wealth. Unaware of René's gaze, she walked to the mirror and turned several times. Her face saddened when, her hands pressed the fabric close to her body tracing the shapes of her breasts and belly. When the candlelight shone through the filmy fabric René was mesmerized at the sight of her enticing curves, her porcelain arms, her perfectly shaped legs. He pulled away. He should not be privy to such an intimate view of his goddess but clearly he was instantly smitten.

"I have never seen such skin, pure as new snow. And her lips are redder and more luscious than winterberries."

The Cardinal nodded with approval. This young man was the right choice. He was honorable and would protect her. "So she looks familiar to you?"

Le Blanc nodded, embarrassed that the Prime Minister understood his passion for the woman in the tableau, but he never dreamed she existed in the flesh. "She is infinitely more beautiful than the painting, Your Excellency."

"From the moment she arrived at Court her startling beauty inspired the Royal Artist Jean-Baptiste Pater to paint her. He imagined her more mature, of course, but quite the beauty." He chuckled. "Jealousy raged in the Court for quite some time after His Majesty hung it in the Hall of Mirrors."

René turned back to the grating. "The Lady's beauty is ethereal. Dare I ask her name?"

The Cardinal complied willingly. "She is the Queen's cousin, Lady Eugenie de Beaufort. And she is also a relation of His Majesty."

René believed his relation to the King and the Lady's to the Queen could not be just a cruel coincidence. Surely their ancestry had ordained their destiny to be together.

The Cardinal snapped the peephole shut and lifted the torch from its wall sconce motioning for René to follow. They retraced their steps toward the stairway. René turned wistfully to look back to the now dark hallway.

De Fleury said, "She is to be betrothed at Court tomorrow."

René's heart sank to the cold stone floor. He leaned against the wall choking his disappointment. The Cardinal looked at him and realized it was his spiritual heart, not the physical one, which caused him pain.

Le Blanc winced as he asked, "Who is the most fortunate bridegroom?"

"Why 'tis you, Lord Le Blanc de Verdure. You shall marry her."

He fell to his knees, bowing before the Cardinal. "Excellency, I am unworthy to be chosen."

"Surely you do not refuse His Majesty's request?"

"No, certainly not. I am always at His Majesty's command in all things. I only meant…."

Cardinal de Fleury interrupted. "So my Lord accepts the King's proposal to marry the Lady?"

René kissed the largest of the Cardinal's rings. "With eternal gratitude, I am your humble servant and that of the King. And she has consented?"

"She shall obey His Majesty's command. But I believe she will be pleased with the match."

René wanted to assure there were no impediments. "If both of us are related to His Majesty…?"

De Fleury waved off his concern, "Not to a questionable degree." He smiled, "However, rest assured we could have obtained a Papal bull of dispensation had it been necessary."

"His Holy Father knows of this?"

The Cardinal put his hands on René's shoulder. "I am here, of course. No one but a priest should serve as Prime Minister for our Catholic Majesty."

"How is it I have never seen Lady de Beaufort at Court?"

"She was presented only this year. You must have crossed her path without realizing."

The young man shook his head. "If so, I would have never left her side."

The Cardinal shrugged and led René up the winding staircase. At the top landing Fleury pulled the lever and the wall panel slid open.

The two men stepped back into the Hall of Mirrors and after de Fleury had closed the wall they both walked down the corridor to stand in front of the large painting.

"Her image is so beautiful she seems not of this world," said Le Blanc. "But why the urgency to marry?"

He took René by the arm and began walking down the long corridor. "His Highness awaits. So much to prepare and precious little time."

René abruptly remembered his profession. "My students! I must arrange a replacement."

De Fleury responded without missing a stride. "It has already been done."

René nodded with a smile. "I should have thought as much."

As the two men walked together, their images reflected through the hall in the opulent mirrors. Sieur René of the royal house of Le Blanc de Verdure was ecstatic. The goddess in the painting hung in the Hall of Mirrors at Versailles Palace was to become his wife. He anticipated giving her the lifetime of happiness she deserved, even if it was away from the Court. He wondered if she would agree to leave Versailles and her friends and family at Court, whoever they might be.

So many questions arose in his mind as he looked at Pater's "La Fête Champêtre" once again. He saw a beautiful Eugenie fifteen years hence, aging gracefully. He looked forward to sharing many years with her and the great number of children he hoped they would have together.

The Cardinal stirred him from his reverie. "Perhaps you have guessed that, as with all matters at Court, there is more." The Cardinal guided René to the painting.

"Tell me what you see."

"Angelic beauty, childlike innocence...."

The Cardinal placed his hand on René's arm. "Surely you saw otherwise in her person?"

René was puzzled. He shook his head. "No, Your Excellency."

"She is with child, of course."

CHAPTER 6
Plague

MARSEILLE and PARIS

leeping on a straw mat in his small cell, Père Rivière was woken by a bell ringing at the entrance to the presbytery. He plodded his way forward, surprised to find a King's courier at the door. The nervous young man handed the priest a letter sealed with the crest of Cardinal de Fleury. Père bowed in thanks, intending to close the door.

The messenger spoke anxiously. "His Excellency bid me to wait until you answer. But holy sir, please quickly. I saw many dead bodies and I aim to leave as fast as I came."

Père Rivière said, "I understand. Are you hungry? Can I prepare a basket of food for your return journey?"

The messenger shook his head and stood stiffly inside the door, looking around as if he expected ghosts to appear.

The Cardinal had written with the great flourish of his hand:

"My Dear Brother in Christ Père Nicolas Rivière,
With regret it has been decided to close your Parish Church. You are requested to take all sacred articles and vestments you can carry and make your way to meet me in Paris at Notre Dame Cathedral by month's end. After the Church formalities and our meeting, a coach will take you to Le Havre where you shall voyage to your new Parish in Grand Pré, Nova Scotia, in the New World. Do not fail to arrive this

month as the ship sails soon thereafter. You may leave the Church unlocked for
those poor souls who seek God's mercy and love.
  God we serve. In God's name we do all things,
  Cardinal André-Hercule de Fleury."

Only minutes later the priest had written a simple response.

"Most Holy Excellency,
With God's help I shall arrive timely at the Cathedral.
Your obedient and humble servant in Christ,
  Père Nicolas Rivière."

Without waiting to seal it, the priest handed the folded paper to the messenger, who slipped it into his waistcoat, jumped onto his horse and stopped for nothing and no one. The sound of galloping soon faded until it could be heard no more.

Père Rivière stood at the door for a while, he did not know how long, remembering the last months of his five-year posting as the priest at Saint Peter's Church. His small waterfront parish was frequented by the dregs of society that included beggars, thieves, harbor workers, sailors, prostitutes, barkeeps and an occasional maritime pilot and crew. The priest prayed for their salvation and gave comfort where he could, though many a confession had burned his ears.

The city fathers did not realize the Black Death, which had taken the lives of nearly half the city's citizens between 1720 and 1722, had reappeared. It was only when victims went to hospitals with blackened tongues that the authorities took action. But by that time, tens of thousands of men, women, and children had fallen victim to the illness. There was no discrimination as to age, status, sex or wealth. Many had tried to reach the Church in time for a final blessing but most ended up on the cobblestones outside. Over the last few months, Père Rivière found that of his hundred or so parishioners, only a dozen attended Mass. Gradually the number dwindled to a handful and then to none.

City inspectors worked with physicians and traced the origin of the Plague back to an infected rat on a merchant transport that had arrived with spices and exotic goods from the Levant. The cargo was unloaded and transported throughout the region, while the crew stayed in the city for weeks. They quarantined crews from disembarking and cargo from entering or exiting the harbor but by that time the Black Death had taken its toll on Marseille and the surrounding region of southern France.

Although no new cases had been reported to the hospitals in the last few weeks, those who had been most recently exposed were still dying in the streets. The quarantine had been lifted, subject to arduous inspections of vessels, crew and goods before anything or anyone was allowed on the wharves of Marseille.

Père Rivière looked out upon the cobblestones and saw the last vestiges of the disease. Even with the smaller number of bodies than usual he repeated his daily ritual. Taking a jar of blessed oil from the table near the door he walked outside among the dead. He made the Sign of the Cross in the cool morning air above the bloated rotting bodies, blessing them with drops of oil for the last time. Administering the sacrament of the dying for victims of the Plague was the most sorrowful duty he had ever performed as a priest. Then he dropped to his knees and prayed for those whose names he would never know.

Private burials were forbidden by the city fathers, who sent carts to pick up the dead. As the carts rolled through the city in the morning before the sun spread the stink of the corpses, Père Rivière had learned to bless the dead early.

When he finally rose, he saw a large man-child lying on the hard cobblestones next to the corpse of a woman. He was unsure if his eyes were playing tricks on him because the boy seemed to be breathing. He walked toward the figure that awoke with a start.

Slowly, a large horse-drawn cart made its way up the cobblestone street. The cart's two occupants, a driver and a cartman, wore red-stained shirts and breeches, large bloody gloves, and cloths tied around their head to cover the nose and mouth. The driver stopped the horses across from the Church. The men stepped wearily from the cart, picked up a body and unceremoniously tossed it into the back of their carriage. Walking to the next body, they saw it was a small child. The driver picked it up over his shoulder and tossed it into the cart.

The other cartman was offended. "You got a child?"

The driver walked to the next body, this time an infant. He grabbed it by the foot and carried upside down in one hand. "Ain't got one, ain't want one."

The cartman replied, "And you got no heart neither. They's just little ones."

"We gets paid per set of bones, big or little. Dead is dead, ain't no matter their size. We gots a job to do. You wants to get paid, shut yer trap and do it."

The cartman knew he had said enough. He needed the money for potions he hoped would keep his wife and two children safe. Without further delay the men cleared the other bodies from the cobblestones, then walked up to the priest and the boy, kneeling beside the body of what was once a comely woman. When the men stooped to pick up the body, the cartman nodded in sympathy to the boy.

"She is with the angels now, son."

Sun nodded teary-eyed, wondering how he knew his name. He remembered something and grabbed a piece of jewelry from the woman's neck, a very unusual necklace. The driver cursed his luck that he did not see it first. That would have made his lady friend very happy.

Père Rivière made the Sign of the Cross over the cartman. "God bless and keep you and your family safe."

The cartman bowed slightly. "Thank you, Père."

The driver nodded to the cartman and they picked up the body, then walked it over to the cart, tossing it on top of the stack. The street was empty and their cart was full.

"A good day's work is what we done here." The driver pulled the cart away as the cartman turned around and waved to Sun. The boy smiled through his tears. Père Rivière took his hand and brought him into the Church.

At the Marseille port, only one vessel had been cleared to leave with cargo -- Captain François Jacques' barge, "La Belle Vie." More than a dozen other vessels, all much larger -- sloops, brigs, and full-masted ships -- sat in the harbor with crew on board, calling out to inspectors, who ignored them as they continued to inspect goods already in the port warehouse. Merchants offered bribes to the customs men who refused the money and only inspected merchandise in order of arrival.

Captain Jacques waited as the inspectors stamped the documents releasing his goods for shipment. That had been done only after they had completed a time-consuming examination of each barrel, carton, box, crate and package, down to letters and wrapped parcels. Finally the Captain received his official clearance to leave port with the merchandise. Elated, he signaled his crew on deck to load the goods onto his vessel.

Jacques regularly carried goods out of Marseille to other Mediterranean ports as well as to those in Portugal, northern Spain and northern France. Sailing to the French port of Honfleur he navigated his small boat to Le Havre from whence he followed the Seine River to the heart of Paris. His flat-bottomed, low-draft vessel gave him a great advantage over the large oceangoing cargo ships. The size, weight and design of those vessels prevented sailing all the way up the Seine. Some could only sail as far as Honfleur or Le Havre. Others were still small enough to reach the medieval city of Rouen and offload their goods to overland transports for delivery to merchants in the City of Light.

This would be his last run from Marseille to Paris, and the most lucrative. He planned to move permanently to Le Havre where his only remaining sibling lived.

The towns and villages in Provence near Marseille had re-enacted their "Black Death penalty" laws originally instituted in 1720 which forbade anyone, on pain of instant death, to transport people or goods from Marseille across the "Plague walls." These walls, two meters tall and seventy centimeters thick, had been constructed around the harbor town to prevent the spread of the disease into the surrounding settlements. Under these circumstances, the only way to move goods out of the city was by water, and then only after a thorough inspection by the harbor. Merchants with fine quality goods had no other means to send merchandise to their buyers.

Since Captain Jacques was the first boat to be cleared the vendors had increased their payment to ten times the normal fee to ship goods to Paris. No crops or seasonal items for him -- the Captain took only the best and most expensive goods and he charged for it. But he was ready to relocate back to the city of his birth, Le Havre. Jacques figured he could earn a good living by making short runs along on the Seine River from Le Havre to Paris and all the towns in between.

As he was getting ready to cast off, Captain Jacques heard a voice crying out to him. "Wait for us, Captain Jacques, please wait." He looked around and saw Père Rivière scurrying towards him, holding the hand of a lumbering man-child, and waving his other arm. The Captain knew the priest from attending Mass at St. Peter's Church when he was in port on a Sunday. Jacques stopped his men from pushing off as the priest ran up to the boat, bending over to catch his breath. The Captain saw the boy crying. He appeared to be dim-witted but he asked him softly, "Can I help you son?"

Sun brightened at another person who knew his name. He nodded slowly. "Maman with angels. Me go with you."

CHAPTER 7
Chambers

VERSAILLES

wo pairs of expensive buckled shoes walked in symmetry through the Hall of Mirrors. Cardinal de Fleury leaned down to Lord Le Blanc. "As His Majesty's Consul and Notaire, you shall escort new colonists to Grand Pré on the eastern coast of what was our French territory in the New World. Since the King ceded Acadia to the English under the Treaty of Utrecht in 1713, you will live as neutrals under British rule. At least for the time being. "

René asked quietly, "So it is true? We are on the brink of war with England again?"

The Cardinal replied thoughtfully, "You shall learn the whole sordid story soon enough."

He urged René to walk ahead of him towards two massive carved oak doors manned by two interior royal guards. They were older and stronger than the younger guards posted on the exterior of the palace and grounds, and they were well-trained in the weapons they carried.

The doors led to the King's public outer chamber, where petitioners from throughout the country waited, sometimes for days, to present their grievances to His Majesty. Walking in the midst of the common folk, he saw farmers, merchants, women with children, a blacksmith with his anvil and many others. Some prayed, some slept curled on the floor and many ate food brought for the journey or bought in the village outside the Palace. And though he read anxiety, fear and concern on their faces, each exhibited a glimmer of hope that the King would make things right again for them.

De Fleury nodded imperceptibly to the guards at the next set of doors, which swung open so that the Cardinal and René could walk into the King's public inner chambers.

At the far end of the room, another set of closed doors was protected by heavily armed guards. There stood long lines of noblemen holding papers or large boxes tied with satin ribbons, no doubt gifts for favors received or to be requested. It seemed each powdered wig and gold-trimmed jacket was more ostentatious and expensive than the last. Elegant ladies boasting tall bejeweled pompadours stood near the men to comfort or flirt, or both. Other lords and ladies without petitions milled about in a genteel atmosphere quite different from the outer chamber. Here servants offered wine in crystal goblets and a variety of meats and cheeses and pastries on silver trays. While a harpist played in the main hall, musicians roamed from one of the inner rooms to another, playing lutes or softly singing tunes.

De Fleury leaned down and whispered to René, "I shall meet you at the next door." He pointed to the opposite end of the room from where they were. Then the Cardinal walked behind a curtain, watching the Court's reaction to René. He thought the noblemen would ignore Le Blanc, not realizing the authority he had, which would soon be increased. Power was the only thing noblemen respected and craved. When faced with an unknown, the better action was to pretend not to see than to confront.

As René walked boldly forward, the nobles turned away, standing their ground. They chose to ignore the obviously inexperienced young nobleman. To their amazement, Le Blanc took out the parchment, feigning reading it. The royal seal was visible throughout the room and the nobles decided to err on the side of caution, not wishing to risk the King's disfavor. They were like bees in a hive, flitting about, soon revealing an open path to the door. When the Cardinal approached, the aristocrats bowed deeply and moved aside to reveal René standing by the ornate doors.

The Cardinal smiled. René has used his wits, he thought, but he will surely need that and more where he is going. The guards opened the doors slightly, enough to let the two men pass. Ladies craned their necks and the taller lords peered past the doors but they were quickly shut, cutting off any view. The bees returned to their places in the hive, closing the path to prevent anyone else from moving ahead in line.

René and the Cardinal walked through the doors flanked by more interior guards. They were in the King's private ministerial chambers. René again reached inside his pocket for his parchment but the Cardinal shook his head. "No need, my Lord. His Majesty expects us."

De Fleury directed René to the next entryway, not wasting time to speak with anyone in the room. The King's ministers made this room their own and each stood and bowed to him. He nodded curtly to the men, who regained their seats on narrow velvet chairs. Their aides, secretaries and couriers sat on wooden benches, awaiting their next assignment. Tables were laden with food and drink but the ministers were above serving themselves. Servants took orders, filling them at the table and returning to the ministers with trays overflowing with tasty dishes and wine.

In this room Laurent Arnaud supervised the wait staff, assuring that each minister was taken care of, chiding a servant for not filling the wine glass to exact specifications or skimping on portions when serving the elite guests. He also made sure that when the servants were not busy they served the lowly assistants on the wooden seats. He was living proof that hard work could result in advancement at the Palace and he wanted as many friendly faces at Court as he could count.

Laurent's fastidiousness and efficiency did not go without notice by the ministers, who appreciated his respect for them and their positions, more so than their colleagues. Laurent found himself being asked to procure certain foods or goods for some of the ministers, and to negotiate a transaction between members of Court or ministers as well. He had built a reputation as a trustworthy gentleman.

They walked toward the opposite wall, where four guards and a herald stood, his trumpet at the ready, at the large carved wooden door with bas relief carved figures trimmed with gold leaf. The herald bowed to the Cardinal, who whispered to him before the trumpeter slipped through the partially open doors. René and the Cardinal heard the trumpet sound and the herald's announcement. "His Royal Majesty's servants present themselves. His Excellency Prime Minister of all France and Cardinal of the Holy Church of Rome, André-Hercule de Fleury, and René LeBlanc, Sieur de la Verdure, Royal Notary."

René strained to hear the response, but instead of the voices he expected, he heard the muted sounds of splashing in a tub and music. He looked at the Cardinal, amused at René's look of incredulity. The herald returned and nodded to the guards, who opened the doors slightly to let the two men in. Once inside the King's private chambers, René saw the King in an oversized porcelain bath, with two effusive manservants fussing over him, one pouring a bucket of hot water and the other holding soaps and towels.

Strolling minstrels played lutes and several harpists struck their chords softly. Nubile young women in Grecian gowns refilled the King's various goblets -- one for champagne, another for Bordeaux and several others on a gold table next to the tub.

"Do come in to our chambers, do come in," smiled the King.

René and the Cardinal bowed to the waist and approached the King.

His Majesty was curious. "Well? Well? What news today?"

René was about to speak of the wondrous Lady de Beaufort but the Cardinal knew the King had more urgent matters in mind. De Fleury made a sweeping bow. "Everything His Majesty requested has been accomplished or acceded to."

René bowed and waited for the King to allow him to rise. The King acknowledged him with a wave, then nodded to his two manservants, who covered him in a robe and lifted him out of the tub. The King, still dripping wet, was followed by the dressers, who wiped his wet footprints from the beautiful parquet floor with its inlaid gold fleur de lis motif.

Louis XV climbed into his bed and reclined. He bid the Cardinal and René to sit on the footstools at the head of the bed. The wine girls presented the King with a selection of bottles, from which the King pointed out a champagne. Opening the bottle, the girl served it to a royal taster. When he did not fall to the floor, she filled goblets and placed them daintily on a tray which she offered to the King. He gladly took two goblets and started drinking one. De Fleury and René were each given a goblet of champagne, which they sipped sparingly.

The King directed all of his servants out and they glided or scampered out of sight into the adjoining room. When he heard the massive door close, he leaned forward and tossed a torn, stained document to de Fleury. The Cardinal perused the letter quickly and looked up, alarmed.

The King nodded. "The English demand allegiance of our French nationals on our land that we discovered with Verrazzano and Champlain. That we discovered! If not for that meddlesome Anne, we would not have English troops on our soil; our soil!"

De Fleury and René nodded gravely.

The King continued, "They demand unconditional allegiance to their mad King George, no less. Their mad King!"

De Fleury quietly remarked. "The English violate the very terms of the treaty that Queen Anne signed. King George claims the treaty is invalid because his ancestor created twelve new positions for a majority vote in their House of Lords. Whatever the reason, this violation cannot stand, Majesty."

Louis angrily repeated, "Cannot stand? This violation *must* not stand. It must not stand."

The Cardinal leaned forward and whispered to the King. "His Majesty's dear cousin is the last hope for peace."

The King looked over at René and nodded, convinced as well. "Yes, the last hope for peace; the last hope."

The Cardinal added. "Lord Le Blanc de Verdure has served His Majesty well as his Royal Notary here. Perhaps if he were named Royal Consul as well as His Majesty's Notaire in Acadia he would have more authority and command more respect."

"Excellent idea, excellent idea. Arrange a ceremony at Court when the engagement is announced. Thank you for your service, André. You have never steered me in the wrong direction." He turned to René, who knelt to kiss the King's ring.

René responded humbly, "I am grateful to His Majesty, grateful beyond words, for naming me Consul and consort to Her Majesty's cousin. I shall seek a peaceful resolution to the English problem without any French citizens taking the unqualified Oath of Allegiance to Great Britain which does not guarantee the freedoms in the Treaty of Utrecht."

The Cardinal raised another issue. "And the Governor-General of New France, Your Majesty?"

The King looked at him, furrowed his brow and then nodded. "Ah, yes, New France. We shall inform the Marquis de Beauharnois in Québec City that our new Consul may call upon him for aid where necessary."

De Fleury hesitated. Louis looked at him. "Well? Anything more?"

The Cardinal replied, "Le Moyne de Bienville? The Governor of His Majesty's Louisiana territory."

"He is in our new settlement of New Orleans now, is he not?"

The Cardinal nodded with a bow.

The King shook his head. "We see no reason that he could be of service to our Consul in the far north." The King nodded. The interview was over.

The Cardinal motioned that René take his leave. The new Consul bowed deeply as he walked backwards out of the door.

When he was out of sight, the King turned to his trusted Minister. "You were right as usual, de Fleury, as usual. A distant cousin of recent acquaintance, hardly known by our Court so they have not had time to plot their intrigues and sabotage before he takes his post. Excellent choice, excellent choice."

De Fleury responded with a bow, "His discretion is our ally, Majesty. And his loyalty is beyond reproach."

When the King nodded affirmatively the Cardinal continued, "He is the man for His Majesty's work in Acadia. And besides, he is already in love with his bride. A man in love is easily manipulated. He is at the command of His Highness as he wishes."

The King clapped his hands. "Even better than we expected, de Fleury; even better than expected."

De Fleury stood to leave but the King took his arm. "And for this you *shall* have your new cathedral."

"Not for me, Majesty, but to honor God for blessing His Majesty's holy reign."

The King then pulled the bell cord. Suddenly, the back room door swung open and a flock of servants entered to serve the King's pleasure. The Cardinal hid a smile as he bowed and walked himself out of the door backwards, as René had done earlier.

The King was quickly surrounded again by doting staff. The lute players and harpists began their music again. The Grecian-robed servants poured more hot water into the bath as the manservants helped the portly monarch out of his robes and back into the tub. A cool goblet of champagne was placed in the King's hand as servants rubbed warm oil on the King's shoulders.

He mused, "De Fleury has come far since being my tutor. He assured us that we would value his teachings of philosophy and the strategy of war, but how did he know those lessons would be applied nearly as often inside the castle walls as outside against our enemies?"

The King made a decision. "Enough thinking and strategizing for one day." Leaning back in the tub, Louis relaxed. The herald bowed, looking expectantly at the King to receive the next petitioner but Louis shook his head. He had finished for the day.

The herald walked out of the chambers with trepidation. He feared telling waiting noblemen to return the following day. They could be as nasty as a mob with torches and pitchforks.

CHAPTER 8
Court

VERSAILLES

nside the Palace, the Petit Royal Chamber was brightly glowing with dozens of candles. A multitude of voices was interlaced with soft chamber music played by the King's musicians. Court members in their finery wanted to see and be seen. Exquisitely dressed Lords observed aristocratic Ladies dressed in silks and brocades. Women's jewels glimmered in the candlelight as they made their presence known. Bobbing wigs bowed to flirtatious fans as voluminous skirts rustled, gliding to and fro, their owners giggling and gossiping in small groups.

Several Lords offered private banter to Ladies while muted voices and laughter echoed through the intimate hall. Gracefully flickering her fan against her face, an aristocratic woman would cover all but her eyes, hinting at mystery and the unknown. Once a noble responded with a nod, a bow or for the very boldest of royals, a whispered word, the woman would snap the fan shut, then quickly flip it open, catching the attention of all around her.

The courtly dance had begun, the eternal game of cat and mouse. No matter how willing, a Lady could never be seen to be the enticer. Chivalry had to remain in effect at all costs, and a Lord was the undisputed master of this domain. This method of flirting through subtle eye or hand movements rather than questions and responses was the first dance everyone learned at

Court, a delicate balance for those whose spouses were also at the Palace. Most noblemen had firmly ensconced their wives and children in châteaus and on estates far from Versailles. Those who lived in Paris were kept in satins and jewels on condition of remaining there, never to disturb their husbands at Court.

Royal Artist Jean-Baptiste Pater seemed oblivious to the birds and bees fluttering and buzzing around him. He concentrated intensely on sketching the scene at his easel, near the royal thrones of King Louis XV and Queen Marie Lecszinka.

Suddenly, the members of Court hushed themselves and bowed deeply. The strains of the musicians' instruments ceased quickly. The Cardinal led a procession through the doorway as the nobility bowed and parted to make way.

In the center of the room, the Cardinal stepped to the side as the King and Queen ignored the parting crowd and swept grandly onto their canopied platforms. The Cardinal quietly followed the monarchs, flanking the King's right side.

The royal entourage was waiting near the throne and upon the King's nod, they joined their respective monarchs. Royal pages fanned them with huge ostrich feathers. Ladies-in-waiting sat on small tuffets near the Queen, with Lady Louise and Lady Véronique seated nearest to Her Majesty. The King's valets and attendants stood behind him. Armed guards stood at the doors and corners of the thrones within three feet of the sovereigns.

Following at a respectful distance behind the monarchs, René escorted Eugenie through the throng. She wore gold brocade intertwined with silver threads and a diamond and ruby necklace at her throat. A collective gasp emanated from the crowd. Several Lords were so struck with her beauty that they dropped their hats in their hands. They were quickly brought back to reality by quick taps of fluttering fans.

Several of the Queen's Ladies-in-waiting whispered jealously behind their fans and edged farther away from Eugenie. Lady Louise whispered to the Countess de Berri, who looked shocked. How did she learn such things? Then she remembered Louise's familial relationship to the Queen. Of course Her Majesty would confide in Louise. Who else could she trust? But why did Louise reveal such a secret about Lady Eugenie? Did everyone know her condition?

Suddenly, the members of Court hushed themselves as they watched René lead Eugenie up to the throne. The whispers began again, this time louder as the audience members looked at one another quizzically, trying to understand the situation. How could they have been caught unaware of this important occasion? Maids and valets whom they bribed for information, such as the news announced today, would be properly chastised after the ceremony.

At the thrones, René bowed and kissed the King's proffered ring. Eugenie curtsied deeply, her eyes cast down to the floor. When she did dare to look up at the King, she felt the Queen's piercing eyes on her and she quickly looked downward again.

After the King slipped a ring from his hand onto René's finger, the bridegroom kissed the King's hand. Then René turned to the Queen, bowing his head. She offered her hand to him, so pale and delicate. As he kissed it, she whispered to him. "You honor the Queen, removing such a harlot, our cousin, from our Court. You alone are welcome in our sight in the future."

René raised his gaze ever so slightly, his head still bowed respectfully. He returned a whispered response. "I thank Her Majesty with all my heart. But if I return, I shall proudly bring my wife with me."

The Queen frowned slightly, nearly cracking the perfectly set powder caked onto her face. She leaned towards the King, but he subtly waved her back. She submitted to his domination, as she always had, with a quiet sigh and improved posture, eyes forward, looking at everyone, seeing no one in particular. If this was how her husband wanted it, he would have it. But she had gotten her way. The problem had been solved.

The King stood and bid Eugenie to approach. Immediately members of Court started quietly buzzing with signs of disapproval, shaking of heads, movement away from Eugenie as she moved forward. The Queen slowly, stiffly, rose at the King's side without so much as a sideward glance at Eugenie. Ladies-in-Waiting gossiped behind their brisk-moving fans. Lords overtly snickered as their bobbing wigs passed the gossip along, until the entire Court seemed to know a secret. Or did they?

The King gently took Eugenie's hand. Their eyes lifted slowly, methodically, to focus on each other. As they drowned in each other's gaze, the King placed Eugenie's hand in René's. "The King grants his blessing and his most fervent wishes for a long and happy union." His Majesty turned from Eugenie's gaze but not before pointedly commanding the pair, "Behold your future husband and wife." The young couple looked at each other. Eugenie's heart sank. René's leapt with joy.

King Louis applauded. The Queen forcibly followed his lead. Quiet but polite applause followed throughout the Court. Cardinal de Fleury stepped forward and covered Eugenie's and René's hands with his.

"His Royal Highness, Louis Fifteen, King of France and Navarre, declares his Royal Assent to the marriage of Lord René Le Blanc, Sieur de Verdure and Lady Eugenie de Beaufort in a fortnight. The wedding shall be a private affair in the King's Private Chapel followed by a marriage banquet. All are invited to the feast processional, after which the Court is admonished to respect the wishes of the King and the privacy of the happy couple with their invited dinner guests."

Tradition and gentility dictated that all the members of Court present a gift to the newlyweds, even if they were not invited to the wedding ceremony or the feast. Those who were not fortunate enough to dine would walk single file past the tantalizing food displays then exit the hall after the gifts were unwrapped. The Cardinal's invitation was no less than the King's command which prompted loud buzzing throughout the Chamber.

René was oblivious to the chatter, consumed in his ardor for Eugenie. She quickly returned his gaze, daring a short smile. Then she turned to the King, who was leaning to hear his wife's whispering soliloquy. The Queen chided Eugenie with her eyes, even as she spoke to the King behind her hand, cupped at her mouth.

Eugenie dropped her eyes and looked no further at either the King or René. Satisfied, the Queen leaned back. King Louis gave more than a passing glance at Eugenie but she did not dare look up. The wrath of the Queen, once so gentle and friendly with her, would be too much to bear. And Eugenie could not risk losing this marriage to not only a handsome man but one who seemed intent on loving her without guise, without demands and without guilt.

Eugenie only moaned to herself that she had not met René a year earlier. René, hearing her moan, reached out his hand to reassure her. She looked up at him and smiled as if to say, "All is as well as it can be under such circumstances."

Cardinal de Fleury bid Eugenie to sit in a chair near the Queen as he motioned to René to kneel on the step near the throne. De Fleury looked to the King, who walked over to René.

King Louis looked out over his Court. He saw them murmuring behind fans and whispering through their teeth and he smiled. They did not have any inkling of what was coming next. Leave it to de Fleury, he thought. The man is a brilliant strategist keeping the nobility on edge. They fear him…and me…because they do not know what we are thinking. As it should be.

The Cardinal, carrying a large bejeweled chest and a rolled document with the red wax royal seal, stood next to the King. De Fleury blessed the box and the scroll, then handed them to Louis.

The King announced loudly, "We proclaim you, René Le Blanc, Sieur de Verdure, in addition to being our Royal Notary, to be appointed as our Royal Consul for all our colonists of Acadia, now Nova Scotia, for as long as you shall live. Take this Royal seal and represent us against our enemies, renew our friendships with our allies the Mi'Kmaq First Nation, and strengthen the faith of our citizens in our name through God's help. Amen." He handed René the box and the document.

René repeated, "Amen."

Then the King looked expectantly at the Court. The aristocrats all repeated the refrain, "Amen."

The Court was in awe. They never expected such an unassuming noble as the Notary to become the King's most powerful ambassador in the New World. Representing France in British territory assured him of the King's ear and support even more so than the governorship of New France or that distant outpost in the Louisiana territory.

Then the buzzing began. Was this a sign that war was imminent? Nobles and Ladies debated the question.

Avoiding talk of politics, Lady Louise whispered to Madame de Prie. Baron Delaveau leaned as far left as his birdlike neck would allow. He leered at overhearing the conversation. Lady Louise Opalińska had never been known to mince words but this? This was juicy gossip indeed. A beautiful and young Lady with child by an unknown father?

The Baron was a gambling man so he proposed a friendly wager with the two noblewomen. The first to learn the name of the father would win all the money.

Louise and Madame de Prie were quick to accept.

Louise had her eye on some new baubles. She knew just the right moment when the Queen would take her sleeping potion and retire to bed. Louise would pose the question while Her Majesty was still coherent enough to answer Louise's query and reveal the secret. Louise planned to win.

CHAPTER 9
Rings

VERSAILLES

ardinal de Fleury lifted his hand from the joined hands of Eugenie and René and turned to them. "Now for the exchange of rings." His words echoed in the eerily silent stone chapel, presided over by King Louis and Queen Marie. The only light came from sputtering tapers on the alter and from the moonlight streaming through the stained glass window of Saint and King Louis IX, the King's royal ancestor.

The light cast shadows on the walls of the betrothed couple at the altar, which made them seem larger than life. Both were attired in splendid garb. Eugenie wore a rose-colored gown of intricately woven brocade and satin with jewels at the neckline and hem, with a full beaded and jeweled train. René wore a gold brocade waistcoat and purple velvet breeches, the royal colors.

Eugenie was pleased with the choice, although she had had to make some alterations herself and had stuck herself with a needle many times. She accepted the Queen's gifts of dresses, which she packed to wear on the sea voyage but did not want to wear a used dress from her cousin for her wedding. She would marry but once and she made certain it was in one of her own dresses. In the end the pricks were worth the sight of her husband's face filled with joy.

The King and Queen, who were never outdone, even at a royal wedding, wore dazzling garments with thread spun from real gold, ermine-trimmed royal purple robes and jewel-encrusted crowns. The Queen also wore a beautiful ruby choker, which sparkled brilliantly in the candlelight.

Eugenie's father, the Count de Beaufort, had been overwhelmed to escort his daughter down the short aisle and kiss her one last time as a single girl. His hopes were pinned on Lord Le Blanc, in which he felt justified when he felt the young man's strong, firm handshake.

As for the groom, Rene had been beside himself awaiting this day. Never before had he been so nervous preparing for an event. He had measurements taken by the royal tailors for his wedding suit and appropriate clothes for the rugged New World. He approved the menu for the wedding feast with the assistant steward Laurent Arnaud and together they arranged food and drink for the sea voyage with the King's cooks and wine steward. He met with the coach builders to design new coaches and a carriage that would be carried onboard the ship for use in Grand Pré. But René's first act had been to design Eugenie's wedding ring with the Court goldsmith. It had to be perfect for his ethereal bride -- elegant yet simple in its beauty. He chose a matching simple band for himself. When the gold rings arrived, they were everything he had imagined.

The only other guests at the ceremony were Doctor Hébert and Christine de Castille, who sat behind the King and Queen. They were present in the event Eugenie had need of their services. The black bag was packed and sat in the pew next to Christine.

Eugenie's belly protruded slightly from the sumptuous gown although the thick folds of the design and the jeweled bodice led the eyes upward. A superbly delicate emerald necklace set in gold and encircled by diamonds shone brilliantly around her neck. On her ears she wore large diamond earrings dropping nearly to her shoulders. Christine admired Eugenie's pride in carrying herself straight rather than cowering to hide her condition. René was elated with the match despite his ignorance of the identity of the child's father.

Once René and Eugenie exchanged rings the Cardinal, in his booming voice, echoing throughout the nearly–empty stone chapel, made the Sign of the Cross, blessing the newlyweds and announcing their union.

"Through the glorious intercession of Our Lord, so it is that Lady Eugenie de Beaufort and Lord René Le Blanc, Sieur de Verdure are now joined together as man and wife."

The Cardinal contentedly turned to the King, who gazed upon Eugenie with longing. De Fleury raised his hands and eyes heavenward, avoiding the gaze of the monarchs. Loudly he proclaimed, "What God hath joined today let no man put asunder."

René stared at Eugenie as if frozen. The Cardinal leaned over to him and gently reminded him, "You may kiss your wife, my Lord."

René dared not lift Eugenie's wedding veil but gazed longingly into her eyes. He did not see her exchange a meaningful glance with the King through the veil. But someone else did.

The King sat motionless on his throne as the Queen glared at him. He felt her stare and squirmed slightly, avoiding turning to his wife. He seemed vulnerable without his entourage surrounding him. He had found that even pages, valets or guards could buffer his wife's stares.

René needed no further encouragement as he lifted the veil. Eugenie recoiled abruptly but quickly regained her composure and leaned forward ever so slightly. René followed her lead and unhesitatingly initiated a chaste brush on her lips. Eugenie reciprocated and they enjoyed a slow, passionate embrace.

Uncomfortable at the sight, the King squirmed in his chair ignoring the Queen's gaze. They stood and the Queen steered the King to escort her past the Cardinal. Kissing the Cardinal's ring, Marie whispered to him. "Make sure all witnesses are on the same ship. We want nothing left to chance."

The Cardinal bowed. "Your wish is my command, Majesty."

Unseen by the Queen during her discourse with the Cardinal, the King smiled softly at Eugenie, who returned the smile.

René was oblivious to the intrigue around him.

But nothing escaped the Cardinal as he blessed the couple. "In nomine patrie, et filius, et spiritu sanctus. Amen."

The Cardinal placed his hand on the Queen's head and whispered, "All is taken care of. Go in peace, my Queen."

The Queen nodded and walked into her private hallway in the Palace, followed tentatively by the King. When he was sure Marie was not watching him, he glanced back into the chapel but saw the couple walking out arm in arm, their eyes locked on each other. They seemed happy, which pleased him.

The Cardinal looked at Eugenie's full figure as she held René's arm and they glided together out of the chapel into a palace hallway. De Fleury glanced at Doctor Hébert who seemed nervous at but gave a nod to the

Cardinal. When the couple had exited the chapel de Fleury took the doctor by the arm.

"You must assure me that Lady Eugenie's condition is healthy."

"Of course, Excellency, she is quite healthy."

The Cardinal, exasperated with a vague answer, revised his question. "I mean to know will she will be able to withstand the voyage and bring forth a living child?"

The Doctor glanced around and seeing no one but Christine, he waved her on ahead of him. She nodded and followed the couple out.

Doctor Hébert said in a low whisper, even though no ears could hear, "The Lady is nearly halfway through her term. If everything were to go right I would tell you there is still a danger, not necessarily of death but of an early birth. However, untold numbers of things go wrong on long sea voyages. Violent storms. Wrecks on the rocks. Poisoned food. Lack of water. Disease. The list is endless."

The Cardinal was impatient for the doctor's final word. "We know of troubles at sea. What of the health of mother and child?"

The doctor bowed. "The midwife will be on board, as will I. We shall do everything in our power to protect both of them. But what if a decision must be made? Which life do we save?"

The Cardinal said, "I wish I could say Lady Eugenie."

The doctor nodded, waiting to hear more.

"But of course it must be the child. Promise me with your life you shall save the infant at all costs. You must do everything to birth a healthy baby."

Doctor Hébert knelt and kissed the Cardinal's ring. "Of course, Your Excellency. We shall do as you say. If it comes to that."

Satisfied, the Cardinal nodded, his robes rustling past the Doctor as de Fleury entered the private hallway used for the monarchs and their Court officers. As Prime Minister, de Fleury had the authority to use that door, although he would have taken it anyway, as a Prince of Rome. He joined the newlyweds and directed them to the banquet hall for their wedding feast.

CHAPTER 10
Navarre

VERSAILLES

No one at Court enjoyed lavish banquets as much as Laurent Arnaud. After a second meeting with the Cardinal, Laurent had been given a promotion inside the Palace to assistant steward in the royal dining hall. He was relocated to a private room in the Palace far away from the guards' quarters, given a handsome increase in wages and assigned a private tutor. All had been arranged by de Fleury. Laurent inquired of the Cardinal the reason for the generosity.

The response the young man received was enigmatic. "It is the least I can do for your father, who aided me long ago."

Laurent, ever considerate despite his brother's treatment of him, asked, "Will you do the same for Claude?"

The Cardinal looked at him and said, "The heir never needs help. It is always the second son."

Thereafter, the subject was never broached again by de Fleury or Laurent, who was elated with his post and his ongoing education.

Laurent's task today was arranging tables for the banquets and feasts scheduled according to the King's fancy and most always with the Cardinal in attendance. Laurent was happy to be away from his domineering brother Claude. His older brother was only too happy to make the new Royal Guard cower as had Laurent.

The younger Arnaud took to his new duties like a peacock to the King's gardens at Versailles. He felt twice his height, no longer embarrassed by his size. Rather than darting here and there it seemed that he glided through rooms. One moment he was in the kitchen talking with Cook, the next he was in the hallway listening to the maître d'hôtel. Then he was back in the dining hall directing the staff to position the enormous oak tables. Often he supervised the placement of the trays, tasting bits and pieces as the food was carried in, watching over the food decorators and floral experts to assure everything was in its place. Usually that was the task of the head steward, who was only too happy to delegate to Laurent so that he could take care of personal business.

Laurent loved a wedding feast and springtime was the most beautiful time of the year for such a banquet. He relished the heady smell of fragrant blossoms and perfumes throughout the Court, the tantalizing odors of soups and all sorts of meats -- veal, roasted beef, mutton and rabbit. And of course a peacock stuffed with freshly laid quail eggs for the King -- his favorite. Oh, and the sweets. Laurent could never forget the multi-layer cakes, the thick fruit-filled pies, the hand-twisted candies. As for the baked breads and buns with butter and jam, his mouth watered thinking of them.

Obviously Laurent would not be the rotund young man he was if he did not anticipate enjoying his favorite food -- overripe, melting cheeses. Some would call their smells more stinky than pungent, but that attracted him all the more. They were cut to be round, square, triangular, shredded and sliced and were always piled so high on the table that they were never completely eaten, despite the aristocratic guests filling their bellies with as much as they could. He could never choose between Camembert, Brie, Roquefort, and even Gouda from the Low Countries, along with the many other kinds of cheeses served in the Palace.

As Laurent's head spun thinking of the exhilarating meal to come, he looked over the banquet scene. Tonight's feast was for his smallest group yet, just over a dozen. According to the name cards the calligrapher had placed on the table, the attendees were only the monarchs, the Cardinal, the wedding couple, the bride's father Count de Beaufort, the Royal Artist Pater, and a small hand-picked group of aristocrats. Oh, and Doctor Hébert and Mademoiselle de Castille, though he did not know why. He rushed around the tables holding his breath, hoping to see the name of his lovely Véronique de Navarre.

Ahh, he released his breath. There it was. She was to sit next to the Queen and across from Lady Louise. He looked at the adjoining place cards and frowned. She was seated next to one of the most notorious womanizers at Court, the Count de Chambéry. He frowned until he realized he would be there to rescue her if anything untoward occurred.

Satisfied that he could protect his Lady, he motioned for the Palace gardeners to add their fresh flowers and greenery for the finishing touch to each place setting. He supervised the wait servants who lit the huge candelabras above the table, careful to ensure the undercups were perfectly placed to catch the hot dripping wax, rather than allowing it fall onto the unsuspecting guests below.

The pièce de resistance tonight was a ten-layer cake in honor of the wedding couple. The magnificent tower was topped by a crystal aquarium with fish in a variety of hues of gold, blue, and red from the Palace fountains. When Laurent asked the reason for it, he received a vague response that the couple was to honeymoon at sea.

The dining room was ablaze with soft light, which displayed the different food arrays to their best advantage. Laurent felt confident and eager to show his handiwork to the King. He walked past every table once more with the final touches -- arranging the boar's head, placing fresh fruit in the pig's open mouth, adding flowers to the cakes, placing bowls of sauces closer to their respective meats and vegetables. He smiled to himself, knowing everything was perfect for His Majesty. Once the diners had promenaded past the food tables, he was certain they would be impressed with the culinary delights offered to them.

Laurent's enthusiasm mounted as he reviewed every detail but he became even more excited when he received the large printed menu boards from the royal calligrapher. His mouth watered when he read the details, even though he, not the head steward, had arranged purchases of the food and knew what awaited the guests. He held up a card and read it aloud:

Marriage Feast

Lady Eugenie de Beaufort and Lord René Le Blanc de Verdure

---

8 Royal Courses, Multiple Dishes, Each Salted.

Laurent continued to review the course descriptions, verifying each dish on the grand menus.

1st course: Entremets – Eggs stuffed with Sturgeon Roe, Artichokes in Melted Butter, Spanish Pates, Asparagus with Lemons, Spinach with Gravy, Cauliflower with Parmesan, Mixed Ragout

2nd course: Entremets – Pheasant Pie, Turkey Giblets in Consommé, Brioches, Thrushes with Cucumbers, Sweetbreads in Papillotte, Ham Omelette

3rd Course: Soups & Potages –Turnip Purée, Large Onions Ouille, Sweet & Sour Birdnest à la Chinois

4th Course: Seafood Entrées – Oysters au Naturel, Sturgeon en Brochette, Boiled Lobsters with Mussels, Marinated Acadian Cod, Crayfish, Fried Trout with Almonds

5th Course: Roast Entrées - Chickens à la tartare, Rump of Beef with Cabbage, Calves' Heads, Spitted Suckling Pig, Filet Mignon of Mutton with Sauce Piquante, Turtle Doves with Truffles, Sirloin Fillets minced with Chicory

6th Course: Game Entrées – Veal Loin with Capers on the Spit, Wild Boar's Head, Guinea Fowl Wings, Duckling with Orange, Fillets of Pheasant en Matelote, Pigeons fried with Eggs and Breadcrumbs, Fried Young Turkey, Partridges with Bay Leaves, Rabbits on Skewer

7th Course: Salads of Lamb's Lettuce, Watercress and Garden Cress with Herbs – Tarragon, Thyme, Sage, Basil, Onion Stalks, Garlic, Shallots, Pimpernel, Chives, Various and Sundry Flowers – and Croutons and Salad Sauces – Wine, Lemon, Orange, Vinegar, Sugar or Oil

8th Course: Desserts – Pudding, Chocolate Profiterolles, Stewed Apples with Cinnamon, Glazed Fruits, Seasonal Berries, Nuts, Cheeses and Breads

Wines and Champagnes

Marriage Cake and Cherry Cordials

Laurent opened one of the dining room doors slightly to place the menu boards outside the entry. The guests would gather soon. He wanted to whet their appetites and delight their senses.

The head steward had no imagination. He had always placed the meal menus inside the doors but when the crowd proceeded into the banquet hall they shoved the cards aside, thus losing the impact of anticipation of that which often had taken the cooking staff many weeks to prepare. Of course, with a shorter period of time to prepare this feast, the King's stores were depleted and the kitchen chefs needed dozens of additional servants to finish in time.

As long as Laurent held his post, he was determined to tantalize the guests. By the time he closed the door, he heard "oohs" and "aahs" from the hall where the Court, carrying gifts of all shapes and sizes, had begun to gather and review the menus.

Laurent nodded to the wait servants, all in uniform and wearing crisp new white gloves. As part of their duties included picking up food particles dropped under the tables, no servant could wear his gloves more than once. Each took his assigned place next to the tables, framing the food displays, readying trays with wine and champagne bottles, or next to the doors.

The young steward looked around the hall at staff meandering here and there. Once he clapped his hands, the wait staff lined up at the table, each holding a chair, ready to assist the guests into their seats. Servers took their positions at the tables next to the serving trays filled with plates and bowls of food. After the guests had walked past the tables and the King had eaten they would carry the trays to the table, where the wait staff would serve the guests their course choices onto dinner plates.

He noted the two tables stacked high with additional dinner plates that would be changed three times during the long service -- after the entremets for the soups, for the meat course and for the desserts. Wine and champagne would flow freely throughout the meal. The drinks were not his domain but he had consulted with the wine steward to coordinate placement of bottles and glasses and the serving staff positions.

Suddenly the head steward walked up to Laurent, a bit flushed but ready to serve. Laurent whispered, "All is in readiness, sir."

His superior nodded. "As it should be."

Laurent was content that he had supervised the organization of the feast nearly single-handedly. He noted the time on the gold pocket watch he carried. Its engraved filigree cover opened to reveal an ivory face with intricate hour, minute and second hands, each made of silver. He had been stunned to find the precious piece upon his arrival when he unpacked his meager satchel in his room at the Palace. Hidden in his clothes, it was ensconced in a velvet pouch.

Pulling the timepiece from the cloth purse, Laurent read the inscription again, hardly able to believe it was meant for him.

"To my son Laurent, Your loving father, Charles."

Not knowing what to make of it Laurent had said nothing, but was careful to conceal it well from Claude. He had planned to question his mother when he returned home at Christmas but she had taken ill and died of pneumonia before the holiday. The brothers had gone home for their mother's funeral to find their father crying in his drink. "I should have treated her better. She never would have looked at him. She would not have done it." The big man finished his grog and passed out at the table.

Claude passed it off as the drink talking, but to Laurent it was the tip of the proof he needed that she had indeed known, and possibly loved, another man, possibly "Charles." He decided to ask the man he knew as his father when he was sober. But the next morning the sons found their father frozen to death, lying on their mother's grave. They buried him and sold the house the same week. Claude divided the money, demanding two-thirds as the elder son and therefore the "rightful heir."

The brothers returned in silence to the Palace and soon after, Laurent had moved to rooms near the dining hall and had barely seen or spoken to his brother since. He might have to speak to him tonight, as Claude was on duty at the entry doors. But that would not deter Laurent from his mission to speak with the lovely Lady de Navarre.

The head steward did his one and only task for the day by signaling the musicians to start the music. Soon lilting strains filled the hall and Laurent was stirred from his thoughts. A few moments later, the King and Queen entered the hall, followed by Cardinal de Fleury, the beautiful Lady de Beaufort resting her hand on the arm of her new husband Lord Le Blanc de Verdure and the Count de Beaufort. Behind them came the other guests.

Laurent searched for Véronique de Navarre, whom he found being escorted by the Count de Chambéry. Lady Louise Opalińska and the stately widower the Duke de Rochefort walked slowly behind while they whispered in conspiratorial tones, unintelligible to Laurent, on a seemingly serious matter. When everyone had entered Laurent gave the signal to the guards to close the dining room doors. Claude scowled, not happy to take orders from his younger brother but he and the other Royal Guard obeyed and closed the doors.

The King had requested Chef La Varenne, employed by the Marquis de Brévard-Lasnet, to work with the King's chefs in preparing this special wedding feast. La Varenne had become renowned for his book of French recipes gathered from the women in his family. He called his publication "Classic French Cooking" and it quickly sold out in Paris, necessitating many subsequent printings.

At Versailles the Queen followed La Varenne's opinion that foods should be prepared to exhibit their natural taste, with hints of additional flavors in light creams or sauces rather than being covered with thick gravies. Louis still adored the thick sauces and blended pastes that his chef poured or patted onto his favorite meats, fowl and fish, but wanted to indulge his wife.

Marie was too busy supervising the nine nannies for their nine children to take much notice of her husband. But she did notice that his visits to her bedchamber had become more and more infrequent of late. She reasoned affairs of state, particularly the nasty English, were to blame for the King's restlessness. Rumors abounded that he had taken a mistress who would soon be presented publicly at Court. Ladies regarded each other suspiciously, trying to ascertain the identity of the mystery woman. Little did they know their monarch had taken another route, one which would follow him to the end of his life.

Once the monarchs were seated, the King invited the engaged couple to sit near him, Eugenie at his right and her father next to her, with René on the King's left. The custom was to never seat married or engaged couples next to one another. That would lead to a dull table with little conversation. The Cardinal waited until several of the other guests had been seated. He had a specific mission in mind and had made certain his name card had been placed at the very seat that would accomplish his purpose.

The Queen took her place at the end of the large table opposite King Louis. She chose Louise and Véronique as her immediate dinner companions on her right and left. Laurent quickly bowed and held the chair for his lovely Lady de Navarre, who looked up at him and smiled. The head steward was relegated to seating Louise, the dowager lady-in-waiting. Louise gave Véronique a knowing glance and she nodded sheepishly. Véronique knew that Madame Opalińska approved and that the task of flirting had begun.

At the King's nod, Laurent motioned that the Guards open the doors and allow the members of Court to enter. The nobility formed a small procession, each Lord and Lady with a gift for the couple which was first presented to the King. At his nod, the gift was unwrapped by a servant and placed on a nearby table. They stretched their necks to see what their rivals had given, each hoping their gift would best all the others.

After the gift presentation the guests paraded in a long procession past the tables groaning with food and drink, exclaiming their admiration at the repast they would soon enjoy. Great applause broke out when they walked past the wedding cake with its unique aquarium and soon disappeared from the hall.

The invited guests were prepared to stay at table most of the night, until the wee hours of morn. But of course they could not eat with the King unless he invited them, and he would not do that until he had the best portions of every dish. A wedding feast did not change the natural order of customs respected at Versailles.

The guests were seated according to their place cards. The Count de Chambéry happily took the place next to Lady Véronique. Next to Lady Louise sat the Duke de Rochefort, who had been widowed for over fifteen years. Once he took his seat the Cardinal slipped into the adjoining cushioned chair and struck up a quiet but earnest conversation with him.

As Laurent supervised the service of each course, he anticipated the moment at the end of the evening when he and the other servants would be allowed to gorge on the remaining foods. Tonight they would not have to eat the standard Palace servant fare. Most often Cook served gruel of ground beans, some vegetables from the small patch near the kitchen, usually asparagus and artichoke, perhaps a piece of meat left from an earlier royal meal, and seasonal berries and nuts.

The servants were given table wine by the wine steward's staff made from pouring water over the grape press after the royal wine was made. The servants' wine contained the mashed stems and seeds, which was irrelevant to them insomuch as they welcomed the taste of the grape. No one drank the King's wine but His Majesty except when served at the royal dining table. And then the King's royal taster took the first sip before it could touch the lips of His Majesty.

It was rumored that the former wine steward, François Bourg, had poured a small portion of wine and was about to taste it in the hallway before a dinner began when the King walked by and dismissed him on the spot. Claude was the guard who booted the man outside without so much as his personal belongings. The steward booked passage on a ship to Acadia in New France, so great was the humiliation that he could not obtain work in France. After that there was no question of testing the King's wine without the formalities.

Unnoticed by the dinner guests, a large black rat peered out from his hole in the banquet room and climbed up the nearest table leg to a tray of desserts. It hid behind the mound of entremets and nibbled away until a waiter removed the tray to serve the guests. At that point the rodent stealthily disappeared behind another tray, where he continued to feast.

This continued for hours, the rat tasting various foods on the trays until they were removed, then scampering to another hiding place. When all the food had been served, the rat crawled down the table leg and boldly scampered straight across the stone floor in the open rather than along the wall. It ran under the dining table directly to a huge hunk of cheese which had been dropped by a nobleman onto the floor. The cheese was as large as the rat, which started nibbling away at its favorite food.

Cardinal de Fleury called Laurent over to him and specifically asked him for the time. Laurent thought the request odd since the King had a timekeeper at all official functions who would provide the hour to anyone who asked. Laurent looked around to ascertain that Claude was not in the vicinity and then he opened his beautiful pocket watch. He saw the timekeeper standing near the door, but the Cardinal appeared oblivious.

The Duke de Rochefort noticed the timepiece and asked if he might see it, whereupon Laurent graciously handed to him. The Duke pressed his fingers over the engraved message on the back of the watch. The Cardinal then whispered in Laurent's ear that he should meet with him the following week to discuss not only his education but also a new position as His Excellency's personal Secretary. Laurent, as always, bowed to the Cardinal and kissed his ring reverently. He felt very blessed that the Cardinal continued to show concern for his future.

Then the Duke returned the watch to Laurent, clasping both of his hands. It seemed that he had a tear in his eye when he said, "Your father obviously loves you very much to have given you such a beautiful family heirloom."

Not knowing the provenance of the watch, Laurent could only politely agree and bow to the Duke. The Cardinal excused Laurent, who walked away a bit confused but elated in anticipation of the new post – working for the Holy Cardinal himself! Laurent walked away, oblivious that the Duke continued to watch him as he spoke in low tones with the Cardinal, who nodded.

Between the seventh and eighth courses young Lady Véronique felt a stirring underneath her petticoats. Something was wrong with her shoe, she thought. It was sliding off her foot. Perhaps she needed to re-tie the ribbons around her foot.

*

Véronique was the only child of Marquis Robert de Navarre. Without a male heir the Marquis set about finding a suitable husband for his daughter. The Marquis firmly believed she would have a son if she married a nobleman. So he had devised a plan, writing to Lady Louise Opalińska, with whom he had dined several times at Versailles. He enlisted her assistance and secured her vow of secrecy in the matter.

Following the instructions in Louise's response, the Marquis had ordered a sumptuous carriage to be built for his daughter's arrival at Court. Then he spent two weeks in Paris where Louise introduced him to milliners, couturiers, lace makers, cobblers, leather craftsmen, fan creators, jewelers, and other designers of women's things. Louise selected the fabrics and trimmings for a variety of day dresses, evening gowns in every color with shoes to match, fans both feathered and unfeathered, hats, gloves, cloaks, capes, shawls, scarves, riding clothes, jewelry, lace underpinnings and an exquisite wedding gown spun with golden threads, all sewn to his daughter's exact measurements taken by her lady's maid.

Months later, everything had arrived in Navarre, including the appointment of his daughter as an assistant lady-in-waiting to the Queen.

The Marquis did not quibble over the astonishing sum that Lady Opalińska had demanded for making the arrangements. He offered her even more to encourage the aging dame to find a fitting husband for his only daughter who would then provide the requisite heir.

On the day of Véronique's departure, de Navarre's staff filled a caravan of coaches with trunks, boxes and satchels. Amidst Véronique's tears of protest, her father kissed her goodbye, closed the door of her carriage and charged her to remain at Versailles under Lady Louise's watchful eye until she was engaged.

He was certain his only daughter's display of wealth would attract a suitable husband and that their union would produce a male heir.

She hoped she would marry the man of her dreams and enjoy Palace life as a Lady-in-waiting to the Queen.

*

Given her fine new wardrobe, Véronique was at a loss to explain why these never-before-worn slippers felt strange. Under the table, the rat struggled with the huge cheese chunk that had fallen on top of Véronique's ribbons. The harder the rat tugged at the food, the more the ribbons loosened until the shoe flew off Véronique's foot and landed on top of the rodent. Véronique happened to look down at the very moment the creature was scrambling to get out from under the shoe while holding on to the cheese.

Véronique de Navarre unceremoniously jumped up onto her chair and screamed, "Rat! Rat!" Pandemonium erupted in the dining hall. The King ordered the staff to lift the Queen onto her chair. Meanwhile, waiters knelt on all fours and the King lifted his legs onto their backs. He took another swig of champagne and watched the show.

Laurent saw this as his heroic moment for his Lady. He quickly armed himself with a nearby broom and began the chase, sweeping under the table as the creature ran in zigzags, trying to elude him. When he swept under one side of the table, the rat scurried to the other side. He ran to the other side to catch the varmint but it had disappeared.

The Count happily assisted Lady Véronique onto her chair, holding onto her tiny corseted waist a bit longer than needed. The Duke de Rochefort assisted Lady Louise by offering his hand as she attempted to climb onto her seat but when that failed Louise looked down and motioned that the Duke push her up by her rather large bottom. Such an emergency was one of the few times nobles were able to touch a woman in public anywhere but the hand, even during greetings or dancing. It was also a rare occasion to see the ankles of a woman whom one did not know, in the carnal sense.

The Queen and her Ladies-in-waiting temporarily forgot decorum and manners, lifting their rustling skirts and exposing their legs in their haste to see if any creature was crawling below. Suddenly the dining room was awash in color as a rainbow of bright stockings came into view.

Chaos continued in the room. Laurent had tracked the rat to the table with the marriage cake and used a silver tray to push the rodent from his hiding place. Other waiters grabbed boxes or empty wine bottles, attempting to trap the wiley rodent. Claude sat back, avoiding any activity, which he thought seemed silly. He preferred to stand his post at the door. Laurent caught a fleeting glimpse of his brother sitting idly by before the younger brother immersed himself in the task once more.

Delightful, mused the King, seeing his Court drop their pretenses and act like peasants, jumping around and raising all those skirts. He watched them closely and found that they enjoyed the reprieve from the restrictive morés required at table. That sparked his idea to create his own respite away from Court in an old cottage in the Palace gardens. He would turn it into a convention-free haven and decided to name it "Parc aux Cerfs," the "Deer Park." He told no one of the secret name until many years later, after he had built a mansion to entertain a long line of mistresses.

The rat took advantage of the chaos and stopped to bite into a large piece of cake. Then it ran straight for the hole in the wall. Laurent followed the icing trail of the cake to the tiny hole, wondering how such a fat pest squirmed through. Thinking quickly, he blocked the opening with the silver tray. Now there would be no access in or out for the pest.

Laurent took this as his opportunity to be noticed by the Court and announced, "Fear not, the rat has been chased back into his hole and we have closed it. It shall not bother you again."

Arnaud bowed deeply to the King then turned his bow to the Queen. While returning back to the other side of the room he passed Véronique and caught her eye. She smiled directly at him, flirtatiously opened her fan then lowered her eyes behind it. She tried to hide her interest but he had piqued her curiosity. She would ask Lady Louise about the young man who appeared to be about her age.

Véronique had been at the Palace all of six months and had purposefully remained chaste for her wedding night. To date she had not been approached by any nobleman and soon she would have to write her father again that she had no marriage prospects. Véronique had approached Lady Louise, whose advice was sought on important matters by all the noblewomen at Versailles. Louise was a cousin of the Queen's father and had been with Marie since she was a child in the Polish Court at Warsaw. The Lady was the one person at Court who always knew what would curry favor with the Queen, or displease her. She knew Her Majesty even better than did the King.

"My father insists I find a husband at Court," Véronique lamented to Louise. They were folding a mountain of gloves for the Queen. "But I cannot determine who is eligible or not. And how to attract their attention."

Louise had been waiting for the girl to broach the subject, having received monthly payments of gold coins from her father. The old woman looked at Véronique with amusement. "First you must take a lover for a night or two, "she replied.

Confused, Véronique asked, "But why do that? Would not the noble want me to be pure for our wedding night?"

Louise stopped folding. She looked at Véronique, trying to determine if she was being coy. No, the girl was serious but after all, she was from the country. Such young noblewomen were always locked away in their father's chateaus and hidden from the pleasures of life so readily available at Court. That certainly explains her naïveté, thought Louise.

"A nobleman wants to impress his wife. If you have no experience, how will you appreciate your husband's prowess in the marriage bed? And do not fear, men are alike everywhere, like dogs, ready to rut. Stable grooms, heralds, guards, waiters, kitchen vendors. Open your eyes. You can find a willing male any hour of the day or night at the Palace."

After last week's conversation with Louise, Véronique decided she would not lose her virtue nor would she settle for an old nobleman. She began to look for an appropriate suitor. After that, anything could be possible, she reasoned. Perhaps she would be married and whisked away from the petty jealousies and competition among the women at Court. Unfortunately, she had to become a blemished woman or marry quickly; otherwise she would be subjected to endless mockery.

Louise sat across the table from her, bantering with the Duke de Rochefort, then with the Count de Chambéry. Men never left her side without feeling entranced, not with her faded beauty but with her witticisms and her ability to make them feel powerful. Véronique thought, "She is as old as the hills but knows more about keeping a man's attention than I ever will."

She turned her head just as she had finished the thought and saw Laurent. A little smile, a flicker of her fan and maybe he would be hooked. She was right. When she caught Laurent's eye, she caused his heart to beat faster and faster. I have met my Lady, he thought and he bowed deeply, offering his hand to assist her down from her chair.

"May I be of service, Lady de Navarre?" he murmured in his most sophisticated voice, praying that it would not crack under such pressure. When she did not respond, he repeated in a panic, "You are Lady Véronique de Navarre, are you not?"

Véronique took Laurent's hand and noticed Louise across the table, still seemingly engrossed in listening to the Duke but motioning to Véronique to put both of Laurent's hands at her waist. Louise nodded encouragingly to Véronique, which the Lord took to mean for him. The girl took Laurent's hands and placed them at her waist, whispering, "Sire, I was unaware that you knew my name."

Laurent was awestruck at the beauty of her face but he took his responsibility seriously and held her tiny waist firmly but gently as he lowered Véronique to the floor. Laurent responded respectfully with a bow, "Anyone not knowing your name should be banished from Court. Your beauty lights the Palace wherever you go." He held out the chair for her as she slowly slid into the seat. He leaned to her and quietly said, "Laurent Arnaud at your service."

Véronique took a liking to him immediately. He had a pleasing face, even with the long scar, though he was not what Louise would consider handsome. And he had a good natural scent about him, not the smell of a woman doused in perfume like so many of the nobles at Court. She abhorred that sweet smell on a man. Give me a man who is sure of himself, like Laurent she thought. She whispered in his ear, "Thank you for your kindness, Monsieur Arnaud. I hope we shall meet again."

He replied with a like whisper, still bowed but with eyes raised, looking directly into her soul, "Milady's wish is my honor to fulfill." Then Laurent floated away to his post near the tables still groaning with platters of uneaten food.

Louise smiled and nodded her approval. She was pleased that her lessons were paying off. But not for merely Véronique's sake. The Marquis de Navarre had promised Louise an exquisite jeweled bracelet in addition to the agreed-upon payments when she arranged a successful betrothal for his daughter.

Louise had carefully ranked the aging noblemen who were prospects. The Marquis had approved her selection and she began to work on the two whose names were at the top of the list: the two high-ranking nobles at the table, the Count de Chambéry and the Duke de Rochefort.

She had approached each aristocrat discreetly and guessed correctly he would drool at the prospect of adding the substantial land holdings of the Marquis de Navarre to his own estate. That the daughter in question was a beauty was more than he could hope for and might even cause him to see a mistress less often. Each nobleman then began to shower Louise with gifts to assure she would push his cause with Véronique. Louise twisted her new pearl ring from Chambéry around her finger. She felt the weight of the cloisonné bracelet imported from China by Rochefort.

A third prospect was her old friend the Grand Duke of Tuscany Gian Gastone de' Medici. Unfortunately, he had died three months earlier but had ordered the gift she wore tonight -- luscious brocade slippers -- from a renowned Venetian cobbler who had sent the shoes to her before the funeral.

Louise recalled she had at first disdained the Italian shoes as similar to cheap Roman charioteers' sandals. But she quickly reversed her opinion when she was told by the Queen's dressmakers they were all the rage in Venice and that it was only a matter of time before Parisians would wear the latest fashion. The ankle ribbons were not to be tied in a single bow but to be wrapped around the leg high underneath the skirts and petticoats, up, up and away.

Louise was an old crone by the Court's standards and she knew it. But even an old lady could live her dreams through a young protege. The young girl could have what Louise never did -- lovers and a husband. As a first cousin to Marie's father, King Stanislaw, Louise had always been forbidden to have male visitors as it was Polish custom that the King's daughter must be the first to marry in her generation. Then and only then could a female cousin in the extended family through the third degree accept a marriage proposal.

Though Marie's union with the King took place at a young age, Louise was much older and by the time of the royal marriage Louise had quickly passed her prime and lost her bloom. Still, the younger women at Court sought her frequently for what they believed to be her wisdom and experience with men.

Véronique shivered as she sat and stared at Laurent. Perhaps she found the knight to save her from marriage to an older nobleman. She hoped her father could accept his status. When Louise turned to her, Véronique nodded towards Laurent, unobserved by others. Louise smiled broadly and whispered across the table, "Well done, my dear."

While Véronique ruminated on her future Louise gave a knowing glance to the Count de Chambéry, who raised his glass to her. Louise acknowledged him with a slight nod, then turned to smile at the Duke de Rochefort. He smiled, hoping he would have a new bride at last after so many years. With two confirmed suitors, Louise had a successful evening and looked forward to collecting her matchmaking fee very soon.

The newlyweds, Eugenie and René, seemed to be in their own world, speaking with their eyes across the table. Eugenie's father spoke enough for all three, talking with René about his estates and inviting him to visit at the earliest opportunity. When they told him about his post in Acadia he was visibly disappointed but even more fearful.

The Marquis wondered to himself what possessed his daughter to agree to such a far-flung territorial home. Besides, too many things could go wrong at sea -- shipwrecks, storms, even pirates. He needed a male heir! He learned later that evening that she might be carrying the requisite son at that very moment. Only then did he relax and enjoy the rest of the feast.

*

"Thank you Cap'n Jackk. Thank you." The boy hugged him at his waist until Jacques gently unlocked the boy's grasp.

Crew members unloaded several satchels onto the bank as the Captain and the priest watched Sun. The overgrown boy with outstretched arms and head thrown back twirled his big body in a circle, crying out with glee, "Parish, I is in Parish."

Père Rivière shook Captain Jacques' hand and tried to pay him. "For my trip and the boy's. It would have been impossible to meet the Cardinal and still board the ship without your taking us with you."

The Captain refused the priest's coins. "'Tis the least I can do, Père Rivière. Poor boy, losing his mother and all alone in this world. He will be alright then? Will the Church take him in?"

The priest patted Jacques on the shoulder. "He will be fine. I shall see to it. He will sail with me to the New World. There is no doubt opportunity in the fields for an earnest young man."

Captain Jacques said, "My brother Philippe sails out of Le Havre but he was not in port when we were there. Would you give him something for me?" The priest nodded as Jacques went below deck and returned with a small envelope. "We had a big family in and around Marseille but since the Black Death no one is left...." The Captain was teary-eyed as he spoke.

Père Rivière nodded. "I shall remember them and you in my prayers."

Then the priest disembarked carrying the Church's sacred articles and holy garments for his new Parish. He led Sun towards the Notre Dame Cathedral. The red and gold streams of moonlight shining through the stained glass windows reminded Sun of his mother in the bloody wagon.

CHAPTER 11
Honeymoon

VERSAILLES

 he King ended the banquet abruptly by leaving after the marriage cake was served. The Queen followed and the room cleared quickly. There was much gossip to spread throughout the Court about such an eventful evening and Lady Louise wished to be the first to do so.

De Fleury brought the wedding couple out of the hall through a separate door and through another winding hallway. They ended up in René's rooms, which he rarely used. He turned to René and said, "Bid your wife goodnight, Lord Le Blanc. We shall all meet again in the morning to board the coaches for Le Havre."

René started, and then said, "But it is our wedding night. Can we not both be here together?"

The Cardinal looked at Eugenie, who knew the only response she could give. She answered, "My Lord and husband, I am very tired and still have much to prepare for the journey tomorrow. If you are agreeable, I should repair to my rooms so I will be rested for our trip."

The Cardinal patted her hand and looked at René. "You do understand, do you not? What is one night when you shall have the rest of your lives together?" He proffered his jeweled ring and René kissed it.

"Of course. I should have thought it myself. Shall I take her to her rooms?" René asked.

"No need. I shall see to it myself."

Then the Cardinal offered his arm to Eugenie but before she took it, she invited René with her eyes. He walked to the door and she nodded. The Cardinal averted his gaze. Eugenie leaned forward, eyes closed and rich plump winterberries pursed. René's lips melted into hers as he touched her cheek, then her lips. Eugenie nearly swooned and leaned against René for support. He looked at her questioningly. She removed his fears by kissing him again. They slowly released each other.

"Until tomorrow, my darling wife." René could hardly breathe.

Eugenie dropped her eyes. "Yes, my dear husband."

The Cardinal placed his hand on Eugenie's back and directed her out of the room. "Come, come. We must get you to bed, my Lady." And with a flourish of the Cardinal's red cape and Eugenie's wedding silks, they disappeared leaving René to his thoughts.

De Fleury whisked Eugenie through a secret panel in the wall so that no one could see that she was not with her new husband. Careful of her condition, he led her down the stairway and into the passage that opened into her own room. On the far side of the chamber near the door stood a man wearing a mask and cape. The Cardinal bowed and disappeared into the secret passage. But he opened the small wall grate to watch.

Eugenie ran to the masked man and reached for his hand. He handed her a letter, then bowed and left the room by a secret door behind the mirror. She watched him exit where *he* used to enter her room. *He*, the father of her child. *He*, who wore a mask and cape to avoid being identified. *He*, whom she would never see again. Eugenie eagerly tore open the letter. It was simple and in his own hand.

"You and the child shall always hold a place dear in my heart. Think of me often as I shall of you. Call on me if you are ever in need."

It was unsigned but she knew it was from him. She held it to her breast, pounding with emotion. She glanced toward the secret passageway where she believed Cardinal de Fleury was watching. Waving the letter before letting it flutter to the stone floor she said softly. "It is done, Your Excellency. It has ended." Then she fell to her bed in sorrow. She knew she would never see him again. For that she cried herself to sleep.

De Fleury slowly closed the grating. It would, no doubt, be painful for both of them, he thought -- Eugenie and the father of her child. But it had to be done. There was no other way.

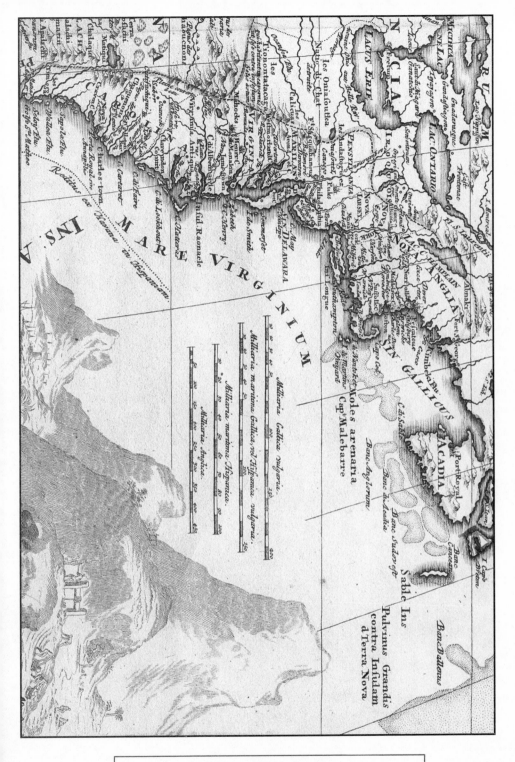

Detail, The New World:
Acadia and Northeast British Colonies,
particularly Massachussetts Bay, 1720
cartographer: Johann Baptiste Homann

Part II
1738 – 1749

"There is no fear in love; but perfect love casts out fear."
- *Holy Catholic Bible, 1 John 4:18*

CHAPTER 12
Preparation

1738 - VERSAILLES

 ené had been awake for hours, unable to sleep after his wife was escorted out by Cardinal de Fleury. As he paced his room he prayed his wife was refreshed and feeling better. He debated whether he should go to Eugenie's rooms or not. He wondered if the Cardinal would bring her back or whether he was to meet her at the carriage. Unsure of the proper etiquette, René waited to be called for the departure to Le Havre when he and Eugenie would begin their new life together.

*

The rat made its way alive out of Versailles despite the efforts on the part of the King's servants to assure it would never enter the Palace again. The road to Paris for rodents and other undesirable creatures was usually fraught with danger and narrow escapes from farmer's pitchforks in hay wagons, rich ladies' grooms that could flatten them barehanded, and wine barrels or vegetable boxes that could fall and cut off part of a tail.

But this time the rodent hopped inside a coach and hid comfortably under the long crimson robes of Cardinal de Fleury. The carriage had rolled out of Versailles many hours earlier, after Eugenie received the letter.

De Fleury headed toward the Notre Dame Cathedral in Paris to handle one more matter before the coaches left for Le Havre. There, the Cardinal finalized Père Rivière's transfer to his new Parish. Together they baptized Sun giving him the Catholic name of "Peter." Then they traveled all night in de Fleury's carriage to the Palace of Versailles. Sun's eyes nearly popped out of his head; he had never seen a house so grand.

*

René chastised himself for not knowing the proper decorum at Court. Then he heard a soft knock. Hoping against hope his wife was at the door, he rushed to open it. Eugenie entered with a small satchel of clothes, firmly closing the door behind her as she stared into René's eyes. René wrapped his arms around her and kissed her with ardor. She returned his passion in kind as he drew her next to him.

Without a word the groom lifted his bride into his strong arms and laid her softly in the silk sheets. Their eyes spoke a myriad of feelings -- love, respect, hope, gratitude, desire. She softly caressed René's face as his trembling fingers removed her dressing robe. The strap of her gown fell from her shoulder. He kissed her soft porcelain skin as his hands, now firm and confidant, unlaced her shimmering nightdress. Her body was more exquisite than a sculpture. Slipping off his nightshirt, he slid into bed next to her, igniting their passion. The two became one and began their new life together as husband and wife.

Outside in the Palace courtyard, blazing torches held by a dozen royal pages streamed light and smoke onto the flurried activity. Travel preparations for the newlyweds had been underway for hours. When dawn broke and the sun rose over the Palace, the torches were doused one by one, to the relief of the pages who had quietly suffered the burning heat.

Royal guards held watch against unauthorized persons entering the yard, whether thieves, gawking servants or curious aristocrats. They were steadfast in surveying everyone although it was difficult to keep track of so many servants, cartmen, drivers, footmen, maids, stewards, and various and sundry laborers. It seemed almost every member of the royal staff was involved in preparing and loading the dozen coaches.

Servants scurried in and out of the coaches with carts and trunks of clothing, fabrics, hatboxes, shoe cases, linens, laces and cloaks. Footmen packed the personal items carefully into coaches outfitted for goods rather than passengers. Cartmen brought loads of furniture and household items for the couple's new home. The horses had been hitched and the drivers and their assistants were perched in the driving boxes, waiting for the signal to leave. All the while, barking dogs followed and jumped underfoot, hindering the work.

The King had sent a contingent of sixteen of his strongest Royal Horsemen, led by Captain Michel Broussard, to assure safety along the overland journey to the port. Le Havre was on the northern coast of France, on the channel between France and its longtime rival, England. The road was a dangerous one, running through woods and near known hiding places of bandits and gypsies. But Broussard had made the trip often, accompanying guests of the King or protecting shipments destined for the Palace. He was the right man for the job.

Claude Arnaud learned of the mission late and he begged the Captain to let him join. Claude believed Laurent had advanced under the Cardinal's guidance as a result of that chance meeting but realized that there was little hope for him. He needed to make a new life for himself away from the Palace. Becoming a member of the Royal Horsemen seemed a perfect fit.

One of Broussard's men took ill a few days earlier so Claude's new post was confirmed with an added assignment to assist the royal couple on the journey and then to travel to Québec City to assist the Governor until further notice. He was jubilant until he questioned whether Laurent had something to do with sending him away. No matter, Claude would escape the shadow of his younger brother, who was much beloved at Court; that is, as beloved as a servant can be.

The Royal Horsemen had mounted their steeds and were circling the courtyard slowly. Their superior, Captain Broussard, gave last-minute instructions. Claude listened attentively, his sword hilt gleaming in the sunlight. He glanced over his shoulder and saw Laurent checking a list of foodstuffs as they were loaded into two carriages. Claude saw that the adjacent carriage had been filled with bottles of fine wine and champagne, no doubt from the King's own cellars. He made a mental note to grab a bottle or two during what would surely be chaos at the dock in Le Havre.

Claude trotted over to Laurent, who looked up and smiled. "Good luck to you, Claude."

Claude was conscious of Captain Broussard's eyes on him so he shook his brother's hand and kept the conversation short. "I am off to make a new life for myself."

"I heard. I hope you find what you are seeking. And I remind you of our wager. I shall marry a Lady and you shall be in service in my house."

Claude threw his head back and laughed out loud. "You have always been such a dreamer, Laurent. We might never meet again so let us say goodbye, brother." Then he rode off without waiting for a response.

Laurent shook his head as his brother rode off. He repeated to himself, 'I shall marry a titled Lady and I know just the one." Then he nodded and the doors were closed and locked, then metal bars placed over the doors of coaches with valuable cargo that could only be opened with a key.

Broussard trotted slowly past the passenger carriages and the clothes coaches. In the next carriages were the household goods -- kitchen items, cooking utensils, pots and pans, hearth implements, grills, knives, spoons, forks and other useful items for the couple's new home. Other carriages carried heavy boxes of silver and gold ornaments and fixtures, and dozens of well-packed boxes of crystal in every shape -- chandeliers, candlestick holders, champagne coupes, wine glasses, and other glassware. Boxes of porcelain figurines and the special set of dishes from the royal factory at Sèvres were loaded. Gunpowder and a cache of weapons -- muskets, swords, handguns, bayonets, knives -- were stored in boxes, covered with linens and utensils and labeled "household goods" to prevent immediate recognition. Each coach carried such box of weapons in the event of attack.

The food carriages came next and the cook and his kitchen staff brought baskets of stores for the trip -- roasted pheasants, braised hams and beefsteaks, preserved jams and jellies, boiled shellfish, oysters and cockles, smoked fish and fowl of all kinds, roasts of all sorts of animals hunted on the King's lands, dried meats, speckled quail eggs, baskets of dried applies, prunes and pears, lemons for good breath, and other delights for the passengers. In a separate basket was placed fresh fruit for immediate consumption. The cook could not risk rotten fruit spoiling the other items meant for the long sea voyage. Sacks of flour, potatoes, and spices and jars of oil were packed as ingredients for soups and bread. Numerous barrels of fresh water were loaded. The royal baker had packed bread, cakes and other baked goods and sweets in many forms and shapes for the journey.

Laurent handed the key to the food carriage locks to Broussard, who tipped his hat and moved on. The wine steward surveyed the footmen loading cases of fine wines, sherries and champagne into its own coach, lined with extra padding and blankets to prevent breakage. The steward had locked the wagon and handed the key to Broussard.

Captain Broussard assigned one Royal Horseman to each coach except for the largest of all, the Consul's carriage, where he placed four of his best men. The additional guard was needed for René's royal carriage, where tens of thousands of French livres for the Consulate in Acadia were locked in strongboxes and hidden in secret compartments for which René held the only keys. Claude was to guard the carriages filled with clothing, jewelry and personal items of the newlyweds. The remaining Horsemen were assigned to guard the unlocked coaches when the passengers stopped at overnight inns, so keys were not required. A thief might steal food and wine without being noticed but someone caught wearing a stolen royal dress or custom shoes or a velvet waistcoat would have been punished immediately.

René's carriage was the largest and most comfortable of all. He and Eugenie would travel with the midwife Christine, who could take care of any discomfort Eugenie might feel. The carriage master had his craftsmen appoint the carriage sumptuously with soft velvet padded cushions on the benches and piles of pillows, quilts and coverlets. He added individual foot rests and a small candelabrum on the coach wall by each seat for reading, with a foldaway writing desk for the Consul.

The bench on the other side of the carriage had been converted to a velvet tufted lounging bed for Lady Eugenie, long enough for her to lie comfortably and sleep. A unique latticework of soft leather straps padded with velvet cushions and affixed to the wall could be stretched over the bed to protect the Lady from being thrown onto the floor when the carriage wheels hit the usual ruts and holes along the way. Drawers had been built under the seats for storing travel necessities, though the carriage master did not know medical supplies would also be stored there.

Doctor Hébert carried two large black bags as the footman assisted him into the second passenger coach, which he believed was his own. King Louis initially regretted losing Doctor Hébert and Christine but he wanted the best care for Eugenie and the infant who might be born onboard the ship. He also hoped their medical expertise would be helpful to the Acadians, who had recently written of remedies provided by the Mi'Kmaq Indians. The King could not imagine Indian herbs could heal and believed a physician would modernize the Acadians.

The physician was surprised to find two other passengers already seated in his coach -- a priest reading his Bible and an overgrown boy staring out of the coach window, apparently mesmerized by the activity around him. Hébert strapped his bags on the overhead rack and took the cushioned bench opposite them. He and the priest nodded and introduced themselves with a handshake.

"Doctor Hébert at your service, Father."

"I am Père Rivière, replacing the recently deceased pastor at St. Charles des Mines Parish in Grand Pré. And my ward, Peter, but he prefers Sun."

"Sun?" Hébert pointed above his head. "Like...the sun?"

The priest nodded and Sun took his head out of the window long enough to grin a wide, partially toothless grin, "Me Sun. Me go to New World. Me be your friend." He reached out his hand, oversized like the rest of him. The doctor shook his hand. Then the boy returned to gazing out of the window as if he had never been interrupted. Hébert thought to himself the lad was dim-witted but nothing he had could cure that.

At the last minute the Court Artist Pater waddled up to the coaches. De Fleury had imparted specific instructions on his mission. "The King commands that you paint important moments of the sea voyage and the landing. Then, after Lady Eugenie gives birth, you are to paint two portraits of the Le Blanc de Verdure family with a backdrop of the magnificent tree grove just beyond the beach -- one for the Lady and an official painting for the King. Once the ship loads supplies and the Acadian exports of cod and striped wool fabrics, you shall return to the Palace with your works of art."

Pater kissed the Cardinal's ring, overjoyed at the prospect of being able to see his beautiful muse for weeks on end. He replied with fervor, "Your Excellency, it shall be my greatest honor."

De Fleury knew of Pater's deteriorating health and was unsure whether he would last the entire journey. When the Queen learned that Pater had gone with the others, the King would contend with, and contain, Her Majesty's anger, as she had insisted there be no witnesses to the secret at Court. Except, of course, the Cardinal himself.

The portly Pater would have fit into Hébert's coach but for all of his materials and supplies. The carriage master quickly converted a supply coach by adding layers of cushions and pillows to the benches. When the artist arrived, it took two footmen and a groom to stuff the man through the narrow door. He squeezed in next to piles of clothing trunks, crates of canvases, paint pots, jars, boxes of brushes and satchels of cleaning cloths. He plopped onto the bench and re-checked that all his materials were there.

While they were readying to leave, Doctor Hébert called for Christine. She joined him in his carriage and together they checked their instruments, potions and pots in the black bags. Each held a leech jar, pulsating as ever. Hébert was content they would be at his hand in a moment's notice if the situation called for them. When they verified they had everything they needed, Christine returned to the royal carriage, awaiting Eugenie's arrival.

When the carriages, stores, horses and passengers were all ready, Broussard rode up to the Palace and mounted the steps. He disappeared inside and returned a short while later to escort René and Eugenie, her hand lightly resting on her husband's, to their carriage. Cardinal de Fleury followed, his hands folded solemnly inside his cape, his eyes watching everything and everyone. He nodded with satisfaction that it was just as the King had wished. He looked back to the second floor windows and caught a glimpse of a tall, powdered wig with strands of jewels glimmering in the sunlight. De Fleury bowed and moved on. He did not want to discuss the King's business with Her Majesty.

Pater, proud of his lustrous locks, always poofed and powdered like a wig, held his hair as he bowed deeply through his window to René and Eugenie as they walked past. He waved to them excitedly. "The King's wedding gift is my painting of your family portrait upon landing in Acadia." He added quickly, "With your permission of course, my Lord."

René bowed slightly as Eugenie blushed but smiled broadly. René's heart jumped to see his wife so happy. "Anything my wife wishes is her command. We are pleased and grateful, Monsieur Pater."

"It shall be a true gift to me to be able to paint the beautiful Lady Eugenie again," Pater responded and bowed again.

Eugenie insisted they review all the carriages and acknowledge the passengers and staff who were making the journey. De Fleury had introduced them to Père Rivière and Sun that morning when they passed the coach where they was sitting. The boy waved to her through the open window. Eugenie pressed her gloved hand to his and, as the priest had taught him, he lifted it to his lips and awkwardly kissed it. She smiled and said, "Thank you, Sun. Are you ready to travel on the big ship?"

Sun smiled, happy the beautiful lady knew his name. "I ready for the big coach, the big ship, the big new world. When do we go?"

Père Rivière and the doctor held their breath, hoping the child was not too impertinent. But Eugenie and René laughed and he assured the boy, "We are leaving just now so take your seat." Sun smiled and lumbered back to his chair where the priest strapped him in to not bounce off the bench.

At their coach, two footmen offered Lady Eugenie their hands. René looked on with concern until Eugenie turned and reassured him with a small smile. "I shall be fine, my Lord and husband."

"You have everyone at your feet for whatever you may need. You must not hesitate to ask us to stop if you do not feel well."

She nodded. "That will not be necessary." Smiling at Christine, she told René, "We shall do quite well, all of us together."

Cardinal de Fleury stood near the carriage as a footman assisted Eugenie to her seat and Christine adjusted her pillows. Satisfied that his wife was comfortable, René turned to the Cardinal, who pulled him aside and guided him to the back of the carriage, away from prying eyes. There de Fleury handed René a faded leather journal. René read the title, *Acadia*, and asked, "What is the nature of the book?"

The Cardinal wiped a tear from his eye. He shuddered when he remembered the contents of the writings. "A lesson to prepare you for the English. They are capable of immense cruelty." Then he gave René a warm, fatherly hug. "You have become like a son to me. I shall pray for your success and for the health of your wife and child. May there be many more."

René responded humbly, "With the help of God, we shall bring honor and dignity to France."

De Fleury nodded. "God we serve. In God we can do all things."

René turned to go, then faced the Cardinal again. "Excellency, is it important that I learn the father's name? Should he not know the child?"

The Cardinal took him by the shoulder and blessed him with the Sign of the Cross. "All in good time. Go with God and have no fear."

René was the last to board. He checked on Eugenie, dozing quietly. Christine nodded that she was fine. He then took his seat and silently thanked the carriage master for the extra cushions and pillows. The long journey would be much more comfortable than he had thought. Le Blanc nodded to the footman, who removed the steps, shut the door tightly and climbed onto the back of the carriage, next to the coachman.

Captain Broussard gave the signal to begin the trip. The driver cracked his whip and the horses lurched the carriage forward.

From a window in her chambers, the Queen waited until the carriages pulled out of the entry before she pulled the curtains, disappearing from view.

The King directed de Fleury to walk with him in the Gardens. "Our Prime Minister has done well. All is now in our cousin's hands."

De Fleury nodded. "His Majesty could have no more loyal subject to carry out his plan."

The King lowered his voice. One could not be too careful. "And Pater?"

"You shall have the most beautiful painting to record the event."

Together, they watched in silence as the carriages disappeared in clouds of dust. The cadre of Royal Horsemen galloped out of the Palace gates alongside the carriages. They had precious cargo to protect.

CHAPTER 13
Journal

ON THE ROAD to Le HAVRE, FRANCE

he train of carriages rolled steadily through the lush French countryside. Dusk was approaching. Captain Broussard rode up and down the line of coaches, pushing the drivers to reach the way station before dark.

Broussard had thought they would be at the ten-kilometer mark by now. He rode ahead, signaling Claude to ride with him. The two made haste, galloping quickly, avoiding the large potholes in the road. Suddenly, they came to the inn and the Captain sighed with relief. He directed Claude to assure the rooms were in readiness for the Consul and his Lady. Then the Michel rode back to meet the carriages.

The innkeeper sheepishly handed Claude the keys, having forgotten their arrival today. He back to drinking his grog while Claude's inspection of the chambers found them very much wanting. Dirty floors, stained sheets, torn windows at the curtains, all discovered upon a cursory review.

Claude found himself wishing Laurent were with him to organize the work to be done but he found that coins worked wonders. Soon he had servant girls scrubbing floors and windows and cleaning the dirty hearth. Another maid had filled jars with fresh flowers from the nearby field. Several other servants had pulled off all the dirty linens and curtains.

Claude decided that the royals could eat in the dining room while he brought fresh linens from one of the carriages.

He cringed at the sight of the kitchen, or so it was named, in the back of the inn. The three-sided shed open to the elements was as filthy as an animal pen, and chickens and pigs roamed freely on the dirt floors. In front of his very eyes, the heavyset cook grabbed one of the cocks and spun it around until the neck broke. Then he slammed it to the wood table and chopped it into pieces with an ax-like knife. He threw all the bloody pieces into one of the many pots of boiling water hanging from a metal rod over the fire in the large stone hearth.

Claude rushed outside and bent over, throwing up everything he had eaten at the luncheon Lady Eugenie had requested. He was determined to see that none of Captain Broussard's charges left this inn with illness from bad food. He gave the cook and his assistants extra money to pour boiling water over the table and all the utensils that they would use. Claude had no idea if it would prevent disease but at least things would be cleaner as the hot water washed away blood, entrails, bones, feathers and other nasty bits.

Down the road, inside the royal carriage, Eugenie had fallen asleep after lunch and still slept soundly. René leaned back and closed his eyes. Christine, satisfied that everyone was asleep, opened her travel bag and pulled out a small book.

René opened one eye and surreptitiously watched her make notes in her booklet. He noted with interest the title imprinted in gold on the cover, "Natural and Herbal Cures." Doctor Hébert had made no secret of his distaste for what he called "modern unproven methods," instead proclaiming the value of leeches. René determined he would prevent the doctor from letting Eugenie's blood, if it came to that. And he made a mental note to talk with Christine about the subject of natural remedies out of earshot of both his wife and the doctor.

René turned to look at Eugenie, who even in her sleep nurtured her unborn child, protectively cupping her hands around her slightly protruding belly. The Consul prayed his wife would give birth only after they had settled into their new home rather than on the ship. He was unsure of the circumstances that might precipitate an early birth but he prayed that no such situation occurred. After all, René reasoned, Eugenie was not even five months into her term and with good winds they might make shore in three months. But he did not foresee the turn of events that would forever change his life.

While he had mused, Christine had fallen asleep. René picked up the well-worn book from de Fleury and opened it to the first page.

"A true account of the unjustified English attack on the French colonists of Beaubassin, Acadia on the thirteenth day of August in the year of Our Lord one thousand six hundred and ninety-six."

The carriage rumbled along the dusty road a bit, then suddenly stopped. René pulled his window curtain back a bit and peered outside. Captain Brossard rode over to him, followed by Claude.

"Monsieur le Consul, we have arrived but we have an unusual request."

René waited expectantly and Broussard nodded to Claude. The young man spoke. "My Lord, we should need fresh linens and blankets for the rooms from your supply coach. I took the liberty to remove the soiled ones and have the rooms cleaned again. It would not do for the Lady Eugenie, or his Lordship, or anyone to become ill from dirty sheets."

René nodded vigorously. He appreciated the boy's quick thinking. "Of course. Perhaps Christine can select something for the Lady Eugenie and take the other things you need. Her Ladyship's health is of the utmost importance. Thank you. I do not believe I know your name?"

"Claude, my Lord. Claude Arnaud."

"Arnaud? Laurent Arnaud organized our wedding feast. Any relation?"

"My younger brother, Sieur Le Blanc de Verdure." He wanted to avoid a prolonged discussion of his brother who was much beloved at Court. However Claude he had a better appreciation of Laurent's talents now, having gone through the exercise at the inn. "Also, the food here appears not to be edible. The cook knows how to prepare but has no fresh stores, so may we take from the stores meant for the sea voyage"

"Certainly, take enough to feed everyone at the inn. Christine, should something special be prepared for Lady Eugenie?"

Christine nodded. "I shall prepare it myself."

Claude assisted Christine out of the coach.

René whispered to Claude, "Pick out the best bottle of wine you can find from the wedding feast. Then set up our supper in our room. I want it complete with candles and flowers. And thank you again, Claude."

Claude and Christine selected the foods and the footmen carried them around to the kitchen. Claude turned to Christine.

"I must warn you about the condition of this kitchen. Blood and animal guts everywhere."

"I suspect not as bloody as birthing children. Could you handle that?" she asked, partly in jest but mostly in all seriousness.

Claude had the urge to vomit again but he willed himself not to.

René stayed in the carriage, not wishing to wake his wife. She would need every ounce of strength she could muster. Eugenie woke an hour later and he brought her to their large room. The wooden floors had been freshly washed and covered with thick rugs. The room was fragrant with the scent of fresh wild flowers, the windows covered with silk curtains and the bed covered with quilts and soft pillows. René pulled out a chair at a table set for two. Candles twinkled on the fireplace mantle and at the table.

"My dear husband, shall we sup here, just the two of us?"

"My darling wife. We are, after all, on our honeymoon. I prefer to spend as much time alone with you as you shall allow."

He kissed the top of her head and she leaned back. He kissed her, enjoying the plump sweetness of her lips.

There was a knock at the door and two serving girls entered, proudly wearing servant dresses from Claude, carrying trays of delicious smelling food. Claude poured a bottle of the same wine served at the wedding feast. Eugenie was touched by her husband's romantic thoughtfulness.

The next day the Versailles passengers were woken at daybreak. They ate a hearty breakfast of fresh breads dripping with butter, sweet jams and jellies, a variety of meats, sauces and cakes. The innkeeper and his wife and daughters, the servant girls, feasted on the leftovers when the royal party departed. But no one saw Claude. He was long gone, riding hard to prepare the next inn in the same manner. He prepared himself to do the same for every overnight stop convinced the inns along this road would all be as disgustingly filthy as the first.

Once Eugenie and Christine were settled in the carriage, René joined them. Captain Broussard asked permission to leave, which René granted. As the coaches began to roll down the road, René took out the Cardinal's journal. He began to read quietly to himself.

"Recorded from an eyewitness account told by Philippe Gaudet to André-Hercule de Fleury, priest of the Catholic Parish of Acadia."

René's heart skipped a beat. How was it possible to be the Cardinal's own journal, he wondered. He continued on, spellbound, reading the entire book.

Then René clasped the journal to his chest and wept silently at the thought of human beings, even political enemies, treating others in this way.

He closed his eyes to blot out the memory of what he had just read but the writing contained so many details that René kept reviewing them over and over in his mind.

The carriages soon arrived at the inn. Within an hour, everyone had eaten and had retired to their rooms. René leaned over to Eugenie, who was so fatigued she had barely managed to stay awake for supper. He kissed her forehead and before he had blown out the candle, his wife was fast asleep.

That night René had a vision about the massacre recounted in the book. He never told anyone that what he saw in his mind's eye that night had actually happened. He knew the vision was not a dream but the true events that were revealed to him so that he would never forget to stay vigilant against the English in order to protect his new charges, the French Neutrals. The vision began with the Acadian shoreline at night.

A large three-masted vessel bearing the English flag was moored in the sea beyond the rocks, protecting the shore. The waves were dotted with small rowboats filled with British troops in uniform, all armed with swords, bayonets, muskets. Many rowboats were already on shore and they were soon joined by the others. Soon English officers led their troops into regimental formation.

An officer in Major's dress with a black eye patch held up the Bible as the troops fell into line. He prayed, "Our holy Queen Anne has ordered daily prayer and forbidden swearing and drunkenness. She has also authorized us to hang French Acadian rebel leaders and sell our prisoners of war into slavery for plantation work in her Colonies. Let us pray for victory and our Queen."

The troops knelt in the sand on the beach, holding their hands in their hands and bowing their heads as the Major continued.

"O Lord, hear your faithful servant Benjamin Church and grant him and his troops the strength to bring the Church of England, our Majesty's true Church, to these heathen French Catholics. And finally, Lord, give us the courage to battle the infidel French without fear. Protect us as we conquer the Acadians in Your Name. To all of this we pray. Amen."

The troops shouted out a loud, "Amen" in response to the Major's prayer.

The wind carried the roar from the beach up a hillside into the treetop where a young Acadian boy of twelve was perched. He had volunteered as the town lookout every night in exchange for free lodging and food during the day at the stables. The boy's name was Philippe Gaudet.

Philippe had been orphaned at age six when his parents died in the hard snows of Beaubassin. They had been tenant laborers, traveling from farm to farm and ending up in Beaubassin. Thereafter the townspeople of Beaubassin treated him kindly, giving him food and clothing.   Soon he became the errand boy for the settlement.

Young Gaudet looked through the trees, down a hill to the beach. How could he have missed all the activity, he wondered. British boats and soldiers had swarmed the beach where French merchants unloaded their supplies. He would learn later that the British had captured one of these French vessels, looted everything they could, then sunk it with the sailors still aboard crying for mercy. The English were not merciful in the slightest.

Without taking the time to climb down the branches, Philippe anxiously jumped from his tree to the ground below, turning his ankle. Despite the pain, he hobbled down the dusty road to warn the villagers. Once he reached the signpost marked, "Bienvenue à Beaubassin," he stopped merely to catch his breath and enter the town. He found all was dark on the main street.

Beaubassin was the largest town in the Acadian province, having been settled in 1630 by French settlers who were not able to obtain land in the sister settlement, Port Royal, the main settlement in the French territory. Yet Beaubassin consisted of little more than stone or wooden buildings serving as shops and houses on a main street of dirt. A great forest was located to the west of the town. At the edge of these woods behind Beaubassin was a gathering of wigwams and bark huts belonging to the Acadians' allies, the Mi'Kmaqs. A large hill overlooked this Indian Village and the town of Beaubassin. Philippe knew it well, having played hide and seek with the other children there.

Back on the beach, the troops were at attention. Major Church raised a red-sealed parchment in front of his troops. He broke the seal and read it quickly. He turned back to the troops. "Orders from our holy Queen. Burn, kill, plunder and destroy. Take spoils wherever we may. Officers, move your troops to the top of the hill, check weapons and await my orders."

The officers obeyed and ordered their troops forward. They quickly disappeared from the beach as they marched up the hillside. The soldiers started singing a battle song, until their officers hushed them for their surprise attack.

Philippe turned back to the road, thinking he heard more shouts, and even a ditty, from the direction of the hill. He saw no activity but knew he had to take quick action to warn the townspeople who had been so kind to him.

A long line of troops marched away from the beach, up a small hill and onto the dusty road. There they halted and made final preparations for the attack.

The officers sent powder boys through the troops, loading muskets and powder pouches. Soldiers sharpened bayonets or knives. Others readied their muskets. Torchbearers lit their torches.

A burly soldier loosened his pantaloons and turned to the torchbearer nearest him, "Those French women act too good for us. I shall show them a thing or two."

The torchbearer responded, "I shall be there with you. Not much longer now."

Philippe ran through the town, knocking on windows and doors but no one heard the boy's cry. He ran for the stables. With a horse he would be able to make more noise and wake up the residents. Once inside the stables he climbed up the ladder to his sleeping quarters in the hayloft. He tucked his Bible in his jacket, grabbed his other set of clothes and started down the ladder.

In his haste and unbeknownst to him, he knocked over his still-burning candle into the hay. Below the boy the horses whinnied and stomped in fear at the smoke filling the loft above their stables. Philippe quickly jumped down the ladder.

At the top of the hill, the officers organized their troops back into regimental formation on the road. Church rode by and reviewed the troops, all at attention.

The Major hacked the air with his sword and gave the order they had waited for. "Attack! Now, forward march!"

"Forward march," called the officer for the first unit as his troops pushed ahead down the road.

The second unit officer repeated, "Forward march," and his soldiers followed the first unit toward the town.

The refrain, "Forward march," was repeated down the line for each of the seven units of troops. Each unit was to carry out a specific task relative to the village and its inhabitants, though many were to be carried out simultaneously to take the village and its environs by surprise.

As the loft began to burn, Philippe saddled a horse and rode out of the barn, opening the doors and freeing the other animals. They scattered in panic, running aimlessly through the streets and out of the town. The boy galloped once more through the town, this time throwing rocks at windows and warning the villagers.

"Get out, get out. The English are coming!" Philippe shouted at the top of his lungs.

The bloodthirsty troops marched forward in an unending line along the road. As they rounded the bend the stables burst into flames and horses burst out of the barn, running directly into them, upsetting their regiments.

The townspeople finally woke because of his cries or perhaps the light of the burning stables or the sound of cracking wood and falling planks in the street.

Pandemonium erupted as Acadians opened their windows and poured out of doors into the street. When they realized the situation, they ran back inside, women gathering children and packing food and blankets and men readying their weapons.

Philippe looked back at the road and saw torches beyond the bend moving forward. He pointed back to the road and cried out to the men, "The troops are on the main road. Leave before it is too late." Then he raced out of town to the Mi'Kmaq Village.

Some families left everything and ran into the nearby woods to hide. Others left on horseback, riding out of town opposite the main entry. These were the lucky ones, only a few.

But most of the townsmen readied themselves for a fight and took vantage points in windows or on top of buildings to fire at the soldiers.

While the Acadian leaders were preparing defenses, Philippe reached the Indian Village, where he found the tribe abuzz. Some of the women and children were already in the woods, dragging their aging and infirm relatives behind them on bark sleds. The Indian chief and his warriors had painted themselves for battle and waved Philippe to move on.

Instead of running up the hill to safety, Philippe hid the horse in the woods and climbed up one of his favorite trees. He had a clear view of the entire town and the Indian huts but was protected from view.

At the edge of town, Church directed the first unit to follow him as he circumvented the town and moved toward the Indian huts near the woods. His officers had each issued their unit the same orders, issued by the King. "Loot and pillage as you will and kill any who resist. Bring us first all females, adult or child. Lock up all the rest of the heathens as prisoners of war."

As the first troop of soldiers followed Major Church to the Mi'Kmaq Village, six other large troops of English soldiers marched into Beaubassin.

Philippe saw everything that happened and remembered it in great detail.

René woke with a start, the detailed images remaining with him. He wept at the thought of the events he had just seen that had befallen his countrymen on that fateful day.

The Consul turned to his sleeping wife and kissed her hand. He was so thankful they were going to a province at peace, even if it was English territory since the Treaty of Utrecht. He resigned himself to remember the tragedy and to prevent it from happening ever again.

He slept fitfully the rest of the night and met Claude before dawn in the dining hall of the large inn. They shared a breakfast from René's stores before the young man headed to the next inn. René woke Eugenie, who refused to eat but walked directly into the carriage and fell asleep again. Christine assured him not to worry but worry he did, all the same.

On the third day of the journey, as his carriage rolled forward, René re-read some of the passages in Cardinal de Fleury's journal that haunted him with images etched vividly in his memory.

"*Major Church and his first unit with a few torchbearers set fire to the bark huts and wigwams. A handful of Indians jumped out from the houses with tomahawks in hand and cracked the skulls of several soldiers. After the initial shock, the English fired their muskets but missed the Indians, who escaped into the woods. Suddenly the English soldiers were pelted with arrows from the woods, many hitting their mark. Major Church decided against following the Mi'Kmaqs into the forest, and instead he led his troops into the town. They marched past the burning stables and joined the second unit.*

The two units knelt in formation in the middle of the main street, each unit alternating to face the opposite direction. The soldiers aimed their weapons at doors and windows, waiting to see the Acadian heathens.

Any of the French colonists who appeared at a window, door or rooftop was hit with shots from dozens of soldiers' guns. The Acadian fighters shot and wounded a few soldiers and killed fewer still. But they were no match for the English soldiers who killed over half of the townsmen in return volleys.

The third unit of soldiers was ordered to plunder. They first broke into the building closest to the entry which housed a store with French imported goods. They looted the shop and filled their sacks with everything in sight. They continued along the street, ransacking valuables and foodstuffs in every shop. When they found cases of French wine, they carried them into the street and passed them out to the other soldiers.

Several of the soldiers in the third unit broke into the Catholic Church, desecrated the altar and stole the gold chalice. They broke all the holy statues and the beautiful stained glass window that had been brought from France by Père Doucet, the parish priest. They hanged him from the balcony of the Church and then set the building on fire.

The Acadians lived on the second and third floors, above their shops. Many had locked themselves into the upper floors. Some tried to escape by the back door during the looting. However the fourth unit was stationed in the rear of the houses and plunged their bayonets into all the males escaping from the back of the house, then brought the women and girls to the seventh unit of soldiers waiting in the town square in the middle of the street.

The fifth unit followed the looters and nailed shut all doors to the town's buildings and houses after they were ransacked to prevent the Acadians from escaping.

Those Acadians who did come out of their houses before they were nailed shut, even those with the white cloth of surrender, were shot on sight by the second unit of troops, who kept their muskets loaded and aimed at the exits.

The sixth unit worked with the torchbearers to set fire to all the buildings. The Acadians had the choices of jumping out of a window, breaking down the door and risking being shot, or remaining inside and being burned alive. As soon as a building was torched the Acadians fired from the roof or the windows but soon were either killed by musket fire or by the smoke and flames.

The seventh troop tied the women and girls hand to hand with rope then half-dragged them to the middle of the main street. The officers had been drinking all morning and were ready for the women. The troops forced the females to kneel and perform unspeakable acts on the officers, who then stripped and raped them, even as young as five years of age. These and other acts of degradation were performed on the wives and daughters of the Acadian men, whose arms had been chained around nearby trees and forced to watch. Any Acadian who turned away or cried out was shot in the head.

After the officers were satisfied, soldiers in order of rank were given their choice of the women. Most of the soldiers took their turn in the street, but the torchbearer and the burly soldier, still drinking from their wine bottles, dragged two teenage sisters behind one of the burnt buildings.

The torchbearer was drunk and fell to the ground, but the soldier was readying to have his way with the younger girl. She had been beaten so badly she could hardly move. As soon as he dropped his pantaloons he let go of his wine bottle. The older sister cracked the bottle on the edge of the house and slit the burly soldier's throat, then killed the torchbearer. Then she dressed herself and her sister in the soldiers' clothes and stumbled together as if drunk, out of the town. They soon passed the burning embers of what was the Indian Village and entered the woods.

The girl collapsed below the tree where Philippe hid. He slid down the tree and helped them into the woods, where several Mi'Kmaq women appeared and assured Philippe they would care for them as their own daughters.

Philippe jumped on his horse and rode to the hilltop behind Beaubassin. Hidden behind a range of tree, he saw the town had been completely burned, all the men shot at close range and the women violated, then killed too. The soldiers had not distinguished between Acadian men, women or children but had condemned all of them to a violent death.

God bless their souls, prayed Philippe.

He saw Major Church round up his officers, who marched their soldiers out of town and back down the hill.

Philippe turned his horse and galloped out of sight in the opposite direction."

René pulled back the curtains of the coach to see the dawn breaking. He closed them again and leaned back, alone in his reverie. Closing his eyes he imagined what the brave young Philippe would have done next and how he met de Fleury.

Philippe rode all day and night but he finally saw lights in the valley below. Exhausted, he led the horse down the hill and they arrived at a small stone Church near a settlement of many homes, buildings and farms.

In the belfry, a handsome young Catholic priest rang the Church bells. Philippe jumped off the horse and pounded on the door until the priest opened it. Philippe staggered in, trying to describe the massacre.

"British attack. Murdered our priest," sputtered Philippe.

"Where, my son? Can we help?" said the priest.

Philippe shook his head. "English killed everyone. Beaubassin is gone. Mi'Kmaq Village burned too."

The priest led the boy into the parish house next to the Church, saying, "Save your strength, my son. First you must eat and then sleep. We will talk when you have refreshed yourself." Philippe was too weak to argue. Food and sleep were just what he needed.

The priest's jovial housekeeper, Madame Trahan, took Philippe's arm and sat him down, refilling his plate several times. "Poor boy. What is your name?"

"Philippe Gaudet, Madame."

"Well you are nothing but skin and bones, Master Gaudet. Just let Madame Trahan fatten you up."

Philippe nodded and asked, 'Where am I? I feel like I have ridden for days."

Madame Trahan replied, "Grand Pré at the Church of St. Charles-des-Mines. We are your family now: Père André-Hercule de Fleury and I."

The priest nodded and Madame Trahan was about to take Philippe to what would be his room.

He said to the priest, "I must tell you what I saw while my memory is fresh, although the images of the massacre will stay with me forever." Then he added. "I cannot write. Will you do so?"

De Fleury nodded. "Of course." He went to his writing desk and pulled out a leather-bound journal. Madame Trahan filled the inkwell and handed him a stack of quills. She took a seat. This could take a while.

Père André-Hercule de Fleury dipped the quill in the ink and opened the journal to the front page. He read aloud as he wrote. "A true account of the unjustified English attack on the French colonists of Beaubassin, Acadia on the thirteenth day of August in the year of Our Lord one thousand six hundred and ninety-six."

So the Cardinal had been the parish priest in Grand Pré, thought René. No doubt he had hand-picked Père Rivière for the post, which comforted René after reading the horrific events in the journal. René put the book away, determined not to read it again until he arrived in Grand Pré. He knew he would never forget the vision but he did not want to divert his concentration from his wife. That night passed quickly and the party left early the next morning.

The fourth day saw storms erupt after lunch and pelt the carriages for hours. The drivers were unable to make much progress. After rolling through mud-filled holes, wheels on two of the supply carriages broke. Fortunately, many spares had been stowed and the drivers and coachmen were able to make the necessary repairs.

In the driving rain the carriages slowed their pace and arrived at the station rooms well after midnight. Claude was waiting for them and, fearing the continuing rain, had built a crude wooden tunnel from the driveway to the front door with the help of the innkeeper and his strong son. René was thankful that Eugenie was not exposed to the elements and asked Claude what he could do in gratitude. Claude uncharacteristically refused. But René, who had seen him eyeing the wine at their suppers, gave him two bottles. Claude was ecstatic and stowed them in the satchel he tied to his saddle before he took to the road.

The rain continued through the night and at dawn René met with Captain Broussard.

"Captain, how close are we to Le Havre?"

Broussard replied, "If we can continue our pace we shall arrive tomorrow, but if the rain continues it could take us two more days."

"The ship sails in three, does it not?"

"Yes my Lord, but Captain Jacques is a careful man. He will be even more cautious with you and the Lady Eugenie on board and will not risk sailing in foul weather."

"Would it be prudent to stay here half a day and see if the weather clears or do you prefer to move slowly forward?"

"Sire, we have leeway of one day so we could wait until midday."

"Excellent suggestion. If the rain continues then we move forward slowly and if not, we will arrive in Le Havre on schedule."

The passengers were advised they could sleep a few more hours until the rain lessened or the weather cleared altogether. The grateful souls, exhausted from the journey, accepted the offer.

Midday saw the rainclouds clear and the carriages rolled toward the port. But within hours, bad weather befell them along the way. Trees had been split in two by lighting, blocking the road two hours distance from the inn. Several hours later the coachmen and the Royal Horsemen had removed the large logs and debris and the drivers had started the horses.

An hour later a band of traveling gypsies had stopped the head coach, threatening to harm the passengers unless they were given gold pieces.

René told Broussard to set up a tent and fill it with food and a barrel of wine for the gypsies. Then he asked that he bring the leader of the gypsies to the nearest clearing after the meal to meet with René. Broussard's men and the coachmen fulfilled their orders quickly. Soon the gypsies filled their bellies with food. They drank the wine and danced until they collapsed, each in a drunken stupor.

René was given a horse and he rode with Broussard to meet with the gypsy leader. The man was a short wizened fellow sporting a long beard and trying to appear dignified in his ragged patched coat. He realized René was an important man, perhaps even a relative of the King. But he also knew the Royal Horsemen with their muskets and swords surrounded his sleeping family. He knew what he had to do, and he bowed for forgiveness.

"Me lord, my family was hungry was all. If we can just get some more food we will be on our way."

René was curious about the man who looked frightening but seemed to be pacified. "What is your name, sir?"

"Karaztyev, me Lord."

René shook his hand and placed a coin in it. "Monsieur Karaztyev, your family shall have food for a month if you promise to leave these woods and threaten no other passengers on this road."

"No, me lord, I means to say yes, me Lord. No more threats. Thank you, me Lord."

René trotted back to the carriage of stores, where he told Claude to prepare a bag of fresh food. Claude looked askance but did as he was told. René reached into another carriage and pulled out some clothes, including a new wool cloak, and put them into another satchel. Claude handed the bag and satchel to Karaztyev, who called out to his family in a strange guttural language. They stood drowsily then clumsily scampered out of the tent and soon disappeared into the woods.

The drivers were able to push the horses forward in the muddy lanes until the tempest turned into a violent thunderstorm. When lightning struck nearby in the forest, the horses whinnied and bucked, refusing to move.

The carriages were stopped for hours. Near sunset, the muddy road laden with broken branches and limbs, René decided they would have to stay in the carriages for the night. The Horsemen took shifts guarding the carriages, with four men riding up and down the line all night in the raging winds and rain.

Finally, the storm broke at dawn and the servants could see well enough to clear the road ahead. While the carriages made their way slowly through the muddy lane, the footmen continued to clear the next stretch of road. There, the way widened enough for a carriage to pass another, the sign of a nearby town or inn.

René leaned out of his carriage. "Captain, let us stop early today at the next station. The trip is taking its toll on my wife and I am certain the others, including you and your riders, need the rest."

Broussard bowed. "There is an inn not two hours ahead. With another approaching storm we should shelter the horses, too."

As Broussard galloped away, René leaned back and closed his eyes. He heard the steady clipping of the driver's team, broken by the trotting of the Royal Horsemen. The wheels rolled in harmony with the horses, and he heard an occasional crack of a driver's whip before he was fast asleep.

CHAPTER 14
Port

Le HAVRE

From the time of the Frankish Kingdom ruler Clovis in the fourth century, the northern coast what was now France had been protected diligently against unwelcome foreigners. Viking marauders, Celtic warriors, English Saxons, Portuguese pirates and Spanish Armada captains all tried to breach the rocky shores to conquer the Kingdom. And though there were some successes over the centuries, French fleets were launched which changed the balance of power so that France became the most powerful nation in Europe.

In times of peace, merchant cargo vessels brought foreign goods and foods into France through Honfleur and Harfleur, northern harbors existing since ancient days. The ports had been some of Europe's busiest for centuries until their gradual silting reduced their utility and affected trade. In 1517, Francis I built a modern harbor which he named Franciscopolis, renamed Le Havre by his successor.

The harbor became the primary departure point of privateers, merchants and explorers, including Giovanni da Verrazzano, who embarked there on his famous expedition in 1524 that resulted in France's expansion into Acadia in the New World.

The trip from Versailles to Le Havre in the cramped carriages had been more difficult than imagined. Sitting in finery and confined quarters for hours on end made even the softest cushions feel as hard as stone. The passengers endured their journey, each in a different way. René's raison d'être was to fulfill Eugenie's wishes. When she was not asleep, they sat close to each other, sharing private conversations or watching the passing countryside together. Christine was bent over her books of remedies, comparing one with another and writing notes in the margins of the papers.

In the next coach, Sun chortled joyfully each time the coach hit a hole in the road, causing him to bounce in his seat. Père Rivière put his nose in his Bible reading, reflecting and marking passages for future sermons. Doctor Hébert had resolved the monotonous situation by drinking a potion each morning, putting him in a deep sleep until he had to be woken for a meal or arrival at an inn. In his private coach, Pater was jostled about and bumped on every part of his corpulent body as his boxes and crates bounced around in the carriage.

Captain Broussard and his men had been trained to ride for hours on end and wore special clothing to prevent or soften the pain of sores; all except Claude, of course, who had not thought to requisition special clothes for the long journey. Because the Doctor was heavily sedated, Claude, with much embarrassment, asked Christine for a liniment to ease his pain.

Christine insisted on a personal examination of the damage and had matter-of-factly told him to drop his pants. Outside the kitchen of the inn Claude had done so, to the hoots and hollers of the cook and his assistants. Even the servant girls had enjoyed the scene. When Christine was satisfied, she dressed his blisters with salve prepared from her Indian remedy book. After that, Claude found physical relief but suffered as the victim of a daily joke among his fellow Royal Horsemen. However, they also gained a newfound respect for the young man who had not complained or asked for special treatment, though the Consul had shown favor on him and his brother was secretary to the King's powerful Prime Minister.

Despite the great discomfort of the coach and her condition, then new Lady Le Blanc de Verdure knew how lucky she was. She had fallen in love with her husband somewhere along the route. Love and happiness were rare among royal marriages, which were arranged most often for political alliances rather than attraction between the bride and groom. She already knew René's quiet strength, experienced his constant care, despite having a doctor and midwife on the trip, felt his tenderness and saw his commitment to fulfill her every desire. She hoped she would be able to deserve his love over the years and vowed to put her heart and soul into pleasing him.

Eugenie regarded her husband with admiration and felt a great sense of calm knowing she and her child would be protected and, most of all, loved by this man. Keeping her thoughts to herself, she noted that both René and Christine were asleep. She would not wake them until they reached their destination, which Captain Broussard had assured would be late in the day.

*

In the stormy harbor of Le Havre, Captain Philippe Jacques had ordered his sailors to batten the hatches, stow the sails and seal the hold of his new ship which had just been christened, *L'Acadie*. As the sun dipped into the water, thunder cracked loudly, bringing with it another deluge. The Captain peered out to the open sea with his spyglass. He saw unending crests of whitecaps, each taller than the last. Looking at the waves and the black skies, he knew they could not get out of port until the weather changed drastically.

Storms had continued for the last week and the Captain did not see any indication of the rains letting up. Since the royal carriages had yet to arrive, he presumed they, too, were caught in storms along the way. The Captain feared it could be weeks rather than days before a smooth embarkation could be had. He had expected his crew would be bustling by now to hoist sails, sweep decks, load stores and lower the gangplank to the waiting passengers in the busy port but they were simply drowned rats, waiting for the signal to scamper off the deck and back to the portside inns.

After waiting until midday, with no sign of the swells lessening or rains letting up, he decided not to set sail until the weather cooperated. He would not risk the life of one passenger, whether royalty or commoner, and gave his crew leave until the following week. The extra time should calm the waves for smoother loading of passengers and goods. Jacques knew most of his crew would end up in the bars in the port, preferring to drink their wages in town rather than attempt treacherous country paths home for a few days. The Captain had given strict instructions to report for duty in a week and he knew his men well enough to know none would risk their jobs by arriving late. But by the looks of the storm beating down upon the port and everything in its path, Jacques wondered if he had been too optimistic to think they could depart in several days.

The Captain deposited a letter for the Consul at the harbormaster's small office, then fought his way through the torrential rains and fierce winds to the Whitecap, a local inn near the port. Thankfully, upon observing the approaching storm clouds he had reserved rooms for himself and his men with an extra chamber for the royal party's staff earlier in the day. As he entered the door of the rustic building, people were accosting the poor innkeeper for shelter anywhere. The man was able to rent places on the stairway and in his barn to stranded visitors and passengers glad to pay anything to have a roof over their heads. He knew his sailors would stay warm with their grog and a barkeep's stool so he went to the dining room to eat before the food was gone.

*

The royal carriages pulled up to the dock in Le Havre and René awoke readily. He looked over at Eugenie who was smiling, comfortably propped among pillows, waiting for her husband and Christine to awaken. Peering through an open slit in the curtain, René saw the faint outline of a ghost ship through the driving rain. He expected to see a lowered gangplank and a welcome party, even in the rain, but instead saw the ship battened down and uninviting. Captain Broussard rode over to the harbormaster's building and after a short while returned to deliver the Captain's letter to René. Then he waited expectantly for orders.

"Captain Jacques has delayed the sailing for seven days and reserved all the rooms at a boardinghouse named Highpoint. He said if your men are willing to sleep three or four to a room there should be sufficient space for everyone."

"That is most gracious of you, Monsieur le Consul. I happen to know Madame Perrine Mercier's house is the best in the town. She is a local widow with two daughters who are excellent cooks and, as I recall, also accomplished in music."

"I was correctly informed, then, that you know Le Havre quite well."

"My men and I have stayed at Highpoint when in Le Havre, the last being several years ago, with full satisfaction and no regrets."

"Do you believe Her Ladyship will be comfortable there?"

Eugenie protested, "My dear husband. Please do not fuss over me. I am perfectly agreeable to such accommodations. Let us install ourselves as the Captain recommended."

René told Broussard, "We shall settle everyone and provide our stores for Madame's daughters to cook. Then you and I shall meet with the Captain. He is at the Whitecap Inn, with a room to house the drivers and coachmen. Let us away before we are caught in a lightning strike."

Broussard nodded. "It shall be as you command, Monsieur le Consul." He signaled his men and they informed the drivers, who cracked their whips. The carriages moved slowly out of the harbor. A small crowd of townspeople had gathered in the pouring rain to see if the rumors were true. And they were -- the King had come to Le Havre!

Carriages bearing the royal crest were rare this far north unless an invasion was launched by sea against the enemy. Since the local inhabitants had not been called to arms, no one understood why the King was in their village. But they were not going to let the rains stop them from seeing what, for most, would be the most interesting sight in their entire lives.

The locals included a few tipsy gents from the Port Tavern who stumbled their way towards the carriages. Behind them were several feisty women who sold fish and vegetables at the street market and, walking alongside them, several tradesmen and a few well-dressed merchants. A brigade of young men dressed in tattered rags, the port thieves, lurked between the vendors and the drunks. They bided their time, looking for bulging pockets to pick but not bold enough to attempt a theft in front of the King's men.

Attempting to blend into the crowd, the Karaztyev family had made their way through the forest to the port. The father saw the familiar coaches and, clutching his warm new cloak about him, determined he would ask for a job...for his entire family.

As the sun began to disappear, Broussard halted the carriages when the port road diverged -- the lower road went into town and the upper road to a hilltop. Madame Mercier's husband, Captain Jean Mercier had sailed merchant ships around the world returning with fascinating tales and exotic souvenirs. He had built their home on the highest point in the village so his wife would be the first to see him sail into the harbor. But unfortunately he had been lost at sea on a voyage to China before their daughters were old enough to have known him.

The Captain's widow had converted the huge house into rooms for distinguished visitors and upper-class passengers awaiting their sailing date. She had high hopes for her daughters to marry good men who would whisk them away to Paris or another great city in France where their talents and beauty would be appreciated. But thus far Madame had only been approached by farmers and merchants, even the local hogsman, who were rejected as suitors before her daughters learned of the offers.

While the carriages were at a standstill, the coachmen carried torches to light lamps to show the drivers' way. The Royal Horsemen each carried a torch, riding on the cliff side of the pathway. It soon proved to be unnecessary, as Madame Mercier had installed large torches along the road which the Horsemen lit to show a wide expanse of road before them. No chance a horse would miss its footing and plunge to the sea below.

The parade of the locals approached closer until Broussard's men formed a barrier to hold the crowd back. The gawkers could not see much except closed carriages, whose windows were covered by thick brocade curtains. Suddenly, one of the pickpockets, Daniel Theriot, made a run towards the last passenger coach, squeezing underneath two horses. It was an innocent move, even for a pickpocket, because he thought he saw a shiny object on the ground.

Just as Daniel ran midway between the carriage and the crowd and leaned down to collect the shining piece, Claude was upon him and flicked his whip. Daniel flew face down into a newly discharged pile of horse manure into which a small coin had fallen. Claude admonished Daniel to rejoin the crowd which he did after he had grabbed the coin. It was easy to keep an eye on the boy after that, as the crowd moved away from the stink wherever he walked. Daniel would say later he learned two lessons that night. First, that royal horse piles stink just as much as those in the local stables he cleaned. And second, never to look for treasure where horses are gathered.

After that incident, the King's Horsemen formed a tighter line of defense against the curiosity seekers. The Royal Family was much beloved here so no danger of assassins lurked but Broussard reasoned it was better to have too much security than not enough.

Soon the royal entourage arrived at the boardinghouse. Madame Mercier and her daughters, Adèle and Claire, warmly greeted everyone at their carriages. Adèle marveled at the variety of foods she would be cooking, some of which were so exotic she had never before seen them. Claude, smitten at first sight, coordinated the relocation of the stores from the coaches to the cooler storage rooms built into the hillside. Then he organized the first week's food, which he had coachmen deliver directly to the kitchen. He planned to woo her with his strength and helpfulness in carrying her future deliveries.

"May I assist you Mademoiselle...?"

"Adèle Mercier, Monsieur."

He kissed her hand gallantly. "I am Claude Arnaud, member of the Royal Horsemen of His Majesty King Louis, at your service."

She tossed her blonde curls and smiled. "And not a moment too soon. I could use some help getting the roasts out of the oven. We took the liberty to prepare a meal, thinking you would be hungry after the journey. But we only learned a few hours ago that so many would be coming. There are too many platters for me to carry."

"Say no more, lovely lady, but give me your orders. I should be honored to do your bidding."

"So I shall, Monsieur Arnaud. Let us begin in the kitchen." He was pleased to be at her side, when not needed by Captain Broussard, from that moment forward. He made it his mission to learn everything about the entrancing Adèle. He discovered that in addition to being an incomparable cook and musician, she was also an accomplished seamstress. She had sewn and embroidered all the linens for the guesthouse and, unbeknownst to Claude, her wedding clothes for the day she would marry. He fell more under her spell every day.

Footmen assisted Lady Eugenie and the other passengers out of their carriages and into the house. Madame made them feel immediately welcome in the well-appointed home. Eugenie and René were given large adjoining rooms used by Madame Mercier on the main floor. Still on his honeymoon, René preferred to share the same bed with Eugenie so the second room became his temporary office. His coachmen cleared the chamber and brought in René's desk from the coaches, then unloaded his parchments, inks and quills. He would write his first letter to Cardinal de Fleury tomorrow after he learned more details of their new sailing date from Captain Jacques.

Madame Mercier made efficient use of the beds, cots, pallets, and straw mats in the house. Adèle moved from her room upstairs to join Claire, giving her larger room to Christine and her mother. The royal status of Pater, Doctor Hébert and Père Rivière required a separate room for each, while Captain Broussard took the attic alcove. The Royal Horsemen divided the remaining rooms in the main house. Sun was happy in the tall pigionière outside the house. Mercier's homing birds were long gone but Sun was enthralled with the view of the harbor, where Madame had watched for the Captain's return.

The final lodgers were René's driver Luc Bourg and his footmen, who slept in the small servants' quarters at the back of the kitchen. Madame had staff when her husband's salary paid their wages but they were let go when he was lost at sea. Thereafter, she raised her daughters to be able to run the boardinghouse themselves, if it ever came to that.

After Eugenie was tucked into bed to rest before dinner and Christine promised to look in on her, René and Broussard walked onto the front deck of the Inn. As they were about to leave, Père Rivière rushed up and handed a letter to Broussard.

"Would you please deliver this to Captain Jacques? It is not good news, I fear, but nonetheless I promised his brother I would."

Broussard took the letter and he rode at René's insistence in the royal coach. They were followed by two other carriages overflowing with the Consul's drivers and footmen. Broussard, with René's approval, met with the innkeeper and the lodgers, who were in awe of seeing an actual Horseman in the King's service. As a result, Broussard was able to negotiate rooms for the servants by paying lodgers the price of their room and new sleeping space on the floor as well as all their meals as long as the Consul's men stayed in the inn.

René met with Captain Jacques in the dining room and they discussed new sailing plans based on his study of the weather and the almanac he trusted, from Belgium. Broussard arrived for the end of the meeting. When René had approved a delay of a fortnight and all the details of the voyage had been discussed, Broussard and René returned to the Mercier house.

Captain Jacques sent word of the new sailing date to all the portside taverns and drinking houses, and his crew members were overjoyed to hear of their new paid holiday. Jacques never docked his crews' wages for weather delays. At the news, several of the married men left Le Havre to return to their families, hoping the roads would be dry upon their return.

At the house, René asked Claude to open enough champagne for all. When the glasses were filled, he surprised the group.

"Captain Jacques has set a new departure date of two weeks from today. He consulted his Almanac liegeois and believes the weather will be right to set sail then. So if Madame Mercier and her lovely daughters will not mind so many guests for so long, shall we drink to their health and to good sailing weather?"

"To your health and good sailing weather." Everyone lifted their glass to the Mercier women, then sipped the King's own stock.

Captain Broussard's eyes lingered on Claire in wishing the Merciers good health. His heart skipped a beat when she looked across the room and gave him a slight nod of her head.

Madame Mercier was overjoyed at the Consul's news, but not just for the income that a full house would bring. She had her eye on a certain physician as a husband for Claire, and a certain Captain of the Royal Horsemen for Adèle. But as she would soon learn, her daughters had minds of their own in matters of the heart. And Dr. Hébert was a confirmed bachelor dedicated only to his work.

Adèle asked Claude to follow her to the kitchen, where he and the footmen carried the large cooking pots to the dining room sideboard. That was the awaited signal and Madame Mercier announced dinner to the group, which was in good spirits despite the weather. Adèle had spooned huge helpings of vegetables, stewed fruits, steamed clams, boiled lobsters and slices of roast into bowls and platters and set them on the tables.

Out of necessity and the lack of servants, Madame Mercier had long ago devised a family style meal where each diner served himself from the heaping bowls passed around the table. Most of her guests were aristocrats, successful merchants or King's appointees who would have found the custom unacceptable in Paris or Versailles. But in the little port town of Le Havre, all Madame's diners found it to be a charming albeit unique practice.

René watched Eugenie's reaction to the lack of servants, but she enjoyed filling her plate with as much or as little of a particular food as she wished. He noticed her plate contained mostly lobsters, which he insisted on cracking himself.

With such a crowd in the rooming house, the guests quickly became a family. They gathered in the large parlor after dinner to listen to Claire sing as Adèle played the piano. Eugenie and René retired thereafter but their staff was on call in the kitchen. Doctor Hébert retired to his room, his potion taking effect soon after every meal. Père Rivière sent Sun to his quarters and walked along the hillside, meditating as he watched the twinkling lights in the town below. The Horsemen, except Claude and Broussard, rode into port for libations and amusement.

Madame Mercier invited two men to join her and her daughters for a game of cards. Then Madame feigned fatigue and left the four young people alone. Claude was not a doctor but he was certainly attentive to Adèle, and the difference in ages between young Claire and the worldly Captain Broussard did not bother Madame in the least. She fell asleep planning two weddings.

While Madame Mercier dreamed of two new sons-in-law, Eugenie dreamed of...what was it? She woke in the middle of the night with an insatiable desire for lobster. René went to the kitchen himself, cracked the lobsters and fed them to his darling wife at midnight. They both toasted her health with the last of the champagne.

Captain Jacques asked to meet with René near the end of the two week period. When they met in the Consul's office at the Highpoint, Jacques hesitated before making his suggestion.

"My Lord, as you see, the rains have come back. The whitecaps are fewer and farther between but if we should wait another fortnight we shall be in early summer weather, which is the perfect time to sail."

René frowned. The closer to Eugenie's time, the more likely she would give birth on board the ship. And Eugenie's health could be at risk. He had to consult with the medical experts. "I shall advise you of my decision tomorrow." Captain Jacques took his leave and hoped that the Consul would agree to wait. He was only too aware of the Lady Le Blanc's condition and hoped he had explained as delicately as possible that sailing would be easier for a woman with child in the coming weeks.

He spoke with Eugenie. "Darling, do you feel strong enough to wait another two weeks to sail? You should know your own strengths better than Doctor Hébert or Christine."

"My dear husband, I feel in better health now than at the Palace, with no complaints except the unusual craving for lobsters. Please do not counter the Captain's advice on my account."

René nodded and kissed his wife's hand. Then he sought the counsel of the medical staff.

Doctor Hébert stroked his long beard. "In two more weeks the Lady Eugenie would have four months remaining and would need to stay in confinement except for a brief daily respite on deck for fresh air. The child would be that much stronger, in the event an early birth occurred."

Christine added, "Her Ladyship gets more color in her cheeks every day. And she has told me our walks do her good. If we continue to do so she should bear a healthy child."

René invited Captain Jacques to join them for dinner, their large meal at midday. Afterwards, the Captain took René on an inspection of the ship and their quarters. When they arrived at the port, Jacques was dismayed to see that the main mast had been cracked, apparently by lightening during the storm the evening before, and the mainsail ripped in half. He was unsure whether the mast could be repaired or if he could find a suitable mainsail in time. He recalled his sailors and sent his best climbers to the crow's nest to assess the damage and report to him.

Other captains of ships docked in Le Havre boarded *L'Acadie* to inspect and discuss the situation. The untenable weather brought forth many idle sailors in the French maritime hierarchy to give an opinion on the mast of the *L'Acadie*.

In the end Jacques agreed with all the others that a new mast had to be ordered to protect the security of the passengers. Fortunately for the Captain, the shipbuilding works of the King's Maritime Master Builder Jehan Hébert were located near the port. The new mast was promised to be delivered within the fortnight.

Hébert was a descendent of a long line of royal shipbuilders for the Kings of France. Their family connections with the sea dated back to Admiral Verrazzano's young aide of the same name who first saw Acadia two centuries earlier. Hébert was fortunate that his oldest son, François, was still in port to help with the work on the very ship that would take him and his family to Acadia. There he planned to open his own maritime works for boat construction and repairs in the region.

Once again Captain Jacques requested a meeting with Sieur Le Blanc and informed him that the new mast should be completed within their two week extension.

With the mast problem solved, Jacques ordered the crew members to ready the ship for the voyage. The royal coachmen and drivers went to and fro as the port laborers unloaded crates, barrels, boxes, furnishings, satchels and parcels galore into the hold of the ship.

Notice of the sailing date was sent to all the passengers who had advised the harbormaster of their address. Captain Jacques also posted a large notice in the harbormaster's office and had a small sign painted and attached to the lifted gangplank at the ship. He did not want to lose any of his passengers to other ships whose captains might not be so cautious.

After reading his brother's letter that everyone else in their family had perished in the Marseille Plague, Jacques realized how important it was to protect the lives in his charge and their faith. He would request Père Rivière to hold weekly Mass for all the passengers no matter the weather. That thought brought him great comfort.

CHAPTER 15
Ceremonies

Le HAVRE

 o René, it seemed the final two weeks in Le Havre passed more quickly than the first two. The weather cleared and the final days of the group's stay at the Mercier house were beautifully sunny. They often ate picnic lunches on the grounds overlooking the sea.

During the four weeks at the boardinghouse, love had blossomed between Michel Broussard and Claire, Madame Mercier's younger daughter. She had grown from the timid gangly young girl he had last seen into a confident beautiful young woman. He was eager to learn more about her and to that end he spent his free time, though limited, with her in the gardens of the Mercier home. They sat on a wooden bench overlooking the sea and he turned, took her hands and proposed. She nodded, tears of joy filling her eyes, and Michel kissed her softly. They sat silently together until the sun disappeared into the sea and lights twinkled in the harbor below.

In a like vein, Claude had fallen in love with Adèle Mercier and asked permission of his superior, Broussard, who immediately acquiesced. Claude took Adèle by horseback to visit the harbor and admire the ship.

She turned to him and wistfully, "How I would love to sail the high seas and make a life away from Le Havre. My father was a great adventurer who left me with a wanderlust that has never been satisfied."

Claude looked at her and immediately he descended from the horse, knelt on the dock and looked up at her. "Mademoiselle you would do me the greatest honor if you would consent to be my wife. Give me the opportunity to fulfill your dreams and take you to Acadia."

The answer was a foregone conclusion but. As he stood she jumped from the horse into his arms and kissed him on the spot, in public. Claude loved that about Adèle -- she knew her mind and followed it, regardless of public opinion. They looked at the beautiful ship *L'Acadie* and simultaneously suggested they be married on it. He knew they would do well in the New World, free of the many formalities in France. Or so they both hoped.

Arnaud approached Consul Le Blanc, who had just finished his last communication to send to the Cardinal for the King before they would sail. "My Lord, may I present two matters for your approval?"

René put down his quill and waited attentively. "Please go on."

"Mademoiselle Adèle has consented to marry me, and Captain Broussard has given his permission. But it would mean a great deal to me if you would also give your blessing, and if you could arrange for us to remain in Grand Pré, rather than going on to Québec City."

René was taken aback. He never expected a man in the King's service to make such a request. "Of course I wish you and Mademoiselle Mercier much happiness. I can make the request of the King but would not be able to assure your future in Grand Pré."

Claude expected as much. "I would not dare presume the Consul had a position for me but I have learned new skills and trades in the King's service that I never knew. I am certain that I can make a home for my wife and future family."

René nodded and clasped Claude's hand firmly, holding his shoulder with his other hand. "Then I shall pay your wife's passage as your wedding gift."

"My Lord, that is far too handsome. But I speak for my future bride and myself in thanking you for such generosity."

"And when shall the wedding take place?"

"We would like a shipboard wedding just before we set sail, so that her mother can attend. Père Rivière has already agreed to marry us. May I respectfully pray that your Lordship request permission of Captain Jacques?"

"Consider it done. And what of the younger sister?"

At that moment Michel Broussard entered. "I can answer that, my Lord. As a representative of the King would you grant your permission allowing me to marry Mademoiselle Claire?"

René nodded and shook his hand. "The rugged King's Horsemen have discovered beauty and love in the King's northern territory. So there are to be two ceremonies?"

Broussard answered first. "With your permission, we prefer the Mercier grounds overlooking the sea, with Père Rivière officiating."

"You have it with my blessing, of course."

René jotted a note on a piece of parchment, folded and held the wax to the candle, sealing it. Then he handed it to Arnaud.

"My request that Captain Jacques prepare for the wedding ceremony on board the ship the day we sail."

Both men bowed, thanking René profusely, then hugged each other as new brothers-in-law and rushed out to tell the good news to their brides.

Lady Eugenie had seen Adèle Mercier eyeing some of her fabrics in the carriages the first day Claude was helping her to select the food for the guests. That evening, Adèle found on her bed a large parcel which contained the very cloth she had admired. The blue silk sparkled with gold threads and matched her eyes, while the piece of handmade white lace was the perfect size for a veil. A similar parcel was on Claire's bed, except it contained shimmering green satin and black lace.

Adèle had begun sewing her own wedding dress the next day using the luxurious fabric for her wedding dress, replacing the plainer one she had previously sewn. She was smitten with Claude and thought he felt the same way about her but if he did not, the dress would keep in her dowry chest. She packed it carefully in the chest to wait for Claude's declaration. Michel had proposed to Claire before Claude broached the subject with Adèle, so Adèle began to sew her younger sister's dress, believing she would wear hers before Adèle would marry. That ended up being the case but for a different reason than she had thought.

Madame Mercier had immediately agreed to the engagements, though she had hoped Adèle would marry first and Claire would wait several more years. In their room, Christine heard Madame Mercier cry herself to sleep but only because she would lose both daughters at the same time. She had prayed that her daughters would fall in love as she did but only one at a time.

The girls were ecstatic and each night they planned how many children they would have and what their names would be. They were getting married!

The day before the *L'Acadie* was to sail, Père Rivière joined Claire Mercier and Michel Broussard in holy matrimony in the Mercier hilltop gardens overlooking the Port of Le Havre. Claire carried a bouquet of her mother's finest roses and wore the shimmering green gown and black veil. When Michel raised the veil to kiss the bride he lost himself gazing into her eyes. She leaned forward, reminding him to kiss her which he promptly did. Then he kissed her again for good measure to the applause of the guests.

René arranged for Michel and Claire to stay in Captain Jacques' room for their wedding night, as Jacques had already moved to the ship. He had to make other arrangements on board for Claude and Adèle since all the cabins had long been reserved.

René had provided the food for the wedding banquet, with his stores replenished with fresh foods for the journey. Madame had insisted on doing most of the baking and cooking, though her daughters could not stay away from the kitchens. Working together gave the three women a last opportunity to laugh at good memories and cry at the loss of future ones together.

The next day dawned bright and clear. At last, the departure date -- and another wedding day -- was upon the royal caravan. At the port, cartons, crates, wagons and carts appeared in the harbor as the laborers, merchants, carpenters, farmers and other French families who were going to settle in Grand Pré anxiously awaited their turn to have their goods loaded onto the ship for the journey. All of Le Havre had looked forward to this day with bated breath. They would finally have the opportunity to see the distinguished royal visitors. A crowd had been gathering since daybreak for the best view of the harbor and especially the ship's gangplank.

While Claude made final preparations for the ceremony with Père Rivière, Captain Jacques and his crew coordinated loading the passengers and their goods. An aristocrat's carriage with wagons and carts of goods stopped on the dock next to the ship. Lord Henri Mius d'Entremont and his young son Gabriel, passengers on the ship, stepped out as a flurry of workers began to unload their possessions.

D'Entremont was anxious to move far away from the memories of his wife, who had died several weeks before, and eager for his son to grow up independent and strong in the New World. He looked forward to meeting with the Mi'Kmaq First Nation with whom he had common ancestry on his father's side.

René, Eugenie and the other passengers were ensconced once more in their carriages. Doctor Hébert rode in René's carriage to allow the three Mercier women to ride with Père Rivière. Claude had found room in a carriage for all of Adèle's clothes, handsewn linens and her dowry chest. He was proud of his fiancée and was nearly bursting with anticipation of their wedding later that day.

Inside the carriage, Eugenie was pressed by Doctor Hébert to drink a vial of dark liquid. "It will give you strength for the voyage," he said. Eugenie complied and drank the bitter medicine while Christine wiped her brow with a linen handkerchief.

Eugenie was gracious, even in her condition. "I am grateful to both of you."

Doctor Hébert opened the jar of leeches and prepared to unbutton Eugenie's sleeves. René shook his head, saying, "I have never believed that leeches remove bad blood. The Lady shall take only the liquid medicines. Thank you, Doctor."

Doctor Hébert knew not to argue with such a powerful man as the Consul. He quickly hid the leech bottle and his disapproval by turning away from René to pack his medicines in his medical bag.

René held his wife's arm. "Everyone is here for your needs."

She smiled at him. "I know, my dearest." She turned to the doctor and Christine. "Thank you for your sacrifice coming on this long voyage to take care of me. I know I am in good hands. Thank you, both of you."

Hébert said, "It is our honor to be of service, Madame."

Christine asked, "How are you feeling, my Lady?"

"Much better, though it is quite warm."

Doctor Hébert whispered to René, "She needs fresh air." René immediately opened the curtains to let the air circulate in the coach.

The crowed roared with excitement. "Look at the royals," Daniel Theriot's mother said. Her wicker vegetable basket was empty except for one half-rotten onion. In her excitement at being in the presence of royalty, she grabbed the withered vegetable without thinking and took a big bite.

The other onlookers started shouting, and Michel Broussard motioned for the other Horsemen to tighten the row of horses between the crowd and the carriage. They stood fast on an invisible line to keep the crowd away. Broussard rode quickly to the carriage and peered through the curtain.

"My Lord, open curtains are not safe with these fools about."

René peered outside and said, "My wife's health is more important. Besides, they look harmless enough. I see no weapons being brandished." The crowd started shouting at the sight of René even though they had no idea who he was. He was in a royal carriage, so he was important.

Captain Broussard replied, "'Tis true they know no better, sire but we must take every precaution for your safety."

René opened the curtains wider and waved at the crowd. The people swelled forward calling out, "Your Majesty" and "Bless you, Majesty."

It was well known that the King gave favors and sometimes coins to townspeople who were lucky enough to get close to him. The poorer citizens of France always hoped one day to meet their King to receive his grace...and his money.

Madame Theriot looked up and, upon spying René's rich garments, she yelled out, "The King! The King at the window," then passed out again.

Two local drunkards started singing a ditty that had something to do with the King meeting a mermaid and taking her with him on a ship for a long journey. They finally came to the end of the ditty, singing in a strange off-key harmony, "Then His Majesty returned to port, with ten little otters and twenty big daughters, and they all lived together in one big fort."

Fortunately, no one else listened, especially the King's men. They had license while on the road to punish whomever they found making comments at the expense of the King or his extended family. Of course the King had mistresses and illegitimate children but it was not for anyone, especially drunks in port towns, to debate, discuss or ditty about. The cacophony of admiration lasted only a few moments as the Royal Horsemen once again herded the crowd farther away from the carriage. Claude thought he recognized a face in the crowd -- was it the gypsy Karaztyev? But the man disappeared into the crowd before Claude could determine who he was.

René waved again, then acquiesced to Broussard's request and closed the curtains facing them. As Michel galloped off, René opened the curtains on the other side of the carriage, out of view of the crowd and nearer the sea. The passengers in the coach soon felt a refreshing cool breeze. They turned their attention to the ship.

The commoners and those in hammocks and benches had been boarding since dawn. Captain Jacques stood in his cabin while his First Assistant welcomed these passengers at the top of the plank. Uniformed sailors directed them to their places below in holds, hammocks or, for the less fortunate, seats in the dining hall. A stream of people walked the gangplank up to the ship -- French families, couples and single men looking for new homes and new futures in Acadie. The passengers hauled what seemed to be a never-ending load of trunks and boxes up the gangplank to the ship.

Dozens of children ran up and down the gangplank, generating a friendly confusion among many families who were related and whose children had the same names. Good Catholic families had at least a dozen offspring, many with sixteen or more. Mothers called out "Marie," "Jean," "Denis" and "Anne," only to find nieces and nephews, rather than their own children, running up to them.

A large bearded man, Thomas Gaudet, carried a heavy box of carpentry tools aboard. Following not far behind him, a petite brunette named Anne Verrazzano reached the ship and looked around in amazement, looking forward to the excitement of the journey. She was thrilled to be following the sea route taken by her ancestor Giovanni Verrazzano who had explored the New World for France. Not watching her step she bumped into Thomas who took one look at the tiny beauty and was smitten. He followed her like a puppy dog, staying near her as long as he could, until the men and women were directed into separate sleeping holds.

All the non-perishable commercial goods and merchandise for buyers in Acadia had been loaded during the week prior to the sailing date. The process was a tedious one but Captain Jacques was fastidious about not allowing any cargo aboard his ship without proper documents showing the King's tax had been paid and that nothing harmful to the passengers was in the boxes or crates. Most ship captains were happy to take merchants' money to carry goods on their ships, ignoring those without the King's tax stamp. But Captain Jacques was unlike those. His most precious cargo, the newlyweds from the Palace of Versailles, were yet to board and he would not allow any goods to risk their health or safety.

By the time René's carriages arrived, nearly all the working class travelers were aboard. René knew the group of over two hundred souls would be his responsibility in addition to the existing French residents once they arrived in Acadia. Moving from the upper deck to the stairs below were farmers with their implements, tradesmen with tools and supplies, loggers with their huge saws, miners in their traditional dress, fur trappers with their traps, fisherman with nets and equipment, and families with large numbers of children intending to till the rich, fertile soil of Acadie or open shops in Grand Pré, the region's center of trade. All the tools and implements were stored in one large room in the hold which was locked so there was no chance of misuse or danger while at sea.

René had a special place in his heart for children, and looked forward to the day his and Eugenie's would be counted among them. He already felt Eugenie's baby was his own. He loved her deeply and knew that he would feel the same love for her child, no matter who the father. Eugenie had never revealed the name and René respected her decision. He knew the man's identify was unimportant since he would not be in their lives. He would learn years later this was not the case.

When all the passengers in the commoner class were in their assigned places, the holds were shut and locked and those sitting on the lower deck were locked into a large room. They would be released to their places once the nobility and their staff had boarded. The decks were separated by gates with locks to which only the Captain and the First Assistant had keys. Even the sailors assigned to the lower decks ate and slept there, forbidden to climb to the upper decks.

The royal foodstuffs René brought were for meals for the passengers on the upper deck only, which included the royal group from Versailles, the Captain and his officers and Sir Mius d'Entremont and his son. The ship's cook was elated to see so many good foods that he could prepare early on in the voyage. Most nobles easily tired of fish, which was the only fresh meal towards the end of the voyage, although the cook had learned a hundred ways to prepare it. Still, it always smelled and tasted like fish. Using the preserves, dried fruits and exotic foods the King had sent, the cook was certain he would be able to please even the most particular palate.

Of the handful of cabins on the ship, the largest was reserved for René and Eugenie. The Captain and Christine each had a private cabin. Lord d'Entremont and his son were assigned one cabin, but Pater and Doctor Hébert shared as did Père Rivière and Sun. Claude and his wife would have to sleep below in the separate holds for men and women. René had made arrangements for them to sleep in the First Assistant's room for their marriage night but would thereafter have to sleep in separate compartments for the rest of the journey.

Christine assisted René with moving Eugenie next to the window. "Is that more comfortable, Lady de Beaufort Le Blanc de Verdure?" asked Christine, using Eugenie's full married name.

Eugenie was quite fatigued but managed a smile and a slight nod. She lifted her ring to the window, admiring it in the moonlight. It was not that it was jewel encrusted. Eugenie had all the jewels she could ever want, and many more than she needed. It was that she now had a husband who legitimized her status and, even more than that, loved her and her child without condition.

Just at that moment, the sunlight faded behind gigantic dark clouds. Eugenie shivered. A nervous feeling enveloped her that something ominous was to happen during the voyage. She turned to René. "Dear husband, I sense something is amiss on this ship. Could we not wait for another?"

René kissed her hand. "We are on a mission from His Majesty. We must travel to Acadia and begin his work as soon as possible."

"But I feel something will go awry," she protested weakly.

René kissed Eugenie's forehead. "Captain Jacques is one of the best on the high seas. Despite his youth, he has proven himself time and again, which is why the King personally appointed him for the journey. Nothing will go wrong, my darling wife." He kissed her hands. "Thankfully, your fever has gone. You must still be feeling the excitement of the weddings and the sailing. But if you do not feel strong enough to walk up, I shall call several Horsemen to carry you."

Eugenie shook her head. "I should very much like to walk in the sea breezes."

"Then let us make our way to the ship."

Eugenie was happy. Whatever foreboding she felt disappeared with her loving husband now at her side. She would make certain he did not leave her while she was on the ship. Then she would be safe.

René told the others his plan to exit the coach. The doctor and nurse nodded in agreement. Christine helped Eugenie put on her gloves, then placed Eugenie's cloak on her, covering the lady from head to toe, protecting her against any elements except the breeze blowing lightly on her face.

Then Christine assisted Doctor Hébert with emptying the coach of the various jars and bottles with remedies used for Eugenie during the trip.

René opened the curtains facing the port once more. The crowd roared with delight and demands for favors. At the noise, Michel Broussard saw the open shades again and, thinking the worst, quickly rode up to René's windows. He asked. "Sire, how may I be of service?"

René handed him a stack of coins. "We will exit the rear of the coach while you distribute these to the crowd. Thank them for their prayers and ask them to return to their homes."

Broussard nodded. "Excellent, my Lord."

While Michel rounded up his horsemen and distributed handfuls of coins to toss to the local residents, Doctor Hébert and Christine exited the side of the coach away from the crowd. René lifted his hand in greeting through the window. Madame Theriot swooned, thinking the King had just waved to her. Her son, the pickpocket everyone was calling "Stinky," caught her in midfall and lowered her to the ground. Then he grabbed the rest of her onion. He was too used to stealing not to keep in practice. Besides, he reasoned, it ain't stealing if it comes from your family.

The First Assistant confirmed to Captain Jacques that it was time to greet the nobility. Jacques looked in his small mirror, straightened his uniform, properly set his hat and stood at the top of the gangplank on the main deck. He warmly greeted each passenger from the Versailles carriages. Père Rivière and Sun arrived first, followed by the Mercier family. A steward was assigned to each upper deck passenger to carry baggage, lead them to their cabins, and provide services during the voyage. Christine offered her cabin for Adèle to change into her dress and prepare for the wedding. Henri and Gabriel Mius d'Entremont shook the Captain's hand as they boarded.

Just as René and Doctor Hébert assisted Eugenie up the gangplank, Captain Broussard and his men flung the coins to the crowd. Christine had joined the others on the top of the deck and she and Doctor Hébert helped Eugenie to her room as René and the Captain waved to the crowd.

The townspeople cheered as each person tried to catch the coins in the air. Broussard shouted to the onlookers. "On behalf of the King, God bless you all. Now please return to your homes. Thank you for your loyalty to the King."

But the crowd did not disperse. Instead they held their coins up and cheered, still believing René to be the King. Their voices rang out with gratitude. "God bless you, Majesty." "Thank you, Your Excellency." "God bless you and yours."

Captain Broussard galloped to the top of the deck where the priest was waiting for him. The wedding could not start without Michel. He was Claude's best man. And he had the ring.

CHAPTER 16
Deck

ON BOARD "L'ACADIE"

aptain Jacques was strong, both of body and character. He was honored that His Majesty entrusted this voyage to him, and he knew that with the special royal guests aboard, this would be the voyage he would remember for the rest of his days. Once he had taken *L'Acadie* out to sea for several days, he began an account of his impressions and the events of the voyage in his journal:

"On our first day as the passengers boarded, I had the honor of welcoming the strikingly beautiful Lady Eugenie de Beaufort Le Blanc de Verdure. Her beauty is only surpassed by her kindness which she shows to everyone, regardless of class. Nobles as well as farmers have remarked on it. We are truly honored to have her and her husband, the King's Consul Lord Le Blanc de Verdure with us."

His writing was disturbed by a knock at the door. "Enter," he said. At the door was his First Assistant Jehan Hébert, descendent of the aide to Admiral Giovanni Verrazzano.

"Captain, you are kindly requested by Lord Le Blanc to meet with him in his cabin."

Jacques complied and followed him to the large suite that had been prepared for the newlyweds. René was waiting at the door.

"Captain, my wife is feeling very well today and asked if you would escort her on a tour of the ship." He lowered his voice, "If you could assuage her fears about sailing that would do much to brighten her spirits in general. I would be most grateful."

The Captain nodded and said loudly, "That is wonderful news about the Lady's health. It is an honor, my Lord."

René led the Captain into the salon and offered his arm to the beautiful Lady Eugenie, who rose gracefully. She smiled at him and he melted in the warmth of it.

"Captain, you must tell me everything about this wonderful vessel. And the weather, I would like to know about the weather. And the size of the waves, and whether you have seen any sea monsters." Eugenie continued to express anxious questions as they walked out of the cabin.

On deck, René walked quietly behind his wife. A steward had joined him, carrying a special lounging chair in the event Eugenie tired of the walk. But she did not. She and the Captain conversed about the structure and soundness of the ship and its ability to handle storms and high seas.

The Captain reassured Eugenie of the solid construction and expressed his confidence that his experience would be able to handle the worst storms, just as he had in the past. Jacques also tried to calm her anxiety, telling her he used the most modern methods, checking almanacs and watching skies and waves and comparing historical weather journals of his trips and those of other seafarers in port. He spent days trying to ascertain weather and sea patterns in order to complete safe crossings. He assured her that this voyage should be quite uneventful. He truthfully explained that he had never seen any sea monsters and had no reason to believe they would encounter any on this trip.

René watched Eugenie's shoulders visibly relax and she tilted her head back to look at the blue skies and enjoy the breeze.

Pater had set his easel on the deck. He bowed deeply to his muse and to the Captain and René. "I am ready to begin your portrait whenever it suits you, my Lady."

She nodded. "Perhaps next week? Would you come to our cabin then?"

Pater bowed as his heart danced with pleasure. "Of course, Lady Eugenie. Whenever you desire." Watching them promenade down the deck, he outlined a quick sketch of the scene where Eugenie had looked upward. In his final painting which he did from memory, she was alone on the deck, drenched in light, basking in the warmth of the sun.

Walking to the other side of the boat, the couple and the Captain were joined by Christine admiring the view from the deck. She nearly ran into a young boy of six running around the corner. A well-to-do noble, Henri Mius d'Entremont, apologized for his son.

"Lord Le Blanc, Lady Eugenie, Captain, please excuse Gabriel. He loves exploring...."

Before he could finish, Gabriel stared at Eugenie's stomach. She did not realize her condition was obvious because the Queen's handoff clothes were so comfortable that she did not notice her growing belly. Henri was horrified and tried to pull Gabriel away but Eugenie smiled at the boy and placed his hand on her dress just over her protruding stomach. They both felt a kick and he jumped.

Then Gabriel smiled boldly, bowed to Lady Eugenie and said proudly, "I shall marry your daughter, my Lady. I hope you will consent."

The adults were taken aback but without waiting for a response, Gabriel ran to meet Sun on the other side of the deck, where they quickly disappeared from view.

Henri called out, "Gabriel?" Turning back to the group, he bowed as he introduced himself. "Henri Mius d'Entremont at your service. A thousand apologies. Gabriel has been without a mother and since her death he is a bit...."

Eugenie finished his sentence for him "Independent?"

Christine said simultaneously, "Rebellious?"

Everyone smiled. Henri agreed, "Well perhaps a little of both." He bowed to the two women and the Captain and turned to René. "Monsieur le Consul, might I have a word when you have a convenient moment?"

"Certainly, Sieur d'Entremont. Shall we walk down the deck?"

As the men excused themselves, Eugenie turned to the Captain. "Thank you for the tour. I should like to rest here a while." The Captain bowed and took his leave as the steward and Christine helped Eugenie into the chair. She thanked the steward, pressing a coin in his hand. He tried to refuse but she insisted.

During the voyage, after the nobility had retired from dinner, the officers had each remarked on one occasion or another of the kindness of Lady Eugenie. All had noticed her genteel manners to everyone, including the staff. That was astonishing, as they had served lesser nobility who had treated them with disrespect and even disdain. Everyone had a special place in their heart for Lady Eugenie.

René and Henri stood at the end of the deck, away from earshot of the other passengers. The women waited with the Captain near the railing, enjoying the view.

Henri asked, "Is it true the English colonies want to expand by taking French land in Grand Pré?"

René responded, "The King has a plan that should ensure the peace. May I count on your help?"

"You have but to call on me and I shall be there."

The two men clasped hands, fast friends already.

Père Rivière came out of his cabin looking for Sun. He passed Eugenie and Christine, blessing them with the Sign of the Cross. "God be with you, my Lady. Christine."

The women smiled in response.

"Have you seen my ward Sun, by any chance? He told me he would be on deck."

Eugenie replied, "He and young Gabriel d'Entremont ran past. They must be getting into something by now."

The priest nodded. "Sun does enjoy his pranks but he means well. Please excuse me. I must find him before… well, he is a kind boy but slow. I must watch him."

Eugenie bowed her head. "Lord Le Blanc and I would like to request daily Mass. Would you be so kind as to come to our rooms? I am not to be allowed to be on deck for any length of time to attend your services, I am afraid." She looked at Christine, who nodded silently.

The priest bowed and kissed her hand. "It would be my honor, Lady Eugenie."

Eugenie, suddenly feeling very tired, replied, "Thank you, Père Rivière. I…." Before she could finish her sentence she felt faint and swooned into her chair.

CHAPTER 17
Christine

SPAIN, MARSEILLE, PARIS

 hristine Galvez de Castille inherited her flaming red locks from her great-great grandmother, Luisa Santángel de Castillo. She and a long line of Santángel women before her were midwives at Court to the Spanish nobility for as long as any of them could remember.

The Santángel patriarchs had been the most successful money lending family in Castilian society for centuries. Luisa's brother was Luis de Santángel, the powerful Minister of Finance for King Ferdinand and Queen Isabella of Castille and León. Luis held his post until the Queen's death on November 26, 1504. But Luisa would be long gone from Spain before then.

By 1490 the Santángels were well-regarded as rich and religious Catholics in the region and were invited to join the royal Court. Luis and Luisa's parents, Carlos and Patricia de Santángel, had great ambition but their son's position with the monarchy had propelled them into the heart of society and raised their social standing to the highest level possible in short order.

Carlos had other reasons for celebration. Their daily presence among the nobility at Court would surely bring more important clients. The family members were ensconced in newly-constructed private quarters in the royal Palacio del Valladolid. As Carlos proceeded to carry on his money lending business, he found he had more prestigious clientele than he had imagined.

Isabella and Ferdinand were pious Catholics who invited all noblemen and Ladies at Court to daily Mass in the Palacio. Their policy, while not an order, guided them to promote only faithful Catholic nobles to the most important positions at Court. Once the Santàngels were at Court they, too, attended the services and, like the other nobles, had a private box in the Cathedral.

Luisa was truly her father's daughter. She was interested in his business and from an early age learned mathematics from counting money. She learned reading and writing from keeping Carlos' business accounts. But she also inherited the desire to heal from her mother. She loved to walk with her mother in the forest surrounding the Palacio, where Patricia taught Luisa about which plants were harmful and which had healing qualities, which could be eaten and which were to be avoided.

Luisa had quickly learned the medicinal properties of these herbs and plants. She was promptly appointed an assistant lady-in-waiting to the Queen's daughter, the Infanta Isabella. Even at her age, Luisa was able to help the Infanta with minor ailments. She could be seen walking through the halls of the Palacio, her thick red tresses flowing freely, framing her pretty young face. One nobleman after another asked Señor Santángel to sign a contract of marriage for Luisa to his son. Luisa's father always refused, because of her tender age and his hope that she would one day marry and move away, out of Spain. He never expressed this desire to his wife or to Luisa but kept it in his heart.

The first client at Court who approached Señor de Santángel for a loan was Count Nurio. He was an aristocrat who was often in debt due to his secretive gambling activities. Naturally, due to the nature of the loan, Carlos included a discretion fee for not disclosing the Count's passion to others at Court. When Nurio agreed without blinking, Carlos realized he would easily double his income, as he was certain everyone at Court would want his silence and be willing to pay for it.

Only a few days later, Señor Santángel was approached by the Count's wife, Countess Inès. She gladly paid the surcharge for funds to buy herself a new ruby ring. She wanted to make her husband jealous enough to return to her chamber, though their marriage had been the truce between two feuding noble families. She had missed not having true love and decided it was not too late to change things.

The new banker's willingness and ability to keep each spouse's loan private from the other established their reputation for discretion and honesty. Soon the Santángels became the bank of choice for the other Court members. Occasionally, when a borrower was unable to pay his loan when due, Senior Santángel graciously extended the loan for the usual costly interest, foregoing the penalty for the first delay. If the aristocrat still failed to pay after the extension, he confirmed the debt in writing in Señor Santàngels little black book, which the banker always kept in the interior breast pocket of his long coat.

At Court, many a nobleman bowed and many a lady curtsied when passing Carlos in the Palacio, at the same time eyeing his coat, which he wore every day. The Court respected him and his family to the point of effusiveness, knowing their secrets could be revealed in an instant if he were treated otherwise. Santángel never broke the confidences of the nobility, and continued lending until he was certain he held enough secrets in his little book to obtain influential positions for his children. Then he called the loans and was promised favors in exchange by those who were unable to pay. He was satisfied the favors could be traded for a noble husband for Luisa and a high-ranking position for Luis.

At this time, the Minister of Finance, Manuel Mendez, had been in his position for decades. He did not bother to hide his taste for things other than his work, including a well-known stage performer who was known to be his concubine. Isabella was displeased with his personal life as well as his views against expansionism of the kingdom. She did not like his decision to keep money idling in the treasury rather than being invested in exploration for new territories.

The Queen had met with the explorer Christofer Columbus three times before and listened to his request to finance three ships to find a new route to the wealth of China. The Finance Minister was present in each meeting and had opposed each proposal. After Columbus left, Isabella had grilled Mendez about his opposition. Each time, Isabella felt Mendez had not given any sound reasoning why the kingdom could not afford to pay for the undertaking. Mendez slyly approached Isabella's personal confessor and convinced him to oppose the venture as not being part of God's plan.

On Columbus' third visit and after hearing his well-planned proposal, the Queen specifically asked Minister Mendez for financial reasons why the kingdom should not seek new lands with great riches by using some of their own riches on hand. Mendez could not answer and immediately realized his usefulness was at an end. He quietly started making plans to move. Isabella never called him into another meeting with Columbus or for any other economic matter. Instead, she asked her husband Ferdinand to consider candidates for a new Finance Minister.

At the time, Luis de Santángel had finished his studies at the University of Valladolid, excelling in mathematics and accounting. He studied under Professor Rodriguez who, as it turned out, was one of King Ferdinand's favorite cousins. But Luis shone most brilliantly during the Friday evening dinners that the Professor held to debate financial affairs of Spain and its far-flung territories.

One evening, unbeknownst to the students, Ferdinand listened to the debates through a peephole in a secret corridor. He was enraptured as Luis challenged traditional methods of accounts recordation. But when Luis proposed an original system of managing finances for distant land holdings and territories, the King kept silent no longer. He burst forth from the hidden room and, to the amazement of his cousin, proceeded to engage Luis in a discussion about finances until dawn.

The next morning a knock came at Luis' door. He opened it to find a King's coach that took him directly to the office of Minister Mendez. Mendez unceremoniously dumped the books of account in Luis's lap without a word. Then he climbed into the waiting carriage and drove off to see Fortuna, whom he called his lady love. Being a widower, he had been granted the indulgence of a concubine by King Ferdinand. However, Isabella terminated the arrangement when she ordered him to marry his mistress or let her go. Mendez could not bear to do either and now he would be with her on his terms, not those of the Queen.

Luis watched the carriage roll away and pondered whether there was more that met the eye in the King's appointment to replace Mendez. He was grateful the King had showered his favors upon him but he did not believe it would have happened had their family not converted. Luis demonstrated his worthiness for the cabinet position by often burning candles through the night to finish his work.

He began with an innocent investigation of records of incoming revenues from all territories. Luis found deposits made directly into the Treasury from the lands in Spain's European borders and the former Muslim kingdom of Granada that Spain had captured after a ten year battle. However, he soon found numerous anomalies in the recordkeeping of Canary Islands revenues. He read letters confirming payments from Islands to the Minister of Finance, but found no corresponding deposits of those funds into the royal treasury. He knew it would not do to accuse a former high-ranking official to the King and Queen without documentary proof. Luis spent the night verifying his work again and in the morning he realized Manuel Mendez indeed had been stealing from the Treasury.

The next morning Luis brought his findings to Ferdinand and Isabella who, after a quick but thorough review, sent their guards to arrest Mendez. The neighbors reported he had packed his carriage to the brim with boxes and bags but had not disclosed his destination. One particularly observant passerby had said that a distinguished-looking man had joined a well-dressed, bejeweled woman inside their coach but could not hear the instructions to the driver.

Luis quickly curried favor with Isabella, accurately determining that she, not Ferdinand, was the real power on the throne, although it was her husband who had appointed him to the Ministry position. The Queen's bold decisions did not go without notice in the Court, particularly concerning one Cristobal Colon, sometimes known as Christopher Columbus, whom many nobles considered touched in the head. The idea of the world being round was unheard of, they scoffed. A walk on any of Spain's rugged coasts showed the earth continued to the horizon in the distance in a flat line. But Isabella had long believed it was round, and she trusted Cristobal.

With Luis in attendance, Isabella called Columbus for a fourth visit, listening again to his exploration proposal. She expressed her interest in expanding the kingdom, while Ferdinand stated his firm opposition of payment from the Treasury. Isabella turned to the young Minister and, before the entire Court, asked his opinion. Luis was ready. Carlos had learned from his clients that the Queen tested her ministers on grave matters spontaneously, without prior preparation or study. He insisted Luis determine a response to the Columbus question which Isabella would surely ask. And indeed she did. But Luis was ready with a bold plan in mind. He expressed it quickly before he lost the attention of the monarchs.

"Your Majesties, I humbly respond with what I hope will be an acceptable proposal. Our beloved Spain under your monarchy has become the richest and most powerful nation that exists today. We also know that to maintain a great position of strength and wealth and to show leadership to other nations, it is imperative to expand its holdings. You have proven success in the Canary Islands and the Muslim territories. Now Señor Columbus proposes to expand Spanish trade routes, which could bring untold riches to be invested again in expansion and more wealth. With all the other financial undertakings you have now, I see but one way to resolve the issue at hand."

He stopped to take a breath and he quickly glanced at the Queen. She gave him an imperceptible nod. He looked at the King, who leaned forward on the throne, wondering what the final proposal would be. Luis could hear murmurs throughout the Court but did not know whether they were for or against him. He knew the next few moments would solidify his relationship with the monarchy and the Court, or he would be booted out with derision.

"We all agree that the plan of Señor Columbus is costly and that even the massive treasury is unable to withstand being partially empty at this moment. When the territorial rents and other payments are received at the end of the year perhaps that would be a solution, but today, unfortunately, it is not a practical one."

He saw the King relax and nod, leaning back in his chair. The Queen held herself more rigidly than before and a slight frown crossed her face.

Luis continued, "To this point, funding for the Kingdom's ventures has been directly from the state coffers. However that is not the only way to finance this important voyage. Value takes many forms other than Spanish coins. Her Royal Majesty is most beautiful and has no need of adornments...." He trailed off and looked pointedly at the Queen's bosom.

Isabella understood he was not being impertinent. She looked at Ferdinand who nodded his agreement. Without a word the Queen stood and took off her jeweled necklaces, bracelets and belts. She held them out to Luis, filling his arms with jewelry and clasping his hands with her ring-adorned fingers. He bowed and then delivered them to Columbus, who fell to his knees in front of the Queen in gratitude. She proffered her bejeweled fingers to the explorer, who kissed them repeatedly.

The Court erupted into great cheers, with loud stomping of feet and clapping of hands. Luis furtively looked at Ferdinand, who smiled broadly and bid Luis to come up to the thrones. The royal couple looked at each other and smiled, then placed both of their hands on his head. The King spoke first. "I knew my instincts were right about you. The Queen and I wish to reward you with a share of the proceeds that come from Columbus' success."

Luis bowed to the floor, and humbly responded, "Their Gracious Majesties are too generous to their humble servant."

Isabella removed a ring, a stunning diamond surrounded by emeralds. She placed it into his hands, "Take this as a token of our personal gratitude to our most astute Minister of Finance ever." She leaned forward and whispered, "We have heard rumors that you may be a Catholic in name but that you secretly practice another religion."

Luis was speechless, stunned at the priceless gift and at her comment. He stuttered, "No, of course not, Majesty."

She continued in a hushed voice. "For your exceptional service we have chosen to ignore these accusations, borne out of jealousy of some at Court." She looked at her husband who nodded. "And we assure you of longevity in this position."

Luis exited the Court amidst cheers and claps on his shoulder, well aware that some of those offering congratulations were the very ones who set the rumors spinning to denounce him. They were loyal to Mendez, he thought and perhaps through them he could find Mendez and the stolen Treasury.

When Columbus returned in 1493, bringing gold and natives from Hispañola, Spain's monarchs continued their active strategy of exploration and colonization. Luis received his reward from Columbus' exploits and was given additional responsibilities to manage the treasuries for the overseas territories, as well.

Ferdinand sent Luis to the Canary Islands for a few months to set up their books of account so that the monarchs could monitor the territorial revenues and assure all the taxes owed to them were paid. While there, Luis met with the unofficial governor of the Islands, Alfonso Galvez, the largest plantation owner providing rents to the Spanish treasury. He had lived on Gran Canaria since he arrived with the first group of settlers from Spain, he told Luis. His younger brother, Padre Antonio Galvez, had stayed in Valladolid as the priest confessor to the monarchs and nobility at the Palacio. Luis gave Alfonso all the news about his brother and the Court. The Governor handed Luis a large chest of coins, revenues from Islands, for which Luis signed an official receipt indicating that the funds would be deposited into the Treasury.

Alfonso offered to show Luis where he could buy inexpensive land in the Islands and how to hire an overseer for the crops, but Luis declined. He was more than satisfied with his remuneration and did not want to have any conflict, real or imagined, with his monarchs. Alfonso shrugged and said that the former Minister of Finance, Manuel Mendez, had moved to a large plantation on La Palma with his mistress after he retired from Court service and wondered if he should have set an appointment with him. Luis could barely contain himself but assured the man it was unnecessary. He did not yet trust the Governor, although he had not mentioned bribes directly.

Upon his return from the Canary Islands Luis reported his findings directly to Ferdinand and Isabella. They were pleased he had found the thief who had stolen from them. Mendez was soon arrested and brought to justice at a trial in Valladolid, where sentences were handed down appropriate to the crime. A starving boy who stole bread once had a finger cut off. Stealing a cow resulted in the loss of a hand. But the Judge determined a trusted member of the royal ministry who took Treasury funds for his own use would have to lose many limbs. After the executioner cut off as many appendages as Mendez had excepting his head, he was still alive, barely, but died a slow bloody death. Fortuna Mendez, who had convinced the old man to marry her, did not appear at the trial. She changed her name and was never seen again in Spain.

While Luis was preoccupied with his work, Luisa was happy serving the Infanta Isabella until she died giving birth to her son, Miguel. Luisa was then assigned to care for Miguel and at his death was appointed royal lady-in-waiting to the Infanta Joanna. The child's bouts of madness left Luisa in an impossible situation. She never knew what the Princess would say or what mood she would be in. Joanna made requests and at first Luisa hurried to fulfill them before Joanna forgot what she had ordered. Once, she asked for five green doves on a flying carpet. Another day she wanted one hundred pair of unicorns. Later, as Joanna became more and more forgetful, Luisa would simply leave the room after Joanna made a request and would return hours later to find Joanna staring out of the window. Perhaps that is why Joanna never beat or berated Luisa as she did her other ladies-in-waiting.

When Joanna was betrothed to the Prince Philip I of Burgundy, son of the Holy Roman Emperor Maximilian I, he came to visit her at Court. Luisa saw why he was called "Philip the Handsome" and wondered whether he knew the Princess had a family streak of madness in her. Luisa determined then and there that she would go to France and find a handsome husband for herself.

Luisa began saving every coin she could for her quest. She knew her father had been asked many times for her hand by the nobles at Court but he still saw her as a little girl and refused to let her marry. But her father died and Luisa feared she would die an unwed children's nursemaid in the Palacio. She might have carried out her plan but for a chance meeting with a Spanish nobleman in the summer of 1504.

His name was Count Pedro de Castillo and he served the King and Queen as their Master of the Cloth, importing fabrics from foreign lands for the Court. Pedro caught a glimpse of Luisa's red mane and her arresting smile as she and other ladies-in-waiting whispered among themselves and followed Princess Joanna into her receiving room. Pedro was waiting with tables covered with new brocades, boxes of ribbons and exotic feathers, and beaded shoes for Princess Joanna.

The Count was immediately smitten with Luisa. Over the next months he arranged "chance" meetings to see the object of his desire. He delivered a forgotten box of ribbons for the Princess and asked her to pick them up. A new shipment of shoes arrived and he requested her to take them to the Princess. He missed taking some measurements of the chairs for new fabric coverings and needed someone to take him to the receiving room. One day, as Luisa was carrying a stack of cartons for the Infanta, Pedro happened to be in the corridor. He saw her approaching him though she was nearly hidden behind the boxes. He stepped out in front of her to help her and she tripped. Thankfully, he caught her as she fell into his strong arms. Their eyes locked and he pulled her into a corner, hidden from what he knew could be prying eyes.

Then he stole a kiss. Not just any kiss. Luisa's first proper kiss on the lips by a man who was not a family member. Pedro kissed her gently then wrapped his arms around her and squeezed her. She trembled with desire she never knew was in her. He looked at her and found her eyes closed, her puckered mouth reaching for his. He showered her with soft kisses on her neck, her earlobes, her cheeks, and when he finally he arrived at her mouth, she was panting with excitement. They hungrily explored each other's mouths, their tongues dancing with each other until she pulled back and looked at him.

Pedro whispered with a kiss in her ear, "Will you marry me, my love?" She whispered back, "Yes, yes, I will." He insisted the wedding be kept secret even from her friends and family and told her they would move to another country, where she would never be able to contact her loved ones again. He held her as she cried but she did not change her mind.

Luisa questioned her fiancé as to his motives, not because of any strong familial duty but out of curiosity. He remained obstinately silent except to inform her that the secrecy was for her protection. She insisted that she know what country they would live in. The young woman recounted horror stories told at Court about explorers being eaten alive by half-animal, half-human creatures in the New World. She made him promise they would not live there. He assured her they would stay on the continent, then relented and told her they were moving to France.

Luisa was elated. Her dream was going to be realized in every way. Not only would she have the most handsome, kind, loving man in the world as her husband but she would be leaving Spain for France. She had no regrets at the thought of leaving her remaining family members, whom she saw only occasionally since moving into the Infanta's apartments. France! She was on top of the world. Pedro reassured her of his love for her and that she would never want for anything. Luisa took a deep breath and leaned forward for another kiss. Her new love did not disappoint her.

The next week, Pedro paid a handsome tithe to the officiating priest, Padre Galvez, to marry the couple secretly at midnight and issue their marriage license under the French name "Pierre and Louise de Castille." With the payment, Padre could finally move to his villa on La Palma in the Canary Islands.

After Spain conquered these Islands, many nobles and government officials, including Alfonso Galvez, migrated and received land grants of hundreds of acres. For others, land was still plentiful and cheap. Alfonso cultivated fields of orchil, which produced a deep violet dye highly prized by weavers and dyers to European royalty.

Alfonso had long urged his brother Antonio upon retirement from the priesthood to relocate and live with his family on Gran Canaria. The priest had refused but agreed to visit. Once he did, he bought a small hilltop tract on La Palma and hired a builder for his private home. Every few months he had sent funds for the construction until it was finished that year. With this latest payment, Antonio could retire in luxury.

Padre Gonzales received approval for his retirement from the Pope and he obtained Queen Isabella's blessing. He left the priesthood and the Palacio without ceremony the next morning at dawn. He was eager to live out his days in relative seclusion, watching the flat horizon off his grand deck on the La Palma coast. Scholars had declared the Canary Islands were all that remained of the lost continent of Atlantis and, being inquisitive, Antonio wished to study the problem.

Immediately after their wedding, Pedro and Luisa disguised themselves as peasants and, with the help of Padre Gonzales, jumped on horses loaded with food and blankets. Luisa had left her beautiful clothes behind so as not to raise suspicion. They set off on the road from the Palacio del Valladolid to the forests that led to the sea and rode for hours, until Luisa could ride no longer.

At the edge of the forest they saw a small inn. Pedro bid Luisa to remain with the horses in the brush while he went into the inn. Soon thereafter he rejoined her with food and drink to find Luisa had cleared underbrush from overhanging foliage and had made a soft bed of grass and leaves, covered with the blankets.   She was hungry, to be sure, but was more ravenous for her husband and the proper wedding night she had anticipated for so long. Pedro smiled at her and their blissful honeymoon began.

The following morning they traveled all day until they reached a small harbor. Pedro peered through a scope, looking until he saw something, or someone, he recognized. They walked their horses to a small boat in the harbor, where the man at the helm slapped Pedro on the back like an old friend.

Pedro said. "Captain Charles Jacques, meet my wife, Louise." He turned to his wife and said, "My dear, Captain Jacques will take us on the first leg of our journey. After that I plan to hire him and his family for my new merchant shipping business."

To this, the Captain nodded and replied, "We must talk, Pedro. We must talk." Then he kissed Luisa's hand and said, "Charming, just charming. My sons will help you get settled on board while I stable the horses. We shall set sail upon the return of my wife who has gone to purchase foodstuffs to cook for your journey."

He signaled to three young men on the boat, each of whom had the tall lankiness and shaggy brown hair of the Captain. They directed the couple to a large cabin below deck, out of sight. Jacques' wife traveled with her husband on board and cooked excellent meals for the couple during the journey, which ended several days later in the northern French port of Franciscopolis.

Monsieur and Madame Pierre de Castille installed themselves in a set of rooms in a small boarding house near the wharf. It was there that Pierre finally told Luisa the truth. Yes, he did import expensive goods and, yes, he was of noble blood. But he made more money working against the monarchy for an Italian mercenary named Giovanni da Verrazzano, who robbed Spanish galleons off the coast of France.

Pedro's routine had been to gather information at Court as he went about selling his goods. Then he would travel to France and meet Giovanni at the Port Tavern near the wharf and provide the schedule of dates and departure ports of Spanish royal galleons. Of equal value was the description of the cargo to be carried on each and how many frigates would sail alongside the galleon to protect the treasurer from corsairs like Giovanni. From this intelligence, Verrazzano was able to determine where to station his own brigs to attack the most vulnerable and most valuable of the Castilian galleons.

Pedro had amassed his knowledge from royal ministers and other aristocrats at Court proud to share their information with one of their own. He had planned to approach Luis Santángel to learn more about the gold shipments, since the Minister of Finance was responsible for transfers of all royal funds. But when he learned Santángel was Luisa's brother, Pedro dismissed the idea. He did not want any connection to her family, lest they be harmed if his secret was exposed.

Back at their rooms, her husband assured Luisa they were out of danger since he had concluded his final mission and their change of name would protect them. Pedro told her Giovanni had provided them with two new cargo ships and crew for his importing business in the Levant, a beautiful villa overlooking the Port of Marseille, and a fortune in gold to last their lifetime. He told her he would keep her wrapped in silks and satins and jewels even more beautiful than those belonging to the Spanish royal princesses she had served. Luisa was only too happy to obey her husband and move to the southern port city of Marseille, France.

Captain Jacques and his sons sailed Pedro's ships and the business soon became so profitable Jacques offered to buy a share of the enterprises. A deal was struck and Jacques and his sons became half-owners.

Queen Isabella died six months later and King Ferdinand turned to other matters. If any man at Court knew of Pedro's whereabouts he did not reveal the secret and no spies were ever sent after Pedro de Castillo.

In each of the next five years Luisa bore a healthy male child. During that time, profits soared and Pedro and Captain Jacques doubled the merchant fleet. That allowed the Captain and each of his sons to sail their own ship. Pedro occupied himself in Marseille with receiving and clearing with the customs officials the many shipments of high-quality goods arriving on their ships from distant ports.

Luisa and Pedro had a happy home life, raising their sons and planning for their future. Luisa had just learned she was pregnant with their sixth child and looked forward to giving the news to Pedro upon his return from the docks that evening. But he never returned to their villa.

While Pedro was inspecting bolts of silks newly arrived from the Levant on a ship sailed by Captain Jacques, a flea-infested black rat bit his hand. The Captain brought Pedro to the hospital but the doctors refused to allow him to enter when they saw blood dripping from his nostrils and heard his sneezing. The hospital had been rebuilt after the Great Plague of 1500 and the administrator refused to risk the lives of the doctors and patients for what they thought was a potential Plague victim. But Pedro was not the last to attempt to enter the hospital. The Black Death had re-appeared in Marseille.

Jacques did not want to expose Pedro's family to the Plague so he placed Pedro on a long table in one of the company storage buildings at the wharf and locked the door. Only then did he visit Luisa. He begged her not to visit her husband for fear that she might catch the dreaded disease. She ignored his pleas, covered herself from head-to-toe with a hat and cloak and tied a cloth over her nose and mouth. Then she went to her husband's side, nursing him for three long days until he died.

Private burials were forbidden by the Marseille authorities for fear of spreading the disease so cartmen hoisted the bodies into bloody wagons headed for a mass unmarked grave. Luisa could not bear to leave her husband in that way and she solicited Captain Jacques in a plan. Luisa covered Pedro's body with herbs and wrapped it tightly in cloth. Then she and Jacques hid the body in a small rowboat which he rowed out of the harbor with Luisa at his aide. As dawn was breaking they tossed the body overboard into the sea that Pedro loved so much.

After the loss of her husband Luisa was distraught and needed solace from the family she had abandoned years earlier. She did not know if Pedro was still being hunted and believed letters to be too dangerous as they passed through too many hands. Captain Jacques agreed to travel to Spain and find Luisa's brother Luis who could send family to comfort his sister.

After many weeks her scheme went as planned and Captain Jacques returned with Luisa's aging mother and gifts from Luisa's siblings. Most importantly, Jacques recounted Luis' assurances that the Spanish Court knew nothing of Pedro's acts and that Luisa could safely carry on her life without fear of retribution.

Despite her comforting mother, Luisa found the memories of her beloved husband too painful to bear. She sold Pedro's share of the business to Jacques and his sons. Then she moved her entire family, including her mother, to Paris.

Shortly after installing themselves near the Ile de la Cité in the center of Paris, Luisa's oldest son Pierre, named for his father, became ill with a raging fever. Fearing the worst, Luisa rushed him to the Hôtel Dieu Hospital near the Cathedral of Notre Dame and tended him night and day for a week. Her next oldest son Jacques, named for their friend the Captain, took care of the children and occasionally came to the hospital for instructions from his mother.

The attending physician Doctor Carlos Galvez, an older gentleman scholar who had taught medicine at the Sorbonne, checked on the patient several times a day and soon became infatuated with Luisa. He told her his ancestors were from the Castile region of Spain and had migrated to Gran Canaria on the first of a series of vessels provided by the Spanish monarchy to populate the island. He then said some of his relations had moved to Paris in recent years after their orchil plantation suffered blight for several successive years, leaving them destitute. She told him her family history, omitting her early family origins, and they deduced they had relatives in the same parts of Spain and France at the same time.

Carlos proposed to Luisa on the day Pierre was released from the hospital in full health. The couple wed in the small sanctuary of Notre Dame before a Catholic priest who did not realize Luisa's condition until he had pronounced the couple man and wife. Six months later he baptized Carlos Castille Galvez, with light pouring onto his forehead through Notre Dame's stained glass windows. The following year the entire family gathered at Notre Dame to welcome the first girl in the family, Christine Castille Galvez. They called her Cassie.

Pierre's sons became doctors at the Hôtel Dieu and Cassie became a midwife, learning the ancient techniques and herbal remedies of so many of her ancestors. The boys married and had children of their own while Cassie remained, attending to patients daily. One night Doctor Galvez brought home a young physician who had just transferred to the hospital, his fourth cousin by a Canary Islander. The two were married within weeks and a year later the Galvez dynasty began.

Two centuries of de Castille and Galvez descendents followed, many in the healing profession. But it was the union of Doctor Pierre de Castille the Sixth with the current Galvez family midwife and healer Louise Galvez in 1722 that produced Christine Marie Galvez de Castille the following year. As soon as she could walk and talk she intently watched her mother treat patients. Little by little she learned to pick herbs with medicinal properties and grind certain stems; on other plants just the leaves and still others only the roots. At age six she was making healing poultices. At eight she learned to mix the potions that would lessen the pain of her mother's patients.

Her father had noticed Christine's ability to learn and he began her training as a nurse assistant to him at the Hôtel Dieu. She quickly learned complicated medical techniques as she watched the doctors perform their surgeries. Her father taught her his methods of diagnosis and remedies. She agreed with most of the practices except leeching. She told her father that patients always seemed sicklier after the exercise than before.

Doctor de Castille became a consulting physician to the King's physician, Doctor Hébert, on difficult cases or when the patient requested a second opinion. As a result, Pierre often traveled to Versailles at Doctor Hébert's request. He decided to take Christine with him on the day that she later said changed her fate and started her in her profession.

After being amazed at the opulence and grandeur of the Palace, Christine was introduced to Doctor Hébert, who had lost his assistant, a silly girl who ran away with the first kitchen supply vendor who smiled at her. Doctor Hébert directed Doctor de Castille to the patient's room and left them to return to his workroom. Doctor Hébert, a serious professional, had no time to waste training another young woman. However, he had agreed to meet with her at Doctor de Castille's insistence, since he had become a favorite at Court.

In their first meeting, Doctor Hébert grilled Christine about her intentions for her future. "How intent are you upon learning our profession and working night and day to comfort, heal and cure where we can?"

Christine did not hesitate. "Sir you have my word you shall never see a more devoted assistant. I am prepared to do anything you need for your patients and their care."

The Doctor was unconvinced. "Harrumph. What if all you do is wash stinking bodies of human waste and vomit? Or clean blood and pus and mucus from their bedclothes and linens?"

"Then I shall do my all to make certain the bodies and linens are cleaned to your satisfaction, Sir. Blood does not make me dizzy or fearful. I have a strong constitution and have never been ill in my life. This is my desired profession."

Doctor Hébert nodded. "What say you to cutting the birthing cord after the baby exits?"

She replied, "I have observed many births, some difficult enough to cut the mother open. Once I had to use a kitchen knife to cut the tail cord when a street urchin had a baby outside the Hospital in Paris. I am proud to say both of them survived the ordeal due to the poultices I made to stop the bleeding. When I gave the mother a potion to ease her pain she relaxed and healed more quickly."

He looked at her and sighed. He disliked the idea of a female assistant but there was no other candidate and he was already short-handed. So many noblewomen and their husbands' courtesans wanted leeching these days. When had it become so fashionable?

He had one final question. "If I were to give you a position to the Court, do you promise never to marry or to consort with a man resulting in a child while in your service here? "

Christine stood up with excitement and shook the Doctor's hand repeatedly. "Yes, Doctor Hébert. Yes with all my heart. I do not plan to marry. I want to work for you and help you in your good work here. Thank you, sir. Thank you with all my heart." She rushed out of the room without giving him a chance to reflect that he had not actually offered her the position. But Christine had learned it was better to make the decision for a man than to wait for him so she acted quickly, all the while acting as if it he had made the final choice. But think about it the Doctor did and he found her to be a brave girl, especially at her young age. She might do. Rather, he thought, she would have to do.

Calling on a servant girl Hébert ordered her to clean out the extra supply closet and bring in bed linens and a chamber pot for his new assistant. Christine would sleep next to the workroom and would learn soon enough they had no life of their own. In fact physicians and midwives at Court were considered but servants at the beck and call of the nobility. Of course the royal family took precedence but they had been a healthy lot of late, touch on wood.

If that continued, the doctor and his assistant would be relegated to relieving Baron Delaveau's overactive bladder due to excessive drinking or lotions for softening a woman's hands. Or the leeching, of course. That went without saying. He sighed. Christine would learn all these things and more but he needed to make sure she would not run off and get married. Perhaps he could put his special medicine in her drink that prevents pregnancies forever. If he told her later, she would not want to marry then because her womb would be absolutely barren. He toyed with the idea but made his final decision to wait and see if she would be true to her word. Then he dozed off to sleep in his luxurious apartment down the hall from the workroom.

Within the week, the fifteen-year old Christine Galvez de Castille had packed her bag with her few possessions. She kissed her mother and gave a special hug to her father, then bounded into the carriage Doctor Hébert had arranged for her so she would not have to walk. The Doctor reasoned she would take too long and be too tired to work if she arrived on foot. He needed her help as soon as he could get her to Versailles.

At Versailles, Christine was a bright student and learned quickly. She remained silent, observed everything and faded into the background for several years. Almost overnight, her childish figure became that of a woman. Christine's independent nature of ignoring personal conversations instigated by aristocrats who visited the medical rooms posed a direct challenge to the nobility. She truly was uninterested in them yet her aloofness placed her on a pedestal as the most desirable female creature in the Palace.

Noblemen at Court placed bets as to who would win her favor first. The thought of burying one's hands in her flaming curls was nearly overwhelming to the younger aristocrats. The older noblemen had been with many of the beautiful temptresses who arrived at Court single and left married. But their impure thoughts as to Christine never became reality.

True to her promise to Doctor Hébert, Christine refused the advances of every man at Court, including visiting noblemen from her ancestral home country of Spain. She was on a personal quest, though she dared not speak it, to become the first female physician at the Palace of Versailles.

Although that dream was never to be accomplished, Christine welcomed the journey to the New World when Doctor Hébert proposed it to her. She had been taught at an early age the story of her ancestors, from whom she had inherited not only her lustrous hair but her desire and ability to heal.

Christine saw her decision to travel to the New World as a tribute to her adventurous ancestor Luisa and a continuation of the family tradition of healing. While her first day at Versailles had been the beginning of her new position, Christine believed her arrival in Acadia would be the beginning of her new life.

CHAPTER 18
Pater

AT SEA

kirts rustled and linens crinkled in the somber cabin lit only by a single candle to reduce the summer heat. The open porthole did not provide much of a breeze as Christine and Doctor Hébert hovered over Eugenie. René watched over her steadfastly. He started when she opened her eyes.

"You gave us all a bit of a scare, my darling. How do you feel?" René whispered.

Eugenie stared at him, then at the doctor and nurse and cried out, "How long have I been asleep?"

René smiled. "Your fever broke last night after a long week. You took some soup and slept soundly until now."

Eugenie nodded, then said in a startled voice, "My baby! Did something happen to my baby?" She rubbed her hand over her belly under the covers.

Doctor Hébert reassured her. "My Lady, the baby is doing well. Christine examined you last night when you awoke briefly."

Eugenie grabbed his arm. "Please do not let anything happen to my baby. No matter what happens, you must promise me the child will be born healthy." She looked from the doctor to Christine and then to René.

"You shall have a healthy child and a long life with your new family." Doctor Hébert bowed.

Christine curtsied and nodded in agreement. "Of course, my Lady."

Eugenie looked at them all and spied a tray of food. She pointed and sheepishly grinned. "I am quite hungry. Thank you for thinking of me." She looked at her husband when she saw a huge red crustacean on the tray. "My dear, you remembered. I do still crave the taste of lobsters."

René helped her sit up as Christine brought the tray. Then René dismissed Doctor Hébert and Christine. The husband wanted to care for his wife in private.

Eugenie insisted on feeding herself. The lobster tasted delicious, full of nourishment and too good to waste even a single morsel. She also ate an entire bowl of soup, wiping the remains from the bowl onto a chunk of bread as she had seen servants do in the Palace. René was surprised, as such a custom was beneath their royal stature at Court. But he was anxious that his wife be happy and inasmuch as they were alone in a private cabin on the ship, she could certainly do as she pleased; even try out some peasant ways.

Eugenie turned to see René staring at her, before he dropped his eyes. An irrepressible grin came over her and she placed his hand under the quilts on her belly. The baby kicked. René's demeanor changed completely. The baby was letting them know he, or she, was a fighter. He had full faith in God that the infant would be born strong. He was not wrong on that point.

A gentle knock was heard at the front room of their cabin. René closed the doors between Eugenie's bed chamber and the front salon. Then he opened the door to find Pater juggling his easel, a sack of brushes and paints, his palette and a canvas.

Pater had become a prolific painter for the modern world though he had been born in the last century in 1695. He was selected for tutelage by the master French artist, Watteau, himself. Pater's prominence came when he was thirty-five years old and began a series of paintings later referred to as the "fetes gallants." His most famous would become the "Fête Champêtre," finished at the Palace of Versailles in 1730 after King Louis appointed him the Royal Artist in residence. He could not have imagined that this painting of his muse as an older woman would become one of the most famous of the period and for years in the future.

*

Pater's art exemplified the Rococo method which he learned under his impatient teacher, Antoine Watteau. However, he was bored with his master's ambiguous paintings and yearned to tell a story that would be clear to the observer, rather than follow the disguised, subtle work of the day.

Pater traveled to the Low Countries, where he was greatly influenced by Peter Paul Rubens, the Flemish artist, who glorified the roundness and plumpness of the royal female figure. Although Pater was given Watteau's commissions at his death, he feared becoming penniless as had so many artists before him. Thus, he created a factory of sorts, re-using the same personages and themes from one painting to the next, rather like an assembly line, in order to complete more works in less time. Pater finished more than six hundred works in his series of fêtes galantes, but his greatest was the painting of Eugenie de Beaufort Le Blanc de Verdure painted on a ship, but later lost in a disaster.

In "Fête Champêtre," young aristocratic couples are seen in a series of courtship tableaus in a lush park wherein they commence by flirting, then dancing, then participating in intimate conversations.   He introduced Venus, the goddess of love, and old-world colors into his modern paintings in order to simultaneously tease the eye and stir the heart.

Once at the Palace, Pater continued his works in the same vein as before, feverishly, almost mechanically, as if to create a legacy while he was still young. His death at age forty-one shocked everyone, as he had endeared himself among royalty, not only to the King but to most of the King's mistresses and the other ladies at Court.

But his choice of Eugenie de Beaufort as his central female figure in Fête Champêtre created unimaginable consternation among the other Ladies at Court who yearned for Pater's admiration. Naturally when the younger, obviously more beautiful Lady de Beaufort was chosen, her competitors' feelings turned to jealousy; rage, even.

Pater could not have chosen anyone else once he set eyes on the beautiful Lady Eugenie. He knew he had found his muse and he meant to glorify her beauty to the Court and all of France. Perhaps all of Europe too, he brazenly thought. In the end, his "Fête Champêtre" achieved the opposite of what he had anticipated, at least at Court. He had fanned the flames of envy harbored by the other Ladies into a blazing bonfire which burned the Lady Eugenie de Beaufort.

Pater had realized, not coincidentally, his bed had been empty in recent months after the painting began. He dared not consider propositioning his muse, but he yearned to be near her in a spiritual way. Thus, he gladly accepted Cardinal de Fleury's offer to travel with the royal couple and return to His Majesty with a series of paintings of the French colony in Acadia.

He would begin with a painting of Lady Eugenie during the sea voyage. He intended to present her with the painting as a token of his great esteem. Little did Pater realize that his gift was not to survive the events that were to occur in later years.

*

But today was a joyous day for the King's artist. To spend months doing what he loved most, painting his muse, was the dream of a lifetime. He had spoken with Doctor Hébert in the corridor, who confirmed the Lady was able to move about and that being on deck would be restorative to her health. Of course, the Lady Eugenie would have to determine the appropriateness of being on deck during the final months of her confinement but the Doctor approved the idea of short visits in the open air.

"The Lady Eugenie is feeling much better, I trust," bowed Pater to René at the door. Even the Court Artist had limits when a lady was in her boudoir, unless he was not working, of course. But his visit was all business. He had the utmost respect for Lord Le Blanc de Verdure and cherished Lady Eugenie, placing her on the highest pedestal of honor.

"Do come in, Monsieur Pater. Would you care for some refreshment?" René held up a bottle of fine wine.

Pater never turned down the King's good bottles. "Of course, my Lord. But just a taste." René poured half a glass. Then Pater motioned with his fingers for a bit more. René complied. Again the fingers, a little more. René filled the glass to the brim and heard Pater's sigh of contentment.

René poured himself half a glass and raised it to Pater. "To art. May it continue to be as beautiful as life."

Pater knew exactly what he meant and raised his glass. "To the incomparable Lady Eugenie."

They sipped their wine, René waiting expectantly for the artist to speak.

"If she, and you, deem it acceptable, I propose that I begin the painting of Her Ladyship on deck. I assure you it can be accomplished in short periods of time acceptable to the Lady's health."

"I see. I pray you excuse me for a moment, sir?" René asked. Pater nodded and as he took another sip of wine, René slipped through the dividing doors and closed them behind him as he entered Eugenie's stateroom.

Pater appreciated that the wine was exquisite, better than most bottles he had drunk at the King's table. And somehow it always tasted better in the morning. He reached over for the wine bottle, nearly tipping it over, but managing to fill his glass again and restore the bottle without spilling a drop. He quickly gulped the expensive wine and awaited the response to his suggestion.

René sat next to Eugenie's bed. "Do you think a bit of fresh air might put color back into your cheeks, my love? Monsieur Pater would like to start his painting, if you agree." He always asked for her decision, rather than telling her what to do, the latter being the custom of most noblemen. Then again, he was not just any nobleman.

She smiled. "That would be delightful. Tell Monsieur we could join him after morning Mass today."

"Of course, my dearest."

René kissed her cheek and Eugenie continued to eat her breakfast. He returned to the salon and gave the good news to Pater. "We shall see you in two hours, Monsieur, if that meets with your schedule?"

"But of course. I shall see you and the lovely Lady Eugenie on deck. Thank you, Monsieur le Consul."

The artist bowed out of the doorway and nearly jumped with jubilation as he walked down the hallway.

The upper deck was for the royal passengers and their staff only. As a result, it was virtually empty. The only passengers allowed on deck were René and Eugenie, Henri Mius d'Entremont, Doctor Hébert, Christine, Père Rivière, the two boys, and Pater himself, in addition to some of the Lord and Lady's attendants. The entry gates on the stairs were locked and guarded by uniformed sailors night and day to protect the peacefulness of the deck for its esteemed passengers. But there was no prohibition against upper class passengers descending to the lower deck.

René was proud of Eugenie, who had started a tradition of a weekly walk on the common deck, weather permitting. She was beloved by the colonists, with whom she sat and carried on lively conversations, as if there were no status distinction between them at all. René admired her since royals and aristocrats only mixed with commoners who were their servants. Otherwise, it was not acceptable at the Palace or anywhere in France. The nobility and the Catholic clergy were considered in their own classes, the First and Second Estates, respectively, and far above the peasants, the Third Estate.

The colonists on the ship knew nobles whose lands they worked as tenant farmers, serfs or house servants. The merchants had occasion to meet with nobility who purchased their goods but no one on the common deck had ever met a member of the Royal Court of Versailles. Each man and woman on the lower deck dreamed of meeting Eugenie and René, never expecting the dream to be realized.

The women were most interested in Eugenie's fashion sense -- her dresses, hairstyle, hats and gloves, and the shoes, what beautiful shoes, a different pair every day. Wives of laborers had two pairs of shoes -- one to wear in the fields and farms and the other for Saturday dances and Sunday Mass, usually what they had worn for their simple wedding. The dresses Eugenie wore were elegant designs. On one walk the dress was a solid vibrant color with lace, netting and embroidery. On the next she wore an overdress of stripes over lace and muted designs followed the following day by a mixture of floral patterns and so on -- each week a new feast for their eyes.

The best part, the women knew, was that Eugenie was completely natural, at ease among them. She had not one pretentious bone in her body. She sat and laughed with the other women as if they had been friends for years. Their daughters were awestruck by the beautiful Lady talking with their mothers. They felt lucky to be in her presence. The young boys were too shy to join their mothers but they admired Lady Eugenie from afar, dreaming of one day marrying a beautiful lady like her.

The men respected René as their government representative, the voice of King Louis XV but found him to be much more approachable. They appreciated his direct responses to their questions that did not involve government secrets. Their primary interest was in the status of the Treaty of Utrecht, what they could expect regarding their demands for neutrality, whether they would be required to take the English Oath of Allegiance, and any restrictions in Acadia that would affect their lives or livelihood. René was forthright where he could respond and clear in explaining what he could not discuss with them.

Their sons looked up to René as a guardian, a protector who made their fathers stronger. They yearned to be old enough to sit in on the mysterious conversations about oaths and neutrality, and something called a "Mi'Kmaq," among other topics that had never been discussed in their homes in France. If only they were older, then they could be real men like their fathers and talk to such a hero as Monsieur le Consul.

Each night, couples compared their impression of the royal couple. Each time the result was the same. Eugenie and René were beloved and respected by the King's subjects.

Today was a bright, sunny day with a mild breeze, typical of mid-summer on that part of the sea. The sails were not as full as they had been when the voyage began, so the afternoons languished and the sun beamed on the top deck. Pater walked onto the deck carrying a small cart with his collection of tools and paints, an easel and a canvas for his work. He looked up and down, finding the deck empty except for Henri and Gabriel at the railing. What were they doing, he wondered?

As Pater moved closer, he saw Gabriel looking upwards to the sky through a magnifying spyglass, the kind used by sea captains. Suddenly, he jumped with excitement and gave the glass to his father, pointing to several winged creatures flying above. Henri nodded as Gabriel sketched the birds on a small writing pad. Henri then wrote a description of their find beneath the drawing.

Pater walked up to them and admired Gabriel's drawing.

"You have a budding artist in your family, Sieur Mius d'Entremont."

Henri smiled with pride at his son. "Gabriel has been drawing since he could hold a quill. I brought his collection with me if you would care to have a look one day."

"With great delight. Carry on, young Gabriel. You have a natural eye for beauty."

Gabriel nodded. "But I lack skill in understanding colors. Perhaps you would teach me?"

Henri chided his son. "Monsieur Pater is much too busy, my son."

Pater interrupted him. "If you approve, Monsieur, it would be a pleasure to take your son under my wing and tutor him. It is rare to see such an innate talent."

Gabriel pleaded with passion. "Father, please agree. This is most important to me."

Henri relented. "But only when Monsieur Pater invites you. Do not follow him like a shadow."

Gabriel agreed with glee, clapping his hands. He was quite astute for being all of six years old.

Pater had work to do. "Pray excuse me, as I am about to begin my painting of the Lady Eugenie."

The two men and Gabriel bowed slightly to each other as Pater took his leave.

Pater set his easel and two chairs at the far end of the deck. He began sketching on a large canvas. The background was taking shape as a beautiful grove of trees on a hillside. The center of the painting was empty, awaiting Eugenie's portrait.

At that very moment, René escorted Eugenie to the painter, who did not conceal his joy. Pater made certain Eugenie was comfortable. René stood nearby with an extra cloak and blanket for warmth if the weather turned or she indicated she had the slightest chill.

The view was extraordinary from Pater's vantage point. The Lady against the deck railing, the sunlight dancing on her face, her smile beguiling any man who looked upon her. Yes, this was paradise on earth for Pater.

René looked over the railing at the lower deck, where the commoner colonists would soon be looking to him for guidance, direction and protection. He was aware that status and employment within this class of passengers determined their hierarchy in France, even to the type of sleeping quarters and meals they were allowed on a ship. He knew that they were all seeking a better life in Acadia, without the stringent class distinctions usual for the common working class.

René had requested a visit of the entire ship after Eugenie had toured the upper deck, as he had not seen the lower decks on his inspection prior to sailing. The Captain had explained the sleeping arrangements necessitated because the design allowed for no cabins on the lower decks. Men and women were separated into various large bedchambers, which were actually holds.

The higher-priced common tickets allowed a person to have a bed, such as it was. Boards were attached to the wall and built one above the other, with barely two feet of space in between. Enough for an adult and a child to squeeze in and lie in the same position all night. Women with infants had to take special care not to roll over their babies during the night. The deaths were explained as "infant breath disease" though the children were smothered to death Though no such tragedy had occurred on any of Captain Jacques' voyages, this sad event had happened more often than imagined on other vessels.

The next lower-priced ticket was a large hold with hammocks hanging from above, which required a ladder for access. Once a person got into their swinging bed he could not get out until the next morning, as the ladder was moved from hold to hold by a sailor until all the hammocks were filled. Families purchased these places for up to four children on one ticket, alternating them in one hammock, head to toe. Because most families had between ten and twenty children, the solution was also economical. And the hammocks prevented seasickness for the young ones as they rocked with the boat, resembling their cradles of earlier years.

Beneath the hammocks, a cheaper fare bought the use of a straw mat on the wooden floor of the passenger hold. The ship rocked to and fro and although the mats were fixed to the wooden floor, their occupants were not. So these passengers rolled back and forth with the others all night long. They no doubt appreciated the swinging hammocks above if they did, indeed, prevent children from being ill on board.

The next cheapest passage was for the "sitters," restricted to males only, age ten and older. The seat was a numbered square on a wooden bench where the passenger slept sitting upright. Many of these were single men or orphans whose occupation was general laborer or farm serf. Some had relatives already in Acadia, descended from early French colonists of the settlement founded in 1603 by the French explorer Samuel Champlain, apothecary to the royal family Louis Hébert, and René's forebear Claude Le Blanc.

Eugenie's ancestor, Guillaume de Beaufort, had also been on the first expedition to Acadia but after being one of the fortunate few survivors of the harshest winter he had ever known, he returned to his family estates in France and never returned. The descendents of these early settlers who remained were now wealthy owners of the largest farms in the territory and in dire need of labor. They had written to relatives back in France calling for cousins, nephews and uncles to work their fields.

The seats for these men were in the large room that doubled as a dining hall. At mealtime, the sitters were pushed out of their benches to the back of the food line, behind the commoners with more expensive tickets. They took their bowl of food and took an empty seat. Usually they were fed only one meal a day, but René wanted his new colonists to be healthy. He had insisted on two and provided the foodstuffs for the cook.

The least expensive ticket of all was for a child who slept on the floor under the wooden benches, strapped under the bench so he could not roll out with the ship's motion and be stepped on by a sitter.

Today René watched the families promenade slowly on the common deck while children ran back and forth, playing games with balls and sticks. A few couples noticed René on the upper deck and bowed respectfully to him. He nodded in response.

René turned from the railing to watch Pater preserving Eugenie's beauty on the canvas. The artist presented the completed painting to his muse, who gave it to René. He was thunderstruck when he saw the artist had captured some of the subtle nuances in his wife's features that endeared Eugenie to René -- her dimpled cheeks, the small brown beauty mark at the edge of her mouth only visible when she smiled. Otherwise the portrait was perfect in every way, perhaps too much so. René hung the painting in the outer salon so he could gaze at it as he sat and wrote in a journal. He had decided to keep a detail of the events of interest to the King relating to the voyage and his administration in Grand Pré.

Le Blanc dropped his quill in the ink pot and silently thanked God they had sailed in excellent weather for the past month and that Eugenie did not have to battle sea sickness usually caused by storms. She was in her seventh month and Christine and the Doctor reported to him of her continuing good health. He shuddered to think what might happen to her if storms overtook them at sea and delayed their landing.

Not three weeks later, his premonition came true. Captain Jacques saw a large black cloud moving quickly toward them, and he prepared the vessel for the impending storm. He ordered the crew to batten hatches, secure the ropes, lower the sails, and seal the food in crates and barrels to avoid spoilage and loss. The crew advised passengers to be ready for the worst and Jacques made an exception to the rule that men and women were separated. He allowed families to be together in the holds.

Père Rivière held a Mass on the lower deck for the passengers before they returned to the holds. The priest then said the Mass for the upper deck in René's salon. Eugenie remained in her bed on Christine's strong recommendation and the door was opened slightly so that she could pray the Mass with the others.

After Jacques made as many preparations as he could, he found L'Acadie soon caught in not one tempest, but crosswise between two black, whirling squalls. The Captain and his crew battled the elements for three days without sleep. The typhoons brought driving rains and whitecapped swells crashing on the decks. The ship escaped the brunt of one storm without major damage but the second tempest sent thrashing rains and forceful winds during the remainder of the week, causing a broken mizzenmast and torn sails. As the rains began to slacken, roaring winds blew the sailor in the crow's nest overboard. He had forgotten to strap himself in and his body was never seen again.

The passengers on the bottom deck huddled together, afraid to sleep. Meals could not be prepared but bread was distributed with pitchers of grog. Many were unable to eat for days due to sickness caused by the unending rise and fall of the rolling ship. The sitters were given ropes to tie themselves to the benches nailed to the floor so they would not be thrown overboard when the waves crashed on their deck and into the dining hall.

On the upper deck, René and Christine kept careful watch over Eugenie, who slept fitfully, moaning occasionally. She was covered with layers of blankets which were carefully tucked and tied to the bed so she would not be thrown to the floor, which might cause fatal damage to the baby and herself. Doctor Hébert set himself up in the large chair in their salon where he snoozed every few hours, his hand firmly holding the black bag next to him.

Henri asked Père Rivière to bring Sun to their cabin, where they prayed together for good weather. Every few hours, Henri sent Gabriel to René's rooms to inquire as to Lady Eugenie's health. Each time the boy returned with no news different from the last visit. She was sleeping restlessly but otherwise nothing else had occurred.

At once the seas became calm. The air was very still and the only sound was of occasional waves lapping against the boat. The whitecaps had disappeared, along with the winds. The ship sat silent and unmoving in the water. Captain Jacques had sailed through hurricanes but had never been caught in the eye, which is where he believed they were at this very moment. He feared the weather they had just experienced for days was small compared to the powerful elements ahead of them.

Jacques dispatched the crew to tell everyone that worse weather was approaching. Panic gripped the colonists, who did their best to protect their children. The Captain ordered the sails hoisted to the fullest to catch as much wind as possible to sail away from the monstrous black cloud approaching. He feared the ship would arrive in Acadia with few living passengers or, worse, would be torn apart if he tried to battle the hurricane. His deduction was that it would be better to sail off course than to stay on this path of certain death and destruction.

Nothing was written later about the bravery of Captain Philippe Jacques and his crew on that voyage. But by his quick thinking and the decision he made, the L'Acadie escaped the worst of the hurricane. They were safe now, he thought to himself. All his passengers will live. Neither he nor anyone else on the ship expected the future to unfold as it did.

CHAPTER 19
Henri

ACADIA

inging Rain was Henri Mius d'Entremont's paternal ancestor. He had been told two explanations of how she came to marry his ancestor, the first Lord Henri d'Entremont, a French explorer who traveled at Samuel Champlain's right hand. D'Entremont had joined the initial expedition to settle Acadia for France after Verrazzano's discovery the century before.

The first story Henri was told was that the Indian maiden was a bride of political convenience arranged by Champlain with her father, Chief Membertou Mius of the Mi'Kmaq First Nation. The Mi'Kmaq tribe had traded Champlain's expedition many furs which would bring a substantial profit back in France. As a show of good faith in their new alliance, Champlain acted as the go-between for Lord d'Entremont as a marriage partner to the Chief's undeniably beautiful daughter. The arrangement was hardly a sacrifice for either of the betrothed.

The second tale was the version that Henri, a romantic at heart, believed. When the Chief concluded a large fur trade with Champlain and the handsome d'Entremont, the Chief directed his daughter to serve the celebratory meal.

The beautiful Indian princess Singing Rain walked into her father's tent and first laid eyes on Lord d'Entremont. The couple fell in love at first sight.

Within days they had obtained the blessing of Chief Membertou Mius and Champlain. The wedding feast continued for three days and forged an alliance between the Mi'Kmaqs and the French that had never ended.

Intermarriage between the French and their native allies was a common occurrence. King Francis I himself had encouraged weddings between his French colonists in New France and Indian maidens due to the singular lack of women and to strengthen the existing alliance with the Mi'Kmaq First Nation. Over a thousand unmarried fur trappers, traders, fisherman, farmers and noblemen had moved from France to Acadia. Perhaps due to the harsh snowbound lands or the failure to find an agreeable bride, the men brought no wives. Thus, many unions took place between French settlers and young Mi'Kmaq daughters.

After their marriage, d'Entremont and Singing Rain traveled to his estates in France in 1607 on the return voyage of Champlain from Acadia. The couple raised a large family of twelve children, of which seven outlived them. The surname on each child's baptismal certificate read, "Mius d'Entremont" keeping the names of both father and mother. Henri's line was direct from Lord d'Entremont's oldest son, who inherited the title, rank and the land holdings of his father, then married and had a son, who had a son, and the line continued from Henri's father to him and from Henri to Gabriel.

Singing Rain began her family tradition by handing down to her eldest daughter a necklace made from interwoven stone beads and porcupine quills. Her mother had given it to Singing Rain to wear at her wedding and to take with her to France to remember her family. From that point forward, the eldest daughter of the eldest daughter would inherit the necklace.

Henri followed the genealogy of his direct line, but not the cadet lines of the family branching from sons other than the eldest. He had not known any ancestors other than his father and mother, so Henri was unaware that his great-grandfather had sired several children other than his grandfather.

One of those children was their eldest daughter, born with long flowing black hair, just as her mother, Singing Rain, had. She was named Whistling Rain Marie Mius d'Entremont. Her siblings called her Rainée.

Rainée refused to marry the nobleman her father had chosen for her. Instead she ran from Chateau d'Entremont to Marseille with Jerome, the son of their local baker. Lord d'Entremont denounced her for her disobedience, removed her from his will and never spoke to her again.

But before she left, Rainée she took the one thing that she held most dear -- the necklace from Singing Rain's armoire. More than just a rightful inheritance it was tangible proof of her heritage. She wanted to give it to the daughter she hoped to have one day.

Rainée and Jerome were penniless but happy. She worked as an assistant in a restaurant at the port from dinner until after midnight. Jerome left shortly after she returned home to seek work in the port with shipbuilders as he could wield a hammer. Since they rarely saw each other, Rainée was overjoyed to discover she was with child and planned to give Jerome the news when he returned that evening.

That morning Jerome had been hired to repair a ship's mast by climbing scaffolding high above the harbor. The builder had purchased thin rope to keep more profits for himself, thus making the scaffolding precarious. Jerome was hoisted on the wooden plank and he began his work. When he leaned over to repair the tall mast, the rope broke without warning, sending Jerome to his death in the murky water below.

Rainée waited all night for her husband. She went to the port at dawn and was told he was in a watery grave. She would have thrown herself in too, but for the baby. The builder gave her Jerome's wages for the time he worked until he fell, then he chased the girl away.

Rainée named her daughter Jeanne Marie Rain Mius. She placed the girl in a basket with the necklace and a note of her ancestry and her name, then tenderly left it on the steps of St. Peter's Church, near the dock. After that, Rainée disappeared. Sailors in the port taverns would later swear they saw the spirit of a woman in Indian dress manifest itself in the harbor each morning just before dawn, looking for her husband.

Jeanne grew up in the Church orphanage and was anything but a model child. The Catholic nuns were exasperated with her unwillingness to study, because she was bright. A few years later, the milk delivery boy took a fancy to Jeanne, and she to him. The nuns gave them their blessing and they were married.

They spent their wedding night in a small cell in the orphanage. While Jeanne was asleep, contented with her new life, her husband took the pouch of wedding money and ran away. Nine months later Jeanne gave birth to a baby boy. She named him Sun Mius.

CHAPTER 20
Baptism

ACADIAN COAST

aptain Jacques sailed to Acadia with the aid of his First Assistant Jehan Hébert and the use of his compass and a new invention called an octant, much smaller and easier to carry than their old Davis quadrant for determining a vessel's latitude.

They followed the maps made by Gastaldi in 1548 and by Champlain more than half a century later. Fortunately, the coastline had changed little since those discoveries for France had been charted. The Captain anchored his ship that day in late August, nearly four months after they departed Le Havre, in a small cove a few hundred yards off the beach. From there, the colonists would walk through a magnificent grove of trees up the hill. From the bluff, they would walk toward a plain surrounded by forests, mountains and dikes to their new home of Grand Pré.

The ship's crew had efficiently loaded the passengers into small landing boats and brought them to safety on shore. René and Eugenie, Doctor Hébert and Christine were the first passengers to arrive on shore. The sailors carried Lady Eugenie in a makeshift bed to avoid her having to wade through the water, quite icy even in late summer, to the beach. René had carefully carried his treasured portrait of her far above his head to protect it. The next boat brought d'Entremonts, Père Rivière and Sun, followed by Pater in a boat filled with his canvases, paints and brushes and other materials, ready to paint the landing for His Majesty. All day the launches carried the colonists from the ship to the sandy beach strewn with stones.

The colonists from the common deck loaded their meager possessions into their landing boat. Once they arrived on shore, the items were easily carried by dividing their boxes and satchels among numerous family members.

Except for small satchels and essentials that could be carried and would fit in the rowboat, the items loaded into coaches at Versailles and René's large carriage remained on board. After the birth of Eugenie's baby, Pater would return to the ship and sail with Captain Jacques and his crew further up the coast to the harbor of Annapolis Royal, where all of the household goods, the coach and the remaining foodstuffs would be offloaded to be carried overland to the new Consulate building in Grand Pré. Jacques would then return to Le Havre with Pater and a cargo of Acadian fish and woolen goods to be sold for the best prices in Paris.

From the moment they landed, the passengers of *L'Acadie* were overwhelmed by the sight of the beautiful trees. They believed the view to be a portent of good luck for their entry into the New World. Père Rivière gathered his new congregation near, and they knelt to give thanks for their safe arrival, their health, and for the soul of the lost sailor, who was the only death during the voyage.

While the colonists were at prayer, the crew set up shelters on one end of the beach, under the trees. Cloth was tied to tree branches and trunks, closed on three sides, to provide an overnight respite and some shelter from the elements. On the other side of the beach, far out of earshot, the sailors had erected several fully enclosed tents with royal insignia which had been brought from Versailles. They were arranged, as were the ship cabins, so that those passengers had a private refuge before they continued their journey on foot to their new home in Grand Pré the following day.

The largest tent had been raised for René and Eugenie under the leafy branches of the beautiful trees at the edge of the woods. It was inside this shelter that Eugenie had been carried in her bed. A table and chairs had been set up for René on heavy rugs that covered wooden planks on the hard ground. The tents for the d'Entremonts, Christine, Doctor Hébert and Père Rivière and Sun were simply furnished with planks on which linens and blankets had been placed, to eliminate lying on the sandy ground. They, too, had rugs, unlike the commoners, who placed blankets on the sand where they and their children would sleep.

Pater was given a small tent to himself, where he stored the materials he would not use until later. He enlisted the help of Gabriel and Sun to carry his easel and small chair while he carried a satchel of paints and brushes and held a large canvas before him. The little parade marched to the shore, where Pater set his easel facing the beautiful trees which the Cardinal had described. They would figure prominently in the background of this painting for King Louis he would entitle, "Arrival in Acadia." While Gabriel and Sun sat at the artist's feet, he began to sketch the outline of his new work. Gabriel watched how Pater made his brush strokes and began to create his own sketch of the unique grove.

The crew assisted Christine by building a fire outside Eugenie's tent and filling barrels full of fresh sea water. Then she hung an iron pot of water over the fire to boil and walked inside the tent with a stack of clean linens.

Doctor Hébert set up the black bags near the bed and took his leave as Christine prepared her utensils and linens. Birthing was a midwife's work, but for wealthy women Hébert always waited outside the woman's chamber in the event of an unforeseen problem. Soon Christine had organized everything as it should be. She had asked Adèle Arnaud to assist her in bringing hot water as needed. Adèle also volunteered to prepare meals when Eugenie became hungry.

Eugenie was placed in the bed and propped up comfortably. René held her hand, kissing it over and over. She suddenly cried out in pain and motioned for him to leave. René did not want to leave although everyone knew it was not appropriate for a husband to stay during a birth. Christine took René by the arm and escorted him to the front opening of the tent.

Eugenie cried out again, this time louder, and René turned back to go to her. Christine insistently shooed him out and closed the flap to the tent. Christine had prepared both a leather strap and a knotted cloth for Eugenie to bite when the pain was too intense but Eugenie pushed them both away. She moaned between loud shrieks of pain.

René could do nothing for his wife, though he prayed for her health and for a strong baby. Men were helpless when it came to childbirth. It had always been like that and probably would always remain so. One by one, the other men from the top deck joined René outside his tent -- Doctor Hébert, Henri, Père Rivière and Claude. Being preoccupied with his thoughts, René charged Claude to pour wine and distribute cigars. The men eagerly partook of the offerings as they waited for the sound of a crying infant.

The lower deck passengers, who had all survived the journey alive, sat under their shelters watching the activity in Eugenie's tent. They knew that René's kindness in providing two full meals a day had actually improved the health of many weak and sickly family members and friends. They owed him and his wife a debt of gratitude and they each began to pray for a successful birth and the health of mother and child.

The men with René shared their experience with successful childbirths. Père Rivière had been present at many, including in fields, at the port and one at the doors of the Church, each resulting in a healthy baby. Doctor Hébert promised that Eugenie was stronger than many women at Court who had given birth successfully. Claude was too young to have experience so he was partly entranced and partly incredulous with their stories of this mysterious womanly power. Henri was silent until René turned to him and asked about Gabriel's birth and the death of his wife. D'Entremont described the long and arduous birth of Gabriel by his wife, Diane. He reassured René that, despite the difficulties, both survived without further incident.

The death of Diane Mius d'Entremont came six years later, when she was trampled by a wild horse that broke out of a fence under repair on their estates. Henri did not tell René she had been about four months with child, a little girl, whom the old physician tried to bring forth alive without success. It still pained Henri to think of it and he had told no one, not even Gabriel. The village priest had blessed the partly formed infant and buried her with Diane at the private funeral ceremony attended only by Henri and the doctor who had eased the pain of Diane's last hours. It was his wife's dying wish that Henri take Gabriel to Acadia to seek relatives of Singing Rain among the Mi'Kmaqs. Henri had promised Diane through his tears, and then she left him. The priest and the doctor agreed to keep the unborn infant's death a secret. They both died of natural causes within weeks and Henri booked passage on the L'Acadie.

Henri believed the move to Acadia would be good for Gabriel to inspire him and instill a sense of adventure. But he also hoped the trip would erase his memories of Lady Diane. Alas, that was not to be. Memories of his wife had floated around him in Le Havre and on the ship. A glimpse of a lady promenading in town. The smell of the same perfume she wore. A feathered blue hat similar to one of hers. A beautiful striped dress in her preferred color. Her favorite dish served by the crew.

Only last night he had awoken drenched in sleepsweat and cried out Diane's name. Gabriel had soothed his father by tapping his shoulder.

"Maman is in heaven watching us. We shall be fine, Papa. She will make certain of it."

Henri vaguely remembered, or had he dreamed it? He thought Gabriel said he was going to marry the baby girl that Lady Eugenie was carrying. No, he must have been dreaming. How would a child know the infant was a girl? And what would cause him to think of marriage at this early age? Jolting himself back to the present, Henri convinced René that all would go well. The Lady Eugenie was healthy and she had been quite careful in her confinement.

René expressed his concerns, "We had planned for the birth once we had settled in Grand Pré. But she is not yet at the end of her term, which will bring the child several weeks early."

Henri responded, "Her Ladyship was strong during the voyage and should not have any problems."

Père Rivière had joined the commoners, who were gathered together at the edge of the tree grove. He led them in reciting the Rosary. "Our Father, Who art in heaven..." Their prayers were interrupted by more cries coming from the tent.

Christine opened the flap to Eugenie's tent and asked Doctor Hébert to enter. But René rushed to her first. "What is it? How is she?"

Christine tried to calm his fears, "It is helpful for me to ask the Doctor for help in measuring, that's all. So far the baby seems to be moving along slowly but without problems. Lady Eugenie is in pain, which is to be expected for any childbirth."

René had become quite worried. "Does a birth usually take this long? It has been hours. Or is there a problem because the child is early?"

"Every woman is different but for a first child a few weeks early or a few weeks late and many hours of labor are not out of the ordinary. Please have patience, my Lord. Now we must attend to Lady Eugenie," Christine replied.

René looked at the doctor, who agreed, "Christine is correct. Thus far nothing is cause for alarm. Rest assured I shall tell you at once of any health concerns." With that, Hébert and Christine disappeared inside.

The colonists continued their prayers, led by Père Rivière. René and Henri walked over to meet them. Le Blanc prayed with the people he would guide. They all prayed for the health of his wife and child.

René returned to Eugenie's tent and sat outside. He needed to be as close to her as he could and he preferred being there than in a warm, comfortable tent of his own. The hours tolled slowly into the early morning just before dawn. Eugenie's cries continued but they were weaker and softer. René went to the tent and questioned the Doctor. He explained the Lady was having normal pains and there was nothing that could be done.

The ship's passengers finally settled in for the night, some laying under the stars, children asleep, but many whispering quiet fears about Lady Eugenie's laborious ordeal.

Henri and Père Rivière walked back to René's side. Cries were coming from inside the tent. None of the men spoke, but all of them had the same thing on their minds. The priest put his hand on René's arm and said, "Let us pray." With that the three men knelt on the rocky ground, bent their heads and followed the priest in prayer.

As dawn broke, the sleeping colonists arose. Some filled bowls and pots with sea water. Others started small cooking fires from hastily built hearths. Children were still groggy but insisted on watching the activity outside. But no matter the age, every passenger on the beach looked toward to Lady Eugenie's tent for news, which did not come.

Eugenie cried out loudly this time as Christine encouraged her to push the baby out. Thereafter René and the men near the birthing tent heard a splash of water and a loud cry. This time the noise was not from Eugenie but from an infant.

René rushed in and saw Christina wrapping a beautiful child in the fresh linens. She handed the baby to him. "A girl, Monsieur Le Consul. Perfect in every way." Then she turned to Eugenie, who was drained and weak. Christine held her hand encouragingly. René sat next to Eugenie on her bed and put the baby in her arms.

"My darling wife, we have a beautiful daughter." Eugenie was exhausted and nodded before closing her eyes and falling into a deep sleep. René cast a look of concern at Doctor Hébert.

The doctor motioned for René to step into his tent with his new baby. There he said gravely, "Lady Eugenie lost much blood in these last moments. We have stopped the running, but she needs her rest. All has been done that is possible. It is a time for prayers as she sleeps. A blessing from Père Rivière would help her now." He bowed and walked outside to the priest and Henri with the news. Gabriel and Sun were waiting expectantly and they ran to tell the colonists about the baby girl.

Hébert pulled Père Rivière aside, whispering to him. Père Rivière immediately joined René, who was walking back into Eugenie's tent and holding the newborn child.

As soon as the new colonists heard the news, loud cheers rang out. The crowd shouted blessings to the Consul and Lady Eugenie for the good fortune of a healthy baby.

Pater and the two boys rushed over to the tent to catch a glimpse of mother and child but the tent was closed and they sadly returned to their painting site.

While everyone else was occupied, Christine and Adèle removed the bowls of dark crimson water from the tent and emptied them out of sight. Adèle asked Claude to bury the bloody towels when no one was watching. He adored his wife and jumped at her every request.

Père Rivière asked René, "Sieur Le Blanc de Verdure, would you like a blessing on your new family?"

"If you please, Père."

The priest raised his hand and made the Sign of the Cross over Eugenie, René and the infant. "May the Lord our God bless and keep you, strengthen you and give both of you the grace and strength to raise this beautiful child in the Word of Our Lord. Amen."

René repeated, "Amen." René sat at Eugenie's side as she slept restlessly. René kissed the infant over and over again on her forehead. Eugenie woke and weakly held her arms out for the baby. The priest exited the tent as René placed the infant at Eugenie's side and together they held their baby girl.

Alone with their child, René kissed Eugenie and the baby. "She is such an angel, a perfect angel, my darling," René said. "And she has your beautiful hazel eyes. What shall you name her?"

Eugenie smiled. "There is but one name for a little angel, my dearest husband -- Evangeline."

René grinned in response. "Evangeline she shall be."

Then the coughing began. René was not worried, as Eugenie was tired and the cough was dry. But she continued coughing into her handkerchief which she tried to hide from René. He took it from her and saw spittle tinged with blood. René was alarmed and called for help. "Christine! Doctor Hébert! Please come at once."

Christine rushed in, and an exhausted Eugenie handed the baby to her. When Evangeline started to cry, Christine rocked her in her arms, taking her out of the tent.

The doctor looked at the red stains on Eugenie's handkerchief and bedclothes and shook his head. He took a vial of dark liquid from his black bag and poured the substance down the Lady's throat as René held her head. He laid her head back and propped pillows around her then covered her with a blanket. She nodded and dozed off again.

The doctor whispered to René, "It will make her more comfortable but the end is near. There is nothing more we can do." He bowed sadly and crept out of the tent.

Eugenie woke with a start and pleaded. "Stay with me, my darling husband. Do not leave me alone, even if I sleep. I must be near you. It will not be long but I need you."

René caressed her hair, kissed her hands and tried to keep his voice as level as possible. "I am here for you always, my love."

They both knew she was dying. Tears streamed down René's face. He had found the other half of his soul and was about to lose her so quickly.

Evangeline's cries were heard just outside the tent. She knew something was wrong. Christine tried to shush her, but she was not her mother.

Eugenie called out, "Let me hold my baby. I need to hold Evangeline."

Christine appeared and placed the baby in her mother's arms. Instantly, Evangeline stopped crying and started cooing, looking into Eugenie's eyes. Christine turned to leave but she felt a weak tug at her sleeve. Christine bent down as Eugenie whispered, then nodded and removed the jeweled cross from around the Lady's neck. Christine tried to place it in Eugenie's hand but the gesture was refused. Eugenie motioned for Christine to bend toward her. Then she whispered to the young midwife.

"I owe you a debt of gratitude more than words can express. Thank you for bringing this beautiful soul into the world. Thank you for caring so lovingly for me."

Christine shook her head. "My Lady, it is an honor to be here for you. I shall remain just outside if you have need of anything." She tried to return the cross but Eugenie insisted that she keep it.

"It was my mother's and, until my marriage and the birth of my daughter, it was the most meaningful thing in my life. But I want you to have it now."

Christine placed the gold chain around her neck, sadly knowing that Eugenie was near death. Christine nodded her thanks,

Eugenie continued, "I know you will care for my husband and my daughter as you did for me. Please do not leave them and return to France. They need you." Christine nodded as she tried to hold back her tears.

"Of course I will do anything for them. We shall all miss you and I shall make certain Evangeline knows her mother is an exceptional woman." Then she hugged Eugenie and exited the tent.

René wrapped his arms around Eugenie and Evangeline, and the three of them remained in the embrace, unmoving, for the longest while.

Eugenie lifted her head and whispered into Evangeline's ear. "I love you. Your Maman shall always love you, darling daughter. I shall watch over you with the angels."

René was heartbroken. His time with Eugenie was much too short. Their lifetime of memories together had been stolen abruptly. The love of his life would be gone soon. How would he survive without her, having succumbed to her, both heart and soul? He did not try to stop the tears flowing unabashedly down his face.

Eugenie continued, now crying salty tears onto Evangeline's hair, as black as night. "René is your father now and he will take care of you but he will also tell you of your true family heritage. And when the time is right, you must help him. Convince him to take a new wife. He deserves so much more love than I could give him. Remember, my little angel, how much I love you. Good bye, Evangeline."

Weakened, Eugenie fell back onto the pillows. René took the infant from her and brought Evangeline to Christine outside the tent. He shook his head to Père Rivière, Henri and Doctor Hébert standing nearby. They nodded in sympathy and walked with the priest toward the ship's passengers on the other side of the shore. They respected his need to be alone with his dying wife.

Christine held Evangeline and followed Père Rivière. The priest bid the colonists to meet them at the shore. Everyone was anxious to see the newest colonist of Grand Pré and they all met at the water's edge, where they admired the baby. But when Henri informed them of Lady Eugenie's condition they fell silent with shock and grief, many falling to their knees as the priest led them in the Lord's Prayer.

Pater was so grief-stricken that he could not join the others but sat at the edge of the shore, crying at the loss of his beloved muse. He stayed in that position with his red tear-stained face until the waves rushed in so fast that they nearly carried him out to sea. Gabriel and Sun helped the artist move his materials back to his tent, where he sat without moving.

Gabriel asked to borrow some of his paper and charcoal to draw and Pater nodded without looking. Gabriel grabbed the precious materials and ran out of the tent. He stood close to Christine as she held the infant and he drew Lady Evangeline from memory, depicting her cradling Evangeline in her arms. Gabriel handed it to his father. Henri was amazed at the likenesses and kept the sketch, planning to give it to René at a more appropriate time. Then Gabriel returned to Pater's tent, sitting on the ground as Pater told stories about his muse.

One of the colonists was a master carpenter, the heavyset bearded Thomas Gaudet. He left the group after the first prayer and walked into the grove of trees. After looking carefully at the variety of hardwoods and softwoods he spoke softly to himself or perhaps to a beautiful tree just behind Eugenie's tent. Stroking the tree as if it were a child, he cut its largest branch and sat on the soft hillside expertly trimming it with his double bladed knife.

Seeing the man she had grown to love during the sea voyage, Anne Verrazzano brought him a cup filled with water. He gratefully drank it and invited her to sit next to him. She did so, silently marveling at his talented hands that seemed to sculpt the wood into a beautiful object.

From the edge of the shore Père Rivière waded waist-deep in the sea and filled a holy chalice with water. Gabriel walked up to Christine, holding the baby. He lifted his hand up and wrapped it around Evangeline's tiny fingers. Gabriel whispered to Christine, "You know she will be my wife one day."

Christine whispered in reply, "Are you not a bit young to think of such things?"

Gabriel replied, "I am nearly six. Would the Consul give her hand now?

Christine stifled a grin. "Not unless marriage comes before baptism."

"I shall wait. But remember this day, Madame, for I shall come for her."

"I shall indeed."

Père Rivière waded onto the beach and took Evangeline from Christine. Gabriel reluctantly let go of the baby's tiny fingers. The priest poured water over Evangeline's head, making the Sign of the Cross. "I baptize thee in the name of the Father, and of the Son and of the Holy Spirit as Evangeline Marie Beaufort Le Blanc de Verdure. We welcome you into our Catholic community of the Saint Charles Parish in Grand Pré, Acadia. Halleluiah!"

Père Rivière then returned the baby to Christine's arms and turned to the crowd, who replied, "Halleluiah" with a mixture of happiness for the new child and sorrow for Her Ladyship, whom they had grown to love. The colonists kneeled on the stones and received their blessing from the priest. Then they rose and gathered around Evangeline, eager to see her more closely.

Gabriel felt protective of Evangeline as he looked on her with adoration. Gabriel looked up at the infant. Her tiny hands stretched out and he took them into his own. Evangeline smiled and cooed contentedly.

CHAPTER 21
Cross

THE BEAUTIFUL GROVE

Inside their tent René and Eugenie heard the cheers down at the beach. She smiled weakly, and he kissed her forehead gently. "Our little angel has been baptized," she said. He nodded, fighting back the tears. Eugenie gently took his hand. "I know you will be a devoted father. Christine will be of great help to you."

René responded, "My love. Stay with me. We still have much to say."

Eugenie smiled and leaned toward René. "No need to speak of what we both know. For my part, I have never been loved purely and completely as you have loved me. I am so grateful for the happiness you have given me."

René shook his head. "You had my heart from the moment I saw you, my love. What else could I do? What will I do without you? I am already lost." He sank his head into his hands until he heard his love cough. Instantly he adjusted the pillows under her head to make her more comfortable.

She said, "Evangeline will be safe with you. But you need to know who the father is to protect her." She bid him to come closer. He listened carefully as she whispered a few words in his ear, and then she coughed again. Exhausted, she added, "You will know when the time is right to tell her but I beg you to guard the secret well. No one must know."

René agreed. "Of course, my love. I shall protect your secret. But please, do not go. Not yet. I cannot bear the thought of life without you."

"Think of me when you see Evangeline. Teach her the right way to live, in our Catholic faith. Educate her so she may be of great service to others. Remember I shall be with both of you always."

Tears streamed down René's cheeks. Eugenie's face glowed and René knew the end was near.

She repeated, "Promise me you will present her at Versailles and marry her to a nobleman but protect her from the pettiness and jealousy of Court. I only pray she will be as happy as you have made me, my love."

"Yes, dearest Eugenie. I promise it shall be done as you ask. But you must stay with me longer. Please, please stay."

He leaned closer to her and she gave him a final kiss, tender, loving, providing all the answers he would ever need.

"Thank you for loving me. I shall always love you, René, my love....." Then she leaned back, closed her eyes, and expired.

René was distraught. He held his wife, weeping bitter tears and remaining next to her for hours. No one entered the tent except Christine, who quietly lit candles around Evangeline's bed so that he could see her in the light. He did not notice the midwife, his face buried in Eugenie's hair, his arms wrapped around her body. He had to warm her chilling body.

Thomas Gaudet walked out of the woods holding the wood object in one hand and Anne's hand in the other. He had carved a cross, but this was not just any ordinary burial marker. His craftsmanship was exquisite, the wood having been smoothed and finished using sand from the beach. An intricate fleur de lis design covered every part of the cross and Lady Eugenie's name was carved in the center, surrounded by a shower of roses.

Gaudet took it upon himself to organize a group of other men to assist in constructing the coffin. Adèle sewed the coffin linens that Eugenie would rest in, covered with green silk to match her unique hazel eyes. Several times Adèle had to stop to prevent her tears from staining the fabric but she managed to muddle through. She added a lace overlay to finish it and then lined the coffin with the soft layers of fabric.

Her husband, Claude, felt helpless and asked Père Rivière, Henri and Doctor Hébert how he could be of service. Henri suggested he ask several sailors to row him back to the ship where Captain Jacques and his crew were waiting for the news. He also asked that they bring back food for evening supper and for the following day as they had not planned to stay this long on the beach. Without ado Claude had selected three strong men to row with him. To Henri's surprise, Claude and his group returned with the Captain and all of his officers and crew who could be absent from the ship overnight. Jacques and his men filled the harbor with their boats. Only a few were needed to bring the necessary supplies but all wanted to pay their last respects to the Lady Eugenie they had come to love and admire.

Once back on shore Claude and the cooks had sent children to gather firewood and men to build fires. The women assisted the cooks in preparing supper in their own pots for a large, family style meal. Many burly laborers were in the group. Each volunteered to dig the grave trench in honor of the Lady who had shown them courtesy and kindness. With so many workers, each took a turn with his own shovel and the sad task was completed in no time at all.

Père Rivière did not wish to be under the watch of Protestant English soldiers for such a private Catholic ceremony as a funeral, so he chose a secluded site at the edge of the beautiful grove Eugenie had admired. While the men worked, Christine sent a group of women to collect wild blooms on the hillside. Though it was the end of summer, a glorious array of sweet flowers was found to fill the coffin, framing Adèle's silk and lace handiwork.

Père Rivière surveyed the arrangements for the funeral. When he found everything ready, he sent the mourners to their shelters while Claude distributed the food. They ate quietly and waited for directions from their Consul, who had not left the tent.

After sundown, Père Rivière suggested the families rest for the evening and plan on the burial in the morning. They complied but no one slept well that night. Everyone felt the pain, though to a much lesser degree, of Lord Le Blanc de Verdure.

The Captain and his men stayed on shore, talking quietly with Henri, the Doctor and Père Rivière. Pater joined them but did not contribute to the conversation. He sat by their candlelight and sketched one drawing after another, trying to capture on paper all the moments with Lady Eugenie he held in his heart.

The next morning most of the colonists awoke before dawn, awaiting the funeral procession to the gravesite. At daybreak, Père Rivière entered René's tent. He stayed a long while but when he exited, he motioned to Christine and Adèle to enter the tent.   Then the priest walked over to Thomas Gaudet and the other men, who carried the coffin to René's tent and waited.

The two women assisted René and carefully dressed Eugenie in her wedding clothes. René covered her in a beautiful cloak so she would not feel the morning chill. He blew out the candles and carried Eugenie's body gently through the opening in the tent. Henri and Gabriel, Doctor Hébert and Père Rivière waited for him there. Christine held Evangeline, who watched René without a whimper.

Père Rivière waited patiently with the entire congregation until René gave the signal. When he nodded, the five men who had been closest to her on the journey, other than René, carried the empty coffin forward -- Henri d'Entremont, Doctor Hébert, Claude Arnaud, Pater and Captain Jacques. Père Rivière asked Thomas Gaudet to be the sixth bearer, as he had made the coffin beautifully with his hands.

René gently placed Eugenie's body on top of the flowers in the coffin, then held her hand and kissed her again. Adèle and Christine laid bouquets of fresh flowers in Eugenie's hands.

Then René nodded to Père Rivière, who led the procession up the hill to the site. There he blessed the body and conducted the Catholic funeral rites. Every passenger and crew member on the ship walked past Eugenie's coffin to show their final respects. Many women tossed flowers into the coffin.

Sun did not understand much but he walked up to the coffin. "My Maman waits for you. She show you the way. No need to be 'fraid. She right here, see?" He pointed to an invisible spirit next to him and then he smiled and nodded to Père Rivière. "She took her hand. She with the angels now. All is good." He skipped away from the funeral and went down to play on the beach.

The colonists who overhead him began to sob louder realizing that Lady Eugenie truly was gone. Père Rivière understood Sun's comments to be signs of his spirituality which he also attributed to his Mi'Kmaq heritage.

Gabriel knelt by the coffin and whispered to Eugenie's now cold body. Only those closest to the coffin, René, Père Rivière, Henri and Christine who held Evangeline in her arms, overhead him. "I shall marry Evangeline and take care of her. Do not worry. I am strong and can protect her." He picked up Eugenie's hand and placed a unique seashell in it, then gently placed her hand back in the coffin. He added, "Something bad will happen on the water. Bring the angels to protect us. Goodbye, most beautiful Lady Eugenie." He stood up and ran to the beach where he sat next to Sun.

When the coffin was closed, tears flowed and colonists sobbed aloud. René was inconsolable and they cried for him as well. Everyone already missed Eugenie's kind face and generous spirit. Père Rivière said a final prayer, then closed the Bible. He nodded and the congregation sang hymns as the laborers dug into the mound of earth. They handed a shovel of dirt to each settler, who tossed it onto Eugenie's grave as a mark of respect. One by one the colonists filed by a second time, wiping away their tears as they bowed to René.

Thomas Gaudet stepped forward to offer René his carved wooden cross with the intricate carvings. René was so moved he put his hand on the man's shoulder. "Whom should I thank for such kindness, sir?"

"Thomas Gaudet, Monsieur le Consul. Anything you wish in wood to be carved, cut, built or repaired, I am at your service."

"Thank you, Monsieur Gaudet. Your work is indeed beautiful. I am touched by your kindness. You did not know her did you?"

Gaudet bowed and with humility said, "I wish I could have actually spoken to the beautiful Lady Eugenie. But I was fortunate to see her when she walked on our lowly deck. She treated us like real people, my Lord, not like servants or worse. We all loved her."

René responded through his pain, "I shall not forget what you did for me in my time of great sorrow."

"Shall I place it here?" Gaudet pointed to the head of the grave.

René nodded and Gaudet buried the foot of the cross at the gravesite.

Once the colonists had paid their final respects, Henri directed them back their tents. It was time for René to be alone in his sorrow. Without noticing that the others had crept away, René knelt at the grave. With tears streaming down his face, he removed his golden neck cross, kissed it, and placed it on top of Eugenie's grave. René slowly made the Sign of the Cross and walked back to Eugenie's tent to grieve.

As Captain Jacques and his crew prepared to row the boats back to the ship, Pater jumped out of the boat and into the water. He splashed onto the beach looking up and down until he found the person he sought. He gave Gabriel his satchel filled with brushes, charcoal, pencils and drawing paper. He hugged the boy and whispered in his ear. "Remember what I have told you. Promise me you shall tell the child all about her beautiful mother, and why she was my muse." Gabriel nodded and Pater huffed back to the rowboat. It took three sailors to pull him in but finally the launch boat moved forward again.

When René moved back to the tent, the laborers finished burying the coffin and left the gravesite. The new colonists walked to the water's edge, waving goodbye to Captain Jacques, Pater and the crew as they rowed back to the ship.

Christine, carrying a now sleeping Evangeline, asked Adèle and Anne to plant wildflowers on the grave to forever remind them of the sweet Lady Eugenie de Beaufort Le Blanc de Verdure.

CHAPTER 22
Summit

ON THE ROAD TO GRAND PRÉ, ACADIA

 alking slowly uphill through the thick tree grove, the new French Consul to Grand Pré, Sieur René Le Blanc de Verdure led his new colonists to the summit of the hill. René used the spyglass the Captain has presented as a parting gift. He thought he saw the figures on the ship waving to him. René stretched his arms waving them above his head. Colonists, too, waved in frenzy to a barely visible ship in the distance.

Fathers lifted sons and daughters on their shoulders hoping to give them a last glimpse of the French ship that had brought them to their new homes. The children shouted and clapped gleefully as their parents gave knowing glances that the only certainty was that uncertainty lay ahead for everyone.

In the Bay below the sailors pulled anchor, raised the sails and prepared to depart. Captain Jacques peered through his nautical glass and saw a faint figure at the top of the hill whom he presumed to be René waving. He waved back, then handed the glass to Pater, who had been sketching the scene.

The artist hoped King Louis would not regret the numerous paintings Pater had made of Eugenie before she…he could hardly finish his thought…before she became an angel. He had secreted a second painting of Eugenie looking at the light, just as in the one he had given to her. It comforted him to know that René would honor Eugenie with his painting in the New World and that Pater would hold Eugenie's memory back in France. Pater waved a final goodbye to the figure he thought was René. He was filled with sadness at the loss of his beloved Lady Eugenie, his muse. He immersed himself in painting memories of Lady Beaufort's beautiful ghost, which he saw everywhere he walked on the ship. And he vowed that her spirit would live in every female figure on his future canvases.

The artist had no way of knowing his life would end shortly after his return to Court. The tragic incident would occur when he brushed away a small rodent from his paint pots near the Versailles south entry gate. Pater would ignore the swelling bite on his hand, intently sketching Lady Véronique de Navarre and her fiancé Laurent Arnaud. That young man would be the one to find Pater's bloated body lying in the foliage of his favorite painting spot. But that was yet to occur.

On the hill Henri d'Entremont was deep in conversation with Gabriel. As usual Sun was at his side. Sun idolized the younger boy and saw it as his mission to protect him though Gabriel was quite capable of taking care of himself. Henri continued his lecture. "You are becoming a young man. You too, Sun. You must learn to be aware of your surroundings." He pointed to the ship and the surrounding Bay. "Learn the land all around you. Even if it is under the sea. Land can provide shelter, food, and safety. Become one with the land and it will be of great use to you."

Gabriel peered intently down at the beach below but Sun, while slow to understand, took every word at its meaning and followed every instruction to the letter. He looked carefully around him and soon spied an unusually shaped rock. He knelt in the grass, found a broken stick and started digging around the large stone. Lifting it, he discovered a patch of earth different from the rest of the dirt. He slowly pushed the stick into the ground until he had loosened the patch. Then he scooped the earth with his hands, watching closely as he let the dirt run through his fingers.

Gabriel moved the sifted dirt away from the rock so that Sun had more room to work. Sun grunted his thanks. Gabriel and Henri were intrigued, watching Sun as he repeated his process slowly and carefully. The third time Sun filtered the dirt, an intricate beaded bracelet caught in his fingers.

"Mi'Kmaq," Sun said, proudly displaying the jewelry to Henri and Gabriel. He pulled back his jacket and lifted the necklace from around his neck that he had taken from his dead mother's body before she was carted away. The bracelet was of a nearly identical design, of beads and porcupine quills.

"Mi'Kmaq?" asked Gabriel.

Simultaneously, an incredulous Henri asked, "Sun, how is it you know this Indian name here in this foreign land?"

Sun knotted his forehead. He could not express his thoughts with words. It was in his memories, a foggy dream in his head that he could not describe. Perhaps his mother had spoken the word. He could not remember.

Sun began slowly. "Maman....beads of Mi'Kmaq." He felt more confident. "Mi'Kmaq my Maman." He placed the bracelet around his hand. He had rubbed the necklace each night on the ship before dozing off to sleep. His last thoughts were always of his mother's face when she was still alive, smiling at him, holding him as a young child, pointing up to the sun and the stars.

Sun was ecstatic at finding another relic with which to remember his mother. It had no other value to him, though he noted Henri eyed the jewelry with great interest. Even at his age Sun knew the beads must be important to the big men and he told Henri that he and Gabriel would return to this spot and uncover more treasure when no other eyes were around.

Henri nodded in understanding. "Your mother wore this jewelry. Who gave it to her?"

Sun was frustrated because he did not know. He shook his head.

"How did you know it would be under the rock?"

How could he explain that it was not just that the earth looked different, it was as if it spoke to him. He thought his mother whispered from under the rock. He knew she would not be there but he was strangely pulled to the stone. She had guided him on how to dig and where to look.

Henri caught Père Rivière's attention and bid him to join them. When Henri pointed out the bracelet to the priest, his eyes grew very wide.

The priest asked Sun, "Where did you find it?"

Sun piped up, "Maman tell me. Beads under stone. Find for Maman."

Père Rivière patted Sun's head and knelt beside him. "I believe your mother's relatives may be here. Do you understand? Your family is here."

Sun nodded with excitement. He misunderstood that his mother was here. He did not know how that was possible but the priest was a holy man and he would help him find her. He ran to find Gabriel.

Henri turned to the priest. "Gabriel and I are also descendents of Mi'Kmaqs on my father's side. We plan to visit the Chieftain of the Village. It is at the edge of the woods just beyond Grand Pré."

The priest was elated. "This explains why the boys get on so well. They are distant relatives. Let us bring them meet their family together then."

Henri nodded in agreement. The men watched Sun clap Gabriel, on the back the way he had seen the big men do. Gabriel slapped him back in a friendly way. The two had become best friends that would last a lifetime. Gabriel planned to ask Sun about the jewelry when they were out of earshot of the adults. Meanwhile Sun was formulating a plan for the two of them to locate more valuable beads.

Christine carried Evangeline and walked up to ask a question of René. "Monsieur Le Consul, perhaps serving lunch to the women and children would provide the opportunity for you to meet with the men and discuss a course of action. Could I assist?"

René glanced at Henri in deep discussions with several other men. Christine's suggestion was well-timed. He nodded and sent her to arrange the meal. Christine enlisted the help of Adèle and several of the wives to lay blankets under a nearby grove. The weary women passengers reclined as their children played in the soft grass.

Captain Jacques had provided baskets of the remaining foodstuffs, which were distributed. His cooks would purchase new supplies in Annapolis Royal once René had approval from the British to enter. Bread from the remaining flour and moldy cheese tasted like a royal dinner to the commoners and bottles of wine from René's personal stores were luxuries.

Henri directed Gabriel and Sun in the direction of Adèle sitting on a blanket with Christine, eating as Evangeline napped. "Go to Madame Adèle and Madame Christine, who will give you something to eat." Sun and Gabriel grinned from ear to ear. They were ready to eat anytime, so it was a welcome sight to see women handing out bread and cheese. They ran to the closest blanket under the shade of several trees and fell onto their backs.

Henri and Père Rivière watched the two boys. Henri spoke first. "The boy you call Sun? Where is his family?"

The priest said, "He said his mother was the only family he had. I found him hovering over her, dead of the Black Death. With the chaos in Marseille my concern was to remove him from any danger, so he became a ward of the Church. He has learned to assist me with Mass and to put the holy articles in their proper places."

Henri nodded in understanding. "You were right to bring him with you when the Cardinal chose you as our new parish priest. Besides, Sun has been a good friend to Gabriel. Now my son will not feel so alone in this colony."

"It seems Gabriel has also been a welcome companion for the poor boy."

Under the trees, Gabriel and Sun began to play a favorite game. Gabriel pointed out a cloud and Sun described what animal it looked like in a strange tongue Sun called "Mi'kmawi'simk." Gabriel presumed his friend had just made up the language. The boys had each collected a large pile of stones. The test of the game was for Sun to create a new name for each creature cloud using his special language rather than their native French. He received a small stone for every word he said. Any that he could not say with the strange sounds meant that Gabriel took a stone from the pile. When all the stones were divided, the boy with the larger pile was the winner. Gabriel tried to stump his friend but Sun won every time, though he could never explain that the words already existed and he just recalled them, rather than making them up.

Before long, the boys were each given a share of crusty bread and moldy cheese. Gabriel removed the mold, but Sun ate it all. He found that was always the best kind of fromage -- bluish-green on the outside and delicious on the inside. He even enjoyed the smell. Gabriel and Sun talked and laughed while munching stale bread they thought had never tasted so good.

Drinking wine from a bottle was relatively unknown to the commoners. Their lot was a sip of homemade grog from a friendly innkeeper in exchange for fresh eggs or a pail of milk, when able to be spared. Times had been hard in the provinces of France. Farm goods were as much in demand as alcohol to dull the pain of not being able to feed a family or having to work their children, from the age of four, in the fields. Wives grew vegetables in small patches to assure their offspring would not go hungry. Decades hence flour would cost a month's wages and many would fight or kill for a loaf of bread, but the situation in France was so difficult that families preferred the risk of a sea voyage for a new life than their present condition.

The passengers who had been on the upper deck had never known the pangs of hunger or seen starvation in the eyes of their children. But René saw the desperation on the faces of his new charges and was determined to give them comfort and earn their trust. He walked among the families, getting to know them better and reassuring them all would be well in their new settlement.

After the women and children had eaten, Adèle distributed bread, cheese and several bottles of wine to the men. They were profusely grateful and quickly ate their lunch while huddled together, murmuring and responding to René's direction. René concluded the discussion of their course of action.

The generosity of their Consul was never more appreciated than their first lunch on the hill overlooking the beach and the sea. In this beautiful country they were confident they would start new lives and that nothing could make them leave.

Thomas Gaudet waited until René had spoken with the other settlers and then he asked. "Monsieur le Consul, may I ask your permission?"

"What would you need it for, Monsieur Gaudet?"

"So's I can wed Mademoiselle Verrazzano, sir, proper like."

Gaudet nodded to a young woman who hastily joined them. She blushed and giggled as she looked at the ground. René joined their hands together.

"You shall make a fine match. Of course you do not need my approval but I gladly grant it and bless you."

He looked over at a group of men and motioned to the priest to join them. Père Rivière looked at the two and knew instantly what he was to do.

"You wish to be married, do you?"

"Yes Père, yes indeed," said Gaudet. Anne kept her head down, just nodding and giggling.

"And what are your names?"

After a brief discussion the priest stood on a tall rock and spoke to the congregation. "Does anyone here have cause to object to the marriage of Mademoiselle Anne Verrazzano and Monsieur Thomas Gaudet?"

The crowd rose to their feet, cheering and clapping. They had admired Gaudet's work, and aboard the ship Anne, being the only single female passenger, had held infants or played with the children when harried mothers needed a moment to rest. The couple was much beloved by the passengers on the lower deck who knew them.

"Then I shall waive the three weeks of marriage announcements and we shall hold the wedding as soon as you like."

Gaudet put his arm around the waist of his still giddy bride. "Here and now Père Rivière, if you please."

The priest looked to René, who gave his consent without hesitation. The short ceremony was held on the top of the bluff overlooking the beach. The lumbering Gaudet lifted the tiny Anne into his arms for the wedding kiss, to the cheers of the crowd. Then he picked up his bride and carried her into his world of woods and trees, far out of sight of the others. He did not plan to wait until evening to consummate their vows.

René turned to Henri. "Gather the men quietly and ask them to meet me there." He pointed out a small clump of trees in a bend across the road, hidden from where the colonists had gathered. Henri nodded and started working his way through the crowd.

When the men had assembled, René pointed to the far end of the winding road ahead. A tall wooden fence with an elevated guardhouse flying the English banner was slightly visible in the distance. René shuddered at the sight of the Union Jack. He wrapped his coat tightly around the precious French flag he had brought with him for his Consulate. The fleur de lis was his strongest connection with France now. It comforted him to know it would soon fly freely in what was enemy territory, although the Treaty of Utrecht had granted the Acadians freedoms as "neutrals." René would soon find out that was a sore subject with the British.

"We are planning a reconnaissance to see what lies ahead. We cannot make any mistakes as we are on English soil now."

The men murmured their agreement. Everyone knew France had been at war with England, on and off again, for the last hundred years. The existing peace treaty had been signed twenty-five years ago, a long time considering the enmity between the two countries. They were nervous and looked to their Consul for direction.

"I shall present my letters from His Majesty to the English commanding officer, Lieutenant John Handfield, who shall accept them for Lieutenant-Governor Charles Armstrong. Though we continue to call this territory 'Acadia' the official British name is 'Nova Scotia.' We must above all respect the English while we continue to practice our Catholic faith and our French customs. There should be no change to either. Lord Mius d'Entremont had accepted the post of Vice Consul and shall act in my stead. If anything should happen to me he knows what to do."

The men congratulated Henri on his position and he thanked them humbly. "I shall endeavor to be worthy of this great honor and to serve you to the best of my abilities."

René gathered the men closer, speaking in a low voice, though the women and children were too far away to hear. "The Mi'Kmaq First Nation lives in the woods past Grand Pré. If any danger arises from the English, hide the women and children with them. They are long-time allies of our King and will battle the English, or join with us if it comes to that. But we pray it does not. My mission is peaceful co-existence with the English. To accomplish this we shall meet again after you have all settled. At that time I shall present my plan to maintain peace and order in the territory. In the interim, do I have your word that you shall not take any act of aggression against the English, but that you bring your grievances to me?"

The men nodded in unison and René released them to rejoin their families where Père Rivière called the colonists to prayer. They knelt as the priest raised his Bible and bowed his head. Parents silenced their children, knowing this was an auspicious occasion for all of them. But paramount in their thoughts were the important questions of survival. How would they feed their families? Where would they live? Could they afford property for their own farm or business? These unspoken questions and more were on everyone's mind as they reverently bowed their heads and knelt on the soft ground.

Père Rivière bowed his head. "Let us pray. For the health and safety of his Holy Christian Majesty Louis Fifteen, King of France and Navarre. For all our brothers and sisters here. For loved ones we have left behind and those we have lost, especially the Lady Eugenie. For holy guidance to our Consul Sieur Le Blanc and his Vice Consul Sieur Mius d'Entremont. For peaceful relations with the English. For friendship with native Mi'Kmaqs. For the freedom to practice our Catholic religion. For prosperity for our families and our professions. And for long lives in our new home of Grand Pré, Acadia." He paused, and then concluded by saying, "All these things we pray to the Lord God Almighty, his son Jesus Christ and the Holy Spirit. Amen."

The colonists responded, "Amen."

The settlers looked down through the trees at the sea from whence they had arrived. *L'Acadie* was now at full sail on its way to replenish its supplies and load its much-desired cargo of Acadian goods for the journey home to France. The settlers bid a silent farewell to their old lives, then turned their back on the sea and looked with hope to the road stretching before them.

As they walked up the road, Père Rivière and Henri flanked René as he led his delegation of new colonists to their new lives. They were trailed by Doctor Hébert and Christine, who cuddled the sleeping Evangeline. Gabriel walked next to the infant, looking up at her every now and again, and Sun lumbered along next to his good friend.

Père Rivière asked, "Monsieur le Consul, the Cardinal advised that Acadia is neutral territory and that we are free to practice our Catholic religion. Is this not the case?"

René responded quietly, "We shall determine the truth of it for ourselves, Père." The priest nodded gravely, pondering the uncertainty of his words and what the answer would mean to his parishioners.

CHAPTER 23
Flag

FORT VIEUX LOGIS, OUTSIDE GRAND PRÉ

lancing out of his office's only window, the heavily bearded man in a crisp uniform, Lieutenant John Handfield, looked up. Despite his appearance as an experienced British officer, Handfield was barely twenty-four years old. As the highest ranking officer of the English King's regiment at Fort Vieux Logis, he was proud to see the Union Jack flying in the breeze above the lookout in the fort.

Actually "fort" was a misnomer. The British spot, called "Vieux Logis" or "Old Spot," had originally been a house built in 1732. It had been fortified by adding two other houses connected with wooden walkways slightly elevated above the marshy ground, quite muddy at this time of year and at other times covered in snow so deep that the walkways were not visible. The fence that surrounded the buildings was made of logs spiked at the exposed ends. An entry gate was monitored by a sole armed sentry. Several other soldiers stood nearby but appeared not to have an official function as they laughed and joked among themselves.

Several years earlier, upon the death of the English King George I, his son, George II, succeeded to the throne. The new monarch had renewed the appointment of Lawrence Armstrong as Lieutenant-Governor of the territory which had been called Acadia until France ceded it to England in the Treaty of Utrecht in 1713, at which time it was renamed, "Nova Scotia."

The Treaty had also laid an obligation, distasteful to Handfield, on Britain's shoulders, to allow French citizens living in Acadia to continue their unperturbed existence. The absurd Queen Anne had even relented in approving a clause in the Treaty that the Frenchies retain their wealth, exercise their heathen religion and continue their friendship with the English enemy, the Mi'Kmaq Indian tribe.

Armstrong wasted no time in dispatching Handfield and other soldiers from the British capital of Annapolis Royal, previously called Port Royal as French territory. They were sent throughout Nova Scotia to proclaim the reign of the new King. They were also charged with "requesting," which Handfield understood to be "demanding" that the French neutrals and the Indians take an unqualified Oath of Allegiance to the new ruler of the land.

With no single French government representative in Nova Scotia, as the Governor in New France's Québec, Acadian deputies elected by the French colonists in each town had unanimously agreed to give an Oath that was conditioned on having their priests in town and being able to practice their Catholic religion and on being free of any obligation to bear arms against France or the Indian allies during a time of war. Lieutenant-Governor Armstrong ordered Handfield and several other English Lieutenants to bring the deputies before the English Council at Annapolis Royal.

Acceding to the Lieutenant-Governor's request, the Acadian deputies went willingly but were advised, upon appearing before the Council, that Armstrong and the Council were displeased with their refusal to sign an unconditional Oath. As a sign of power and a message to the other Acadians, Armstrong marched the deputies to jail. Within a matter of weeks they were released, however, and Handfield was requested to escort them home. Several months later he found himself posted to Fort Vieux Logis.

Within the confines of the fence not far from the command post, the small house that Handfield lived and worked in, were the "barracks" for the troops, set up as tents with wooden tables for sleeping bunks. Even though the set of ramshackle buildings did not resemble a fortress of protection, it was symbolic. This was *his* Fort, Handfield reminded himself. *His* sentries paced back and forth, saluting *his* lookouts armed with *his* muskets surveying *his* road below outside *his* Fort at Grand Pré. Handfield had made all ready to teach the new French Neutrals *his* method of English governance once they arrived.

Vieux Logis offered a lookout perch from which to survey the goings-on in the town of Grand Pré and the Minas Basin region where the French Acadians lived. The location was so high that on a clear day one could see from the landing point and the beach where ships arrived into the region, to the dikes that surrounded farms, to the woods where the Mi'Kmaq Indians lived, to the plains beyond and all the way to the cliffs of the Cobequid Mountains.

Handfield desired to rebuild the Fort upon receiving funding he had requested from Lieutenant-Governor Armstrong. But thus far he had not received a response except an order to deliver the Oath of Allegiance signed by every Acadian, including the new King's Consul. Handfield firmly believed that once the new French leader understood *his* rules Handfield would succeed where all the other British officers had failed. The French colonists in Acadia would sign the Oath or Handfield or Armstrong himself would die trying to coerce them into doing so.

Because Richard Philipps, the Governor appointed by King George I, had returned to England years earlier, Armstrong was the governing authority in all of Nova Scotia. After being in the King's service since his miraculous survival after a shipwreck in 1711, Armstrong had proven a loyal and faithful officer to the Crown. He intensely disliked the French colonists in the settlement which he administered for many reasons. They practiced their ritualistic religion, which confused him. They refused to speak English, though many understood it well, which angered him. They did not offer food but willingly sold their surplus crops for his troops, which cost him.

René had brought the colonists to rest at the top of the bluff at the edge of the tree grove. Several hundred paces down the road, past the entry gates to the town of Grand Pré, stood the English Fort Vieux Logis. Soldiers milled around the barracks talking to one another, entering or exiting the buildings. None of them appeared to take any notice, if they saw the Acadian delegation.

As René was to find out, Handfield did not need the space of an entire house but he brooded and sought his privacy when he did so. That meant that his hundred troops were squeezed into the other two houses and the tents. Handfield did not request more troops because the pitiful budget from Armstrong could barely support them now.

René walked up to the entry gate of the Fort. He noted on the small posted sign that the British replaced their letter "S" with the letter "F":

ENTERING GRAND PRÉ, MINAF BAFIN
TERRITORY OF HIF BRITANNIC MAJEFTY GEORGE II

Below, a crude note was added as if written by a child's hand:

Prefint Bordurr Paffef & Idyntity Papperf
Englifh onlie talket Heere

René translated it to read, "Present Border Passes & Identity Papers. English only talked Here."

The Cardinal had instructed him well with English border requirements at entry points. Lieutenant-Governor Armstrong had instituted the policy in Nova Scotia identical to that of the other British colonies regarding official entry papers and the requirement to speak English. A pass signed by the Governor or highest authority of each territory was required at the border, whether English or foreign.

As René acted for King Louis, he was qualified as a foreign government representative to sign passes for the entry of the colonists into Nova Scotia and, more particularly, the Minas region and the town of Grand Pré. But because this group of settlers had disembarked from a French ship without such signed passes, a verification process of identity papers was required to enter Nova Scotia.

Handfield was diligent in requiring English as the official language in communications. However he translated all orders into French so there could be no mistake of what was expected of the Neutrals. He cursed his inability to control the inhabitants of the Indian Village. His superiors had ordered him to refrain from any acts against the Mi'Kmaqs and to buy their loyalty with goods which could sever the alliance with the French. The tribe had befriended the French since the first settlement in Acadia a century and a half earlier and many families had inter-married since that time, the Mius d'Entremonts being the first.

Handfield was unaware of these long-term relationships when he met with the Chief, Mahtook Mius. The Chief and his Council met with Handfield and his officers and accepted their gifts. The next time the Lieutenant rode up to the Indian Village he was turned away. The Chief was unable to meet with him. After that Handfield became wary of the tribe, believing they would never become a true ally of England.

However, few Mi'Kmaqs spoke English, or let on that they did, except their guides, who sometimes worked for English soldiers transporting official correspondence. As of yet Handfield had not found bi-lingual Acadians willing to work with him and his troops.

René asked Henri to collect the identity papers from each family. Then the Consul kissed the forehead of his daughter, asleep in Christine's arms.

Henri handed the Consul the identity documents just as the entry gate to the fort opened. Turning to look at the English flag, René's heart beat faster beneath his jacket, where he had placed the official papers. In a strange way, he felt as though he were entering enemy territory, although their two countries were at peace. The feeling gave him great unease.

René warned the settlers to remain on the other side of the road quietly until he returned. Père Rivière again blessed René as he walked through the entry. The French settlers caught a glimpse of English soldiers milling about inside the checkpoint area. Every pair of adult French eyes focused on the British weapons. Their concern heightened when they realized that the armed soldiers were boys not older than sixteen or seventeen, the age of some of their children.

René entered the Fort craning his neck to see above the fence but the only things visible against the wood pickets were thick woods and grey skies from smoke rising within the trees. He surmised it was from the Mi'Kmaq Village, though he could not see the Indian wigwams or bark huts. René had planned to meet with the Chief after settling the colonists in town and on farms.

"Wait here. Someone will be getting yer." A sentry lifted the gate and pointed to a checkpoint area.

"Papers?" A second guard held out a grubby hand. René presented his documents but kept his hand tightly on the precious papers. The guard looked but could not understand French so he shrugged and told him to sit on the bench. "Someone will be coming to meet yer."

A young soldier, Nathan Turnbull, rode up to René and held out his hand. "Papers."

Le Blanc stood and spoke in a bold voice, "I am Consul to His Majesty King Louis Fifteen of France and Navarre. Your commanding officer expects me to present my official documents to him in person. Please take me to his headquarters."

Turnbull replied, "Nobody gave no orders to let a Frenchy pass. Wait here." He trotted to the checkpoint gate and the guard lifted it. Then René watched as the young soldier rode toward the building flying the Union Jack.

Handfield's reverie was interrupted by a sharp knock. "Enter," he barked, impatient for the French Consul to arrive. Turnbull saluted. "The French Consul is at the gate with his colonists," he informed his superior, who adjusted his hat.

"Show him in but keep those other Frenchies out. There are too many of them and we do not need any altercations."

Turnbull saluted and exited the building. But instead of going back to the checkpoint he stopped in the next house.

René saw his moment. He did not know what the young soldier was doing but he knew his position as French Royal Consul outranked him. Le Blanc hesitated only a moment when the guard left the checkpoint post, then René hurriedly cleared the gate. Turnbull was still nowhere to be seen so René pushed ahead, closer to the Fort headquarters.

Turnbull came out of the building and mounted his horse but seeing René gone, he whipped around. Then he saw the Consul walking quickly to Handfield's office.

The Sentry cried out, "Halt! You there." Le Blanc ignored him. His own business was with the soldier's superior.

Turnbull then called out to the soldiers in the area. "Extra whiskey rations to the one who grabs that worthless Frenchy." Two other soldiers, Wicker and Greenfield rushed after René.

Wicker warned, "Stop or I shoot this here musket." But René continued toward the office steps.

Greenfield muttered under his breath. "Bloody Frenchman. What did you expect?"

Wicker looked at his fellow soldier in astonishment. "I thought he would be afraid of me."

"Have you loaded any gun powder in it?"

Wicker looked sheepish. "Ain't got no powder to load."

"Precisely."

Oblivious to the chaos outside his office, Handfield read over a letter. Before he could affix his signature to it, he was interrupted by a loud scuffle outside. He pulled the curtains from the window to see Wicker jam a small knife into René's pantaloons.

René rushed into Handfield's office and slammed the door, bolting it behind him. Handfield was so taken aback he was speechless.

Outside, on the porch of the office, Wicker and Greenfield beat on the door to open it, without success.

Handfield demanded, "What is the meaning of this, this outrage, sir?"

René calmly pulled the knife out of his leg, bowed and presented his papers.

"*Sieur René Le Blanc de Verdure presenting my official papers as Royal Consul and Notaire to His Christian Majesty Louis Fifteen, King of France* and Navarre." René remained standing, knowing that the English officer before him would test his patience, wits and strength of character. Though blood dripped on the floor, the wound barely grazed René's leg through his formal dress worn for the presentation occasion.

Handfield casually lit a cigar and crossed his legs on top of his desk. "French titles mean nothing here. You shall direct the French settlers to sign our Oath of Allegiance to Holy King George if you all wish to enter our territory in freedom and remain here."

"Your Queen Anne granted us religious freedom and neutrality status when our Holy King ceded the territory to her. In the Treaty of Utrecht as you recall."

Handfield waved him away. "You bore me with dusty paperwork signed thirty years ago by someone with no vision. A woman at that, even if she was English. It is well-known she had to appoint twelve new lords to the chamber for a sufficient number of votes to pass that vile Treaty. Her act means nothing here."

There was a sudden crash as Wicker and Greenfield broke through the door with their bayonets. Turnbull rushed in and aimed his musket at René, addressing the Lieutenant. "Has this madman injured you, sir?"

Handfield ignoring him turned to René. "My overly zealous First Lieutenant was just leaving." Handfield waved him away.

Turnbull saluted and begrudgingly exited. Handfield stared at the papers and touched his burning cigar to royal documents.

Nonplussed, René reached onto Handfield's desk, picked up his diary and proceeded to lay the brittle pages face down onto the fire. He knew the act would confuse Handfield long enough for René to determine the next move in this dangerous chess game with this peacetime adversary.

Handfield roared, "Not my journal! That is property of the King!" It was then that he realized he had met his match in this brash but polite Frenchman. Theirs was a stand-off but with mutual respect, at least for the moment.

With his journal, Cardinal de Fleury had slipped a dossier providing René with a great many details on the British military leaders in the New World. The information was so intimate in some cases it could only have come from a spy working at the highest level of the English armed services. As a result, René learned that many of the English officers were religious zealots and that some, including Bostontown colonial officers William Shirley and John Winslow, as well as Lieutenant John Handfield standing before him, were said to be Protestant fanatics. He had not determined how that information could be used to benefit his mission until now.

René continued the conversation that had begun before Turnbull appeared. "We shall sign no Oath that disrespects the terms of the Treaty. That includes our right to practice our Catholic religion and release from taking arms against our mother country or our Mi'Kmaq allies. No reasonable man would forego freedoms previously granted, would he?"

Handfield became angry although he had expected the Consul's response. "Is that all, Monsieur le Consul?"

"We agree to live peacefully as neutrals. We are practical men. Can we not agree to do so, Lieutenant?" René gazed evenly at him as he pulled a large bottle of the King's best wine from his satchel.

Taken aback, Handfield chomped on his cigar as he accepted the wine without thanks. He did not like the Frenchy but fine wine from his country was hard to come by these days, especially on a Lieutenant's wage. He motioned for René to be seated while he reviewed each of the identity papers, one by one. His French was not perfect but he understood their meaning and he accepted René's official posting.

Handfield stood to end the meeting and returned the partially charred stack of documents. "Consul, take the settlers to your Church opposite the main square in town. It has been empty since your last priest died. An unfortunate accident."

René looked at him quizzically. "It was not a natural death, then?"

Handfield waved his hand at such a trivial matter. "He was being released from prison with a group of Acadian deputies last year, when he stole a guard's gun and...accidentally shot himself. We understand you brought a new preacher with you."

René looked him squarely in the eyes. "Yes, Père Rivière. Did the priest's death pertain to the Acadians' objection to the Oath?"

Handfield became suddenly frustrated. That blasted Oath. When would it ever be signed so this subject would be done with? "The very same."

René shook his head. "But the colonists agreed to sign an Oath with the terms as specified in the Treaty."

"Yes, yes, but our King George Two finds these are too many demands. Simply unacceptable. So we are once again at the same question. Will you direct your colonists to sign the Oath?"

René looked at him. So it began. The dance of English force to pressure the French neutrals to relinquish their treaty rights. "We shall review what you propose and discuss it with you at the appropriate time."

Handfield rose to his feet angrily. Before he could say anything, René pulled a small Bible from inside his jacket. "We both worship the same God. Shall we both reflect in prayer before we meet again?"

That seemed to mollify the English officer, at least for the moment. René returned to their former subject. "You were saying about our housing?"

Handfield sat down and continued, "The church's benches and floors can provide temporary sleeping quarters. Turnbull will show you to a building that will suit for offices. Upstairs are spacious private quarters. It was kept for the fort's military leadership but I prefer to be here with my men. Repairs will be needed, at your expense, of course."

"I am sure it will meet our needs, at least for now."

"And then there is the matter of a price. England does not give her property away."

"That is only to be expected. You do accept French monies?"

The Lieutenant nodded arrogantly. Then he pulled out a rolled paper, spreading it open on top of the desk. "The King's properties for sale." He pointed as he spoke. "Available farms and empty lots of land here. Vacant shop buildings with rooms above there." Then he rolled the map and handed it to René. "When your colonists have had time to inspect the sites and buildings, we shall negotiate the purchase."

René looked at him. "At a fair price."

Handfield smiled for the first time since he set eyes on the Consul. He was counting the money that could be spent at his discretion. "We are quite civilized here, as you will see."

René nodded in relief then responded, "I was certain of it."

René gave a courteous bow and Handfield chomped on his cigar again, bowing slightly, just enough to be considered polite.

Outside, René was followed every step of the way back to the outside of the Fort by Turnbull. His horse trotted so close to René he felt the heat emanating from the animal's nostrils.

As the sentry closed the gate behind him René looked back once more at the Union Jack. He shook his head and rejoined the settlers, first wiping away the sense of foreboding from his face. He hoped that he would be able to keep the peace. And if all it took was a bottle of wine from time to time, he would assure that his own cave was well-stocked to keep the English Lieutenant placated.

For the next year René was able to successfully skirt Handfield's continued demands that the Acadians sign an unconditional Oath. But the year after that an incident brought the Oath to the forefront, at least in

René's mind. Nova Scotia Lieutenant-Governor Charles Armstrong killed himself with a single shot to the head. No note was ever found and the British military were at a loss to explain it. René surmised the troubled man committed suicide because he was unable to coerce the French Neutrals into signing the Oath of Allegiance, something he had promised both the old King and the new one. He was right.

The event brought relief from the tension the French had lived under for two years when Handfield was recalled back to the capital in Annapolis Royal. One day the Fort was active and the next, Vieux Logis was emptied of its British presence, closed and locked. At that time in 1738, it seemed that Grand Pré and all the French Acadians had been all but forgotten by the British military.

CHAPTER 24
Communications

GRAND PRÉ

ené was often frustrated by the distance between Acadia and France. It seemed as time went on that greater delays occurred in exchanging information, letters and royal correspondence with the King through Cardinal de Fleury. What had taken only three to four months had of late taken eight months and, once, a year, with the ever-increasing military strength of England's blockades or seizure of French ships on the high seas.

French brigantines and other military vessels were banned from entry into British territory so they sailed across the seas to New France. From there, French coureurs du bois carried official documents from the King and French government officials to Acadia, then traveled to northern French territories of St. Pierre and Miquelon and Île du Roi. There the vessels would sail with the coureurs back to New France, bypassing Acadia and the English territory, to wait for the next ship from France. Then the cycle would repeat. A coureur traveled light, with the King's pouch and a weapon, usually a handgun and a saber at his side. But still it took weeks for a single rider on the overland route to reach Grand Pré from Québec in good weather with fresh horses at French forts and way stations along the way.

Even with the communication system as efficient as could be arranged, René still did not receive communications from the King and the Cardinal for months at a time. There was no way of knowing until much later whether a vessel had been captured or sunk. Over two hundred French frigates, brigantines, corvettes, sloops and other military vessels been captured by the British, their documents seized and analyzed by British authorities and their crews either hanged, forced to walk the plank into the sea, or burned alive on the captured ship.

Captains of French merchant transports disliked entering the English capital of Halifax. They complained of long delays and expensive bribes to customs officials to release their goods. Then there was a British tax for every signature on the voluminous border passes. As a result, goods, and packages and letters from loved ones in France did not reach the Acadians for many months. They were usually brought by sea to New France, then offloaded onto wagons or coaches in Québec and brought overland to Acadia.

In the winter months passage was next to impossible so Acadian families were only able to receive or send letters and packages in the spring and summer. They eagerly anticipated this time of year which enabled the arrival of letters and packages, some of which had been sitting in New France waiting for rivers to thaw or snows to melt.

During the especially long winter of 1743, Evangeline was a precocious child of five and René was adamant that her education should commence. He was determined that she should be well-versed in languages, the classics, philosophy, mathematics, astronomy, theology, taught by the Catholic priest in the parish, and other subjects. René also planned that Evangeline would be skilled in riding, hunting, swimming and sailing, though typically girls did not have this type of training. Christine planned to teach Evangeline medical skills, midwifery and intimate knowledge of healing and poisonous plants. She would assemble bakers, cooks, vintners and farmers from the region to instruct about food and wine from the seed to the table.

René wanted Evangeline to learn everything he had been taught as a young noble growing up in France. He knew his daughter would marry into nobility or royalty for which such knowledge and skills would be desirable, but unusual, traits. Realizing such an education would take years, he and Christine together had charted the lessons and experiences that would be taught over the next ten years of Evangeline's life. She would spend half a day in a classroom in the Le Blanc home above the Consulate, and the other half day out in the world, always supervised by Christine and taught by the most knowledgeable Acadians in the region. Never before in Acadia, or in France for that matter, had such an ambitious plan of study been devised, and that winter Evangeline embarked on an educational journey that the wealthiest noblewomen of Europe would envy.

Her first outdoor lesson was learning to ride a pony, which Henri d'Entremont himself taught her at his stables. As Vice Consul, Henri often brought Gabriel with him to the Consulate. As he had been when Evangeline was born, Gabriel was protective of the little girl and her riding lesson was no different for the boy who was now eleven years old. While his father walked alongside Evangeline, Gabriel led the pony around the field, turning back every few steps to ascertain that Evangeline was alright. He need not have worried. Evangeline took to riding as he had not seen boys do at his father's stable. She was unafraid and kept trying to push the horse into a trot.

Gabriel watch his father who had turned away for an instant. Gabriel winked to Evangeline and then pulled the reins quickly. Suddenly the pony galloped away with Evangeline bouncing in the saddle. When Henri and Gabriel finally caught up to the animal, Evangeline was laughing as hard as she could. She held out her arms to be lifted from the horse but when Henri tried to pick her up, she shook her head defiantly and pointed to Gabriel. When he took her off the pony, she hugged his neck and whispered to him, "Go again. Make my horsie go faster." Gabriel smiled and whispered, "Perhaps next time." That seemed to satisfy Evangeline. She nodded and clutched Gabriel's fingers with her chubby hand until they reached the house where Christine waited in René's carriage.

That evening Gabriel received ten lashes on his legs with the longest branch his father could find. Henri made him promise not to endanger Evangeline again. But secretly Gabriel knew that she was never in danger, and that she would become a fine horsewoman. For years afterward, Evangeline and Gabriel would talk about her first riding lesson and how she loved the feeling of freedom when the student and her "horsie" ran away from her teachers.

*

In the spring of 1744 that news arrived in Grand Pré of the death of the man to whom René owed his daughter and position, Cardinal de Fleury. René learned the great man had died a year earlier which explained why he had not received responses to his many letters during that time. René had thought the lack of letters resulted from the Cardinal's great responsibilities as the King's Prime Minister. René wept bitterly, knowing France had sustained an irreplaceable loss and he had lost his greatest confidant in the Court of Versailles.

Two months later, Claude Arnaud received a letter from his brother bearing the seal of the Cardinal. It was dated the previous year and had traveled from Versailles to Le Havre to Québec and then to the cart of a merchant who carried it to Grand Pré. Upon opening it, a stack of French currency bills fell to the floor and Claude was taken by surprise to recognize Laurent's writing. His brother wrote in a strong, bold hand:

"15 February 1743. Dear Claude,

I realize it has been years since we last spoke in the Versailles courtyard upon your departure to Le Havre. Much has happened since, but first I must tell you that the man to whom I owe my good fortune, the saintly Cardinal André-Hercule de Fleury, died last month. I thought you would want to know. You must have suspected that the Cardinal arranged my promotion, but after you left he appointed me as his secretary and I served him faithfully until he died. The Royal Artist Jean-Baptiste Pater sought me out at Versailles to tell me of your marriage and your decision to move to the New World. Bravo to you both. Pater unfortunately died soon after he returned to the Palace, but not before he painted a portrait of my wife and me. More about that later in this writing.

Now sit down, for what I have to tell you may astonish you, as it did me. Through the Cardinal's good graces and his network of information agents in France, he arranged before his untimely death for my real father to acknowledge my birth. Yes, does it not now make sense why Claude preferred you, and our mother showed favoritism to me? And why we are so completely different, not only in temperament but also in physical appearance and attributes?

I must confess I went to our father's house, that is, your father's, after our mother died not to curry favor for an inheritance in his will but quite the opposite; to inquire if I was the child of a union between my mother and another man. Of course it was too late then. But upon my return the Cardinal inquired about the gold pocket watch I wore. Our mother had slipped it into my bag when I was sent to Versailles. I hid it from you because the inscription reads, 'To my son Laurent, Your loving father, Charles."

Some time later the Cardinal told me the story of my real father, the Duke Charles de Rochefort, and how the Cardinal had been watching over me like a guardian angel since Claude was in service at the Palace. Your father had brought our mother to Versailles where she gave birth to you. But soon after, Claude drank too much one night and nearly beat her to death. She escaped with you and was found on the road outside Versailles by the Duke, a widower at the time with three sons. He and his servants nursed her back to health and watched over you until she had recovered. The Cardinal assured me she willingly submitted to the Duke with the understanding he would acknowledge the child with a substantial inheritance, though the Duke's title would pass to the Duke's eldest son.

Maman lived with you in the Duke's home in Paris until I was born and only then did she return to Claude. He had been injured by the poacher and sent home from the Palace with a small pension. He knew I was not his own but I suppose he tolerated it because our mother brought you back to him and took care of both you and him. She gave me all the love I could have hoped for and I pray you feel the same about her. God bless her soul.

So, dear half-brother, as it turns out I am Laurent de Rochefort, son of Duke Charles de Rochefort. He recently passed away, leaving me a sizeable sum and a château in Provence in the south of France. And, most importantly, he acknowledged me as his fourth son in his handwritten testament. He also left a letter which is meaningful only to me so I omit those details having to do with our conversation at Versailles that I believe was orchestrated by the Cardinal so my father could meet me in person without arousing suspicion.

While he granted me more money that I should need in a lifetime, the main point of the story is that the Cardinal convinced the Marquis de Navarre, father of my beautiful Lady Véronique, to accept me as her husband since I am of noble blood. (You remember her, do you not, at the Consul's marriage dinner, when the rat scurried under her skirts?) We were married in June of 1738, several months after you left and are so happy, with four healthy children (three sons and a beautiful daughter) and at this writing another to arrive later this year. As it turns out, my father-in-law is so pleased with his male heir and the two other boys that he has promised to...."

The rest of the page was a series of illegible ink smudges, which piqued Claude's curiosity. But try as he might, he could not make out any of the words and reluctantly turned to the back of the page.

"I hereby return the money you gave me after Claude's funeral, with interest. It is rightly yours (you recall you gave me one-third and kept two-thirds for yourself). I ask you to come to our château and be my valet, which you promised to do if ever I married a Lady. Which I did. Best wishes to your wife and your children, if you have any, from your half-brother and my wife Lady Véronique and our children.

Kindly, your half-brother, Laurent de Rochefort."

That evening Adèle returned from the seamstress shop where she worked for Madame Dupont. She found Claude completely drunk with the crumpled letter on the table and hundreds of French notes on the floor. Here was her husband, a former King's Horseman and a friend of the French Consul to the King, crying his eyes out that his brother was noble -- the son of a Duke, no less -- and he was nothing.

Adèle read the letter, her eyes tearing up that her husband's brother, or, half-brother, had four children where she and Claude had none. Then she wiped her eyes and dunked her husband's head in a bucket of water until he was coherent.

She made Claude tell her everything, not forgetting the part about his promise to be his brother's valet.

CHAPTER 25
Bounty

MINAS BAY REGION

fter Verrazzano's discovery but well before the founding of Grand Pré, French fishing boats began operating in the Grand Banks off the Acadian coast in 1501. By 1519 they were drying their catch ashore and trading with the indigenous Mi'Kmaq First Nation. Soon, over four hundred fishing vessels from various European nations operated in the waters there during the summer months. Yet no permanent settlements had been established.

In 1532, French explorer Jacques Cartier tried to establish a colony in Acadia which failed, due to scurvy and harsh winters. By 1581, Norman and Breton merchants had started a brisk fur trade with the Mi'Kmaq tribes. When beaver hats became the fashion rage in Paris, the business became so profitable that French King Henry III gave a monopoly on the fur business in the new world to a group of French merchants.

Upon the King's assassination his successor, Henry IV, appointed Pierre Du Gua, Sieur de Monts as Lieutenant-Governor of the French territories of the New World in 1603 with the exclusive rights to the fur trade The following year, leading an expedition with the Royal cartographer Samuel Champlain and seventy-three settlers, de Monts founded the first permanent colony in North America, on Île St. Croix in the Baie Française – the French Bay -- of Acadia.

Among the colonists was Louis Hébert, the Parisian apothecary to royalty, whose vast knowledge of medicines and plants assisted the colonists through their first harsh winter. In the spring of 1605, the settlement was relocated and named the Habitation at Port Royal on the south shore of the Bay. While the other colonists immersed themselves in the fur trade, Hébert preferred to cultivate the soil and he became the first farmer in Acadia.

In 1607 the English settled Jamestown and began to eye the French territory. They led a raid in the fall of 1613, destroying Port Royal, setting the French colonists and Jesuits adrift in boats and selling captured Mi'Kmaqs into slavery. The French were rescued by the remaining Mi'Kmaqs who had hidden in the woods and who provided food and shelter throughout the winter until the French took back Port Royal. They rebuilt the Fort which was again burned in 1619 by the English. Undeterred, the French constructed a new fort once more.

Cardinal Richelieu obtained for his cousin, Isaac de Razilly, the appointment as the King's Governor in Acadia. The new official expanded the settlement by bringing three hundred new French colonists to the territory. They settled mainly along the Bay of Fundy, near Port Royal. This group, which included forty large families and many single men, founded a new town, Grand Pré. They built homes near the Bay and on the rises above the plains rather than clearing the forests and intruding on Mi'Kmaq First National lands. This sign of peace and friendship by the Acadians continued the harmony with two peoples without the necessity of a treaty during the entire time the French lived in the territory.

The struggle between the French and English continued but in 1632 the Treaty of St. Germain-en-Laye restored France's territories in Québec, soon named "New France," and in Acadia. By 1635, Acadia's Governor Isaac de Razilly had greatly expanded Port Royal, now thriving. He had brought his cousin, French nobleman Sieur Charles de Menou d'Aulnay to join him. D'Aulnay's father was a high ranking official in King Louis XIII's Court and d'Aulnay used his family relationship to obtain financing for ships and crew. The colonists, mainly from d'Aulnay's own estates, were recruited by the promise of their own tracts of land in Acadia. Their industriousness and letters to relations in France greatly enhanced d'Aulnay's ability to colonize the territory.

Free passage and ownership of a plot of land in Acadia was part of d'Aulnay's enticement to new settlers. He brought over a hundred additional colonists, mainly families working his own estates in Vienne in southwestern France. But he had a never-ending supply of laborers on his lands, so he could afford to be generous. He wanted to see the colony of Acadia grow and he knew free land would be more tempting than working the land of another, as the colonists' parents had done. He also knew that unmarried men from his lands would find a spouse on the boat or in Acadia who gave them reason to stay. He was right on all counts.

Upon Razilly's death in 1635 the King named his brother, Claude de Launay-Razilly, the new Governor, who appointed Lord d'Aulnay as his lieutenant in Acadia.   D'Aulnay erected a new Fort at Port Royal and oversaw improvements to the territory, which now included other towns named Grand Pré, Les Mines, Pisiquid, Cobequid and Beaubassin. D'Aulnay ordered dikes to be built to drain marshlands for farming and mills to be constructed for their crops. Devised in the Saintonge region of France, the Acadian dikes added an important aboiteau system. This hinged water gate allowed fresh water to run off into the marshes when tides were low but it prevented the salt water of the surrounding rivers from flowing back into the cleared farmland at high tides. The large earthen mounds created the most fertile land in the region.

Lord d'Aulnay also imported French miners for the regions's copper and iron ore deposits. He commenced logging operations, not only for use in erecting wooden homes and shops but also for building small fishing and cargo vessels. All of these industries, with the fishing and fur trades, made Acadia a profitable territory for France and made the Grand Pré colonists a prosperous lot.

The Acadians' peaceful existence was destroyed when the English Puritans from the Massachusetts Bay colony captured Acadia in 1654, until England returned it to France in 1667 with the Treaty of Breda. Yet the British continued to attack, sacking Port Royal again during King Williams' War in 1690 though it was recaptured by the French in 1692. The British began Queen Anne's War in 1701 and tried to get control of the prosperous Acadia by attacking Port Royal again, once in 1701 and twice in 1707, all of which the Acadians repulsed.

After a long siege, the French surrendered in 1710, but the Treaty of Utrecht in 1713 ended that war and ceded Acadia to England. That treaty, however, protected the Acadian citizens by granting them status as "French Neutrals," with the right to practice their Catholic faith and with exemption from bearing arms in any future battles against the French or its allies, the Mi'Kmaqs.

Finally at peace, the French Neutrals of the Minas Bay region, particularly the prosperous Grand Pré Acadians, believed the English would honor their Treaty obligations. Within their closed society and in a confined geographic space, progeny of the large Catholic families of the region intermarried into other Catholic families in the locale and their population grew steadily. Indeed, the only change from French to British rule seemed to be the renaming of the main Fort from Port Royal to Annapolis Royal.

From time to time the British asked the French to sign their loyalty Oath to England, to which the Acadians responded they would be only too happy to oblige if the Oath included the treaty protections. Since the English demanded an unconditional Oath and the Acadians did not wish to lose their rights under the Treaty of Utrecht, the issue of the Oath was at an impasse from 1713 through the subsequent forty-two years.

*

King George's War began in 1744 between the French and English as the War of the Austrian Succession to determine who would rule that country. While the war was raging in Europe, French troops from New France unsuccessfully attempted to retake Port Royal, which had been named Annapolis Royal by the English after the Treaty of Utrecht. William Shirley, Commander of the Colonial Forces in the British North American territories, and Governor of the Massachusetts Bay colony, captured the French Fort at Louisburg in New France, on the other side of the Bay from Nova Scotia. But the Treaty of Aix-la-Chappelle resolved the War and returned Fort Louisbourg to the French.

The Acadians of Grand Pré remained neutral, honoring the terms of the Treaty exempting them from bearing arms either against France or England. Though uninvolved in the battle near them, the French Consul was kept abreast of the fighting by the Mi'Kmaqs who aided their allies in New France. He and his Vice Consul, Henri d'Entremont, often burned candles late into the night reviewing documents from their allies or the French couriers who traveled overland between Québec and Grand Pré.

Gabriel, now nearly thirteen, often accompanied his father to the Consulate and though he helped his father in the office for most of the day, he always took time to talk with Evangeline during a break in her studies. At six, she was reading the classics in French, and would soon learn Latin.

One day they discussed her favourite poem, which happened to be his as well, the pastoral sonnet "Arcadia" by Sannazaro. Evangeline had a greater grasp of the meaning of the poem than Gabriel had imagined and he had enjoyed their conversation. When Gabriel left to return to the office downstairs, Evangeline stared after him. Christine reminded Evangeline to rejoin her teacher. At the classroom door Evangeline turned back and jolted Christine's memory of the day Evangeline was born and what Gabriel had told her.

"Gabriel is handsome. I want to marry him. Can I?"

Christine shooed her back into the room and shook her head. "Perhaps one day, Evangeline, perhaps one day."

*

In 1749, Nova Scotia Governor Edward Cornwallis brought over two thousand five hundred British to settle a new city, Halifax, which was the new capital of Nova Scotia. To build the city, Mi'Kmaq land was taken without authorization. The action violated the 1725 Treaty of Boston with the Mi'Kmaqs but Shirley had his fill of Mi'Kmaqs and declared them to be "rebels" rather than "enemies of war." By not declaring war, he proclaimed the rules of civilized warfare did not apply. Cornwallis and Hopson justified their decision to take Indian lands in order to place the government seat closer to the French Acadians. However, the resulting Anglo-Mi'Kmaq conflict continued with no decisive victory.

Shirley instituted a Scalp Bounty within his troops, offering ten pounds for each Mi'Kmaq scalp or prisoner, which he increased to fifty pounds the following year. But an unheard-of bounty of one hundred pounds had been promised for capturing alive the Jesuit priest Jean-Louis Le Loutre, who aided the Mi'Kmaq tribes.

When few scalps had been presented for payment, Shirley dispatched raiding parties to hunt down the Indians. However, the increased bounty was so tempting to underpaid soldiers that many scalps were turned in with clear European characteristics.

British headhunters had been killing innocent Acadian women and children for the bounty. Yet British paymasters looked the other way and accepted all scalps without question.

CHAPTER 26
Village

GRAND PRÉ

he settlement of Grand Pré was named for the large prairie resulting from diking the marshlands for farming. The land was the most fertile in the region and produced multiple crops each year. The crops yielded too much for local residents to use so they exported grains and produce as well as cattle, sheep, hogs and other animals they bred, to other communities in New France as well as to the English colonies along the Eastern seaboard.

Grand Pré was both a major town and the center of the geographic area south of the Minas River leading through the Gaspereau River to the Bay of Fundy. Most sailors who knew the Bay chose not to operate in it, due to the phenomenally high tides. The entire territory was referred to as Minas Basin or the Region of Grand Pré. The Basin was fed by several streams and rivers and then it flowed into the Bay. Hills in the distance beyond the forests rose to expose their red clay cliffs of mountains. These stretched for fifty miles along the Bay, reaching heights of four hundred feet above the level of the plain holding the fertile farms, fields and orchards of Grand Pré reclaimed by the Acadians.

The Acadian landing beach was not an actual harbor as was the one built in the English capital of Halifax. It was located half a mile from the broad outlet leading towards the Bay. The low tides of the landing place accommodated small transports, fishing boats and Mi'Kmaq canoes. Tides took their vessels from the Gaspereau River out to the Bay where more powerful tides swept them out to the Atlantic for shipping of crops, animals, fish, textiles or other merchandise to New France, the British colonies and beyond.

Acadian animal husbandry skills resulted in annual cattle and sheep drives destined for the slaughterhouses and drying stations as well as for live animal sales at the markets. The Acadians were able to feed their animals throughout the winter months thanks to the salt water hay they found in the marsh. By drying the hay on tall wooden beds, they would have plough animals and fresh milk during the winter when the English colonists were eating their cattle as dried beef sticks.

Acadian boat builders used their skills to construct excellent schooners for those who relocated north to the fishing banks. Most moved from Grand Pré to settle on the French Islands of St. Pierre and Miquelon and Île du Roi off the northeastern coast of Nova Scotia. They fished offshore, running lines for cod. The most attractive fish were gutted, salted and stored in the hold until they were moved to barrels of brine. French and other European merchants imported the important barrels containing about five hundred pounds of fish. Other small boats were built for the Grand Pré fishermen who tossed lines in the rivers and streams. Their fish, much smaller, would be cleaned, salted and dried on racks for enjoyment all year long. Grand Pré cod, whether barreled or salted, brought substantial prices in the market and made many a bachelor a prize catch in the region.

The British relied on the fertile Grand Pré farms as the primary food source for their growing colonies along the Atlantic seaboard. Of all the Acadian settlements, Grand Pré had long been considered the main breadbasket. These particular farms yielded so bountiful a crop of vegetables, fruit, wheat and corn that the Acadians' overabundant supply of food was shipped to the seaboard colonies. Demand from the English colonies for agricultural products was growing as their cities grew and farmland was converted to lots for buildings, roads and factories. Grand Pré farmers became so prosperous that they supported a flurry of new businesses in town opened by incoming settlers.

The town boasted shops with imported French merchandise in stock such as books, wine, lace, candles, gold jewelry, carriages, glass, porcelain, tableware, oil lamps, and other desirable goods that could not be found in the area. The town also offered the services of a dressmaker and tailor, baker, cobbler, rope maker, blacksmith, carpenters, a builder and furniture craftsman, and other tradesmen, as well as a physician and veterinarian. Each non-farming family generally owned a plot of ground to grow their own fruits and vegetables or bartered other goods for those foods.

"Lâche pas la patate" was the Acadian motto to waste nothing, use everything and be ever vigilant of their environment. They pickled and preserved fruits and vegetables while salting and drying fish and surplus meat for the winter. They even made beer from fir and spruce trees.

Equal to the impressive crop output from Grand Pré were the quantities of high-quality textiles, clothing and bolts of cloth woven by the women of the region. While raw wool was also available from the sheep farmers, the woven fabrics tempted the wives of the colonial maritime captains, traders and merchants.

Grand Pré was known throughout France and the English colonies for its brightly colored striped cloth made into aprons, caps, gowns, skirts and vests. The Acadian women went beyond simple weaving to incorporate unique patterns and stripes in their cloth, which was in demand throughout the colonies. Grand Pré was especially famed for its rich hues of deep purple, scarlet and "Grand Pré royal blue." Even the governor of a colony could rely on a new dress in Grand Pré purple or royal blue to make an unhappy wife forget an unpleasant discourse. The care taken by the women of Grand Pré to comb the flax, then card, spin, then weave the wool was evident in their beautiful cloth, exported mainly to Europe and the colonies.

In addition to their famous colored and striped fabrics, Grand Pré women were also known for their quilts. A dozen women would gather at an Acadian home at night and cut up old clothing to reuse in extraordinary new ways by making patchworks with bold colors and unusual textures next to each other. In time the local men joined in by singing tunes to set the pace for the women to sew, starting off slowly and ending with rousing marches and folk songs as women's needles and thread flew through the pieces of cloth. The end result was always a unique piece treasured in many a girl's chest for her dowry and a family heirloom to treasure for years.

The clothing that the Acadians of Grand Pré wore consisted of multiple layers. Women first put on a cotton shift that might also serve as a dressing gown or nightdress. The shift was followed by a petticoat which was covered by a skirt and an apron. For the top, the women wore a bodice and a mantelet of either wool or cotton depending on the season. A linen neck scarf and for Mass or special occasions a headpiece called a caline finished their ensemble. Their jewelry was simple -- usually only a gold Catholic cross on a chain and, if married, a gold wedding band.

Men began their dressing ritual with a suit of long underwear, usually wool, on a year-round basis. Then they put on a linen or cotton shirt and a wool vest that buttoned in the front. Their pants were loose fitting with a front opening covered by a flap. They usually wore a wool cap of grey, blue or red. Adults and children alike wore woolen socks dyed blue or grey and moccasins or wooden clogs. For special occasions such as a marriage, some wore imported shoes like those of the French Court made of satins and silks with patterned designs and raised heels.

The Acadians were French Catholic and for generations each family had as many children as a wife could bear. Fifteen to twenty offspring were the norm, and many an Acadian widower took a second wife, often still of childbearing age, if a prior spouse died in childbirth or otherwise. Some unfortunate Acadian men who had lost two previous wives married a third time. Orphans were taken into families and raised. Widows with children were not left to fend for themselves. If they were not married to eligible widowers or older bachelors, the community helped them with major home repairs and other chores. Grand Pré, like other Acadian towns and villages, consisted of large families who inter-married with others in the region, creating a close-knit society closed to outsiders, especially the English.

With such large families, young Acadian men and women of marriageable age found themselves with a wide choice of potential spouses. In Grand Pré, the notion of a bride selecting her own husband was unheard of, as her father made the best match for her with the father of a preferred young man. The parents generally sought an acceptable match for daughters once they reached age fourteen or fifteen, and sons who had attained their sixteenth year. But before that ritual began, certain technical skills had to be mastered by the young adults of marriageable age.

A young Acadian girl was required to weave and dye wool into a bolt of cloth before she was allowed to marry. Many a young girl of suitable age displayed her talents in the multi-striped gowns or brightly-colored aprons she wore proudly. These girls began learning to weave as soon as their feet could reach the floor from the spindle stool, sometimes as early as age six or seven. The color of a young Acadian girl's striped tunic, apron, or skirt often showed her level of expertise. The first colors learned, and the easiest, were brown or black. The next level of difficulty to master was purple, then scarlet, then the bright French blue, the color of the royal fleur de lis that gained a wide following and created the reputation of Grand Pré women as skilled weavers and dyers. Their royal blue bolts of cloth were prized by women all along the Atlantic seaboard and resulted in comfortable fortunes and livelihoods to the Acadian families whose daughters mastered the difficulty of the color.

Similarly, an Acadian young man had to prove he could build a wagon and repair its wheels before marriage was allowed. The young men of Grand Pré began their training on family farms or shops as soon as they could carry a board or a sack of nails without falling over. Families taught sons to be skilled carpenters, farmers, merchants and maritime builders. For the most part the young men were quick learners. The priest taught them to read, write, do their ciphers and give the proper coins in change to customers at family shops or at the weekly open air markets.

Once the technical aspects of the rite of passage of young adults had been mastered, a young man's father would approach the father of a potential bride to discuss arranging a marriage. The amount and kind of the dowry was always discussed, but equally important were the professions of the two patriarchs and how they could build alliances for trade and wealth. Once an agreement was made, the young man would then meet with the girl in public several times before making a declaration to her of his intentions. If she agreed, the courtship would continue until he gathered the courage to ask for the girl's hand, which was rarely refused. If she disagreed the potential groom's father moved on and the ritual commenced again.

Marriage contracts were different in France, particularly for an aristocrat who sought the heir of a higher-ranking nobleman as a husband for his daughter, and where the eldest son's father chose beautiful, young daughters of royalty, no matter how distant the familial relationship to the royal family. If Evangeline had been at Court in Versailles she would have been sought after by every noble family with a son, as both of her parents, many members of Court believing Sieur Le Blanc de Verdure to be her father, were of royal blood. And although his daughter was not in France, René intended to keep his promise to Eugenie to wed Evangeline to a worthy French nobleman.

Evangeline followed the Acadian traditions, mastering the arts of weaving, dying and sewing intricate striped gowns and aprons. Christine only allowed her to wear her hand-made clothes in the house, preferring Evangeline were the expensive designs of Madame Dupont more suited to Evangeline's station. Even without class distinctions in Grand Pré, Christine made certain Evangeline acquired the elegant taste and ways of her mother.

Part III
1754-1755

"Love does not consist in gazing at each other, but in looking
outward together in the same direction."
- Antoine de Saint-Exupéry

CHAPTER 27
Evangeline

August 22, 1754 - GRAND PRÉ

lowers, fresh flowers. Shall you buy some lovely posies today?" the teenage girl asked of the well-dressed men and women walking along the bustling commercial street. Many were intently involved in conversations but shook their heads. Others went into one of the many shops on Main Street in Grand Pré. Thus far no one had bought any flowers.

"Who would like to buy my beautiful flowers? Fresh picked today for someone special? Will you buy, sir?" she called out as she nodded to a gentleman passing in a carriage. He politely tipped his hat but the horses clopped by her.

Béatrice Gaudet stopped at the corner and looked across the street at the park in the town square. The sun was quite warm and she was tired of standing and holding the huge flower basket. It would be cooler there.

Just as she made her decision to step off the sidewalk into the street, she squinted into the light to see a well-dressed officer moving towards her. He appeared to be in his mid-twenties and wore a bright blue uniform with gold tassel epaulets, engraved brass buttons and a tight-fitting waistcoat over crisp white pantaloons and shiny black boots. The color and the fleur de lis design on his sword handle told her that he was French, as was she.

What a handsome gentleman she thought, and a welcome sight after the rough-mouthed English soldiers. They bought posies from her for their special ladies who lived in the fancy house in the English Quarter outside the town gates. Each night, after she had prayed for her deceased siblings, she blew out her candle and sat at the third floor garret window, looking out at the town.

When the shops closed, Grand Pré streets emptied as Acadian men returned home to supper, storytelling and nightly prayer with their families, thanking God they lived in the prosperous town of Grand Pré. But the British sector was active until dawn, with soldiers going in and out of the tavern and that house all night. When the large wooden door opened and cast firelight on the English officers Béatrice caught the faint tinkling of piano music and laughter. She began to think about finding a husband.

The girl's father, Thomas Gaudet, had come to Acadia on the *L'Acadie* seventeen years ago with nothing but his carpentry tools and a heavy heart. He had buried his childless first wife in Le Havre only two weeks before the sea voyage, during the delay caused by enormous storms. All he could procure was stairway space to sleep in a drafty Le Havre inn, where she caught the chills and died suddenly. Thomas had decided to move to Acadia anyway, as he had nothing left in France.

On the ship he had met Anne Verrazzano, a distant cousin of the famous explorer Giovanni Verrazzano who had first discovered the region. Like her relative, Anne had a spirit of adventure and as an unattached young woman had decided to make a new life for herself. She could bake pastries exceptionally well and had heard that Grand Pré was growing with the many new families emigrating each year. She hoped the town already had a bakery that would let her sell her pies and cakes in a corner of the shop.

After their marriage, Thomas and Anne wasted no time raising a family. In the seventeen years since their arrival, Thomas had sired fifteen children, of which all but two had succumbed to the pox, measles, and other diseases. Only Béatrice and her younger brother Pierre, whom Thomas always called Pine for Thomas' favorite tree, remained. Béatrice failed to comprehend how she did not suffer from the pox or the measles when she slept in a bed with her ill sisters, or how Pierre had escaped the fate of the other boys on their large straw-filled mattress. She did not understand but she was grateful.

When Béatrice was twelve her mother nearly died giving birth to a stillborn. Papa said it was another boy. But for Anne, losing another child was too much to bear and she retired inside her own world. From that day forward Anne had only gurgled nonsensical language. She lost her wits and Grand Pré lost the best pastry cook the town residents had ever known. Béatrice tried to bake as her mother had done but the cakes were lopsided and the pie crusts never had the right thickness. She sold her mother's recipes to the baker, whose wife followed them to the letter. The shop's customers said they were as delicious as the ones Madame Gaudet had made but Béatrice knew there was never as much loved baked into them.

After that, Béatrice became mother to Pierre and housekeeper to her father, cooking the meals and keeping their rooms clean. Her mother sat on the floor day after day, making unintelligible sounds and Thomas became more and more despondent. He slowed his work to a trickle, rarely accepting new carpentry commissions except when the French Consul placed an order. Then Thomas set to work immediately on the new job, putting any other work to the side. He was devoted to the Consul and would most likely have done anything for him.

With the small family in dire straits, Béatrice turned to selling flowers to make ends meet. She eagerly anticipated walking in the woods and fields early in the morning picking wildflowers just as their blooms popped open. She enjoyed her quiet stroll back into town when she observed the town slowly come alive as the streets filled with merchants, vendors and customers.

But this particular morning Béatrice forgot about her family, the town, and their money woes. She looked directly at the handsome man who strode over to her and said, "Your flowers are beautiful."

Béatrice curtsied and smiled, speaking in a clear voice with self-confidence. "How kind of you to say, sir."

The man continued, "They match the beauty of a young noblewoman I know. I shall buy all that you have if you can deliver them now."

The girl was so filled with gratitude she kissed his hand and curtsied, losing her composure in the gesture. "It will be my pleasure Your Grace, er, Your Excellency."

He filled her hand with coins and said, "Gabriel Mius d'Entremont, but Gabriel will be fine, Miss…?"

She was tongue-tied but managed to sputter her name. "Béatrice Gaudet kind sir, but you can say just Béatrice, that is all, sir."

Gabriel asked, "Your father is the carpenter Thomas Gaudet?"

She nodded without speaking.

He continued, "I have just been appointed Vice Consul to Lord Le Blanc. We need new furniture for our office. Please ask your father to meet me there tomorrow. You know the location?" he queried, pointing down the street to the building flying the French flag.

Béatrice was enamored. The Vice Consul, no less she thought. She nodded. "Yes sir, I know it. Everybody knows it. I love to see our beautiful French flag fluttering in the breeze."

He leaned down to her and whispered, "Deliver them to Mademoiselle Evangeline Le Blanc de Verdure. But the Lady is not to know the flowers are from me. Shall you keep my secret?"

"Yes sir. Of course sir."

"Good girl," he said and he handed her several coins.

"But sir this is too much," she protested.

He reminded her, "For your silence. Our secret, remember."

Béatrice nodded. So you got paid more if you kept a secret, she thought. That is good business. She would be on the watch for more secrets to keep. She watched him disappear around the corner and soon galloped past her on a beautiful black horse heading for the woods past the south gates of town.

She whispered, "Gabriel," as she merrily skipped in the other direction, careful to avoid the carriages of important townspeople and the men on horseback trotting to and fro. Narrowly missing a steaming pile of horse manure, Béatrice passed their Catholic Church, Saint Charles of the Mines. She quickly made the Sign of the Cross and hurried to the next street. After the church came a series of shops with apartments above, including her family home. She was giddy with the money she had made so early in the day but decided to wait until she returned from the delivery to give her father the good news. She walked quickly down the street and brightened at the sight of the French flag. She was nearly at her destination, near the north gates of Grand Pré.

When she was one street from the French Consulate she heard angry English voices coming from around the corner. She hid behind a post and stared at three English officers arguing with Madame Dupont in front of her shop. Madame was the seamstress in town, designing and sewing the most beautiful gowns and hats for wealthier women. Of late she had been exporting her designs to Québec City and Bostontown. Her assistant was Madame Adèle Arnaud who sewed women's clothes and also tailored men's attire, including intricate military costumes. After a while the British sent all their uniforms to Madame Dupont's shop rather than to Halifax or Bostontown.

Béatrice had seen these Englishmen before. She tried to think of their names. She knew the tall thin one in charge of the others was a Captain Turnbull, a cruel man that the Acadians avoided. Climbing on his horse with ease was the largest of the three, a huge bear of a man with an unusual shock of red hair. The others called him Wicker. And the short squatty one with a round face was unforgettable. He had one eye that circled around and around and made her dizzy just looking at him. He had a name with a color. She furrowed her brow. What was his name? A color of some kind. Brown? Red? No, she suddenly remembered. It was Green. Greenfield.

The Captain held up a jacket with a loose button and shrieked at Madame Dupont. "Do you call this acceptable? You were paid to stitch this button and here it is loose as the day I turned it in to you."

When Madame tried to look at it, Turnbull took the jacket and ripped both sleeves off. He told Wicker and Greenfield to take off their jackets and the Captain ripped them as well. Then he said, "You are to repair these jackets as they should be. Each seam shall be straight and in perfect alignment with the others. And all buttons shall be sewn tighter than the day they were made. You shall deliver them by dawn tomorrow."

The seamstress was distraught. "But Captain Turnbull. My assistant Madame Arnaud began her confinement today and cannot take any sewing. My eyes are not what they used to be. I do not know how in one day I can complete this work." She dropped her head and tears stained her cheeks.

"That matters not a whit to me. You have been well paid but have not given us our money's worth." He walked to the railing and untied the reins of his horse, mounting it in one quick leap. The other men did the same. "And do not expect payment for this work."

Madame Dupont pleaded with him. "Please sir, please let me provide you with something in my shop. Pick out anything you wish. But please relieve me of this burden."

Turnbull glared down at her. "Do it or I shall press a charge against you of stealing money from the King."

When the men had galloped out of sight, Béatrice came out of her hiding place. Madame Dupont had closed the shop, no doubt to labor over the odiously unfair demand. She knocked on the door. Madame did not respond. Béatrice determined to return and see how she could help.

But before the girl walked away she leaned against the window as if it were a sweets shop, both hands pressed against the glass, her nose as close as she could get without fogging the window. She loved looking at the bolts of imported French cloth in the window -- rich burgundy silks, the palest blue satins fit for a princess, delectable green wisps of fabric as dark as the forests outside Grand Pré. After she did her usual visual inventory she turned to the shop's other window and stopped short. She gasped.

A new dress was displayed on a form in the window. But not just any dress. This was the dress of her dreams -- a long crimson gown embellished with crystal beads at the décolleté neckline and painstakingly applied on the skirt to look as if they had been simply tossed there as an afterthought. How long had she dreamt about a formal gown that was beautiful, sparkling...and red. It had to be a deep rich red hue to match the depth of the love that she was ready to give to a husband. *If* she could find one.

She had filed the image into her memory never thinking she would have any occasion for it. Now after meeting Gabriel, she thought, she had to buy it. It was the only way to turn a man like Gabriel into a suitor. She vowed she would sell as many flowers as she could until she could acquire the dreamy confection. But how much did it cost, she wondered? She would return to ask Madame Dupont after she delivered the flowers for Monsieur Gabriel.

Poor Madame. Her husband, who imported European luxury goods including beautiful fabrics for his wife, had died of a musket wound under mysterious circumstances. Béatrice had heard her Papa talking about it not so quietly with some of his friends over a bottle of wine one night when he thought she and Pierre were sleeping. Monsieur Dupont's killer was never caught even though French witnesses sent written statements to the Lieutenant-Governor in Halifax. They reported they had seen Lieutenant Turnbull in a verbal altercation with Dupont the evening before he was found dead. But her Papa said the British authorities dismissed the complaint saying Frenchmen could not be trusted and that their word had no validity at all. Turnbull was privately chastised to refrain from public disputes with a French Neutral. But that day he was furious that his seams were not straight so he risked a quarrel with the dead man's wife.

Béatrice arrived at her destination on the corner of the next street, a tasteful wooden building of three floors. Other than the church it was the largest building in Grand Pré. Above the main door hung a sign painted with the royal fleur-de-lis. She could not read every word but she slowly mouthed the letters:

CONSUL and ROYAL NOTAIRE to HIS MAJESTY
KING LOUIS XV of FRANCE and NAVARRE
SIEUR RENÉ Le BLANC de VERDURE

A painter had just completed an addition to the sign and walked away with his ladder and paintbox. Béatrice stood there trying to mold the letters into words. Her spelling was less than adequate but she instinctively justified her lack of mastery of the words as being too long. Béatrice looked at the sign for a while.

VICE-CONSUL GABRIEL MIUS d'ENTREMONT

Suddenly it came to her and she read the word "Gabriel." Her heart skipped a beat when she realized that was the name of her benefactor. She whispered it again. "Gabriel." She wondered if he was moving into what was commonly known as the "King's Consulate." That she knew the man and how to spell his name could be important for her in the future. She memorized this information, hoping it would prove fruitful one day.

Before her mother had become ill she had attended lessons with other French Catholic children at the school run by their priest, Père Rivière. He had taught her to read some words so she was able to decipher "René" and "Gabriel." Though Béatrice did not know, the two floors above the Consulate office constituted the LeBlanc residence. The family rooms and the Consul's chamber were on the second floor and the rooms for the Consul's daughter and her governess who had become the family housekeeper were on the floor above.

Béatrice walked up to the door and was surprised to see dozens of small bouquets already lying there. She compared them to the posies in her basket, confident the Lady would prefer her wildflowers. She pulled the brass knocker and a young brunette beauty of seventeen, Evangeline Beaufort Le Blanc de Verdure, peered from the third floor window to the front door below. She saw a small girl holding a very large flower basket. It seemed from above that she stood in a field of flowers. Where had such a profusion of color and perfume come from, Evangeline wondered.

Béatrice waved to the Lady above and placed her large basket on the stoop. She was proud because it looked so grand compared to the other bouquets. When she looked up at the window again it was empty. She was unsure of what to do but after only a few moments the door opened and Evangeline reached for the basket.

"Thank you. They are indeed very lovely," said Evangeline who appreciated their natural beauty and scent. "But where is the card? I must know who presented me with such a generous gift."

Béatrice smiled and said, "That, sweet Lady, is a secret I cannot reveal. The gentleman insisted. I do hope they bring you pleasure."

Béatrice was crestfallen, realizing Gabriel's heart already belonged to Evangeline. But the Lady was so kind and, of course, very beautiful. She thought to herself that he would have to be mad not to be in love with her.

Evangeline smiled. "They are for my birthday. Would you happen to be the master carpenter's daughter?"

Béatrice curtsied and nodded. "Béatrice Gaudet, my Lady."

Evangeline nodded. "And your mother? How is she feeling these days?"

Béatrice shuffled her shoes and looked at the ground. "She mostly remains in the house. She is quite ill, you know."

Everyone in Grand Pré knew about Anne Gaudet. "Well, we must both say prayers for her then. Thank you, dear Béatrice." Evangeline tried to press a coin into the girl's hand but she declined.

"Oh no, I could not take anything from you, my Lady. The gentleman paid me more than enough."

"Papa is holding a dance tonight and you should come. Seven o'clock at the Church hall."

Béatrice queried, "Will he announce your betrothal? Perhaps to a certain gentleman?"

Evangeline dismissed the notion. "This is my sixteenth birthday celebration only. Papa thinks I am too young. He is much too busy to make any arrangements for me. In any case, when the time comes I shall be the one to choose my own husband. All girls have that right. I hope you remember that."

"Please enjoy the gift and the dance, Lady Evangeline." Then Béatrice was off.

Evangeline called into the house. "Christine. Could you please help? I can only carry the large basket, not all the other bouquets." Evangeline drank in the perfume of the flowers in the basket. She wondered who had sent such a lovely gift.

Gabriel rounded the corner so quickly he bumped into her, causing her to drop the flower basket. Gabriel lowered his gaze. "Please forgive me, Lady Evangeline." He bent to pick up the basket and several of the other bouquets. "Shall I assist and bring these into the house for you?" They shared a lingering glance as their eyes met.

Evangeline said softly, "Thank you kindly, Monsieur Mius d'Entremont. Or should I say Monsieur Le Vice Consul Mius d'Entremont?"

Christine appeared at the door, nodded to Gabriel and started to gather the rest of the flowers from the doorstep. Without taking her eyes off Gabriel, Evangeline handed the bouquets to Christine. Understanding the situation, Christine filled her arms with most of the bouquets and took her leave. "I shall fill the vases for tonight." Her absence was not missed. Not even the sound of the door closing was heard by the entranced couple.

Evangeline pointed to the remaining bouquets and the basket. "Which of these is from you? I should like to thank you properly, Monsieur."

Gabriel answered indirectly. "Please, we have known each other for all of your life. Long enough for you to call me Gabriel. If you so desire." He bowed and kissed her hand.

She blushed and rearranged the flowers in the basket, leaning down to take in their fragrance. "If that is to be, Gabriel, then I pray you call me Evangeline."

He stole a furtive glance at her. Clearly they were attracted but hid their feelings from each other.

When Evangeline looked up, he cast his eyes downward. "I wish you the happiest of birthdays, Lady...I mean Evangeline."

Evangeline was agitated. "Does this mean you will not attend my party?"

He looked up to see her disappointment. He felt that was a good sign. He shook his head. "I must finish my work. I am to ready the office for Monsieur Gaudet." He grinned sheepishly. "Your father wants new furniture for me. I told him the old desk would do but he insisted."

She nodded. "Papa thinks very highly of you. He has told me so." She added shyly, "He also says work comes first but even he is taking the evening to dance with me. Will you not steal away for a few minutes?"

Gabriel bowed deeply. "Please accept my apologies. I am to complete some urgent work for your father and than I have a prior engagement. I do hope you will forgive me."

They both started to open the door, their hands on the doorknob simultaneously. When they pulled back instinctively out of respect, Evangeline lost her balance and leaned into him. He dropped the flowers and caught her arm, helping her to right her position. Then he bowed and opened the door.

"Please allow me, my Lady...Evangeline," he bowed.

"Thank you," she murmured quickly, embarrassed as she rushed inside. He followed, his arms filled with flowers. She was flushed but smiling as she walked ahead, her back to him.

Gabriel followed her inside and closed the door behind them. He walked with her to the bottom of the stairs. She took the flowers from him with a smile and walked up to the landing. Gabriel waited until she turned so that he could give her another bow. Then he exited the building. He is always working, thought Evangeline, like Papa. Indeed, she repeated, he is just like Papa.

Outside Gabriel trotted away on his horse, passing the corner where Madame Dupont had opened the door to Béatrice. The young girl told her she had overheard Turnbull's demands and offered to help. The seamstress showed Béatrice how to remove thread without tearing the fabric. The young girl watched carefully, thinking she might better support the family with this kind of work than selling flowers, or perhaps she could do both. There were at least eighteen hours available each day for work if one used a candle in the evening. She promised herself she would learn this new trade as quickly as she could. Madame Dupont was happy to have assistance while Adèle Arnaud was indisposed. This could work well for them both.

In the Le Blanc salon, Evangeline walked in to a room scented with bouquets on all the tables. Christine had filled every vase with profuse blooms. The two women stood back and admired the room.

"They must be from every eligible Acadian man, not only in Grand Pré but the entire province. You shall have your choice of suitors," said Christine.

Evangeline brushed off the remark. "I am only interested in one man who does not know of my existence."

Christine asked, "Would he be Gabriel?"

Evangeline turned with a quizzical look on her face. "How did you know?"

Christine shook her head with a smile. "Do you not think I have seen the look in your eyes when he is in the same room as you?"

Evangeline grinned sheepishly. "Can you see it so clearly?"

Christine took her hand and spoke with all seriousness. "That young man has loved you your entire life. "

"But he ignores me every time I see him with Papa in the office."

"Give him time to show it in his own way. Surely the flowers are a good beginning."

"But he did not ever admit the basket was from him. Béatrice would not divulge the name of the person who bought them."

"Come now, how did he appear just as the flowers were delivered?" Christine wrapped her arms around the young girl and hugged her dearly. "We must hurry to reach Madame Dupont's shop before it closes. It would not do for you not to wear the dress you ordered for your own birthday. Your gown should not only attract his attention but hold it as softly as a floating butterfly all evening."

Evangeline said, "But he said Papa has assigned work for him until late tonight." She begged Christine, "Can you not ask my father to release him early? You have his ear."

Christine shook her head. "You know I cannot interfere in the Consul's work. Perhaps Gabriel will attend after all, at least briefly, to extend his best wishes for your birthday."

Evangeline replied, "I only hope that is the case. Now I must change."

Christine looked at her. "You look perfectly fine. I see no need to change your dress to meet the dressmaker."

Evangeline rushed up the next flight of stairs to the landing and looked down at Christine. "But what if I meet some of those suitors? How shall I make Gabriel jealous if the others do not vie for my attention?"

Christine choked a smile as Evangeline disappeared from view. The girl she raised from an infant had become, seemingly overnight, a young woman. She already understood the wiles of the fairer sex. Christine gathered her shawl and descended the stairs to the front entry hall. She knocked on the door of the office.

"Come in," said René.

Christine entered, leaving the door open so Evangeline would join her. Sometimes, she thought, women could take matters into their own hands without saying a word. Evangeline rushed down the stairs and breathlessly reached the bottom of the main stairway. She wore an exquisite hand-embroidered dress of deep blue silk with lace collar and sleeves. The bodice showed off her firm breasts and a narrow black belt cinched her tiny waist.

She entered the office. Gabriel stood, peering over René's shoulder. They intently studied a parchment map. Christine stood back, dusting the lamps on the table. Evangeline took in the entire room and the adjacent annex. The room previously had been filled to the brim with crates of files, dossiers and documents but now it was empty in anticipation of being refilled again, this time with Gabriel's office furniture and records. The room in all its emptiness looked so much larger than it had as a storage chamber.

Evangeline looked at her father, nearly thirty-seven years old. She mused to herself, he had to use his spectacles more often these days. And he became more easily fatigued. She had seen him in the afternoons sipping a glass of wine with Christine when she had returned from shopping or visiting her friends. She thought nothing of it but now that her Papa was getting older he should take a new wife. And Christine seemed the perfect woman for him. At only thirty-two, she was still within her childbearing years. And it would be nice to have some young children in the house.

She adored Christine, the only mother she had ever known. Evangeline had observed Christine and René over the years. They seemed to have a silent language between them, perhaps even a form of mental communication, knowing each other's tendencies and nuances. She certainly knew his favorite foods and clothes, as she set out his suits every Sunday for Church and washed his things weekly. He, in turn, thanked her after each meal, always stood when she entered a room, and was generous with payment to her for whatever she requested. Christine had never asked for anything for her own use or pleasure. She spent René's funds on fresh foods, beautiful clothes for him and Evangeline and on decor and maintenance of the home as it should be, inside and out. He insisted from time to time that she meet with Madame Dupont for new gowns, but otherwise Christine lived to serve the Le Blanc de Verdure family.

It was Christine who had insisted at their arrival in 1738 that René hire Thomas Gaudet to renovate the entire interior of the Consulate building. She did not want Evangeline being raised where there was any remnant of English soldiers or society. René worked out of a makeshift office downstairs where he also slept but he insisted on renting rooms for Christine and Evangeline from the boardinghouse run by Monsieur and Madame Jean Lambert.

The Lambert's daughter, Jeanne, was Evangeline's age and the two girls began a friendship that would last a lifetime, first playing together as infants. The construction took much longer than anticipated because Gaudet insisted on selecting, cutting and planing every piece of wood himself rather than hiring laborers. He convinced René no one knew the trees of Grand Pré better than he did and that knowledge would translate to a residence and Consulate befitting the royal French Consul.

After five years the house was finally completed and the result was a home as grand as any château in France. Christine had arranged a comfortable design so the rooms flowed from one to the other without long hallways except in the bedroom wings. She had also installed Pater's painting of Eugenie in the center wall of the dining room, flanked by hanging candelabras which brushed soft candlelight onto Eugenie's face. In the flickers, Eugenie almost appeared alive and often René would stop in the middle of his meal and stare at her picture for long periods of time, oblivious to his daughter and Christine.

René was so grateful to Christine for her work that he broke down in her arms, remembering that fateful day, his last with his darling Eugenie. Christine understood. He was not ready to move on while his heart was still broken. Christine's heart was heavy with sorrow but pledged to bide her time. She had fervent hopes that he would one day soon look upon her in a loving way different from that of his child's nursemaid or his housekeeper.

When René, Christine and Evangeline installed themselves into their new chambers, Thomas undertook to reconstruct the offices. The rooms themselves did not take nearly as long, but Gaudet insisted on carving new desks, tables, chairs and document cabinets for the Consulate. The furniture was delivered and Gaudet spent hours showing René the various intricacies of secret drawers and spaces, moving parts that released levers that dropped wooden boxes where treasures could be hidden. Gaudet did not trust the English and he himself had built a small hidden room behind a wall in his workroom where he hid valuables and sacks of coins. He told the Consul in case anything should ever happen to Thomas but asked him to keep the knowledge to himself. Not even his wife and daughter knew his secret.

It seemed to Evangeline that her father loved Christine, but she wondered if Christine felt the same. She was ever polite and caring but the girl was not sure this was out of duty or it if was something more. Evangeline determined to broach the subject with Christine soon. Her father was so involved in his work that he had probably never considered marrying again.

But Evangeline did want to marry, so long as she wed a man she loved, and start her own family in her own home. She knew Gabriel should be her husband. But when considering a union between her father and Christine, a dreadful thought popped into her head. What if neither her father nor Christine wanted to marry and they both ended up living alone for the rest of their lives? She would not be able to bear two such loving people not sharing their love.

No, she decided, they must wed each other. It is the only thing to do. Then another thought arose. Is this my will, trying to arrange things, or is this a selfless act for the two people I love most in the world? She wrestled with those thoughts as she descended the stairs. As if Gabriel had read her thoughts, he looked up. When he saw Evangeline in a dress that revealed her perfect figure he let out his breath, which became an involuntary whistle. He had never seen her look so ravishing. He suddenly remembered himself and stepped away from René's desk.

René looked up from his stack of documents and proclaimed, "Daughter, you shall not leave this house in that dress. Cover yourself with your shawl."

Evangeline walked over to her father. She kissed his cheek and gently chided him. "Come now, Papa. Madame Dupont created this in the style of the latest Paris fashions. You would not want your daughter wearing last year's old rags, would you? Besides, Christine and I must collect our party gowns before Madame closes her shop for the evening."

As she walked away she feigned innocence and dropped her small embroidered bag at Gabriel's feet. She murmured. "How clumsy of me."

Gabriel instantly retrieved it, and looked up into her eyes from his kneeling position. She waited expectantly as he rose slowly and handed her the purse.

"Lady Evangeline," he said, locking his eyes on hers.

René did not see the incident, so intent was he on studying the official document. But Christine noted everything that went on. Good for Evangeline, she thought. She knows now she has his attention. René waved his daughter and Christine out. "We have much work to complete. Do you need anything else? Payment for the dresses?"

Evangeline lowered her eyes and tilted her head downward to hide a small smile of triumph. At last, she thought, Gabriel has noticed me. She shook her head, "Thank you, Papa. But Madame will send you the bill as she usually does. Goodbye."

René grunted, "Goodbye daughter. Christine, please see that she does not tarry in that clothing of hers."

Christine smiled at René, but he had already turned back to his work. Without feeling rebuffed she replied, "Of course, you know I shall."

Christine preceded Evangeline into the entry hall. At the office doorway Evangeline turned to see Gabriel still staring at her. When she caught his glance he looked down and fumbled with some papers on the desk. Evangeline was pleased and glided out of the room.

Once outside the earshot of René and Gabriel, Christine turned to Evangeline. "Well? Was my intuition correct?"

"You have been my lifelong teacher, Christine," began Evangeline. "I only wish you would teach me how to understand men. I mean one man. Gabriel, that is."

Christine said, "That, my dear, will require a lifetime of study." They grinned at each other and exited the building with linked arms.

When the women had closed the door, René confided in Gabriel. "What a fool I am to have put my work above Evangeline. She has grown into a beautiful woman and will soon marry, leaving me alone."

Gabriel asked him, with more than a touch of concern, "You have not already accepted a proposal for her hand?"

René shook his head. "Nearly each day a different Frenchman asks me to accept his son, a fine young man. But how can I tell them I cannot choose any when I have already made inquiries at Court among the nobility?"

Gabriel replied quietly, "There are indeed many fine Acadian men around you. Even close to you."

René ignored him, intent on his own thoughts. "I must decline them all tonight."

"You have not already accepted a proposal?"

"Not as of yet. But I do anticipate receiving several offers on the next ship from France."

Gabriel realized how much he cared about Evangeline. Still, he was not ready to discuss the subject with René. Instead he said, "Your daughter is the most beautiful young woman in the entire region, in the country, even. Perhaps she will make the choice of her own will."

René was suddenly transported away, with a distant look in his eyes. He nodded slowly. "She does have the same independent spirit as her mother. No one could tell Eugenie what do to, except the King. And I never tried, so lost in love was I."

René opened a metal box and took out a parchment document, handing it to Gabriel. "I must prepare for my daughter's ball. Make copies for me to circulate among our Acadian Commission members at our meeting tomorrow. Then replace the original in the strongbox in its hiding place."

Gabriel nodded. He had devised an emergency plan to protect their royal documents and sensitive information in the event of an English raid. Gabriel was convinced it was a matter of time. René would not believe the English would deceive him or seize private government documents but agreed to be prudent just in case. Gabriel was also concerned that in the vast British network of agents it was possible to have a traitor in their Acadian midst.

"Men do desperate things in desperate times. Some of the Acadians might have reason to sell information or access to it," reasoned Gabriel.

"I refuse to believe that any French subjects could betray the King." René hesitated then added, "But I shall nonetheless accept your suggestion."

He and Gabriel built a hidden compartment into the base of the sideboard cabinet in the dining room of the residence. No one else knew about the hiding place for their sensitive documents -- not Christine or Evangeline, or Thomas Gaudet. Better to keep this precaution to themselves, they reasoned, which would give them the time and opportunity to move secret papers out of the building in the event of an unexpected British search.

Though the British had not conducted such a raid René had a foreboding that a turn of events could happen any day. He and Gabriel had become more wary of the English and their unpredictability in military matters without changing their appearance of peace toward them.

In 1749 the British Fort Vieux Logis at the gates of Grand Pré had been completely rebuilt with new fortifications. Then in the spring of that year the Fort was inexplicably abandoned and locked by the English, though Captain Turnbull and a small contingent of one hundred troops remained in lodgings they had built. The act lulled most of the Acadian Neutrals into believing they would live free of British troops in their daily lives from then on out. René and Gabriel did not change their peaceful outward appearances but they watched every move the English made.

This political face was difficult for Gabriel, who had endured the sight of Turnbull and his henchmen insulting his friends. But he had agreed with the Consul to take no action. He planned to keep his promise. At least for the moment.

Walking in town, Christine and Evangeline were within eyesight of Madame Dupont's shop when they saw it was closed. The women looked worried but Christine knocked at the door. Madame Dupont peered around the shade and opened it, whisking them inside.

"Has something happened?" asked Christine upon seeing the tear-stained face of her friend. Madame Dupont shook her head. "It is nothing. But I shall not be able to attend your ball. I must...." She broke down in tears and could not finish. Béatrice peered out from the workroom and told them the entire story. Evangeline and Christine promised to speak with René about Turnbull's cruelty, over Madame's protestations.

Madame Dupont forced herself to put thoughts of Turnbull aside and brought out two gowns. She and Béatrice assisted Evangeline into a stunning evening dress of deep green satin matching the color of Evangeline's eyes – hazel like her mother's. As Madame arranged the long full skirt, perfect for twirling on the dance floor, Béatrice was awestruck by the elegance yet simplicity of the handiwork. The low-cut neckline was trimmed in simple green crystal beads which were also sprinkled throughout the dress. The Lady is as beautiful as an angel, Béatrice thought. She whispered a quick prayer to look half as pretty when she wore the red dress and married the man of her dreams, whoever he would be. Madame Dupont had agreed to deduct some of Béatrice's wages each week to pay for the gown, which would remain in the window until she owned it.

Madame Dupont and Christine circled Evangeline, who nodded in great appreciation at the design. The dressmaker stated, "It is even more beautiful on you than I could ever imagine, Lady Evangeline."

Evangeline asked Christine, "He will like it, will he not?"

Christine nodded unhesitatingly. "He will be blinded by your beauty, no matter what you wear." Then she stepped behind a hand-carved wooden screen and tried on her new dress, a beautiful creation of deep rich gold silk with a hand-beaded bodice and a long skirt. She could surely turn a man's head yet she was still unmarried, which was a conundrum to Béatrice who believed every woman should marry before she was too old to have children.

Evangeline admired her dress in a series of three long mirrors arranged to show the various angles and sides of the dress. She hugged Madame Dupont and whispered, "Thank you. It is perfect. Your work is so lovely, I shall come to you for my wedding dress."

Christine walked out at that moment in her new dress and looked at Evangeline questioningly. The dressmaker turned to her in wonder, "So you have accepted a proposal? Who is the most fortunate bridegroom?"

Evangeline shook her head. "No one has actually asked for my hand. But when I accept a proposal from the man I love, you shall make my dress, simple but elegant, of rich blue satins and silks with cream trim and handmade laces." She turned to Christine. "Would Maman have approved?"

Christine hugged her. "She would have chosen exactly the same."

Evangeline changed clothes behind the screen then walked to the door. "I shall wait for you outside, Christine. Thank you again Madame."

The two women nodded. Christine turned approvingly in the mirror. "Madame, you always make such lovely creations. I am so grateful." She returned behind the screen to change into her daydress. The seamstress stared at Christine, who seemed to be in love, but with whom? Christine would tell her when she was ready so she held her tongue and completed her work of wrapping Evangeline's dress in paper and a large box tied with a green silk ribbon. She took the dress from Christine and packed it in the same way. Christine emerged from behind the screen and picked up the two large dress boxes, thanking the seamstress. "We hope to have another happy occasion to order new dresses. Goodbye, Madame."

Madame Dupont waved to her favorite customer. From the moment Christine had first arrived and ordered baby clothes for Evangeline through the death of Monsieur Dupont until the present day, Christine had been a loyal friend. Madame pulled the shades and closed the shop. She sighed then returned to the workroom and lit large candles. She told Béatrice, "We have a long night ahead of us." The young girl gasped at the extravagance of the candles but nodded in agreement. She moved closer to the candlelight, not daring to stop working on the English uniform in her lap.

Outside, Christine found Evangeline surrounded by handsome young Acadian suitors all vying for her attention. Evangeline was polite to all of them while showing no particular interest in any one. Gilles Cormier, the son of the local wine merchant, whispered into her ear. "Did you receive my flowers, Lady Evangeline?"

Evangeline nodded and smiled. "Thank you, kind sir."

"May I ask for a dance tonight?" he continued.

Evangeline said, "It is only for you to invite me. Thank you."

Another suitor, Nicolas Hébert, whose father owned the largest farm in Grand Pré, murmured, "My Lady, I hope you approved of my bouquet and shall accept my dance offer this evening."

Before she could answer, Christine walked over to her and interrupted. She led Evangeline away, thanking the suitors but leaving them to admire her from afar.

Cormier turned to the other young men and said, "If her betrothal is announced, her husband shall be a happy man indeed."

Hébert asked, "My father is a member of the Acadian Commission close to Lord Le Blanc's ear but he has heard nothing."

"So we wait and learn who is to be the lucky man," said Cormier.

The suitors each prayed he would be the chosen one. But Evangeline had ideas of her own. For her there could not be marriage without love. In these modern times she hoped her father would not resort to the old-fashioned custom of an arranged match for her. She had set her sights on one man. All she needed to do was let him think it was his idea.

CHAPTER 28
Arrangement

GRAND PRÉ

fter searching high and low without finding what he needed, René walked from his office into the hallway and called up the stairs, "Christine, do you know where my spectacles are?"

In the dining room Kitok had been teaching Evangeline and Christine to speak Mi'kmawi'simk. They had requested a lesson each time he came to the Consulate to meet with Gabriel. The women enjoyed learning more about their Mi'Kmaq friends on each visit. Today Kitok had instructed the women on his Mi'Kmaq family ancestry and the names of all his current family members.

Evangeline was most intrigued about the Mi'Kmaq intermarriage with the French d'Entremont line many generations ago and asked questions incessantly about the Mi'Kmaq genealogy of Gabriel's ancestors, the Mius d'Entremont nobility. Kitok politely answered the questions he could, but seemed particularly anxious at the mention of Gabriel. He continued to look downstairs hoping to see Gabriel. They had urgent matters to discuss.

Evangeline turned to him. "Kitok, shall you attend my birthday dance tonight?"

Kitok declined politely. "My father requested I meet with him. Please accept my apology."

"We shall save some cakes for you then," she said gaily.

"Thank you. Now I should excuse myself and meet with Gabriel." He nodded to the two women, who smiled in return. They did not know the real nature of Kitok's meeting with Gabriel nor would they until each woman discovered it in her own way.

As Kitok hurried down the stairs, René called again, "Christine? Have you seen my spectacles?"

Christine walked downstairs and into René's office. She opened his side desk drawer and handed them to him. He smiled up at her with gratitude. Then she left quietly. She was loyal and deferential, never interrupting his work or entering his office uninvited but always ready to help at his call.

René was thankful Christine had agreed to stay in the Consulate after Eugenie's death. He appreciated Christine's help and knew he could not have raised a daughter alone, considering his responsibilities to the King and the Acadian colonists. René appreciated the unspoken friendship they had. A mere look or glance spoke their thoughts louder than words.

As of late however, Christine had become difficult to understand. She hid her feelings well behind a mask of calm acceptance. He was determined to ask her if all was well when they both had a free moment. He shuddered at the thought that she might be ill and he might lose her. For a fleeting moment he felt his heart race as it did when he married Eugenie. He wondered if his feelings for her were stronger than those of mere friendship.

Christine had done an excellent job of instructing Evangeline in her numerous lessons as well as in the unwritten rules of Court and royal etiquette at Versailles. As a replacement mother, Christine had always been by Evangeline's side to help her. She even managed to teach her to control her willful nature.

From Christine, Evangeline learned to bestow acts of kindness on the colonists and their Mi'Kmaq friends. They brought food to the aged and helped midwives with new births. For the sick they prepared Christine's herbal healing poultices which had been vastly improved by learning other natural cures from the Mi'Kmaq medicine woman, White Bird. The colonists adored both Christine and Evangeline. The Acadians who had known Eugenie had all loved her, and they saw many of the same fine qualities in the daughter as the mother.

René was proud of both women and looked forward to the ball that evening. He decided to speak to Christine about her health during a dance with her. Then he buried himself in work again. He broke the red seal of a thick parchment stamped with the King's insignia and began to read intently.

Gabriel stood patiently at René's side until he laid the document on the desk. René removed his glasses, pinched his eyes and, then turned to Gabriel.

"King Louis has received information that the English Council in Halifax has plans to expand their colonies along the Eastern seaboard," René said, pointing to the document.

Gabriel nodded. "The British continue to attract more settlers. The Acadian farmers informed me that Grand Pré is now the largest supplier of foodstuffs for many of the colonies, particularly Massachusetts."

"For us this is a double-edged sword. Our colonists have become very wealthy but our colonial neighbors have become envious. The British have never been content to have an imbalance of power in any form -- the sea, settlements, food sources, or wealth. It is only through our peaceful trade negotiations that they have been kept satisfied," stated René emphatically.

Gabriel responded, "But they must respect the Treaty of Utrecht. It was designed by their own Queen in taking possession of Acadia. Surely that is enough for them?"

René shook his head. "King George Two is a far different ruler than his father or Queen Anne before him. I do not believe he will respect an old parchment, particularly with his thirst for worldwide expansionism. And with Charles Lawrence in Halifax as Acting Governor we must be increasingly vigilant."

Gabriel concurred. "Lawrence has the reputation of a cunning fox. He shall soon appoint someone new to carry out such a strategy right under our noses. But who shall it be? Captain Murray at the nearby Fort Edward seems inexperienced and Turnbull is too much of a hothead."

René chided him. "Gabriel, we cannot lose seventeen years of peace over your dislike of one English Lieutenant, no matter how sinister he may seem."

"Far beyond that, Turnbull is a madman with the power to carry out his evil deeds free of interference. I overheard him chastise Madame Dupont on the street for a loose button on his jacket. And I still believe the man was responsible for her husband's murder."

"That was quite an unfortunate incident. Both Christine and Evangeline asked me to investigate. I asked Madame to meet with me but she sent a letter requesting that I please not look further into the matter. She fears she will lose her livelihood without the uniform repair work that Captain Turnbull and his men send to her."

"And your response to her, my Lord?"

"Gabriel what else could I do but acquiesce? I understand her dilemma. Ours is a difficult line to follow but we must respect the Treaty and maintain the peace without relinquishing our neutral status or our freedom of religion."

"How is peace-keeping justified when the English do not respect our King, our religion or your position as the King's representative in Acadia?"

René said firmly, "Political enemies are best kept close at hand. You would do well to remember that, Vice Consul." Then he pointedly changed the subject.

René pulled out the Cardinal's worn leather journal. Handing it to Gabriel he said, "I have shown this to no one since Cardinal de Fleury presented it to me on our departure from Versailles. It is time for you to read it. Then we shall discuss a strategy with our Acadian Commission."

Gabriel said in a low tone, as if the walls had ears. "Kitok is waiting for me. The Mi'Kmaqs have been tracking English movements and await the Chieftain's request for a meeting tonight. Shall you be there or should I represent you in your stead?"

René sat quietly without responding for several moments. Slowly he said, "I was absent during my daughter's youth working for the King, whose service I proudly accepted. But tonight I cannot break my promise to dance with her on her sixteenth birthday." He dipped his quill in ink and wrote a brief letter to Chief Mahtok Mius. He then pressed a roller across the ink to prevent smudging and folded and sealed the document with red wax and the royal Notarial crest.

He handed the document to Gabriel. "As Vice Consul you already have the credentials and with this I hereby grant you the authority to represent the King on my behalf. Please give my personal thanks to Chief Matok."

Gabriel responded, "Thank you for your faith in me, Monsieur le Consul."

"You have much work to do before you leave this evening. Evangeline will be disappointed that you cannot attend but if such a meeting is called, ask for me at the ball and advise me on your way to the Mi'Kmaq Village. Then you can give your best wishes to her for a moment. Now I must dress for her special occasion." Then René left through the back door of the office which led to the stairway to his private rooms.

Gabriel opened the front door to the office to find Kitok. The two men talked in hurried tones. Gabriel asked, "What news on the English front?"

Kitok replied, "I have just returned from Halifax. The English Council is taking grave action. We must move quickly. Should I tell my father the Consul will attend?"

Gabriel nodded. "He appointed me the honor of meeting with the Chief and the Council."

The Mi'Kmaq said pensively, "These will be difficult times my good friend. We must be prepared and stay ever vigilant."

"My men are ready and waiting for the word. We look forward to victory over the English and soon."

The two men hugged each other as brothers. Indeed they were distantly related through the inter-marriage of Princess Singing Bird Mius and the first Henri d'Entremont. Then Kitok took his leave and Gabriel locked the office door. He took a piece of bark from a hidden compartment under his desk. With his knife he etched a message and slipped it into his jacket. Then he began working on the stack of documents René had assigned him.

Upstairs, Evangeline sat in her boudoir before a mirror. Her eyes shone brighter than ever, reflected in the green satin dress. Christine, in her party dress, decorated Evangeline's long black tresses with flowers and greenery from the fresh bouquets.

Evangeline did not mask her disappointment. "Gabriel is not coming tonight. He did take note of me but only because I was a step away from him."

Christine chided, "Now, now Evangeline. How can he not notice you? Why, at your Baptism he announced he was going to marry you."

Evangeline turned to her. "Why have you never told me of this?"

Christine turned the girl back to her first position so she could finish her hairdo. "I doubt an intelligent young man such as he would forget such a declaration. I sense he remembers his vow and knows I would hold him to it if you wished me to. He may still need time to accomplish...other things."

"What things? Politics?"

She frowned until Christine adjusted Evangeline's hair decorations and turned her face to the mirror. Evangeline kissed Christine on the cheek.

"Thank you for making me look beautiful tonight. I hope he changes his mind. If we could dance but once, perhaps he would never let me go."

Christine smiled with a sigh. "You remind me so much of your mother. So striking, yet so humble. She never realized her own beauty until your father convinced her of it and accepted her for who she was...." She paused.

Evangeline urged her to continue. "What did he do for my mother? You must know how important this is to me. Please."

"Your mother was not well-admired at Versailles. She was, as some women said, too beautiful, and they were green with envy. Vicious in their rumors, they were always deferential to her in person. After all, she was related to the Queen."

Christine hesitated but Evangeline took her hand and encouraged her. "Please go on."

"Lady Eugenie heard some of the gossip bandied about at Versailles and believed she was beneath the station of the other noblewomen although her father's rank exceeded most other family patriarchs. Eugenie walked behind them or stayed out of their sight until the day she was betrothed to your father in the presence of King Louis and Queen Marie. I will never forget the looks on the faces of those jealous felines."

Christine grinned broadly to Evangeline. "Your father was somewhat of a mystery himself, with his royal lineage in the King's family and having been hand-selected over all the other nobles to marry the beautiful Queen's cousin. A handsomer couple was never seen before at the Palace, although no one dared mention that to our monarchs. But it is true that your mother was more beautiful than Her Majesty."

"It is surprising that Papa never discussed this with me. I find it fascinating and shall ask him about it," Evangeline said, mesmerized with images of her beautiful mother outshining the other noblemen's wives. And even the Queen!

"There is not much more to tell. But I never saw your mother smile until she was married to your father. She told me many times on the voyage from France that she felt free for the first time in her life and that she owed it all to René. It seemed she had finally been accepted for her inner beauty as well as her looks. That made all the difference to her."

Evangeline reflected on the story and asked, "And how did she die?"

Christine shook her head. "Any more you should ask your Papa. Now come, this is a happy occasion. We must not be late for your own sixteenth birthday."

Downstairs, René was dressed and waiting on the two women. He looked dashing in his French uniform with a sash of the royal fleur de lis pattern, given to him by the King.

Gabriel spoke in low tones to René, continuing an earlier conversation. "My Lord, despite the political unrest it would be premature to betroth the Lady Evangeline to a nobleman across the seas. She is still young, although she matures more every day. But you are needed here and surely she will not marry without you being present."

René nodded. "You may be right to wait on a betrothal for Evangeline. At least until the unrest is settled. But her mother wished her to marry French nobility and my promise to her is one I intend to keep."

Gabriel was visibly relieved. He said, "I must tell you that tension grows among the young Acadian men. Turnbull instills more hatred in his men for us. Thus far the incidents have been mere taunts or mean acts."

"And what would these particular acts be?"

"Monsieur Gaudet received horse manure in a large pouch meant to contain furniture orders. My father found the stirrups cut on two new saddles. Old Grandfather de la Tour Landry's hearing horn was broken in two and replaced on his mantel. Farmers have found their aboiteau hinges broken or holes dug in the dikes. If they had not been diligent the salt water would have flowed and killed the crops. Then we would have had a famine on our hands. And there is more."

René looked at him askance. "Did you not think it most urgent that I be informed of these incidents?"

Gabriel said, "You have had many issues of great importance. When you appointed me Vice Consul I believed my role was to carry some of your burden. Please forgive me if I overstepped my bounds, Monsieur le Consul. It shall not happen again."

René shook his head and clasped Gabriel's shoulder. "No, you are right. As Vice Consul you have done well. Please have the colonists sign statements of these acts and let us keep the list locked in the secret compartment. If British acts continue or become more violent we shall have ready proof for the Acting Governor this time. And you should institute a monthly visit to each farm and outlying town in the region. Other acts may have occurred which the colonists have kept to themselves for fear of retribution."

Gabriel nodded, eager to carry out this mission.

René turned his shoulders to face him. "Remember, we are to do nothing and say nothing that would anger the British. We shall maintain peace and order, but prepare for the worst."

Christine and Evangeline slowly walked down the stairs, their dresses sashaying down the hall. Midway to the front entry door they saw the Consulate office door was open and overheard the ongoing conversation.

Gabriel responded, "I have heard a secret militia is being formed to take English matters into Acadian hands."

René quickly advised him, "A resistance? We all know the punishment for sedition is death. The British shall execute them without a trial. Tell me who these dissidents are. You and I must stop them before it is too late."

Gabriel shook his head. "It is only a rumor. But French dissent is growing."

Evangeline furrowed her brow as she and Christine entered the room. Gabriel was first to see Evangeline. He was so stunned by the vision before him he could say nothing. He drank in her beauty and her natural manner that said she was unaware of the effect she had on men, particularly him.

René took one look at his daughter and for a moment he saw Eugenie. He blinked several times and lost his balance, holding onto his high-backed chair for support. Christine joined his side as he regained his composure. He smiled at her and squeezed her hand in thanks.

Turning to his daughter, René directed her. "Close your eyes." Evangeline looked around the room. Christine looked at her slyly, knowing what was to happen. Gabriel was as naïve as Evangeline to the secret. Evangeline dutifully did as she was told.

She felt René clasp a heavy piece of jewelry around her neck. She opened her eyes and looked down on an exquisite gold necklace of large emeralds encrusted by diamonds. From a small box hidden in her purse Christine pulled out Eugenie's large diamond drops and affixed them to Evangeline's ears.

Her father said, "These pieces belonged to your mother. They were gifts from the King that she wore on our wedding day. It is time they are yours." He hugged her to him and whispered, "You are the image of Eugenie, my darling. She would be so proud of you tonight but not any prouder than I am at this very moment."

"Thank you Papa. I wish I had known her. The portrait is beautiful but it is not enough," she replied. He nodded with understanding but choked on his next words.

"I love you, Evangeline and I know she is looking down on you from heaven with love."

He held her hands, then twirled her around slowly. "So beautiful, do you not agree Gabriel?"

Evangeline blushed. "Papa." But she turned a second time, this time more slowly to let the satins and lace swish against the wooden floor. Her heart was beating quickly. She wanted to know what Gabriel's reaction would be when she turned. She need not have wondered.

Gabriel was awestruck. Slowly he took her hand and kissed it, looking into her eyes as he whispered. "The jewels pale in comparison to your own beauty, my Lady."

Evangeline smiled graciously, trying to hide her inner awkwardness. He reacted as she wished, but what should she do now? She looked to Christine for help but it was René who interrupted the moment.

"Our carriage awaits, ladies." He turned to Gabriel. "Remember what we discussed. Bring the information to me as soon as you have it."

Gabriel nodded. "Tonight would not be too soon to begin, then?"

René waved his hand in approval. Then he escorted the women outside to the royal coach stationed outside the Consulate.

Evangeline said, "Papa, we can walk the few streets. The carriage is not necessary." Christine tapped Evangeline's hand and shook her head. Evangeline blushed, realizing her father wanted to shower her with attention tonight. The costly dress, handmade satin shoes, Maman's jewelry, and now the coach. She blushed when the royal footman assisted her into the carriage. She knew Papa was wealthy but she preferred the simple to the ostentatious. Still, he held the highest French government post in the territory and he did have to maintain the family image so she relented to his wishes.

When she was seated Evangeline looked back through the little window to see Gabriel staring at her from the darkened doorway. Her heart skipped a beat, realizing how much she loved him. But how long would she have to wait until he felt the same way, she wondered.

Gabriel brooded that he could have lost his love if René had accepted any of the Court propositions, or even chosen a local Acadian. He decided he would go to the dance but only for a few minutes, to speak with his Lady Evangeline. He knew he loved her but his heart was also heavy with his many responsibilities as Vice Consul. And, of course, there was that other matter with the Mi'Kmaqs and the Acadian resistance.

Once Christine and René were in the carriage, it rolled down the street, past the square to the St. Charles Catholic Church. Lights and music poured out of the large Parish hall next door. René had funded its construction to provide a gathering place for the Acadians after Mass and for occasions such as this. But he never expected it to be so enchanting. The hall was decorated as a night garden, filled with flowering plants, silken ribbons and twinkling candles in lanterns. Evangeline's bouquets decorated a gazebo at one end of the room, furnished with several benches piled high with gifts near a series of stuffed royal chairs from Versailles, moved from René's sitting rooms for the occasion.

At the other end of the huge hall were long wooden tables groaning with food and bottles of René's best French wines. Young Acadian boys and girls served the wine and food to the guests as musicians played nearby. Couples danced in the center of the room as their old relatives sat on nearby chairs clapping and stomping their feet to lively folk songs brought to Acadia by their ancestors from France over one hundred fifty years earlier.

Suddenly the musicians stopped and the floor cleared. The musicians played a royal entrance song as René escorted Evangeline on one arm and Christine on the other. The three walked to the gazebo under candles twinkling overhead like stars. René assisted Christine to a chair. "Rest assured I shall return to ask for a dance."

Christine replied coyly, "In that case I must save one for you."

He bowed to her, then escorted Evangeline to the middle of the dance floor. The Acadians in attendance burst into great applause. He acknowledged them, nodded to the musicians and took his daughter's hand. He expected it to be dainty, like the little girl he always considered her. Yet she clasped his hand with the strength and gracefulness of a woman, as Eugenie had held his hand at their betrothal at Court. Their little angel had grown up and he had missed it, he thought wistfully.

The entire audience hushed in anticipation of this very special moment. The musicians took up their instruments and began the strains of a lovely waltz. René slowly twirled his daughter around the room in a great circle. He was cognizant that many hopeful suitors followed them to obtain a closer look at the beauty.

René whispered to Evangeline, "My dearest daughter, you are more beautiful than ever. You have surely become a woman without my realizing it and for that I will never forgive myself."

Evangeline looked up at him and smiled lovingly, knowing that he realized she was of marriageable age. She teased him. "So does that mean that you shall owe me a favor of some sort?"

René looked at her sheepishly, not realizing that she was making a joke. "Of course, daughter. Tell me what I can do. Another new dress? Do you want a new stallion?"

She shook her head and spoke softly. "Papa, I blush at the cost of this new gown. And Maman's jewels. You are already far too generous with me. I only meant...."

He kissed her forehead as he said, "You are the belle of the ball, and of my heart. You only have to ask and if it is within my power, I shall grant your every wish."

"You must know your seeing me as a woman for the first time means more to me than any material thing."

"Yes and with your womanhood comes the responsibility to marry and give me grandchildren."

"Papa!" She was not prepared to discuss such a subject with her father.

"Dozens of Acadians have offered a match with their sons. Fine young men, all of them, but I have not chosen them. Nor would I."

"Thank you, Papa, but I have no interest in any of them."

"It is only right and my obligation to plan for your future."

Evangeline replied a bit too abruptly, "I do plan to marry, Papa, but when I do, it shall be to a man who loves me for who I am, not how much of a dowry I have. Someone who interests me and is devoted to things much more important than dancing. And I have much to accomplish before a wedding and children."

As Evangeline opened her mouth to continue speaking, the music grew louder and faster. René whirled her in the center of the floor, as the guests tapped their feet and clapped to the beat. She relished this rare opportunity to have fun with her father and did not have it in her heart to spoil what was for René one of his proudest moments, showing her off to the French citizens of Grand Pré.

At the end of the lively tune, René bowed to Evangeline's curtsy. Evangeline's eyes sparked as brightly as her jewels. They turned to the gazebo where a line of suitors awaited an opportunity to dance with the beautiful young woman, even if only for part of a dance. Custom allowed a man to interrupt a dancing couple and if the lady accepted he would whirl her around until the end of the music.

Walking back slowly, Evangeline kissed her father's cheek. "Thank you so much, Papa. Now, about my birthday wish that only you can make come true."

René whispered, "You shall have anything I can give. What is it?"

Evangeline asked, "Agree that I shall make my own decisions about whether to marry, to whom and when. Please say that you do promise. It is the only thing I ask of you."

René quizzed her. "If you are certain this is best for you?"

She nodded breathlessly. "Yes, it is, Papa."

"Then of course I shall do as you ask. Gabriel and I..."

Evangeline pulled her head back. "You discussed this with Gabriel?"

René shook his head. "I had considered an arrangement."

Evangeline glared at him. "Without speaking with me?"

"Hear me carefully. I thought, and still believe, you should be married. I wrote to friends at Court about potential matches. I did not want you to remain here when you could live at Versailles or in a château married to a nobleman."

"Papa, money and position have no meaning to me."

René looked at her with sadness. "It was your mother's wish that you marry a French nobleman of royal blood. To assure you were taken care of."

Evangeline felt faint. She could not breathe. She held on to René's arm. She was to be shipped off to France, away from her friends? Away from her love?

"Gabriel convinced me to wait. There are sensitive matters, political issues that must be handled first."

Evangeline said, "But you shall keep your promise that I choose my own husband when the time comes."

René kissed her forehead. "Of course, my dear daughter. But you must promise me that you shall not choose the son of a local family without first being presented at Versailles. If you find none of the noblemen meet your standards then you may return here and marry for love."

Evangeline smiled, "Oh thank you, Papa, thank you. I love you, you know." She kissed his cheek and René's eyes clouded a bit as he walked her back to the gazebo. Just before they entered it, Evangeline whispered, "Christine looks beautiful tonight, do you not agree? You would make a fine couple on the dance floor."

René looked at Christine clapping in time to the music as she watched couples on the dance floor. She was a lovely woman and he did agree. His daughter did not need to prod him. "Yes, she has assisted greatly with the preparations for your party."

Evangeline looked at him and said, "She has done everything for us selflessly. I love her, Papa. And she loves me. She loves both of us."

He said, "Please show the suitors your kindnesses. Do not reject them so quickly. It could deter their spirit."

She blushed as she nodded and accepted the hand of the first suitor in the line, Nicolas Hébert.

With a deep bow, René invited Christine to dance. "May I have the pleasure of this dance, Mademoiselle de Castille?"

Christine curtsied and said, "It would be my pleasure, Sieur Le Blanc de Verdure," and they glided out to the dance floor.

Other French couples in their finery entered the dance floor and swirled to the music. As Evangeline was dancing with Nicolas, Gilles Cormier tapped his shoulder. Evangeline nodded with a smile and she finished the dance in his arms.

Wishing to spend as much time with Evangeline as he could, Gilles escorted her back to the gazebo, where she was immediately swarmed with suitors seeking her favor. Nicolas sat on her right and Gilles claimed the left seat. Suitors appeared offering champagne and cakes or fluffing the pillows on her chair.

She was quite polite to all the men, though she often looked past them to the door as if she were waiting for something...or someone. The candles burned brightly, focusing on the guest of honor in the gazebo and her long line of suitors.

René escorted Christine to a chair at the side of the room and said, "May I ask you something, dear Christine, that I have been thinking of a great deal of late?"

She responded quickly, "Of course René, what is it?"

They were interrupted by Nicolas Hébert's father Daniel, who asked René, "May I speak with you, Lord Le Blanc?" René nodded, excused himself from Christine and walked with Daniel but after a brief conversation, René shook his head and returned to sit next to Christine.

Christine reminded him. "You wished to speak with me?"

René nodded. "Have you been feeling unwell of late?"

Christine shook her head. "No. I am quite well, other than being a bit fatigued with preparations for the ball. Why do you ask?"

Before he could respond, Monsieur Cormier and his wife walked up and asked for an audience. René excused himself again from Christine and spoke with them. René listened, then shook his head and they bowed and separated, the Cormiers going to the dance floor and René returning to Christine.

A continual stream of colonists approached René, some fathers bidding for their suitor sons and others couples paying their respects to their Consul. All who spoke with him privately left disappointed that the beautiful Evangeline was not to be their daughter-in-law. Piles of gifts were delivered to her at the gazebo.

Evangeline barely finished one dance before another young man bowed for the next dance. Evangeline was courteous and friendly to each but looked over the shoulder of each man towards the door. Still no Gabriel, she thought, hoping that he would still come in the last hour of the ball.

A weary Béatrice Gaudet walked from Madame Dupont's shop to the church hall, pleased that she had helped Madame Dupont finish the uniform repairs and that she had not missed the dance after all. She climbed onto a stack of crates and looked through the window, which had been opened to release the heat from all the candles and the dancing.

Strains of the music floated out to her and she watched Evangeline dance in the beautiful garden room. She tried to mimic the Lady's movements and swayed to the sounds. Suddenly the crates wobbled and Béatrice lost her balance. Out of nowhere, a horse galloped towards her and a pair of strong arms caught her, one of the hands holding a single red rose.

Béatrice looked up into Gabriel's eyes. She smiled and shyly placed her arms around his neck as he descended his horse and lowered her safely to the ground. Gabriel peered through the window to see Evangeline curtsying at the end of a dance to one of her suitors. He watched as Nicolas Hébert escorted her back to her chair in the garden gazebo. She was the center of attention, surrounded by a line of suitors. Nearby, the benches and tables were laden with gifts and bouquets of flowers. Yet Gabriel detected a note of sadness, as if the evening had not met her expectations. He thought he saw Evangeline look towards the front door as if she were waiting for someone. But he could have imagined it, so entranced was he watching her.

Gabriel turned to Béatrice. "Mademoiselle, would you honor me with this dance?"

Béatrice curtsied. "They say I am too young for a dance. But I know how. Well, I just learned watching Lady Evangeline. She is so beautiful."

At that Gabriel lifted Béatrice in his arms and waltzed her around to the door of the hall. Then he whispered into her ear and gently placed her down on the ground, handing her the rose. Béatrice gaily ran into the building, holding the flower in her hand. Gabriel paced nervously outside the building until he saw Evangeline laughing as she walked out of the door. She held the flower as Béatrice led her outside by the hand.

"What game are you playing, Béatrice?" asked Evangeline.

Béatrice saw Gabriel, who nodded. Béatrice dropped Evangeline's hand and then slipped into the nearby shadows. Oh, if she could only meet someone as handsome as Lord Gabriel.

Evangeline glowed at the sight of Gabriel and coyly asked, "Gabriel, do you send a child to do your bidding? Shall you not join me...everyone... inside?"

Gabriel smiled. "I would be old and gray if I waited in line. My father taught me that a smart man always finds the shortest route to his destination."

Evangeline teased him. "I am a location now, am I? A mark on a map?" She involuntarily shivered, feeling a chill after the exertion of dancing, then feeling the cool night air.

Gabriel covered her shoulders with his jacket. His hands lingered on the epaulets and he whispered. "I wish you the happiest of birthdays, dear Evangeline." She drew the rose to her face and inhaled its scent, moving to the strains of music coming from the building. "May I have the honor of this dance?"

Evangeline smiled broadly, forgetting her coquettish ways, and then curtsied. Thinking they were to dance inside, she stepped toward the door. But Gabriel ignored the formalities. He simply took her hand in his, encircled her waist with his other hand, and slowly whirled Evangeline around to the music. At the end of the dance they stood captivated, gazing deeply into each other's eyes.

At that moment Christine called out. "Evangeline are you there?" She walked out and saw the couple in an embrace. They quickly parted.

"Hello Gabriel. Have you come to join the party?"

Gabriel said, "Unfortunately, I must take my leave."

Christine told Evangeline, "Your father has been asking for you. I shall tell him you are on your way." She smiled and re-entered the ballroom.

Evangeline returned Gabriel's jacket, then walked toward the ballroom. She turned back to smile at him and lingered.

Gabriel could not let the opportunity slip by. He walked back toward her and asked, "Would you be free to ride with me tomorrow?"

She smiled with delight. "I would indeed, sir. And I shall prepare a picnic basket."

Gabriel had an afterthought and said, "Of course Madame de Castille is invited as well."

Evangeline giggled a musical, lilting sound. "I believe I am old enough to not need a chaperone any longer, Monsieur le Vice Consul. Until tomorrow."

She disappeared through the doors as Gabriel mounted his horse and repeated to himself. "Until tomorrow."

Béatrice watched from the shadows as a handsome Indian brave a bit younger than Gabriel rode up to him. Béatrice was intrigued and wondered why she had never seen him before. But then, the Mi'Kmaqs did not often go into town, preferring to stay in their own Village beyond Grand Pré. She heard that Père Rivière held a private Mass for them there every week at the Chief's request because St. Charles Church was too small to hold all the Acadians and the Indians at once.

The Indian told Gabriel, "I have looked everywhere for you. It is time."

Gabriel nodded. "I must speak with the Consul first, Kitok."

Kitok replied, "Do so quickly. The Council has been called."

Gabriel said, "We have long awaited this honor to speak with Chief Mahtok, though I wish the circumstances were different."

Gabriel rushed into the building and saw René alone with Christine. The musicians played a slow waltz as the end of the ball drew nearer. Evangeline was dancing with Gabriel's close friend, Marc de la Tour Landry. When Evangeline saw Gabriel, her heart jumped. She would have walked off the dance floor but could not be rude so she continued dancing, trying to position herself to see Gabriel. Marc saw Gabriel as well and they exchanged a knowing look.

Gabriel whispered to René, who excused himself from Christine. The two men walked swiftly to the door but not so fast as to alarm the party guests. Outside, René spoke quietly with Kitok as Gabriel mounted his horse. René and Kitok shook hands. Then René took his leave and rejoined Christine at the dance.

"Shall we continue our discussion tomorrow? All of the suitors have been rejected, which is an unpleasant task as their parents are such good people."

Christine said, "Of course, I understand. I should like to discuss something with you as well. But it can wait until we have more time and without the excitement of the ball."

The music ended and the crowd clapped, enviously watching Marc de la Tour Landry bow to Evangeline and whisper in her ear. "Shall I give Gabriel a message for you? I am meeting him later."

Evangeline whispered teasingly. "Thank him for risking my father's wrath to dance with me. And thank you, Monsieur de la Tour Landry. Now off with you. I am certain you have more urgent matters than a dance."

He smiled. If Gabriel were not his best friend he would have put forth himself as a suitor for the beautiful Lady Evangeline. Marc's family came from a long line of French nobility with lands in France and a successful boat building business in Acadia which had generated immense wealth for generations. But his friend was powerfully smitten with the Lady, perhaps even in love with her, though Gabriel kept such things to himself.

The final dance was announced. Everyone waited expectantly as René made a final toast in honor of his daughter's birthday and escorted Evangeline to the dance floor. This time neither was talkative, both thinking of the same thing -- Gabriel and his meeting with Chief Mahtok.

Marc walked over to the woman who had captured his heart, Evangeline's best friend Jeanne Lambert and he bowed, inviting her to dance The Lamberts had moved to Acadia and operated a small boarding house, the profits of which they had parleyed into buying and rebuilding properties throughout Nova Scotia. They owned many shops, inns and residences, as well as farms which they rented to incoming settlers. Their family wealth was substantial and although Marc did not need a dowry, he knew Mademoiselle Jeanne would certainly have a large one. She curtsied to him and smiled. They had discussed their mutual feelings though they had not disclosed it to either set of parents. Marc was waiting until Jeanne was a year older. He believed her parents would accept him on her seventeenth birthday so he only had to wait until the following year, 1756. He could do that. They whirled around the floor, content in each other's arms.

Outside the hall, Kitok smiled at Gabriel. "You know I am a Prince. Perhaps you should bow to me."

Gabriel flicked his reins and pulled his horse next to Kitok. "Well, Prince Kitok, my political appointment and my royal lineage require a bow as well. Even more so, seeing as our paternal roots are the same several generations back."

The two men simultaneously lowered their heads to one another, both grinning broadly. Then Kitok took off in the direction of the Indian Village.

Gabriel was about to follow Kitok when he saw Béatrice still standing in the shadows. He bid her to walk over to him and handed her a coin. "Thank you for your help tonight. Will you keep this meeting with the Prince as another of our secrets?" She nodded. She liked keeping his secrets. And getting paid for them.

Then she watched Gabriel gallop out of town following Kitok's trail. She whispered to herself, "Prince Kitok. Monsieur Prince and Madame Béatrice Kitok."

CHAPTER 29
Mi'Kmaq

GRAND PRÉ

ahtok Mius became youngest Head Chieftain, sometimes called Sakmaw, of the Mi'Kmaq First Nation at sixteen. His father, Chief Santok Mius, had been a living legend, old enough to be Mahtok's grandfather. He had married a young Indian princess when his loving wife had died and Matok arrived the next year.

At Santok's death the other elders of the Council chanted until dawn as they circled the corpse laid out on a hand-woven death blanket. His wife had made it in anticipation of this day, weaving beads and dyed and painted porcupine quills in bright colors of ochre, blue and green. She included the rattle of a snake she killed with her bare hands. The rattle would waken the gatekeepers of the spirit world to let her husband in. Then the Council members removed the headdress from the Chief's body and placed it on Mahtok, naming him their new Sakmaw.

The Indians called themselves a band or the "First Nation" and spelled their name a variety of ways over the past centuries -- Mikmak, Mi'gmak, Mikmaq, Migmak and finally Mi'Kmaq or Micmac. Their language Mi'kmawi'simk was originally written in pictographs similar to the ancient Egyptian and Mayan hieroglyphics before it became an alphabetic language.

Long after the Mi'Kmaq had lived in what was to become Acadia, Jesuit missionaries arrived from Paris in 1625 and converted the Nation to the

Catholic Church. After their baptismal rites had been performed, the Jesuits began to teach the Mi'Kmaqs to modify their native pictures to the alphabet and to speak and write the French language. Despite their conversion to Catholicism and their faithful practice of the religion, they retained many ancient customs, including the death ritual.

The Mi'Kmaqs became a prosperous Nation trading with the French and encouraging intermarriage, thus solidifying their alliance with France against the British. The women of the tribe were skilled in artistic design and were known throughout the province and France for their porcupine art. Their unique clothing and jewelry interwoven with beads and quills were items much in demand in Paris.

They lived in one room dwellings, cone-shaped wigwams or huts covered with animal skins or bark. Their chief food source was from the sea and they were expert canoemen. Their boats were prized by Mi'Kmaqs and French alike along the waterways surrounding the peninsula on which the town of Grand Pré sat.

Tonnok Mius was Chief then and he sat Santok beside him at every meeting of the Mi'Kmaq Council. Santok watched his father when he met with Daniel d'Auger, Sieur de Subercase, the Governor for the French King. The Governor had consulted Chief Tonnok before agreeing to the terms of the turnover to English rule in 1713. Tonnok assured Lord Subercase the Mi'Kmaqs would remain loyal to France after the British government was in place. When he died shortly thereafter Santok as Sakmaw sat his young son Mahtok at his side in every meeting with the French and the English as well. Young Mahtok did not understand the words of the white men but he had a general sense of the discussion. Tonnok sat his son Santok down; later Santok fathered Mahtok and trained him as well.

After the French delegation departed Chief Tonnok asked not Santok but his grandson Mahtok for his opinion. Mahtok's response had impressed his grandfather, who arranged for a tutor working for the French as a coureur du bois, an Englishman named Simon Bancroft. Not only did Simon teach Mahtok to speak both French and English fluently but he also taught the boy a variety of methods to obtain secret information from the English for the Mi'Kmaq's French allies.

Mahtok took Singing Bird, the loveliest Indian maiden in the Village, as his wife and Princess. She loved him with her whole heart and faithfully bore him twelve children. Unfortunately, all were daughters. Mahtok's ancestors, before their conversion by the Catholic Jesuits, had taken many wives. But as far back as Mahtok could remember, the Chief of their Nation had only taken one, true to their Catholic beliefs.

Matok was torn between his faith and his desire to protect his people with an heir. He asked the Grand Pré Catholic priest, Abbé Chevreaux, for a blessing on his wife. Abbé prayed with Singing Bird and Mahtok and blessed them. "In the Name of the Father, and of the Son and of the Holy Spirit, Amen." Then he told them to be patient for one more year.

Singing Rain was happy without the burden of a lacking son on her heart. She began to sing nearly the entire day long. One morning she woke and rushed outside. The Chief thought nothing of it until she returned and knelt on their thick bearskin rugs. She took his hand and gently placed it on her belly. Nine months later the heir was born. They named him, "Kitok."

The Chief's Catholic faith had become only stronger through the years and no one grieved longer for Abbé Chevreaux upon his death than Mahtok. So when he learned that a new priest was to arrive on *L'Acadie*, Chief Mahtok made preparations for a great banquet, so anxious was he to greet the new pastor. But when Père Rivière arrived, it was the Chief who received the greater honor.

The priest introduced a young boy named Sun to the Chief and Singing Bird and their family. The boy held up his hand, not for a handshaking, but in a sign of greeting the Mi'Kmaq way. Singing Bird examined Sun's quill bracelet and necklace and his curious resemblance to Singing Rain. Her family had bestowed the primary name "Rain" on the firstborn daughter of every generation in honor of their ancestor who had first married the white man Sieur d'Entremont.

The Chief invited the big boy to sit with him and he asked about his family. When Sun said his mother's name was "Rainee" the Chief was overjoyed. Here was a long-lost son of the First Nation, and a firstborn son to Singing Bird's family. The Chief honored Sun as Rainee's firstborn son in their tribal tradition by adding the letters "o" and "k" to the end of Sun's name and rechristening him "Suntok."

Matok, Singing Rain and their twelve daughters took Sun into their care, which pleased Père Rivière because the boy barely noticed when he was ready to leave. Sun was home, with family.

Mahtok knew Kitok had been sent by God as his son and successor to lead their Nation and arranged for Père Rivière to say Mass every week in their Village praising God for their future Chieftain. Sun was treated exactly the same as his new siblings, with love and kindness and much patience as he slowly learned to speak the words that circled in his head. Older than

Kitok he became the young boy's fiercest protector, never leaving his side, as he had watched over Gabriel during the long voyage from Le Havre to Acadia.

Over the next years the members of the Chief's Council trained Kitok and Suntok in the ways of the coureurs du bois. They were amazed at Kitok's quick study of details, hiding places and traps in the woods. And Suntok surprised them all with his innate understanding of nature and his love of birds and wildlife.

Thereafter, Suntok was put in charge of returning to the forest the small animals that inadvertently wandered into the Village. He studied the calls of the birds which flew overhead and within months he was a master at the cries of the hawk, the ringed owl, the crow and others. Suntok taught the calls to the other boys in the Indian Village and soon Kitok and Suntok were able to find each other in the forest by shrieking a bird cry.

To complete their education the First Nation's ancient medicine woman, White Bird, taught Kitok and Suntok about plants in the forest -- which to eat, where to find water in roots, and what poisons could be made from certain plant parts to use against his enemies. She gave him valuable lessons on curing ailments with herbs and roots.

At age ten Kitok, as the future chieftain of the Mi'Kmaq tribe, was sent to live in the forest for a month, required to subsist on leaves, berries and other edibles he could find in the woods. He was not allowed to have Suntok at his side, which the slow boy could not understand. He cried himself to sleep each night and no one could console him until Kitok returned safely.

Kitok learned languages easily and before long he could speak English, French and Mi'kmawi'simk interchangeably. In his fifteenth summer the Council accepted Kitok as the heir apparent to lead the Mi'Kmaq Nation upon the passing of Chief Mahtok.

On this particular night in August of 1754, the Chief had called a meeting of his Council on a grave subject -- the increasingly aggressive behavior of the English and its implications for the Mi'Kmaq and their Acadian French allies.

Mahtok knew well the history of the Mi'Kmaq First Nation, which was handed down from one Chief to another, including the massacre of some of his ancestors at Beaubassin in 1696. He hoped to avoid a similar unwarned attack but he feared the probability of such an event, because no Mi'Kmaq had been able to trust the British.

The Council decided they should hold a conference with a representative of the French government. They dispatched Prince Kitok to invite Vice

Consul Mius d'Entremont, not only because of his familial relation to the Nation but also because of his bond with the future Chieftain. The Council members arrived wearing rich ceremonial robes decorated with colored beads and porcupine quills painted in an array of colors. The Council members then dressed the Chief in their most ornate robe and the Nation's only feathered and beaded headdress, which had been handed down through the generations. Everyone took his place in a circle around a fire in the center of the bark wigwam.

When Kitok and Gabriel arrived, Princess Singing Bird ushered them into the hut and was about to leave when Mahtok grasped her hand and indicated she sit next to him. At first, the Council members were taken aback but a Chief's action was never questioned. The Chief decided to explain his action out of respect for the Council. Because the decisions to be made concerned the entire Village and since nearly half the tribespeople were women, Singing Bird's opinion on their behalf was important.

The Princess sat on her husband's left side and Kitok to his right, the circle completed by the Council members, except for the open place of honor opposite the Chief.

Gabriel bowed to the Chief and his family and then to the Council, saying, as Kitok had instructed him, with his head lowered, "Great Chief Mahtok Mius of the Mi'Kmaq First Nation, Princess Singing Bird, Prince Kitok, and Most Honorable Members of the Council. I bring you greetings of peace and assurances of continued friendship and alliance from His Most Christian Majesty King Louis Fifteen of France and Navarre. Our noble Lord and Consul Sieur René Le Blanc de Verdure sends wishes of long life and prosperity from your friends and allies in Acadia and France."

The Chief looked at his wife. Princess Singing Bird responded, "Our hearts and hands are joined as we welcome you. We are grateful for your friendship to our Nation. We are also proud that the Consul has chosen you, one of our own family, as his voice."

The Chief nodded, pleased with his wife's greeting, and he said, "The Mi'Kmaq First Nation thanks His Majesty King Louis and Lord Consul Le Blanc and heralds France as our great friend. Together we shall continue our long alliance and shall work to vanquish those who seek to disturb our peace and friendship, including our common enemy, King George Two and his kingdom."

With the greetings extended, Chief Mahtok bid Gabriel to sit across the fire from him and the discussion began with the Chief's first words. "Kitok has been guiding the couriers for Lieutenant Turnbull." At this Gabriel nodded.

Mahtok continued, "You know the British have tried to turn us against you. So we began a ruse. Kitok instilled trust in the couriers and when they slept he read their secret documents and maps. He discovered the English plan when he guided their main couriers from Halifax to Grand Pré."

The Council members and the Princess nodded, aware of the situation. Gabriel was anxious to know more. "What was this information you learned?" Gabriel asked.

"The English Governor Hopson has been too ill to serve. In his place Lieutenant-Governor Charles Lawrence called a meeting of the English Council. The King issued an Edict to force the French Acadians to take a new oath of ultimate loyalty to England," reported Kitok.

Gabriel's response was immediate. "The Consul has orders from the King to reject any oaths that prohibit our colonists from worshiping freely as Catholics or that require our taking up arms against our mother country or our honorable allies, your First Nation."

Kitok said, "According to the report of the meeting, the subject was heavily debated. But no final resolution was made as to the consequences if the Acadians refused the demand."

Gabriel turned to Kitok and asked, "How is it that the English took you on the trip? Surely they would guess you would read their documents at night?"

Kitok shook his head. "I speak very few words in English to them so they think I am a heathen who cannot read."

Gabriel looked questioningly at Kitok about another matter. Kitok understood his concern and nodded. "My father granted permission. You may discuss it."

Gabriel said quietly, "Kitok and I have been organizing the French resistance. My men await your word. They are prepared to fight."

Chief Mahtok looked at him. "And Consul Le Blanc? Does he know of this?"

Gabriel shook his head. "I believe he has guessed that it exists but he does not know the names of any members. I chose not to inform him for his own protection. He is completely honest and truthful when negotiating in good faith with the English. And the resistance consists of many sons of members of the Acadian Commission. They are protective of their fathers, who would be punished or killed if they knew their sons' secret."

The Chief nodded slowly. This Vice Consul was protective of the Consul and respectful of the Mi'Kmaq. He would have a long career. Then Mahtok unrolled a map of Acadia on the rug. Signed by Gastaldi, this was the most complete territorial map the Mi'Kmaq had in their possession. It detailed the waterways, hills and forests which could serve as refuge in time of battle.

Kitok marked several locations on the map. "English troops plan to bring men and weapons to a cove far from Grand Pré. Then they must cross these points overland to reach us. We will be waiting."

The Chief whistled. A dozen Mi'Kmaq Indian braves entered and bowed to him and the Council. The Chief murmured a few words in his native tongue to them. They bent over the map, looking at the markings and grunted knowingly.

The Chief told Gabriel, "They are my family and will support Prince Kitok to lead your resistance to positions of advantage and safety. Trust them as you do me."

Gabriel nodded to each brave and they returned the gesture, then studied the map again. The braves knew what they would be called to do and they were ready. They had not shed British blood in their lifetime. They thirsted to be the generation of honor that would avenge the murder of their ancestors at the Beaubassin massacre. All the while Gabriel prayed for a peaceful resolution without bloodshed and was determined the Acadians would not be the aggressor against the English.

The next morning the sun broke through the clouds, promising a beautiful day. Gabriel tied two horses to the post outside the Consulate and knocked on the door, expecting Christine. Instead, an eager Evangeline rushed out of the door, carrying a basket filled to the brim.

He gently took the basket and bowed. "My Lady Evangeline."

She responded gaily. "My Lord Gabriel. You chose a fine day for an outing." She handed him a bottle of fine French wine that she pulled from beneath her cloak. He rolled it in the blanket in his saddlebag.

They heard René call out to her. "Evangeline? "

She smiled at Gabriel. "Yes Papa. We shall not be late." Then without waiting for Gabriel, who was about to jump off his horse, she put her dainty boot in the stirrup and swung on the horse. Gabriel was suitably impressed that she could be so elegant the night before and so comfortable in boots and, were they her father's pantaloons?

He laughed out loud, causing her to look at him quizzically.

"Your riding clothes suit you very well, my Lady," he teased.

"These? Old things of Papa's I found in the house," she replied, also in jest. Then she looked at him with a sly grin, pressed her stirrups hard against her horse and took off. Gabriel bolted right behind her.

They galloped side by side and soon were riding at a comfortable pace in the flower-filled fields and hillsides above Grand Pré. Gabriel stopped several times to show her different points of interest, though it seemed to her that he was always looking around for something.

They stopped in a beautiful meadow in front of a small natural lake. Gabriel set out his blanket and Evangeline opened the basket, offering a vast array of foods. He opened the bottle and they enjoyed the wine in beautiful crystal glasses Evangeline had brought. They shared the picnic talking and laughing at times, and staring into each other's eyes at other times. She packed up the remaining food and he led her back up the hill. They trotted behind a grove of trees near a ledge with a vantage point of the cove below.

The harbor was busy with activity. Silently they watched as troops of English soldiers rowed their launches to and from a British military vessel in the middle of the cove. The ship's deck swarmed with activity.

Gabriel pulled out his spyglass and pointed it at the vessel flying an English flag. He saw sailors carrying boxes from the hold and handing them to the troops in the small boats. On the ship's deck Lieutenant Turnbull directed the activity, cracking his whip at slow-moving sailors. Gabriel then lowered his spyglass to the beach and saw Sergeants Wicker and Greenfield direct troops unloading the boxes. Greenfield opened one of the cases and when Gabriel saw the contents, he frowned.

Then he put away his spyglass and turned to Evangeline. Their eyes met and they smiled, finally acknowledging their mutual affection. He reached for her but suddenly Evangeline spurred her horse to take off across the hill. She laughingly said, "Catch me if you think you can before I reach your father's stables."

Gabriel shouted out in response. "I can and I shall."

She galloped around the bend and out of sight but before Gabriel could follow, Kitok rode up to him.

"I thought I would find you here. She does not know?" asked Kitok.

Gabriel shook his head. "I have not even told the Consul yet. Your information was accurate. Preparations for battle are well underway."

Kitok asked, "And the boxes?"

Gabriel said, "Filled with weapons, powder and other munitions."

Kitok replied, "We have no time to waste. I shall inform the Chief."

Gabriel said, "Leave the message for me before Mass tomorrow morning. The usual place."

They rode off in opposite directions, Kitok to the Mi'Kmaq Village and Gabriel to chase Evangeline. Back at his family stables outside the gates of town, Gabriel found his father Henri talking with Evangeline, sharing a comfortable conversation as if they were father and daughter. The sight warmed his heart. Gabriel had never seen Evangeline in the same type of conversation with René. He knew Henri adored Evangeline and had talked many times about the voyage and Lady Eugenie's kindness to him.

Gabriel had asked his father to recount stories of their adventures on the ship and their arrival on the beach. Henri's eyes always became moist when he spoke of Eugenie's death but he always concluded with Gabriel's declaration to marry Evangeline. And then Henri would turn to his son and ask, "Is today the day you propose to her?" Gabriel would shake his head and tell his father, "Soon, Papa, soon the time will be right. I shall ask for her hand then."

Evangeline saw Gabriel arrive but ignored him. She and Henri continued to brush her horse as Gabriel trotted into the barn. She turned to Henri, "Your son said he would be able to keep up with my riding but I see he has only just arrived."

Gabriel pleaded, "You must give me a second chance. The delay could not be helped."

"*Must* is a strong word Gabriel," teased Evangeline.

Henri commented to his son. "I believe you have met a woman with your determination to succeed."

"Father, please do not encourage her," Gabriel replied.

Henri threw up his hands in jest and walked out of the stables. Evangeline fed the horse an apple, whispering into its ear. She enjoyed the moment before responding to Gabriel.

"I shall think about it," she replied teasingly. "But now I must return before Papa and Christine begin to worry."

He looked at her in a new light. He knew he had been in love with her for years but he finally believed she loved him too. He leaned over to her and took her face into his hands.

He hoped she would not try to run away again. She hoped he would not wait any longer to kiss her. All of their hopes were realized as their lips met, softly touching, softly brushing against each other.

Gabriel wanted to pull her to him but also wanted to maintain their decorum. Their position and rank dictated restraint and he did not want to go too far too soon. But without thinking he found he had wrapped his arms around her and kissed her harder. She responded but only for a moment, then broke away, flushed yet smiling.

Gabriel lifted his love on the back of his horse and escorted her home. With her arm around his waist, they rode to the other end of town to the Consulate without a word between them. At the door he descended from the horse and gently let her down, then gave her the picnic basket. She entered the house, then turned once more to him. She was hoping he would kiss her again. She lingered in the doorway. "Thank you Gabriel for the most enjoyable day I can remember."

He bowed. "The pleasure and honor were all mine, I assure you. And now please excuse me for I must speak with your father." They both entered the building, Evangeline up the stairs to the residence and Gabriel into the open doorway of the office to see René.

*

Sunday Mass at St. Charles des Mines Catholic Church in Grand Pré was a much-anticipated event each week. Its beauty did not rest on any one particular facet of the service; not just the Latin prayers or the tall, burning tapers. Not only the hauntingly beautiful organ music played by Claude and Adèle Arnaud's daughter Pauline, or Père Rivière's always moving sermon. Not merely the fresh flowers placed in the Church by Christine and Evangeline every week or the songs sung by the Acadian community together. Not just the sunshine streaming through beautiful stained glass windows made by master craftsmen in France and brought to the Church years earlier by the Abbé Chevreaux.

Sunday Mass at St. Charles was a combination of all these things but it also presented an important opportunity for the Acadians to gather after services in the great hall. It was then that they felt the love of their friends and family after spending the other six days in the week toiling and laboring, often under English surveillance. Families on farms were able to see their relatives who lived in town. Relatives and friends met to exchange news from letters abroad or from family in other Acadian communities. Women exchanged recipes, discussed new herbal cures, learned who was with child, and planned wonderful bees to sew quilts or spin their famous striped cloth. Men discussed politics, potential marriage arrangements for their children and, of course, the continued demand for the oath.

That morning, Evangeline and Christine greeted Père Rivière outside the Church. René talked with Henri and Gabriel in low tones. They nodded to other Acadian families as they entered the carved wooden doors of the

Church. The skilled carpenter Thomas Gaudet had painstakingly carved the doors to honor Saint Charles and a litany of angels and other saints.

The men finished their conversations and Gabriel offered his arm to Evangeline, who smiled as they walked in together. René raised his eyebrows to Christine at Gabriel's boldness. He offered Christine his arm and they followed the young couple in. Christine longed to gaze longingly at René but she hid her feelings, not knowing how he felt about her at all.

The Church filled quickly with the Acadian congregation who left the front pews open for the nobles in their community. René and Christine were seated next to Gabriel and Evangeline in the first row. Henri Mius d'Entremont sat behind them next to the other noblemen, the large de la Tour Landry family. The Lamberts, including Jeanne, always sat in the middle of the Church near the Arnauds. Today Claude came without his wife, still in her confinement, and escorted the aging Madame Dupont. Béatrice Gaudet had brought Thomas and Pierre to the Mass and they took a seat near the rear. She had tried to brig her mother once but Anne could not sit still and insisted on gurgling loudly in gibberish during the prayers and the sermon. After that, Béatrice locked Anne in her room so that she would not hurt herself on the hearth fire.

Père Rivière began his sermon to the faithful. "In the name of the Father and of the Son and of the Holy Spirit, Amen. Today we live together, French and English, as one family. But a family can only have one head and all members must speak the same language. That head is God. The language is the Catholic faith. Let us pray that with our King Louis we spread that language throughout our family here in Grand Pré."

As the sermon continued, Gabriel heard a noise at the window. He saw Captain Turnbull angrily turn his horse and he led two officers with him, Wicker and Greenfield. They rode away from the Church.

The congregation was not disturbed as they responded to the priest, "Amen."

The priest distributed the Holy Eucharist to the parishioners and concluded the Mass. Before the ending processional, Père Rivière raised his hands to regain the attention of the congregation. He nodded and a fifteen year-old boy stepped up to the altar next to the priest.

Père Rivière proudly announced, "One of our own young men here in Grand Pré has heard God's call for vocations and has answered it. Let us welcome François de la Tour Landry, who will begin his studies for the priesthood in Québec, and will take his final vows here next year."

The congregation stood and clapped enthusiastically though more than a few young girls showed their disappointment. François was the second son of this French noble family who was of marriageable age. The young women knew that most second sons in French noble families either went to sea or took religious vows, but they thought that was an outdated custom. This wealthy, handsome man who would soon wear the black robes of a priest had been considered one of the town's most eligible young bachelors, after Gabriel and François' older brother Marc who had of late been seen courting Jeanne Lambert. But the girls clapped politely as they turned to look at the other promising young men sitting with their families in Church. Ah, Nicolas Hébert, and over there, Gilles Cormier, were still potential husbands. And gazing over the crowd the young women found there were even more fish in the Acadian sea.

The priest led the processional song and exited the Church, followed by François and the members of the Parish. Gabriel escorted Evangeline to a group of her friends and said his goodbyes. Then he slipped away to the side of the altar and out the back door. In a narrow alleyway he looked around, then pulled out a loose stone from the building. He put his hands into the cavity and found a piece of bark etched with a note. He replaced the stone, then again checked around him to assure that the passageway was empty.

He looked at the note and read it silently. He realized the mission was being carried out at that very moment. He had to find René and give him the news. But when he reached the doorway, he had a surprise waiting for him.

*

Kitok had planned to implement the mission while the Acadians were still in the Church. He and the braves were dressed as English soldiers, some on horses they took from the English over a period of months. Others drove wagons from the area. Kitok had been preparing for this day for quite some time.

The Mi'Kmaqs watched a repetition of the scene Kitok and Gabriel had seen. An English Brigantine was anchored in the cove. Sailors on deck loaded more boxes into the small boats. Other troops on shore emptied the landing boats and loaded the cartons into large stacks. Wagons drew up and their drivers waited as troops filled the wagons from the stacked boxes.

Lieutenant Wicker was satisfied that the first wagons were fully loaded. He climbed aboard the wagon next to the driver and gave the signal to move away from shore.

Kitok signaled his Mi'Kmaq braves. They quietly divided into small groups heading in different directions -- some rode slowly down the hill to the beach and others positioned themselves in the hills above the approaching wagons.

*

At the Church, when Gabriel reached to open the back door he found Evangeline standing there. "Does this concern the wagons we saw yesterday?" she asked.

Gabriel pulled her inside the back door of the Church and closed it. He looked around the small room, stored with candles, jars of oil, prayer books, and religious vestments. No one else was present. "I would not have brought you there but for the urgency."

She was petulant. "So our outing was a ruse? You used me to discover what the English were doing?"

Gabriel pleaded with her. "Please, you must believe me. Being with you, not just yesterday but today and every day, means more to me than you know. But for now please keep this secret. It could put you in danger."

"Are you involved with the Acadian militia? So it *is* true. I thought it was but a rumor. Why did you not tell me before now?"

Gabriel tenderly lifted a lock of hair that had fallen across her eyes. "I would never let anything happen to you."

"Then we must make certain the information is guarded. No one else shall know from me," she assured him.

Without saying a word, Gabriel placed Evangeline's arm in his and he escorted her out the door to the front of the Church, after feigning showing her some lovely flowering bushes on the side of the Church.

Evangeline smiled to herself. He must love me to entrust me with such a secret, she thought. Finally, he is beginning to share his life. It was the foundation for a life together she had prayed for.

CHAPTER 30
Plan

April, 1755 - HALIFAX

ova Scotia Lieutenant-Governor Charles Lawrence admired his image in the mirror. He repeated to himself, "I am nearly at the top...nearly at the top." He was proud to have risen so close to accomplishing his lifelong dream. He was fully convinced he would soon become Governor of the Province the French still called Acadia, though the name had been formally changed in 1713 to Nova Scotia with that blasted Treaty of Utrecht regretted by the English today.

Most importantly to the French living in Acadia, the Treaty guaranteed them the status of French neutrals, with free exercise of their Catholic religion, exemption from bearing arms against France and its Mi'Kmaq First Nation allies, and the choice to either remain in the territory with ownership of their possessions or to leave with all their goods and proceeds from their property sales.

But the English consistently ignored the Treaty, demanding that the Acadians sign the King's Oath of Allegiance which took away those freedoms. The prevailing English sentiment was resentment that the fertile Acadian lands yielded abundant crops sorely needed in the British colonies, which were expanding industrialized cities and reducing farm output. Such rich lands should be farmed by English, not the heathen Catholic French.

The expansionist theory was agitated steadily by the Massachusetts Governor William Shirley along with the Nova Scotia Governor Peregrine Thomas Hopson, who shared his views.

Hopson had returned to England after contracting an illness. He tried to resign but the Boards of Trade in London who supervised the colonies would not accept it. With Hopson's assistance they appointed Lawrence as Acting Governor in his stead. This was a bittersweet victory for Charles Lawrence, as he received the full salary but not the title of Governor. He was still an official subordinate to the Governor, but exercised full administrative control over Acadia, albeit still in Hopson's name.

Still, Lawrence believed that if he could accomplish the task envisioned by Shirley, Hopson and his predecessor, Edward Cornwallis who had left for England in 1752, the governorship would be his. All Lawrence had to do was convince or, if necessary, force the Acadians to sign the Oath. Lawrence had devised several alternatives of how to handle the "Acadian question" if the French Neutrals refused. He was ready to present his proposals to fellow members of the English Council for their approval. From there, he prayed His Majesty King George II would approve the plan and issue the necessary orders.

English colonial leaders had been discussing the Acadian question for nearly one hundred years, during wars and skirmishes against the French in that territory. Yet no resolution had been reached and all the while more French colonists and Catholic priests had settled in Nova Scotia.

After the Utrecht accord, the Treaty of Aix-la-Chappelle was reached in 1748 to end the War of the Austrian Succession and determine the balance of power amongst the great nations of Europe. This Treaty did nothing to benefit the French Neutrals of Nova Scotia who had not been aggressors or given the British any reason to fear an attack. However, leaders like Shirley and Lawrence knew the Acadian farms were vital to support the future growth of the other colonies and they could not afford to let the farms rest idle for even one season. The colonies would be impacted by lower food production and might even risk famine if their own crops failed at the same time.

Besides, thought Lawrence, the Acadians were led by a clever and certainly most intelligent Royal Notary and Consul René Le Blanc de Verdure. He was responsible for the colonists' consistent refusals to sign the Oath. Yet he maintained calm among the Acadians despite malicious wrongdoing of the British soldiers, which Lawrence continually denied. It was immaterial to the Acting Governor that Le Blanc had offered a petition of over one thousand signatures of Acadians on their modified oath which they referred to as the "Treaty Oath." Lawrence was perturbed that the French Consul had sent letters to every Nova Scotia Governor since arriving in 1738 reminding them that the Treaty Oath specifically enumerated the freedoms and conditions previously granted by the English. It was written in legal terms, like the lawyer that Le Blanc was.

Lawrence chafed at the idea that the old Treaty could still be enforced. Times were drastically different. Nova Scotia was not an insignificant outlying territory any longer. The Lord Justices of Trade had taken notice that Lawrence had organized the orderly settlement of over two thousand five hundred new English farmers, and built government buildings in the beautiful new capital of Halifax. He had also arranged that the province, particularly the region surrounding Grand Pré, become the major food supplier to the colonies. He made certain he was given credit that the seaboard cities, especially Bostontown, continued remarkable growth and industrialization, sending more goods and taxes back to England. All because he threatened to imprison any customs agent demanding a bribe to load and release transports carrying produce, grains, fish or beef from Acadian suppliers to the English colonies.

The decisions to be taken at the English Council meetings over the coming months would set the course of Lawrence's future. His preparations for the meetings could assure the right outcome and that the King would approve the Council's plan. Once that was accomplished, two important goals would be achieved. First, it would end the Anglo-Mi'Kmaq War raging on since 1749 when the English established Halifax on Indian treaty land. Secondly, and more importantly, the Acadian question would be finally answered.

Satisfied with himself, Lawrence turned his thoughts to the preparations underway for the meetings, banquets and rooms for a fortnight of hospitality he offered his fellow English Council members. He adjusted his ostentatious powdered wig until the curls framed his oversized jowls just perfectly. Then he gingerly placed his plumed hat on top of the pompadour and descended the stairway to the main entry of the mansion he had assumed from Governor Hopson. He always referred to it that way, though its official name was the "Nova Scotia Meeting Hall."

Lawrence had hired dozens of extra staff to clean every nook and cranny in the overwhelmingly large house. From the stairs he watched with approval as a flurry of maids and butlers passed. They moved in all directions carrying brooms, brushes, dustbins, candlesticks and all the necessaries he had demanded.

Walking back to the noisy, bustling kitchen built in the back of the official building, he met with the cook to review the menus for the Council banquet that evening. Foodstuffs were still being delivered to the back door. Freshly caught fish flapped in tubs of cool water next to a huge barrel of cod in brine, fowl squawked in their cages, a huge turkey sat in an iron pot hanging over the fire, oysters were piled near a bucket for cleaning and opening. Every table in the huge room was laden with baskets of eggs, fruits, vegetables and salad cresses and herbs of every shape and color. Sacks of potatoes lay in one corner of the room where a young girl sat on the floor and patiently peeled one after another. Lawrence chuckled, watching as a young boy chased an escaped chicken around the kitchen. Feathers flew everywhere until the boy knocked it to the floor with a large butcher knife, then chopped off the head, spurting blood everywhere. In iron cauldrons, soups and sauces bubbled over open fires.

In the next room where the brick ovens were, bakers rolled mounds of dough for breads, loaded them onto flat wooden paddles known as peels and flipped them onto the oven floor, quickly closing the door. Muffin dough was kneaded and put into pans before loading into the ovens. Pastry chefs shelled nuts and cut fruit for pies and chocolate desserts. The chief steward poured tastings for Lawrence, who approved each bottle of wine for each of the dozen courses that would be served at the dinner.

Walking briskly to the front of the house, Lawrence nodded approvingly. The new furnishings he had ordered had been installed on lush new rugs and carpets. Every nook and cranny was filled with elegant, expensive items, but none of them added up to good taste. Lawrence had a seemingly endless budget, due to the frugality of his predecessors, and he intended to put it on display.

He nodded again as maids carried fresh linens and flowers upstairs to the guest rooms. He inspected chamber pots for cracks and residual matter before sending them upstairs. New cloak and hat racks were set near the front entry door. And when all had been inspected, he directed a long crimson carpet to be unrolled down the entry walk, awaiting the arrival of the carriages and their powerful passengers who could determine his own future in government.

Lawrence was determined no fellow Councilor should want for anything during his stay at the mansion. The meetings were too important, the votes too crucial to his promotion. He stopped himself. What he should have thought was the great significance of their decisions to Nova Scotia, the colonies and England. He could not afford any distraction from their vital task -- to devise a plan that would resolve the Acadian question.

Governor Hopson and Lawrence had often discussed Nova Scotia's status as the breadbasket of the English seaboard. The other English continued to industrialize and expand their cities, converting farms to towns and plantations to new technology in mills and factories. Thus the crops grown and animals raised by the French Acadians had proved to be crucial sustenance for a large part of the other English settlements.

Finally, after Lawrence was assured that each and every detail had been completed to his satisfaction, the morning of the all-important conference dawned. The results of this day would tell where his career was to go. He had butterflies in the pit of his stomach, so anxious was he to obtain a unanimous approval of his answer to the Acadian question. In his mind this meeting would be the first of many that would seal the fate of the French Acadians and catapult Lawrence to the coveted governorship.

Looking around the room, he noted in satisfaction his servants immaculately dressed in the new uniforms ordered for the occasion. They stood at attention with their heads held high, awaiting his orders. Lawrence was a stern taskmaster who forbade any of his staff to speak to him unless he first addressed them. A strict authoritarian, he enjoyed control over all in his domain from servants to, he hoped, the members of the Council to respond in the manner he desired.

That morning a steady stream of Councilors arrived in carriages, each one more gilded and ostentatious than another. The sole exception was the simple black coach hired by the first man to arrive, Lieutenant-Colonel John Winslow. He took his duty seriously but he was only recently appointed as the newest Councilor. A simple, God-fearing man, he always insisted on pounding the brass knocker of the Meeting Hall. The gesture was completely unnecessary as Lawrence had stationed a butler outside and inside the house to open the door and relieve each Councilor of their heavy coats, hats, and baggage.

Though not officially part of the English Council proceedings, it was understood that the members had free license to stay in the Governor's guest quarters. Each man was escorted to a suite of rooms by a butler furnished by Lawrence. While the period could be several days, several Councilors, notably Lord Whitecliffe and Lord Dulcy, were known to require "rest days" for a fortnight before returning home to their shrews and their unending complaints.

Acting Governor Lawrence personally greeted each man after the wine steward had offered him a libation. Thirteen Councilors, including himself, and two invited guests from the British Admiralty, were present today. The Council, comprised of nobility and provincial leaders in commerce, law and military, was formed to supervise the affairs of the colonial Governor and to send their recommendations to the English Lords of Trade in London for transmission to the King relative to important issues in Nova Scotia. The number in attendance this day was impressive, and many more than usual. British military leaders had been quite active over the past few months and the presence of an Admiral and a Rear-Admiral would emphasize the importance of today's vote on Lawrence's proposal.

Lawrence wanted the honor of being the sole drafter of the proposal, but Massachusetts Bay Governor William Shirley co-authored the plan due to his substantial military knowledge. They had agreed to work together on the passage of their plan. Although he was President of the Council in Nova Scotia Governor Hopson's absence, Acting Governor Lawrence was also the meeting host. Thus, protocol required him to defer the main presentation to Shirley.

Glancing over the meeting room, Lawrence was pleased to see it was filled with important decision-makers. Lawrence looked around the table at each man, remembering their vital information in files that he planned to use as it best suited him. Now, all that information would come into play, as Lawrence needed every vote.

He had set a leather journal with a copy of the notes from the last meeting and a sheaf of papers, an ink pot and several quills before each member. Very few ever did any writing, since the Council had an official Secretary, but Lawrence was always fastidious in providing the journals nonetheless.

To learn about the Councilors in greater detail, Charles Lawrence had requested months ago that the Crown provide a complete dossier on each member. His excuse was that the Governor had left the Province with all information. A thick packet of materials had arrived on the next naval vessel from London and Lawrence set about learning everything about the men that he could -- their strengths, weaknesses, likes, dislikes, family histories and careers. He knew them well before they had arrived for their first meeting, which had been held three months ago. Half the men were in the British military service and the others were nobles, judges, and the overbearingly pious John Winslow who, though an aging Lieutenant-Colonel, seemed to put himself above or at least to the side of politics.

While Lawrence sat at the head of the table, the foot was reserved for a philosophical enemy, Judge Jonathan Belcher. The man had been appointed the first Chief Justice of the Nova Scotia Supreme Court the year before, in 1754. No doubt this was the result of his family connections in politics and commerce in the colonies. His grandfather had been a Lieutenant-Governor of New Hampshire and his father a prior Governor of Massachusetts and New Hampshire as well as, later, New Jersey. Belcher was a lawyer and was called to the Bar in England, but his family was not influential enough in the country for him to become successful at the chief bar in London so he turned to government work. He worked for five years gratuitously in a lowly position in Ireland until he was given the Nova Scotia appointment. Immediately thereafter he had set about creating a legal court system in the province, which brought him into conflict with Lawrence.

The two men had worked together on an issue presented by the English courts as to whether the English Council in Nova Scotia had authority to legislate for the province in the absence of an elected assembly. In January Belcher had agreed with Lawrence that the Virginia colony's precedent allowed legislation without an assembly to be valid. Belcher had issued his legal opinion as Supreme Court Justice to that effect. However, the Lords of Trade had disagreed, ordering Lieutenant-Governor Lawrence to work with Belcher and create the means to call an assembly.

Lawrence did not want anything to interfere with ridding the province of the French so he intentionally delayed moving ahead. Belcher proceeded without him and presented a plan to the Lords of Trade, which created a grave rift between the two. At present no assembly had been called and Lawrence hoped the Acadian question would be settled once and for all before it could be turned over to an elected assembly in the future.

On Lawrence's right sat the man he thought the most important in all of the American colonies, Massachusetts Governor William Shirley. His political connections in England showered him with commissions and appointments, including the governorship twice. Lawrence had spoken with him on earlier occasions about their common interest in the Acadian question and found in Shirley a comrade with the same intention as himself.

Next to the Governor sat an invited guest, the Third Sea Lord and Controller of the Navy, Savage Mostyn, who recently had been named Rear-Admiral. Lawrence believed he was a significant part of the plan because he controlled procurement and material in the British Royal Navy. He also ran the business of the Navy Board, so he was in a position to know the location of all vessels in the fleet at all times. He had come from a long line of English navy officers, including his grandfather, who had been an influential member of an earlier English Council. He had led the discussions to eliminate the French from Acadia when the question was first raised.

His adjacent seatmate was also an important guest, Vice-Admiral Edward Boscawen, who had only received his appointment two months earlier in February. The third son of the First Viscount of Falmouth, Boscawen distinguished himself early in the Royal Navy while his brother became a Colonel of the 19th Regiment of Foot at Fortress Louisbourg. He was known for his aggressive victories against the French, and was nicknamed "Old Dreadnaught." He was often quoted by captains engaging in battles at sea: "Never fire, my lads, till you see the whites of the Frenchmen's eyes."

Next to him sat Admiral Thomas Temple, who had held a particular interest in the Acadian question since he was a small boy. His grandfather had been a member of the English Council years earlier and had instructed Temple on the many debates the Councilors had on the issue of the French Acadians without resolving it. If they had, Lawrence thought angrily, the Province's wealth would be in the hands of English settlers rather than French Neutrals, who would have ceased to live on these lands generations ago.

The next man seated at the table was Erasmus James Phillips, a noted soldier and munitions manager for the English troops. In the spring of 1727 he had been assigned by Lieutenant-Governor Lawrence Armstrong to administer the Unconditional Oath of Allegiance to the Acadians of Beaubassin. Although he was unsuccessful, Phillips was rewarded for his efforts with an appointment to the Council in 1730. Lawrence knew he could count on him for a correct vote.

Next was Captain Alexander Jeffries, a former British lieutenant who advanced his career by marrying a daughter of the King's cousin, who was rumored to be his favorite. Jeffries was ordered to the colony of Mary Land and became its Lieutenant-Governor. Always at odds with the Governor, Jeffries was relocated to Halifax and appointed to the Council. Lawrence correctly surmised the appointment was to keep Jeffries him from meddling in established colonial business. Lawrence had been ordered to put Jeffries to work, which he would soon do in exercises in Nova Scotia harbors unloading and storing weapons for British troops.

The last seat on that side of the table was occupied by Lieutenant-Colonel Robert Monckton, the son of English nobility who enlisted at age fifteen, saw action in the War of the Austrian Succession and rose quickly to earn his rank at the tender age of only twenty-six. He returned to England to take his deceased father's seat at Parliament but soon missed military action and accepted the post as Fort Lawrence commander in Nova Scotia. He had earned the confidence of both Shirley and Lawrence, no easy feat, and became renowned for his strategic cunning leading to victory in battle.

On the other side of the table, seated at Lawrence's right was Benjamin Green, a former merchant who served as secretary and finance manager for the British military and was then appointed Nova Scotia Treasurer and concurrently a Judge of the Admiralty Court at Halifax. The English Council had voted him as their Secretary five years earlier in 1750, which had proved to be an excellent decision. Treasurer Green was thorough and detailed, and had excellent writing skills, making the notes of the meeting easy to read.

Next to the Treasurer and Secretary was William Cotterell, a notable from Halifax who kept to himself, made no speeches or objections and appeared to be easily influenced. Lawrence had befriended him since he had been named a Councilor and hoped that gesture would be repaid today with an approving vote.

Seated adjacent to Mr. Cotterell was retired Army Officer and Halifax Justice of the Peace John Collier. Though he had only immigrated to Halifax at its founding in 1749, Collier became a Councilor when Governor Cornwallis appointed him. Collier was known to have important connections with nobility and military leaders back in England, which could have influenced the appointment. However, his abrasive personality had put him at odds with Lawrence on earlier occasions, and he had butted heads with Judge Belcher over every legal argument, even the most minor points.

Lieutenant-Colonel John Winslow sat in the next chair, aloof, usually engrossed in the large Bible he always carried on his person. A newly-appointed Council member, he was a God-fearing man who carried his Bible with him and read it daily. He placed it with a loud thump on the table in front of him and took a seat midway between the head and foot of the table.

Lawrence disliked Winslow but not because of his religious ideology, as Lawrence was also a member of the King's Church of England. His contempt of Winslow was due to the man's loyalty to Governor Shirley. Winslow came from a founding Pilgrim family, of whom two had been Governors of the Plymouth Colony, but he had proven on the battlefield to be an excellent strategist.

Winslow still had close ties to Governor Shirley, who had promoted him to Lieutenant-Colonel of militia the year before and put him in charge of eight hundred troops. His success in that mission resulted in his new appointment by Shirley as Lieutenant-Colonel of a provincial regiment to serve in Nova Scotia. Lawrence was to find out that he would be Winslow's superior and when he did he would have to take care not to reveal anything to Winslow he did not want Shirley to know.

The remaining two Councilors present were first cousins -- Lord James Peregrine Dulcy and Lord George Naultin Whitecliffe. Their appointments to the Council were due primarily to their family connections. They married sisters who were their third cousins and who were both related to King George. The two nobles always enjoyed the food and fine wine at the meetings but they amused themselves much more while away from their wives.

Lawrence nodded to Governor Shirley who rose from his seat. Within the Council he was respected by some, feared by others and considered his fiercest competitor by Charles Lawrence. Both men shared the same philosophy of keeping this enemy as close as possible while at the same time engaging in an alliance for the same cause -- ridding the Nova Scotia territory of those heathen French Catholics to make way for new English settlers.

However Lawrence's strategy was fraught with problems. He was basically a fixture in Halifax as its Acting Governor. He had less reason to travel and so much deskwork to do -- a never-ending stream of documents to prepare and send to England for approval, budgets to draw up, supplies to requisition for the military, staff to oversee. There was no time for trips throughout the Province to build alliances with other colonial leaders.

Meanwhile, Shirley roamed all the colonies freely under the guise of establishing relations with the other colonies while his Massachusetts Bay grew wealthier and more important to England. Lawrence had no doubt that much of Shirley's travel was to improve trade for his own colony while eyeing Nova Scotia for expansion into new lands and greater wealth. Lawrence knew he had to maintain as close contact as possible with Shirley without raising suspicion.

William Shirley cleared his throat. The room was hushed. Not even old Admiral Temple complained about his hearing horn.

"Gentlemen of this Honorable English Council, I call upon Lieutenant-Governor Lawrence to open this meeting."

Shirley nodded to Lawrence, who hid his irritation. The Governor would have his moment to shine soon enough. He should not take charge of the Council President's meeting. Lawrence stood, briefly hitting his gavel upon its wooden base. He looked at Shirley, who had not taken his seat. That meant he wished to speak after the meeting formalities were complete.

"Hear ye, hear ye, this meeting of the Honorable English Council of His Majesty King George Two is hereby called to order at ten thirty o'clock in the morning of the seventeenth day of the month of April in the year of Our Lord one thousand seven hundred fifty and five. All ye who have business before this Council shall now approach or be silent."

Lawrence cleared his throat and turned to the Judge. "Will the Honorable Judge Belcher call for a vote to approve the notes of our last meeting recorded by Mister Secretary Benjamin Green?"

The Judge stood slightly and said, "I do, Excellency." Turning to the members of the Council, he stated loudly. "All those who approve the notes of the last meeting please signify by saying, 'Aye'."

Belcher went around the table, looking at the members, each of whom nodded and orally affirmed their approval. Belcher turned to Lawrence and reported, "A unanimous thirteen votes in favor, no opposals and no withheld votes. The notes for the last meeting are approved, Honorable President Lawrence." He bowed and sat down.

Lawrence bowed in response. "We thank the Honorable Judge Belcher. And now, our first speaker. The Honorable Massachusetts Bay colony Governor William Shirley." Lawrence took his seat and motioned the Governor to begin speaking.

"Ah, thank you Acting Governor, Lieutenant-Governor and Honorable Council President Lawrence."

Lawrence sat unmoving, waiting for Shirley to present the plan that Lawrence had thought of, drafted, revised and worked on for so many years, waiting for the opportune moment to present it. And now it had come down to the more respected, and feared, Council member presenting the plan, *his* plan.

Shirley began his address. "Honorable members, grave military matters must be imparted to you now. You will recall at our meeting last year this English Council unanimously approved a recommendation to His Majesty that we take steps to protect our borders from the French, if any encroachments should occur. We received a general directive to do so, taking measures of the greatest force, if necessary. Acting Governor Lawrence and I started arranging the details to attack the French Fort Beauséjour. Our own Lieutenant-Colonel Monckton, commander of Fort Lawrence across the Missaguash River from Beausejour, spent the winter with me in Bostontown making preparations. For the last two months we have been building our fleet."

Old Thomas Temple interrupted in a loud voice to compensate for his loss of hearing. "Governor Shirley, begging your pardon sir, but what does the attack on French boundary pushers have to do with the Council? Methinks those at Beauséjour are the Québec French, not the French Neutrals. That is two different Frenchies." Temple grabbed his ear horn and turned it in Shirley's direction to hear the response.

Before Shirley could answer, John Winslow spoke up. "Yes, do tell, Governor, what business do we have today with Beauséjour? Has a secret war been declared we are not apprised of?"

William Shirley bowed stiffly to Temple and then to Winslow and responded. "Gentlemen, if only the matter were that simple. Whether free French from Québec or Neutrals from Grand Pré, they are French and thus our enemies. Do we not agree on this point?"

As Temple and Winslow watched, the other Councilors clapped and cheered to indicate their agreement.

"Acting Governor Lawrence and I reflected that with support from other colonies we could forestall any other threats by simultaneous attacks on multiple French installations. I am pleased to inform you that on the fourteenth of this month I assembled a Congress at Alexandria with fellow Governors from the colonies of Virginia, Pennsylvania, Maryland, New York and North Carolina. They have pledged their troops to assist us."

Whitehall spoke up. "But sirs, are the attacks on peaceful French settlements in compliance with the King's directive?"

Dulcy quickly added. "Would we not need a full declaration of war?"

Shirley held only administrative power in his own Massachusetts but he was highly respected by most of the other colonial governors. He needed the support of the Council so that if anything went wrong, the blame could be shifted away from him. He could not afford to lose the status he held as he sought even greater power. His goal was to replace General Edward Braddock as Commander-in-chief of the Colonial Forces.

Shirley gazed evenly at each Council member. "You surely recognize that we cannot wait until the French actually relocate and build in our territories. It is unimportant that they have not actually breached our borders. That they are only meters away from English soil is a great enough threat that must be eliminated."

Mostyn asked, "Which settlements do you propose to attack?"

Collier chimed in quickly. "Who can lead the charges on each fort?"

Shirley relaxed his taut smile. This Council would soon be eating out of his hand. "General Braddock shall lead the charge against Fort Duquesne and Colonel William Johnson at Crown. I shall attack Fort Niagara, and of course Lieutenant-Colonel Monckton will take Beausejour."

Winslow looked up. "Would you have need of my service, Governor?"

Shirley appreciated Winslow's vast military experience; however, he might undermine Shirley's plan and receive the accolades for his success. He reasoned it was better to send Winslow away from the action. He looked to Lawrence to respond.

Charles Lawrence took the hint. "Lieutenant-Colonel Winslow, we are preparing an important mission for you to command additional troops in Grand Pré. The French Neutrals there have, of late, appealed for a meeting to discuss signing a conditional oath. We shall incorporate you into our plan to keep order in the region."

Winslow nodded, and then returned to his Bible.   Shirley continued describing the plan of action, but Lawrence turned his thoughts away. He knew Shirley wanted a leading military post, having been quite successful as the Massachusetts Bay's leader. But power was Lawrence's addiction and he never considered he would not ever be named Governor.

In comparing the two men, John Winslow would later say Shirley abused his office to benefit his own Massachusetts Bay colony and that Lawrence usurped the authority of his office to further his own career. No one took notice of John Winslow, who would soon see his last engagement in Nova Scotia before he was sent back home to Massachusetts.

Lawrence recalled his prior conversations with Shirley, who assured him the other English colonial Governors were anxious to increase their coffers with additional taxes from new settlers. The Eastern colonies had attracted streams of English immigrants to claim land grants. But the results were a near disaster -- overpopulation on existing British lands, the dearth of land grants, and an ever-increasing need for other territories for growth.

Nova Scotia, on the other hand, was rich with available lands, abundant farmlands, bountiful forests, fish-filled rivers and access to the colonies and the sea routes for trade to and from England. It did not take long before the leaders of the other colonies began to think as Shirley did, eying Nova Scotia as necessary for their own expansion.

Lawrence was aware of the motives of these other power-hungry colonial administrators. He had heard that Massachusetts Governor William Shirley was decrying the shortage of land in his territory. Rumors reached his ears that Shirley claimed he should like to rid the northern territories of the French.   Though Lawrence knew his position aligned with that of the Governor, he also was acutely aware that other colonial Governors were equally ambitious for the growing influence of England and its leadership in the New World.

Nova Scotia under English rule had had no formal lawyers or judicial officers until now. Governor Hopson organized an elaborate ceremony to install Belcher as Chief Justice and at the same time as a member of the Nova Scotia Executive Council. Hopson and Shirley had long discussed the Acadian question, as Massachusetts Governor Shirley wanted to assure that the legal system was in place so that any decisions proposed to the King would fall within constitutional guidelines. Nova Scotia Governor Hopson, who had already planned to move back to England and did not wish to be in the territory when the Acadian question was resolved, merely wanted the Supreme Court to take over his legal duties.

Though their desired results were divergent, their plans had been realized when in 1754 Belcher arrived and instituted a new legal system, including a Supreme Court, over which he presided. As the Chief Justice, he established that his court would issue proclamations of acts passed by the Council. As a member of the Council he was now in a position to write an act that, when approved by the King, would become a legal proclamation.

The Councilors rose to their feet, cheering and clapping, as Shirley retook his seat. Lawrence was pulled out of his reverie by the loud chants of the Council members. "Call for the question. The question, sir."

Lawrence spoke to Benjamin Green but intentionally loud enough for the entire table to hear. "Mister Secretary Green, we must hear the proposal in its entirety. Do read it back to us, we pray."

Green stood up and in a clear voice, read slowly and distinctly.

"The proposal of the English Council of Nova Scotia unanimously recommended to His Holy Majesty King George Two to resolve the Acadian question once and finally forever by deporting all French Neutrals from our soil by English transports as may be readily available to colonies along the Eastern seaboard; and further, that all possessions or lands that they own be forfeited to the Crown except as they may carry with them on board; and further that females of child-bearing age shall be boarded on separate transports than males age ten and older including children and spouses, to prevent them from banding together as families to return to Nova Scotia and reclaim their lands and possessions; and further, that all lands thus forfeited shall be available to be issued by grant to new English settlers, farmers and planters once the French Neutrals are removed from the territory. Thus voted by the Councilors who sign herebelow on this the thirtieth day of April, etcetera, etcetera."

Green looked up and down the table. "Of course this is presuming the vote is unanimous."

More loud cheering by the Councilors as all hands were raised in favor.

"Of course it is unanimous," said Admiral Temple.

"Yes, yes," repeated the noble cousins Whitecliffe and Dulcy.

Their sentiments were echoed by Captain Mostyn.

Winslow looked up from his Bible and nodded. "Agreed."

Charles Lawrence took a deep breath before speaking. "I wish to add but one clause prior to the vote, that being as follows. Before deportation we shall give the French Neutrals one last opportunity to sign the unconditional Oath of Allegiance to our great and holy Majesty King George, and if they do...."

A loud cry ensued from most of the Councilors – Shirley, Mostyn, Temple, Whitecliffe, Dulcy, Collier, Jeffries and Philipps. "Deport them anyway," Shirley said. "Send them away," said Mostyn and Temple. Whitecliffe and Dulcy cried out, "They must go." "We need their land," said the rest.

Winslow said quietly. "I am in agreement with the ends but not the means. The French Neutrals will sense something amiss if they see a sudden increase in vessels, weapons and soldiers in their villages." He looked for encouragement to continue from Lawrence and Shirley. Both men nodded. "It is my humble suggestion to hold meetings with their Consul and representatives in the coming months with the appearance of conciliation. The entire while our contractors, Althorpe and Hancock, can arrange transports while we devote our time to recruiting and training troops at Bostontown until we have the means to deport all of the heathens at the same time. Then we send in troops for repair works, nothing out of the ordinary, and take them by surprise before they can unite against us."

Monckton was the first to respond. "An excellent strategy, Lieutenant-Colonel. The element of surprise is crucial in a battle where we are outnumbered, as we would be here."

Lawrence regarded Councilors murmuring agreement. "And we shall deport them anyway."

The Council members stood and cheered, the applause lasting a good five minutes. Lawrence motioned to his wine steward, who arranged a waiter with a wine tray and glass behind the chair of each man at the table. Lawrence basked in the attention. Then he stood with them and said "With this additional clause, Honorable Councilors, please cast your vote."   He turned to Judge Belcher who was about to stand and said, "I shall request the vote at this time, Your Honor."

The Judge nodded and lowered himself back into the chair. It was the prerogative of the presiding official of the Council, the Nova Scotia Governor or person acting in his stead, to defer the vote counting to a legal authority at the table or to do so himself.

Lawrence could feel the thrill in his voice as he proceeded to name each Councilor from one end of the table to the other, calling for his vote. To the man, each responded, "Aye."

Lawrence raised his hand and said, "And my 'Aye' makes it a unanimous recommendation to His Majesty."

Lawrence signaled the wine steward and servants to fill the wine glass in front of each man. Everyone stood and awaited Lawrence's toast. Lawrence turned to Green. "Mister Secretary Green, please record a unanimous vote of thirteen for the proposal." Then he gazed at the Councilors facing him at the table and lifted his glass. "Gentlemen, this is the answer to the Acadian question. Your ancestors and your descendants thank you for putting those worthless French heathens in their place, which will not be on English soil much longer. Raise your glasses!"

The men all joined in the toast and gulped the wine as if it were of utmost urgency. The servants scurried, refilling many of the glasses. But by that time John Winslow had returned to his seat and opened his Bible. When they tried to refill his glass he placed his hand over it, refusing any more wine.

Lawrence told Green, "It is time for you to retire to the library and finish writing the official act for all signatures to send to the King." Green nodded and a servant led the way out of the room.

The main butler rang the dinner bell. Charles Lawrence turned to the other men. "Gentlemen, dinner is served." The men cheered and slapped each other's back in congratulations, following Lawrence into the expansive dining room.

The men entered the room, ablaze with candlelight to see a veritable feast laid out before their eyes. Fish and fowl, salads and vegetables, breads and desserts, with an abundant supply of wines. The effect was exactly as Lawrence had envisioned.

The Councilors clapped vigorously, waiting for Lawrence to take his customary seat of honor at the head of the large table. Then they ensconced themselves in the leather chairs and began to enjoy the banquet in earnest.

CHAPTER 31
Oath

July, 1755 - HALIFAX and GRAND PRÉ

harles Lawrence banged the gavel once, then again once more. The din had become unbearable as other members of the provincial English Council and invited guests from the English Admiralty animatedly conversed with each other. The Nova Scotia Councilors were eager to hear the news from England and the seaboard colonies and Admiral Boscawen and Rear-Admiral Mostyn were only too happy to oblige.

When the din still had not ceased, Lawrence banged his gavel powerfully on the table. "Order! Shall we have order to begin the proceedings?" The men had formed groups in the various corners of the large meeting room. When Lawrence stood and hit the gavel a third time, they sheepishly ended their conversations and took their seats.

All eyes were suddenly focused on their Council President, acting for Governor Peregrine Hopson. "Thank you gentlemen," Lawrence announced with great gravity. "This meeting of the English Council of Nova Scotia is now come to order at eleven o'clock on the morning of the third of July in the year of our Lord one thousand seven hundred fifty and five."

Lawrence pushed through the formalities of the meeting, then turned to Benjamin Green, seated to his left. "Will our Council Secretary please record the notes of this meeting?" Green duly nodded, his quill already dipped in the inkpot and waiting.

The meeting was attended by some but not all of its members. Those present included Lawrence, Green, John Collier, William Cotterell and Chief Justice John Belcher. Because the King's response to the Council's recommendation sent in April still had not arrived, this meeting was purposefully going to be short. Lawrence did, however, prepare rooms for all the attendees who were invited, as always, to remain in the mansion up to a fortnight after a Council convocation.

At this meeting, Lawrence held a letter for the members and guests to see. "Our Captain Murray in Grand Pré received this Petition from the French Royal Consul Le Blanc de Verdure. It has been signed by his Deputies and more than one hundred French Neutrals from Grand Pré and the surrounding region they call 'Les Mines.'"

With this, Lawrence looked up and said, "That is the 'Minas Bay' region in the King's language. We shall now read the text of this letter."

"The Tenth of June, one thousand seven hundred fifty and five Anno Domini, To His Excellency Charles Lawrence, Lieutenant-Governor of the province of Nova Scotia or Acadia, etcetera, etcetera, Sir,

We, the inhabitants of Grand Pré, Mines, Pisiquid, and the River Canard, take the liberty of approaching His Excellency for the purpose of testifying to our sense of the care which the government exercises towards us. It appears, Sir, that Your Excellency doubts the sincerity with which we have promised to be faithful to his Britannic Majesty George Two."

Lawrence looked at the members of the audience carefully listening to the letter. He cast his eyes downward and continued reading.

"We most humbly beg His Excellency to consider our past conduct. See that, very far from violating the Treaty Oath we have taken, we have maintained it in its entirety, despite the solicitations and the dreadful threats of another power. We still entertain the same pure and sincere disposition to prove under any circumstances, our unshaken fidelity to His Majesty, provided we shall be allowed the same liberty that the Treaty of Utrecht has granted us. We earnestly beg His Excellency the opportunity to present our Petition to him and if desired to the Council members...."

Lawrence looked up, removed his spectacles and tossed the letter onto the table. "Etcetera, etcetera, etcetera. The French Neutrals insist on repeating their same arguments. They offer to sign a conditional Oath to which they have given the moniker 'Treaty Oath' but refuse the full Oath of Allegiance that his Majesty demands. Now they wish to make their entreaties to the full English Council while ignoring the King's command."

Chief Justice Belcher picked up the letter and reviewed it carefully.

Lawrence queried the Chief Justice. "Shall you make a proposal to this Council for a vote?"

Belcher bowed. "With pleasure. We are completely on firm legal ground to dismiss this letter and its pathetic entreaties. However, I propose otherwise – that this Council invite the Neutrals to make their presentation at our next meeting and that we send a new written demand that all inhabitants of the region sign the Oath of Allegiance to England and His Britannic Majesty, on pain of loss of all property. Once they present their proposal, if they have not yet signed the Oath, we shall decide their fate at that time."

Lawrence nodded to Belcher, who called for the vote. It was unanimous.

*

In his office, Consul René Le Blanc de Verdure dipped his plume in the ink pot on his desk. He reflected on what was to become one of his last letters to His Majesty King Louis XV, unbeknownst to him at the time.

As had become customary, whenever the New France Governor received shipments of official correspondence for Acadia, he sent his personal coureur du bois Philippe Melançon to deliver to René the documents bearing the unmistakable red royal seal and to await his response. Philippe usually remained several days in Grand Pré at the homes of various Melançon cousins, exchanging news and giving him letters for their Québec relatives.

Philippe waited to be called to the Consulate to collect the official response. This time he would not travel beyond Grand Pré to the islands of St. Pierre and Miquelon but was instructed to return immediately to the Governor's office upon receiving the Consul's response. A French full-rigged ship sat in the Québec City harbor ready to take the correspondence to the King. Philippe had stayed but a day in Grand Pré because René was prompt in his response. Diligent in the details of his letter to the King's official for New France and, since the Cardinal's death, his superior, René wrote:

"To the Secretary of the Marine for Overseas Territories and Acadia:

It is my solemn and sad duty to inform you, for further dispatch to His Royal Majesty King Louis, that last month British Captain Murray, who oversees Fort Vieux Logis at Grand Pré from his base at Fort Edward, disseminated the Governor's new order. Our French colonists were commanded to ground all seaworthy vessels, even canoes and barks used for fishing and to carry goods and transport families between our towns, and to cease the transport of foodstuffs from one port to another due to the corn embargo which of late has been extended to all provisions out of Nova Scotia.

This naturally causes heartache among the families to lack news of their relations and also brings economic distress to the farmers and fishermen whose families depend on sales of surplus produce, animals or sea catch. The week following the order, twenty-five Acadian men from Piziquid on the other side of the Minas Region from our Consulate sent a gentle and reasonable petition, respectful in all manners, to Lieutenant-Governor Lawrence in Halifax pleading to retain their fishing vessels for food and assured that no embargoed crops would be transported therewith.

Upon receipt of the petition, the Lieutenant-Governor ordered Captain Murray to find their vessels and destroy them by all means necessary. Such fires have never been seen in these parts, and when the troops completed their job the only remains were so charred as to be unrecognizable. I had not been informed of the petition, though I would have supported their sentiments, and was only made aware of their actions when Captain Murray informed me by letter.

Unfortunately, our countrymen had surrendered Fort Beausejour to Colonel Monckton only shortly before. As Lieutenant-Governor Lawrence was victorious was of no mind to listen to pleadings of our people, even relating to those protections of the Treaty of Utrecht of 1713. According to an extract of the minutes sent by the Lieutenant-Governor explaining their actions, the men 'were severely reprimanded for their Audacity in Subscribing and Presenting so impertinent a Paper' although they had 'Presented it with Great Submission and Repentance.'

The interminable unqualified Oath of Allegiance to the Crown of England is, in our opinion, is at the base of all actions by the British. The English do not relent to allow our people to sign a qualified Oath as provided by the Treaty which allows us to practice our Catholic faith and which relieves us from bearing arms against our mother country of France and our allies the Mi'Kmaqs.

We are mindful of the document delivered to Governor Edward Cornwallis on the eighteenth of September 1749 which was signed by one thousand of our men, under my direction and approval. In that paper we informed the English authorities that we would leave Acadia before we would sign the unconditional Oath of Allegiance as demanded. The Governor demanded his Oath be signed within the month, during which time many of our families determined to relocate to French lands in New France near Québec City, the Chignectou region and Île Royale and Île Saint Jean. Governor Cornwallis became adamant that if any Frenchman left he should leave all his possessions except the clothing on his back. The French Jesuit priest Jean-Louis Le Loutre led an exodus of nearly half of our people to these regions. The British named the priest 'Moses' for the biblical similarities and placed a substantial bounty on his head, but he is protected and well-hidden from them.

And we cannot forget the acts of the previous Governor Richard Phillips who, in 1720, ordered the Acadians to sign the unrestricted Oath or leave the territory without their possessions within four months. We discussed at length with the late esteemed Cardinal de Fleury that when the Acadians began to build a road to exit Acadia, English troops stopped the works and ordered them back to their homes. Thereafter, the Governor accepted the oath issued with the Treaty protections, with his verbal assurances that our colonists would never have to bear arms against France and her Indian allies. To my knowledge that assurance has never been given since or in writing. The Cardinal referred to such British acts as 'English treachery.'

As of today, despite my numerous written requests to the Lieutenant-Governor, we still have no further news as to whether they shall allow our colonists to build new boats for their livelihood. No entreaty to English authorities brings results.

The Fort here at Grand Pré is absent a commander on the site; it being surveyed by Captain Murray from time to time when he travels throughout the Minas region from his base at Fort Edward. To us we hope this is a sign that the English have finally decided to honor the Treaty of Utrecht and shall leave us be as they did during the calm period from 1740 to 1749.

Therefore, mindful of our mission to maintain peace for the French Neutrals, we requested a meeting with the English Council to once again offer the Treaty Oath and have been granted an audience by month end. I ask for guidance and orders, should His Majesty so desire, as to any actions we should take relative to such 'treachery' as referred to by the Cardinal and any other actions in this matter...."

*

After the Consul sent his letter, Charles Lawrence sent a report to the Lords of Trade in London on the eighteenth of July 1755 relative to the French Acadians.

"The Inhabitants have since earnestly desired to be admitted to take their Treaty Oath of Allegiance. But I am determined to bring them to a full compliance with His Majesty's Oath, or rid the province of such perfidious subjects, the latter being the unanimous vote of the English Council of April this year and the third of the present month, subject, of course as always, to the will of His Majesty our King George."

In anticipation of a response from the King to this, the third letter relative to the Acadian problem, Lawrence issued the request to the Council members to meet again during the last week of July.

*

It was not unprecedented. The King's Consul had spoken before from the Church pulpit when there were important issues to inform all the French inhabitants of Grand Pré. Being Catholic they all attended weekly Mass so it was certain that everyone, except those too sickly or old to attend, would hear the news at the same time. But this had not been done in recent years.

On this twenty-second of July in seventeen hundred fifty-five, the parishioners of St. Charles des Mines Catholic Church were understandably slightly anxious when their pastor made an unusual announcement after he read the Gospel. "Rather than a sermon today, we have an important lecture from our Royal Consul. Please give him your full attention. Thank you."

The Church was silent. Even babies, who usually broke the silence with their gurgles or cries, were conspicuously quiet. René looked over the vast sea of faces. He saw friends, neighbors, and, hopefully soon, future family members. He wanted to protect them at all costs. He had promised his King. He had prayed for guidance from God. Then he spoke.

"As you know, ever since our arrival here in seventeen hundred thirty and eight the English Governor and military commanders in Nova Scotia have demanded that we sign their Oath of Allegiance and forego all freedoms granted to us in the Treaty. It has been decades and yet they still persist."

The Acadians all nodded gravely. What he was about to tell them sounded ominous.

Their Consul continued slowly. "And you are aware that we have acted on your behalf advising the English authorities of our adamant refusal to sign such an unconditional Oath of Allegiance."

The men and women and their children who were old enough to understand murmured in agreement, waiting to hear more.

"We have previously advised the English authorities time and again that every man, woman and child in Grand Pré and in the entire Les Mines region is agreeable to signing a modified Treaty Oath that includes the Utrecht protections granting us religious freedom, exemption from bearing arms against France or our allies, the Mi'Kmaq First Nation, and the choice to remain here with our homes and goods or to leave with profits from the sales of our properties."

At hearing these words relating to goods and properties, most of the men instinctively leaned forward to hear René's news. They prayed it did not involve property in which they had invested their life's blood, not to mention their savings.

"Recently I received another demand to sign the unconditional Oath. But this time there was an important difference. This time the letter was signed jointly by Lieutenant-Colonel Lawrence acting for Nova Scotia Governor Hopson, and by Massachusetts Bay colony Governor Shirley, whom I have learned was recently appointed Commander-in-Chief of all the Colonial

Forces upon the death of General Braddock during the battle against our French countrymen at Fort Duquesne."

The men murmured among themselves. This was disquieting news. Never before had two colonial leaders demanded that they, the French Neutrals, sign the unconditional Oath. Everyone had questions but no one was quite sure if it was proper to ask the Consul in Church.

Henri Mius d'Entremont looked around and heard the quiet buzzing and sensed the uncertainty. He stood, echoing the thoughts of the other men. "Do you think this is a sign of foreboding, that such high ranking officials make this demand?" He sat down again.

Gabriel rose next to his father. "Does this mean Lieutenant-Colonel Winslow is going to be replaced? If so, Captain Turnbull would likely be placed in charge. His cruelty knows no bounds. We would have to protect ourselves because his intentions are for war." He sat and looked around the Church at his fellow patriots, who were nodding vigorously, agreeing with his statements. He looked at Evangeline, who smiled with encouragement. He nodded to her and promised himself he would not fail her, no matter the cost.

René saw the panic in the faces of the women and children, and the anger in the men's faces at the English insult. He tried to calm everyone's fears.

René spoke quietly. "We do not yet know what this demand means. However, we responded that a delegation from Grand Pré shall present our response in person to the English Council in Halifax. Of course they still refer to us as 'French Neutrals' so I did the same in our request."

The men nodded in understanding and appreciation for the guidance, protection and generous spirit of their Notary in looking after their interests.

Evangeline rose to her feet. "It would be an honor to participate in the delegation if you would allow it."

Gabriel stood, too. "We know the voyage to Halifax is a long, dangerous ride by horseback. Only men should hazard the trip."

Evangeline retorted, "I ride as well as you or better, Monsieur Mius d'Entremont. Ask your father how many races I have bested you coming off the bluff."

Gabriel smiled, now more relaxed. "One, Lady Evangeline, only one. And you started before I did! But we shall race again soon."

Evangeline waved him away with a coquettish smile, a bit embarrassed but pleased that he was proud of her. She had started the race before him, it was true. But she had been determined to beat him at his favorite sport at least once. And in any event, no one contested that she was the best horsewoman in the region.

The congregation laughed softly at their banter, relieving some of the tension.

René looked pointedly at his daughter. "We shall discuss this at home."

Evangeline sat down with a pout. She had every right to be a part of the delegation even though she was not a man. She started formulating her arguments to convince her father.

René concluded his speech. "Our intentions are best displayed by a show of strength so we invite the first one hundred men ready to sign the Treaty Oath to join us in the delegation. Keep in mind the travel risks are great. And we do not yet have permission to present our Petition in person to the English Council. However, I believe that the authorities in Halifax will be fair and listen to what we have to say. Those who will join us, please step forward and sign this document." He stepped down from the pulpit and signed the document.

Père Rivière stepped forward and signed, then waved to the men to come up to the altar. Gabriel, Henri and Claude joined him, quickly followed by Marc, Gilles, Nicolas and other young unmarried men. Many of the older Acadian men spoke with their wives first, then filled the rest of the document with their signatures. There were signatures by fathers and sons of many families, including those named Cormier, Bellivau, Hébert, de la Tour Landry, Bourgeois, Lambert, Melançon, Broussard, and others.

René brought the completed Petition back to the pulpit and held it up to the applause of the parishioners. "Thank you all. Please join us at our offices tomorrow to prepare the details for the trip. God bless everyone. Vive la France. Vive l'Acadie."

The congregation repeated his words in a joyful chorus.

Père Rivière waited until René rejoined Evangeline in their pew and then the priest completed the Mass.

After the service Gabriel and Marc quickly exited the building. As they did so, René and Henri walked out together, discussing their concerns. Christine and Evangeline walked closely behind them.

Henri spoke first. "You did the right thing to include many men, rather than a small delegation."

René shook his head. "Then why do I feel such trepidation? I can only pray that this is our best course of action."

At the end of the street Henri prepared to mount his horse and ride to his home in the opposite direction from the Consulate. He added, "It may be our only hope to keep the peace." René nodded and shook his hand. Then the men turned toward their individual homes.

Evangeline and Christine walked in step with René. Evangeline looked at him and spoke in a quiet voice. "Papa, the English shall never agree to change their Oath. It is they who will make the demands, using trickery or forcing you to sign what they want. Kitok said their French translations of documents are not even the same as the English versions."

"My dear daughter, I do know there is risk in everything. But the risk is worth keeping the peace."

"Does this mean, Papa, that they will declare war if we do not all sign their written Oath?"

René looked off into the distance."Only God can answer that, my dear."

As they approached the front door to the Consulate, Christine began to worry. She turned to René. "Is this trip a safe one to make?"

He replied gravely, "There will be no safety if we fail to respond to the Council." He did not let them reply but opened the door for Christine and Evangeline. "Come, my dears. It has been a long day and you must be quite tired. I need to gather files and documents in preparation for the trip."

They linked arms and walked into the Consulate.

CHAPTER 32
Council

July 25-28, 1755 - HALIFAX

his was the week that Nova Scotia's Lieutenant-Governor Charles Lawrence would remember for the rest of his life. The time had finally come, and he could hardly remain calm. After the April meeting of the territorial English Council, of which he was de facto President while the Governor remained in England, the Council had voted to recommend what would later be considered an ethnic cleansing. The Councilors unanimously wanted to rid Nova Scotia once and for all of the French Neutrals and bring in new settlers from England and the colonies.

Lawrence had sent an official document, quite lengthy and with all the ribbons and seals that his office as Lieutenant-Governor and English Council President allowed, to King George. Of course, Lawrence had used poetic license and his literary skills to fabricate acts and attribute them to the French Neutrals thought they had never committed such acts.

The Council had no facts to present that French neutrals had actually violated the Oath they had taken years earlier or had broken the peace which began in 1713 with the Treaty of Utrecht. However Lawrence, William Shirley and Justice Jonathan Belcher had concocted a plausible story describing various and sundry treasonous acts of the French, with great embellishment, that had never occurred. They had no doubt the French had, at a minimum, treasonous thoughts to take back the territory from England, and in their minds that was justification enough.

Lawrence had written much about the need for the rich agricultural holdings of the French Neutrals, and that the colonies needed that land for growth and expansion, and that hundreds of planters from England would relocate to the colonies but for the lack of land grants. He enclosed the unanimous Council recommendation for immediate exile, forfeiture of goods and properties and severe separation of families to prevent the French Neutrals from reuniting with what would surely be a vengeance against the new English settlers planned for the Acadian lands. Lawrence added a final petition that the King issue immediate deportation orders.

Before sending the missive to the King, Lawrence had included input from Massachusetts Bay colony Governor Shirley and Supreme Court Justice Jonathan Belcher. That was in April. It was now July and Lawrence was amazed to receive the King's orders in such a short period for such an important matter.

Earlier in the week Supreme Court Justice Jonathan Belcher had sent a note to Lawrence, informing him the King's reply had arrived, apparently with an official Edict and orders favorable to their cause. Lawrence was overjoyed. He also was very proud of himself. He smelled a promotion to Governor, his lifelong ambition. This mission would end in glory for him...and for King George, of course.

Inside the imposing building Lawrence pulled aside the brocade draperies of the great meeting room to watch the arrival of the Councilors and their invited guests. The first was always the nondescript black carriage that Lieutenant-Colonel John Winslow hired for each Council Meeting.

Soon thereafter several coaches, each marked with the British insignia of King George II, pulled into the carriageway. Lawrence took his place at the head of an immense table he had purchased for the dining hall, with a matching table used for the Council meetings in the meeting room. He had purchased extra thick seat pillows in rich brocade without buttons or tassels. He could not take the chance on a member being uncomfortable in his seat.

The butler waited respectfully for Winslow to hit the brass knocker on the door as he always did, and graciously opened the door, ushering him into the dining room. Winslow ignored the expensive items that decorated every nook and cranny. Had he noticed, he would have considered none in good taste in any case. He believed the government should spend its funds not on fancy housing or furnishings but on the best marching boots and weapons money could buy.

After Winslow, a steady stream of English aristocrats and military men filed into the dining room, took their seats and began conversing with each other. A long parade of cooks filled the table with platters of meats, cheeses, vegetables and fruits. Bakers followed, setting out a variety of freshly baked breads, sweets and pastries of every kind. Previous meetings were strictly business followed by a large dinner. This time he spent a considerable budget to assure that the Council members and guests were refreshed and well-nourished before beginning the meeting.

Winslow ignored the goings on, preferring to keep his nose in his holy book. When all eight men had arrived Lawrence interrupted Winslow to give the blessing. He prayed as the members stood and bowed their heads.

"Oh dear Lord, we pray Thee bless this food and wine. Make it holy for our hearts and strong for our bodies to make deliberations according to Thy will and that of His Britannic Majesty George Two. Amen."

The men repeated, "Amen" and took their seats.

Lawrence nodded to his servants who began to serve the guests with expensive wines and rich foods. The wine steward poured wine into each goblet and continued to refill them as the Lieutenant-Governor had ordered.

Musicians played in the corner though the tunes were drowned out by the din of the crowd. Since the men all knew each other but only met several times a year they had much to discuss. They continued conversations they had begun several weeks ago. Some of the Councilors had never left the residence, preferring to enjoy Lawrence's hospitality at his expense than to endure a long carriage ride home and back again. Their topics spanned news of home, primarily London or the seaboard colonies, including births, deaths, marriages, promotions, mistresses, their sons' education, court-martials by the military and their favorite humorous, if somewhat bawdy, stories.

Lawrence had eaten little and drunk even less wine, only a toast to the success of the meeting. He wanted this conference to be the crowning point in his career. To do that he had to be clear-headed and quick thinking, especially with the uncertainties surrounding Winslow.

Once the men quenched their thirst and filled their bellies, the main butler led the men into the meeting room. Lawrence stood and with great gravity made his important announcement. "This meeting of the English Council of Acadia shall come to order." When the din still had not ceased, he banged his gavel powerfully on the table, declaring, "Order! Order, members and gentlemen. The meeting of the Council is now in session."

His excitement was too great as he chirped the news. "Finally the royal proclamation has arrived. What we have all wished for these many months, and what our ancestors prayed for over these many years, is at long last in our grasp. We have awaited your arrival at this meeting to proclaim the King's Edict on the Acadian question."

The men around the table cheered and clapped; all except Winslow, whose nose was still in his Bible. He looked up and asked simply, "And His Majesty's pleasure?"

Lawrence intended to make the moment as momentous as he could. "Our fine Chief Justice Belcher received the official edict." At that point Lawrence made a sweeping bow with his hat and relinquished the head chair to Belcher. The Judge, whose powdered wig was even grander than that of Lawrence, slowly placed his spectacles on his protruding nose, broke the seal of the Royal parchment and loudly read the proclamation.

Belcher began slowly, as if he listened for an echo of his own voice. He loved to hear himself speak.

"Hear ye, hear ye. Our Britannic Majesty having determined the French Acadians to be traitors to the Crown for refusing to sign an Oath of Allegiance...."

At this point, the Chief Justice adjusted his spectacles again. Lawrence became impatient, tapping his writing quill on the hand-hewn table, dotting it with ink drops until Belcher's voice continued.

"And for various and sundry treasonous thoughts and deeds...."

Further reading was drowned out by cheers led by the two Admirals, who jumped from their seats and clapped the other members on their backs with great gusto. Amidst the chaos, the refined Belcher replaced the document on the table without finishing the reading.

Lawrence banged the gavel on the table for silence until the members subdued their glee and retook their seats. Not being able to contain his curiosity and too impatient to wait for Chief Justice Belcher to re-adjust his glasses again, Lawrence seized the proclamation and read it aloud hurriedly.

"The French Acadians heretofore considered as the 'Neutral Colonists' and forfeiting such neutrality by their own actions are hereby ordered to be driven out of Acadia and to forfeit all their possessions and lands to the Crown."

Lawrence inhaled deeply before continuing to read.

"We further order that such Acadian properties are to be granted to English colonists loyal to the Crown in expanding the colonies as the English Council

esteems fitting and just. Further, that Lieutenant-Governor Charles Lawrence and his troops shall make known this Edict in all Acadian towns...."

Lawrence looked about the room, which was in near pandemonium. He banged the gavel several times until the Council members calmed themselves and turned their attention back to him. He smiled knowingly at the naval officers Mostyn and Boscawen for their upcoming crucial role in the matter. Then he returned to the reading of the document.

"...and thereafter imprison all males above the age of ten whilst the Royal Admirals arrange transportation by sea to remove the French from Acadia and to disperse them among the various English colonies, the leaders to be brought to England for hanging and all families to be divided so that they shall not know the destination of the others in order to reunite against England again."

Lawrence looked up and with a flourish of his hand proudly finished.

"Signed by His Majesty George Two, et cetera, et cetera."

After a moment of stunned silence the Council members erupted into loud applause, forgetting the decorum of their station. Each was celebrating while calculating how he could benefit financially from the King's decree. Perhaps he could obtain new lands for his family or arrange, for a fee, grants to his friends of the valuable Acadian land, animals, and houses, essentially everything the heathens would be unable to carry with them when shipped out.

More than one Council member eyed others around the table, wondering who would be able to obtain the greatest benefit. Many of the men wondered who would have to be bribed to obtain these valuable grants.

Slowly but surely all eyes passed from one to the other of the most powerful men at the table -- Chief Justice Belcher and Lieutenant-Governor Lawrence. Massachusetts Bay colony Governor Shirley was not present but he, without a doubt, would be a force to be reckoned with. The silent consensus seemed to be that one or all of these men had the authority, and if not they would be able to justify the power, to enrich their fellow Council members -- at a price, of course.

Then Lawrence motioned for Admiral Boscawen and Vice-Admiral Mostyn to join him at the head of the table. "We shall now determine the strategy and operations. How and when do we rid the colony of the heathens?"

In unison the men at the table shouted a response. "As soon as possible!"

Lawrence continued, "And there is the question of tides and weather, food stores, and troops required on the ground to keep the peace until we surprise the dirty Frenchies with their just desserts."

Boscawen spoke first. "We will reset the naval schedule to send the contractors all transports not already scheduled for new colonists. But we have very little time, sir. Most likely we will only have transports for animals and goods, without any passenger comforts or accommodations."

Lawrence replied coldly, "The French will get as they have given. If they must be dumped into cattle dung in the holds, so shall it be done. Ours is not to provide the same quality transport as we do for our loyal subjects. The French are traitors and should be treated as such."

Mostyn said, "Lieutenant-Governor Lawrence, we shall await your accountants to distribute monies to buy foodstuffs for the journey. Even bread and water shall be costly for ten to twelve thousand French persons...."

Boscawen jumped up. "Twelve thousand heathens? Are you certain? But how shall we ever find enough transports to deport them all?"

Mostyn nodded. "Or pay for the food to give them on the voyage? Is that the correct population count?"

Lawrence turned to the Admirals and tried to reason with them. "The last census was eighteen thousand, but we think the census takers counted the same families twice so the actual number should be much lower. Confusion abounded during the count with so many families having the same last name -- Hébert, Broussard, Le Blanc, Melançon, Gaudet, and such."

Mostyn nodded thoughtfully. "We could certainly procure cheap provisions like old potatoes and dried pork to ration every other day."

Lawrence agreed. "Yes, and let us not forget that many of the elderly and infirmed Acadians have probably died since they were counted. Surely more will pass away in the cold as the loading will take place at the onset of winter. Thus, you should finally ship several thousand less than expected."

Boscawen said, "But many more have no doubt been born to take their place. Those French families breed like wild rabbits. When one of their little ones dies of a fever they have two more."

Belcher retorted, "All true. I have heard the average Acadian family has fifteen children. Those are deep roots that must be pulled out at the core and separated forever."

John Collier, who rarely spoke at a Council meeting, quietly asked, "How does one determine who is related to whom? Are they not incestuous breeders? It seems they are all related to each other. Putting a cousin on a transport with an uncle hardly seems like dividing families to me. They will still be bound together by blood."

Lawrence responded, "The plan is to separate the men from the women, as the women will not be likely to resist. Then we shall pull fathers from sons and brothers from each other and dispatch them to different colonies. After the men are shipped out, we shall bring the transports back for the women, young children and the aged. The same separation process will occur. In the end, each shall be unaware of the destination of his relations. This shall make it nigh impossible for those large families to reunite and return with a vengeance to reclaim their lands."

Around the table loud applause and cheers rang out from the members as Lawrence turned to the Admirals. Mostyn spoke up. "You should be able to expand the capacity of the holds by adding additional floors within the same space to double or triple the size...."

The Chief Justice interrupted. "Are you saying you can rebuild the holds to fit three times the heathens as animals in the same space? Pray tell, explain how that is so."

Lawrence nodded. "Yes, we must be assured they cannot escape and return to repopulate lands that our planters need."

Winslow asked, "How much room would they have to move around, relieve themselves, and such?"

Mostyn turned to him. "Have no fear. The Acadians will not be able to move, much less escape, as none of the boxes will have windows. The only entrance and exit will be the door of the hold, which shall remain locked."

Lawrence looked to Boscawen and Mostyn. "The Admirals, having more familiarity with the dimensions of cattle ships, should be best suited to give us more information, I believe."

Boscawen and Mostyn huddled together, whispering, drawing sketches on paper, and alternately nodding and shaking their heads. After a few minutes, Boscawen addressed the Council first. "The wooden feed and water troughs in the holds at present are not necessary. Or the bulkheads. They can be removed, which will add about twelve feet to the length of the hold of an average animal transport."

Mostyn picked up where Boscawen stopped. "We can build two additional floors within each hold by reducing the height of each level to four feet or so. Essentially we would create three boxes, each about twenty and four foot wide by sixty foot long, after removing the troughs."

Winslow looked at his fellow Council members, aghast. He pressed his Bible close to his heart inside his jacket. "Gentlemen, we must remember that the prisoners deserve our sympathy. They may be heathens and thus, lesser creatures, although they are not exactly animals. Surely to box hundreds of men in a cramped four-foot high windowless box with no separate places for eating and relieving themselves is the equivalent of a death sentence. If one were to become ill, or be boarded while sick, they should all soon pass away from the same disease."

Lawrence peered at Winslow. "Sir, if I did not know better I would think that you did not have the iron will to be the military commander that you are."

Belcher gazed directly at Winslow from above his spectacles. "I should think you could cipher that an epidemic in a cell should provide more room for the living. No harm in the strongest animals surviving."

Mostyn nodded in agreement. "We are dreadfully low on stores this winter. Fewer mouths to feed should not be a bad thing."

Lawrence grunted approval of his supporters. "What we do not have to spend on foodstuffs for the heathens shall bolster our coffers here. We must make you gentlemen comfortable when you attend our Council convocations, as you can see." He motioned for the waiters to serve more wine.

Winslow shook his head rapidly. He did not want to lose his rank or his future pension. "Sirs, please forgive me. I have misspoken ruminations that were clearly confusion on my part and meant to be kept silent."

Lawrence asked Winslow, "So you shall take no issue with being charged to carry out the King's Edict?"

Winslow bowed. "It would be my honor to serve, Excellency."

The Admirals nodded. They were not used to implementing such cruel treatment but they intended to carry out their orders to the letter. This was a mission close to the King's heart and they would do all in their power to aid in its success.

Lawrence turned to Winslow. "If your men provoke the young hot-blooded Frenchmen to physical altercations, that is reason enough to justify hanging them for legal cause. Respect of the King's officers and the safety of the English living in Grand Pré are of utmost importance, are they not?"

Winslow scowled and mumbled, "This business is very disagreeable to my natural make and temper."

Lawrence overheard the complaint and turned to address Winslow. "We have heard much about one Turnbull in the King's service in the region. Perhaps he has the constitution to best handle these matters?"

Winslow shook his head silently. "I am your man, sir."

Lawrence continued, "Then we shall send our Captain Adams with a contingent of troops to assist you in the preparations. Once the first ships have sailed exiling the men from Grand Pré, Captain Phinneas Osgood shall replace you."

Winslow bowed respectfully. He did not want to be cast off after a lifetime of service. "Shall I report directly to you, Lieutenant-Governor?"

"Most certainly not. You shall serve under Lt. Colonel Robert Monckton. It is he who shall keep us apprised of your activities. Perhaps that journal of yours can come to some good use then? Keep uppermost in your mind this is the most important mission of your career. His Royal Majesty has commanded it!"

Winslow started to argue that Monckton was decades younger, an insolent puppy that had no experience with the French Neutrals. Yet even as the youngest commander, he had been the sole success in the Council of Alexandria's four battles only two weeks earlier. Winslow knew he had an ally in Governor Shirley should any problem arise so he responded with a bow. "Of course I shall be honored to carry out the orders given to me, sir."

Lawrence nodded haughtily. "We thought as much."

Mostyn raised a glass and the others followed his lead. "To our future Governor Lawrence."

Lawrence feigned humility but drank to the toast. Then he responded in a loud voice saying, "For the glory of our King, here is to our Great and Noble Scheme."

The men stood and repeated in unison, "Our Great and Noble Scheme."

Chief Justice Belcher raised a legal issue. "The seditious criminals should be hanged in the most public place, do you not think, such as the Westminster Gatehouse, for all of London to see? Surely the King would approve showing the power of England over the French."

The men pounded their fists into the table in agreement. "Hear, hear," they cried out together, "Hear, hear."

Winslow stood to make a different point. "Governor Shirley of the Massachusetts Bay colony met with me in Bostontown. He requested that we send them more labor for their plantations. Most indentured servants are about to be released and the Africans they imported for work have not been able to survive the harsh winters. Would it not be sensible to ship the Frenchies to Bostontown?"

Lawrence pondered before he answered. Clearly Winslow still had close ties to Governor Shirley, who had appointed him Major-General the year before and put him in charge of eight hundred troops to build forts and prevent French encroachment on English territory. His success in that mission resulted in his promotion by Shirley in less than a year to Lieutenant-Colonel of a provincial regiment. And it was Shirley who had chosen Winslow to execute the deportation in Grand Pré.

Lawrence nodded to Winslow. "Yes, thank you sir. We have begun preparations to resolve that very problem. Our friend in the Colony, Jonas Cornhandle, has arranged to sell as slaves the Acadians who are shipped to Bostontown. By law, persons of the Catholic religion are not allowed in the city, so he has set about building auction blocks on the wharf. The heathens will be stripped so buyers can see the wares they are purchasing. Then they shall take their new French slaves directly to their plantations without affecting the sensibilities of the citizens in town."

Winslow asked, "This Cornhandle. Would he happen to be any relation to the man running the general store in the Grand Pré English Quarter?"

Lawrence looked at Winslow. What did it matter who was related to the slave trader? The point was that the Nova Scotia would finally be rid of the abhorrent Acadians, who would finally get their due. If they survived the sea voyage, that is. Lawrence was anxious to move forward so he answered quickly. "It is possible, yes." Then he turned to Admiral Boscawen. "And to continue, Admiral, have you additional information for us?"

Admiral Boscawen stood and the men gave him their attention. "We suggest sending one group of prisoners directly to France, depositing them on one of their outlying islands before we sail to England. The strength of our Navy would be proven by entering French waters undetected with a boatload of their own citizens and then departing secretly before their King Louis even learns we have been there."

Lawrence nodded and looked to the others. "The idea is appealing to us." The other Councilors murmured their agreement to one another.

Belcher agreed. "These heathens should not have refused our Oath of Allegiance. But even if they agree to it at this late hour they are still guilty of treason and should be punished moreso than simply being driven from their homes. Lieutenant-Colonel Winslow, if you and your officers bring me proof of French acts against the Crown in Nova Scotia, I assure you my justice shall be swift."

Winslow ignored him but the rest of the Council members approved the plan by acclamation, hammering their fists on the table, some of them quite drunk on the wine. Lawrence signaled his waiters to pour more wine since he was meeting no resistance on the Acadian question by those who emptied their glasses. Then he raised his glass and made a toast. "To success in our greatest mission for His Majesty's glory."

The men responded, "To success and His Majesty's glory!"

Lawrence brushed his hands together, glad to be rid of the matter. He nodded and Winslow bowed his head to pray.

Lawrence was interrupted by the butler, Simon, who bowed and whispered in the Lieutenant-Governor's ear. Lawrence quickly interrupted the prayer. "My apologies, gentlemen. It seems we have visitors. The very heathens we have been discussing are at the door. Please carry on in my absence and close out the meeting."

Raising his Bible above his head, Winslow prayed piously. "King George, the head of the one true Church has ordered us to rid our lands of the Romanists. We pray for the courage to carry out this mission for King and country."

The members of the Council finished the prayer. "Amen."

In the hallway Lawrence followed Simon, who turned to him in apology."Forgive me Lieutenant-Governor Lawrence, but I felt it best to keep these, these dirty...."

Lawrence filled in the word for him. "French Neutrals?"

The butler nodded, "...to keep them in the room off the kitchen rather than in the receiving salon until I had your permission."

Lawrence patted the man on the shoulder. "You are a good man, Simon. But we wish to see them in the Council meeting room. Please escort them in. However, no food or drink for those heathens, do you understand?"

Simon smiled. His superior was quite cruel but he would follow him to the ends of the earth if requested. Simon waited until Lawrence had entered the meeting room then he closed the door and returned to the kitchen. He made sure he was wearing gloves. He did not want to catch the diseases he heard those dirty Frenchmen carried.

In the meeting room, Lawrence addressed the group. "Gentlemen, this should amuse you. I ask your indulgence for a few minutes more. The French Neutrals have brought a Delegation of one hundred men led by their Consul, René Le Blanc de Verdure. They beg your permission to present their Petition."

The sound of merry laughing exploded as the Councilors and the invited guests enjoyed the thought. Belcher waved his approval. There was a knock and Simon entered leading dozens of French Acadians from Grand Pré into the huge Council room.

The Consul presented his French papers from King Louis XV to the Acting Governor Charles Lawrence. Le Blanc bowed out of respect, Lawrence out of custom. He would not have bowed to a dirty Frenchman for any other reason. But no one told him he would have to like diplomacy.

In a loud clear voice, Royal Consul Le Blanc de Verdure presented the Petition.

"Today Your Excellency and most honorable members and guests of the Nova Scotia English Council, today you have the opportunity to change the course of history forever. We are one hundred of the most notable men in Grand Pré, including our French officials representing His Majesty Louis Fifteen, King of France and Navarre, praying that you please hear and favorably accept our Petition. We present you with this Treaty Oath of Allegiance signed by us, to which shall be soon added the names of each man, woman and child in the territory old enough to sign or make a mark.

We hereby sign this Treaty Oath of Allegiance to His Britannic Majesty King George Two, pledging our undying loyalty and friendship as neutrals residing in the English territory of Nova Scotia, with the free exercise of our Catholic faith, our exemption from bearing arms against our mother country France and her allies the Mi'Kmaq First Nation, and the ability to live peaceably with full ownership of our lands and possessions or, at our choice, to remove ourselves from this territory with our movable possessions and proceeds from the sale of our lands and properties, all as guaranteed in the Treaty of Utrecht executed by Her Britannic Majesty Queen Anne in the year of Our Lord one thousand seven hundred and thirteen. We humbly pray thee accept our Petition and allow us to continue living peacefully and shipping our crops and animals to your Eastern seaboard colonies while we all live in harmony. This we pray."

The Consul handed the Petition to Lawrence and gazed at the men around the room. Many faces were hardened, some even glared at him, and others appeared bored. Le Blanc had a foreboding of imminent danger.

"Your Excellency, what is your pleasure in response to our Petition?"

Lawrence responded coldly. "Wait outside. We shall send our response to you."

Le Blanc bowed, as did all the members of the Acadian delegation. Simon sniffed as he led them out of the building just as they had come in, by the back door. He could not risk having important people in Halifax seeing such a mish-mash of dirty heathens on their front porch. What would they think of him?

Outside, René spoke quickly to the other Acadians. "Gentlemen, I thought this may be dangerous but now I am convinced of it. I believe they intend to harm us while we are here in Halifax, imprisoning us at St. George's Island or worse. I beg you all to begin the ride home post haste before evil befalls you."

Gabriel addressed the group of Acadians. "The Council members certainly are not to be trusted. I agree they may soon try to punish us. But Monsieur le Consul should not be alone during the Council's discussions. I shall remain with him as well."

René pulled him aside as the others in the group milled about the back of the great building. The Consul shook his head. "It is most important that I stay as our King's representative but you should return to office duty in my absence. Take your militia with you. No one knows what the British might have done at home during our journey here."

Gabriel reluctantly obeyed and turned to the young men in the group. These were the men he had trained and worked with in his secret militia. "Men, we shall ride immediately. We must return home. Mount up and follow me." The young patriots hurriedly followed their leader. René urged Père Rivière to join them, which he did. Within a matter of minutes all that remained of the group was a fog of dust from galloping out of town.

René stood apart from the other men as he watched Gabriel lead more than half the delegation away. He motioned to Henri Mius d'Entremont, who joined him.

René asked, "Would you coordinate the provision of supplies for the rest of the men? We must prepare to leave immediately upon receiving the response."

Henri queried, "What plan have you in mind if they reject our Oath?"

René shook his head. "I fear this may mean impending war, but it might take hours for the Council to debate our request. I have heard they spend days and even weeks over matters raised in their meetings."

Henri asked, "Whom do you wish to stay with you?"

René said, "It is safer if I remain here alone. The English dare not harm the King's official representative here."

Henri left René to his thoughts and rejoined the other men whom he divided them into groups to buy food and drink for the return trip. He remembered René's last directive to meet back at the main harbor in two hours, with or without the provisions, as there was no time to dawdle.

Simon had hidden himself near the doorway, out of sight of the Acadians. He overheard all conversations but the one which René had with Gabriel, as they had walked some ways from the building. When he saw many of the Frenchmen leave in groups, he slipped back into the building. Once there, he walked from the kitchen back to the Council meeting room. After the formalities of knocking and being admitted, Simon whispered quietly to Lawrence, who nodded and dismissed him.

Lawrence turned to Belcher. "Chief Justice Belcher, would the court condone an arrest of these heathens? They had no permission to leave their homes or to disrupt our meeting but now that they are here and we are deliberating, they wish to leave against the wishes of this Council."

John Rous added, "I heard them make threats against the Crown and its colonies. It is proven here in their own hand."

Winslow nodded. "Their document states that unless we let them live peacefully they will cease sending crops and animals to our colonies in desperate need of these foods, especially Massachusetts Bay."

Councilor John Collier spoke up. "And they promise violence against our helpless women if we do not let them keep their possessions, which includes tax money. The Crown must have their taxes but they intend to steal them here."

Belcher briefly perused the document. "Indeed, those threats have been made. The law considers these to be criminal. Should they be arrested, any court in our land would uphold such action."

Lawrence leaned back in his chair, nodding with pleasure. "Then they *should* be arrested. And they *shall*." He nodded to Winslow. "Good Lieutenant-Colonel, please do the honors and round up the heathens who had the audacity to propose their Treaty Oath in direct refusal of the King's orders."

Winslow rose, bid his adieu to the other men and exited the meeting room. An uproar ensued among the Councilors and the admiralty present. Men clapped each other on the back and shouted to each other creating an unintelligible din. The noise became so great that Lawrence banged his gavel a number of times. The only way he was able to hush the crowd was by ordering his wine steward to fill every glass. A few more thumps of the gavel and all eyes were on Lawrence, awaiting his toast to their great success.

"Gentlemen, a toast. Long live the King!"

A resounding chorus from the other men repeated, "Long live the King!"

In the harbor, about forty Acadian men waited for Henri and the other men to return with the necessary supplies. Nearly two hours had gone by when from one end of the harbor Henri and his men appeared, riding hard. Henri shouted to the other men. "Mount up and ride out of town. We must hurry!" The Acadians started to climb onto their steeds but it was too late.

Suddenly, a regiment led by Winslow marched into the harbor blocking the exit of the Acadians. With their muskets loaded and aimed, the soldiers waited for Winslow's order. But his orders were to imprison the men, not to kill them, unless they tried to escape.

When Henri turned his group around to ride off, Winslow issued the order. "Fire on the escaping Frenchies. Do not let them get away alive." Volleys of shots rang out, disturbing the quiet harbor.

Several men cried out, some wounded but able to ride away. Others fell to the ground, Henri among them. The Acadians in the harbor began to help the injured and dying when Winslow ordered them not to move.

The troops herded the uninjured Acadian men into an orderly line and chained them together, then pushed them toward the dock from where they would be taken to the prison on St. George's Island. British soldiers quickly dragged the bodies into the light where a medic could conduct an examination.

Winslow asked, "Are any alive?"

The medic said, "I count five men still breathing, sir."

"Will treatment save their lives?"

"No, sir. Each shall die in the next few moments. Neither musket balls nor medicine should be wasted on them."

"Thank you, sir. Your work is finished here."

The medic saluted and left the group to return to town.

Winslow's voice rang out clearly in the evening stillness. "Who can identify these men?" Antoine Bourgeois, the butcher in Grand Pré, raised his hand.

"You there, tell us who these heathens are." Winslow motioned that a soldier remove Antoine's chains and drag him over to the bodies.

Antoine walked up to each body, knelt and quickly made the Sign of the Cross on the man's forehead, then identified the person who had either died or was left to die. After Bourgeois provided the names of all the wounded and deceased, he was chained again to the other men still alive.

Winslow issued an order. "Sail to the island and deliver the prisoners to the warden at St. George's gate."

Troops forced the chained Acadians to move into a small boat which set sail toward St. George's Island where the prison was located. Within a matter of minutes the harbor was empty except for the bodies of the dead and dying. The British troops had quickly dispersed, having done their duty.

At the Meeting Hall, Charles Lawrence told René that the Acadian Petition had been denied. Then Lawrence handed him a parchment with the King's Oath, ordering that it be signed by all French citizens in the region and returned to him with Rene's official seal within a fortnight.

René quickly mounted his horse and rode to the harbor, dreading what he would find. But even he was not prepared for the sorrowful scene. Every Acadian man who had been shot was dead except Henri, who was still holding on to life by a thread.

René jumped to the ground and lifted Henri's head. "Henri, you shall be fine. I shall find a doctor here."

Henri looked up at his friend and weakly grabbed his jacket. "You must return home. They will kill you, too."

René, tears in his eyes, tried to be strong for his oldest and dearest friend. "Then we shall return home to our wives together."

Henri sputtered as he spoke, coughing up blood and spittle. "Tell Gabriel to sell everything I have and return to France. Make a new life with Evangeline. I would have liked to have seen their children grow up."

René brushed his tears away. "Stay with me, old friend. We shall find Gabriel on the way home and you shall tell him yourself."

Henri winced in pain as René lifted him up onto his horse. René kicked his heels into the sides of his stallion and away they went. He rode like the wind, seeking Gabriel and the other Acadians. But the young militia men had left hours earlier. There was no hope of catching them.

At the edge of the woods near Grand Pré René stopped and turned to Henri. "We are home, my friend."

He heard Henri cry out, "My dearest Diane, I am yours." With that he breathed no more and fell against René. The Consul dismounted and laid Henri on the ground, praying and holding him in his arms for several hours.

Kitok rode by on his way to meet Gabriel. He told René, "I shall bring the priest and Gabriel if you wish to stay."

René nodded as tears filled his eyes. A senseless death at the hands of the English. And all because he and all the others had tried to do the right thing. Because he tried to keep the peace. René decided the militia must stay secret but they had to be prepared from this day forward...for anything. For war.

Henri Mius d'Entremont's funeral was a most somber occasion. The church was overflowing with mourners. Père Rivière's sermon was quite emotional, taking its toll on the priest as well as the parishioners. But when Gabriel rose to the pulpit and spoke of his father's exemplary life no dry eye remained. Behind Henri's closed coffin, dozens of other candles glowed in memory of the other Acadians who had been killed in what Gabriel had termed the "Halifax Harbor Massacre." A funeral had been held for them the day before but the candles continued to burn in their memory. Additionally, Père Rivière had set up a side altar honoring those captured and whose fate -- death or life in St. George's -- was unknown.

Evangeline stood by Gabriel throughout the ordeal. Christine supervised the women who had cooked for the wake and the funeral. Thomas Gaudet had hewn the most beautiful wooden cross for the grave, where Gabriel knelt throughout the burial service. He spoke to no one, instead praying for his father to avenge his killers.

Evangeline waited patiently for Gabriel, not joining in the funeral supper with René, Christine and the others. She understood Gabriel's feelings of hopelessness and anger. She knew this was a major turning point for all the Acadians, who now saw the English as cruel, bloodthirsty warmongers that violated the peace Treaty based on their whim and caprice.

Written requests by the French Consul to the prison warden for visitation with the prisoners went unheeded. Letters sent to the Acting Governor at Halifax received no replies. A small delegation of brave Acadian men led by Claude Arnaud rode to Halifax then took a boat to St. George's Island. However, they were turned away at the gate with no news of their imprisoned friends and family. The Acadian prisoners were not heard from at all. René prayed that they were still alive in prison. But he thought it more likely that they had either been sold into slavery in Bostontown or had been summarily executed.

Thereafter, Nova Scotia Supreme Court Chief Justice Belcher issued an official opinion that the Council's decision was legal and binding, based on the Order of King George II to deport the Acadian neutrals.

Nothing was mentioned of the Acadian Delegation of One Hundred or of their Petition or of the Halifax Harbor Massacre.

The legal opinion was not questioned.

Part IV
August – October 1755

"No man is an island...Each man's death diminishes me.
For I am involved in Mankinde. Therefore, send not to know
For whom the bell tolls, It tolls for thee."
- *John Donne*

CHAPTER 33
Winslow

GRAND PRÈ

 ieutenant-Colonel John Winslow had arrived at the old "Vieux Logis" Fort of Grand Pré without any fanfare on the nineteenth day of August. The Fort had fallen into great disrepair since its last active use the year before. Winslow had obtained a small budget to refurbish the Fort for what he estimated would be six weeks from his arrival. He fully intended to rid the territory of the French Catholic population by the end of September. So Winslow allocated most of the budget to weapons and temporary housing for the soldiers he was assigned for the deportation -- all four hundred of them, which, together with Captain Murray's six hundred troops at Fort Edward, should be sufficient to subdue the French colonists.

A temporary village of tents to house the troops was being constructed by soldiers led by Turnbull. To spur the officer's efficiency, Winslow had procured the commission of Captain for Turnbull, whom Winslow knew was status-conscious and eager to rise in the British military system.

Winslow had heard rumors that Acting Governor Armstrong had killed himself out of honor years earlier because he could not convince the French Consul Le Blanc de Verdure to order his Acadians to sign the Oath of Allegiance upon his arrival. Winslow wondered if the Consul would create havoc within what was to become Winslow's very ordered world. Nova

Scotia was his domain now and he would not tolerate anyone or anything upsetting his plans.

As Winslow rode in his carriage on the route to Grand Pré, he longed to be settled so he could preserve his thoughts in his journal. He reflected on the last English Council meeting he attended the month earlier. The other Councilors had enjoyed leading on the Acadian Delegation, hinting that the Council would actually entertain the Petition's preposterous idea to modify the King's Oath.

It was an impossible mission -- no one could ever suggest modifying the royal order. After all, their Britannic Majesty had issued the order that the Acadians sign the Oath of Allegiance many years earlier and many times. Armstrong had tried, Shirley had followed him, Lawrence had worked hard to achieve it, and the Council had made diligent efforts. All to no avail. The heathens refused to take the King's requisite Oath of Allegiance, instead relying on the Treaty still in effect which King George preferred to ignore.

Winslow could not fathom the Frenchmen's lack of understanding that they sealed their fate by refusing the King's order. Oh, they talked of the Treaty of Utrecht and the grant of their religious freedom. But treaties were only written words. Honor and loyalty were based on acts, not words. And the Frenchies had done nothing to show their allegiance. No, Winslow reasoned, those heathens would sign the Oath under his very eyes due to one simple difference between himself and the other English officers who had attempted to accomplish the task -- spiritual beliefs.

Winslow's faith was stronger than that of his superiors, or anyone on the Council. That faith and his adept knowledge of the Bible would help him to convince the Frenchies who were so tied to their religion that this was God's work, not the work of man. He would have to tread carefully since His Majesty King George II was also the head of the one true Church, but so long as he was surrounded by trusted officers he could accomplish it. And, he thought, if that did not work then the old-fashioned methods of beatings and imprisonment would.

The Frenchies had done the unthinkable by refusing to obey the King's order. They lived and raised crops and animals on his lands. Their handsome, dare he say it, wealthy lifestyle was on the King's lands. And if the King only asked for loyalty in exchange for such wealth and success, who were the French Neutrals to refuse?

Today Winslow felt nothing but an inexplicable lack of understanding towards the actions of the Acadians in refusing the Oath. Winslow believed that the head of the Acadian Delegation at Halifax, their Consul, had no doubt concocted the last-minute personal appeal as a scheme to refuse the required Oath. But there was no logical reason to do so. They already practiced their religion in their church building. Their friendship with the Mi'Kmaqs was tolerated, mostly for their inter-marriages, which produced skilled trackers who worked for the English troops against the Iroquois and other invaders from outside the territory.

This Disagreeable Business would soon be over, he thought. Then he would gladly turn over the business of new colonization of the area to Captain Phinneas Osgood while he enjoyed his next post back home with his family in Massachusetts. Or so Commander Shirley had promised him. Little matter that Lieutenant-Colonel Lawrence asked that Winslow be re-assigned to a fort on the border of English and New France territory in Québec, where Winslow would never leave alive. That was what the jealous Lawrence wanted, so eager was he to become a confidant of Shirley. But Winslow had bet his career on Shirley and it was on Shirley that he relied.

Winslow had his orders and though he did not intend to cause bloodshed before he loaded the French onto ships and out of the territory, he was not squeamish. He might have his subordinates carry out the orders but he could live with blood on his hands. He would have to do so.

Winslow anticipated his meeting with the head of the colony he was to describe as "filled with heathens." He continued to denigrate the French, despite their wealth and farming importance to the other British colonies along the Atlantic coast. Acadian settlements continued to expand inland nearly encroaching on land of the Indians, the other heathens who might become alarmed and cease being allies of the backwards French. But Winslow had high hopes of converting the Roman Catholic colonists to his Church of England, a dream that saw not one convert, despite his efforts.

Winslow was soon followed by several hundred troops from his regiment in Halifax. They had built the Fort there to protect the English government's new capital in Nova Scotia. Prior to his arrival Winslow had relied on the officer assigned by Lawrence, Captain Turnbull, to begin to implement his plans. Turnbull had relocated troops from regiments of Captain Handfield and Captain Murray. He situated soldiers in Acadian homes as "temporary visitors" awaiting Winslow's arrival.

Turnbull lived up to his reputation as a taskmaster. He had directed the troops proficiently in the short time allotted to his mission. They had cleared the town square of everything but the outermost paths and shade trees. Troops had piled logs, muslin and other materials and supplies, awaiting Winslow's orders. As Turnbull had lived among the Acadians for quite a few months now, he knew the town better than anyone in the English forces. He had stayed out of sight while putting his best trackers and spies to watch young spirited Acadians and their whereabouts.

Turnbull rode his horse through the square, cracking his whip to push his troops to work night and day. The fence pickets had been hewn and installed so that his vision of a tent city was becoming a reality. Satisfied they would continue working without his constant supervision, Turnbull galloped out of town and down the road to the Fort.

Just in time. As he rounded the bend in the road, John Winslow's carriage pulled up. Winslow exited the coach to find Turnbull saluting him and escorting him through the gates of the fort.

"Impressive, Captain Turnbull. Very well done."

"Welcome and thank you, sir," Turnbull replied.

"Your reputation as a taskmaster precedes you but this is indeed a most agreeable refurbishment. Do tell. Was much work involved?"

"Yes sir, Lieutenant-Colonel. We built new palisades all around and new quarters for you. The guard house was mightily repaired."

"Indeed. But where are the housing and dining areas for the troops?"

"At present, sir, they reside with families in town."

"French families, you say?"

"Exactly, sir."

"How ever do they communicate?"

"I dare say there is little communication as our troops work from before dawn till after dusk. Then we grant them short leave for relaxation before roll call, at which time they return to their hosts' homes."

Winslow entered the log building that he would call home, but hopefully not for too long. He anticipated the business would be completed in September; that is, if Admiral Boscawen and Real-Admiral Mostyn were true to their word. At the last Council meeting they had appeared to be unsure if they could procure all the vessels in time. But Commander Shirley had informed him the ships would arrive since the lands had already been assigned. Many English farming families had committed to relocate to the Minas region and agreed to continue supplying food to the Eastern seaboard.

Shirley was pushing the admiralty to get rid of the French neutrals so their land could be granted to the new English colonists. The commander had coined a name for them. He called them the "English Planters." His associates in England had sought out agricultural tenants and rural residents in the countryside of England, staying clear of London and other large towns where government spies could upset their land grant scheme.

"When you wish, sir, I shall present you with the plan for our new Tent City."

"And I wonder how you derived that name, Captain?"

Turnbull started to answer, then remained silent, realizing his superior had a droll sense of humor. But in fact it was the French Neutrals, who always had their own words for everything, who were the first to name the housing project as "Tent City." Soon the troops began using the phrase.

Turnbull was confident his superior would soon see how well Turnbull had organized the troops. While they were more afraid of his whip than of him, the result was the same. They had a choice of hard work or brutal punishment. Turnbull had only inflicted his remedy for laziness a handful of times but that was enough to dissuade any other troops from shirking their duties.

A new guard entry house and ten-foot tall log palisade had been built around the fort, as well as sentry points at the corners of the palisades and a new officer's quarters for Winslow. He entered and looked around. He saw a large office area with his desk, work tables and other chairs with not one but two blazing fireplaces. The next room was a dining room with a large table set with a dozen places. He noted a door at the back of the room, which he opened.

From the door, a covered walkway connected to a small kitchen building where cooks and their aides were bustling about. The smells were nothing short of wonderful after the long journey. Winslow realized he was hungry but also wanted to see the remainder of the building. Turnbull was never more than a few feet behind him. Winslow walked to the other side of the room and found a long hallway, at the end of which were several sleeping rooms.

He walked into the largest one, in which the fireplace burned brightly and warmed the entire room. He sat on the huge four poster bed with red cloth curtains. "How unusual," he said. He reached for one of the curtains and rubbed it to his cheek. It felt soft and thick but it also felt very warm. Turnbull informed him local girls had made the cloth and the town's dressmaker Madame Dupont had sewn the curtains. Turnbull had vast local knowledge which Winslow would use to his advantage.

He walked back into the main office. Though the building itself was a bit spartan for his taste, he knew he would not live there long enough to import goods from England. He would commandeer what he needed from the capital in Halifax.

"Yes, this will do, Captain Turnbull. This will do quite nicely." Winslow took a seat at a large wooden desk and laid his feet on top of it. He leaned back and looked through the window as troops manned the entry station and the lookout towers.

"I thought…that is to say, Lieutenant-Colonel, I ordered dinner for you. Some refreshment after your long journey?"

"Yes, that sounds right. Let us eat. Then afterwards I should like to see my new Tent City."

Turnbull saluted and disappeared from view into the dining room and out into the kitchen.

Winslow took his seat. In a matter of minutes the dining table was laden with food. He invited Turnbull to join him and the serious conversation began. He needed to rely on Turnbull to execute this dirty business.

Turnbull had assigned troops to build temporary sleeping bunks, a large dining hall for the troops, officers' quarters and storage facilities all with wood and tenting. Many of Winslow's troops had been installed in rooms of Acadian families throughout the town, but often they were found asleep on the floor of the parlors and other rooms of the brothel run by Hetty Phipps.

The troops and other officers knew Hetty's best girls were reserved for Captain Turnbull but he was ready to defer to Lieutenant-Colonel Winslow. But he refused to set foot in the woman's den of iniquity. He wanted to ban his troops from such licentiousness but he decided to ignore it as the mission would be completed and he would be gone in a few weeks.

Winslow's introductory meeting in his offices with the French representatives, the Consul and his Vice Consul, was uneventful. From René's perspective it was quite different than that of his arrival in 1737 when Handfield had immediately demanded the Acadians sign the unconditional Oath of Allegiance or leave the territory.

Actually, Winslow had been quite civilized, inviting René and Gabriel to dine with him and Captain Turnbull. The Lieutenant-Colonel had insisted his chef cook use only local ingredients, which were abundant and that his wine steward serve only French wines, which flowed like water.

The French were quite wary of such an impressive show and realized it was to hide the actual intention of the meeting. That became evident after dinner when Winslow's servants offered cigars, which the French politely declined. Winslow took a great deal of time selecting exactly the right cigar, clipping it at exactly the right place and lighting it at exactly the right moment, just after he presented René with a document.

Nonchalantly Winslow said, "In the event the document was misplaced that you received from Lieutenant-Governor Lawrence. For your colonists to sign. We ask you to provide the notarial seal of the Crown of France by each signature, or a mark if the colonist is unable to write."

René stood and bowed. "As advised by His Holy Christian Majesty King Louis Fifteen of France and Navarre and on behalf of all French colonists living in Grand Pré and in Acadia, we are knowledgeable of such an unconditional Oath and we respectfully decline."

Winslow's face turned as red as beets. Furious, he stood at the table ready to pounce on René verbally or physically. But Turnbull took the document and ripped it in half, giving Winslow time to calm himself.

Winslow regained his seat and turned to the two Frenchmen. "You do not know the gravity of your fate as a result of your decision tonight."

René responded, "We repeat to you as we have to your predecessor and all English military leaders that every Acadian of age ten and above is prepared to sign the Treaty Oath that respects freedom of religion allowing us to practice our Catholic faith."

Gabriel added, "And does not require us to bear arms against France or the Mi'Kmaq, our allies."

Winslow sneered. "You cannot mean this is your last word."

René nodded. "You have it, sir."

René and Gabriel began walking to the door. Turnbull placed his hand near the gun at his side. Gabriel opened his long coat and placed his fingers on his gun.

Winslow puffed on his cigar, apparently unruffled by the rebuff. "Monsieur le Consul, you are aware that treason is punishable by death, are you not?"

René said without responding directly to Winslow's comment. "When you are prepared to add freedom of religion and exemption from bearing arms against France and its allies, we are ready to sign such an Oath. Thank you for the delicious meal. We bid you good evening, Lieutenant-Colonel Winslow. Captain Turnbull."

Winslow's butler waited for a signal from Winslow to assist the Frenchmen but instead he continued smoking his cigar. The two Frenchmen retrieved their hats and coats and let themselves out of the door while the butler stood idly by.

When the door shut, Winslow turned to Turnbull. "You must keep a special watch on the young Vice-Consul. He is a fighter while the Consul is the peacemaker. Give me a report on d'Entremont's activities every week."

Captain Turnbull stood and saluted. "Yes Lieutenant-Colonel."

Winslow said, "That will be all."

"Yes Lieutenant-Colonel. Good night sir."

Winslow waited until Turnbull had left, then he dismissed his servants. When the dining room was empty, Winslow took the papers and angrily threw them into the fireplace. "You heathens shall get what you deserve even earlier than planned if I can arrange it. I shall not fail in my mission."

*

The next morning, in the Mi'Kmaq Village, the medicine woman White Bird had laid on a blanket the variety of plants, flowers and mushrooms she and Christine had cut in the forest near her wigwam. The medicine woman's limited knowledge of French and English and Christine's inability to speak Mi'kmawi'simk had not hindered the two in understanding each other until now.

The Mi'Kmaq woman held up an odd-shaped flowering bush. "Stop red river," she said.

Christine looked puzzled and shook her head. "Red river?"

White Bird took the knife they had used to chop the plants and roots. She quickly sliced the blade across her finger. Blood poured profusely from the cut.

Christine jumped in surprise but the medicine woman was unperturbed. She took a leaf from the odd bush, bit it to open the leaf veins and pressed the white fluid oozing from the leaf to her wound. The bleeding stopped instantly.

Christine nodded. "Red river. Blood. I understand."

White Bird grunted. "Warpaint and red river plant, Warrior come home. No plant, warrior not stay living."

Christine responded, "I will pack the red river plant when…if…our men must fight. Thank you. This is a very valuable plant."

The medicine woman picked up the next plant, which had red-tinged leaves. She pulled a leaf, spit on it, and then placed it on a flat stone, grinding it with a wooden stick until it became paste. Christine was fascinated with the resulting white creamy mixture.

White Bird explained, "Make paste, put in food. Man sleep for long time. No hurt, just sleep." She handed Christine a leaf and the stick, urging her to spit and make the paste. Christine successfully passed the old woman's test. Her paste looked nearly like White Bird's.

The old crone smiled with approval. Then she ran her clawlike nails ran through Christine's red tresses. "Fire hair. Mans love fire hair, no?"

Christine laughed. "I would not know. I have never been with a man."

White Bird looked at her in surprise. "No man?" She clapped her hands and a handsome brave of eighteen entered the wigwam. He wore only a loincloth and his manhood was visible as he bent over the old woman. He kissed her forehead and said, "Honorable grandmother" in their language. She muttered some words that were incomprehensible to Christine except she thought she heard "fire" in Mi'Kmaq when White Bird touched Christine's head.

The young man knelt on the blanket next to White Bird and said in French, "I am Sitting Fox. My grandmother presents me to you." He held out his hand to Christine, who did not move. She did not know this custom.

White Bird impatiently placed Christine's hand in Sitting Fox's, pointed to a closed off sleeping area of the wigwam and pushed them in that direction. Christine realized what was happening and pulled her hand away. White Bird took it again, slapped it hard and put it back.

Sitting Fox gently prodded Christine to walk with him to the room. She acquiesced to take time while her mind raced. Her heart was with René. She could never be with another man. How could she extricate herself without offending her generous teacher and the handsome young man, she wondered. White Bird waited until they sat on the blanket, then she pulled the thin wool curtain. Christine heard her retreat to the other side of the hut.

On the blanket Sitting Fox whispered quietly, "I only touch you if you wish. If Honorable Grandmother hears no love noises she get angry I not make you happy."

Christine said softly, shaking her head, "I am sorry. My heart belongs to someone else. I am waiting for him to love me. Do you understand?"

Sitting Fox nodded sadly. "You are beautiful woman. We make some noises now but I res...respect you. No touch."

She said, "Thank you."

He lay on the blanket and rustled his clothes then motioned for her to do the same. She followed his lead. Then he moaned in a low voice and moved the blankets. Christine arranged her skirts noisily and made a groaning sound. Then Sitting Fox motioned to stop suddenly.

They heard White Bird on the other side of the blanket. She grunted loudly with approval and said, "Mans love fire hair."

When Sitting Fox escorted Christine out of the wigwam she had a glow about her although he had only kissed her hand with respect. A virile young man found her, a maiden over thirty years of age, quite beautiful and desirable. This tribe had long revered women of age, and Sitting Fox's attraction to Christine was no exception.

Christine felt a renewed self-confidence that had slipped away over the years. She promised herself she would express her feelings to René when they were alone. She wanted to marry him and live with him until a ripe old age with children and grandchildren...as many generations as God willed she would see in her lifetime.

She knew René would make her a very happy woman. What she was unsure of was the secret to his forgetting Eugenie. She nodded her head, wishing she knew the answer but nonetheless firm in her decision. Yes, she would declare her secret love for him and pray that he accepted it.

*

In his offices that morning, John Winslow dipped a fresh quill in the inkpot and began to write reading aloud as he scribbled the letter.

"Dear Mother Winslow,
I am eating very well in my new post at Grand Pré in Nova Scotia. The lobsters have claws big enough to...."

He stopped at hearing a din outside. He had stationed additional troops outside to assist with the incoming supply wagons so he gave it no further thought.

He took a brief respite to enjoy a glass of expensive French wine and took a long, slow sip. He looked at the label. Ahh, he did enjoy the fruits of the Bordeaux vineyards and all the pleasures afforded by his station, no matter if British or French. Good wine had no political ambition, he reasoned. Besides, he knew the fate awaiting the French Acadians, after which they would no longer have ownership or possession of their imported goods. Placing the container back on his desk, Winslow continued writing.

"...to hold a bottle of wine. And the swordfish are as big as cows. The place is small but suits my nature, as did Bostontown, though the citizens here are not as agreeable."

More noises outside the window. Again Winslow stopped but decided to ignore the sounds. He dipped the quill again, then finished his writing.

"I continue to read the Bible daily but have not yet converted the French heathens to the one true religion. This shall be done even if God's wrath must be brought down on them.

Your devoted son, John Winslow."

Winslow sealed the letter with hot wax, then stamped his insignia with his ring. The din had become so loud he walked to the window and looked out to see wagons passing the sentries at the gate. The sentries inspected the wagons and boxes, and then directed them down to the gates of the town. He knew Turnbull would efficiently unload the wagons and stack the supplies and materials in the tents recently erected in the square.

More stores and weapons for the transports, he thought approvingly. He would not let any obstacle prevent him from fulfilling the King's orders. Governor Shirley had already a list of new English Planters ready to take ownership of the French farms and plantations. Winslow scowled when he first read the list -- so many had the same last names as members of the English Council. He deplored the English system of family favoritism, since he had earned *his* promotions on merit. But the land must be farmed at all costs.

He shrugged. By the end of August his troops would have more than sufficient weapons necessary to imprison and subdue any heathens who disobeyed the Edict. He planned a surprise announcement in the Catholic Church, which would become their prison until all the transports arrived. It should be simple to herd them to the shore and into the vessels, after which his mission would be completed and he would return home to Massachusetts with honor.

At Tent City Turnbull and his Lieutenants Greenfield and Wicker supervised the unloading of crates and materials into the square. Captain Jeffries directed teams of soldiers to build a fence around the square. Then Winslow rode back to the Fort without being seen by any of his officers.

Satisfied with the work thus far, Turnbull then headed for Winslow's office. The Lieutenant-Colonel had approved additional works for Tent City to house the supplemental troops expected to arrive in September before Winslow announced the Edict to the Acadians.

Winslow contemplated what his new mission would be from Governor Shirley, now Commander in Chief of the colonial army. Through the window, he saw a beautiful woman walk by, whose tousled red tresses were flying wildly in the breeze. She hummed a tune unknown to Winslow as she strolled past the Fort smiling to herself, carrying a basket laden with fruits and plants. Spellbound, he dropped his wineglass on the wood floor.

At the sound of breaking glass, Turnbull knocked and quickly entered and saluted. "Lieutenant-Colonel, is something amiss?" Spying the shards on the floor he collected them with his gloves. "Are you hurt, sir?"

Winslow was glued to the window and ignored the presence of his newly promoted officer. Turnbull followed his gaze to see Christine's petticoats flouncing as she passed the Fort and walked toward the town gates, her hair still dancing in the wind. Turnbull decided to curry favor with his superior and arrange a chance meeting.

Turnbull suddenly remembered why he had walked toward the office. "The works are nearly completed. We are ready for inspection at your pleasure, sir."

Winslow waved Turnbull away and he saluted, then exited the office, the broken glass tinged with red wine cutting through his gloves. Turnbull discarded the glass and rushed back to meet Jeffries and his other main officer, Lieutenant Greenfield. The officer needed to finish his work to get on with personal business. Tonight he planned to visit Hetty's best girl, Gertrude. He affectionately called her "Gertie." He was thankful his Captain Turnbull had no interest in her though he failed to understand why.

Christine walked into the Consulate building. She looked toward the office but the doors were shut tightly. She went upstairs to her private room to create an encyclopedia of cures like the one she had brought with her from France eighteen years ago. First, Christine outlined the leaves of each plant White Bird had given her. Then she wrote the plant name and a description of the powers, good and bad, of each plant. Finally, she listed common sites where the plant could be found.

In the Consulate office below, Gabriel paced. He dropped supplies, misplaced papers and spilled the glass of wine René had requested. René looked over at Gabriel before he could clean up the mess.

"Are you unwell?" he asked Gabriel.

"No sir, not at all," responded Gabriel. Then he added a question of his own. "Do you have any additional work for me today?"

"No. All of our reports are completed so you are free to go."

Gabriel bowed. "Thank you, sir. I am to take your daughter boating."

René said, without looking up, "By all means, she should enjoy herself. And you too, Gabriel." Then he went back to his work as Gabriel slipped out of the office.

Back in the square, Turnbull watched the buzz of activity among the troops. Out of the corner of his eye he saw the Consulate door open. He turned and saw Gabriel exiting and hurrying away from the building. He scowled and called Lieutenant Wicker over to him.

"Follow d'Entremont and report on his activity. I do not want him out of your sight. Tell me everything he does, down to a shite in the woods."

Wicker saluted. "Yes sir. With pleasure, sir."

Turnbull added, "And Wicker, he must not see you trailing him."

"Of course, sir. That is, of course not, sir."

Turnbull walked over to Jeffries and they consulted as they followed their units of troops. The first unit was busy completing the fencing of land for the Tent City in the Grand Pré town square. The second unit unpacked cartons of materials, which were additional tents. They began to pitch the tents inside the fence. The third unit continued to unload boxes of ammunition and weapons from wagons and store them in the shed. The fourth stored food supplies in the new dining hall.

Turnbull kept looking for his trusted Lieutenant Greenfield whom Winslow had sent to Halifax several days earlier. Greenfield had not yet returned and his absence was missed in their ongoing works in the square.

Outside his office Winslow mounted his horse and trotted into the town square. Turnbull called the troops to attention and they stopped what they were doing. Jeffries stood next to Turnbull and saluted as Winslow passed. They watched anxiously as the Lieutenant-Colonel inspected the works of the troops thus far.

Winslow reprimanded the third unit on a precarious stack of boxes. He flicked his whip on the neck of several of the troops, drawing blood. Continuing to inspect the fencing, Winslow found the line to be uneven. The tents were not erected so as to minimize space between them. He called Turnbull to him. The Captain quickly reported to Winslow with a salute.

"Yes sir, Lieutenant-Colonel."

Winslow cracked his whip hard against Turnbull's face.

"Captain, do not call me again to inspect your troops until their works are completed in accordance with my exact specifications."

Turnbull turned beet red with anger, but he saluted his superior officer and remained at attention.

Winslow rode back to his office. Only when he had closed the door did Turnbull allow the troops to break formation and return to their assigned duties. Then Turnbull wiped his bloody jaw, avoiding the looks of his men and his counterpart, Jeffries.

*

Near Grand Pré, Gabriel dipped a pair of oars into a shallow river, propelling the canoe forward. The small boat was Mi'Kmaq, made of bark which floated lightly on the water. Since the Acadians' fishing boats had been seized by the English, Gabriel had arranged with Kitok to borrow the only boat available. He and Evangeline sat opposite each other on small wooden seats built into the canoe. She held a parasol in one hand and ran her other hand through the clear water. She suddenly closed the parasol and put it away.

"Will you show me how?"

"I was unaware you were interested in boats," he said as he pulled the oars out of their harnesses.

"My preference is to learn many useful tasks to care for myself. It is better than relying on others who are always at work." Evangeline smiled and teased Gabriel with her remark.

Gabriel moved the oars into position for her to row. He leaned forward and placed her hands on one of the oars, showing her the movement. Then he moved in back of her, distributing the weight evenly but making sure he could take the oars if need be. They paddled smoothly until they neared a bend.

"Careful now as we make the turn. The currents are faster."

He leaned forward, stretching the oar to turn the canoe. Evangeline tried to follow but the currents pulled the oar out of her hand. As she leaned forward, the weight shifted and the canoe overturned, throwing both of them into the water.

On the sandy beach not far away, Lieutenant Wicker watched behind a clump of foliage. He wondered why Turnbull took such great interest in this Frenchman who was only trying to impress his lady friend. But he did not do that very well, he thought to himself. At first he thought he should seize the canoe but clearly it was Mi'Kmaq and not within his purview of authority. Only after that did he remember Turnbull's instruction to remain out of d'Entremont's sight so he hid deeper in the foliage.

Evangeline flailed her arms in the water, or so it seemed to Gabriel. He swam to her and placed her arms around his neck, then started to swim to shore. She surprised him by releasing her arms but he caught her and kissed her softly. She smiled at him, tightening her arms around his neck. He kissed her again and again until she broke his embrace and started for the beach. Gabriel swam after the canoe, uprighting it and towing it to the shore as he swam.

Wicker stole away from the bushes and took the path past the Indian Village to Grand Pré. He did not think Gabriel could have noticed him.

As Evangeline was swimming toward the shore she noticed a man in an English army uniform scurrying away from a row of bushes. She thought she had seen him before and thought she would be able to find him in Tent City. Hundreds of troops had arrived but she was sure he had been there before the new soldiers came to town.

She was lost in her thoughts and did not hear Gabriel swimming strongly behind her as he dragged the boat along. When she did, she picked up her speed but they both reached a sand bar at about the same time, where they were able to stand and wade to the beach. He carried the light bark canoe over his head and rested it on the shore.

Later, as their cloaks hung drying next to a roaring fire on the beach, Evangeline broached the subject of the soldier. "I am certain I have seen him before. If I could only remember his name."

"Can you describe him? What kind of uniform was he wearing?" Gabriel asked with alarm.

Evangeline shook her head. "I know it was an English uniform -- an officer -- perhaps one of the men I saw unloading boxes from the Brigantine the day we went riding."

Gabriel shivered, but not from the cold. It was a warning. Why would the English send someone to follow the French Vice Consul unless they were plotting a scheme? He would consult with Kitok and the militia.

Evangeline tossed her now dry, lustrous hair which did not go unnoticed by Gabriel. "But a resistance is dangerous, is it not? Papa has always insisted on keeping the peace."

"The Halifax harbor massacre confirmed my greatest fears. None can be trusted. Though Winslow may be diplomatic Turnbull is bloodthirsty. When Kitok learned of an English plot against Fort Beausejour we tried to stop them. The Mi'Kmaqs believe the English are planning to destroy all French presence here. We cannot sit back."

"Surely Papa can help. I want to do my part too, Gabriel." She looked at his face, which did not approve of either option. She persisted. "Let me go with you to convince him. Papa is reasonable. He respects you."

Gabriel took her hands and looked into her eyes. "Please do not speak to him of this. He would report the soldier and I do not want to see you in danger. Please promise me you shall remain silent." He pleaded with his eyes.

She nodded, lowering her eyes. Why had she not swum faster so she could have identified the English officer, she wondered. Then she could have helped the man she loved.

Gabriel helped her to her feet and they put on their dry coats. He embraced her again and they kissed eagerly and hungrily. It was Gabriel who pulled away this time. Though it was not yet dusk he lit a torch and she carried it as he lifted the canoe and walked her into the Mi'Kmaq Village. He left the canoe outside Kitok's large wigwam where they mounted their horses and he escorted her into Grand Pré.

*

That night, Kitok slowed his stallion to a slow pace as he guided Lieutenant Greenfield ahead on the trail. The Englishman was on a skittish horse and after drinking whiskey all day Greenfield could barely balance himself.

As Kitok rode his horse through a narrow clearing he heard loud sounds behind him. A wild wolf, without warning, had attacked Greenfield's horse. Baring its sharp teeth, the animal clamped onto the horse's leg, bit a large chunk of it, and pulled the huge horse down. The horse whinnied loudly but could not release itself from the wolf's grasp. Greenfield fell on the side opposite the wolf without as much as a whimper. Watching the wolf, Kitok verified Greenfield was alive. When he felt the man's breath on his hand he grabbed his rifle.

Intending to scare the wild wolf away, Kitok fired his weapon straight into the trees above. He could not kill a wolf. They were brothers. Kitok rode up and down the path searching for rest of the pack wolves usually traveled in but saw nothing. This wolf was alone. Something was not right.

The wolf gnawed on the horse's leg but otherwise was unmoving. Kitok dismounted, leaving his horse a safe distance away. He walked slowly to the wolf, holding his rifle at his side. The wolf looked at him, and then leaned down licking his other foot hidden in the brush. Kitok realized he was trying to do something but what? The downed horse whinnied again as it tried to right itself. Greenfield was still motionless.

Walking nearer to the wolf, Kitok peered through the brush to see the wolf's foot was caught in a hunting trap. English soldiers must have placed it there. He knew the Acadians and the Indians killed wild game when food was needed, or to store for the winter. They did not set such traps to check later, leaving unsuspecting travelers at risk. But then, the English soldiers did not know much about living in this territory. Many had been shipped in from England or the colonies, no doubt thinking they would catch bears for warm coats or skin rugs. But bear hunting took place in higher terrain and other territories, not here in the woods outside Grand Pré.

Kitok picked out a series of leaves and herbs near the path, chewed them and spit on them to make a paste in his hand. Then he carefully applied it to the wolf's leg, which twitched. Yet the wolf did not make a sound, watching Kitok's every move but remaining docile.

Kitok nodded to the wolf and carefully released its injured foot from the trap. He patted the rest of the paste on the horse's leg but the wound was too deep to heal. Kitok turned back to the wolf, signaling it to return home. But the wolf merely limped over to Kitok and stood beside him. Kitok picked it up and put it back into the woods then walked back to check on Greenfield again. The man had not moved but was still clearly breathing. That he had imbibed so much on the trip back home from Halifax might have been his saving grace.

When Kitok turned around, the wolf had returned. It was sitting on its haunches but eyeing the horse. Kitok shook his head and motioned for the wolf to stay sitting. It did not move.

Kitok seized the opportunity and ripped open Greenfield's satchel. He pulled out a series of documents tied with royal red ribbons rather than having been sealed with wax. While intermittently checking on the status of the wolf, the dying horse, and Greenfield, Kitok managed to read every page. He re-read the last few pages again, unsure if he correctly understood the English words. If what he read was true, he had to meet with Gabriel and share this ominous news.

He heard Greenfield moan. Kitok rearranged all the documents, re-tied them with their proper ribbons and placed them back in the saddlebags. He looked toward Grand Pré and the Acadians, and back to the Indian Village. Then he walked towards Greenfield, stood over his inert body and pointed the rifle down at him. Greenfield moaned slightly, but still did not move.

The horse whinnied again and again tried to stand up but failed. Kitok withdrew his gun and walked over to it. The wolf followed him without making a sound or a move, but occasionally lifting its injured foot. Kitok knelt by the horse, rubbed its mane and whispered in its ear. The horse whinnied and reared its head back. Kitok brought it back down, laying it on the ground, and continued to whisper to it. As if the horse understood, it lay still and turned its head away from Kitok.

With a tear in his eye, Kitok fired his weapon once, putting the beautiful animal out of its misery. Then he pulled the saddle off the dead animal and placed it onto the bare back of his own stallion, Winddancer. He soothed his horse as he strapped on the saddle, knowing it would not enjoy the tight leather belts but that they would not hurt him. The Fort was not far down the road once they exited the woods so this was only a temporary inconvenience.

Then Kitok tied the dead horse's legs with a rope, mounted his own horse and dragged the animal into the woods. The wolf followed, keeping a respectful distance from Winddancer and Kitok.

When Kitok returned, Greenfield moaned loudly and raised his arm to his head. "Where am I? What…?

"Have pain? Want medicine woman?"

Greenfield shook his head. He winced as he tried to get up.

"Must complete…my mission. Help me to my horse.…"

He looked around but could not see his steed. With a dazed look on his face, he turned back to Kitok. The Mi'Kmaq lifted Greenfield onto Winddancer then jumped on in front of him.

"My satchel. Where…?"

Kitok pointed to the bag tied to the saddle. Greenfield nodded in relief. He leaned over the side of the horse and vomited. He wiped his mouth with his proper English uniform, nearly losing his balance.

Kitok wrapped Greenfield's hands around himself and tied them with ropes to steady the Englishman. He did not want to have to explain an accidental death. Not after the documents he had just read.

"I take you to fort now." With that Kitok nudged Winddancer to break into a slow trot. The wolf managed to follow, keeping the pace even with its limp.

Kitok's eyes were as hard as steel. He was impatient to deliver Greenfield and then bring Gabriel the astonishing news of what he read. He needed Gabriel's political insight to help him determine what it meant to their respective peoples.

When he had delivered Greenfield and left a message behind the brick in the Church, Kitok returned to the Mi'Kmaq Village. He descended his horse and found that the wolf was still limping behind him.

Kitok nodded to the wolf. The animal howled softly in response, then sat on his haunches. The beast never took its eyes off Kitok who pulled a blanket aside and entered his wigwam.

Only then did the wolf lie on its paws outside Kitok's home. During the night Kitok exited the wigwam to relieve himself and sleepily patted the wolf's head as if it were his personal pet. When Kitok returned and lifted the blanket again, the wolf immediately stood at attention.

Kitok gazed back at the animal and patting its head again, he said, "Good night, Courage."

The wolf waited until Kitok had disappeared into the tent, then let out a long howl of acknowledgement.

The next morning when Kitok exited the tent Courage was nowhere to be seen. Walking through the Village Kitok could not find the wolf. He jumped on his horse and returned to the woods. There he finally found the animal lying cold and dead near the dead horse. The wolf had died of a musket wound, its paws cut off.

Kitok had heard English soldiers kept animal paws for luck but he had never seen the results, which made him both angry and sad. Kitok carried the wolf into the brush. He dug a small hole then carefully laid Courage in the grave. Covering the wolf's body with dirt, branches and leaves, Kitok brushed a tear from his face and looked in the direction of the Fort. He wondered if Greenfield had come back and discovered his dead horse had been attacked by Courage. Regardless of whether it had been the Lieutenant or someone else, Kitok knew the British were to blame.

The Mi'Kmaq did not know how or when but he vowed to avenge such a senseless killing.

CHAPTER 34
Attack

GRAND PRÉ

 udbowls. The streets of Grand Pré had become mudbowls since the summer storms began a week ago. Day in and day out, the rains continued to drench the few townspeople who dared to take to the streets.

Instead, the villagers preferred to remain in the shelter of their habitats. Most of the shop owners lived above their stores so they were only too happy to walk downstairs when they heard a knock on the door below their quarters. A few brave souls were scurrying along the boardwalk that ran the length of each street of shops and houses. No need to risk ruining what was, for many, their only pair of shoes. But sometimes the necessity of buying a cut of beef, bottle of wine or sack of flour justified the trek.

Even Tent City was unusually inactive. Neat rows of canvas tents stood at attention as their inhabitants lay inside. For many, the rains were a welcome respite from drills and marches. They used the time to write to loved ones back in England. This new territory was so far from home and the Frenchies were so strange. They were committed to their religion, without a doubt, and they were always polite when they passed in the street. But still, they just were not like the English.

Alone in his tent, Lieutenant Bancroft began to write in his diary.

"The village girls are comelier than the ones I have seen in Londontown, Rumors have passed through the tents that we might be brought here for more than security. Our superiors may be planning an attack on the town of Grand Pré."

"Drat." The quill broke. He checked in his satchel but there were none to be found. He slowly opened the flap of his tent. The rain flew into his dry space and he quickly closed it again. He finally put on his cape and ventured outside to the troop supply tent. The English government issued quills, ink and small leather journals to all troops to keep them occupied when not in battle or military exercises. When he exited the tent, several quills inside his cape, Bancroft heard thundering hoofs and saluted as Captain Adams galloped by him, saluting quickly and riding to the other end of town.

Captain Adams pulled his horse to a stop outside the gates of town at Hetty's, or the "pleasure palace" as the troops called it. Hetty kept a candle burning in the window day and night. She and her girls were always open for business. Hetty loved her coins and bestowed special favors on the girls that brought in the most.

As of late Gertrude had become the most asked-for girl in the house. Gertie, as Hetty affectionately called her, was in demand day and night and probably would have worked for days straight if Hetty had not made her sleep a few hours each night. Men were always bringing Gertie special little gifts to keep her happy, and to remind her of them when she was with someone else.

While Winslow settled into his quarters and chose not to participate in the pursuits of the ladies of the evening, Turnbull and the other officers enjoyed the fruits of their labors, visiting the brothel as often as Winslow's new evening curfew would allow. Hetty had been issued an order by John Winslow himself to prevent the soldiers from imbibing to the point of inebriation, so she made certain the drinks she offered had juts enough alcohol to let the men feel a slight kick but not enough to bring out their violent side.

*

That afternoon the parishioners of St. Charles des Mines Catholic Church had finished their dinner and socializing. They began to exit the hall. English troops watched the French families through the open flaps of their tents on the square opposite the Church building.

In the officers' tent Turnbull ordered more grog for his officers. They had done a good job and deserved their reward. Turnbull noted with particular interest how the Consul's daughter had grown into a beautiful woman. He turned to Captain Adams as three Lieutenants, Wicker, Greenfield and Bancroft, enjoyed their drinks.

"What is the name of the French Consul's daughter? With the long brown hair. Look, she just walked by."

Greenfeld took a long swig of grog and swirled it around his gold teeth. "Dunno but the likes of me would sorely like to find out."

Wicker glared at him. Did the man not learn anything from seeing the results of Turnbull's whipping? Clearly the Captain was attracted to the young woman. "Seeing as youse is so interested how's about a friendly wager then?" Wicker looked at Greenfield and tossed several coins on the table.

Turnbull placed a handful of money next to Wicker's coins. "I shall take the bet."

Wicker bowed slightly to the Captain. "If you can get the likes of her to talk with Greenfield, then by the tides of Fundy, these coins are for your purse." Wicker should not have put near his entire wage at stake. He would have to forfeit the money to his superior officer whether Greenfield succeeded or not.

Greenfield harrumphed loudly. "Watch and learn." He walked out of Tent City directly to the sidewalk where Evangeline stood alone. She had lagged behind her father and Christine to peer into the church alleyway, hoping to see Gabriel there. But he was nowhere to be seen.

When she looked back to the walkway she was startled to see an English officer standing in the street next to her. He tipped his hat to her and bowed slightly. "Good day, Miss. I was wondering, Miss, if you could tell me what has been going on today. All the people milling about and such."

Evangeline looked at him curiously. Was this the man she had seen at the beach? The uniform looked the same, but on second thought she believed he was a different officer. To hide her thoughts she smiled at Greenfield. "Of course, sir. Do you have an interest in the Catholic Church?"

Greenfield smiled sheepishly, anxious to keep up this little game. He was certain she knew he was joking but he kept it up anyway. "Well, Miss, I have thought about it. Could you recommend something for me to read? Like that book in your hand, for starters?"

He slipped the Bible out of her hand, believing that, as most books were rare, the name of the owner would be written on the inside of the cover. Births, deaths, and marriages were generally recorded in the back of the Good Book.

She was taken aback but thought he was genuine in his interest so she talked while he open the Bible and looked at her signature. He had learned to read, which enabled him to rise in Turnbull's service. Turnbull refused to promote anyone who was not literate. But he had not learned to read curved letters, only printed ones. So he could not decipher her name.

Evangeline gently took the Bible from his hands and showed him the divisions of the text. "Sir, this is the Roman Catholic Bible, which contains both a New Testament and an Old Testament. Do you see?"

"Oh yes, Miss, I do." He took off his hat and bowed. "Lieutenant Greenfield at your service. And your name would be?"

Evangeline gave a slight curtsy. "My name is Évangeline Le Blanc de Verdure. The French Consul is my father. His office is just over there." She pointed to the Consulate building.

"Please call on our priest, Père Rivière, for any theological questions. He is much better prepared to answer them. Now please excuse me. I must go. Good day to you, sir."

He grinned. "I shall keep that in mind. And if I can ever help, I can be found just there," said Greenfield, pointing to Tent City.

Evangeline walked hurriedly to catch up with her father and Christine, who were entering the building. Evangeline was pleased she learned the officer's name. It would be important to Gabriel.

Greenfield watched her from afar then returned to the officers' tent. When he entered, he saw a pile of coins on the table where the officers were sitting. Wicker had a stupefied look while Turnbull was amused.

Turnbull looked at him. "Well, did you win for me or did she convert you to her heathen religion?"

Greenfield saluted. "If I were not a loyal Englishman true to our Holy Majesty, her beauty could cause men to do whatever she commanded. But yes, sir, you have won the wager. Her name is Evangeline, daughter of the mightiest Frenchman in the region."

"Drat it all," said Wicker. He did not believe a brute like Greenfield could ever have convinced such a beautiful girl to speak with him much less give him her name. He scowled and walked out leaving his money on the table. Turnbull took it and flipped one of the coins to Greenfield in thanks.

*

There was no other brothel in town but Hetty knew of large houses in the rich southern colonies of Massachusetts Bay and Mary Land. She had overheard young officers like Bancroft and Captain Adams talk about them when they first arrived. Hetty felt she was too old to relocate again but she could not afford to lose her most expensive, and profitable, girl to another colony. She laughed out loud every time she remembered picking up the waiflike ragamuffin from that dirty London street. Was that only six years ago? Time in Grand Pré surely flew by.

After Greenfield's long trip from Halifax nothing was more at the forefront of his mind than his favorite wench Gertie. Drat, he thought. What a livery stable in front of Hetty's today. Every soldier in the region must have tied his horse to the posts. He could find no place to hitch his own. No matter, he thought. He needed to buy his girl some hair ribbons anyway.

Gertie had new delights for him every time he visited, in the form of stories. The girl could spin a yarn that mesmerized him. When he asked where she had learned so many different tales she just waved him off and ended their session.

Gertie had hatched the idea of story-telling from a book she obtained from the wizened English mercantile dealer Timothy Cornhandle. He was a short little man who lived with his mother, a cripple who never left their rooms above the store. With three huge warts on his nose, he was a repugnant sight yet his store always seemed to be crowded with troops and Hetty's girls.

Cornhandle always believed his English customers preferred his merchandise to that of the French shops – except Madame Dupont's shop; she was the only one who carried ribbons and frilly lacey things. Cornhandle's mother forbade him to have such signs of debauchery in the store and since she paid all the bills he acquiesced. But the most likely reason was convenience. Cornhandle had the only store in the English Quarter of Grand Pré, which happened to be door to Hetty's where nearly every English soldier stopped at one time or another.

Gertie did not understand why the man's shop was so successful until she went into the store to see for herself. She learned he was able to procure special goods not found in any of the French shops. And as the only English shopkeeper in the area, Cornhandle would open the store after hours to anyone with coins to spend. But the soldiers were wary of him. Once, Lieutenant Bancroft told Gertie that Cornhandle would sell his mother if he could find a box big enough to put her in.

When Timothy Cornhandle saw Gertrude walk into his store, his heart melted. He was in love, true love, not lust like those rich soldiers. His warts shuddered with excitement. How could he make her his own? He waved her over to him.

"Good day to you, beautiful lady."

"Good day, sir."

"Timothy Cornhandle, your servant." He bowed nearly to the floor, which was not so difficult for him because he was only four feet tall.

She saw his trembling nose as he leaned his head gently against her thigh. She laughed and patted his head.

"I am Gertrude Lattimer."

"Is there some item of particularity you seek today?" he asked as he ran his beady eyes over her entire body.

"Your goods are unknown to me. What do you offer?"

"Of course, beautiful lady, this is your first visit. I would have recognized your bountiful features the moment you set your lovely foot in my humble establishment." He rubbed his hands together, eager to run them through her beautiful long tresses.

Gertie looked at him. The little old man was so nervous his whole body was trembling as he spoke. "What about a book?"

"A book would be fine. I aim to better myself with some more book learning."

"What kind, dear lady? I carry a variety to choose from." He pointed proudly to a rickety bookshelf with a handful of dusty volumes. Apparently no one in Grand Pré was interested in books, at least not the ones in his shop.

The French citizens of the town had two reasons not to buy his books. First, they were in the English language which some Acadians knew but preferred to read in French. And next, they would not support a British merchant. They gave their money to their family and neighbors who owned shops in town. As for the English men in Grand Pré, most were soldiers who could not read. The only English women were at Hetty's; they were either uneducated in that sense or they had no interest in books.

"Something not so difficult. No long words. Maybe with pictures?"

"Perhaps a novel of adventure would be of interest?"

"A what?"

"Well it is a new way of storytelling to capture your imagination and take your thoughts to a foreign land. What do you say, milady?"

"I think…yes, yes of course. I should like to have a…what you said."

"Novel of adventure."

"Yes."

"Beautiful lady, this is your special day. I have such a book but cannot show it to you now. My shop is filled with customers and I would like to take the time to explain this special book to you."

"That would be grand. When should I come back?"

"If you can return at dusk I will be closing and we can spend the time we need without interruption. I will keep the door closed even if late customers arrive so we can concentrate on your book."

The unsuspecting Gertrude agreed to return. Looking back, she did not regret what she had to do for the book because it had raised her stature with her employer, Hetty, and increased her demand. It was just that she liked direct talk. She did not like to go around the square to end up at the same place she started. But Timothy Cornhandle was not a straight talking man. He enjoyed the intrigue of walking around every tree in the square before getting to the point.

That evening, when Gertie returned, Cornhandle was waiting for her. The store was empty and after she entered, he drew the curtains and locked the entry door. His hair smelled like grease. Indeed, he had found some old cooking stuff to slick back his hair. His shriveled yellow teeth shone in the lamplight as he took her hand. The hairs on his three warts wiggled a greeting to her as he grinned widely.

Gertie willingly followed the ugly little man. A book about princes and princesses in foreign lands would be wonderful. She had only seen one such book in her life, in the London orphanage where she grew up. It was a picture book. She strained to remember and vaguely recalled the orphanage director read a little of the storybook every night, telling the tale of a servant girl who fell asleep for a thousand years. She was woken by the kiss of a handsome foreign prince who had found her missing slipper then he married her. They lived happily ever after with many children in a big shoe, and a wolf tried to blow the roof down but three little pigs, or maybe it was three blind mice, saved the day. She really loved that storybook.

Timothy brought Gertie into the outhouse and showed her the book. The outhouse served as a room to smoke meats, with a large hole in the ground for waste -- human and otherwise -- and boxes stacked in the corner covered with old wool blankets. She asked him what was in the boxes and it was the first and only time he had ever gotten sharp with her.

"Them's for an English officer. No sticking your nose where it ain't belonging, missy," he growled.

"I see nary a book so I will just leave now." She turned on her heels and marched angrily back into the shop.

Cornhandle scurried after her. "No. Wait. I have it. Please do not leave. "He slowly retrieved it from his filthy apron pocket, blowing the remaining dust off the cover. Salivating at the thought of touching the beauty standing before him, he opened the book to the first page and read the title.

"The Life and Strange Surprizing Adventures of Robinson Crusoe, of York, Mariner: Who lived Eight and Twenty Years, all alone in an un-inhabited Island on the Coast of America, near the Mouth of the Great River of Oroonoque; Having been cast on Shore by Shipwreck, wherein all the Men perished but himself. With An Account how he was at last as strangely deliver'd by Pyrates."

Once she heard the title of the book she knew she had to own it. But when she asked the price, he told her he would take trade only, not money. His price was steep -- Gertie's services, once each month for a year. Twelve times, she thought, twelve long times with the ugly stinky man. But the more she looked at the book, the more she decided he was no different than some of the smelly soldiers who came to her without boiling their uniforms or washing their hands or picking the grease and gristle out of their teeth. Thank goodness for the no kissing rule. Gertie made sure Hetty told every customer, new or repeat, kissing her girls was forbidden. Gertie could not tolerate bad mouth odor.

A few moments later Gertie and Cornhandle were back in the store. He opened the book to the last page and marked an "X" with his quill. He handed it to her saying, "Bring this with you each time you visit me. When there are twelve marks, your debt is paid. Each time you forget to bring the book, another month is added to the price."

"I shall remember to bring the book each time." Gertie did not want to extend her services beyond twelve months.

Gertie was anxious to escape and frantically pulled on the latch but it would not budge. Cornhandle sauntered up and unlocked the door with his key, twitching with excitement as she rushed out.

Today Gertie had opened the book and counted the marks he had made in the book. Eleven. The first time was last summer. As of today she only had to make one more visit to his outhouse and would never have to see him again. She had tried many times to buy out the remainder of the bargain, offering Cornhandle more than the cost of the book. But the little wart-faced man always refused, preferring her company to money even if for only a few minutes in the outhouse.

As Gertrude read of Robinson Crusoe's adventures, she began to devise her own stories but added more romance. She told one of her stories to Greenfield, who paid her extra. She told a different story to the visiting Captain Murray and he did the same. Soon, after a chat with Hetty, Gertie charged the highest prices in the house. Just for *talking* to a man, telling him made-up stories. A girl had to plan ahead, she thought. She had a steady clientele and she liked their attentions. But she liked their money even more, and was determined to keep the men coming back.

For each client, she wove an adventurous tale which left the hero and heroine in desperate predicaments at the end of the session, promising to reveal the ending the following week. But when the gentleman returned, the main characters found themselves in different perils at the end of that session.

As Gertie's stories continued, her clients increased and her pile of coins grew. Gertie had saved nearly enough to move to Bostontown where she would work in a respectable shop, marry her prince and live happily ever after. Cornhandle had given her the idea the month before.

"If you are interested in a position in the new colonies, I could help you." Cornhandle's eye rolled as he leered at her. The thought of her being in his debt was almost too much to fathom. Oh, the things they would do. To convince her he began to embellish his abilities and connections.

"I have no intention of moving, as I am very content here," Gertie said, hiding her interest. Then she strengthened her bargaining power. "You know our arrangement terminates next month?"

The little man nodded, furrowing his brow at the thought of not seeing her again in that way. "My cousin, Jonas Cornhandle, is well-placed in Bostontown. He works at the port and knows the captains and ship owners."

She ignored him, although she was dying of curiosity. He sensed he had whetted her appetite for adventure so he grabbed her hand.

"I could arrange passage for you and then my cousin would place you in a higher station there."

"How does your cousin know such important people?" She was thinking of befriending the cousin in exchange for an introduction to a rich ship owner.

Cornhandle's three warts twitched with excitement. He hoped she would agree to his plan. "He has become very rich and very powerful. He even knows the Mayor of Bostontown, because he trades in slaves -- especially white ones."

Her eyebrows shot up when he mentioned slaves.

Cornhandle continued, "He says trading is brisk in whites. Plantations are in dire need of labor and not many indentures are coming in from England."

"What is that...indent...?"

"Indentured slaves. They sign up to work on the plantations without pay. Farmers pay their passage and get free labor for seven years. But those plantation owners are smart. They charge the slaves for everything, even water and hay for their bed. So they mostly have to work another three years to pay off their food and shelter."

"Why do they not simply run away?"

"Penalty for runaway white slaves is death."

He leaned toward her and whispered, "The English Council is looking around here for new sources of white slavery."

"How do you know this? What does this mean?" she sputtered.

"You ain't heard it from me but Frenchies might make for good farm workers, being as they have experience on their own. If they decide to fight, there might not be a Grand Pré for you to work in."

"Oh poppycock. I heard you detest the Frenchies because they are too much competition for you."

"I swear this information is true. Swear on my mother's life. Comes straight from Governor Shirley himself. My cousin had a meeting with him in Bostontown last month."

She stared at him. "What of the town? What does he say it is like?"

"Not like here. They's got streets paved with stone cobbles. Shops all have big windows. Houses are tall and made of bricks. Not like the wood and stone houses here."

She ruminated on the thought that her beautiful dresses and silk shoes would not get muddy. Cobblestone streets would be a dream come true. And rich clients, not soldiers.

"So's you interested?"

She nodded cautiously. "That would depend on the details. See if you can get them for me next time we meet."

He grinned. He would box up his mother, marry the girl and take them both to Bostontown. And with Gertie's skills Timothy calculated he would not even have to work.

As Cornhandle mentally schemed, so did Gertrude. Yes, she would move to Bostontown and live in a civilized world, not like the forgotten territory of Grand Pré. She might even wed his rich cousin or, if he was already married, then she would become his mistress and have all the new dresses and ribbons she wanted.

Gertie thanked Lieutenant Bancroft for the coins as he exited her room. Then she absentmindedly looked through the lace curtains outside. She smiled when she saw her regular customer Greenfield down the street at Madame Dupont's shop. Everyone still called it Madame Dupont's even though Madame Arnaud ran it most days. My, my, she thought. That book was worth it in the end. She wondered if she could double her prices in Bostontown. The villagers here were well off but the Bostonians must be even richer to have stone cobbles and brick houses.

*

Gertie had often thought of that picture book through the years. The images and the story gave her hope when the orphanage turned her out at ten into the big, dirty city of London. Parents like hers in difficult financial straits could not feed all the hungry mouths at their table, so children too little for the workhouses were left at an orphanage. When more and more young children arrived the older ones were forced out to make room. On her first night alone, Gertie slept in a dirty alleyway near the orphanage. She was determined not to cry so she dreamed about the picture book.

Early the next morning she dusted herself off and walked into the street. She bumped into Hetty, causing the older woman to drop her basket full of food. Gertie was stunned, not by the lady's beautiful dress but by the variety of beautiful foods. Cheeses, meats, funny fruits and vegetables of all kinds and, of course, a large round bread. Gertie wanted to grab some food and run but she had visions of being a princess and this lady looked like a queen to her.

Instead, Gertie picked up all the food and loaded it back into the basket, then did her best imitation of a curtsy and looked up at Hetty. "Your queenship, would you happen to need a housemaid in your castle?"

Hetty laughed so hard she tipped over the basket herself. Gertie dutifully replaced all the foods and looked down at her feet. How would she ever get to be a princess if she could not convince the queen to take her to the castle?

"What do they call you?"

"My given name is Gertrude…but Gertie is fine, dear queen lady."

Hetty shook her head and continued to laugh. "No, girl, I am no queen, though some of my customers say I treat them like a king. You can call me Hetty. How would you like to live with me and learn to be a lady?"

Gertie was at first confused about the talk of customers and kings but understood Hetty was asking her to live in her castle. She was overjoyed and wrapped her skinny arms around the well-endowed Hetty. "Yes, Queen Hetty, I would like that very much. I will be your servant and then become a lady and marry a prince and live happily ever after."

Hetty laughed again. "That is what they all say at first, Gertie; that is what they all say." Hetty took Gertie under her wing, buying her pretty dresses and new shoes, and teaching her to read and write. That might come in handy as the girl's features faded. When Gertie turned thirteen and finally had curves, Hetty put her to work, making sure she got a very pretty penny for Gertie's first time. Hetty needed to get her three-year investment back.

When the English military advertised in London for "special lady friends" to move to the Nova Scotia territory, Hetty had jumped at the opportunity. She reaped the benefits of being the first and, as it turns out, the only vendor of female companionship in response to the full page in the *London Gazette*, which announced:

"A Riche City in the British Lands of Neuwe Scotlande populated by the King's Troopes needs Speciale Ladie Friende Services for which Payement shall be Prompte and in the King's Coin. Sea Transporte provided."

*

Hetty liked military men, both soldiers and officers. They spent their money willingly, especially before a battle, as they never knew what the outcome would be. Hetty never regretted the move and had built up such wealth by the summer of 1755 she was planning to move back to London and sell the business to Gertie. She hoped Gertie would be more selective with her gentleman callers, as she looked so tired of late.

Gertrude was as unaware of Hetty's thoughts as the madam was of Gertie's idea to move out to Bostontown. Gertrude's steady clientele showered her with gifts to make them more memorable among all the new troops clamoring for her favors, of which the soldiers had heard stories night after night, in Tent City. After all, Gertrude had only so many hours in the day and night. With hundreds of well-paid soldiers she knew Greenfield realized he could not risk her tiring of him. But she was tiring of his little trinkets. She would demand more expensive gifts like jewelry and, of course, more money. She needed to build her treasure chest for her move to Bostontown. That is where she was convinced she would find her prince and be happy forever after.

Down the street, Lieutenant Greenfield pounded his fist on the door of Madame Dupont's dress shop. He was anxious to get his gift for Gertie and then get into her soft bed with its secret delights. Time was a-wasting. Why did the Frenchies close their shops during the day? Where was that woman?

The thunder clapped loudly and the downpour began in earnest. Greenfield saw the stacks of silk ribbons in the corner and was about to break the window when Madame Arnaud opened the door.

"What can I do for you today, sir?" she asked politely, waving him in.

"Some more of them silk streamers you sold me last week."

Adèle nodded knowingly and led him to a table. She laid out rolls of ribbons in all the colors of the rainbow. Silks in soft yellows and pale greens melted into a sea of blues that merged into lilacs and pinks. She pulled out the blues in every shade from the palest azure to the darkest midnight.

Greenfield grunted. He did not know what to choose. The selection was much too vast. "I should have to think about this. I know she likes pink...." He hesitated because he was color blind. The only reason he knew she liked that particular color was that Madame Arnaud had suggested it on his last visit. He remembered how Gertie had shown her appreciation to him. He remembered how odd it seemed that she kept repeating pink was the "princess's color." So he knew she liked that color.

Sensing his predicament, Adèle Dupont cut several ribbons in varying shades of blue and shaped them into a beautiful hair bow. She affixed a pin and said, "You bought the pinks last time. Perhaps these shades of blue would be to her liking?"

Greenfield grunted again, uncomfortable at seeing all the lacey things around him. The only time he liked to see those things was when he took them off Gertie and threw them on the floor. Once he ripped her bodice so quickly that he had to give her money to buy a new one. He presumed she bought it from this shop but did not want to ask. He grew angry at the thought of her wearing those lacey things for any man but him. He was determined to marry her and make her his for all time. When Adèle handed him the package, he sheepishly left some coins on the table and quickly exited the shop.

Adèle locked the door behind him, scrutinizing his actions. He seemed erratic, even angry, she thought as she watched him untie his horse.

Greenfield took a long swig from his flask and looked down the street to Hetty's. He could see nothing but dim candlelight shimmers due to the blinding rain. He starting thinking of Gertie, his Gertie, with another soldier, with many soldiers and became angry and jealous. He had to possess her. He opened his flask again and downed the rest of the grog. He wiped his mouth and, with a dazed look in his eyes, he put his foot in the stirrup. At the very moment he was mounting his horse, lightning struck and a loud thunderbolt cracked. The horse reared in fear, throwing the officer to the ground.

Swearing loudly, Greenfield pulled himself up out of the mire, a brown smelly mixture of horse manure and mud. He tied the horse to the post and walked down the street. He passed Bancroft riding toward the Tent City. The men saluted each other though Greenfield's was more of a drunken wave than a military sign.

In her room, Gertrude retied the ribbons on her lingerie. She loved the embroidery on the lace imported from France that was sold at Madame Dupont's. Even if the men could not appreciate the handiwork because of their haste to get their hands on her body beneath it, she reveled in feeling like a princess each time she wore the handmade creations.

Downstairs she heard noises, shouts and scuffles. She and the other girls ran out of their rooms and looked over the railing to see a drunk Greenfield reeling. He grabbed collars of soldiers and screamed at them, "Have you been with Gertie? My Gertie?"

Each man shook his head quickly and rushed out of the room. Greenfield made his way to the stairs, tripping over chairs and tables.

Gertie looked all around but Bancroft was nowhere to be seen. Lieutenant Greenfield looked up and saw Gertie. He waved at her. "You are not to see any man but me. Nobody else."

Gertie tried to placate him. "Lieutenant, sir, come upstairs. Let us have a talk about this." She did not see Hetty anywhere.

Greenfield started taking the stairs two at a time, yelling at her. "You're mine, Gertie. Nobody can have you but me." At the top of the stairs he wheeled around and shouted to the soldiers, "Do you hear me? Nobody is to see Gertie as of this moment. Only me. Do you understand?" He looked over the crowd of men. They all nodded, some in fear, some chuckling under their breath.

"Who is that I hear laughing at me? I am your superior officer. What soldier is that mocking me?"

By now Greenfield weaved along the railing and stood next to Gertie. He took her hand and kissed it. Several soldiers laughed again. The girls took their clients back into their rooms.

Greenfield turned to the soldiers, "You who mock me. I know who you are and I will punish you. Mark my words."

Gertie grabbed his hand and tried to pull him into the room. At that moment Greenfield slapped her so hard she fell to the ground. Several soldiers started up the stairs but Greenfield warned them. "This is not your concern. Go back to the tents. All of you."

The soldiers of lesser rank obeyed the officer and left the brothel. Only a few officers were left in the main room below. They were awestruck at Greenfield's lack of decorum and his jealous rage.

Hetty appeared out of nowhere. "Gentlemen, follow me into the music room. I have opened my best bottles for you to enjoy. Compliments of the house, of course." She pointed the way down the hall and looked at Gertie questioningly.

Gertie nodded that she had things under control. Hetty followed the men into the other room. Music was playing and glasses were clinking. She shut the door.

Gertie managed to get Greenfield into her room and lay him on the bed. He mumbled incoherently and tossed the hair ribbon at her.

"For you, my darling Gertie."

"Mister Greenfield, I have wished to speak with you."

"You're mine, Gertie. No more men."

"We need to talk. I leave Grand Pré for Bostontown soon."

"No!" He grabbed her hand and pulled her on top of him on the bed. "No, you will never leave. Not without me."

"You have been a wonderful gentleman caller."

"Caller? I am but a *caller* to you?" He sat up on the bed, enraged.

"That is not what I meant. You are more than that, of course. You are a friend, a very dear friend. And I am hoping that my darling friend can provide me with more money now to leave."

"Not without me I said. You cannot leave. You are mine."

She shook her head defiantly. "I must go, I am sorry."

"*NO! NEVER!*" He grabbed her by the throat.

Trembling with fear, Gertie slowly unwrapped his fingers from around her neck as she gently stroked his cheek. "I think you should go and get some rest now. We shall talk tomorrow."

"We shall talk now or never talk again." He pulled her up by the hair and she screamed. Then he wrapped his arms around her. "I love you, Gertie. I want you to be my wife."

She pulled his arms away from her and tried to urge him to the door. He did not budge.

"Are you going to marry me or not?"

She shook her head. "I am sorry, you are a friend but I am set on marrying a man in Bostontown. I have made arrangements to leave in a fortnight."

Furious, Greenfield grabbed her by the arm and slapped her so hard she went limp. He picked her up and tossed her onto the bed. She was moaning but no one was present to hear her. He leaned over to kiss her and she weakly said, "I will not marry you. Please leave me be."

Greenfield became enraged and slapped her again. When Gertie tried to put her hands in front of her face, he tore them away and punched her with his fist. She was silent, unmoving. He whispered, "Gertie, wake up. Gertie?" He took his handkerchief and wiped her bloody face, caressing the bruises he had inflicted.

When she did not move, he continued, "You look so tired. Just sleep, then. We will make arrangements tomorrow to get married. You are not going to Bostontown." He kissed her lips, then weaved his way down the stairs to the entry room which was empty.

As he exited, Greenfield became angry again, ruminating on Gertie's words. How dare that woman think of going away. And without him. What was it she had said before she went to sleep? Oh yes, she wanted more money. So all she thought about was his money. Well, he would find another lady friend. He walked through the rain towards his horse.

On her way back from meeting with Père Rivière Evangeline passed in front of Madame Dupont's shop. The priest had offered without success to escort her home but Evangeline insisted she preferred to walk alone the few streets to her home. She saw Greenfield's mount tied outside the shop, next to a dark alley. Evangeline petted the horse and looked down the street for its owner but saw no one. Suddenly from the shadows Greenfield grabbed her, covered her mouth with his hand and pushed her into the alleyway.

Evangeline was overpowered by Greenfield's strength, but she kicked and bit his hand. He pulled out his knife and placed it near her throat. He stumbled a bit and accidentally nicked her neck, drawing a few drops of blood.

She pleaded with him. "Please just let me go. I will not tell anyone...."

Greenfield clamped his mouth again on her throat. "Shut yer trap, little wench." He swayed, still drunk and she shuddered but did not kick or bite again. He slurred his speech. "You are mine now. You are not going to Bostontown and you are my property to do as I wish."

She mumbled through his hand. Clearly terrified of his knife, she whispered. "Please sir. I have but a few coins but please take them all."

"I said shut it. Tell me where is that friend of the Injun Kitok...the traitor Gabriel? I seen you with him riding your horses through town, taunting me." His head dropped and he steadied himself by leaning the hand with the knife against the wall.

"Sir, please remove your hand so I can speak to you."

He took his hand away but replaced the knife at her throat. "If you scream, you are a dead girl."

She nodded slowly and carefully because of the knife. "Do you speak of Kitok the Mi'Kmaq guide?"

"No guide I heard of ransacks papers. He is a Frenchie agent." His eyelids close briefly and he nearly keeled over but regained his senses. He grabbed her and pushed her against the wall. "And d'Entremont is no patriot. Where are they?" He pressed the knife closer to her neck.

The rain slackened up and Evangeline desperately looked into the street for help. She could not risk a scream, not with the knife at her throat. But it would have been futile; the streets were empty. The Acadians were all in their homes saying their night prayers or already asleep. She saw no candles burning in windows, no troops roaming the streets.

Evangeline resorted to her wits since the man had easily overpowered her. "Sir, I have no information that you request. Please just let me know what you want and this will be done with."

"No!" He sneered at her.

"Here," she proffered her purse. "Take everything in it but I beg you to let me go. My Papa is...."

"I know who he is. I am guessing you have no memory of doing a tease on me after your church several weeks ago, missy. Well your paw ain't nowhere around, is he? Neither is that Acadian spy you have been seen riding with."

Evangeline struggled but his grip on her was tight and rough. She was about to scream, regardless of the risk when she felt his huge hands pressing down on her mouth and throat. She could hardly breathe.

"Now you are mine." She bit his hand as hard as she could manage. He yelped, "Ouww, why you little...." Evangeline gasped for air. She tried to scream but no sound came out. She did not see his huge hand but felt a hard knock on the back of her head. She was instantly thrown into the mud and landed with a soft thump.

"Better than the likes of you deserves, little heathen hussy. You commenced to toss those long locks at me and showed me those big French eyes and then you ignored me every time you passed the tents? No woman gets away with that no matter who she is. Not with Greenfield here."

Gabriel was walking down the street and heard the drunken voice from around the corner.

Greenfield slit the ties on Evangeline's bodice with his knife then tossed it deeper into the alley and ripped at her clothing. Quite inebriated, he fell over just as Gabriel ran into the alley.

Seeing Gabriel and needing a weapon, Greenfield scrambled up and stumbled down the alley in search of his knife. He saw a shiny reflection near a stack of crates.

Gabriel grabbed a large rock to chase the English officer but stopped when he saw Evangeline lying as if unconscious in the muddy path. For the moment Gabriel forgot about the English officer to help his love. He knelt over her and tried to revive her while keeping an eye on Greenfield down the way. He was slumped over and looked like he had passed out from drinking.

Finally Evangeline opened her eyes and on seeing him, she wept for joy.

He kissed her softly and whispered. "Are you hurt?"

She shook her head.

"Wait here a moment and let me make sure the attacker will not harm you ever again."

Evangeline grabbed his hand weakly. "Please do not hurt him. He is an English officer named Greenfield. There could be consequences." She debated about telling him more so she added. "He was intoxicated. I do not think he shall remember a thing."

Gabriel responded abruptly. "I will not be but a moment. Close your eyes and rest. Then I will return to take you home."

Too weak to argue, she did as she was bid. Gabriel held his rock tightly as he walked toward Greenfield, but the man had not moved since Gabriel last saw him. His mouth was white with a foamy substance which from a distance looked like he had vomited on himself. As Gabriel walked closer he saw a large snake slithering away. He was surprised, as he had always believed the snakes in these parts were not venomous. But he saw puncture wounds on Greenfields's hand -- the one he had stuck behind the crates seeking his knife. Perhaps something in Greenfield's body had reacted to the reptile's bite. Or it was possible he had choked on his own vomit. In either case, an evil man had gotten his just desserts.

Gabriel ran back to Evangeline, who was still moaning softly but very much alive. He covered her ripped dress with his jacket, then checked her hands. He saw scratches but no fang marks. He kissed the scratches and gently lifted her to him and held her close.

"Can you wrap your arms around my neck?"

Evangeline opened her eyes. "Gabriel. The officer…is he?"

"Yes, you will have no more trouble from him. But did he hurt you?"

She shook her head slowly. "It is nothing. But he said things…."

He shushed her with a kiss, at first tender which became more fervent. They pulled away from each other, afraid of their mutual passion. Knowing Greenfield was no longer a threat, Gabriel carried Evangeline to the street.

"He knew about you, Kitok opening his document satchel, all of it. Please tell me what you are doing and how I can help."

"You are the most beautiful, intelligent woman in Grand Pré. But these things are better left to the men."

She pulled away angrily but fell back against him, still too weak to walk on her own.

"You took care of me. You will take care of the English. Why is it always you taking care of everything?"

"Of course I did not mean…."

"How many ribbons and dresses can I buy, or cakes can I bake, or quilts can I sew without feeling utterly useless? I am meant to accomplish more important things. I had hoped I could do so with you."

Gabriel softly took her shoulders with his hands.

"If Greenfield thinks you know of the resistance then his superiors must believe the same about you. And if Turnbull thinks you have information about the resistance not even your father could protect you. Conspirators are slowly tortured to reveal even the slightest details. I would not dare put you in that position."

"It is my choice. And I am willing to take the risk if we can work together."

Gabriel looked at her and released her shoulders, taking her hands into his.

"If this is what you want."

She nodded emphatically. "I assure you it is, Gabriel."

"Then we shall both work closely for our cause against the English."

They embraced and kissed longingly until Gabriel broke away.

"You must leave now and not wait for me to move the body. Do you feel safe returning home alone?"

She nodded. "After our conversation I feel I can do anything. Thank you my love."

She hurried out of the alley. Gabriel looked protectively after her, and then finished his work. He dragged Greenfield's body to the end of the alley and pushed it behind the crates. Perhaps the snake would remain there and feed on its prey.

As the rain continued to pour, unseen by anyone, Gabriel set Greenfield's horse free, giving it a gentle tap on the haunches. The horse trotted out of the city gates and stopped in front of Hetty's pleasure palace. The hitching posts were empty at this late hour. The troops respected the Lieutenant-Colonel's curfew.

Inside the brothel, Hetty had discovered Gertie moaning softly in her room. The girl had not been able to lift herself out of bed and was too battered to cry out for help. Her face was a bloody pulp and several teeth had been knocked onto the bed linens, now stained dark purple.

Hetty cleaned Gertie's face and dressed her in a clean nightgown before tucking her in for the evening. She detested the through of losing her best girl but she had grown to love Gertie like a daughter. And her little girl had to be protected.

Closing Gertie's chamber door behind her, Hetty made her way into her boudoir. She sat at the immense hand-carved wooden desk, a gift from that nice Governor Shirley. He had allowed his officers a brief respite at Hetty's establishment during an inspection of the Fort. Shirley had shared conversation and a glass of wine with the madam while his soldiers' partook in more lively activities upstairs.

Purposefully, Hetty pulled a page of notepaper from the desk drawer and dipped a quill into the inkpot. She began to write the letter that would at once sadden her with the lost profits but also fill her with maternal pride at protecting her favorite girl from harm.

"Dear Madame Taylor,

Are you still looking for new girls for your second house in Bostontown? I believe I have just the right one for you. I dread her loss for she has made me a pretty penny as she will you, I dare say. But still I ask that you care for her as a daughter, as she has been to me...."

CHAPTER 35
Raid

GRAND PRÉ

 rom a distance the couple appeared to be merely young lovers enjoying each other's company at a private picnic. But the man's eyes drifted over the bluff to the sea quite often. The woman followed his gaze, understanding but saying nothing.

The couple, Evangeline and Gabriel, munched the last of the luncheon as they lay on a blanket he had strategically placed under a grove of trees on the bluff overlooking the harbor below. They enjoyed a long discussion of theological philosophy. They applied religious theories to their concerns about the political situation between France and England, the resistance, and the killing of enemies in war as opposed to taking prisoners.

Evangeline had stressed the importance of kindness to the enemies. She espoused not taking an eye for an eye but, rather, turning the other cheek and affording English troops the opportunity to work with the French Neutrals to resolve differences.

Gabriel always contested her philosophy. He described the atrocities that the British soldiers had committed on their fellow Acadian countrymen, women and children. He reiterated French history of battles instigated by the bloodthirsty English, and their bounty placed on scalps of the Acadians' Indian allies resulting in Acadian deaths, too.

Gabriel held Evangeline's hand as he challenged her. "How can you justify another opportunity to English troops after they have burned so many French villages, massacred innocent families and scalped our Mi'Kmaq friends?"

"Gabriel, you speak of acts occurring many years ago. There have been no such burnings and no proof of widespread killings in many years. Papa was just saying at dinner that Lieutenant-Governor Lawrence wrote him about a possible release of the captured prisoners in Halifax. That means they are all alive. And he indicated his willingness to negotiate rather than to declare war over the demand that we sign the King's unconditional Oath. This is the proof you seek that the English have turned a new page on their past."

"But Greenfield...?"

"Please do not try to raise that issue. We both know he acted quite independently of any military orders."

Their discussion on the subject always ended in a stalemate. Each firmly believed the other's way was an alternative but not the best resolution to the problem. And each failed to convince the other of the "right" position.

After their lively debate, Evangeline and Gabriel ended their respite reluctantly. She shivered as he whispered in her ear.

"My darling Evangeline, the time is coming when there will be no room for philosophy or kind words, merely survival and protection of our own against the English enemies."

She had tried to protest, but he kissed her lips softly with a promise of more. "We must be vigilant for war is in the air now. More troops are arriving every day. Look at the Bay. Do you see vessels on the horizon?"

Evangeline had squinted and was not sure if the shapes she saw were the partial outlines of rigging and masts or low-hanging clouds. She shook her head.

"What if those are just animal transports loading more cattle to sell in the colonies?"

He shook his head. "If so, that is not their true purpose, I assure you."

She looked at him with concern in her eyes. "What shall we do?"

Gabriel smiled grimly. "We have some time, but very little. Those vessels that remain nearly invisible will be brought in under the cover of darkness. I am certain the English are the enemy and they are a grave threat to all of us. Please prepare a small trunk or satchel with all your valuables and a change of clothes and have it ready. Warn Christine as well. I may come for you both at any hour to carry you to safety."

"But should we not talk to Papa about this?"

They walked away from the cliff. "Let me choose the time to discuss it. Kitok and Marc and other patriots are waiting for me, but rest assured I could not miss being with you, even for such a short while."

"Nor I, my love," Evangeline replied.

He was disappointed that he could not spend more time with the woman he adored, but he had to lead the secret militia. They were devising a plan to keep the Acadians and their Mi'Kmaq allies safe from the English, whom they knew were dangerous. One look at the actions of Governor Shirley or Lieutenant-Governor Lawrence or Captain Turnbull said it all.

Gabriel kissed Evangeline passionately, holding her in an embrace as long as he dared. Then he lifted her onto her horse and handed her the reins. They rode down the hill together. He escorted her to the Consulate's stables and helped her dismount.

Then he kissed her and said, "Remember. Pack your things." He pulled a small box out of his waistcoat and said, "There is one more thing, Evangeline my love."

Her heart leapt. Gabriel pulled a gold locket from the box and clasped it around Evangeline's neck. He opened it to reveal their images, each on one side of the locket facing each other.

"I had hoped it would be ready for your birthday but the artist took longer than expected."

She interrupted him and kissed him firmly on the lips. "It is exquisite. Thank you so much." Then she grinned slyly and kissed him again.

When he looked at her quizzically, she said, "That was for the artist. You really should paint more often. Your work is beautiful."

Gabriel nodded. "The Versailles Court Artist Pater told me I had the makings of a painter at age six." He looked up. "That was the day you were born." He suddenly had a faraway look in his eyes, remembering his pledge to marry her.

Evangeline leaned her head against his chest. "Do you miss not going to Versailles? Whenever Papa or Christine talk of it, Court seems like a paradise." She looked up at him. "Perhaps we shall go one day?"

He kissed her tenderly. "If I had done so, I would not have been with you. And that, my love, would be the opposite of a paradise." Then he looked at her solemnly. "If anything should happen to me, go at once to the house and look behind your portrait." He pulled her into his arms again, holding her tightly to him.

She touched the locket. "God is at your side. Nothing will harm you."

"All the same, promise me that you shall do it."

She nodded rapidly. "Of course, you know I shall. But God shall keep you safe."

In his office, René was entrenched into his work. Evangeline burst through the back door from the stables. She beamed and hugged herself. Then she ran into the office, kissed René's cheek and asked, "Papa?" He waved her away without a word. She dropped her head in disappointment and left the room, closing the door behind her.

As she approached the staircase, she saw Christine give her an encouraging look. Evangeline skipped up the stairs and gaily grabbed Christine's arm, linking it with hers. The young woman smiled uncontrollably but did not say a word until they had walked down the hall and up the stairs into her room.

Christine and Evangeline sat on the bed. Christine took her hand. "Forgive your father. He has pressing political matters that leave him time for nothing else. But your eyes shine with happy news. You must tell me everything. Is it Gabriel? Did he ask you...?"

Evangeline quickly interrupted her to pull the locket from under the bodice of her dress and display it proudly.

"How did you know his feelings for me? They are so much stronger than I had dared to hope. My love for him is such that it fills my heart to overflowing."

Christine smiled when she saw the miniatures. Like a loving mother, Christine hugged the girl she had raised from birth who was a girl no longer. Silent tears streamed from both women. Evangeline laid her head on Christine's shoulder.

Christine stroked Evangeline's hair as she had done when Evangeline was a little girl. "When love is right you feel it with your entire being. Sometimes it comes crashing in like the tides or a waterfall. But often it flows within your heart like an ongoing stream with no waves but a strong current just the same."

Evangeline pulled away from Christine. "Is that how I should feel? A burning ache when I am with him and an even stronger longing for him when I am not?"

Christine kissed the top of Evangeline's head and opened the locket again. "Love is a sword that both hurts and protects. You must understand Gabriel is a passionate man. But he is devoted to his faith and belief in his political cause. That fervor and zeal are much stronger than any ardor he could offer you."

Evangeline huffed. "What do you know of love? You, a spinster who has never known a man's devotion. What gives you the right to intrude on my happiness?"

Christine felt the sting as if Evangeline had slapped her. She stood and walked to the door, then turned back. "You are right. I am not your mother. But I fear your disappointment at expecting something Gabriel is incapable of. You could have any man you desired. Yet you have chosen someone who has already committed his life and his dying breath to his country. Look into your heart and determine if what he can give is enough for you."

Evangeline refused to look at her, caressing the locket. "I love him with my whole heart. And I know he loves me, in his own way. That is sufficient for both of us."

At the door Christine looked at her and said. "Your supper will get cold." She closed the door after her.

Evangeline leaned back on her bed, staring at the locket. She was too overwhelmed with joy to eat. That would have to wait until tomorrow.

Back in the dining room, Christine heard an impatient knock at the front entry of the building downstairs. She looked down into the entry hall from the landing as René opened the door. Turnbull and Wicker roughly pulled him outside.

"What is the meaning of this treatment? How dare you approach me this way. Lieutenant-Colonel Winslow shall hear of this and it shall not be to his liking, I assure you."

"He is the one who gave us the order. Go with us peacefully or follow in chains. Your choice."

"I am readily available to meet with him at any time. Guards are unnecessary. He has but to ask."

René called to the women inside. "Christine? Evangeline? I am going to the British Commander's office."

Christine leaned over the railing, questioning him with her eyes, asking if everything was in order. René responded with a nod. "I shall return soon. No cause for concern."

He exited and closed the door behind him. Christine anxiously peered out of the window and watched him stride proudly ahead of the military escort. Wicker pulled him back as Turnbull scowled at René's display of confidence and independence.

Inside Winslow's office Turnbull walked ahead of René to stand in front of Winslow's desk.

Rene turned to Winslow. "Please inform Captain Turnbull…."

But Winslow interrupted him. "Silence! Your diplomatic status has no effect in this investigation."

"Investigation?"

"Who murdered my officer?"

"What murder? When? I know nothing of any murder." René was genuinely confused.

"We found Lieutenant Greenfield's body crumpled in back of an alleyway today. No doubt the dirty work of the Acadian militia. Yes, it is a secret no longer. Who is the ringleader? Tell me and save the lives of the others."

"John, I swear to you...."

"*On the Bible*! Swear on the Holy Book."

René dutifully placed his hand on Winslow's Good Book.

"I swear before God and on the Holy Bible that I have no knowledge of any officer's death or a secret Acadian militia. If I did, I would personally end it, so strong are the desires of our good Catholic King Louis for peace and my intentions in respecting his wishes."

The two men glared at each other.

"I have sworn it to be true. You must believe it is so, knowing how much my faith means to me." René was adamantly telling the truth.

Winslow scowled. "You would not declare a falsehood before God. But someone else must know of this."

Turnbull responded in his stead. "We are watching your men. Any act against the Crown is treason and shall mean an immediate public hanging."

"You have no reason to worry."

Winslow waved him away. "I bid you good night, Consul."

"Good night, Lieutenant-Colonel."

René exited. Once the door closed, Winslow turned to Turnbull.

"Carry out the next phase of our Great and Noble Scheme while they are in their Church supper on Sunday. It is only fitting they should be punished on the day they practice those heathen ways."

Turnbull saluted. "We are ready and shall execute your orders on that day."

The next morning René had just reached the bottom of the stairs as Gabriel entered the front door. René turned and addressed him contritely in the hallway.

"I owe you an apology. The tension is indeed as severe as you warned."

"What has happened?"

"An English officer was found dead. Do you know anything of it?"

Gabriel hesitated but René continued without realizing Gabriel had not responded.

"John said he was murdered. He believes an Acadian is to blame. I was almost unable to contain their anger. I have no doubt they plan a reprisal if the guilty man does not step forward."

Gabriel then spoke. "Monsieur le Consul, might I first inform you of what I am here to say?"

René looked at him. "What is it?"

"I have organized a group of young Acadian patriots to fight the English. Chief Matok is with us and Kitok has brought his braves to our cause. "

"How many are you?"

"About a hundred men my age. Père Rivière, who also leads us in prayer for the cause. The Mik'maqs, of course, led by Prince Kitok. But English troops still outnumber us. One word from you would recruit all the remaining men."

"This path guarantees death."

"The English shall suffer as well. Liberty always demands a price."

"Gabriel, you are like a son to me. But I will not jeopardize the lives of my daughter and the other French Neutrals. We have worked too long to continue the peace."

"But surely, Monsieur le Consul, you understand they are making plans to attack us. We have not many details but it is inevitable."

"Give me the information and I shall write at once to inform the King asking for his guidance."

"And the militia?"

"I shall say nothing for the moment. But bring me the news."

"Yes sir. I shall do so, sir. Kitok should have more for us shortly."

From the second floor landing Evangeline eavesdropped on the conversation below.

René continued, "If this is your mission, I insist you choose between being my Vice Consul or the resistance leader. You cannot continue as both. I am certain you understand why."

Gabriel looked up to see Evangeline at the top of the stairs, encouraging him. He nodded at her, then led René into the office and closed the door. Gabriel shook nervously.

"Sir, I am in love with your daughter and intend to marry her. With your blessing, of course…and if she will have me."

"Gabriel, I must ask. Have you spoken your intentions to her?"

"No sir. Many times I have nearly made my declaration. I wanted to wait for your approval…and for the military situation to be resolved."

René paused thoughtfully. "You know you shall not be a husband to anyone if John Winslow hangs you for sedition."

Gabriel nodded quickly.

René asked, "Has Evangeline made her feelings known to you?"

"We have not spoken directly, Lord Le Blanc. But I believe she shares the same emotions. We believe in the same ideals of freedom and hope, a rare quality in a young woman, even one as spirited as Evangeline."

René looked up at him sharply. "Have you enlisted her to aid your resistance movement?"

Gabriel quickly shook his head, anxious to convince his future father-in-law. "Please believe me when I say I disclosed nothing to her. But you must know your daughter is quite intelligent. She deduced the strategy herself after seeing activity in the harbor and the increase in English troops." He was eager to turn the tables and change the subject. "Did she speak to you of this subject, sir?"

René responded curtly. "As to you and Evangeline, marriage is out of the question. As we discussed last year, she is to be presented at Versailles as her mother wished, where she will no doubt have her choice of noblemen. The plans are already underway. Family redemption of sorts."

"But if the purpose is to marry a French nobleman I can meet Lady Eugenie's standards. After the Halifax Massacre, I inherited my father's title and estates in France, along with our holdings here. Though I sold the stables to Monsieur Langlinais after Father died, he is aging and should be amenable to selling them back if that is your desire. I have the income to provide Evangeline with anything she desired."

"Gabriel, there is certainly no question of your nobility or of your wealth. You are a good man and have served His Majesty and myself well. But with your activities and the most likely outcome, she would feel a lifetime of pain by losing a spouse at an early age after only a brief period of marriage. I could not forgive myself if she had to suffer as I have."

"Is there nothing I can say, sir?"

"I insist you make your choice."

"I must respectfully choose our cause as the best way to honor my King and to protect our citizens. His Majesty shall be better served with me in the militia than in this office and I shall continue to perform above the call of my duties. But I shall pray that you allow me to marry your daughter."

"Reluctantly, I accept your resignation. But I must have your promise that you shall not see my daughter as long as you are part of this militia."

Gabriel looked at the man who had taught him all the politics he knew. Ignoring the request he responded, "I have asked for your daughter's hand. Are you rejecting me as a suitor to Evangeline?"

René chose his words carefully. "Evangeline is more precious to me than you know."

"I pledge my undying love and protection to her. I assure you that her life is not in danger nor would I allow it to be. I could live with the Mi'Kmaqs out of sight of the English. With your permission, perhaps we could report you have sent me to New France on a mission for the King. Père Rivière would communicate with you as our go-between."

"We should not raise English suspicion to a greater height that it already is. So for the time being you shall remain as Vice Consul but have no public activity in Grand Pré."

"I should like to ask Lady Evangeline to marry me before I secret myself. With your blessing, my Lord."

René looked at the young man filled with love and sincerity. He remembered his promise to let Evangeline choose her own husband. She might see Gabriel only as a friend and reject him as a husband. Or she might agree to marry him. But he had promised to let her make the choice.

"Very well. It is her decision, after all."

Gabriel shook his hand over and over. "Yes sir, thank you, my Lord."

René opened the door to the office for Gabriel when the younger man returned to the subject of the dead man. "On the matter of Lieutenant Greenfield...."

"I did not mention the name of the officer. How is it that you know? Did he die at your hand?"

Gabriel shook his head. "I heard a shout coming from the alleyway..." He decided it better to forego the details about the attack on Evangeline until he asked her permission or she divulged the matter to her father.

"I saw a snake slither away from Greenfield but the man had convulsed to death before I could take any action. My only thought was to remove myself so that I was not accused of it. Though it seems indirectly I have been, despite my precautions."

Gabriel waited a few moments, which seemed like an eternity, for a response from René. Hearing none he continued, "If you check the body you should see the fang marks."

René nodded slowly. "I believe you. I also understand the unfortunate circumstances you were in. There is no easy way to reveal that information. You are already suspect in the minds of the English."

"Particularly that cold-blooded Turnbull."

"I could inform John but he would question how I have come by the details." René was pensive.

"The English are looking for any excuse to make an example of a French Neutral. That is the truth of the matter, which I entrust to your judgment."

"Perhaps the easiest way is to make this knowledge readily available to everyone by happpenstance."

"What is your plan?" Gabriel already felt relieved.

"I shall ask to examine the corpse myself. In checking it I will discover the wounds and they will have their answer."

"Thank you, Monsieur le Consul. I am eternally grateful."

"My prayers are with you Gabriel. Take careful attention to what you say and do from here forward."

"Thank you, my Lord, I shall do so." Gabriel walked to the front door of the Consulate.

René ushered him outside as he searched the empty streets for soldiers. Seeing none, he spoke quietly. "And Gabriel?"

The Vice Consul nodded waiting for the Consul to speak.

"I have changed my mind. There is no need for your resignation if you remain quiet here and in the Mi'Kmaq Village. And if Evangeline consents to marry you, then you both have my blessing. I shall see you in the morning. Good night." René purposefully shut the door without waiting for a reply.

Outside, Gabriel hopped on his horse and galloped back toward his home. The most beautiful and intelligent woman he could ever imagine was to be his wife. But he still had to propose to her before their betrothal would be official. He began to prepare a plan for making his declaration to her. He prayed she would accept him.

As was the case every Sunday, the Catholic Church of St. Charles des Mines of Grand Pré was filled to overflowing with all the French Acadians of the region. Mass was an opportunity to ask for spiritual guidance, to accept the Holy Eucharist, and to pray for a myriad of requests -- relief from suffering of a sick neighbor or a dying relative, a good harvest, a healthy new child, profitable sales of goods, or all of these things.

And it seemed every week more marriage banns were announced as an Hébert was betrothed to a Cormier, or a Broussard girl was to marry a

Dugas boy. But it was also a social occasion for the townspeople to visit with friends and family who lived on the farms far away from town.

Each week the Acadians anticipated dressing in their finest and attending the service. On this sweltering Sunday, the parishioners were thankful for the high ceilings and windows which were opened to let a slight breeze into their beautiful church. But women still adjusted their bonnets and fanned themselves with sturdy plant leaves or large pieces of bark while the men stretched their collars and loosened their neckties or wiped their brows.

During the service Evangeline looked for Gabriel, who customarily sat either in the d'Entremont family pew or next to her. But today he was unusually late. She wondered where he could be. As her thoughts wandered, she said a silent prayer for him.

At that moment, out of her view, Gabriel had slipped into the Church and stood by the rear door near his closest friend, Marc de la Tour Landry. He caught the eyes of a dozen other Acadian patriots his age who heard the door creak. When each turned back to look at him he responded by a nearly imperceptible nod of his head.

In the pulpit high above the altar, Père Rivière gazed over his flock. He nodded to Gabriel and watched as some of Gabriel's friends, the ones he referred to as "patriots" had quietly walked to the back of the church. He was not certain of their plan but hoped it had nothing to do with the English troops marching in formation that he saw through the church's stained glass windows.

The priest took a deep breath and began to preach, though he was not certain it would be one of his most popular sermons. He read from his text so that he did not deviate from his carefully prepared message. As a member of Gabriel's militia, he was in a position to garner public support without revealing the secret.

"God's heavenly kingdom awaits those who preserve and protect our faith. Those who endure persecution for religious beliefs. Those who fight for the freedom to exercise our Catholic faith...."

The priest looked around the Church. Heads that might have customarily nodded off during his sermons were alert. Everyone understood this was something new, a daring subject that the priest had never broached before. Suddenly the tension in the air became taut as a rope. Every man and woman craned their heads to the pulpit as their spiritual leader walked them through their obligations to God and countrymen, replete with metaphors to the political climate in Grand Pré. Père continued to read in a clear, strong voice.

"The day is coming for each of us to heed God's call. We are all soldiers in His army and no one lives but through Him. No one lives but for Him. We cannot allow others not of our faith to dictate our beliefs in God...."

He paused and saw many parishioners murmuring to each other, and a number of other members of the Church nodding in agreement with him. He knew the timing was right for the crescendo.

"The English have attempted for many years to force us to sign an unconditional Oath which would not protect our religious rights and that would force us to take up arms against our mother country and our First National allies. We all know this is not the will of God. We all recognize that we cannot accept such Oath, as ours is the kingdom of God, not of England, and the kingdom of God protects holy King Louis and all His Majesty's subjects, including all of us here and throughout the region, the French Neutrals of Acadia. May God bless and keep each and every one of you. Amen."

With that, many parishioners jumped to their feet, shouting their approval and raising their arms in support. The church was in an uproar, and Père Rivière noticed the English troops had stopped their drills and were approaching the Church.

Quickly, the priest hushed the crowd. "Please take your seats. We should not wish to attract the attention of the troops in their practices outside the Church."

Understanding his meaning, the Church became silent, except for a few cries of hungry babes in the arms of their mothers. Then the crowd stood to recite the Creed. Père Rivière led them in the prayer. "I believe in one God, the Father Almighty...."

Captain Turnbull had stood outside the window nearest the priest's pulpit and heard the sermon. Beside him stood Adams and Hobbs, who nodded to Turnbull. Turnbull led them back to Tent City and asked, "What do you think of the priest Rivière now?"

Adams responded, "If you need a witness to the traitor's words and actions I am here."

Hobbs agreed. "A more treasonous sermon I have never heard."

Turnbull said, "Then of course I am bound to report him as a member of the secret militia inciting the Acadians to riot against peaceful British."

They laughed heartily as they walked off.

Adams added as an afterthought, "You might consider sending him to Bostontown where Catholic prisoners have been placed into slavery. Indentured servants on their farms and plantations."

"No doubt Lieutenant-Colonel Winslow would enjoy assisting the citizens of Governor Shirley's colony," agreed Turnbull.

In the Church the priest concluded the Mass. "Let us pray. O Lord hear us, your children. We are your most humble servants asking for guidance to serve You as You wish us to do. We offer our hearts, our minds and ourselves to you, for your praise, for the preservation and protection of our faith and for the strength to carry out Your will should that day come. Amen."

The parishioners stood and heartily repeated, "Amen." Then they began to sing the processional and Père Rivière left the altar, entering the adjacent sacristy. Gabriel nodded to Marc near the other end of the Church, who signaled the patriots to exit in small groups amidst the other worshippers leaving the building. Gabriel could not afford to raise additional doubts with the English.

René watched the parishioners, making careful mental note of the young men who had been talking to or signaling Gabriel and Marc. He recognized most as sons of the members of his Acadian Commission, pillars of the local community who discussed political issues with René before he made his decisions and sent his correspondence to the King. René had selected representatives from both town and farm to the Commission. There was no division by class or status as back in France and all were welcome at table and René's political discussions in Grand Pré.

Evangeline watched Gabriel leave the Church nodding but not speaking to her. She was disappointed but clearly understood he had important business to attend to. She would be supportive to him in all his endeavors, even if they took him away from her.

Christine looked at René, worried for him and concerned about his reaction to the exit of Gabriel's friends. She knew something was underway and she meant to find out what it was. Evangeline knew more than she was telling. She had asked Christine to trust her and pack a satchel in the event they needed to move but refused to say more. The two women walked with René, following the rest of the congregation to the adjoining hall for their weekly social and family-style meal.

While catching up on the latest news, the Acadians tasted a little from each of the dozens of dishes prepared by the women of the parish for all to enjoy. The farmers and their wives talked about their crops, the weather patterns, the dikes that they built and rebuilt, and the level of the river near their homes. The women discussed fashions, their gardens and the latest imported goods, sharing recipes for meals and remedies for children's diseases and aging parents' aches and pains.

After polite conversation with wives and children, the men gathered in the far corner of the room to discuss politics. Chairs were pulled into a circle so each man had the same standing to speak, ask a question or raise an issue.

The women put the older daughters in charge of the younger children as preparation for marriage and motherhood. The young girls helped children fill their bowls with food and watched over them, or fed their infant siblings with the milk or soft gruel they had prepared before Church.

With their children taken care of, the women sat at the other end of the hall. Each Sunday one or two women would make an educational presentation to the others. The subject might be how to cook a certain dish, cut a new hairstyle, accomplish an intricate embroidery pattern, grow certain plants, or cure an ailment.

Today Madame Dupont and Adèle Arnaud took the floor. Béatrice Gaudet, who had been working with them as an assistant seamstress, helped the two ladies. Madame pulled from her little drawstring bag a series of drawings of the latest fashions from Paris and explained them as they were passed from one woman to the next. Swatches of new silks, satins, laces and other cloth that had arrived from France by way of New France drew admiration from the women. Nearly every wife, and several brides-to-be, made an appointment for a fitting and reserved their favorite fabrics before they were sold. Adèle duly noted the fitting dates in her small journal and smiled, content that they would be quite busy in the coming months taking measurements, sewing fabric and pleasing their clientele with new frocks and even several wedding gowns and veils.

Many times Adèle had offered to purchase the shop from Madame Dupont who, despite her failing eyesight, always politely refused. But as the merchant goods took longer to arrive Madame Dupont found her store nearly bare after only a few months. Lacking additional funds to order more stock, she sold half the business to Adèle. Claude Arnaud was very proud of his wife's business talents and willingly gave her the money from his father's inheritance. That year the two women were able to order a year's worth of fabric at once rather than their usual three-month supply previously ordered four times a year.

Adèle instituted other practices to benefit the store. Madame Dupont, who abhorred the English, particularly the odious Captain Turnbull, had at first refused Adèle's request to sell to the English in their Tent City and at the Fort.   But at Adèle's insistence she reluctantly agreed. When Adèle visited John Winslow he agreed upon the payment of the requisite goods tax in French luxury products, such as wine or cheese. Adèle was able to trade some ribbons and a bolt of French lace to the wine merchant for his wife in exchange for several cases of his best bottles. In the end the true cost of the tax was very little and the shop was not out any actual money.

The first day Adèle and Béatrice appeared outside Tent City with French laces and streamers they sold everything in their small satchel. It seems every young soldier had a sweetheart or sister or mother who could appreciate such fine things. On the next payday the two women returned with a large cart and it emptied quickly while their purses filled and their profits soared. Madame Dupont was only too happy to take the Englishmen's money and order another year's supply with their profits made in only two months.

In a corner of the large hall away from the women and children, the men of Grand Pré listened attentively as their Consul Le Blanc discussed new events that had taken place during the week. They had all seen increased activity at the British Fort, new vessel arrivals and troop training exercises. They were cautioned by René to continue to remain calm in any contact with the English. Their discussions always concluded with the subject of the Oath. Today was no exception.

After discussing politics and the Oath, the invariable topic of matchmaking arose. Fathers with daughters rose to furnish details of their girls' ages, virtues and dowries, and pointed them out among the women. Men presented their sons to the group, expounding on their skills, education and Catholic faith. Then each family head compared their genealogical lines, written in their family Bible, to assure that consanguinity would not require special dispensations. When all the cards were placed on the table and each father had his eye on several potential spouses for his children of marriageable age, the men began negotiating in earnest just as they would have in their own settlements. But the overriding sanctity of the adjoining Church made them much more serious and committed to finding the right person for the child for a happy marriage rather than merely negotiating dowries, skills and business partnerships.

While the parishioners were at Mass and at their social dinner afterwards, the streets were deserted except for troop drills. If someone had walked down the wooden walkways at that time of the morning he would have had nothing available to him. Shops and stores were closed, their window shades drawn. Homes were shut tight. Barns were barred from the outside to prevent animals from roaming.

The main square was empty except for a few English soldiers milling about in Tent City. Those who had finished drill repetitions had filed into the dining tent. The clinking of grog cups and the strains of a fiddler could be heard from the street.

Gabriel, Marc and the young patriot militia had met after Mass outside the southern gates of town, away from prying eyes of the British military, or so they thought. They trotted out of town, some to farms, others toward the hills and a small group led by Gabriel to the Mi'Kmaq Village.

Turnbull watched from behind his tent flap in the square. When the horses were gone and the streets were empty again, he exited Tent City with a band of troops following.

Stealthily, Captain Wicker and Captain Adams led their troops throughout the main streets of Grand Pré. Wicker concentrated on the bottom floors, where the shops were. Adams led his soldiers to the upper floor residences, where the shopkeepers' families lived.

One after another, soldiers entered the rows of unlocked shops and houses. The French Acadians were trusting of their neighbors and had no custom of locking doors. As he opened the door of the wine shop Wicker thought to himself, the French heathens deserved everything they got and more. He wondered what orders his superior Captain Turnbull would issue next. First he supervised the arrival of muskets and ammunition from Bostontown. Now he and the other soldiers removed all weapons from the Acadians' homes and stores. It seemed that the next step would be an attack on the large French population, who would be defenseless and would surely surrender.

Wicker picked up a splinter of wood from the ground while surveying his troops. He picked at his rotting teeth with the wood chip. An attack was just what he needed to make him feel better about losing his best friend, his only friend, Greenfield. He could never talk to Bancroft in the same way, although they did enjoy good times at Hetty's he thought. But that still did not make up for the loss of Greenfield.

Captain Adams ran into a two-story Acadian house taking two steps at a time. He watched approvingly as his soldiers ransacked cupboards, overturned furniture and pulled clothes and linens out of tall wooden armoires. They filled their cloth sacks with guns, knives, swords and tools that could be used as weapons.

In kitchens located outside the buildings and houses, soldiers stole all the knives, cleavers, and axes they could find. They had been used for chopping, carving, cutting, and slicing the various animals and vegetables the Acadians raised and grew for food. Henceforth they would be used no longer for sustenance of life but for its destruction.

From the sheds, barns and outbuildings, the troops confiscated garden tools and heavy farm implements. No matter that the Acadians could not grow any other crops or tend any gardens. They would be soon gone and the food would go to British colonists reserving passage in England at that very moment. The English Planters would reap the benefit of nearly one hundred sixty years of toil and the ingenuity of the Acadians' unique dike system that rendered these farms the most fertile and productive in all the English colonies.

Hastening down the main streets of Grand Pré, teams of soldiers moved from house to house and shop to shop. Their sacks grew bulkier after exiting each building until they could hold no more. At that point the soldiers marched with their sacks through the north gates of town, past the English Quarter to Fort Vieux Logis. Their drills had served them well and they arrived at the Fort in short order.

Once the soldiers passed through the checkpoint they delivered their sacks to Turnbull, who waited for them in a large tent. He had surrounded the arsenal with a new picket fence that could be locked and he also posted guards night and day. Turnbull could not risk losing any weapons. A long line of soldiers formed, each man carrying a large sack filled to the brim with arms or arm-like items. Some bags contained hammers, nails and other carpentry tools for constructing or repairing houses. Others had planting implements to grow food, remove weeds and pests and harvest crops. Still others held vast collections of knives and other sharp objects removed from Acadian homes.

When a soldier emptied his looting bag, each weapon was duly recorded in Turnbull's register by his clerk, and then handed to another soldier. He checked the weapon for ammunition, which was removed, then hand-carried to a box of like items. There, a third soldier cleaned the weapon, making sure it would be ready to use when needed. He then laid the piece down as gently as if it were a baby. He had been rigorously instructed by Lieutenant-Colonel Winslow to carry out the cleaning and storing with extreme care and precision. The weapons were to be ready on a moment's notice and no time would be available for cleaning or advance preparation.

Adams' troops joined the back of the line. Their sacks were full of muskets, pistols, balls and powder taken from the general store and the other shops. The Acadians used their arms to hunt wild game for food or to protect their crops from animal intruders. Adams reflected on what a peace-loving people the French Neutrals were. They refused to take up arms for any reason, whether for the English or against the French or to aid their Indian friends.

Turnbull watched as the last of the soldiers emptied their sacks and were dismissed. Adams and Wicker reported to Turnbull, who commended them on their successful mission. Together, the three men reviewed the long inventory. The troops had taken hundreds, perhaps thousands, of guns, knives, clubs and swords and that was before counting building tools, kitchen utensils and farm implements.

Turnbull had insisted on confiscating household and crop tools over Adams' objections that the Acadians needed them for their food and meals. Adams argued that removal of these implements would reduce the crop output, which would result in fewer stores for the troops to whom the Acadians sold their surplus. However, Turnbull believed the harm was worse than the benefit. Turnbull knew that an innocent-looking garden digger could gouge a soldier's eye. A kitchen knife could slit a throat. A poultry cleaver could slice a man's chest if applied with enough force. No, Turnbull would not take any chances that the Acadians could use farm articles as weapons to stave off their impending doom.

Turnbull was also motivated by his military ambition. As the aging Lieutenant-Colonel Winslow consistently assigned more responsibilities to him, he relished his greater sense of power and authority. Turnbull was ignorant of the reason for Winslow's actions. The Colonel's guilt had grown to such a point that he could not accomplish any additional dirty deeds himself. Yet he knew they had to be done and believed Turnbull's malevolent nature would not be deterred from any orders Winslow gave him. Winslow felt it was one thing to be the commanding officer responsible for an act to be done, and quite another to do the act himself. He had thusly interpreted a Bible passage which comforted him, though that was not the true meaning or intention of the scriptures.

Turnbull scrawled notes on the lists indicating the owner of the house, shop or barn where the weapons had been found. Turnbull's notes indicated those with the greatest number of confiscated items. They became his suspect list. He knew most of the names on his list, who unless one-legged or blind, would be the Acadians under surveillance by his special troops.

He crossed his legs on top of the table, as he had seen Winslow do many times in his office. He grunted with satisfaction as he read the descriptions of the arms and itemization of the kinds of musket balls, powder kegs and pouches and other sundry items obtained by his troops. Weapons were Turnbull's children and violence was their education. He leaned back in his chair and clasped his hands behind his head. "A very good raid, indeed."

Winslow did not understand how Shirley found out about the Greenfield business so quickly. The Governor had ordered Winslow to send a full report on the matter. Shirley was not so interested in the Lieutenant's death, which was easily explained as a snake bite. He was annoyed because his own officers had not done a thorough investigation on the body. The truth had only come out when Consul Le Blanc asked, out of curiosity, to see the body. And if he knew more than he was telling there was no way to find out. One did not torture a King's representative for information that would lead to nothing except trouble. Even if Shirley did want a war for his restless troops, Winslow was certain that neither of them should be the cause of it.

And now Winslow's superior wanted an investigation into the disappearance of one of Hetty's girls, the one named Gertrude. Shirley had enjoyed the pleasure of her company one night when he was in Grand Pré before Winslow took his post. Winslow talked with Hetty's other girls. One had heard Gertie arguing with Greenfield about her moving to Bostontown. Winslow's next visit was to Cornhandle, who owned the only mercantile store in the English Quarter.

"What do you know of transporting one of Hetty's ladies to Bostontown?"

The beady-eyed man smiled and held out his hand. "Sir, as you know I am but a poor merchant, not subject to military orders. Of course I would be pleased to provide what little information I know in exchange for your appreciation."

Winslow was too pressed to argue. This was an investigation and he could put the repulsive little man in prison but he had no time to waste. He placed a coin in the man's sweaty, chubby fingers. Cornhandle bowed and brought him outside to the outhouse. The stench was overpowering. Winslow grabbed his handkerchief to his nose. Cornhandle was nonplussed.

"My cousin named Cornhandle in Bostontown who is a, well...."

"Spit it out man, what is he?"

"A slave trader, Lieutenant-Colonel."

Winslow was so completely taken aback he dropped the kerchief and took Cornhandle by the shoulders, shaking him.

"Did you sell her to the highest bidder?"

The little man was frightened. He bent his head and clasped his hands together. "No, sir, of course not. That was only the preface to my story."

"Come to the story and quickly or I shall put you in the stocks." Winslow released his grasp and Cornhandle rushed into the outhouse, locking himself in the smelly room. Winslow was too disgusted to follow him into the stench. "Out with it."

"Yes sir. Jonas, that is my cousin, trades in slaves in Boston Harbor. He does business with the Governor and obtained an exclusive license in exchange for...."

"What? Speak up, you obstinate little man. What is his trade with Governor Shirley?"

Cornhandle hung his head, "I do not know the details. Only that my cousin Jonas, who is very wealthy, said he would be twice as rich if he did not have to keep paying for his license. And only in gold coins."

"Did he tell you he pays the Governor?"

Timothy shook his head. "Not in so many words but he said he must make a payment every time a boatload of slaves arrives. And he was assured in a matter of months he will have hundreds of whites to sell, including young girls. White skin is more in demand than red or black. But young white girls fetch the greatest prices of all."

"And why is that?" grunted Winslow.

"You know, sir, this fathering business. White slave women can bear the plantation owner's children and the mistress of the house has no worries of local gossip. But a half red or a mulatto baby or worse, a coal black one, makes the wives very unhappy. Apparently the plantation mistresses have forbidden their husbands to buy any female slaves but white ones. And they demand only white males too. This means the Massachusetts Bay plantations that do not acquire the African slaves have a labor shortage producing few crops and buying fewer goods."

"I see now. Governor Shirley's tax coffers are half empty."

Winslow reeled with the knowledge that his superior was going to benefit from the Acadian question in two ways. Now his colonists and friends would get the Frenchies' rich lands and farms and payments from the slaver Cornhandle when they were sold in Boston Harbor, not to mention more taxes from the plantations. "So the Governor has encouraged this white slave business, then?" Winslow spoke uneasily.

Cornhandle's beady eyes glimmered. Perhaps there was a way to bring himself good fortune after all. "Oh yes, sir; yes indeed, sir. Perhaps I could be of service to you in some small way, sir?" Jonas had written to his cousin in Grand Pré that Shirley had said on signing the contract, "Soon those heathens shall have a purpose in life, working in our plantations and filling our coffers rather than theirs."

Winslow nodded. Cornhandle lifted the filthy wool blanket off one of the boxes in the outhouse and nodded to Winslow. "And if your troops need more weapons...." Winslow's eyes widened at the sight. The box was filled with muskets, bayonets and knives. He nodded. He would return and make an arrangement with this smart little merchant.

But at the moment, Winslow was remembering his most recent letter from Shirley. It had alluded to a new position for him in Massachusetts when he concluded the Acadian business. At last Winslow had the makings of a sure promotion back to his wife and family.

Winslow's exodus from Nova Scotia would not be a moment too soon for him. His guilt was beginning to keep him awake at night.

CHAPTER 36
Engagement

GRAND PRÉ

he English troops in Tent City heard a series of shrieks and cries coming from the Acadian homes and shops. Adams, Turnbull and Wicker were back from the Fort. They drank grog in the officers' tent and congratulated each other. Lieutenant-Colonel Winslow had found the raid "well-executed."

Inside the Consulate, René surveyed the damage. His desk drawers had been opened and papers strewn all over the rooms. He checked the secret compartments hidden underneath the desk. Fortunately, all his private communications with France and his personal weapons -- musket and pistol -- and ammunition remained untouched. He had had the foresight to have the compartments built in the desk rather than in a cabinet or locker. He had not thought of a raid but of protecting his daughter. There were things she should not know for her own safety.

He rushed upstairs to check the secret compartment he and Gabriel had installed in the sideboard. The drawers had been pulled out but the base had not been touched. He breathed a sigh of relief. The maps and larger parchments from the King were safe.

Evangeline walked into her father's office. She had been in the back garden and held a few broken garden hand tools. "Most of my tools are broken, and the others are missing."

René straightened the desk, replacing the drawers and drying the ink running onto the floor. "Nothing was taken here but unimportant papers. My own weapons are still safe."

"That is good news, Papa."

Christine rushed in, breathless. "All of the kitchen knives are gone."

René nodded sternly. "Obviously the English have been planning this for some time. Our relations have deteriorated much more than I anticipated after Halifax."

Evangeline looked at her father with concern. "Have you still not heard anything of the prisoners since then?"

He shook his head. "It leaves me baffled and helpless. No war has been declared between our countries yet the English have treated them as prisoners of war without releasing any information. At least they could report whether they were still alive, for their families' sake."

"Will the new commander respond to your entreaties at all, Papa?"

"He claims he must follow his chain of authority, which is a lengthy process. John informs me he must write to Governor Shirley in Massachusetts who is commanding the English troops, who then contacts the Lieutenant-Governor in Halifax, Charles Lawrence. He should, though he might not always, write to the Governor in London who then arranges a meeting with the Lords of Trade there, who may discuss the matter with the King's Prime Minister who obtains permission from the King. Then the cycle reverses back to Halifax and Massachusetts before arriving here again. I believe he is simply biding his time before he is to return home."

"If this Winslow leaves who would be put in his position?"

René put his arm around Evangeline. "We do not know but as Gabriel often repeats, let us pray it is not Captain Turnbull."

"Gabriel asked to meet me this afternoon with your permission."

"Of course but after you help Christine put the house in order. We still do not know the meaning of this. "

He rang a bell and his driver appeared at the back door to the office. "Take this to the Fort and deliver it to Lieutenant-Colonel Winslow personally."

"Do you wish me to prepare the carriage?"

"No, I shall not be going out today, Luc. Take one of the horses. Thank you."

"Yes sir, right away." The man who had been René's coachman since the trip to Le Havre, Luc Bourg, was a son of the King's former wine steward who had immigrated several years ago to Grand Pré. René had offered Luc the position as a means of returning to his family in Grand Pré but was so pleased with his services that he kept him in his service. News of Luc's father's scandal at Court had certainly reached Grand Pré, yet the Acadians never once raised the subject to Rene's knowledge.

Old mistakes in France had remained buried in the intrigue of Versailles, the transgressors forgiven and washed clean during their passage to the New World across the sea. The townspeople of Grand Pré, of which only a few families were noble -- Le Blanc de Verdure, Mius d'Entremont, de la Tour Landry, among them -- had more important concerns, especially since the British raid had occurred.

Christine complained, "What shall we do about the kitchenware and the gardening tools?"

At hearing frantic knocking on the door, René hurried them upstairs. "Let us try to do without for the time being."

Christine and Evangeline walked slowly upstairs. Christine commented. "It is not proper to eat without a knife. How shall we ever be able to eat our peas?"

Evangeline took her arm and laughed. "We can use spoons or simply forego serving that vegetable until we have the proper utensils."

Christine was still upset when they turned at the landing to see who was at the front door. A group of Acadian men and women were frantic. They wanted to inform René of the raid and find out what he knew. He led them into the hallway and asked one at a time to enter. Béatrice Gaudet was the youngest so she was invited first.

René looked at her. "Yes, Mademoiselle Gaudet. What is your purpose for being here?"

"Monsieur le Consul, they, the English soldiers, sir, took all our farm tools and our kitchen utensils. We have nothing to dig our vegetables out of the ground or stir our soup save if we can find a twig or a branch." She began to cry. "They unlocked Maman's door and took her spoon from her hands. When I returned from dinner she was lying on the floor with her thumb in her mouth. She would not say a word, not even her usual gibberish. I fear they may have…taken liberties with her."

René took her back into the hall and told her, "Wait here, child. We shall help you." He called upstairs. "Christine? A moment, please?"

Christine dutifully descended the stairs, nodding to the long line of Acadians waiting in the hallway. When she entered his office he closed the door and explained what had happened. Christine was first shocked, then outraged. She nodded and climbed the stairs, then soon returned to the office with her black bag and an apron filled with ladles. She looked at René and opened her apron. "Spoons we have a-plenty, if you need them, but no knives." She smiled and left the utensils on the desk, then took Béatrice by the hand and walked out of the front doorway.

René sighed as he picked up one of the large utensils and called out, "Next. Please enter."

Outside the Consulate building Christine handed Béatrice a spoon and then said, "Let us examine your mother and make certain she is not hurt."

The girl beamed. "Oh, thank you so very much. I do not know what Grand Pré would do without you. I did not know Doctor Hébert very well when he died but Papa said he was a good man. Still, I trust you to take care of my mother. I think she remembers you." She held the spoon with care. "And now she will not have the taste of wood in her soup."

Evangeline finished cleaning the residence in Christine's absence and walked slowly up the stairs to her room. Looking out of the window across the treetops and down to the sea, she thought she saw tall masts and rigging on the horizon. It could be her imagination but her eyes watered remembering Gabriel's warning.

She loved Gabriel as a man of principles not afraid to stand up for his beliefs. And whether his predictions were accurate or not, his arguments seemed very convincing to her now. Was there a threat of imminent danger to her family and friends in Grand Pré and the Mi'Kmaq Village? Would they one day witness the burning of Grand Pré? It was too much for her to bear. She wept silently for her own indecision, wiping her tears with her handkerchief. Should she speak with her father and Christine, or secretly aid Gabriel in his cause?

Evangeline watched from her window as her father said his goodbyes to several Acadian couples. They looked relieved as they walked across the street to return to their homes. If her father had spoken with all the concerned French residents, she thought this would be the best time to speak with him about the militia. But first she needed to gain his empathy. She walked downstairs and knocked on the partially open door.

"Yes?" her father said.

"Papa, there is something I need to tell you."

"Come in, come in."

"Gabriel did not want to worry you. But that English officer Greenfield...."

"The one who was killed? What do you know about him?"

"Gabriel had nothing to do with it. At least not with the man's death. The Englishman...I was walking and he grabbed me and threatened...."

Teary-eyed, Evangeline could say nothing more. She buried her head in his shoulder.

René was angry at first. "Did he hurt you?"

She shook her head. "He ripped my clothes and Gabriel rescued me before he did anything else. But the English officer threatened to expose Gabriel and his secret militia. Please join him and the patriots before it is too late. You must, Papa."

He hugged Evangeline tenderly for a long while without speaking. "I presumed as much but did not want to know the truth. I fear English reprisal against you. Against all the Acadian women and children."

"But Papa, our safety means nothing if we are not free to worship at Mass and to refrain from pointing a weapon at a fellow countryman or a Mi'Kmaq."

"No doubt you have been studying the issue for some time."

"These past few months I have thought of little else but this subject and Gabriel. How can I card wool or enjoy myself at a quilting bee or even practice writing in foreign languages when more important things are at stake -- life, liberty, freedom from British tyranny?"

"You make a strong case, my daughter."

"Perhaps it is time to use tactics other than diplomacy."

René did not respond. He simply nodded to Evangeline, kissed her on the cheek and returned to his desk.

Evangeline and Christine ate a quiet supper, just the two of them, again. René was too occupied to join them. He pulled the sensitive documents from his desk's secret drawer he had received just before the raid. He scoured them again for information which might help him with decisions to be made for the citizens of Grand Pré and the Minas region. He found an excerpt from a 1745 report by the Governor of New France discussing British threats to deport the Acadians. It had been folded in with some other documents and sent, possibly in error. He was stunned as he read the words aloud.

"We cannot imagine that they could entertain the idea of removing those people in order to substitute Englishmen in their stead, unless desertion of the Indians would embolden them to adopt such a course, inhuman as it may be."

René recognized "they" were the English King and his troops in Nova Scotia who were plotting to exile the Acadians so that new English colonists could take over the homes and properties of the French Neutrals.

René wondered why he was only receiving this news now and if French authorities had known this information long. Were the politics so different at Versailles that after the death of the Cardinal the Acadian colony was pushed to the side and forgotten? King Louis had been in discussions ten years ago with the Québec Governor about possibly losing the Mi'Kmaq alliance to the British and losing the Acadians through exile. René had to believe that if Cardinal de Fleury had been living he would have advised René of such devastating news at once.

René realized at that moment their fate had been sealed long ago. All he could do now was work with Gabriel and his militia to prepare a defense against the English. And they had very little time, by the looks of the transports in the Bay.

The next morning when Gabriel arrived, he took Evangeline aside before he entered his office. He whispered to her, holding her face in his hands. She nodded and they kissed passionately.

Père Rivière and René were deeply engrossed in conversation. The priest was informing the Consul of the militia activities being planned and their need for more weapons. René reached into his desk and pulled out a sack of coins. The priest blessed him and slipped it inside his cassock.

Gabriel entered René's office while Evangeline climbed to the landing, straining to hear the conversation. René stood and told Gabriel, "I have but one thing to say to you, young man." Then he hugged him. "Thank you for saving Evangeline. I cannot express my gratitude for your courage and protection of her honor." The two men separated. Père Rivière looked on with a broad smile.

René continued, "Forgive me. I was a fool thinking I could help John Winslow keep the peace. Now I know he never intended to do so. All my years in this political post left me blind to the danger while you understood the British far better than I could ever hope to."

Gabriel was speechless. It was not what he had expected but he was grateful because his next conversation would be easier, or so he thought.

Suddenly Evangeline appeared at Gabriel's side, beaming and whispering to him. "Speak to him, Gabriel. Tell Papa. It is the right time now."

Gabriel nodded to her but René spoke first. "Gabriel, you now have my complete support. Père Rivière has the funds you need for more weapons. Can I do anything more to help your militia for our cause?"

Gabriel responded thoughtfully, "Could you convince Winslow that you are making progress on signing the King's version of the Oath? That would give us time to complete our plan with our Mi'Kmaq allies."

René nodded. "I shall do my utmost to convince him. I shall not place my hand on the Bible or make false statements to him. However it is true I am making progress on signing the Oath -- the modified Treaty Oath that His Majesty has approved for decades."

Père Rivière added, "God shall forgive you in this time of crisis, René, should it be necessary to say otherwise. How many of the older men can you bring to the cause?"

René grinned at him. "Does this count you as well?"

"I have been a part of Gabriel's militia for quite some time."

René looked at Gabriel. "And your father, Henri? Was he involved?"

Gabriel nodded. "He was my greatest support but he never let it interfere with his duties to you or his responsibilities to the King."

René murmured. "I never knew."

Père Rivière interjected. "We are all in agreement and must make use of the time we have before the element of surprise is gone."

Evangeline looked at Gabriel, who nodded encouragingly. But she surprised him with her boldness. "Now that this has been settled, Papa, Gabriel and I are in love. I accepted his proposal and pray you grant permission to marry. I daresay Maman would approve this match to the man of my hopes and dreams and everything she wished for me."

René turned to Gabriel. "Is this still your intention for my daughter, in light of our conversation?"

Gabriel nodded. "She will make me the luckiest man in the world now that she has accepted my proposal. I shall strive to deserve her and thank God she has agreed to be my wife."

René looked back at his daughter. "You know the English penalty for treason is death. Are you prepared to wed him under these circumstances?"

Evangeline reached for Gabriel's hand. "If we were to be married only for one day, my answer is still yes, a thousand times yes."

She smiled up at Gabriel who kissed her hand. He called for Christine and whispered something to her. She smiled and excused herself back upstairs. Soon she returned carrying a tray with five crystal glasses and a bottle of champagne.

René turned to the priest. "Père, it is appropriate you are here as it seems we shall have a wedding. Would you please select a date, the earliest possible after the formalities, of course, on a Sunday so that everyone in the region, both town and rural, can witness this joyous occasion. My little girl is going to be a wife now, Père. What do you think of that?"

Père Rivière pulled out a black register from his cassock. "It would be my greatest pleasure to marry these two young people who have grown into beautiful adults, spiritual and loving with great concern for others."

He perused the register, silently counting out three weeks. "We must announce the marriage banns publicly for the requisite three weeks, which makes the following Sunday," he said as he pointed to his calendar, "the seventh of September."

Evangeline smiled at René. "Less than a month and I shall be a married woman, Papa, and you shall have Gabriel as a son." She whispered to him, "Thank you for not insisting I go to Versailles for a husband. I met my own French nobleman right here in Grand Pré. But I would love him even if he were a tenant farmer or a fisherman."

René hugged her. "My dearest. I am so proud of you and am certain Eugenie would feel the same way. I love you more than you know."

Father and daughter stood there motionless, their eyes clouding for a moment.

Christine broke the silence and asked, "Shall we say five o'clock in the evening? That will give us ladies time to prepare a large wedding banquet after Mass that day."

Evangeline beamed as she and Gabriel melted into each other's eyes. They both nodded readily. René spoke for them. "Five o'clock it is."

Then René turned to Evangeline and nodded towards the door. "We have work to do for the militia."

Evangeline turned to Gabriel as if looking for support to stay. He shook his head. "It is for your own safety. Please."

She pouted, then realized this was a great victory for him. He needed to meet with René without her. She squeezed his hand and nodded, then turned to her father once more. "Thank you again, Papa."

René grunted, his head already in the maps he had spread on the desk. As Evangeline closed the door, the three men were huddled over the papers, discussing strategy against the English.

At noon, Evangeline and Christine ate quietly except when Evangeline broke the silence with a question. "What were they doing when you brought their dinner?"

Christine sighed. "I have told you. René and Gabriel are reviewing papers and maps. They spoke to Père, who wrote some things in his journal."

Another short silence. Then, "But what were they working on?"

Christine looked at Evangeline. "I simply do not know. They did not tell me. Did they ask you to stay or to leave?"

Glumly Evangeline said, "Leave, of course. Being a woman."

Christine shook her head. "That is not the reason. Gabriel wants to protect you. Did he not say that if you knew more about the militia it could be too dangerous for you?"

Evangeline replied, "Yes. I only thought he was trying to spare my feelings."

Christine took her by the shoulders and said softly, "Have you ever thought what would happen if Winslow or, worse, Turnbull caught your father or Gabriel? You would be the first person they would question. And I the second. We are very close to them. That is why it is so important that we know nothing."

They heard the front door open quietly and both rushed to the balcony to see Père Rivière leaving. When he had shut the door, Gabriel motioned for Evangeline to join him downstairs. Christine disappeared from the landing. As Evangeline slipped downstairs, she heard her father's office door close. She and Gabriel were alone in the hallway.

He held and kissed her. He whispered, "My love, I must leave Grand Pré for a time. Your father has finally decided I should stay with Kitok. You shall not see me as often but we shall be together as much as possible."

She frowned, so disappointed. "Must you go now, darling?"

Gabriel kissed her again and wrapped her in his arms. "You know our mission is at hand."

Evangeline clasped her locket in her hand and nodded bravely. "This will not delay our wedding?"

"Nothing shall interfere with our promise. And because of your influence with your father we now have a patriotic militia with the full support of King Louis."

She whispered to him. "God is at your side. He will protect you and the other patriots."

"I shall see you soon, my love."

"And I wait for your safe return when I shall become your wife."

He kissed her and she returned the kiss longingly, happily wrapped in his strong arms.

He whispered, "I am sure Madame Dupont and Adèle Arnaud shall be very busy making you the most beautiful wedding dress ever seen, not only in Grand Pré but in all of France as well."

She smiled. "I know exactly what it shall look like. I have dreamed about this for a long time."

Gabriel acted surprised and looked at her. "And I thought it was my idea all the while."

They kissed again, this time as if they would never let go. Finally he released her and disappeared outside, shutting the door behind him. She leaned against the door, giddy with love for Gabriel, holding the locket tightly until the sound of his horse's hooves fainted into the night.

René walked out of his office, hugged his daughter silently and trudged up the stairs. She noted he looked much older than before, as if he had the weight of the world on his shoulders. And the colonists' lives in his hands.

Outside the south gates, Gabriel galloped into the woods and stopped when he reached a tree marked with a red feather. He then slowed his horse to a walk. When he heard a strange bird call he turned and suddenly Kitok dropped from the tree above to the ground. He led the horse to a small clearing not visible from the main path, where Kitok's horse rested.

Kitok handed Gabriel a document, the list made by Turnbull. "These are your Acadian weapons and ammunitions taken from the English storage tent. Turnbull assigned one young solider as the night guard. He found the rum mixed with a potion from White Bird and was asleep after a few swigs."

Gabriel patted him on the back. "Everything is safe in the hiding place?"

Kitok nodded then added, "Look at the names that are circled."

"René, Marc, Père Rivière, me? It seems to be a sort of target list, but it contains nearly everyone in our militia. How did he know?"

Kitok said, "I see names circled next to the houses where the largest supplies of arms were found."

Gabriel thanked his friend. "This is valuable information. It shall save many lives, my friend."

The Mi'Kmaq brushed away thanks and asked, "The plan?"

Gabriel nodded. "Done."

Kitok said solemnly, "We also learned other news." He handed Gabriel an English document with a broken seal. Gabriel looked at it and nodded. The two men rode in different directions -- Kitok toward the Mi'Kmaq Village and Gabriel back to town.

After dinner René had planned to retire but he heard the back door open. He went downstairs to find Gabriel. René chided him. "Why risk returning? No doubt the English are watching your every move now."

"I was careful not to be followed. Kitok learned Turnbull's plans for a secret attack. We must stop them. It must be tonight."

"Very well. Contact Père Rivière and alert the men in the militia. Assure they take strict precautions to avoid being seen together."

Within the hour, a dozen older Acadian men had arrived separately and entered through the back door of the Consulate building. They were involved in a serious discussion with René. Père Rivière kept watch, peering cautiously through the curtains of the window every so often.

It was Gabriel's turn to address the men. "Gentlemen of Grand Pré. Welcome to the Acadian resistance. I recognize your faces and you should know that most of your sons are already in our secret militia."

The men murmured among themselves, now understanding why their sons were mysteriously absent every now and then.

Gabriel continued quietly. "The most important quest is to restock our weapons. Most anything can be used. Check carefully for anything left behind in the English raid. Even old tools can be useful. The iron from farm implements, old rusty knives, clubs for tanning hides, fishing traps, rope, fence wires, wooden pickets and, of course, any guns and ammunition. Bring whatever you have to the Mi'Kmaq Village during the course of the next week. Ask for Prince Kitok or Sitting Fox. Be wary of any English soldiers roaming about They must not know what you are doing or see what you are carrying."

René added, "Remember, these weapons are for our defense only. We have all agreed not to harm the English unless they strike first. We shall only take imprison aggressors for an attack. The authorities in Québec City will take care of them once we send them there."

Gabriel instructed them. "We send all future messages through the Consul's office here unless soldiers are posted nearby. In that case, use the Church stone. Tonight is the first night of our fight for religious freedom and for our country. Vive le Roi. Vive les Acadiens."

The Acadians all murmured softly so as to not create a noise heard on the street, "Vive le Roi. Vive les Acadiens."

Suddenly Père Rivière turned from the window. "Everyone must leave. Now. Not a moment to waste."

No sooner had René ushered them out the back door then he, Gabriel and the priest heard a loud banging on the door.

They heard Turnbull shout, "Open up! D'Entremont we know you are in there. Turn yourself in or we will break the door and get you ourselves."

René made sure the scene was staged properly. The other men nodded and René slowly opened the door. Turnbull barged in and opened the door of the office. Père Rivière and Gabriel sat at a table reviewing the priest's black register.

Turnbull sputtered angrily. "We heard members of a secret militia came in here. We shall tear this building apart until we find them unless you reveal their hiding place."

René responded, "Under the Treaty of Utrecht you have no authority to enter this office and my residence, which are French territory. You know it and your superiors from Lieutenant-Colonel Winslow to Acting Governor Lawrence know that fact quite well."

Père Rivière calmly turned to Turnbull. "You are disrupting our plans. We are making wedding arrangements."

Turnbull was incredulous. "This time of night?

Gabriel answered, "Time is short. The Lady Evangeline and I are to be married in a mere three weeks."

Turnbull, spying Gabriel, foamed at the mouth like a madman. "There is the ringleader. You treasonous Acadian." Turnbull attempted to push past René and the priest for Gabriel. René blocked him and flashed the French King's ring. Turnbull ignored him and lunged for Gabriel's throat. Gabriel was man for the task and reached out to grab Turnbull.

René and Père Rivière pulled the two apart. Turnbull's soldiers were frozen, waiting for orders. They knew they had no authority within the French Consulate but they feared Turnbull's whip. In their hesitation, René pushed Turnbull outside.

From the door, Turnbull hissed to Gabriel, "Your day of reckoning is coming and I will be there." Then he directed his troops back to Tent City.

René bolted the door. The men breathed a collective sigh of relief. After the English were out of sight, René urged Gabriel to leave in haste, without stopping to speak with Evangeline. Gabriel nodded and exited by the rear door. He moved in the shadows, as he had learned from Kitok, careful to avoid the main street. Kitok was waiting for him behind the Church.

Gabriel said, "There is something ominous about this Edict that the English are to announce. Keep the boxes of weapons nearby." He stood at the edge of the Church looking for any sign of Turnbull or his henchmen; then they rode to the Mi'Kmaq Village. Gabriel had assembled his group of young Acadian resistance fighters and Kitok his braves in a large bark hut.

Gabriel spoke to his men. "Your fathers have joined our resistance and are fully committed. If you discuss plans with them please make certain no one else in the family is listening. We cannot let the women or children know, for their own safety and to prevent our business from being discussed on the street or when socializing. Winslow's men are everywhere. Turnbull has pledged to watch our every move."

The men nodded in agreement with Gabriel's warnings. He continued, "We know now the transports in the harbor are to send us away from our homes and lands."

The young men in the militia began to speak all at once, creating a din of voices until Gabriel raised his hands for silence. "It is only by working together quietly that we shall overcome the threat of British tyranny."

Marc added, "The English Council that rejected our Treaty Oath and imprisoned so many of our compatriots just last month is sending more troops. This time they will not prevent us from leaving, they will force us out unless we are submissive to their orders."

The men in the room were furious and demanded action. Gilles Cormier asked, "Where are we to go?"

Kitok calmed them and responded. "We do not yet know the destination. We presume it will be one or more of the colonies. We are prepared to help you escape the slave auctions if Bostontown is the destination."

Gabriel added, "And there are the dreaded English jails, where prisoners are said never to escape alive. The two we have heard of are Westminster Gatehouse and Liverpool Prison."

Marc attempted to lighten the charged atmosphere. "Then we can all be sure we shall be together in one of those two English jails."

Claude Arnaud added, "Do we have enough weapons and food stores if we move before the exile?"

Gabriel replied, "Evangeline and Christine are working with Princess Snowbird to begin stockpiling food stores. And Père Rivière now has more funding for arms. Work with him on this question."

Claude nodded and, as the tension in the hut released, all the men gathered around the table. Kitok brought out a large map of the region, showing water, land, woods and mountains. Gabriel drew marks on the map as if he were a general preparing for battle. "We have devised three courses of action so that if we are forced to abandon our preferred plan, we shall already have another ready to implement."

Marc and the other men looked at Gabriel with increased respect and admiration. He was a born leader -- selfless, intelligent and with immense foresight. Not many of them would have thought of a second plan but Gabriel had three different strategies, each designed for their capabilities and number.

With Gabriel's leadership and the help of the Mi'Kmaq braves, they would save their families, friends and neighbors, not only in Grand Pré but the entire region.

That is, if one of Gabriel's three plans came to fruition.

CHAPTER 37
Militia

GRAND PRÉ

 nside the confines of the Fort, Turnbull looked up to see Wicker saluting him. Turnbull scowled in response, barking a question. "Where is the new shipment of arms from Bostontown? We need to add the list to the inventory of the raided Acadian weapons." Without looking up, Turnbull held out a key which unlocked the weapons tent.

Wicker saluted and exited the office, then walked past the guard at the weapons tent. He unlocked the bolt and in he went. At first he did not believe his eyes. The boxes of arms from the raid had been broken into and emptied. Every musket, handgun, bayonet or other actual weapon had been taken. The boxes of rusty metal and farm tools remained but the kitchen utensils were gone. In a panic, Wicker turned to the large boxes which they had unloaded in the cove. He opened the first one, expecting to see the muskets from Bostontown in untouched condition. But the box was empty! Wicker frantically opened the next box to find it bare as well. He rushed outside and grabbed the guard by his collar, dragging him into the tent.

"Soldier, I demand an explanation. Who has entered this tent and who authorized the removal of our weapons?"

The young soldier was stunned at the sight. He stuttered a response. "N-n-n no one, sir, except officers came in, sir."

"Officers? Which officers?"

"Cap'n Adams, Cap'n Hobbs and Cap'n Turnbull, sir. And youse, sir."

"Any other guards with you?"

"No sir, but I am relieved by the night duty guard."

"Where is this man? Take me to him?"

"Begging your pardon sir but Cap'n Turnbull says I cannot leave my post even to enter this tent. He might whip me for being in here with you."

"His name? Do you have a name? And his barracks?"

"Me thinks it is Duncan, sir. He sleeps in yonder tent, there. All the night watches do, sir."

Wicker thrust the boy out of the tent and he quickly resumed his post, looking fearfully around to make sure no one had noticed his absence. The few soldiers milling around were joking with each other, paying him no attention whatsoever. Wicker stomped over to the tent and pulled it out by the stakes. The sleeping soldiers, all boys barely seventeen, were woken by the shining sunlight in their eyes.

"Wake up! Which of you is Duncan?"

A bleary-eyed soldier stood and saluted, though still in his long underwear. "Duncan, sir. What can I do for youse, sir?"

"Get dressed. You shall come with me." The soldier quickly donned his uniform and spat in his hands, then slapped his hair down with the spittle. Without another word, Wicker led him to the weapons tent and took him inside, grabbing the soldier's ear. "Open the boxes. Every last one."

Duncan did as he was ordered in as fast a pace as he could muster. He stood back. All the boxes were empty.

Wicker seethed. "Well? What do you have to say for yourself?"

Duncan was as shocked as the day guard had been. "Sir, I done never seen the likes of this. Me thought there was weapons in them there cartons. Who did this?"

Wicker boxed his ears. "That is what I am asking you. Who did you allow in this tent?"

"Nobody, sir."

"Nobody? Not a Captain or a Lieutenant of my troops? Nobody?"

"Not so long as I watched this tent, sir. On me dead mum's soul, God bless her, not a man entered this tent in the night on my watch."

Wicker peered at the cowering boy. He boxed his ears again and the soldier ran out of the tent. Wicker knew he was telling the truth but who was to blame? Suddenly Wicker knew the answer. Winslow would hold Turnbull responsible and Turnbull would...he would kill him! If the weapons were not here then either those filthy Frenchies had them or them redskins had crept in and stolen them right under their British military noses. He would have bet money on the latter. Them Mi'Kmaqs could walk past you in the night without you seeing anything. He believed in spirits and convinced himself the Injuns had used their magical powers of invisibility to steal the weapons.

But they were not his problem. Turnbull was. Wicker flipped each box over finding only one item on the ground. He stuffed it in his coat and walked pensively back to Turnbull's office. His superior always punished a messenger who brought bad news. Wicker stood at the door and almost ran away. He thought desertion would be better than Turnbull's whip. But he owed it to his King to plough forward. He knocked on the door.

Turnbull readied his whip, imitating Winslow's style. "Enter." When he saw Wicker shuffling his feet he shouted, "Out with it man. Where is the list?"

Wicker blurted out, "Them boxes came straight from ship to shore. We loaded them into our wagons without opening a one of them. Today there was nary a gun or pistol in any of them cartons. There ain't nothing there."

Turnbull looked at him seething with anger. "There ain't nothing there? Nothing there? Do you think Commander Shirley lied when he said he sent us a boatload of weapons? Do you?"

Wicker looked at his feet without a response. Turnbull continued to berate him. "Well who took them? Ghosts?"

Wicker lifted his eyes to answer. "Yes sir, me thinks them Mi'Kmaq ghosts stole every last one of youse arms."

An incredulous Turnbull dropped his whip to the floor and fell into his chair. He turned to Lieutenant Bancroft, who often assisted Turnbull with writing reports and recording details in his journal. Of late, Bancroft seemed to be a more reliable subordinate than Wicker. "Well, what do you say for yourself? Both of you return empty-handed? How do I explain this to Lieutenant-Colonel Winslow or Commander Shirley?"

Bancroft gulped, then said, "We brought our strongest troops and watched them unload every crate onto them wagons. That is the sure truth, Captain."

Turnbull glared at both of them, then focused his gaze on Wicker again. "And why are you so certain Indian ghosts took our arms?"

Wicker reached his hand into his coat and pulled out a Mi'Kmaq feather headdress. "This was in the last box I opened. One of them ghosts left it there to haunt us."

Without hesitation, Turner grabbed his whip. Wicker did not even try to move. He knew what was coming. Turner flicked the whip across Wicker's face so hard he fell on the wooden floor, his face bleeding. "You fool! You had one task only. How is it you cannot follow a simple order?"

Wicker picked himself up and mumbled, "No one can fight them Injun ghosts." He scrambled to get out of the office but not before Turnbull had struck his neck, drawing more blood.

Bancroft was dumbstruck. He longed to run after Wicker but his instincts told him he must stay and get his punishment as well.

Turnbull cracked his whip on the floor and the walls and Bancroft feared he would be next. Turnbull looked at him. "Fools. Both of you. If you was wearing my boots what would you do?" But before the man could respond, the truth hit Turnbull so hard he slumped into his chair. He waved him out and the man disappeared in an instant.

Turnbull held up the headdress. "D'Entremont and that Mi'Kmaq Chieftain's son Kitok! They stole my guns! But how on earth did they do it?"

Outside, Wicker rubbed his face. Dang, that whip did some damage and it smarted so much more than he thought it ought to. Bancroft walked over but avoided Wicker's eyes. "Was this the first time?"

Wicker shook his head. "Hell no, and it ain't no ways going to be the last. Only one thing that makes it better. I knows from experience. Follow me." He got on his horse and galloped out of the Fort. Bancroft was not far behind.

They ambled into the officers' tent in Tent City, where grog flowed freely if a man was not at his post or on a mission. Winslow could not afford to release his best men to the amusements and intellectual pursuits of Halifax for several days at a time. He needed them near the Fort at all times but understood their needs in what the English found to be barren territory.

After taking a long swig, Wicker poured the rest on his scratched face. "Aaaaggh," he yelped. That surely stung, although he knew Turner used the whip as much as a form of humiliation as punishment to cow his subordinates into submission.

Wicker mumbled. "It will be you giving our commanding officer any unwelcome news in the future."

Bancroft laughed. "There will be nary a distressful report to give from here on out. I shall make certain of that myself, even if we have to station our entire troops when we expect a shipment. No Frenchie or Mi'Kmaq will get anywhere close to our weapons again."

That did little to reassure Wicker. The Frenchies and their Indian friends were clever, they were. And with the help of them ghosts, well, Wicker could only shake his head with foreboding.

Back in his office, Turnbull continued to stew. "No matter, the thieves shall be thoroughly punished. But not a quick death, oh no. Not hanging or axing the neck. There is no pain in that. No, no. Stealing weapons is treason, quelled only by the pain and agony of drawing and quartering. That will keep the Frenchies in their place and scare them Mi'Kmaqs away to some other territory. They shall learn that treaties are papers that do not last forever. They have no claim to our lands that are needed for English settlers. I must find the weapons and capture the traitors."

Turnbull opened his desk. He pulled the cork out of the bottle with his teeth and proceeded to swig and swallow and slosh himself with nearly a full jug of grog. He staggered out of his office and tried to mount his horse. After failing to put his feet in the stirrups and falling to the ground, a nearby soldier saluted and lifted him onto his mount.

Turnbull rode slowly to Tent City, where he dismounted. Then he walked behind the Church and hid in the shadows, where he had seen Gabriel and Kitok the day of the raid. Soon he was rewarded for his stealth. An unusually short Acadian removed a loose brick and pulled out a curled piece of bark. Not seeing clearly and thinking the person was Gabriel, Turnbull rushed him from behind. Full of rage, he slit the man's throat without mercy. Then he turned the Acadian over and saw he was merely a young boy of about ten.

With no remorse, Turnbull grabbed the bark from his victim's still warm hand and read it. Even in his stupor he knew this information should have been known only by the few officers reporting to Winslow. He began to suspect Adams and Hobbs, and now Wicker who always seemed to be their shadow. One of those men was the traitor. All he needed was the proof for Winslow and an early promotion would be his.

Turnbull sneered. "This is for you, Greenfield. One dirty heathen does not come close but it is all I have for you at the moment. Gabriel d'Entremont shall be next." Turnbull dragged the dead boy and dropped him on the front steps of the Church. Then he slipped into the officers' tent in Tent City, where he drank disgusting grog for the rest of the night.

Later that evening, Père Rivière exited the Church to find the boy lying in a pool of his own blood, like an animal sliced open and drained. His name was Christophe de la Tour Landry, the youngest brother of the patriot

Marc and François, who was at his seminary studies in Québec. The shock caused the priest's knees to buckle as he knelt on the steps beside the boy.

He verified the boy was not breathing, then he slipped into the Church and returned with a vial of holy water. He knelt on the step and lifted Christophe's head. He sprinkled the water on his forehead and blessed him with the Sign of the Cross, administering the Last Sacrament. "May God Our Father, His Holy Son Jesus Christ Our Lord, and the Holy Spirit welcome you into the kingdom of heaven where we pray that the Holy Trinity watch over your child Christophe, an innocent victim of English violence." He carried the boy into the sacristy and laid him there. The undertaker would arrive and prepare the body. Then the priest rushed towards René's office.

He knocked urgently on the door. Despite the late hour, René was still working. He answered it to find Père Rivière extremely distraught. The two men walked into the office talking in very low tones as the priest described the horror of the boy's death.

René quizzed him. "Did you see anything? Anyone at all?"

The priest shook his head. "My guess is Captain Turnbull himself or one of his soldiers ordered to perform the deed in his stead."

"Yes, that is his mark. Gruesome cruelty without justification."

Père Rivière told René, "Kitok told Gabriel of rumors of an upcoming attack but still does not know exactly what they are planning or when, except it will no doubt be soon."

René went to his desk and pulled out the Cardinal's diary. He looked at the back of the book where he had added several entries. "The English have made more than twelve unprovoked attacks on Acadian settlements since the massacre at Beaubassin in 1696. You believe their new plan is imminent?"

Père spoke up. "The attack at Fort Beauséjour this summer was a near massacre, together with the siege at Fort Louisburg and supply blockades, capturing over two hundred French military vessels. Though short of a formal declaration, it certainly looks like war at the hands of the English."

René said, "Arrange a meeting with the leaders of Gabriel's militia and Chief Matok. We must set our plans." The priest nodded then took his leave.

That evening, in the Consulate dining room, an exhausted René sat at the table, finishing the meal of venison, potatoes and vegetables. "How could John look me in the eyes and lie on his Bible?"

Christine replied, "It was the English Council as much as Winslow. And they all take orders from the King."

"Stay in the residence when we hold our militia meetings. I should not want to involve you or Evangeline in the resistance. It has become far too dangerous."

"Of course. I understand."

She stood to leave for her room. He took her hand suddenly. "Wait, Christine. I have wanted to say something to you for a long while."

Her heart started pounding. Was he finally going to express his love? She hoped this was what she had been longing to hear.

"Thank you for raising Evangeline into such a fine young lady."

She responded, "I truly love Evangeline but I did this for you."

He brought her to him and kissed her slowly, first chastely then hungrily with a passion neither knew had existed. She returned his kisses, hoping he would broach the subject of his feelings for her. She could not wait much longer to tell him how she felt. Suddenly René pulled back.

Christine was visibly crestfallen. She had hoped he felt the same as she and did not want him to see the tears swelling in her eyes. She looked away.

"Are you feeling unwell?" René was concerned.

She shook her head. "It is late and I should retire."

He nodded. "Perhaps we can speak more when we are both rested?"

She nodded then walked to her chamber as quickly as she could without raising his suspicion. Closing the door behind her she fell onto her bed and cried herself to sleep.

René went back to his office, working until the candles extinguished themselves. He knew he had feelings for Christine but he had never expected such powerful emotions. He was in a quandary but decided to put his feelings aside and concentrate on the political issues at hand.

That night Kitok return to the Mi'Kmaq Village with information and an invaluable document. He had learned of Turnbull's plan to attack the Mi'Kmaq Village three days hence. The map for the battle had been left on Winslow's dining table rather than locked in his satchel before he retired for the evening. It was the quickest entry and exit Kitok had ever made in the English commander's offices.

Gabriel's plan to live in the Village had worked well, as he and Kitok coordinated strategies. They seemed to understand each other without speaking, due not only to their mutual ancestral heritage but also to their long friendship, respect of the same ideals and distrust of the English. They worked late into the night in Kitok's bark hut, reviewing the map and designing one battle strategy after another in the dirt floor beneath the rugs.

Kitok and Gabriel worked out their plan, then Kitok's braves rode to advise the militia leaders in outlying areas and on the farms. Gabriel advised Père Rivière and René who contacted the older militia. Then Gabriel met with Marc and Claude who informed the other young militia members inconspicuously in town. The plan was on!

That night at supper René ate nervously. Evangeline and Christine knew he had important matters on his mind but finally Evangeline could stand it no longer. "Papa, what has you so tense? Is it the militia?"

Christine chimed in. "Yes, René, please tell us. Surely we can be of some service to you."

He looked at the two women and calmly said. "The British are planning an attack." The women became fearful and he continued, "The Mi'Kmaq Village on Friday."

"Two days?" asked Evangeline. "What can we do in such a short time?" She was worried but ready for the challenge to help Gabriel and the militia with her father's blessing. But what could she do?

Christine looked quite worried. Would René put himself in harm's way? He was too valuable to the King and the Acadians…and to her. She chided herself for not expressing her true feelings to him last night. Regardless of how busy he was, she was determined not to wait another evening. Events were unfolding too fast that might take him away. She decided to speak with him as soon as he was free, but she only asked, "Do you have a plan for us?"

René nodded. "Christine, you might remember Claude Arnaud has a brother who was at Versailles? He organized the wedding feast for Eugenie and me."

"Yes, of course."

Evangeline listened with fascination. She loved hearing stories of her mother and the Court of Versailles, though she mostly heard them from Christine. Her father rarely spoke of her mother.

"His brother became a secretary to Cardinal de Fleury and was well-informed of our state of affairs from my letters and the responses he wrote for the Cardinal. As it turns out, he is the son of the Duke of Rochefort who acknowledged him and left him a sizeable inheritance. He used part of it to buy weapons in Québec through an intermediary and he had them shipped overland to Claude."

Evangeline was enthralled. "But how did the weapons get past the English border guards? I hear they check every package and parcel most fastidiously."

René laughed. "Here, dear daughter, is a story that should be to your liking. Madame Arnaud's fabrics have of late been shipped through Québec. Laurent arranged her supplier to meet his merchant, who hid the muskets by wrapping them in bolts of cloth. Adèle knows the checkpoint guards and had given them several streamers for a mother and a sister, I believe. When Adèle's goods arrived, she was waiting at the border and had them delivered to her shop without inspection. Who would suspect a woman?"

Evangeline grinned and pointedly looked at her father. "So you see, we can help the cause without being in danger."

René smiled in agreement. "Precisely why I wished to speak to you both. Can you organize the wives and other women to sew two pouches for each militia man -- one for powder and one for musket balls, with a tie for each so they can be wrapped around the waist, easily accessible? Shall we say, two hundred pouches by tomorrow night?" He reached into his pocket and handed her two small packages, one of balls and the other of powder, to use as model samples.

Evangeline nodded as she looked at them. "I shall work with Adèle and Béatrice and coordinate enough women to complete the job. What else did you have in mind?"

René and Christine smiled. Evangeline was born to serve others and she took her calling to heart. "Nothing more tonight, dear daughter. I should like to speak with Christine, if you do not mind."

Evangeline wanted to stay and discuss the plan that Gabriel had no doubt initiated but she noticed the look in Christine's eyes as she gazed at her father. Perhaps Christine did have feelings for her father after all, though she had kept them so well-hidden Evangeline never caught even a hint of them until tonight. She kissed Christine on the cheek, then kissed her father. "Until tomorrow, Papa. Night, Christine."

Christine and René nodded. "Good night Evangeline," they said.

Christine was filled with emotion for René and did not know how to begin. Fortunately he spoke first.

"If Evangeline had not been born, would you have stayed this long in Grand Pré, here with us, with me?"

Christine saw that their relationship seemed to be on his mind as well. "I cannot say. It was my destiny until now. But Evangeline is about to be married and needs me no longer. And you have always been quite self-sufficient. If you wish time to find a replacement housekeeper, I shall assist you until you do. Then, I plan to return to France. I must leave soon, before the overland route is too snowbound to travel."

"No one could ever replace you. If you wished me to hire someone for the household duties, I told you many times I was quite willing to do so." He paused and took her hand, looking into her eyes. "You must know I have grown quite fond of you over the years, Christine."

Christine lowered her tear-filled eyes and said so softly it was nearly a whisper, "If you ask me, I will stay. This time for you, not Evangeline."

He stood and pulled her to him, kissing her softly, murmuring her name. "Christine, so beautiful, so kind." She responded to his kisses, allowing him to draw her near and embrace her tightly. They began to kiss harder and more passionately until he suddenly released her and cast his eyes down. He looked at Eugenie's portrait before he took his leave. "I cannot. I am sorry. I am so sorry." He rushed downstairs to his refuge, his office.

Christine slumped into a chair, crushed. Her pent-up feelings released in a flood of emotion as she covered her face with her hands and sobbed uncontrollably.

*

The largest Mi'Kmaq settlement in the region dating from the 1500's was referred to as the "ruins." It was little more than an abandoned site, with half-standing walls, broken stone fireplaces and burnt barns and huts, the results of an attack by the English in the prior century. The tribe kept the ruins as a reminder to never break their alliance with France for the untrustworthy English. The Mi'Kmaq tribe in Acadia had always lived in a settlement near the ruins, closer to Grand Pré but still at the edge of the forest.

The wigwams and bark huts of the First Nation, led by Chief Matok, appeared in the moonlight. Smoke curled through the chimneys like sleepy volcanoes. Everyone appeared to be asleep in their huts. But if any eyes had been carefully watching, they would have seen shadowy figures scurry from the woods to a large bark hut at one end of the Village.

Inside Chief Mahtok's large bark hut, Gabriel's Acadians were being brought to the tent several at a time where they were painted and dressed in full Mi'Kmaq warrior dress. In a flurry of activity, Princess Snowbird and her daughters applied colorful war paints made from crushed berries and plants to Marc's skin. Sitting Fox taught Claude how to wear the leather breeches and thongs. Kitok's aunts placed a feather headdress on each member of the Acadian militia, adjusting it in place.

Evangeline trimmed Gabriel's long hair and braided it Mi'Kmaq style as he watched her lovingly. She smiled. "I could not sit idle while you brave men fight for our beliefs. I had to do something. You were right all along about the English. Can you ever forgive my naïveté?" He kissed her hands in response, content that she was at his side at such an important moment for their people and their country.

Gabriel anticipated a heavily-armed Turnbull and he wanted to be ready. He hung a handgun in one belt loop and his knife in the other, then tied the pouches around his waist and held his musket. He was ready. He and Kitok nodded approvingly as they made the final adjustments to each man's appearance.

When the hundred or so young Acadians were dressed, Kitok handed each Acadian a knife and musket, which many refused. The dissenters relented only when Gabriel reminded them they might have need of a weapon in defense of themselves or a fellow patriot or Mi'Kmaq. Then old White Bird handed each man the pouches with powder and musket balls and a small sack of red river plant paste. As she had done with Christine, she cut her hand and showed them how to apply the paste to a wound.

Kitok and Chief Matok distributed weapons to the braves, who had been dressed and ready before the Acadians arrived. Each received a flint to sharpen his knife and a quiver of arrows for his bow. The arrow tips had been dipped in poison made by White Bird.

When Kitok nodded, the Chief offered the blessing which his ancestors had learned from the Jesuit priests generations ago. "May God be before you to guide you, above you to watch you and beside you to protect you."

Gabriel spoke for the members of the militia, who bowed to the Chief and said, "It is our great honor, Chief Matok, to stand with your braves and protect your First Nation, our allies."

It would be hours before the battle would commence and the men were beginning to get hungry. In anticipation of their needs, lovely Mi'Kmaq Indian maidens had laid out blankets with food outside the bark huts and wigwams, in a forest clearing. No doubt more than one match would result from the sparks that flew that evening, but not as a result of the fires that had been lit.

Kitok and Gabriel ate in the hut with Chief Matok, Princess Snowbird, White Bird and Evangeline. During the meal, René arrived, followed by the young men's fathers, uncles, and grandfathers. The older men were taken to other huts and wigwams, where the same rituals were undertaken -- clothing, war paint, headdress, weapons, pouches, red river paint. The older Acadians assured René, as their sons had promised Gabriel, they would not to take the life of any English soldier except to defend an Acadian or a Mi'Kmaq.   After several hours, the militia patriots had become Mi'Kmaq, numbering not one hundred but several times that.   They were ready for the attack.

René's surprise at seeing Evangeline was overcome by her display of emotion as she hugged him. "Thank you, Papa. A hundred times thank you. Your belief in Gabriel means everything to me."

"He is already a son to me. Thank you for opening my eyes to his courage and leadership."

They hugged each other and returned to their appointed tasks.

After the Acadians and Mi'Kmaq had shared the meal, the hut emptied but for the Consul and the Chief, who spoke together in low tones.   They briefly talked about the upcoming battle, which had been well planned by Kitok and Gabriel. They agreed to meet again in the Village once Kitok and Gabriel had more specific information about the vessels in the harbor and their relationship to the Acadians and the Mi'Kmaqs.

The English plan was to sneak through the ruins and attack the Village early in the morning. To counter the British strategy, Kitok, Gabriel and René posted their men in pairs before and throughout the ruins and on the edge of the Village. The younger Acadians were stationed at intervals behind the ruins to take the initial prisoners. René's men positioned themselves on either side of the pathway, hiding behind wigwams and bark huts. The Mi'Kmaqs hid in the woods ahead of the pathway and inside the houses at the far side of the Village. They planned to snare the enemy in their trap. In place before midnight they anticipated that the British would appear at dawn, their usual time for surprising the enemy while they slept. But this time, the surprise would be Turnbull's.

As the men waited in place for the English, White Bird led the Mi'Kmaq women and children to safety in the hills above. They had prepared comfortable lodgings in low-lying caves with bearskins and blankets, dried food, fruits and herbs and toys for the children in the event of a lengthy battle or siege. The First Nation willingly risked losing their wigwams rather than dismantling and moving them which would have alerted the English to their plan.

At sunrise Turnbull appeared, leading perfectly formed, horizontal rows of soldiers in typical British military fashion towards the ruins. The Acadians waited in small groups on either side of the main pathway where the soldiers had to march in order to reach the wigwams. The militia hiding in the ruins waited until the formation had marched by.

Then a pair of Acadians rushed behind each soldier on the last row, the first binding his mouth and the second his hands, then one holding the soldier and the other covering his head with a cloth sack, all before the prisoner knew what had happened. Taken by surprise, the soldiers never uttered a cry as they were hauled off into the woods and lifted into a large farm wagon hidden from view of the Village.

The next row of soldiers, which was now the last, kept their eyes facing front and were unaware of what had happened to their rear support. They were captured quickly and in the same manner, with bindings on their mouth and hands and a cloth over their heads, then taken into the shadows.

The prisoners, still very much alive and breathing in the large cart, were guarded by Sitting Fox and Princess Snowbird and her daughters, each proficient in the use of a knife. Sitting Fox ordered the soldiers to sit motionless without making any noise. The women then bound their feet to prevent them from running away, though the women would not have hesitated to use their knife if any soldier had attempted an escape.

The troops could not see or speak and were much too frightened and too young, at age sixteen or seventeen, to attempt anything as irrational as escape. When Sitting Fox sensed their fear, he told them no harm would come to them if they made no noise and remained silent. The soldiers visibly relaxed but did not dare disobey the order as these were the bloodthirsty Injuns that Captain Turnbull had warned them of.

The Acadians repeated their actions until the only English remaining were the front rows of soldiers and the officers, including Turnbull. The English were approaching a series of wigwams and bark huts where smoke rose into the dark sky. Mi'Kmaqs in huts and the surrounding woods initiated bird calls. The nearby Acadians who had delivered their captives to the cart returned to hide in the ruins and responded, their mutual signal that they had completed the pre-arranged plan.

At that point the English soldiers were trapped, although Turnbull did not yet know it. Behind them were the Acadians in the ruins and along their sides were the Mi'Kmaqs in the huts and wigwams. In front of them, Kitok and his braves waited in the dark woods.

Turnbull turned around to give the order to charge but was confused. Where were all his troops? He fired and his handful of remaining troops began to shoot indiscriminately. The Acadians hid deeper in the ruins, looking to Gabriel or René for the signal to fire. Both shook their heads adamantly. The Acadians would not be the cause of bloodshed.

The Mi'Kmaqs felt musket balls whizzing in their direction. They defended themselves by shooting a barrage of poisoned arrows from the wigwams and the woods, many of which hit their marks in the young English soldiers. When the guards next to Turnbull fell, he screamed the command that the Mi'Kmaqs and Acadians had hoped to hear.

"Retreat, retreat! To the Fort at once!"

Turnbull and his remaining soldiers left the dying troops and disappeared in the direction from whence they had come. The militia had left only one possible route open to the English -- retreat. And the English had taken it, scurrying away like rats from a sinking ship.

*

Back in his office, Winslow whipped his riding crop across the unscarred side of Turnbull's face. The cut was vicious and bloody. "You should be sent to Halifax or London and court-martialed for this. An English officer never retreats until the last blood is shed. The Mi'Kmaqs knew about the attack in advance. Find the source of the information and cut it off. And find the bodies of all those young soldiers. It shall be you who writes the letters to their sobbing mothers."

Turnbull saluted and muttered to Adams, Wicker and Bancroft on the way out. "D'Entremont is the snake. Find a way to bring him to me but make sure he is alive."

Even as Turnbull was plotting his revenge, the captive soldiers had answered all the questions Gabriel had asked without being harmed. The boys' fear led them to spill everything they knew, secret or not.

Over one hundred prisoners rode in the farmer's cart, hidden under piles of hay, on the overland route to New France. In Québec, they would all arrive alive to be held in a secret prison known only to the Governor and his closest aids. They would not be tortured or killed, which would have been the result had the tables been turned and had the English been the captors of Acadian or Mi'Kmaq.

The militia had won its first battle removing one-fourth of the troops at Grand Pré without firing a single musket. And unbeknownst to either side, the captured British soldiers would become prisoners of the war soon to be declared between England and France.

CHAPTER 38
Citation

GRAND PRÈ

This business is very disagreeable to my natural make and temper, Winslow thought to himself as he began to write yet another letter to his mother. He repeated over and over again the same words he had spoken to anyone who would listen at the English Council meetings earlier in the year. He did, that is, until Lawrence had threatened to remove him from his commission.

The disagreeable business was Winslow's assignment to remove the Acadian Neutrals from their lands during peacetime, in direct violation by the English of their Treaty of Utrecht with France in force since 1713. Winslow was charged with the organization and coordination of a myriad of details preparing for the deportation. Weighing heavily on his mind was the possibility of a spy in his ranks. He confided his fears, as always, only in his mother.

"Dear Mother Winslow,

Tis the first of September now and I have just received ugly news.   The Acadians we were to round up from Annapolis Royal fled into the woods and have not been found. Those unpredictable heathens even took their belongings with them."

Winslow shook his head in disgust, lifted his spectacles and rubbed his nose. Then he returned to the letter, reading aloud as he wrote.

"How they could carry furniture, linens, iron pots, and whatever weapons we did not confiscate is beyond my comprehension. The only answer is a turncoat within our ranks who warned the French of our scheme for their removal from these lands. That gave them the necessary time to make their preparations and leave, probably to New France."

Winslow pondered what he just wrote. A traitor. But who?

"I must say with bewilderment I believe these Frenchies seem to have a certain degree of intelligence. My fellow officers call them 'animals' without a brain and certainly without a soul, not being loyal to the Church of England. Yet I sense the opposite in my daily observances of them and communications with their Consul."

He laid down the quill, removed his glasses and leaned back in his chair. The idea of a turncoat was quite bothersome. Then he dipped the quill to continue writing.

"I tell you this because I fear reprisal would be taken against me if I uttered such words to any of our English loyalists. My Captain Turnbull recently confided that his troops harbor hateful feelings toward the French and attempt to provoke the heathens in order to justify killing them. Tensions are indeed high, but do not worry your lovely head of curls about me, Mother. This business will soon be over and done with and I shall return home. All the better, as it begins to weigh heavily on my conscience. Not always but sometimes enough to cause my heart to hurt."

He ended abruptly as always.

"Your loving son, John Winslow."

No sooner had Winslow completed his letter than his three Captains, Turnbull, Adams and Hobbs, arrived for the dinner meeting, as arranged. Once they were seated, a lavish meal was served. Winslow's stipulation had been that they partake of no more than one bottle of wine until their business was completed. As the wine was always the finest import, the officers were only too pleased to oblige their superior officer. They would sparingly savor the first bottle, complete their work and then proceed to partake of the other bottles.

Winslow ate hurriedly, impatient to complete their preparations. He scowled, waiting for the men to finish gorging themselves. Captain Adams was still eating and Captain Turnbull still drinking the last of the wine when

Winslow directed the stewards to clear the table. Then he unrolled a large map of the Minas region and began to describe troop activity, beginning with Grand Pré.

"Admiral Boscawen advised that the first of the transports shall begin arriving today or tomorrow and shall anchor here until all have arrived and we are ready to ship them away." He pointed to the Bay, out of view of the Grand Pré coast.

Winslow looked to his officers to ascertain their understanding of the plan. "Tomorrow I take Captain Adams with me to meet Captain Murray at Fort Edward. We shall arrange sufficient troops to move from there as support in the event of runaways. We cannot afford a repeat of Annapolis Royal, where the Acadians disappeared into the woods before we were ready to deport them. Or Turnbull's miserable failure with the Mi'Kmaqs. It is because of you that we need these reinforcements."

Turnbull was embarrassed but decided to take a bold approach. "We cannot allow these heathens to hide until the transports leave. We must root out the enemy before they unite against us for an attack."

Winslow looked directly at him. "The Frenchies know their forests as well as do their Indian allies. Entering their woods is a death sentence for our troops."

Adams and Hobbs agreed. "Yes, sir." Turnbull reluctantly acquiesced.

"When we have completed our scheme in all the other towns and the transports have left, those Acadians will believe they are safe and they will return. We will simply mount a second campaign thereafter and cleanse our lands of them, once and for all."

Turnbull pounded on the table with delight. "I would command troops willing to sacrifice their lives for the opportunity to find the missing Acadians."

Winslow peered at him. "Your troops would rather slaughter them than bring them in alive. You shall do as I command. No searches for Acadians in any woods. Their time will come soon enough. We have thousands of others to get rid of. Many thousands more than we originally thought. The Admiralty, or their contractor, must either send us more transports or build additional holds in the crow's nests."

Turnbull agreed vigorously to the stupid remark, not wishing to cause any displeasure to his commanding officer. Winslow was renowned for painful punishment and even more painful humiliation. Winslow handed Turnbull a roll of parchment documents.

"Deliver the Citation to the French inhabitants in the Minas Bay region. This calls all men to the Grand Pré church four days hence."

Turnbull nodded gravely. "And boys, sir, shall they also be included? Those old enough to hold and fire a rifle at our troops?"

Turnbull thought back to his own childhood. As the second son of an aristocrat, he had not handled a weapon until his father hired a master gunsmith to instruct him. His mother had cried, knowing he had begun his inevitable preparation for his military career and that once he left she would never see him again. She died shortly thereafter, some said of a broken heart for her favorite son. Turnbull chided himself silently. He could not think about that now but of the sons of the Acadian men who had been taught to be independent, even those with titles. They learned to hunt at an early age, much earlier than his genteel upbringing. And they were equally dangerous as their fathers.

Winslow nodded. "The Edict is written to include all males ten years and older." Then he returned to the map, using a quill to point out planned troop locations and movements.

"You, Adams, shall be responsible for coordinating troops with Captain Murray and shall bring his reinforcements here to the Fort. Hobbs, you supervise the arrival of the transports and the loading of foodstuffs. Turnbull, when you have delivered the Citation you shall organize the men in Tent City then work with Hobbs on the stores.

"Naturally you must not reveal the true nature of this mission to your troops and, of course, not to any Acadian. We must protect ourselves against these clever French heathens."

Turnbull spoke up. "Do you believe they are still a danger to us? That they have weapons other than those we took from their homes?"

Winslow rebuked him sharply. "They have long been our enemy and remain so, even in peacetime, with or without weapons."

Winslow was anxious to finish the deportation and leave the rest of the mission to his replacement, Captain Phinneas Osgood, after the first transports set sail with the men and boys only. Osgood, a loyal British army officer, would arrive thereafter to ship off the women, children and the aged and, if the British were lucky, Acadian stragglers returning from the woods.

Shirley believed there would be no further need of an officer in the Grand Pré area above the rank of Captain since, by then, the dangerous French Neutrals would be gone. Winslow surmised Osgood would be granted a promotion after the women were removed, followed by an orderly re-settlement of the land by new colonists, the English Planters. But

Winslow was even more pleased that his mentor, Commander Shirley, had confirmed Winslow's re-assignment back to Massachusetts, though it had no mention of white slaves.

With his orders issued, Winslow dismissed the three Captains. They immediately departed, leaving him in solitude. Winslow motioned that his stewards bring a selection of fine wines, which he proceeded to enjoy until he fell asleep at the table in a drunken stupor.

*

Three small animal transports arrived in the Bay of Minas and set anchor just off the Grand Pré coast. Several Acadian men waded in the chilly coastal waters, trolling for fish and crustaceans with their nets, a necessity since their boats had been confiscated by the British. They threw and hauled nets for seafood at high tides and set wire traps for crabs and lobster. One Acadian waved to the English soldiers on the ships trying to attract his attention. Another called out to the crew, asking about their mission. But the fishermen received no reply. Either the ship's crew members were too far away to hear the cries, or they chose to ignore the Acadian queries.

From the bluff high above the harbor, Kitok and Gabriel watched until the soldiers disappeared below decks. Kitok assigned two braves to continue to monitor the harbor and report any activity immediately. Then he descended the bluff to the tree line. When Gabriel rode away, his last view of Kitok was the image of him quietly slipping into the water, unseen by the fishermen on shore and the crew on the vessels.

*

In town, Evangeline and Christine walked to Madame Dupont's dress shop. There, Evangeline tried on her wedding gown, a stunning creation of rich blue satin studded with pearls and an embroidered lace overskirt. The layers of petticoats were trimmed in the same pearl-studded lace, scalloped at the edges. She had foregone a long train. Keeping true to Evangeline's taste, the gown was simple, yet elegant, and too beautiful for words. The two older women stood with tears in their eyes.

Christine hugged Evangeline softly. "You are such a beautiful bride, as I knew you would be, my dearest. If only dear Eugenie could see you now."

Evangeline asked, "Do you think she would approve?"

"In every way, my dear. In every single way."

Evangeline smiled modestly and twirled the dress to see all the luscious bits and pieces that the dressmaker had sewn. The décolleté neckline had a unique design. Evangeline touched her fingers lightly to the dress and Christine clasped Eugenie's necklace around Evangeline's neck.

Adèle and Béatrice gasped at the sight, not of the stunning necklace but at Evangeline's aura. Madame Dupont said, "You are the most beautiful bride ever to grace my shop. Truly, you will mesmerize the lucky groom." Her eyesight for sewing was gone but she directed Adèle to make nips here and take tucks there. This creation would be their crowning glory on the perfect bride for her perfect day.

Evangeline hugged Madame Dupont. "I adore it. You have created this perfectly to my style. Thank you, thank you so much."

Christine admired it as she walked around Evangeline. "The pearls and stones, and all of that French lace. It is simply magnificent. You have both outdone yourselves."

Adèle gave a slight bow in thanks. "I dare say Consul René would be proud to escort his daughter to her groom if she wore a potato sack." At this the women burst into laughter that turned into tears of joy.

Madame Dupont added, "But I do hope our work shows him how much respect and love I have for your family."

Evangeline watched as Madame Dupont placed a hand-embroidered lace veil over her head, which trailed to form a long train down the back of the dress. When Adèle held up a glittering tiara, Madame Dupont shook her head. Evangeline did not need anything else. She, herself, was the sparkle. Now she looked like a bride and she would awe Gabriel with the vision.

Evangeline bent down to kiss the two dressmakers. "It is everything I dreamed of Madame, Adèle. Thank you."

Christine asked, "Is it my turn to try on my dress now?"

The women laughed as Adèle brought out another creation, then helped Evangeline out of the layers of satins and lace. As Christine modeled her new gown, Adèle boxed the wedding dress and veil. The women merrily left the store, each carrying a new dress box.

That evening, news of the transports quickly spread throughout the town and by the morning all the shops were abuzz. Acadians buying meat in the butcher shop thought the boats were to take the extra animals to market in Bostontown before the winter snows. René sent a messenger to the largest animal breeding farm. He returned with the response that no ships were expected until spring and that the existing stock had been reserved for the Acadians for the winter.

French women shopping in the bakery discussed among themselves that the English were about to buy more grain or wheat for the colonies. But none of the farmers had been contacted to buy more crops.

Some of the bolder Acadian boys called out through the pickets of Tent City, asking the purpose of the transports. The soldiers told them to go away, without divulging any information.

At the dining tables, the English soldiers staying with Acadian families were questioned as to the reason for the vessels in the harbor. Yet every soldier honestly replied he was not assigned to any maritime duty and knew not the reason for the activity.

Some Acadians learned that the ships had bought some provisions from local merchants and farmers. With that, the Acadians felt secure that the transports had merely anchored for stores on their way to other English colonies.

Early the next day, while mounting his horse inside the English Fort entry gates, Winslow issued final instructions to Turnbull. "After you deliver the Citation, monitor all French activity. Post a guard outside the Consulate but at a discreet distance away. No need to let the Consul see we are watching him."

Turnbull asked, "Should I send spies to the Mi'Kmaq Village?"

"That shall not be necessary. The French are our concern. Besides, it shall soon be winter and the Indians shall move away to higher ground for hunting and shelter from the impending snows. They will not be here to protect their heathen allies."

"Yes sir, Lieutenant-Colonel."

"Your job is to make certain the Acadians do not suspect what is to be done with them. Watch for any activity out of the ordinary at the harbor and along the coast as well as in town."

Winslow rode with Hobbs and Adams to the harbor, where a sloop awaited. They boarded and set sail on their short journey to Fort Edward.

Turnbull waited until his commanding officer was out of sight, then he signaled his troops to follow him. They took the opposite direction from Winslow. Turnbull led his men inland. They were to deliver the Citation to the French working the farms in the area.

On his boat, Winslow turned to the two Captains, Adams and Hobbs.

"There is a particular reason why I asked you both to join me today, in addition to the meeting with Captain Murray."

They nodded politely, waiting for him to continue.

"I have reason to believe there is a traitor in our midst. One who informed the French Neutrals of Annapolis Royal of their impending deportation and one who warned the Mi'Kmaqs of Turnbull's raid."

They both gasped in shock. Who among them would dare commit treason, and for their enemy, the French?

"I entrust you with a secret mission to observe troops and officers in Grand Pré. All of them. We must make certain that the same fate does not befall us there. We cannot make any mistakes."

They nodded in unison.

"Our Great and Noble Scheme must succeed at all costs."

Adams nodded and Hobbs spoke quickly. "Yes sir, Lieutenant-Colonel."

Winslow nodded. "This is not to be discussed with any other officer. With no one but me, you understand?"

Adams responded, "Of course, Lieutenant-Colonel. We shall report any information to you."

Hobbs added, "And only to you, sir."

"And Captain Adams?"

"Yes, sir."

"You are to arrange to board an additional one hundred support troops within the Acadians' homes. They are to sleep there and eat there, if you can arrange it. Tent City cannot accommodate all of the Halifax reinforcements."

"Of course Lieutenant-Colonel. Should this be gratis?"

"Since it is for such a short time, arrange payment from my office by the month. The heathens should all be removed after one payment. We must not alarm them."

"Sir, what explanation should I give?"

"Only that these troops are in training exercises and we have no more tents. That should suffice. The French Neutrals are a trusting and honest people. They will not question it but will be accommodating as ever. Their Consul wants to keep the peace at all costs."

Adams said under his breath, "Everyone knows they should have learned not to trust us by now."

Winslow was content with his plan to move forward. Now, if only Murray cooperated. The boat dropped anchor and they were rowed in to meet the Captain, who greeted them on the dock with a salute.

"Welcome to Fort Edward, Lieutenant-Colonel. Your wish is our command. Where would you like to begin? Something to eat and drink after your journey? A short rest?"

Winslow snapped angrily. "I should like to begin with finalizing the preparations for this disagreeable business. Much remains to be done and I must return as soon as possible. Let us get on with it, Captain."

Captain Murray led the way into the Fort. There, the men worked the better part of the day on the deportation plans. Winslow had worked through dinner, their main meal of the day. He had accepted only light refreshment and one glass of wine to sustain him during the tedious planning session. When Winslow rose from the table to leave, he knew how many troops Murray would send and when they were to arrive. Murray and his officers were sworn to secrecy and forbidden, on pain of court-martial and imprisonment, to discuss the plans with their own troops or other officers.

Outside the pickets of Fort Edward, Captain Murray accompanied Winslow back to the dock. Adams and Hobbs advised Murray's aides where to stow provisions for the return trip. Murray wanted to leave his commanding officer with a lasting impression of skill and organization. That would not happen if he had hunger pangs on his way home, although it was his own fault for refusing Murray's hospitality.

*

In Grand Pré, from the bluff above the beach Gabriel and Kitok gazed at the shore through the tree line. They saw a waiting group of English soldiers looking to the horizon. Their horses stomped and whinnied. It was then that Gabriel saw three horses were riderless. That meant three officers had gone to the boats. Winslow's boat was anchored in the nearby waters. Winslow and Captain Adams were rowed ashore. Hobbs had taken another rowboat heading out to one of the large transports.

Watching these actions, the Mi'Kmaqs in the trees and Gabriel and Kitok on the bluff instinctively sensed troubled. However, they were not in a position to learn the meaning of what they saw. The braves regarded the beach and the tree line below. To an untrained eye, the area seemed empty of human life. Acadian boats that had been smashed into ribbons or burned on the beach by the English resembled old skeletons which had been half-buried in the sands washed ashore by the tides.

No one was visible. But the sharp-eyed braves saw four of their brother braves hiding in the trees closest to the shoreline. Kitok had wanted as many eyes on the English as could be hidden from them.

Winslow and Adams alighted from the rowboat, mounted their horses and took off in the direction of their Fort. The braves in the trees below were no longer visible, even to the Mi'Kmaqs above. The English contingent rode through the trees and started up the bluff. The hooves of their horses thundered at the top of the hill, riding past trees in whose branches Mi'Kmaqs had secreted themselves.

Beyond the shore, Captain Hobbs moved to the first transport. The crew lowered a rope ladder, then pulled Hobbs aboard. He disappeared below deck, where he remained for some time. After a while, Hobbs reappeared, was led down to the rowboat and then brought to the next vessel, where he repeated the procedure. Unbeknownst to the Mi'Kmaq observers, Hobbs had boarded each ship to inspect the rebuilt holds and review the food storage and cooking areas.

Each ship captain confirmed with Hobbs their destinations to offload what they were told would be a shipment of animals. The captains knew the ships had been rebuilt with extra holds too short for most animals and food stores larger than needed by a crew, yet not one questioned whether the animals were actual human cargo. The pay for this particular voyage was double the usual rate for a trip between Nova Scotia and the colonies and the captains did not want to lose this lucrative assignment.

Winslow had charged Hobbs with determining how many Acadians could be stuffed into the four-foot high cells and to determine what foodstuffs were needed and where they could be stored for the voyage. No one knew Hobbs' true mission and he did not enlighten them.

Later that evening, Gabriel, Marc and Kitok entered the Consulate through the back entrance. Luckily for them, Turnbull had neglected to assign a watch to the rear of the Consulate, instead assigning troops at the corner across from the front door. The soldiers were to report anyone going in or coming out. But he was apparently unaware of the rear door not visible from the street. Inside the Consulate, René met with the men.

"Could the boats concern the mission referred to in Greenfield's Halifax documents that Kitok read?" asked Gabriel.

René nodded thoughtfully. "The transports in the Bay are too numerous to be peacetime merchant vessels. Yet you confirmed they are for animal cargo."

Gabriel commented, "Lack of a declaration of war does not mean the English are not making preparations for one."

René added, "I have heard rumblings that the seaboard colonists have crop shortages, and with the embargo on corn, they may have petitioned King George for more food."

Gabriel said, "Or lower taxes to buy food, which surely is more costly there now."

Kitok said slowly, "When our lookouts saw nothing I swam out to the first vessel. No English were on deck except one. He dumped loads of animal dung and dirty hay into the water."

Marc blurted in response, "They consider Grand Pré their greatest food source. If they are cleaning out their storage holds are they planning to load their ships with seized crops?"

Gabriel added, "And our livestock? Just as winter is coming? Surely that is not their intention."

The next morning, Hobbs surveyed the coast and saw the additional transports that had arrived. This time Hobbs waved and talked to the Acadian fishermen on the shore. He wanted to calm their fears and create a feeling of trust and security. Because some of the ships were transports for crops and others for animal cargo, he fabricated a partially truthful story that refurbishments were needed before being sent to the colonies for use there.

That seemed to reassure the Acadians. They would report to the Consul and then to their wives, who would tell their parents and sisters, who would tell their husbands, who would tell their friends and so on. The large Catholic families had inter-married with each other for the last hundred and fifty years, retaining their spoken and written French from the sixteenth century and creating a tight-knit community that rarely admitted a non-Acadian by marriage. The Acadians all had close familial ties to births, deaths, weddings and, of course, any news. Naturally, word traveled quickly.

Today was the start of the harvest. Most of the able-bodied men, women and children from town had gone to the farms to aid their relatives. This year had been especially good and the crop yield was plentiful, necessitating the need for extra hands. Turnbull rode into the middle of a large wheat field where Acadians were harvesting the crop. The children saw the troops first and hid behind their older siblings or parents. Turnbull would have preferred to take them all prisoner now but he obeyed his commander's orders.

"Gather round. We mean you no harm. You know we are the peacekeepers. Come quickly and hear what we have to read to you."

The adults stopped their work and walked over to Turnbull. Several fathers carried sons on their shoulders, while mothers held young girls in their arms or by the hand.

"Come closer. That is right." Turnbull forced a smile to attract the Frenchies, of whom he would soon be rid.

When they had all gathered near his troops, Turnbull held up the parchment for all to see. "You shall hear the Proclamation to the Inhabitants of the Minas Bay region." He began to read in English but many of the Acadians could not understand. Though most of the farm hands had been taught to read the Bible and write short letters, they learned on farms, not schools, and in the French language, not English. Turnbull pulled out the French version and began to read aloud.

"To the inhabitants of the district of Grand Pré, Minas, and places adjacent...."

Turnbull began reading, then looked from the paper to the French families standing there, assuming they understood what he said. Everyone was clearly attentive to his words and he continued in French.

"Whereas His Excellency Nova Scotia Governor Philipps, desiring that the previous matters with you should be satisfied of His Majesty's edict and intentions, has ordered us to communicate the same in person; We, therefore, order all old and young men, as well as the lads of ten years of age or older of the above-named district and of all the other districts, to attend at the church at Grand Pré on Friday the Fifth of the instant month at three o'clock in the afternoon, that we may impart what we are ordered to communicate to them, declaring that no excuse will be admitted on any pretense whatsoever, on pain of forfeiting goods and chattels, in default of real estate and all other possessions, and on pain of death for treason."

He looked at the Acadians briefly as he rolled the parchment and finished reading the document.

"Thus are communicated the orders of His Britannic Majesty King George Two and His Excellency Governor Philipps. God save the King."

The Acadians started to question Turnbull all at once and to plead for an explanation of the Edict, but the officer ignored them all. Women wailed and children cried but Turnbull and his troops thundered out of the field, leaving the Acadians to question each other.

Turnbull and his men rode back into town from the farms and the residences near the dikes. He halted the small group outside St. Charles Church. Père Rivière was admiring the repairs made to the front doors by the carpenter Thomas Gaudet and his son, Pine.

Without a word to the Acadians Turnbull watched as Lieutenant Bancroft nailed the French and English versions of the Citation to the huge wooden doors. Bancroft returned to his horse and Turnbull directed them to remain in front of the Church.

The priest and Thomas Gaudet began to read the Citation when René happened to walk out of a nearby shop. Evangeline and Christine were with him, and they followed him to the Church. René quickly read the parchment and turned to the English officer while Evangeline and Christine were still reading it.

"Captain Turnbull, what do you plan to do in our Church that you must threaten us? We are all honorable citizens of this great province. Please ask Lieutenant-Colonel Winslow to meet with me this afternoon on this matter. Captain Turnbull?"

Turnbull ignored him, instead leaning over and joking with the subordinate officers.

Evangeline and Christine felt the stares of the Englishmen on them. Evangeline turned to Turnbull. "Surely you are a man of good breeding, Captain, who would enlighten us with your knowledge."

Turnbull looked at her, his face expressionless. She took that to mean she should continue. "Would you please explain the meaning of this...this Edict?"

Turnbull was amused at her feisty nature. He instantly felt attracted to her. She would be quite a filly to tame. "Well, Miss, it is for your men to learn several days hence."

She continued boldly, although Christine tried to pull her back. "You do not imagine it will take longer than the evening to impart this Edict, do you, Captain?"

"Why ever do you ask, Miss?"

"I am to be married this Sunday coming and as this Edict reading is Friday, it is naturally a question to pose."

"Well, Miss, I know of no Edict that has ever taken three days to impart." He laughed aloud and his men joined in with him as he directed them to ride out of town in the direction of the Fort.

Evangeline looked around and ignored the glare of her father as she and Christine took their leave. On the way back, Christine leaned over to her and whispered in her ear. Evangeline pulled away and told her, "I shall ride to find Gabriel." She turned in the direction of the stables where she kept her horse. Christine continued walking home. Food had to be prepared, clothes washed and the house cleaned. Someone must maintain a semblance of order during these unusual times.

The sight of English troops in front of the Catholic Church had piqued the curiosity of Claude Arnaud and several other Acadian men at the other end of town. They walked to the Church to learn the reason for the gathering crowd. They were surprised to read the notice on the door.

"Consul, what is the King's Edict?" asked Arnaud.

The Acadian men turned to René for guidance. He was equally at a loss. "I have not heard a word of this from Lieutenant-Colonel Winslow and Captain Turnbull refused to send him my message. I am returning to the Consulate to send a written request for a meeting. I shall get to the meaning of it all."

Père Rivière asked, "What should we do in the meanwhile?"

René looked at him quizzically. It still seemed odd to him that in political matters he was the shepherd of all the colonists, including the priest, as his flock. At least he worked night and day to be the best leader he could in guiding the French settlers on a peaceful path. But little by little he was realizing that peace was not a possible solution.

René attempted to reassure them. "This may be a repeat of the English Council's demand that we all sign the King's Oath of Allegiance, giving up our freedoms guaranteed under the Treaty of Utrecht."

Arnaud responded, "But many are still missing, hopefully at least alive in prison, in Halifax for not signing that Oath."

Père Rivière added, "Some of us were fortunate to escape although we signed the petition we presented to the Council. If they had wanted to arrest all of us, they know our names if they can read them."

Marc thoughtfully said, "I do not believe that is what the English want. Who would bring in the crops or raise livestock for the colonies?"

The men murmured among themselves in agreement with René, who continued, "You should know His Majesty King Louis formally advised Britain's King that we are fully prepared to sign the Treaty Oath that recognizes our freedom of religion and exempts us from bearing arms in the war against our mother country or allies."

Thomas Gaudet spoke up. "But this threatens death and forfeiture of all our property if we fail to appear. Is that not much more serious than ever before?"

René nodded. "That is to ensure all men are present." Then he turned to the priest. "Will you hold a prayer vigil for us just before the Edict is read? We should give thanks to God for our freedoms and for all the blessings He has bestowed on us."

Père Rivière nodded. René turned to Marc and Claude. "Can you organize a group to inform all heads of household of this reading?"

The men readily agreed and began to discuss it with those sitting nearby.

René added, "Remember to contact widows with sons at least ten years of age. The English keep a census and know who lives in each home."

The men all nodded but continued to talk among themselves. René raised his hands for quiet and they complied. "Please leave quietly rather than congregating here. The English watch us carefully. Any disgruntled attitudes could cause a reaction that…well, it would be best to return to your homes. I shall prepare a new Oath for all to sign before the meeting. Père, may I leave it with you here at the Church? All male citizens ten and older are to sign before the September fifth reading date."

The priest nodded. "Of course, Monsieur le Consul. I am happy to oblige."

"I shall present the signed Treaty Oath to Lieutenant-Colonel Winslow and perhaps avoid any nasty demands."

The men agreed and they each went their separate ways to spread the news.

Back in his office, René sat glumly at the table, writing notes on a page marked "Edict." Christine set a supper bowl with piping hot soup and a platter of ham chops, salad and vegetables before him. He mused, more to himself than to her, "How could John not have met with me before posting the notice? I must learn the meaning of this Edict before the reading on Friday." He added as an afterthought, "Please stay upstairs for the rest of the evening, for your own safety."

Christine nodded. She would have replied but he turned back to his writing. She sighed and then slowly walked up the stairs to the dining room. She ate in silence and sat as the candle slowly burned.

René entered the room and placed his empty bowl and plate on the table. He did not sit but walked to the wall where Eugenie's portrait hung. His fingers softly outlined the beautiful face and hair.

Christine looked at him with love and sadness. She hung her head in sorrow as she walked away from the table to the hallway. At the stairs to her room she turned to look at René, who had not noticed she was gone. Later, at her dressing table Christine looked at herself in the mirror. She was still an attractive woman, her red hair still its natural flame hue. But she had spent years of her life waiting for a man who barely spoke to her and considered her a housekeeper rather than a future wife. She decided she would go back to face him and speak about the matter most pressing to her. Perhaps he really did love her. His kisses had revealed his passion for her.

But could his obsession with his deceased wife be overcome? There was but one way to find out.

René touched the winterberry lips of his bride's portrait, trying to recall his short marriage with Eugenie so many years ago. René realized he had looked at this painting for seventeen years and had only tonight understood it was not the image of the woman he married. Although René had always been entranced with her beauty, this portrait was something else. It was saintly, otherworldly, perfect. But it was not his Eugenie.

Pater had painted his vision of her, perfect in every way. To be sure, the artist was talented beyond measure and everyone at Court had clamored for his services. But the painter had captured his muse as he wanted her to be, a flawless angel. As René ran his fingers along the facial features of the image he saw that the portrait missed, or intentionally omitted, nearly all the nuances and imperfections that René had so loved about Eugenie. Where was the little crooked tooth René caught a glimpse of when Eugenie had smiled? He saw but a row of impeccably straight teeth without any defect, even such an endearing one. And the wayward strand of hair she used to push back from her face was missing from her perfect coiffure.

René smiled, remembering Eugenie had always complained that her nose was too full. Yet this portrait depicted a faultless aquiline nose, streamlined and slender, but not hers. The change was slight, for Eugenie's nose had never been bulbous, but René was taken aback that he had never noticed it until now. He looked at the image of her hair but did not remember it ever being that golden. He remembered their rare walks on deck when her hair shimmered in the sunlight. But this painted image shone like a soft halo.

He traced the painting's eyes, brilliant with flashing hazel green and brown. Then he remembered how Eugenie's eyes were sad and dull with pain. He fell onto his chair remembering her eyes red from crying after losing her meals. Of course, that happened only when René convinced her to eat at all, knowing she would not keep the food down very long.

For the first time, he realized that he could not remember what it felt like to touch her. He had forgotten the enticing curves of her body which had struck him with awe. He could not picture her actual face although he remembered parts of it. He hung his head, then looked up to see Christine back at the table. She waited for him to acknowledge her. He looked at her as if noticing her for the first time that night.

She stood to leave, dejected, knowing he would lever let Eugenie go. René grabbed her hand suddenly. "I have been remiss in not telling you something very important." Suddenly she felt a spark of hope that he was about to say what she had been longing to hear.

He grabbed her and kissed her with abandon, holding her to him and kissing her. Then he cried out softly, "Christine, I want you to stay but it must be your decision."

He pulled her to him once again and kissed her lips softly again and again. He smoothed her hair, kissed her forehead and took her face into her hands, kissing her with respect as if he were restraining himself against his passion.

She pulled away and knew she had to tell him. "René, I love you. I have been in love with you for years. Can you not see me? I am not a ghost or a painting. I am real. I am here. And I love you. Please, dear, dear René, if you have feelings for me at all, please ask me to stay for you. For us. And I shall."

He shook his head. "Please forgive me for not being able to give you what you truly deserve."

Christine looked at the painting, then back at René. Their eyes met and he knew he would lose her. But still he remained silent. She said, "I shall depart after Evangeline's wedding. It is best for all, I believe."

René nodded, and slowly descended the stairs to his office. He looked back up at her. "Christine, I shall regret losing you more than you know. If you are ever in need of anything, you know you can call on me."

She turned away, unable to speak, standing near the painting until she heard René close the door to his office. Then Christine looked up at the image of the ghost who had haunted her all these years.

She grabbed her empty wine glass and angrily threw it at Eugenie's portrait. Glass shards flew everywhere.

Then Christine looked sadly down toward René's office and whispered, "René, why did you not ask me to stay and become your wife?"

CHAPTER 39
Edict

Friday, September 5, 1755 - GRAND PRÈ

 s morning broke, sunlight streamed into Evangeline's third floor bedroom window. She felt for her locket and opened it, smiling. "Only three more days, Gabriel Mius d'Entremont. Then you shall be married to the person who will make you the happiest man in the world. As you shall make me the most joyous woman."

She walked to the window, tightly wrapping her woolen shawl about her. The winter winds had begun to blow. The snows will come early, she thought. She looked beyond the rooftops of the other buildings, mostly single story homes and a few stores with housing on the second floor.

Evangeline's gaze continued beyond the tree line to the shore. For several days, thick fog had hidden the water from view, until today. And what she saw caused her great alarm. She rushed out of the room.

In René's office Gabriel, Kitok, Marc and Père Rivière huddled together. Kitok gave them the grim news. "I overheard Turnbull ordering one ship captain to prepare for at least one thousand. He responded he had place for only six hundred. Then Turnbull drew his bayonet to the officer's throat and threatened him, telling him he had better find the space."

There was a silent shudder in the room. The men were stunned. Did they hear Kitok correctly?

Gabriel spoke first. "So the cargo is neither crops nor livestock, but human. A thousand Acadian souls will be crammed on a small transport meant to carry a hundred animals or barrels of cod? It is unthinkable."

René said solemnly, "They intend to take us first and then our farms and animals. But how can they possibly fit more than a few hundred persons on board an animal cargo transport? There is not enough room in the hold and on deck for that great a number. It should hold no more than two persons per ton, which allows one hundred to one hundred fifty people on each, not one thousand."

Marc added quietly, "Kitok, where is the intended destination of the ships?"

Kitok responded, "The orders I found addressed to Winslow only said 'colonies.' That could mean any of them or all of them."

Gabriel asked, "How were you able to read the orders without alarming the English?"

Kitok said, "Rumors have spread that Winslow fears a traitor within his own troops so he carries his important papers with him at all times. Several of my braves dug a tunnel under the fence near his house. While he was sleeping I entered the tunnel and found the documents under his pillow. I was able to read the documents quickly by the candlelight in his other room and return them before he awoke. But he may hide them next time for his fear of a turncoat in his midst."

Gabriel nodded and advised, "Kitok is right. We should plan our strategy based on the information we have without knowing if any other details can be obtained."

The men nodded and murmured their assent.

Then Gabriel turned to René. "How are we to advise King Louis? We have no boats large enough to reach France."

René shook his head. "It is far too late for that. We shall send a letter by messenger to New France to send to the King for us. We shall also ask the Québec Governor for troops to reinforce our militia as it is rumored that Lawrence has over two thousand troops at Halifax. The French forces are not near that number. It would be senseless slaughter to send our untrained settlers to fight the experienced British, even with our large numbers. We can only hope the Governor sends what he can in time."

He looked at the other men. "As soon as the Edict reading is over, quietly assemble the men in Mi'Kmaq Village. It might take all night but make sure not more than two travel together and then only those who would customarily do so."

Kitok, Père and Marc left quickly by the back door. Gabriel looked to René. "Should we alert Evangeline and Christine?"

René shook his head. "They are both asleep and they will need their strength."

At that moment, Evangeline burst into the room. It was unlike her to open the door without knocking. "Please excuse me, Papa, but something most urgent has happened." She looked at René who nodded and she continued, "Three or four large vessels are in the Bay. It is difficult to tell because of the fog, but I could see faint outlines of men working on the decks and...."

René dropped his head.

"What is it Papa?"

Gabriel answered for him. "Kitok learned the purpose of the ships." He reached for her hand. She unhesitatingly gave it to him. "They are to remove us from our homes and lands."

She was stunned. "Why? And where are we to be sent?"

Gabriel replied, "We have not yet learned the destinations other than the colonies."

Kitok added, "I am trying to learn but the soldiers do not speak loosely. I believe Winslow guards the secret himself, but we have not located his hiding place."

René said, "It is possible that only the captains of the vessels know where they are sailing."

Kitok added, "Perhaps they will be told only when all of your people are on board."

Evangeline looked at Gabriel, then at her father. "What shall we do? Surely we cannot sit on our hands and do nothing."

Gabriel responded by taking her hands and pulling her to him. "Your father shall speak to Winslow at the reading of the Edict this afternoon. After that, if he does not agree to the Treaty Oath and allow us to live here in peace, then we are prepared to fight for our freedom."

"Fight, but how? Most weapons were taken in the raid and you have no large seagoing vessels."

"We have weapons."

"But how...?"

"It is better that you know nothing of it for your own sake, my darling."

"All the more reason why I must. Please tell me."

Gabriel nodded.

"What should I do?"

"Kitok has stored the arms in a safe place. Go to him if your father and I…if we are not here when you need us. But you must tell no one."

She nodded and looked from Gabriel to her father to Kitok. She realized they had just learned the devastating news when she interrupted them and that their plans had not been finalized. She made a quick decision, caught her breath and spoke calmly. "If you shall allow us, Christine and I shall organize the wives and older girls while you and the other men and boys are in the Church. What do you need us to do?"

Gabriel was hesitant, remembering his promise to René to avoid Evangeline's involvement. But René sought her help enthusiastically. "Ask them to gather and prepare as much food as they can. Do not tell them the actual reason or I fear they will try to hide their children or escape into the woods. If they do, they will starve or the English will hunt them down and hang them for treason. Either of those choices end badly."

Evangeline responded quickly. "Yes, we can gather the food. Shall we bring it to Kitok's family? Would they hide it for us until we are ready to move?"

Gabriel said, "They have stored our weapons and they can do the same with the food. Tell them the food is for our wedding banquet. Bring bread, cakes, preserved fruits, dried meats, salted fish, nuts, herbs, vegetables, grains, flour, spices and salt, anything you can find that will last a good while. Dried meats, potatoes and pickled goods are also good choices if we must hide in the woods or in the mountain caves. Try to get as much food as you can carry that will keep. I fear that the soldiers will attempt a raid on our cellars for food. First they took our weapons, preventing us from hunting for food and killing animals destroying our crops. Next, they confiscated our boats, which closed our fishing businesses. The only thing remaining is our food supply."

Evangeline looked at Gabriel with a mixture of love and fear in her eyes. "Shall this affect our wedding?"

Gabriel held her closely to him. He spoke to her but looked directly at René. "I shall not let anything change that." He kissed her solemnly.

On her way out, René got up from his desk and hugged her. "Hurry! We have not a moment to lose."

Evangeline rushed up the stairs to wake Christine. They had much to do in such a short time. Within a matter of minutes the two women had left the building and mounted their horses. Soon they were on their way to meet the women leaders of their community. The first women they asked to spread the word were Adèle and Béatrice. Together they would provide strength and sustenance for their men, hopefully by providing more than food.

Père Rivière tolled the bells of St. Charles at one o'clock that afternoon. The Church soon filled with young men and their fathers, old men and their male grandchildren, and single men.

The women were absent, though no one took notice. Their men believed they were preparing the wedding feast and the English soldiers and officers had called only for men to present themselves in the Church. They did not want crying women and babies to distract them from their duties.

From the officers' tent in Tent City Turnbull remarked to Adams and Hobbs, "The Frenchies seem anxious to be driven out. They are two hours early." Adams and Hobbs raised their cups to toast their fellow officer, all the while considering he might be the traitor.

Still in his office in the Fort, Winslow was unsure of when he could execute the departure plan. His troops were low on food supplies and no provisions ship had been seen by any forts along the route from Bostontown to Grand Pré. He knew the Acadians outnumbered his force of one hundred in town and some reinforcements from Murray when the Acadians were to be sent out. But he was worried his troops would be overtaken should an uprising occur. His only solace came from writing in his journal. Dipping his quill into the ink pot Winslow scrawled his thoughts onto the page.

"Things are now very heavy on my heart and hands. I wish we had more men, but as it is shall I question not to be able to scuffle through?"

He was comforted by holding his Holy Book and remembering that he had the element of surprise on his side. The French heathens knew not what was to befall them so they could not unite and withstand his forces. He would make them believe he had many more troops than had arrived.

Inside the Church, the young men in Gabriel's militia came up to talk with him, under the pretext of congratulations. They were informed of the plan to meet in the Mi'Kmaq Village that evening. The older men congratulated René on his daughter's upcoming wedding and then listened to plans for the gathering later that evening. They murmured in whispers, nodding when René spoke.

Then Père Rivière stepped down from the altar and walked among them. He spoke quietly of the plans made by the militia. He prayed for their strength. René set out the parchment with their modified Oath of Allegiance as provided by King Louis to King George II and to René for signature by the French Neutrals. The priest led them in prayer as each of the hundreds of men signed his name to the modified Treaty Oath which René planned to present to John Winslow at three o'clock.

Suddenly, the doors slammed. Soldiers bolted the doors, then stood at attention, with bayonets pointed at the Acadians. Fathers comforted their boys, who had begun to cry but the men were equally as fearful.

Captain Adams directed his troops to secure all doors and windows from the inside. Captain Hobbs sent his force outside to shutter the windows and to nail wooden boards to reinforce them and to prevent any escape.

Captain Turnbull occupied his troops in the church setting up a large table and a high-backed chair on the altar for their commanding officer, Lieutenant-Colonel Winslow. Soldiers placed a box filled with ink pots and quills on the table as Winslow walked to the front of the church, set a sheaf of documents on the table, and took the pulpit.

Winslow nodded, and Turnbull and Bancroft grabbed Père Rivière, tore the Bible from his hands and cuffed his wrists with metal rounds. They dragged him in front of the table.

René and the other members of the congregation were outraged. René spoke for them all when he stood and addressed Winslow. "Lieutenant-Colonel, what is the meaning of this? The priest has done nothing unlawful. He is not a military man but a man of God. A man of the cloth. Surely you understand that."

Winslow turned to René. "You have no rights here. Sit down and say nothing." He looked at all of the men in the Church, nodding to his soldiers. They raised their bayonets in unison. The men realized that their fate was in the hands of a madman, Winslow, and they all took their seats.

Winslow picked up the first parchment and read it aloud. "For crimes of treason, including inciting the French Neutrals to riot against His Britannic Majesty, the Catholic priest named Nicolas Rivière is hereby arrested and condemned to a life of slavery in the Massachusetts Bay colony."

René jumped up from his seat and bounded over to the table before any soldier could stop him. He whispered, "John, please do not do this. My daughter is to be wed in three days. Please release him and allow him perform the marriage and our religious ceremonies. Do not send him away, I beg of you."

Winslow looked at him and said with a sadistic grin. "You beg of me? Is that what you do? Well, Monsieur le Consul, as well I beg of you, to direct each man and boy seated here today to sign this Oath of Allegiance to King George and to join his one true church. Then you shall have your priest perform the wedding in three days, though he shall still be sent off to the slaver thereafter. What say you? Would you betray your citizens for the love of your daughter? An Oath for a wedding?"

René looked at Gabriel. He understood. René slowly but firmly shook his head. "You know I cannot. I shall not. But I do present you with a signed Oath by each male present and accounted for here today, being the same Treaty Oath our King Louis sent to your King George." He handed the document to the British leader with a flourish.

Winslow replied tartly, "Being the same Oath which was modified from the orders issued by His Britannic Majesty decades ago, which unmodified Oath has been refused ever since then." Winslow motioned for a solider to bring one of the burning Church candles to the table. He then touched the newly-signed Treaty Oath to the candle and watched it burn. "Now, shall we get back to business?"

René called out, "Where are you sending our priest?"

Winslow shrugged. "To the Bostontown plantations in dire need of plantation labor. He can join the other whites on the slaver's auction block."

The Acadians were incensed. How could the British leader in Grand Pré, who claimed to be God-fearing, send away this holy man to work in a slave camp?

Père Rivière reached his cuffed hands out to René and spoke to him in French. "Bless you my son. Fear not for me or our Acadian brothers and sisters. God is on our side. I promise you we shall meet again in Bostontown, alive and well."

Winslow, looking much as Nero must have while playing his fiddle as Rome burned, shouted, "No French spoken here! You are on English soil. Take him away."

One brave Acadian, Jean Theriot, tried to grab the priest from the hands of the British. But Turnbull was at the ready. He butted the head of his gun against Theriot, who fell to the ground, dead of a gash to the head. The troops carried on and exited through an opening in the ranks of the troops guarding the door. Theriot's son began to cry and Turnbull glared at him until the boy was removed from his sight by his uncle who had been sitting next to his father.

The heavy wooden door slammed shut again and the troops regained their intimidating formation, bayonets thrust forward. They wanted to assure the men that any Acadian who tried to escape would not get within ten feet of the door before being fatally stabbed.

Turnbull looked to Winslow, who waved his hand nonchalantly. "Any other Acadian man who dares to come within two feet of our troops shall get the same, except it shall be only after drawing and quartering. Step up to me if you wish to die for your countryman now." Boys cowered in their seats and men turned their eyes downward.

René and Gabriel laid the body onto a pew then quietly sat down on either side of Theriot's lifeless body as if to protect him from additional English violence.

As Père Rivière was taken out of the Church, he blessed the parishioners in French as he passed them. "En nom du père, du fils et du saint esprit. Amen."

Bedlam ensued in the Church as men and boys tried to reach out for their priest until soldiers roughly pushed them back to their seats. The doors slammed shut and soldiers barred every exit, standing at attention with bayonets pointed at the Acadians. Tension was taut in the room, the Acadians unsure of the soldiers' next move. René and Gabriel directed knowing glances to the Acadian men and militia that they would be in a position to act later that evening.

At the pulpit, Winslow raised his hand for quiet. The Acadians subdued their voices and René reluctantly took his seat. All eyes were on Winslow as he unfolded a royal proclamation. Winslow cleared his throat so there would not be any impediment to his speech for all to hear. He held up the document he had thrust at René -- the original Oath of Allegiance to England.

Winslow commanded them. "Silence! Sign this Oath of Allegiance to our King, our country and the Church of England and I will intercede to His Majesty for leniency. After I read the King's Edict you shall pray to do so, but it shall be too late." He waved the document in front of them. "Who will sign this Oath or forever be condemned to His Britannic Majesty's orders?"

René rose and looked steadily at the crowd of Acadians. Gabriel d'Entremont, Marc de la Tour Landry and his father and two brothers still in Grand Pré stood to join René. Slowly, every French man and boy in the room rose to their feet in defiance of Winslow and the as of yet unknown Edict.

René turned to Winslow. "As the Consul to King Louis Fifteen of France and Navarre and on behalf of his subjects, inhabitants of Acadia, the unconditional Oath shall not be signed. Everyone refuses. You should have warned me as representative of our Christian King to the contents of this Edict."

Winslow screamed back with anger, "You and your men are traitors to the Crown. Obey my orders or I will have no choice but to arrest the whole lot of you and send you to George's Island with the rest of the treasonous French captured in Halifax after the Council meeting."

He peered at the crowd, seeming to stare into the hearts of each Acadian. "Many of you were no doubt there, and for that you shall *ALL* now reap what you have sown."

Winslow motioned to his soldiers, who marched up to the pews and held several of the young boys at bayonet point until René directed all the men to regain their seats. Winslow cleared his throat and began.

"I have received from His Excellency, Governor Charles Lawrence, and have here in my hand, the King's Edict which contains His Britannic Majesty's orders. You are convened to hear his final resolution in respect to all of you, the French inhabitants of his province here of Nova Scotia."

He stared at René specifically and continued, "For almost half a century you have been granted more indulgences than any of His Majesty's other subjects in any other part of his dominions. What use you have made of it, you yourselves best know."

René began to protest but thought better of it and Winslow spoke again.

"It is now incumbent upon me this duty which, though quite necessary, is very disagreeable to me, as I know it must be grievous to you who are of the same species. But it is my business to obey such orders as I receive and therefore, without hesitation, I shall deliver to you His Britannic Majesty's orders." With that, he picked up a parchment and spoke in a loud voice.

"That your lands and tenements, cattle of all kinds and livestock of all sorts are hereby forfeited to the Crown together with all of your other effects, saving your money and household goods such as you shall carry, and that you yourselves are to be removed from this province."

Winslow cleared his throat again, for effect this time, though the Acadians in the Church were silent, some in prayer, others in shock and all hoping to know the reason for the cruel edict. Winslow spoke again.

"Thus it is peremptorily His Majesty's orders that all the French inhabitants of Grand Pré and the other districts be removed, and through His Majesty's goodness I am directed to allow you liberty to carry with you your money and household goods as you can take without discommoding the vessels you shall be put in. I hope that whatever part of the world your lot may fall that you may be faithful subjects and a peaceable and happy people."

The men in the Church began to rise and shout out objections to Winslow and to the Edict. The din was too loud for Winslow to continue. He patiently motioned for the soldiers to move their bayonets closer to the pews. When the Acadians saw the threat of danger they quieted themselves, protecting the younger men by moving them to the middle of the pews.

Winslow adjusted his jacket and then began reading the orders again.

"I must also inform you that it is His Majesty's pleasure that you remain as the King's prisoners, arrested for treason and in security under the inspection and direction of the troops that I have the honor to command. You shall be given instructions when your ships are ready."

Again the Acadians started to stand up and ask questions. Again the bayonets came ever closer, crowding them into the centers of the pews.

"Captains?" said Winslow.

Turnbull, Adams and Hobbs saluted. "Yes, sir."

"Inform your troops that there is to be no killing of any livestock or robbing of fruit from the orchards or vegetable patches or other pillaging. The lands and possessions of all the French inhabitants are now the property of the King. If you have need of me, I shall retire to the presbytery where the priest lived. It shall be closer to our duties."

René called out to Winslow. "Lieutenant-Colonel? Sir? John? What is to become of our women and children?"

Marc called out, "How long shall we remain in the Church?"

Gabriel added, "When can we return to our loved ones?"

Gilles asked, "When do your transports arrive?"

Pine Gaudet was already hungry. "Shall you ask the women to bring supper?"

Winslow ignored their entreaties and exited the Church with his troops. At the door, Turnbull issued the final directive of the day.

"You shall remain imprisoned here until we deport you from here forever. Anyone attempting to escape from here shall be drawn and quartered in the square. Anyone refusing to board or caught returning to Grand Pré or any of the King's territory of Nova Scotia shall be burned alive as a warning to others that your lands belong to our colonists now."

Turnbull exited and the doors were shut and barred from the outside. Leaving open the possibility for troops to enter at will, soldiers were stationed at the doors but they were not nailed shut as were the windows.

Some of the Acadians rushed the doors to no avail. Others knelt in their places and prayed for deliverance and mercy. Still others, believing the futility of action against the British, wept in their seats.

Gabriel and several of his militia rushed to the windows and saw the shutters had been nailed. Marc was about to break the stained glass windows when Gabriel stopped him. "We do not know how long we are destined to remain imprisoned. The glass will stop some of the winter chills."

Jeanne Lambert's father Antoine and several of his friends walked up to the altar to exit by the door into the presbytery but that, too, had been nailed shut and barred. They had not known their prison was being sealed, as was their fate, while they sat as loyal French Neutrals listening to the Edict of the King of the territory in which they lived.

René and Gabriel walked from pew to pew, consoling the boys and talking softly with the men. René walked to the middle of the main aisle and gathered the Acadians.

"We shall overcome the odds against us. When we learned of the English plot, we asked Chief Mahtok to send a coureur du bois to New France. We trust they will send troops to our aid."

The son of Jean Theriot they called Little Jean leaned over his father's body and asked plaintively, "But what happens to us if they do not?"

The men exchanged looks. No one wanted to think of that possibility. René spoke softly to Little Jean. "We must pray for God's help." The boy nodded though his sobs.

*

Settling into the presbytery, Winslow kicked off his boots and fell back onto the comfortable four poster bed. He gazed around the room. The room was even more austerely furnished than his quarters but he appreciated simplicity. He also appreciated the warmth brought to the cold wooden floors by thick rugs in brightly colored stripes, including the rich scarlet, French blue and purple jewel tones for which Grand Pré weavers were acclaimed in Europe and the colonies.

The wood walls of the priest's rectory were covered with tapestries representing Biblical scenes -- Adam and Eve in the Garden of Eden tempted by Satan, the snake, and John the Baptist baptizing Jesus. From the bedroom he could see the small dining room where a tapestry of the Last Supper hung on one wall, and the Resurrection was near the entry door. The priest had excellent taste in art, he thought.

A pre-dieu with a small wooden kneeler hugged the corner of the bedroom. The Bible was missing from the pre-dieu. Then Winslow remembered the priest had it with him. So he was in that respect like Winslow, carrying his own Good Book with him. He took it from his heavy uniform jacket and placed it on the pre-dieu. Then he stooped to the kneeler, trying to place his knobby knees on the hard wood plank. He cried out in pain. Other than that, a table with a large pitcher and bowl for morning and evening ablutions, and a large wooden armoire and a large wooden crucifix were the only items in the room.

Winslow sat up in the bed and stared at the prie-dieu for a long while. He could not pray. His guilt was too powerful. He knew he was doing wrong but he had committed to following orders. He needed the promotion to return to Massachusetts. Otherwise, he feared Shirley would assign him to the hinterlands out of retribution.

John Winslow and his troops were to carry about the first and most horrendous act of ethnic cleansing of a race in North America -- the French Acadians, whose only faults were their staunch Catholic faith and undying loyalty to King, country and their Mi'Kmaq allies.

CHAPTER 40
Potion

September, 1755 – GRAND PRÉ

eturning from the Mi'Kmaq Village, Evangeline and Christine galloped into Grand Pré at five o'clock in the evening. Reining their horses to a slow gait as they passed St. Charles Church, they saw troops standing at attention at the front door.

Evangeline turned to Christine. "They have boarded the Church! Why so many guards? Do you think…?"

Christine replied, "We must pray the men are not locked inside and this is merely the English attempting to dissuade us from our religion. But if they closed the Church, where is Père Rivière?"

"I shall ride to Gabriel's home and find out what I can."

Christine agreed. "Hopefully René is back at the Consulate."

The women separated and rode in different directions, Evangeline to find Gabriel and Christine to seek René at home.

Evangeline rode to the d'Entremont stables that Monsieur Langlinais now owned and which were next to Gabriel's residence. He had not wanted to sell the family home and Langlinais was happy, at his advanced age, to sleep in the annex to the stables. But everyone in town still referred to them as the d'Entremont stables. She saw a blood trail leading to the closed barn doors. Jumping off her horse quickly, she spied a pitchfork on the ground. It was coated with blood, but she took hold of the handle and turned toward the barn. She pushed open a door wide enough to peer inside.

The stables appeared deserted except for several skittish horses. They whinnied and bucked in their stalls.

Evangeline opened the door wider and led her steed into an empty stall, where he began to feed. Then she walked slowly from one stall to another, calming the other horses. She was concerned. It was unlike Gabriel to leave his horses unattended. She had expected to cross paths with the men outside the Mi'Kmaq Village but she and Christine had not seen any Acadians on their ride back into town.

Evangeline turned toward the house and started closing the barn doors. At that moment she heard a soft cry emanating from an empty stall. It sounded like a small animal or a child. Just to be safe she held out the pitchfork as she approached a mound of hay. She called out loudly, "Who is there? Show yourself."

As she moved in closer, the head of a small boy about eight years old popped out of the hay. His eyes were red from crying. She rushed in and helped him out of the hay, brushed him off and held him in her arms. He broke down and sobbed deeply.

"They had big muskets and long swords. One soldier asked me if I could shoot a gun. I said 'of course.' My Lady I have never done so, but I have held muskets for Monsieur Gabriel. Once he took me on a hunt in the woods so I could tend the horses and the camp. That was the time a wolf pack chased one of the horses while I was cooking dinner at the campsite. Then they told Maman I had to go with them."

Evangeline asked, "English soldiers?"

He nodded, still sobbing and holding on to her for dear life.

"Did they hurt you?" She held him away from her and checked his clothes, his head, and his arms. She saw no blood and felt no broken bones. "There, there. No one is going to take you away. What is your name?"

"Francis Melançon."

"And your mother? Where would she be?"

The boy pointed to the large pile of hay in the corner. "Alls she said was they could not take me if I was only eight years of age. But I wanted to go with them like the big boys." He sat there, sobbing as Evangeline saw a bloody arm protruding from the haystack. She uncovered the dead body of a woman covered in blood from stabs wounds. She covered the body again and turned to Francis.

"Is Monsieur Gabriel in the house?"

He shook his head, avoiding the side of his mother. "He went to the Church and never came back, my Lady."

He whimpered, looking at his mother.

He looked afraid to tell her anything more. She urged him, "Trust me. Tell me what happened."

"I lied to the soldiers and said I had shot many guns. They argued with one another. One said 'Captain Turnbull, what shall we do?' and he said 'You know my orders. Bring in all boys who can shoot, no matter their age.'

"The solder started to lift me onto his horse until my mother grabbed that thing you are holding and stabbed the man. I ran away and hid in here."

He turned and looked sadly at his mother. Evangeline looked at the bloody pitchfork and imagined what came next. "Before I closed the door I heard Maman. She was screaming. I turned and saw a soldier was dragging her by the hair as he rode across the yard. The Captain laughed and threw the pitchfork into my Maman. Not even the dying horse attacked by a wolf pack sounded like that."

"I am so sorry, so very sorry."

He continued in a dreamlike voice. "After that, the soldiers set a line and passed the pitchfork from one to another. Each time the soldier dragged her by, one would throw the fork into her. That is when I ran inside and covered myself with the hay. It seemed an eternity before her screams stopped. Then I heard the horses ride off. I looked outside and found her, so I brought her here."

Evangeline regarded the dead woman, solemnly hoping the English troops had disobeyed orders. She prayed that the other women and children on the farms and outlying properties would be safe. But she had her doubts.

Francis continued, as if he were speaking from far away. "If I was ten she would not have fought for me. Then she would still be alive. Why did I have to be a little boy?"

Evangeline hugged him. "You are no longer a little boy but a brave young man. You protected the honor of your mother."

He looked up at her through his tears. "But I did not save her."

She nodded. "You did the right thing, Francis. Remain here. I shall be back."

He grabbed her hand to stop her. He was now fearful of another attack. "I am only going in the house. I will not be but a moment." He let her hand go and curled up in the hay.

She rushed into the house. It had been ransacked. Tables were overturned, cabinets opened and its contents thrown to the floor. She moved from room to room and found the same damage in each.

Walking into Gabriel's bedroom, she saw her portrait sitting on his bedside table. She remembered her promise to her love. She picked up the portrait and found the frame was loose. When she pulled the backing away, the small painting and a slip of parchment fell onto the floor.

She gasped when she read the paper.

"My darling fiancée Evangeline,

If you find this then know the English have taken us. We hope the Edict is nothing more than a reading and that we shall continue our mission this evening. But if not, remember my thoughts are with you always and that I repeat my promise to you that we shall be married.

All of my heart is yours, with love forever. Gabriel."

Every drawer in the table had been thrown to the floor, contents strewn about. The armoire had been emptied. The mattresses on the bed had been upturned and the rug had been pulled off the floor. It was fortunate they did not find the note.

Evangeline wondered what prompted the soldiers' search. Then she realized the English believed Gabriel was hiding weapons. That would explain why several floorboards had been ripped up. She was certain they had found nothing. Gabriel had delivered to Kitok every weapon that remained after the raid. She re-read the piece of paper in her hand. Gabriel knew she wanted to aide him in the resistance. Perhaps the message had a secret meaning. She tried to recall what he had told her when they went to the bluff and he pointed out the ships. She thought back to their most recent conversations. But nothing came to her mind with the same words of the letter. She put the letter over her heart. Perhaps it was merely a love letter. He had been adamant that she open the portrait frame. She felt in her heart he was also trying to tell her something else but she could not determine what it was.

She peered into the room where Henri d'Entremont had slept. Gabriel kept it just as it was before his father left for his fateful trip to Halifax. The wooden floor was intact. Other than opened drawers and the contents of his armoire, personal clothing and linens on the floor, nothing had been moved in that room. That meant the English did not suspect him to be a member of the Acadian resistance. She walked out, and then it hit her.

She re-entered the room and looked under the bed. She thought she saw something bulky in the linens under there. She tried but could not reach what she saw. She attempted to slide under the large wood frame but could not fit.

Evangeline rushed into the barn and grabbed the young boy's hand. "Come with me. We must make haste."

"Yes, my Lady. What is it?"

She led him through the house. His eyes opened wide. Monsieur Gabriel would wonder why his mother had not kept the house clean. But then he remembered his mother was in heaven now. Then he understood the soldiers were the ones that had done the damage.

In the house, Evangeline bid Francis to lie flat on his back. She propelled him under the bed. There was little room between his head and the wooden bed frame. "Reach into the linens above the bed boards and tell me what you feel."

Francis did as he was told. "Nothing."

"If you feel a groove in the board, please move your hand inside it. Anything now?"

He answered excitedly. "Yes I feel something. Cold and hard." He moved his fingers along the barrel of a musket. "It feels like a big gun, like the English soldiers carried."

"Very good, Francis. Can you take it out carefully?"

He turned his head to her. She had knelt on the floor and lowered her head to speak to him. He looked dubious. "How shall I do that, my Lady?"

She gave him directions to move his hands until he had pulled out the musket. Once that was removed, another fell into its place. He took that one as well. Then another, and another. He gingerly handed each weapon to Evangeline until there was a small stack of weapons. As he was crawling back out he happened to see a muslin sack bulging with bits and pieces. He grabbed that and brought it with him as he slid out from under the bed.

When Evangeline opened it, she found numerous packets of powder and musket balls for the guns.

"Gabriel is a very smart man," thought Evangeline, "but only now did I realize he had revealed secret resistance information without saying as much." His ordinary conversations with her gave her vital information that could prove to be their saving grace. In doing so Gabriel had given her the greatest gift of all -- respect for her intelligence. He had all too casually once told her that some of the militia cut grooves into their wood bed frames to hide a few of their weapons as a precaution. After the raid occurred he said those were their only remaining muskets and that their prudence could prove crucial to their survival. But only now did she recognize his hint that he had cut his father's bed, rather than his own. She thanked God for Gabriel's message that relied on her intuitiveness, just as she had asked him to do.

Evangeline loaded Francis onto her horse, and then went back into the house. She wrapped the guns in linens and hid them under the house, away from Francis' prying eyes. Turnbull would not send soldiers to check a house after he had been there so they were safe. Then finding some rope, she tied a gun and the powder sack underneath her voluminous petticoats. She managed to mount her stallion and took off for the Mi'Kmaq Village. The weapons had to be protected at all costs. She did not know what awaited her back in town but she knew that even one musket could mean life or death. She was more determined than ever to prove her loyalty to Gabriel's cause. To their cause.

*

Christine arrived at the rear of the Consulate and looked around for Luc. Then she remembered he would be in the Church with Gabriel and Papa. She quickly dropped off her horse to the young stable boy in the barn. She asked him, "Have you seen Monsieur le Consul?"

He shook his head. "He left this morning after you, Madame. Never seen him since."

"Has anyone tried to enter?"

He shrugged. "I was sleeping till I heard your horse."

"Then he could be in the house?"

"Supposing so, Madame."

She walked out of the barn to the back door of the Consulate. She poised her large key and pushed it into the lock but the door was already unlocked. The door opened. She rushed in.

René's office door had been torn off its hinges. Someone had been bold to invade French territory, such as the Consulate, in this time of peace. His desk drawers were opened and papers appeared to be shuffled and discarded onto the floor.

She looked to the floorboard beneath the desk and breathed a sigh of relief. They had not been touched. His government secrets were safe.

She then ran up the stairs and looked through the house. Other than René's room having been ransacked, nothing looked out of place. She checked the cupboard where she kept the silver. It had not been found in the raid. But this time the entire set had been taken, even the spoons. She looked around and realized other items were missing including expensive vases and crystal. Even the bottles of wine and champagne that were in the dining room had been plundered by the British.

Kitok's words rang in her ears. "English troops are the wildest of savages. They revere the King as head of their church, then take pleasure in carrying out his orders to plunder our villages and rape our women."

Christine fell into a chair at the dining table. "Where could René be?" she wondered aloud. "And what is taking Evangeline so long? She must be with Gabriel this minute. Perhaps they are going back to the Village to meet René. But we saw no one on our trip. And I am certain she would have advised me before leaving town."

She held her head in her hands. "What should I do? How can I find René?"

She wrapped her cloak around her and slipped out the back, careful not to let the stable boy see her. She walked furtively behind the back of the rows of quiet Acadian houses and shops, all shut tightly. When she reached the back of the Church she found it empty of soldiers, though the door had been bolted and sealed. She crept to the adjoining presbytery and peered into the window. To her shock, she saw Winslow in Père Rivière's home. He sat alone at a small wooden table, drinking wine and writing in his journal. The priest was nowhere to be found. She continued silently to the other side of the building. She heard voices approaching and she slipped behind the row of foliage under the window.

The voice of a man, probably an English soldier, said, "Our stores are running low. We need the Acadian women to provide us with more food."

The second voice, which she recognized as Turnbull, replied, "I shall resolve that tonight. Do not raise the question with Lieutenant-Colonel Winslow. He has other worries on his mind. Not enough transports have been confirmed to send out even one-third of the heathens."

A third voice said, "And the troops from Captain Murray have not arrived. I fear we must delay their departure for another month."

Christine gasped, and then covered her mouth with her hand, hoping they had not heard her. She remained motionless behind the bushes. They knocked at the presbytery door and were greeted at the door by Winslow.

"Captains Turnbull, Adams, Hobbs, right on time. Do come in. We must recalculate a more efficient use of the transports."

Once she heard the door shut she came out of her hiding place. Looking back, she glimpsed a faint light through the Church shutters. She pressed her ear to the window, hoping to hear the Acadian men in the Church.

*

Evangeline, with Francis riding in front of her, rode past the Church to the Consulate. Without going into the stables, she told Francis to stay on the horse at the front door. She fumbled with the key and was finally able to open it and enter the building. She saw the state of her father's office and rushed up the stairs calling out, "Papa? Christine? Gabriel, are you here? Is anyone here?"

Finding no one, she ran back down the stairs and locked the main entry door. She hoisted herself in back of Francis, covering him with her cloak and rode to the other end of town, not daring to slow her pace as she passed the Church. Through cracks in the shuttered windows Evangeline saw flickering candlelight. English sentries walked back and forth in front of the Church but were not interested in her or her hidden cargo.

She looked back once to see if the message stone had been discovered. She saw only a pile of rubble at the corner of the building where it had been. Sadly, she rode on. Near the outskirts of town she stopped at Thomas Gaudet's house, dismounted and assisted the boy to the ground.

When she knocked softly on the door, Béatrice opened it. Evangeline saw Anne sitting on the floor of the great room. She played with the large spoon Christine had giver her. Spittle drooled down her vest onto her dirty apron and skirt.

Evangeline introduced the boy. "Béatrice, meet Francis Melançon. His mother used to keep the house and cook for Lord d'Entremont."

Béatrice was just like a little mother, fussing over the boy. "Sit here. My name is Béatrice. Are you hungry?" She spooned a delicious-smelling broth with chunks of vegetables and meat into a porridger. Before she could say a word, he grabbed it and began to slurp as if he had not eaten in days. Of course, that was not the case but Evangeline was relieved he had forgotten about his mother, at least for the moment.

Henri d'Entremont had always served his household staff the same food that he and Gabriel ate. Gabriel maintained the tradition. Many farm workers vied to work for him because he served premium meat at every meal, something the farm workers rarely had. They ate the poorest cuts of cattle and sold or traded the best cuts for clothing, tools or farm implements.

While Francis ate greedily, Evangeline talked with Béatrice. "Have you heard from your father?"

Béatrice shook her head. "I saw him leave this morning before first light. He had a satchel with him and he grabbed the leftover bread from the hearth. I fear he has run into the woods."

Evangeline was shocked. "But you know what the English soldiers shall do to him. They have threatened to burn men alive or punish the families who do not present themselves."

Béatrice hung her head. "I am so ashamed of his lack of courage. And I fear for my brother, Pine, who went to the Church. I do not know what to do."

Evangeline said, "We must find him. That is what we must do. I fear not only for his safety but also for Pine and for your entire family."

Béatrice nodded slowly as tears welled in her eyes. "I was afraid to tell his secret." She hugged Evangeline for dear life. "What can I do? I am just a girl."

Evangeline wiped the tears off her own face first, then took her apron and wiped Béatrice's face. "No, you are a strong young woman. You can do what you set your mind to do. Now, what is it that you wish to do?"

Béatrice pulled her shoulders back and gazed directly at Evangeline. "I shall find my father and bring him back."

"And if you cannot find him?"

"Then I must convince Winslow to spare Pine."

"Excellent. I shall gather some other women to help you."

She shook her head. "No, I must go alone. He will come if he sees me...or smells a pot of my soup. He might think it a trap if others are with me."

Evangeline hugged her as she left. "Please take good care of Francis."

Béatrice nodded. "As if he were my own son. He will be safe here with Maman when I go into the woods." She surprised herself with her maturity. Perhaps she was ready to be married and have her own children. She very much looked forward to that day. But first she had to find her father, bring him back and face the frightening Lieutenant-Colonel Winslow begging forgiveness for her errant father Thomas.

*

Christine pressed her ear against the Church shutters, straining to hear discern the sounds from within. She was overjoyed when she recognized René's voice. "What was Turnbull's response?"

A voice that Christine recognized as Gabriel responded, "He refused to provide food. The younger boys and even some of the men are becoming despondent."

René added, "We must not let them become weak. Then all hope is lost. We must get word to Christine and Evangeline to send food."

Gabriel asked, "How shall we do this? No one is allowed to enter or exit the Church."

Christine could hear the men muttering among themselves, but their speech was unintelligible. Then René said, "Break a window and try to slip a note through the shutters. The spaces between the boards would allow for something."

Gabriel spoke next. "But if the soldiers patrol the Church they could find it first."

Marc said, "We do not know if any women would walk back here or, if she tried, if she would be allowed to do so by the troops."

Gabriel replied, "We cannot sit idly by. We must do something."

Christine looked right and left but saw no one about. She tapped faintly on the shutters. No response. She tapped again. Nothing. She removed the scarf from around her neck and tried to push it through the boards but no opening was large enough. She ripped the scarf then tried again with a smaller piece but the wool was still too thick. She then stuffed it under the shutters, hoping it was large enough to see through the stained glass windows she knew were behind the shutters. Then she tapped again as loud as she dared.

René saw the scarf. "That is Christine's scarf." He put his lips to the glass and asked, "Christine, are you there?"

She was overjoyed. "Yes, René, I have but a moment. Soldiers and Captain Turnbull just entered the presbytery. Is Père Rivière with you?"

René responded, "No, he has been imprisoned. But all the other men and boys are well, though they are hungry and cold. How are you my dearest?"

Christine put her hand on the shutter imagining René's hand was on the other side. "I am well, dear René. What can I do to help?"

Gabriel asked, "Where is Evangeline? Is she safe?"

Christine responded, "Yes, she went to your home searching for you. Do you have a message for her?"

Gabriel joined René at the glass and said, "That I am hers forever and we shall find a way to be married soon."

Christine started to say something but she heard the door opening. "Say nothing more. They are returning." And then she hid in the bushes again.

She heard three sets of boots and three sets of slurred voices of the English officers.

"I shall visit my favorite, Penelope. Who shall join me?"

"You know I shall join you, Turnbull."

"Count me in, too, Hobbs."

As their voices drifted away Christine waited. She heard their horses ride off and only then did she stand and rap on the shutters again. "You must know Winslow intends to ship us out and far away on the transports. He is worried they will not hold all of us so they plan to load many more than they should contain."

René said gravely, "Yes, the King ordered us removed from the province. Our lands and possessions have been forfeited to the Crown."

Christine responded, "How can the women provide assistance?"

René looked to the Acadians. They shook their heads. It was a dangerous mission. Gabriel spoke into the window. "Evangeline can proceed with the plan. She knows what to do and Kitok shall help. Please be careful."

René added, "If you can organize the women to bring food to the Church every day perhaps the troops will allow us some of it. Above all, take care of yourself, Christine. God bless you."

She replied, "I shall try to return tomorrow and, if not possible, then each night following at this same time with news and for your instructions. God bless you and all who are in the Church."

Then she crept to the back of the Church, retracing her steps back home. She dismissed all thoughts of leaving Grand Pré and returning to France. Even if it were possible to travel to New France, which was doubtful, she was determined that she would be at René's side wherever they were sent. But this time she would be his wife.

Upon entering the residence, Christine looked around the dining room. Luckily, her jars of herbs stood untouched on the sideboard. She had filled them with fresh plants and leaves after her weekly visits to the woods with White Bird. The soldiers had not thought the jars worthy of taking or destroying. Little did they know she hoped the contents of the jars would be the downfall of the English plan. She opened a drawer. There, under the linens, remained her marble pestle and mortar that she had brought with her on the sea voyage from France to Grand Pré nearly two decades earlier. It had all been so mysterious and exciting then; the challenges of uprooting herself from the known world of Versailles for the unknown in Acadia.

Staring at Eugenie's portrait, Christine remembered she had been younger than Evangeline was today when Doctor Hébert gave her the pestle to grind herbs and mix mysterious liquids. She had enjoyed learning to make medicines for seasickness and birthing pains and everything in between. The doctor had congratulated her on a remedy for the baby

Evangeline to sleep through the night instead of incessantly crying. Christine felt it had been caused more by missing her real mother than an actual baby illness.

Twirling the pestle in her hand, Christine began to devise an idea. If it worked, this could help René. This could help all the Acadian men. Then, perhaps, her love could open his heart to her. She prayed that he would.

Later that evening, a light snow fell, signaling the coming winter. The main street of town was deserted. Shops were closed. Faint glimmers of candlelight flickered behind shuttered windows in homes and apartments above their owners' stores. Tent City was quiet. Soldiers had retired early to their tents.

Inside the security of his offices in the Fort, Winslow had released his staff, eager to walk quietly in the first snow. He decided he would work from his new home in the presbytery until the Disagreeable Business was done. He packed his satchel of clothes, his Bible and a stack of documents, several with the King's red wax seal.

He wanted to reflect on the Acadian question, which was becoming more difficult every day. Captain Turnbull had informed him that at least one Acadian man, Thomas Gaudet, had not reported to the Church. He knew his orders were to hunt the man and burn him alive. But he faltered in his resolve, not because of a failing sense of loyalty to his King George, but because it might incite a riot among the Acadians. They could still overpower his meager forces of only four hundred. They numbered in the thousands and if they believed in their cause, he knew they would not hesitate to give their lives for it. He needed a release from his woes. He knew one thing that would cure him. He mounted his horse and trotted past the sentries saluting him.

*

After leaving the Gaudet home, Evangeline avoided the main street and took a circuitous route to enter Grand Pré through the front city gates. She stayed as far away from the brothel as she could. At any moment drunken soldiers might exit the place and try to do her harm, as had Greenfield.

Near the city gates she saw a figure galloping in her direction. She nudged the horse into the shadows of a nearby building. The rider stopped at the pleasure palace. She identified him by his uniform before she saw his face in the lamplight. Without a doubt, it was Lieutenant-Colonel Winslow. The grating in the peephole opened and the door was opened wide. Winslow was invited in but he refused. He talked to Hetty and she closed the door. Winslow did not budget. When the door opened again, Turnbull, Adams and Hobbs appeared and followed Winslow.

Evangeline could not risk being seen so she led her horse quietly to the back of the Consulate. The stable boy was nowhere to be seen. Evangeline started to jump off the horse, but her boot stuck in the stirrup. Out of nowhere, a man's rough hands grabbed her and pulled her down from the horse. She screamed but the hands covered her mouth. The man turned her to face him and released his hands from her mouth. It was Turnbull.

Evangeline blurted her question. "You? What is it you want?"

Turnbull looked up at Adams and Hobbs, who leered at Evangeline, thinking she would be enjoyable to tame. Turnbull turned back to Evangeline. "Well, Miss, methinks you know what I want." He started to grab at her skirts. She was fearful the gun would be discovered, and she slapped him, then ran to the door.

He rushed after her and pinned her against the wall his drunken breath covering her like a smelly blanket. Thankfully, the gun was on the side of her skirts so he was still unaware of it. She knew she did not have the time to use the gun but prayed he would not discover it. He held her neck with one grimy hand. As he attempted to fondle her, Evangeline slapped his hand away. The officers laughed heartily at Evangeline's expense.

Evangeline said calmly, "I may be only seventeen but I am engaged to be married. You know my fiancé, Lord Gabriel d'Entremont. If he were here he would challenge you to a duel. And he would win."

Turnbull laughed. "Without a priest methinks there shall be no wedding. And your precious Gabriel is my prisoner now."

She used all her might and pushed herself away from him, turning to face him. "What have you done with him, and with my father? Where are all the Acadian men?"

Turnbull's rough fingers stroked her face softly. "Locked in the church under my supervision until we ship the lot of you off." Then he grabbed her hair. "How your fiancé fares will depend on how you treat me. If you want to see him alive again you should remember your manners and be nice to me."

Adams added, "To all British officers."

Hobbs agreed. "Yes, to all of us."

Turnbull nodded and mounted his horse again, leaving Evangeline angry. He noted her animosity. "Remember, Missy, your man's fate is in my hands."

"What can we do? I cannot give myself to another man. But short of that, is there anything else we can do?"

Turnbull looked at her. "Bring food to the prisoners every day, with enough extra for the sentries. We do not need to waste our stores on prisoners and that will save us time and money."

Evangeline gazed into his eyes evenly. Turnbull realized she was not afraid of him. She sensed what he was going to say, then motioned for Adams and Hobbs to leave. "Wait for me in the main street. I am just coming."

"I am not afraid of you Captain Turnbull. I know that whatever you say, you shall never disobey your orders. You will not risk a war between our countries by dishonoring a French diplomat's daughter. I will keep our bargain for the food and you shall keep Gabriel safe. I saw the transports in the harbor and now I know their purpose. But I ask you to tell me when this will happen."

Turnbull laughed and kicked his horse roughly. "When I am ready to do so."

Turnbull rejoined Adams, who asked. "Why did you not just take her then and there? She seemed willing enough, no matter what she said."

Turnbull grabbed Adams' reins and pulled him toward him. He leaned over to within an inch of the other man's face. He looked to Hobbs then breathed into Adams' face. "Not a word of this to Winslow, understand? I was just having some harmless fun. But know this. Everyone who lives in this house including that wench are off limits."

Turnbull realized Evangeline was feisty, which was tempting. But she was the daughter of the French consul and rape was not a legal possibility for him. But he did have two possibilities. He could threaten to harm her fiancé and she could willingly give herself to him, though he believed she would rather die than submit to a man before marriage. Or, if they were actively engaged in war she would be the enemy and he could take his prize. British troops were encouraged to rape and plunder after capturing an enemy. Turnbull sighed. With their deportation only weeks away, he would have no opportunity, as the French were still Neutrals. Not even their status as traitors by failing to sign the King's Oath changed that.

Adams cowered in front of Turnbull, a huge man who instilled fear in those who angered him. "Your secret is safe with me."

Hobbs tried to calm the men. "Now, shall we raise a cup to celebrate?"

Adams nodded and Turnbull smiled. "We shall."

They trotted past the Church, checked on the sentries, and then rode into Tent City. They dismounted at the officers' tent and sauntered in.

Evangeline walked slowly up the stairs to the residence. It was eerily quiet. In the light of a small candle she saw Christine mixing herbs on the dining table. Christine looked up with surprise.

Evangeline queried, "Are you ill? Can I help you prepare a remedy?"

Christine shook her head. "Please do not ask, dear. Only know that whatever I do is for all of us."

Evangeline fell into a chair. "Winslow and Turnbull have imprisoned Gabriel, Papa, all the men in the Church."

Christine nodded. "I spoke to René and Gabriel...."

Evangeline blurted. "Gabriel? How is he? And Papa? Did they say anything?"

Christine repeated Gabriel's words. "Gabriel said that he is yours forever. He was concerned about your wedding but assured you it would take place as soon as they were released. He was in good spirits but he delegated the mission to you and Kitok. He said you would know what to do."

Evangeline said, "He took me to his recent meetings with the Mi'Kmaqs. Kitok heads their enemy resistance." Then she paused and blurted, "Turnbull threatened to harm Gabriel if I did not cooperate with him."

Christine rose but Evangeline waved her back. "I was shamed but he did not inflict actual pain. What hurts is that we are to be sent from our homes forever."

"René said that was the crux of the Edict. He asked we organize the women to provide the men in the Church with food. What else can I do to help the cause?"

"I promised Turnbull I would feed our men. It pains me to think that he called Gabriel, René and the others his 'prisoners.' We will need the help of other women to cook enough every day for the hundreds of men in the Church. If you can organize that, I will meet with Kitok and formulate a plan. "

Christine looked out of the window and saw a lone horseman plodding down the street. She rolled the paste mixture into a ball and put it in her drawstring sack. Absentmindedly, she responded, "Of course. If you inventory our stores in the cellar tonight, I will spread the word to the women in town."

She stood and started to put on her cloak of the rich French blue wool that Grand Pré weavers had become famous for throughout Europe. Instead she took a cape of lighter wool, of alternating stripes of grey and scarlet stripes, the fabric unique to Grand Pré sought in English territories for its bright red shade. Ordinarily she would have worn her blue cape but tonight she had a special purpose for wearing the other.

Evangeline withdrew the musket and powder sack from under her skirts. "Gabriel had hidden weapons in his home. At least now we can protect ourselves." She hid it and the powder sack under the linens in the sideboard cupboard. She could not get the drawer closed so she kicked it with her foot. Suddenly the base of the sideboard came unhinged and she saw a secret storehouse within.

"Christine, do you know about this?"

Christine looked down and together they emptied the large drawer. They saw documents with the King's seal, a sack of gold coins, maps and the worn diary Christine had seen René reading when he thought she was asleep in the carriage to Le Havre.

She closed her eyes and envisioned the trip. That was when she had first become devoted to René, for his extraordinary care of his wife. The husbands she had seen at Court wanted to be as far away from a wife as possible during the birthing process. But if she had not pushed René out he would have held Eugenie's hand throughout the entire ordeal. Yes, she may have been a bit in love with him then but those little seeds grew into a full heart for the man.

She helped Evangeline replace all the items in the hidden box and together they pushed the hinges back in place. If one did not know of the existence of the secret drawer one would not have noticed anything different. Christine made a mental note to remember how to open it so that she could read the diary for herself. She had always wondered what would cause a strong man like René to weep after reading a journal.

Christine then gave Evangeline a hug. "Make a list of the recipes you want to cook. I shall be back late so do not wait up for me."

Evangeline said, "I shall see you tomorrow morning. Be mindful of the soldiers in town. They can be dangerous."

As Evangeline walked downstairs to go into the cellar, she was distracted by a shimmering light. At the window she saw young Francis Melançon shimmy up a lamp pole. Béatrice stood below the pole, true to her word to protect him as if he were her own child. Evangeline tapped on the glass. Francis saw her and grinned, pointing to the lamp he had just lit. She smiled and clapped for him with admiration, then watched as he lit the lamps along the street. While Evangeline was proud of Francis, she was sad because he had replaced Pine Gaudet, who was locked inside the Church.

When Béatrice waved to her Evangeline felt an eerie sense of déjà vu. Had it really only been a year earlier that Béatrice had delivered the flowers from Gabriel for Evangeline's sixteenth birthday? Evangeline waved back and watched as Francis slid down to the street, took Beatrice's hand and walked with her to the next pole.

*

Winslow had left his horse at the presbytery so that he would walk alone. He relished quiet time out of the office to reflect on things far from the pressing Acadian question. He slowed his pace in front of Madame Dupont's window. He gazed with appreciation at a silk cravat, apparently the latest from Paris, which lay in the window. He would send Turnbull to fetch it for him the next day. He was much too tired to order troops to break into the shop. He preferred to be civilized though he was certain the woman would offer it to him as a gift.

Christine exited the back of the Consulate. She pulled the hood of her cape over her flaming red hair. She was cold, to be sure, but it would not do to be recognized, especially considering her plan.

Down the street, Francis heard Winslow's heavy stomping along the boardwalk close to him. He had heard boots like that the day his mother was killed. He fearfully disappeared from view into the shadows of a nearby alley.

*

At the Consulate, Evangeline was in the cellar making note of their foodstuffs. She prayed aloud for Gabriel and her father and the other Acadians. "Dear God, please protect our men and keep them safe from harm. And grant the gift of courage to your humble servants to bring hope and comfort to our men during this time of uncertainty and tribulation. Amen."

She was strengthened by her prayer and her determination to further Gabriel's cause, the cause of all Acadians. When she returned from the cellar, she made the list of the items on hand.

*

Christine heard the footsteps. She quickly lowered the hood of her cape and tousled her hair. Just in time, she thought, as she passed Winslow on the street. He tipped his hat as she passed. She nodded with a soft smile. There was her quarry. Now, how could she trap him, she wondered. She did not have to wait for he turned to her.

"You should not walk alone at this hour, Madame. Sometimes my soldiers imbibe...."

"I assure you I can care for myself, sir."

All Christine carried was the bag with its precious secret but she coyly let it drop to the walk. She prayed the drawstrings were tight enough to keep the contents from falling out.

He bent and handed the sack to her, looking up to see her flirtatious smile.

"I see the lady is both beautiful and willful. Perhaps if you have no other plans you would care to share a glass of wine with me tonight? It would warm the winter chill." Winslow offered his arm.

Christine choked back the disgust she felt and smiled in response. "It would be my honor, sir."

She took his arm and walked with him. She lowered her head as they walked on the side of the Church to the presbytery. She was surprised there were no guards at his door until she saw them cross the street and enter Tent City, probably for their supper. Winslow unlocked the door, and then bowed as she entered.

"Thank you kindly, Lieutenant-Colonel Winslow." She let her tongue linger on his title hoping he would think she was impressed, though she was not.

"You must call me John."

She echoed, "John."

And where, pray tell, did you develop such a beautiful English accent, Madame...?"

"Mademoiselle. It is Mademoiselle Galvez de Castille. But please call me by my Christian name, Christine."

"Well, certainly."

"I studied at school in France. And I practiced, of course, working for the Consul."

He knew that. He had surreptitiously watched her shopping or doing her errands in town. He had been intrigued by her flaming red tresses, wondering about her ancestry as the Acadians, for the most part, had raven hair. Now he knew it was due to her Spanish heritage. "You are quite a mysterious creature, Christine. Shall I take your cloak?"

"No wait servants?"

"Not when I have lady company...um a lady of such stature as yourself, that is."

Christine untied her cloak tassels and the wool cloak fell into his waiting hands. She felt as if she had his attention where she wanted…and needed it to be.

"Shall you sit near the fire, my dear? The winter chills are coming early this year. We cannot have you catching your death of cold."

"You are too kind, sir."

Winslow poured a glass of his finest wine and offered it to her. She smiled and sipped as she gazed around the room. She had never been in the Père Rivière's personal sanctum. It was not proper for a woman to be present in a priest's private rooms, even if for conversation. She warmed her hands before the fireplace. Winslow stayed behind, enjoying the firelight flickering on her beautiful red locks. He could stand it no more and his great hands touched her shoulders. When she did not flinch they lingered until she turned and sat across from him. She lifted the glass.

"I see you appreciate the finer things in life, sir. But French wine?"

"Yes, we are quite civilized and recognize that some imported goods are better than others."

He drank his glass a little too quickly while she merely sipped. The wine was excellent but she had more important things to do. When he noticed his glass was empty he started to stand. She rushed to him, gently touching his arm.

"Please sir, allow me to serve you. After all, that is a woman's duty."

He grinned and thought to himself that he did not know aristocratic French women at all. He heard they were independent and that their men placed them high on a pedestal, catering to their every whim. But this one was different. She was his sort of woman. Beautiful but docile. Willful, but in a gentle, subservient way. Yes, he would like to know her better.

While he tended the fire he had not noticed she took her bag with her to the wine table. She tore off a piece of the herb ball and stirred it into his wine glass, making sure the particles were dissolved. Then she emptied her glass halfway. As she served Winslow, she tipped the glass to her lips, which remained closed. But it appeared her glass was half empty.

"Come now, you cannot allow me to have more wine than you, sir. You must drink at least half a glassful."

Winslow complied and lifted his finger as if to make an important point when his eyes closed and he fell to the floor. He was sound asleep, snoring like a contented baby.

Christine opened the small desk. It contained a Bible, ink pot, quills, blotters and parchment papers. Carefully watching Winslow, she looked around the room. Where could one hide important papers?

She walked into his bedroom and gave it a cursory glance. The sparse furnishings were spread throughout the large room. She looked under the bed and in the armoire but found nothing that could provide her with information. The small bedside table held nothing but another bible. She was about to walk out of the room when she turned to the prie-dieu. It was unusually far from the wall.

Christine walked closer to the prayer kneeler and found the satchel hidden behind it. She laughed aloud, thinking of Winslow's need for security with all of his guards and sentries and aides. Yet he had placed his most sensitive orders in the most obvious place for one who was known to be serious about the King's religion.

Suddenly Winslow snored and Christine ran to the room, ready to continue her charade. But he dropped his head again and began to breathe heavily again, in a deep sleep.

Christine did not want to lose time so she ran back into the bedroom. Without moving the satchel, she untied it, pulled out the stack of papers and began to read. The royal red wax, now broken, indicated the most important documents, which she read first. She sometimes looked at a sentence or phrase more than once to be certain of the exact meaning, particularly since English was her third language after Spanish and French. She had a sense that Winslow was an organized man and would notice if any papers were out of order. She took the time to replace the papers in their exact positions before returning to the salon.

She took a sip of wine as she pondered what she had read. This man was not a Christian. No God-fearing human would be able to carry out the orders he had been given by the King. No, he was not a man. He was truly a devil of the worst kind -- an evil one cloaked in the robes of a Bible-reading Christian. Yet as distasteful as that was, she knew she would continue her pretense in order to spy on the English and learn the fate of the Acadians.

With a loud snore Winslow woke to see Christine talking to him and sipping her wine. He shook his head and suddenly felt very tired.

He stood and brought her cloak. "My dear, this has been a delight. Shall we dine together tomorrow night? I shall have a special supper prepared."

She turned her back, holding out her hands for the cloak. He again pressed on her shoulders and this time leaned forward to kiss her cheek. She nearly jumped, so disgusted was she, but she avoided his kiss, instead turning and offering her hand. He kissed it and led her to the door.

"I shall count the hours until we meet again, my dear Christine."

"Until then, sir."

Fearful Winslow might try to kiss her again, Christine covered her head with the hood and left Winslow standing at the door. After a few steps she turned around and nodded to him. He nodded as if he had been waiting for her to acknowledge him. She walked slowly past the Church shutters. Her love René was behind them and she longed to speak with him. When she turned to look for Winslow, he was still watching her. She shivered, but not because of the weather. Winslow's eyes had turned beady as they stared at her.

She forced herself to ignore thoughts of René and she walked to the front of the Church where troops now stood. When she looked back one last time, Winslow waved at her again. Only then did he close the door to the presbytery but it was impossible to return to the side of the Church without being seen. She hung her head believing the Acadians would consider her a traitor. She hoped they would understand. She prayed René would know she was enduring this for his sake.

The snow flakes had become flurries. Staying in the shadows Christine rushed to several houses, spreading the word of the plan to feed their men in the Church. Each woman agreed to meet the next morning at the Consulate with as much food as they could carry.

Inside the Church, René had gathered everyone around the altar. After a prayer he bade them to listen as he brought up young Pine Gaudet. At first the boy was nervous but René encouraged him to speak.

"Papa went into the woods but I came here to do my duty for me and for my family. I was telling Monsieur le Consul that we, that is my Papa and me, worked for Père Rivière over the past months in the cellars." He pointed below the stone altar.

Even Gabriel was stunned at the news."Cellars? You mean there are crypts below the Church? Below this very altar?"

He nodded. "My Papa and I repaired the stairs. Some of the stones were broke or missing."

René asked the boy, "Tell them what else you know, Pine."

"The priest told Papa a tunnel could be dug in one part of the crypts that was of earth, not stone."

Gabriel and the members of his militia looked at each other. "Show us where to dig and we shall begin the work now."

Marc asked, "Did you leave tools behind?"

Pine nodded. "Père Rivière paid us for all the digging tools we had or could buy."

Marc asked, "So was this before the raid?"

The boy said, "Yes. After that, Papa just sat on the floor with Maman except to help the priest or you, Monsieur le Consul."

René said, "Your father is a good man. Can you show us how to enter the crypts?"

Pine pointed to the wooden planks directly underneath the altar, a large stone work with an archway carved on the interior in an upside down "U" shape.

The men combed the Church for metal or a wood piece to be used as a lever. Gabriel found a cache of long metal nails near the door, apparently forgotten after the repairs were finished. He and Marc simultaneous placed the nails between two floorboards and were able to raise the first board. They removed it to the side. Gabriel held a candle to the dark cavern below.

René looked into the sea of faces, his friends and neighbors, his charges and his King's subjects. "Because of the danger involved and certain death, if you are caught I can offer the possible escape by tunnel only to unmarried men. Those who have served in the militia shall be first. Who would like to dig your way out?"

Nearly two dozen hands went up, all unmarried men -- Marc de la Tour Landry, Gilles Cormier, Nicolas Hébert and several of their friends. Claude stepped forward and said, "My wife and I have taken risks for all of you and my brother has sent weapons. I should like to be allowed to leave."

René assented. "As long as you know the risks. You must take Adèle and Pauline with you, for it would be certain death for them. Because you have no other family here I will make this exception for you. Do you accept my conditions?"

Claude said, "Of course, Monsieur le Consul."

René asked several times if others wanted to escape by tunnel, but the remaining men preferred to be loaded onto the transports, believing they would then be reunited with their families.

"Here are my terms. Once you descend these steps you cannot re-enter the Church. When we get food we shall lower it to you, then close the opening again. We cannot risk the English finding it. As soon as you get out of the tunnel run directly into the woods. Do not tell anyone and do not return to your homes because you will jeopardize not only the lives of your family but of every Acadian in this Church praying for your escape."

René stopped to look each young man directly in the eye to emphasize the gravity of his next words. "No matter what you hear or see, do not return. If you are caught, everyone here would be charged with treason. And you know the punishment is death, so that must not happen. We shall inform your family once we are all on the ships."

Claude stepped forward and René acknowledged him. "How can we send a letter to let our family know what we are doing?"

René replied, "We shall try to obtain paper and ink before you leave, perhaps in the food brought by the women. Finally, when you exit the tunnel run to the Mi'Kmaq Village and ask for Prince Kitok. He has provisions for you and can help you get to the mountains or lead you part of the way to New France. You should travel light, with only warm clothing, dried food, and a musket and ammunition. After that you are on your own. These are grave responsibilities. Do you accept them?"

Each man agreed.

René led the men in prayer, the Our Father, and everyone in the Church quietly prayed for the success of the young men's escape. Then Pine pointed out the removable floorboards and Gabriel and Marc lifted them. Pine scampered down the stairs and René descended, following him while holding a candle high above him. Gabriel stayed in the Church with the older men and young boys in case the British soldiers entered. They all knew Gabriel by sight and he knew he would never be able to leave the Church by the tunnel.

René followed Pine into the crypt and, after him, the young patriots also followed. With so many candles in the crypt, the main tunnel was visible ahead, branching off into rooms and other tunnels in several directions. In the first room they saw the tomb of Abbé Chevreaux, which had aged over the years. The dank and humid crypt caused lichen and other plant growth over the stone sarcophagus. The circumstances of the Abbé's death had never been fully explained to René's satisfaction. Gabriel held the English responsible for the death of the priest and René silently agreed.

Père Rivière publicly preached forgiveness on the anniversary of the Abbe's passing. But privately he commiserated with René and Gabriel that the British were at fault. Abbé preached the importance of remaining loyal to the French King and to the Catholic religion, and against any unconditional Oath which did not protect those beliefs. René believed English soldiers had learned of his entreaties to the French neutrals and they had begun surveillance with the intent to imprison him or, worse, hang him as an example to the colonists. The Acadians considered Abbé their martyr.

René reached the main tunnel underneath the presbytery and put his finger to his mouth, motioning to be silent, pointing above him. René heard muffled voices of a man and a woman who sounded like Christine coming from the room above. But surely it could not be. How could she even talk to Winslow after she learned of his plan to ship the Acadians away from their homes?

He pushed the idea as far out of his mind as he could. The nagging thought still remained, but she had asked for his trust. Then he realized that he had more than just a twinge of jealousy. He had buried his feelings for Christine by holding on to the spirit of Eugenie. is wife had been his dream but Christine was his life. He promised himself he would make his feelings known to her as soon as he was released; that is, *if* he was released.

Pine never lost his sense of direction but lead the men down a long, narrow passageway. The men followed it in single file until they reached a large, cavernous opening, where they marveled at the sight before them.

Thomas Gaudet had left stools, tables, some boards for beds, blankets, candles and flints and a set of tools where he had been working. On the walls he had affixed iron holders for the candles. But, most importantly, laid on one of the tables was a large map with an escape tunnel drawn meticulously to the proper dimensions. Everything was ready to dig their escape. Gaudet must have had a premonition of what was to happen. In any case, the men looked at each other and each took a tool. They began to work silently.

René shook the hand of each man and whispered good luck to them. He gave them each several gold coins, which he had intended to give to Kitok at their meeting to have been held after the Edict reading for more arms for the militia.

He whispered to Claude, "Good luck. I know you will do well. Give your brother Laurent my best. He must have been a great comfort to Cardinal de Fleury in his last days." Claude nodded, too emotional to speak. René patted his back and then waved to all the men silently. They had already distributed the tools and had begun to dig.

René walked back with Pine through the tunnel, praying for the brave Acadians on their trips overland to New France or by sea to French territory or to other destinations. They were all young, energetic and bold. They should go far in life. He had high hopes for them.

That evening, as the sun went down a light snow fell again. Christine walked nonchalantly in the back of the buildings on her way to the alleyway in back of the Church.

She needed to assure that the sentries did not see her. She knew she was too far away from Tent City for the soldiers to recognize her. Her only problem was how to get past the guards at the presbytery and to check the Church shutters for word from René.

She was certain Winslow would not send his guards away a second time, even with the Acadian men under lock and key and even with the sentries on the other side of the Church. But when she walked up, the deck was empty of troops. Knowing her identity was protected, she walked up to the shuttered window and tapped on it. A note was pushed through which she quickly hid in her purse.

"René?"

"Yes, Christine."

She pushed through a paper with scrawled writing on it. "Here is a summary of King George's orders -- as much as I could remember."

"Where did you obtain this? Not even Kitok was able to come by this information. He said Winslow's office desk was empty."

"He has moved his work to the presbytery."

Winslow watched from the window, peering from behind a thick curtain. He had a view only of his front deck, not of the side of the Church. He thought he had seen the red-headed goddess so he went back to his chair to calm himself for her knock on the door. But no knock ever came. He was puzzled so he walked to the door. Again he looked out of the window but did not see her.

Winslow unbolted the door. Christine was close enough to hear.

René asked. "How did you enter?"

Christine whispered loudly. "Please do not ask. I must go."

She rushed to the door, stepping out of her shoe purposefully to give her time to explain. The man must have furtively watched her. She prayed he had not seen her at the shuttered window. That would dash all of their plans.

Winslow opened the door to see her adjusting her shoe. He looked angry but soon softened as she touched his arm.

"Please excuse my delay. I stepped into a patch of rough ground and lost my shoe."

"I am sorry to hear it, my dear Christine. Perhaps I should have had an officer escort you...?"

She interrupted by placing her hand gently on his. "No need. I am quite capable. It was a silly mistake and shall not happen again."

He smiled. "Please come in. I have a special evening planned. I trust lobsters meet your fancy?"

"Nothing is more to my liking." She suddenly remembered how much Eugenie enjoyed the crustacean. And that reminded her of René again. She would have to concentrate on the job at hand.

Winslow closed the door, and repeated the routine of the previous night. He took her cape and offered her a glass of wine near the fireplace. Then he led her to the dining room, ablaze with candles. He had managed to find flowers in early winter. No doubt he sent troops into the woods, for White Bird had shown her that these blooms grew only in the forest.

A lavish banquet was spread on the table. Not only huge boiled lobsters but also fish and crustaceans of every kind were laid on huge trays. Venison and beef were cooked with vegetables. Lavish platters of fruits, cheeses and breads were set in the middle of the table.

The display was overwhelming to Christine. When she thought of the men without any food in the Church, she felt guilty. But she was fully committed to her purpose. Winslow raised a wineglass and she followed. "To new beginnings, my dear Christine."

"New beginnings," she said as she took a sip. She was dismayed because he had not let her move from the table. She thought she would have the opportunity to put some of the herb mixture in his food but he would not let her out of his sight. Everything, including the wine, was already at his fingertips. He did not need to ever leave the table.

Just then she thought of a way to create a diversion. She dropped her wine glass to the floor, purposely missing the rug. It hit the hard wood floor and shattered into dozens of pieces. Feigning shock, she stood up. Her dress was stained with wine and the floor was wet.

"Sir, please excuse my clumsiness. Now I fear I cannot remain, for my appearance is displeasing and unsightly."

"Nonsense, my dear. We are friends, are we not?"

She acquiesced as gracefully as she could bear. "Of course we are."

"Then you can feel free to change into something more suitable."

Christine had not thought he would attempt to bed her so soon, but she knew she could take advantage of the situation.

"Certainly, sir. Could you suggest something for me to wear?"

He disappeared and she stirred the mixture into his wine glass brimming with deep red wine. When he returned he offered her a long satin nightdress and robe.

"Sir, you flatter me with your intentions. I shall be but a moment."

Christine disappeared into the bedroom. She wanted him to drink the wine but not be so drunk that he could not make it to the bed so she changed her clothing quickly.

He spoke to her from the dining room. "My dear lady, I am not a young man and thus I have no illusions about courtship. I have a wife in the Massachusetts Bay colony. A good woman and comely, though she is not the beauty you are. Alas she is not here, and you are, you see."

"I see. I am here. And you are here." She coyly re-entered the room wearing the clothes he gave her, making certain he saw her in the robe.

He gasped. She was beautiful in his clothes, the firelight dancing on her red hair and red robe. She covered the clothes with her cloak.

He took his wine glass and offered to fill her glass, but she shook her head. "You would not want me to be light-headed, would you?" She took his glass and bade him to drink. She would not release the glass from his lips until he had drunk at least half of it.

He stood to lead her to the bedroom but she took his hand and led him back to the salon. She was waiting for the wine to take effect but the large meal had apparently delayed the process. She would have to change her plan to draw out his desire before he fell asleep so she could read his documents again.

"My dear, I thought we had an understanding."

"Monsieur Winslow, surely you do not think of me in that way? What kind of woman would I be, after our first dinner together? We are only beginning to know each other although I must say I do enjoy your company. Do you enjoy mine?

"Of course, of course, dear lady."

"But we might come to some bargain if you like."

His ears perked up. "Bargain? What kind of a bargain?"

"One might call it an exchange."

"And what does that entail, exactly?" He was getting somewhere and grinned from ear to ear. The rotten and missing teeth explained why he rarely smiled with an open mouth. He started to slur his words and Christine believed the concoction had finally taken effect. He realized what his mouth looked like and he put his hand to his mouth, opening his eyes wide in embarrassment and chuckling loudly.

"You believe you can buy everything and everyone that you want but my proposal does not involve money or jewelry."

"Tell me, dear. You have piqued my interest."

'You shall release the Consul and Vice Consul until the transports arrive and you agree to keep our arrangement secret from them. And if you do these things I shall agree to come to you once a fortnight until I presume you shall send me away too. "

"You take me for a fool? I would be the laughingstock of my troops if I released the two most dangerous prisoners."

Winslow's speech was still articulate so she pushed the wineglass to his lips. He drank greedily. She thought it would not take long before he became more docile.

"You can justify their release as diplomats. In addition, you must release twenty other Acadians each night to visit their families and they shall return to the Church the next evening. In that way you can say that you have done your Christian duty while complying with your orders. A fine line, to be sure, but this would do so."

Christine pulled out a parchment and a quill dripping in ink. She had written the agreement in advance. She handed it to him and he signed it quickly. "Tomorrow is Friday. Remember your agreement."

She took the document with her.

Winslow nodded and fell fast asleep.

Christine was disgusted with him. Torn with guilt, she knew no other way to achieve what she had done. Her heart and her body were reserved for René. She knew that she would rather die than do anything of the nature Winslow had expected. It would require a stronger herb mixture in the wine to assure he fell asleep each time she visited him to make certain nothing happened.

She pulled out his satchel and carefully read every document in it before replacing it behind the prie-dieu. Then she dressed in her soiled gown. Before leaving she left him a note so he would remember his agreement. She was thankful for her experience as a midwife because she otherwise she would not have had the courage to lift his shirt and write his name on such a whale's hairless underbelly. The ink would stain so that he would see it each time he dressed, or undressed. She wondered if he would keep to his agreement. She prayed he would.

CHAPTER 41
Woods

September, 1755 - FOREST NEAR GRAND PRÉ

o untrained eye could detect any movement in the thick forest beyond the settlement of Grand Pré. The trees had turned colors earlier than usual. Bright combinations of red and black maple, golden aspen, yellow and grey birch trees, and red oaks broadcast the early advent of winter. Some of the trees, jack pines and eastern hemlock in particular, had begun to shed their needles.

Suntok crouched in the bough of a thick sugar maple and looked through the foliage at Kitok lying prone on a large branch in the adjacent white spruce. Chief Matok and Princess Snowbird had raised Suntok as their own. Kitok's parents realized the two boys were as close as real brothers and that, despite Suntok's relative slowness, he learned much from Kitok. Suntok smiled, remembering how Kitok was his first true friend and although he was younger, he taught Suntok to be one with nature. Kitok had always surpassed Suntok's skills, whether digging for ancestral relics, hunting black bear, or climbing trees, but he had taught Suntok well.

The boys had played in the forest when they were young and assisted the braves in the Mi'Kmaq band, polishing flints, carving arrows and applying paints to various parts of the braves' bodies signifying status, events and causes of the First Nation. Once they were initiated as braves they continued to roam the forest but for other purposes. They hunted, fished and, on occasion, released animals from cruel traps set by English soldiers.

On the day the Citation was circulated among the Acadians of the entire Bay of Minas region, Gabriel held a meeting with Kitok which Suntok also attended. Gabriel told them. "I have met with our Consul. He asked you to send braves throughout the woods to search for runaway Acadians after the Edict is read. He and I anticipate some men or young boys may try to hide, rather than present themselves in the Church."

Suntok signaled to Kitok, who interpreted for Gabriel. "Suntok wants to know what we do when we see such a man."

Gabriel responded, "Bring him to the Consulate. That will be a safe haven, not the Mi'Kmaq Village. The English threaten to burn alive anyone caught who violated the Citation. And if that is not enough, their families will be punished as well. We shall endeavor to protect their relatives from English cruelty but we must know who has escaped to the woods in order to do so."

As Gabriel rode off, Kitok gathered dozens of braves and explained the plan. On the day of the Edict reading they would all travel into the forest and then separate to create a circle within the woods. They would be able to see much, if not all, activity in the woods, being stationed at each major pathway in the forest.

Before dawn on Friday September fifth, the braves left the Village and entered the woods. Kitok and Suntok climbed their respective favorite trees nearest Grand Pré. Other braves perched in trees throughout the woods and scoured the woods for hours. Kitok occasionally sent a coded bird call to the next nearest brave who was several hundred yards away to his right. That brave sent his own bird signal to the nearest Mi'Kmaq within earshot, who continued the procedure until all the braves in the circle had signaled whether they had seen an Acadian or not. The messages circled the forest until the last reached Kitok. No one had seen an Acadian runaway.

In their first few hours of watch, Kitok and Suntok had seen no one enter from Grand Pré. However, they were finally rewarded for their efforts. Sitting Fox, one of the braves in the woods, signaled Kitok that a large group of people had passed underneath his hiding place in a tall tree as they walked through the woods. The nearest brave to Sitting Fox signaled the group was approaching him.

Signaling to Suntok to keep watch for Acadians, Kitok descended the tree. He jumped on his horse and rode through the forest until he met with the group walking deeper into the forest from the direction of Minas Bay, but not from Grand Pré.

Over a thousand men, women and children were laden with packages and boxes. Some dragged carts and wagons behind them, in which children or pregnant women or nursing mothers with infants rode. A number of people rode on horseback while leading pack animals loaded with bags, foodstuffs, tools and a few weapons.

The leader of the group, a big Acadian man with long flowing brown hair, rode over to him. He gave a great welcoming smile to Kitok, whom he recognized.

"Kitok. It is good to see you again. Your Mi'Kmaq families have been valued allies to us for so long."

Kitok grinned. "Joseph Broussard? Why come into the forest? And who are your charges?"

Broussard pointed to the group behind him. "They call me 'Beausoleil' now. Seems they credit me with bringing some sunlight into their lives by helping them escape. My sons spread the word among the Acadian families in nearby communities that we would protect those who left with us rather than stay for the Edict reading. "

Kitok looked at the sea of faces. "How many have you brought?"

"Well over a thousand. Several hundred joined us from Annapolis Royal. They fled into the woods when their paid agent, a British officer, learned they were to be deported on the first transports last month. We brought some women about to bring forth newborns. For obvious reasons, we dare not leave them behind in their condition."

Kitok reflected. "Move them together in wagons with midwives nearby. Our medicine woman will help."

Broussard looked back at the sea of faces and sighed, feeling his heavy responsibility. He gave the instructions to a handful of strong men near him: his sons Jean, James, Paul, Marc and François. They gently urged their horses into the crowd, asking for the pregnant women to move forward.

Beausoleil continued, "A group from the other side of Minas Bay asked to join us after soldiers burned nearby villages and ravaged all their women."

Kitok nodded. "The English are restless for battle even as an uneasy peace continues between our country and theirs."

The Acadians within hearing distance murmured their agreement. Kitok addressed them.

"Your Consul Le Blanc de Verdure wants you to hear the Edict with orders from the English King."

The Acadians looked to Beausoleil. He said, "We know the requirement to be in the Church on Friday. But everyone here is determined to leave, instead."

"Lord Le Blanc has concern for English wrath on Acadians left behind. Are all family members together?"

Beausoleil turned to the group behind him. Everyone was attentive, waiting for instructions. He looked at Kitok. "Entire families, and in some cases, even whole villages. Many even burned their homes and barns to prevent the English from taking them."

Kitok said, "That will anger the British. But the choice to leave is yours. We will help you to safety in the mountains. It is too dangerous to remain here."

"Kitok, you know I am ready to fight injustice on a moment's notice. But the Citation has a sinister undertone leading us to believe the Edict is a pretext for their real mission. No one trusts the English to obey peaceful orders. We fear they will imprison or kill those in the Church."

"Your actions may save you from the transports. The Consul...."

Broussard interrupted him. "Transports? What do you mean?"

The Acadians listening to the conversation again, murmured among themselves. They had no news of any transport ships.

"English ships for animal cargo transport entered the Bay near Grand Pré. Sources confirm more are to arrive in coming weeks. The Consul learned that the King's Edict orders all Acadians to be deported by sea."

"What is the destination? And when do they leave?"

Kitok shook his head. "Exact details are unknown. But we believe the known resistance members will be sent to Liverpool or Westminster Gatehouse prisons, and strong Acadians as well as young girls will be shipped to the slave markets in Bostontown."

Broussard nodded slowly. "So our greatest fears are to come true. New English settlers will take our lands and homes. Perhaps everything should have been burned."

The word spread quickly throughout the Acadian group and an outburst of questions and shrieks of fear ensued.

Kitok suggested. "We must move quickly. English soldiers will search for runaways in these woods shortly after the Edict is read."

The Acadians cried in horror, anxious that they not be found by the English. Everyone understood that meant a death sentence without any formalities of judge or trial. Beausoleil raised his hands to quiet and calm them.

"We must listen to Kitok. Every bit of his information is vital to our survival." He turned to Kitok and asked, "What plan does the Consul have?"

Kitok responded, "He sent messages to New France's Governor-General Pierre François de Rigaud for military support. His Troops de la Marine are not as numerous as the British soldiers quartered in Massachusetts Bay and other colonies, but are greater than those at the Fort and in the new Tent City."

"How many English troops are located in Grand Pré now?"

"Only about four hundred. De Rigaud's troops could overpower them unless the English send reinforcements. They have at least two thousand troops in Halifax and the same at Fort Edward. And the Governor has not been at his new post long so he is unfamiliar with the terrain and the difficult seas in Minas Bay."

"Where was he formerly?"

"He governed the French territory of Louisiana."

"Could Gabriel Mius d'Entremont not mount his resistance? We pledged to support him until we learned of the Edict. The safety of our families comes first. But once the women and children are safe, then our men will work again with Gabriel."

"We have worked closely with Gabriel but the British weapons raid took everyone by surprise. We were able to obtain a load of English muskets but powder and balls are in short supply. And when we were able to retake their weapons again, the English imprisoned the men including the militia."

Broussard replied. "The English stole our weapons as well. We should have realized their vicious plans, but England had not declared war against France. Not one of us imagined they would violate the Treaty of Utrecht during peacetime."

"What was the final straw in your case?"

"English soldiers forced themselves upon several of our young girls, taking unspeakable liberties. We could not risk going to hear the Edict and leaving our women unprotected to face more possible atrocities."

Kitok nodded with understanding. "Anyone who so touched a woman in our First Nation would be scalped alive."

"During the night we passed Fort Edward and we can confirm over two thousand troops. Captain Murray has of late organized them in maneuvers with muskets and new cannon, as if preparing for battle."

Kitok warned, "If that is the case, travel to New France is too dangerous without French troops in support. Winter is nearly upon us. Food and shelter will be difficult with so many families."

"We had hoped to make camp here in the woods. The English fear the wild animals that we have hunted our entire lives. They would not think to look for us here, as they could not exist on berries and leaves and an occasional animal in the wintertime."

Shaking his head, Kitok disagreed. "Higher ground is best. Mountain caves and natural barriers covered in snow will prevent the English from finding you. We can establish your people in camps until troops arrive from New France."

Beausoleil nodded and then turned to talk with the heads of the families. After a brief discussion, they reached a consensus, which Broussard brought to Kitok.

"We are ready to climb."

Kitok held up his hands. "Be silent and move quickly. You are safe for now, but soldiers will hear your voices."

Broussard said pensively. "No doubt many, like my family, have relatives in Grand Pré. One of my own sons married and left our village to live with his wife and her family there. He would be in the Church today but one of his brothers told him I was on my 'deathbed' so he brought his entire family with only their travel clothes. I am sad we had to hide the truth but we could not risk them packing as if they were leaving -- for their sake as well as our own."

Kitok took a stick and drew a map in the dirt for Broussard. They discussed the various routes and mountain passes to take. When they agreed, Kitok brushed the dirt markings away with his leather moccasin. He mounted his horse and directed Sitting Fox to leave his post and join Suntok at the entrance to the woods. The brave rode bareback through the trees, pushing low-lying branches out of his way and soon disappeared in the thick foliage.

Kitok nodded to Beausoleil who then called out to the Acadians to follow them onto the mountain trail. Kitok said. "I will advise the Consul when next I see him. Now we must go. It will take hours to reach safety."

Broussard nodded. Kitok signaled his braves, who started herding the families into order. Broussard then waved to the families whose migration would end in the mountains before them. There was no Red Sea to part, no Moses to lead with a staff. Yet the faith of the Acadians was so great that nothing else was needed. Each prayed silently, following the footsteps of the person in front.

The next morning, Suntok woke early. Sitting Fox was hidden to all but Suntok in the adjacent tree. He had woken earlier, evidenced by two sacks of wild berries tied to a nearby branch. He untied one and tossed it to Suntok, munching the delicious breakfast while watching below. This was an important day, he thought, the day of the Edict. If anyone is to run into the woods it will be today, most likely this morning.

At that moment Suntok observed a man walking into the woods carrying a lumpy burlap sack. He was not an English soldier but rather a middle-aged man wearing dusty clothes and a carpenter's apron. Was this Gaudet, the one who worked miracles with wood and created such beautiful furniture that he was months behind in his orders?

Suntok looked over to signal Sitting Fox, but he was nowhere to be seen. Unbeknownst to Suntok he was foraging for food for both of them. Suntok did not know what to do except observe the man. Suntok watched Gaudet walk through the forest, careful to stay off the well-worn paths. This was a man who knew the woods and the trees. He stopped every so often to touch a tree and whisper to it. Suntok thought he had imagined it until he saw Gaudet do the same thing a few minutes later. Then Gaudet hugged several trees near the path and walked deeper into the woods, finally disappearing from view.

Suntok peered through the woods looking for any movement in the brush, limbs pulled back or vines cut but there was nothing. It was as if Thomas Gaudet had disappeared into the foliage. He continued to watch the rest of the day but there was no other activity in his line of vision.

Suntok watched the sun drop in the sky and Sitting Fox finally returned. He had brought a rabbit, caught, skinned and cooked by his own hands. He showed it to Suntok, who clapped quietly. Then Sitting Fox tore the rabbit in half and put one part in another burlap sack, which he threw to Suntok. Suntok easily caught the sack and tore into the meat, signaling his gratitude to Sitting Fox.

Shortly thereafter, Suntok felt his tree shaking. He looked below to find someone climbing up towards him. Peering down he saw long brown tresses and a bulky oversized jacket. Then he saw the face of the tree intruder -- it was none other than Béatrice. She grinned at him, then turned and waved slightly to Sitting Fox.

Suntok was anxious to hear what news she brought. Béatrice spoke in a very low voice; so low Suntok had to strain to hear her. "They have locked all the men and boys above age ten in the Church. When I walked past I saw the doors were bolted and sentries were guarding the place."

Suntok was alarmed. "What is to happen to the men in the Church?"

She shrugged that she did not know. Then she added, "My father left home early this morning. Did you see him pass?"

She looked at Sitting Fox, who shook his head. Suntok nodded. "He walked beneath my tree this morning, talking to trees and holding them."

Béatrice understood. "I know where to find him."

"Do you want me to walk with you? I can watch out for bears." Suntok had been told as a young boy that bears roamed the mountains. Princess Snowbird had told him this with the best of intentions so that he would be too frightened to go into the woods without an adult. But Suntok's brain never understood that the bears lived only at the highest altitudes. He was always fearful of the animals whenever he walked or rode a horse in the woods. That was why he liked staying in trees.

The girl shook her head. "Thank you, Suntok. But this is something I must do alone. I shall give him his last night in the forest he loves so well and return in the morning. He must return to the Church."

She hugged Suntok, which brought tears to his eyes. He had not known the touch of a female since his mother had died so many years earlier. The softness he remembered. The face he had long forgotten.

She turned to Sitting Fox. "Please send someone to tell me if you see my father leave the woods."

The brave nodded, as did Suntok. She saw the tears in Suntok's eyes and she hugged him again for good measure.

Thomas Gaudet had made an excellent living from the woods. He was considered wealthy by Acadian standards for his talent, craftsmanship and diligence. He worked every day except Sunday, when he dutifully took his entire family to Mass, until his wife, Anne, lost their baby and she became touched in the head. Then he was as kind to her as he was to a baby. If he left the house, he made sure one of the children watched Anne at all times. He did not want to risk her burning herself again by pouring hot soup over her head.

As to his profession, Gaudet was a knowledgeable and proficient carpenter. He knew what kind of tree to cut for a dining room table, or for a baby's cradle. He knew just where to find a tree with the right burl for the Consul's new desks. He had an eye for duplicating any design from any material into wood.

Thomas had borrowed Christine's mortar and pestle and copied their design in wood. Finely honed to prevent any splinters, they became indispensible items in every Acadian household. The women loved to grind herbs and spices to create tantalizing dishes. The dinners on Sundays after Mass became a tasting delight for the men, who often became more amorous on Sunday evenings. Young girls listened to wives who extolled the virtue of the tools, and begged their mothers to teach them the skill. So in not so small a way Thomas Gaudet was responsible for the large population growth in Grand Pré after his arrival with Consul Le Blanc.

Seventeen years later, Gaudet had a foreboding that his fate was tied to the reading of the Edict. He sensed that fear would emanate from it and that he would never again see his beloved woods. That was the impetus behind his final decision. He had wrestled with the choice to stay or leave but believed he was right in not going to the Church on Friday, September the fifth.

Early that morning, he packed his sack full of potatoes. He awoke his wife, who always slept in the same bed with him. She looked at him and smiled. He held her and kissed her as though they were young sweethearts. She did not remember how to kiss but merely drooled as a tear fell from her eye. He kissed her forehead and closed her eyes. He waited until she went back to sleep, then he looked at Béatrice and Pine sleeping near the hearth. He put all his money on the table and walked out of the door.

Gaudet was surprised to find no one stirring before dawn in the main street of Grand Pré, not even soldiers sleeping off the prior night's drink. He walked without haste into the woods and took his favorite path, stopping to say good-bye to one or another of his favorite trees.

When he arrived at the tree where he had brought Anne for their wedding night he remembered the soft bed he had made of gathered pine needles over which he had laid a blanket for his love. It was still the most joyous memory of his life, for their act produced his first son nine months later. He and Anne named him Pine, after the amazing tree. He hugged the tree, thanking it and expressing his love for everything it had meant to him. Their joy was short-lived, however, when the baby died in his cradle. Thomas gave the same name to the next male child that Anne bore, but that son was stillborn. The next Pine lived nearly four years but died of a fever Thereafter, Pierre was born, and this time Anne insisted that she choose his name. Thomas reluctantly agreed but he always called him Pine. Béatrice was born a scrawny little bird, but she survived illnesses and Thomas considered her his little fighter.

Thomas disappeared deep into the woods, not stopping until he had arrived beside his favorite brook. Then he collected armfuls of pine needles and made a bed, where he would sleep at night. He sustained himself with wild berries and fish from the brook. Ever so often, he took a bit of a raw potato. As if his mind suddenly clicked off, he began talking Mi'Kmaq gibberish to himself. He did not know their language but from his mouth words started to flow. Thomas Gaudet was home and he felt content.

The giant man revered the trees in the forest, not only for the comforts they brought his family when he sold his handcrafted pieces, but also for the joy he felt when he saw their profusion of color during his walks, when it became too cold for cutting wood. He had taken Pine into the woods as soon as he could walk and talk. He taught him how to differentiate between hardwoods and softwoods, how to spot variations and where to cut the sweetest spots, or the strongest, or the most pliable. He would gather pine needles fashioning mats for them to sit and listen to the trees swaying in the wind. Pine told his older sister, Béatrice, their father talked to the trees as if they were people and he expected Pine to understand tree language. Pine pretended, thinking it was a game, but when he realized his father was serious Pine became worried because he could not speak to the trees.

Fiercely protective of her sibling, Béatrice begged her father to take her in place of Pine. She assured Thomas she wanted to learn the lessons of the trees and that Pine was needed to keep the fire burning at home while Thomas was gone. He relented, although he thought Béatrice would never have the stamina to climb the hills and cut the underbrush on their walking tours. She had ended up being the more interested of his two children and a valuable assistant. After a while, she was able to lead him to just the right type of tree to cut for a new commission.

Béatrice knew the woods like the back of her hand, as if she had an indelible memory. Once she took a path, she was always able to find it again. She knew which trees could be found on which side of the hills, and she knew which parts of the woods Thomas preferred. They usually ended up sitting by a mountain brook under a canopy of fir trees, where he told her stories of his courtship with her mother, Anne. Béatrice considered the place magical. On the last trip they made together, Thomas confided his secret to her in this special part of the woods: that he had been a Mi'Kmaq brave in an earlier life. From deep in his foggy memory, he pulled several First Nation words, though he did not remember their meaning.

Thomas Gaudet was not the least bit surprised when Béatrice found him on the morning of September 6, 1755. He had slept soundly on the bed of pine needles at the edge of the brook he loved. He expected something to happen.

She walked up and saw him bending over the brook. When he turned, she saw his face painted with a paste of wild red berries. He danced around her, waving his arms and singing an unintelligible mix of Mi'Kmaq words and Anne's gibberish.

She waited patiently until he had finished. Then she hugged him and took him by the hand. Thomas Gaudet followed his daughter dutifully, their roles reversed. She believed she could save his life by pleading to the Lieutenant-Colonel. She would learn John Winslow's true nature upon her return. She could not have dreamed what their fate was to be.

Walking back through the woods and circling the town on that overcast Saturday morning, Béatrice managed to avoid anyone seeing her and her father. She opened their cellar door outside the home and helped him gently down the stairs.

"Papa, you must be quiet. No dancing or singing and no talking. No one can know you are here. Pine's life depends on it. Do you understand?

He nodded, whispering his gibberish. Then Béatrice climbed the cellar stairs and bolted the door from above. She worried what would happen if anyone found out where he was. She feared the soldiers would be the ones whooping and hollering, those bloodthirsty British madmen. Assuring herself that her mother and the boy Francis were in good spirits playing with the spoons in the main room, Béatrice left the house.

Béatrice boldly walked to the Fort. Her head was held high but by the time she arrived, her heart was pounding. She later admitted to Evangeline she was quite afraid. However, she carried on her commitment to save her father from certain death. The sentries were laughing at one of their fellow soldiers, who had fallen into a mud hole. They did not see the girl slip under the gate and walk up to the office. There, the guards looked out on the yard from the other end of the front deck. She walked into the building through a partially open door.

The office buzzed with activity. Soldiers pored over maps on several desks, and never looked up as she walked past them to the large table in the next room. With all heads buried in maps and charts, no one took notice of the young girl.

"I am here to see Mister Winslow." She sounded calm but her throat felt constricted and her head was about to burst with fear. She looked back at the door, ready to make her escape. She doubted she would be able to run out as easily as she had entered.

The men still did not see her. Apparently she had not spoken a word, but merely thought she had. She cleared her throat and cried out.   "I said…I am here to see Mister Winslow. If you please, sirs. Which one is he?"

At that, every man in both rooms lifted his head and stared at her. Winslow was amused. "Yes, yes, here I am. How the devil did you get in?"

Béatrice remembered her manners and curtsied. The men laughed but she stood proudly and answered. "The door was open, sir."

The men laughed again. Winslow bit his tongue to prevent laughing this time. "Well, out with it, girl. What do you want?"

"My father, sir. And my little brother, Pine. Please do not kill them, sir. Please. We need them to get wood for my mother. She is mad, you see, and they are the only ones strong enough to break the branches because, sir, we have no axe, and you will not kill them, will you? My mother only speaks gibberish and…."

He held up his hand. "Silence, girl!"

The men who had laughed so heartily saw Winslow's patience being tried. They bent their heads over their work and tried to ignore the intrusion, despite their curiosity. That little girl was a brave one, alright.

"Where is your father now? And this Pine?"

"Yes, he is in the Church just as you ordered."

"And your father? Did he follow my instructions?"

She shook his head. "It is not his fault. He is touched in the head, as mad as my mother."

"My orders specified any male ten years of age and older. How old is this Pine?"

"Ten years and two months, sir. And my father is ten years of age and older, though I do not know exactly."

The officers in the room with Winslow appeared deeply engrossed in the maps at his table but still managed to snicker under their breath. Winslow glared at them, then turned back to her.

"Well then, what is your request?"

"Please do not kill either one of them."

"Well, there is no reason to kill your little brother as he presented himself in the Church, did he not?"

She nodded. "And my father?"

"Is he in the Church?

"No sir but…but I can bring him to you…if you promise not to burn him alive."

"Hmm, how did you hear about the last bit, the burning alive?"

"I can read a little, sir, and I read it on the church door."

Winslow looked at the officers. Turnbull, Adams and Hobbs feigned a review of their maps. At another table, Lieutenants Wicker and Bancroft kept their eyes to the table where they appeared to pore over other documents.

Winslow asked his men, "Did one of you threaten a burning?" They shook their heads quickly and returned to their maps.

He turned back to Béatrice. "We shall do the following. You bring your father here and I shall not burn him alive. How does that sound?

"Oh yes, sir, that sounds just wonderful. Thank you for your Christian charity. He is mad you see. He thinks he is an Indian."

"Well, I should like to see that for myself."

He turned to Wicker and Bancroft. "Ride with her to pick up her father. What is his name?"

She curtsied again. "Thomas Gaudet. The carpenter."

Wicker said, "Yes, sir. He built the furniture you see in here."

Winslow looked at the finished table, the polished wood desks. "Very well made. He could not be mad if he can make such fine furnishings." Then he turned back to Béatrice.

"I shall see you and your father shortly."

The young girl curtsied. "Yes sir, thank you sir."

Winslow made a point to look at Wicker. "Lieutenant, you are to make sure nothing happens to the girl or it is your head."

Wicker cursed the fact that he had a reputation for misusing young girls and that Winslow knew it. "Yes sir, of course, sir. I mean, of course not, sir."

Winslow grunted, then turned to back to the maps. Bancroft and Wicker escorted Béatrice out of the office. Wicker lifted her onto his horse, closing his eyes and remembering the trouble he had gotten into in Bostontown with the eight year-old daughter of the scullery maid at his parents' house. He had not thought about that in the five years since it happened. His father had dragged him to the home of a British officer who often dined with them and before he knew it, Wicker had been commissioned as a Lieutenant serving under Winslow. His father disowned him and forbade him to ever return home. When he entreated his mother, she shed not a single tear and closed the door in his face.

Within the hour, Wicker had returned to the Fort with Thomas Gaudet on the back of his horse. Gaudet was covered in white powder, having dipped his head into the flour barrel in the cellar. His painted face resembled a mask, the berry paste thickened with flour. Wicker half-dragged the Acadian into Winslow's office, Béatrice following nervously behind.

Winslow took a quick look at Gaudet and motioned to Wicker. "Take him into the prison tent and hold him until I authorize differently. Is that understood?"

The sentries saluted Winslow and pulled Gaudet to the ground. He continued to wobble his knees and drool, saying nonsensical Mi'Kmaq phrases, jostling some of the flour paste from his head. The sentries understood the man was mad and for that reason his life had been spared. They propped him on a horse and led him to Tent City.

*

Evangeline called to Christine from the window. Lately Christine spent so much time mixing and grinding her potions and medical treatments that she seemed to have little time for anything else.

Evangeline remarked, "How odd to see Lieutenant Wicker taking Thomas Gaudet into the Tent City."

Christine asked absentmindedly. "Was he let out of the Church?

Evangeline turned from the window and sat at the dining table and laughed softly. "Looks like she was able to convince Winslow after all."

"Who was able to do what?"

"Monsieur Gaudet's daughter, Béatrice. She brought him out of hiding in the woods and Winslow agreed to spare his life."

Christine responded, "He did, did he? We may need her help if she is as clever as that."

"I could not agree with you more."

*

Kitok bid goodbye to the Acadian refugees, whom he had helped settled in several caves in the mountains beyond Grand Pré. The Acadians preferred being cold and hungry to bearing the brunt of any additional British humiliation or punishment. They had seen far too many a cruel streak in the English troops.

Beausoleil and Kitok had led the men on a successful hunt using crudely-made traps and the few weapons that had not been confiscated during the raid -- they had been well-hidden even without advance knowledge of the British plan to seize all weapons. Bears would provide meat and warm bed coverings for those who had none. Venison from the deer would be dried to provide food throughout the snow season. The midwives scoured the forest floor, unearthing herbs and healing plants beneath a soft blanket of new snow.

Kitok was content no one would go hungry or freeze during this winter. Beyond that he could not think. The future was too unpredictable. With the knowledge that the Grand Pré Acadians would soon be gone, his own family was making plans to leave their Village and relocate to New France, close to their French allies. They could not trust the English. The Mi'Kmaqs might be their next target.

As his Mi'Kmaq friend left, Broussard thanked him profusely. They promised to meet again in the spring unless they heard English troops nearby. Kitok provided his friend with the route to New France, where he would find the Mi'Kmaqs after their relocation.

*

In her bedchamber, wearing her wedding dress, Evangeline placed the veil on her head and held it there. "Gabriel my darling. With God's blessing I consider myself your wife. There shall never be anyone else for me. I will expend my all to release you and Papa and the others from the Church. We must fight to prevent them from sending us away forever."

She looked at herself in the mirror. The handiwork on the gown was magnificent. Madame Dupont had truly outdone herself. She knew that she might never get another opportunity to wear her wedding clothes and she wrapped her arms around herself tightly.

But she realized she had to take action to help Gabriel. She tossed the veil on the bed, then slipped out of the dress. Carefully replacing them in the large box she mused, "Gabriel means more to me than any finery. I would marry him in a woolen sack if Père Rivière were to be released." She sighed. "Gabriel needs me. Papa needs me. It is time to put away my dreams and continue their work."

She went into René's room and picked out several pairs of trousers, shirts and boots. She gathered them into a large sack and descended the stairs. Grabbing her cape at the bottom of the stairs, Evangeline headed out of the building.

*

While René and his small group were inside the crypt, the other Acadian prisoners had begun introducing themselves to each other. They had come from many different villages in the Minas Bay region, though some already knew each other through blood or marriage. Tears of joy were shed by all upon finding relatives -- brothers, cousins, uncles, sons-in-law, nephews, grandsons. Most every village in the region was represented.

The men talked politics, and could not, would not, believe the English would do anything untoward in a time of peace. Prisoners were only taken after a formal declaration of war, so they naturally believed they would be released to rejoin their families. If they were to be sent to the colonies by sea, they wanted to take advantage of participating in the largest peacetime Acadian gathering in their history.

The direct entry from the presbytery was reached through a door next to the altar in the front of the Church. Winslow had apparently barricaded the door shut from his side. René had noted there was no trap door or other opening from the presbytery above as he led the men forward through the dank tunnel. It reminded him of the underground passageway he took those many years ago beneath Versailles Palace when he first glimpsed Eugenie. He closed his eyes, trying to picture her but he sighed, knowing that she was only a fleeting memory now, the details forgotten except when he looked at Pater's painting.

René realized he had been foolish to ignore Christine. She was a loyal woman, very pleasing to the eye, who had supported his every endeavor without question or complaint. She truly loved him, René knew that now. And without a stirring of surprise, he knew he loved her. He knew what he had to do, and the sooner the better.

Suddenly they heard Pine's voice. "Monsieur René, you must return. The doors are opening!"

René rushed up the stairs into the Church, followed by his men. They had barely replaced the wooden planks when Captain Turnbull was visible as the huge wooden doors were opened by soldiers. Glimpses of the Acadian women could be seen, as they raised arms and handkerchiefs and called out the names of their family members. "Jean. Charles. Christophe. Antoine. Pierre, Claude." The men and boys clamored to the doors to see their mothers, wives, sisters, daughters. Fathers raised sons on their shoulders, who cried out upon recognizing a loved one.

Pine stood on a pew bench and looked for Béatrice or his mother, or his father. Sorely disappointed when he saw no one, he hung his head and walked to a step near the altar and sobbed.

Evangeline called out to Gabriel, Christine to René. Both men stood on the pews nearest the doors and raised their arms in greeting. The women blew kisses to them as they waved joyfully through their tears.

René looked at Christine and mouthed, "I love you," bringing tears to Christine's eyes as she repeated the same words.

Evangeline held up her locket to Gabriel, who gazed into her eyes with his hand on his heart. They nodded slowly to each other, with no need for words. They knew they were for each other, for all eternity.

Lieutenants Bancroft and Wicker laid baskets of food and jugs of wine at the Church entry. No one paid any attention, so set were they on seeing their family members outside. Then, just as suddenly as the doors opened, they were pushed closed and bolted back in place.

Outside the Church, women started singing hymns in French to their men. Inside the building, the men and boys sang the chorus of the songs. Even considering the circumstances, it was a joyous occasion.

Turnbull turned to Evangeline. "Where is the food you promised my men?" Evangeline pointed to the group of women carrying trays of food into the Tent City dining area. He realized she was true to her word.   He could not help but show his pleasure when she pulled a bottle of French wine from her cloak and handed it to him. As he eyed his prize, she joined Christine and the two women quickly walked toward the Consulate.

"That was a grand success, Evangeline," Christine complimented.

"I am so thankful that horrid Captain actually allowed us to feed the men. I thought he wanted to starve them and keep all the food for himself and his men."

"Why would you think that?"

"You were the one who told me they did not have enough vessels for all of us. They could squeeze together more gaunt starving men than robust ones."

It did not take Turnbull and his bully soldiers long to order the women back to their homes to prepare meals for the following day. Evangeline and Christine quietly slipped away before any more demands could be made on them.

Unseen by anyone, Kitok had been watching the entire scene from a high tree above the Church. He slipped down during the soldiers' fight over the women's delicious-smelling meals and crept into the foliage in back of the building. Then he jumped on his horse and rode to the Indian Village.

Turnbull returned to Tent City and entered the officers' tent. There he found Thomas Gaudet tied to a post, his fellow officers tossing darts at him. The wild-eyed Gaudet was still covered in flour and gagged with a handkerchief. His head and neck were bleeding and pocked with holes within a series of red concentric circles painted on his face. Each time a dart came his way he would close his eyes and try to move his head, which was nigh impossible as it had been affixed to the post. The officers had been enjoying grog and the Acadian women's meals but decided to have their fun and use the crowd's cheering to cover Gaudet's screams and moans.

Turnbull raised his hand for them to stop. Gaudet visibly relaxed but he was soon to regret ever coming back from the woods. Night had fallen and Turnbull directed the men to swing a rope from the tree directly opposite the church doors. Thomas realized what they were going to do and he tried to pull away. Turnbull hit him on the back of the head with his musket and Gaudet went limp and fell to the ground.

The rope was soon in place and the soldiers tied it around Gaudet's neck. They tied a crudely-printed note to his hands reading "TRAYTOR." Then they strung him up and placed bets as to how long it would take for him to die. They stood beneath him drinking grog as they watched him gasp for breath and kick his feet. He vomited into his mouth gag and twisted his head so violently he nearly broke his own neck. Within moments the kicking stopped and the officers returned to the tent. The officer who had placed the winning bet collected the spoils.

Unaware of the events near the presbytery, Winslow closed his Bible. He cried fervent tears. "Why are the Acadians so submissive? Is their faith stronger than mine? Is their God stronger than mine? How I pray that this overwhelming guilt be removed."

Turnbull knocked on the door.

"Enter." Winslow looked up as his second in command walked in.

Turnbull said, "The traitor is dead. Hanged by your orders."

Winslow nodded. "He knew the consequences of his action. I can do nothing about it. The others would find me weak and they would cause trouble." He stared into the fire. "I am fatigued. Write my letter, will you?"

"Certainly, sir." Turnbull took the place at the desk and dipped a quill into the inkpot. "When you are ready, sir."

"Dear Lieutenant-Governor Lawrence,

Please send the remaining transports as soon as you can. We can ship out too few of the heathens with what we have in the harbor, just the men and boys and only by tripling the anticipated capacity on each. I await the ships so I am able to withdraw from the most painful post I have ever held.

Your faithful servant, et cetera, et cetera."

Turnbull finished with a swirl, handling the quill to Winslow. Winslow scratched his name on the paper.

"Conduct the census and confiscate the animals from the outlying farms as planned. That should supply the troops enough meat for the winter."

Turnbull said, "Yes, sir, Lieutenant-Colonel."

"Fine, Captain. And another thing."

'Your orders, sir?" Turnbull asked.

"Let the French Consul Le Blanc de Verdure out of the Church until the transports are ready to sail. D'Entremont is to be released each weekend from Friday sundown 'til Sunday eve so long as he remains in Grand Pré."

Turnbull's face turned red with fury. Gabriel? How did he regain his freedom? Did that fiancée of his...? No, Winslow would never have turned to her. He avoided Winslow's gaze and nodded compliantly. "Yes, sir, of course Lieutenant-Colonel."

Winslow guessed Turnbull's thoughts and added, "They are still representatives of the French King and until our King declares war we shall not imprison them. The others, yes, even the aristocrats. But for the short time they have left in the province they shall be allowed to represent their King. That should also bring the voice of reason to any resistance."

Turnbull turned to leave.

"One more thing."

"Yes, sir?"

"Release twenty Acadian men every night for twenty-four hours. They may see their families but must return the following evening before you release the next twenty."

This could prove interesting. "And if any of the men fail to return?"

Winslow looked at him. "If they have no honor, then hunt them down like the animals they are and string them up in front of the Church. If appropriate, you can choose to flay or scalp them as well."

"Appropriate, sir?"

"If they laid a hand on any of our troops, punishment in addition to hanging is appropriate, do you not agree?"

Turnbull grinned and saluted. "Yes, of course, sir."

Winslow waved him away. "Now leave me in peace."

A scowling Turnbull turned on his heels and shut the door as he exited.

*

Christine ate nervously. Evangeline politely ignored her anxiety.

"I have something important to tell you but please do not ask how I learned of it," Christine said.

Evangeline looked at her questioningly.

"The English plan to divide the families, sending the men separately from us. We are all to be shipped out in animal cargo transports or worse. The rations will be limited and of the lowest quality, possibly already rotted or diseased from rats."

"But how are we to know who is to be sent to which destination? Where can we plan to meet?"

Christine got a faraway look in her eyes, thinking of René. Evangeline tried to get her attention. "Christine, we must form a plan."

"The older men are to be locked in rotten hulks and sunk once they are at sea. I fear René may be among them."

"What can we do? Can Kitok help mount an attack? Shall the New France troops arrive in time?"

Christine shook her head to all the questions. "The French in Québec are too far away. We have no weapons."

"But we do. Kitok and Gabriel have a large supply. They used it to fend off the English at the Mi'Kmaq ruins." Evangeline clasped Christine's hand. Christine was non-responsive, as if she had given up all hope.

Evangeline paced back and forth, ruminating on a plan. Cattle boats! Ships sunk at sea! Rotted food! She had to devise a new plan. But what, she wondered.

Suddenly they heard the door to the Consulate creaking open downstairs. They looked at each other knowing only the two men in their lives had the other keys to the building. Together they rushed to the balcony to see who was entering. Each woman held her breath, hoping to see her true love and praying to see both René and Gabriel for the other woman's sake.

Suddenly they saw both men enter the door, looking haggard and wearing filthy clothes. The men took the stairs two at a time as the two women descended to the landing. Everyone met and exchanged hugs and kisses all around.

Gabriel picked up Evangeline and carried her up the stairs into the salon. Gazing deep into his eyes, Evangeline led him down the hall and up the stairs to her bedroom. She closed the door. Gabriel held Evangeline, kissing her hands, her cheeks, her nose, and finally her luscious lips. He held and kissed her as if he would never let her go.

René gently took Christine's hand and led her down the stairs into his office. He closed the door, took her hands and kissed them. Then René wrapped his arms around Christine. She leaned onto his shoulder and as he lifted her chin, she looked deeply into his eyes, knowing this time he would not pull away. He kissed her gently and pulled her to him. Then he kissed her hungrily, passionately. She pressed against him and they melted into each other's arms. She finally pulled away, tears of joy streaming down her face.

*

In the misty distance, the British cattle transports tossed and turned on the waves but their anchors held fast.

Two rowboats approached the shore, a high-ranking officer sitting as a second man rowed. In the launch closer to the beach, Wicker turned to Turnbull. "Lawrence said the Council is going to replace Winslow."

Turnbull looked at him, half in shock and half with excitement. But he contained himself. "How did you come by this information?"

"In the latest pouch I carried from Halifax."

Turnbull was about to slap him when Wicker stopped him. "The letter had no seal. No one knows I read its contents. I have been a courier to Halifax for a long while. It surely would not be in your best interests if I were caught or reported. This could be your golden opportunity."

Turnbull nodded. "It is time for a change."

"No one has been here longer than you, Captain. No one knows Grand Pré and the Frenchies better than you."

Turnbull grunted. "Row faster, man. We have much work to do and cannot risk the chills." Then he changed the subject, speaking in a low tone even as distant as they were from shore.

"Did you do a proper job on the old hull?"

Wicker nodded. "I assure you, sir, those feeble men will sink as soon as the old hulk rounds the corner of the Bay into the sea."

"That had better be the case because I removed all but one day's rations from the boat."

The two men jumped into the water as their boat grounded. "Blast that icy water." Wicker tried to run the remaining few yards to the shore. Turnbull grabbed him by the arm. "Speak to no one of our talk."

"Of course, Captain. I only pray that you improve my status in your company when you take charge of this heathen business."

Turnbull responded absentmindedly. "Yes, of course. You shall have your commission." He felt wet droplets on his face and looked up. "Already snow flurries? We must finish the deportation quickly, before the full of winter is upon us. Now get some young recruits to load the boats. Rations have been delivered to the shore."

Turnbull waded patiently through the water, his high leather boots keeping his feet dry. The other rowboat grounded and several young British soldiers ran past him in a hurry to pull the boats onto the beach.

Wicker joined Bancroft on the beach, where the soldiers had wagons loaded with goods. Once on shore, Turnbull turned his attention to inspecting the food. He showed no surprise at finding dead rats in flour sacks, bugs in water barrels and mold on sacks of potatoes. Upon opening a drum labeled "meat" he found a half-filled barrel of dried meat mixed with an indistinguishable mixture of hay and another substance remarkably resembling animal turds, no doubt from animal stalls rather than from feed grain piles.

Turnbull grunted his approval and issued his orders to waiting soldiers. "Wicker and Bancroft, you supervise the troops. They are to load the stores onto the launches then offload onto the transports. Divide them as best you can so each has an equal amount of each type of food."

The men began to scurry to divide the barrels and boxes of stores among the various small rowboats, readying the foodstuffs to go to the large transports.

Adams directed his troops to fill half-empty flour sacks with sand. Turnbull walked up to Wicker, who was responsible for putting the flour sacks onto rowboats. Turnbull opened the last one placed on the boat. It was short by about two inches. He ripped it open and dumped the sand and flour on Wicker's head. Then he took his whip and cracked it across Wicker's face.

"You Lieutenant should know better than to load a half-empty container. We are limited in space and rations were calculated using full barrels. Every inch must be filled. To the top, Lieutenant."

"But we have no more flour."

"You have an unending supply of sand do you not?"

Wicker cowered. "Yes sir, Captain."

Turnbull looked to the rowboats, which were nearly full. He watched as a young soldier, a boy of no more than fifteen, tried to lift a barrel of the smelly meat mixture but the odor got the best of him. Unfortunately for him, he dropped the barrel, spilling half the meat on the beach. Turnbull strode to his side, cracked a whip against the boy's neck and drew blood from underneath his jacket collar.

"You, there. What is the problem with the meat?"

The young soldier had heard of Turnbull's hot temper. He had to get away from him so he answered quickly, "Nothing, sir." He tried to pick up the meat but Turnbull kicked him into the mixture in the sand. When Turnbull cracked his whip on the boy's head, he covered his head with his hands and cried out. The sadistic Captain continued whipping the boy's hands until they were bloody pulp. Then Turnbull pushed the boy's face into the mess in the sand, holding it there as the soldier struggled to get free.

But Turnbull was unrelenting and held the boy's face in the mixture of dung and hay until the boy could breathe no more and died.

Turnbull turned to the other men, who had gazed on in horror. They immediately stepped up their pace, avoiding Turnbull.

"Someone put the meat back into the barrel and get it on the transport." He glared at all the troops. "Now! Now! Now!"

Five soldiers ran to the barrel. They pulled the body away from the mixture and scooped the meat with sand and the dead boy's blood back into the barrel. Then they hurriedly stowed it in a rowboat.

Turnbull grunted, then motioned for his horse. A soldier helped him mount. The Captain looked down and ordered, "Toss the body in the sea. And be quick about it. We have more work to do yet." Then he rode off the beach into the trees up the hill.

When he was out of sight, Wicker turned to Lieutenant Bancroft. "Regardless of the commission Turnbull promised me, if I could get away with it, I would kill that bloody bastard."

Bancroft added under his breath, careful not to let Captain Adams hear him, "And I would help you do the dirty deed. That madman must be stopped."

*

In the Consulate office, René took Christine's hand and led her to sit at his desk. He took his handkerchief and dried her tear-filled eyes.

Christine said, "René, I hope that when you learn what I have done you will not be disappointed."

He said, "How could I ever be so with you? You mean everything to me. I was just too blind to see it." Then he fell to his knee and proposed. "I love you. I have felt this way for the longest time but was afraid to let my feelings for you go, as I feared they would overpower me. I pray that you agree to be my wife. Will you, my dearest Christine, consent to be my wife?"

She kissed his hands and pulled him to her, both rising to stand together. She buried her face in his shoulders, holding him close to her. "Before I respond, you must hear what I have to say. Then, if you still want to marry me, I shall give you my response."

She cried softly as she told him about her agreement with Winslow. She showed him the herb ball and then sat with her hands in her lap, her eyes cast downward, waiting for his answer.

He took her hands and lifted her from her chair, embracing her softly, kissing her cheek and forehead. "I love you all the more for the great risk you took. I know you would never dishonor God with your actions and yet you risked being dishonored by friends and neighbors for your selfless actions to help them." He lifted her face to hers and kissed her reverently. "I have loved you for so long but only just let myself believe it, hoping you feel the same. My dear Christine, will you be my wife?"

She flung her arms around his neck. "Yes, of course. I have wanted nothing else but this, my darling."

He whispered to her, "But I cannot let you continue your sacrifice. When I return to the Church, I shall remain there. I must."

She looked at him. He had tears in his eyes. She shook her head. "No, please stay, my darling. Winslow shall never know me because of the potion. And I would still have access to his confidential orders."

René kissed her again passionately and held her tightly. He shook his head, determined what he had to do to protect her honor at all costs, even if it meant leaving her. "Let us share these few days and determine how and where we shall reunite and build our life together." They walked arm in arm up the stairs to René's bedroom and slowly shut the door behind them.

In her room, Evangeline looked deep into Gabriel's eyes. She slowly stood up and untied the ribbons on her outer apron, letting it fall to reveal her day gown sitting over mounds of petticoats. The sleeve of the dress dropped, baring her shoulder, which Gabriel kissed softly with his lips. He looked at her for permission to remove his jacket and when he read her eyes, he took it off and laid it on the chair next to the window. She drew the curtains and stood in the muted light dancing on the curtains from the streetlamp below.

He took her hand and slowly led her to the bed. He lifted her chin and kissed her, firmly but softly. Then their lips broke apart, their eyes met and they pressed their lips and bodies to each other, falling on the bed in their passionate embrace.

Downstairs, British troops beat on the front door until they broke it open. Turnbull rushed in, his fat face puffed and red with anger. He raced into the Consulate office but he saw no one. Suddenly Wicker and Bancroft entered the hallway. Other soldiers stood outside the door.

Turnbull looked upstairs and took the stairs two at a time, screaming angrily, "Where is that traitor?" He was quickly followed by Wicker and Bancroft who kicked doors wide open, searching the hallway. They were unable to open René's room which was locked. Then they ran up to the third floor.

René heard noises at his door of stomping boots and Turnbull's rants. He quickly dressed, grabbed his musket and ran out of his room. Fearing what Turnbull would do, he advised Christine to lock the door behind him. She dressed quickly but ignored his warning. She would regret the decision.

René had heard of Turnbull's cruelty towards his own troops. What would he do to Gabriel? The Consul rushed after him but he and the other officers were already on the third floor, near Evangeline's room.

René yelled out, uncharacteristically, "Captain? *Sir?* This Consulate and my home are both property of the King of France. You have no right to enter here. What is the meaning of this?"

Too late. Turnbull was on the third floor and he lunged at the door to Evangeline's bedroom. But it was not locked, as Evangeline had nothing inappropriate in mind when she invited Gabriel in. After all, kissing was acceptable behavior for a publicly engaged couple about to be married.

Evangeline and Gabriel lay on her bed, holding each other tightly and kissing with such ardor burning in their hearts. The door burst open and Turnbull fell flat onto the floor, his head missing the thick rug and hitting the wooden planks instead.

As Turnbull righted himself, Gabriel jumped off the bed in shock and pulled Evangeline to his side. She subtly pulled her dress back onto her shoulder. Nothing untoward had transpired though the two young people were in a state of disarray. But more telling were their flushed faces and short quick breaths.

Wicker and Bancroft had followed Turnbull and waited apprehensively in the hall. They knew what to do but did not know how far Turnbull would go. But they knew their superior despised d'Entremont, diplomat or not, and they had their orders. They grabbed Gabriel, using all the strength they could muster to force him out of the room and into the hall.

The two lieutenants pushed d'Entremont against the wall. As he was about to fight his way out of their clutches, Turnbull unsheathed his knife and placed it at Gabriel's throat. Gabriel dared not move a muscle.

Turnbull screeched, "Traitor. I have got you now. What do you say to that?" He inadvertently moved his knife nicking Gabriel's neck and causing blood to drip onto his linen shirt.

Gabriel replied calmly so as not to agitate Turnbull to a greater degree. "I have done nothing wrong. What do you accuse me of doing now?"

Turnbull heard a noise and saw that René was carrying a musket aimed at *him*. Turnbull was confused. Where the devil did he get that? He thought all the weapons had been confiscated.

René, keeping his voice as level as he could, issued a demand to Turnbull. "Remove the knife from my Vice Consul's throat or I shall have no choice but to defend French territory...to the death."

Turnbull seethed as he stared into Gabriel's eyes. Gabriel returned the gaze, well aware that one false move could result in his own death. Bancroft was fearful of the consequences but he tapped Turnbull's shoulder attempting to ask for orders. Instead, Turnbull slowly gave him the knife. Turnbull was still angry but seemed to come to his senses.

René kept his musket trained on Turnbull. "Toss the knife under the bed." Bancroft was paralyzed and fearful that Turnbull would inflict punishment on him for René's actions, which were none of his doing.

Turnbull looked at Bancroft. "You heard the Frenchy."

Bancroft nodded and tossed the knife into the bedroom, where it landed on the bed.

Evangeline turned to René and running to Gabriel's side she screamed. "Papa! *Do something!*" Then she grabbed Gabriel's hand and cried out to Turnbull. "You cannot take Gabriel. Lieutenant-Colonel Winslow approved his release just this evening."

At the sound of screaming, a third soldier had rushed up the stairs. He poked his musket into Evangeline's back. René saw a fourth soldier was marching Christine up the stairs at musket-point. She tried to appear calm, straightening her dress and tying on her apron, but her frightened eyes were pleading with René for help. Immediately Le Blanc handed his gun to Turnbull. "Let the women go."

Turnbull gave the musket to Wicker and nodded to the other soldiers. As they withdrew from behind Evangeline and Christine, René gently directed the women into Evangeline's bedroom. Christine grabbed the knife from the bed and hid it in her apron. Just in case.

René said forcefully. "Captain Turnbull, you have no right to take our Vice Consul. I shall speak with your commanding officer about this."

Turnbull simply shrugged. He stood in the bedroom, turning his gaze from Gabriel to Evangeline.

Gabriel asked, "What is the meaning of this? Where are you taking me?"

Wicker ignored him as he tied Gabriel's hands behind his back while Bancroft menacingly held the knife toward the prisoner.

Evangeline seized the opportunity and knelt before Turnbull, with her arms outstretched. "Please do not take Gabriel away. He is allowed to be here for two more days. "

Turnbull's eyes turned even colder than when he had stared at Gabriel. "If I had the time, I would take care of you as well. It seems your fiancé has not done a proper job of it." He looked at Gabriel and sneered as Evangeline cried, her face covering her hands.

"Never, Turnbull. You shall never touch my fiancée. Do not even think it." Gabriel lashed out, trying to kick Turnbull, but he was too far away.

Evangeline lifted her head, realizing that Turnbull was trying to induce Gabriel to hit him, which would be treason. Gabriel could be hanged, or worse, drawn and quartered without a trial for hitting a British officer. She wiped her eyes and rushed to Gabriel's side. She kissed his cheek before the soldiers could push her away and whispered softly.

"My love, you know I can care for myself. Turnbull is baiting you to commit treason by attacking first so he can justify your death. Ignore his taunts and Papa will have you set free again."

Gabriel looked at her, then at Turnbull, then back at her. He realized she was right and he immediately became docile. "I demand you take me to Lieutenant-Colonel Winslow at once so we can resolve this matter. He will find me innocent of any false charges you might attempt to bring against me."

Without responding, the soldiers pushed Gabriel down the hall and down the stairs, not stopping until they reached the entry below.

Evangeline rushed behind them, followed by René and Christine. They all watched as Turnbull pushed Gabriel outside the building. She stood steadfastly at the open door. "Gabriel, remember I love you. We shall be together again soon."

Gabriel nodded, "And I love you with all my heart."

Wicker pushed Gabriel onto the soldier's horse and Turnbull turned to Evangeline. He said pointedly, "I shall look forward to more French wine." And with a slap of Turnbull's whip, he took off toward the Fort. Wicker and Bancroft rode toward the Church, the other troops returning to Tent City.

René turned to the women. "Lock all the doors. Evangeline take my musket and go upstairs. I shall return when I have spoken with John."

Evangeline nodded. "Please take care not to let them take you, Papa."

He kissed her forehead. "You have nothing to fear. Now go."

She acquiesced and left her father and Christine by the door.

Christine took René's hand. "My prayers are with you."

He held her face in his hands, looked deeply into her eyes, kissed her passionately, then buried his face in her hair. "Pray for all of us, my dearest. Our tribulations are just beginning, I fear. But we shall face them together. I love you and look forward to marrying you soon." Then he exited the back door to the stable. Within moments Christine heard his horse galloping around the Consulate toward the town gates.

Christine slowly trudged up the stairs to find Evangeline staring at the musket which she had laid on the table. Christine pulled the knife from her apron and laid it on the table. The two women stood in front of the weapons, holding on to each other, staring at the dried blood on the knife. It could have been Gabriel's, or theirs. The both prayed silently for their men and for the Acadians. Their fate was sealed yet Evangeline refused to surrender without a fight.

"Kitok and I will are developing a plan to free the men from the Church."

Christine shook her head vehemently. "It is far too dangerous. Turnbull stations guards at the Church day and night. One call for reinforcements and the entire Tent City militia would fire on every Mi'Kmaq and…they would spare no one, not even women and children."

Even as René was riding up to the Fort to demand Gabriel's freedom, Turnbull's soldiers had roughly pushed the Vice-Consul into the Church. The other Acadian men were surprised, but pleased, to see him. However, their emotions turned to anger against the English as Gabriel explained their fate.

At Fort Vieux Logis, René demanded that the sentry open the gate. "I must speak with Lieutenant-Colonel Winslow. It is a most urgent matter."The young sentry was about to let Le Blanc through when Turnbull rode up. Turnbull looked at René. "No one is to interrupt the Lieutenant-Colonel today. For any reason. Strict orders." Turnbull nodded at the sentry who shrugged to René then lifted the gate so Turnbull could enter. He trotted past the two men, never looking back. René looked around but could see no other entry into the Fort. He had no choice but to return home. There he would waste no time with Christine and Evangeline devising their strategy for reuniting after the deportation.

On the ride back he remembered every detail of Christine's face, the touch of her hands on his face, the taste of her sweet lips, the scent of her thick tresses as she lay in his arms. Despite the impending exile and the English acts of tyranny and violence, for the first time in decades René felt absolute joy. He relished the feeling on the short ride home. He was in love and was determined to marry Christine and raise a large Catholic family with her, no matter where they lived.

CHAPTER 42
Vow

October, 1755 – GRAND PRÉ

T he master of the English sloop, the *Elizabeth*, held his nose as his crew emptied the last of the dung and hay from the hold and emptied it into the sea.   Nathaniel Milbury was not used to carrying animals. He sailed passenger ships, accustomed to the gentility and cleanliness of English settlers immigrating to the colonies.

But a month earlier, the Bostontown mercantile firm of Apthrop and Hancock, contracted by Lieutenant-Governor Lawrence, had offered him substantially greater wages than customary to command a different kind of vessel -- an animal transport. Milbury now realized the higher pay was to compensate for the stench of the hold. Indeed, many of the cattle, sheep, goats and other farm animals bred and raised in Grand Pré had been loaded onto this very sloop, and others like it, for sale at harbor markets all along the Eastern seaboard.

In a typical animal cargo transport, such as his, the beasts were herded into one large hold with open area measuring about twenty-four feet wide by forty-eight feet long. The animals were quite comfortable with a tall ceiling on the hold of about fourteen feet. Six-foot wide wooden troughs were affixed along to each side, the entire length of the hold and filled with water and feed for the animals. Hay was pitched daily to cover the dung and its stench. Voyages from Grand Pré to the colonies could take months rather than weeks, depending on the winds, tides and frequency of storms, so pilots of animal cargo transports had to be prepared for anything, including putrid-smelling holds.

The English Admirals Mostyn and Boscawen had contracted Althorp and Hancock to rebuild the cattle boats for a different configuration-- for human cargo. As an early October freeze chilled Grand Pré, several sloops and schooners had arrived in the waters off the Grand Pré beach. Althorp and Hancock had followed the Admiralty's specifications to the letter, providing three windowless box holds per transport about twenty-four feet wide by sixty feet long and four feet high.

Without any space for movement, all human waste would remain in the same spot with the Acadian who would sleep and eat there as well. But the meals would be less frequent than usual, even for prisoners, since the British had woefully underestimated the number of French neutrals to exile. As a result, the food would be rationed to one piece of moldy bread or bug-infested potato and a piece of dried pork once a day or every other day and one pitcher of grog or water, if available, for those in each cell to share.

The transports had been outfitted to allow more than the advised two persons per ton, so that Winslow and his troops could deport all the Acadians by stuffing them into the low-ceiling holds and piling the sick and dying onto a corner of the deck. They reasoned it would be easier to toss the bodies overboard than having to pull them out of holds that would soon become filthier and more stench-ridden than when the vessels transported animals. They did not imagine the horror that awaited the prisoners when disease spread quickly in the holds without fresh air or water, and more Acadians died in the hold than on deck.

*

At dawn on the 5th of October 1755, René woke Christine with a kiss and held her in his arms a long while before he dressed and presented himself to the troops at St. Charles des Mines Church. The soldiers were surprised but they let him in, oblivious to the fact that the deportation was to take place the following day at dawn. René had been forewarned by Christine of the deportation date and he wanted to meet with the French colonists imprisoned in the Church to organize a plan of action for reuniting.

The Consul met with the men and boys as a group and talked about their impending fate of being sold into slavery in Bostontown, or exiled in one of the colonies or imprisoned in an English jail. He gave them information about the Governors of New France and the Louisiana territory as well as directions how to reach Québec and New Orleans and suggested that they reunite in one location or the other to retain their religion, customs and language. Then René met with the members of each family, giving them strength and encouragement. He gave every man and boy a gold coin reminding them to hide it so the soldiers did not steal it from them.

At the end of the day when the Church doors opened and the women delivered the meals, each man appeared mentally strong though the lack of heat, food and contact with their family had taken a physical toll on many of the older men. René organized a final prayer session reminding the men to place their faith in God.

At midnight all was quiet inside St. Charles des Mines Church. While most of the men and boys slept soundly, Francis Hébert had just closed the crypt after Gabriel and his friends had finished filling in the escape tunnel and had returned to the sacristy of the Church. All the young men had escaped but Gabriel did not want to risk the English finding the route, in the event the escapees needed more time. Pine Gaudet helped him pound, as quietly as they could, the nails of the trap door in place.

Gabriel shook Francis' and Pine's hands when they finished. "We have done our best to give the young Acadians the best hope for their future."

Pine nodded in agreement. "I pray they can escape and make it through what promises to be a long cold winter."

Francis looked over the Acadians, crowded together to share their bodily warmth in the high-ceilinged Church. Winslow had refused to allow any firewood and, without a fire, the days seemed as cold as the nights.

Francis and Pine separated to their pews on opposite sides of the Church. It seemed to Francis he had barely closed his eyes yet several hours had passed and dawn had arrived. Suddenly, without warning other than wood creaking and soft daylight spilling into the Church, the doors were unbolted and opened.

Winslow's heavy boots marched up the center aisle of the Church. Captains Turnbull and Adams stood at the back door, flanked by soldiers with fixed bayonets on their muskets. Clearly they meant business and René believed it was now the time to board the ships.

The men and boys had woken. Loud murmurs were heard throughout the Church until Winslow motioned to Turnbull.

"Silence! You shall listen to Lieutenant-Colonel Winslow."

Inside the Church, Winslow addressed the Acadians. "You are to be released from the Church. We shall take you to the ships and then, of course, your families shall follow."

Winslow continued, "Follow my troops and maintain orderly lines. And lest anyone be tempted to escape through the woods or jump from his transport into the water, my troops have orders to shoot. If the escapees cannot be found, their families shall be hanged in front of this very Church. Disobeying the King's Order is treason punishable by instant death. Does anyone not understand?"

Winslow motioned to Captain Adams, who recited Winslow's orders in more or less passable French. When he asked if anyone did not understand, Pine Gaudet stood up.

"Exactly where will our families meet us? I ask because my mother is touched in the head and is not able to walk very fast."

Turnbull started to answer but Winslow shook his head. "We will make certain that every Acadian in the Grand Pré region is brought to the beach and boarded on the ships. Except those that we must kill for disobeying orders."

Silently gulping, Pine sat down.

No other questions were asked. The orders were clear, the message was received. The faces of the Acadian men visibly whitened and, their spirits dampened, they heeded the order to march.

Winslow exited the Church, followed by Turnbull, playing on Winslow's guilt. "Lieutenant-Colonel, when the prisoners arrive on the beach, do I have the authority to take the acts I think necessary to carry out the mission for the head of our one true Church? Surely you are too occupied with higher military matters for such things."

Winslow responded, "You have it but leave me in peace. I shall not know what you must do."

"Sir?"

Winslow turned, weary of Turnbull's questions. "More questions?"

"Just one, sir. If you prefer to take another posting, rest assured that I stand eager to complete this business for you."

Winslow narrowed his eyes and looked at Turnbull. Did he know of Winslow's request for a transfer? And if so, how? Or should he give him the benefit of the doubt?

"We shall see it through to ship out all the men and boys, though it shall be a mathematical conundrum to squeeze so many on so few vessels. We shall retire to figure how to make them all fit."

"Did the Admirals not promise enough transports?"

"In the end, they were previously allocated for the new settlers for exporting colonial goods before winter. And the blasted census was incorrect by thousands. Then the mercantile company could not hire enough private vessels. Which leaves us in our current position."

Turnbull gave a slight bow, partly to hide the smirk on his face. "If the heathens continue their rebellious nature, the population will shrink as a result of your command to kill any escapees. There shall, no doubt, be quite a few who shall take that risk…and lose."

Winslow waved his hand, indicating that his patience had run and Turnbull should remove himself from his sight. Turnbull complied, returning inside the Church.

From the presbytery, Winslow watched the church doors open. Thousands of Acadian men and boys poured out into the main street of Grand Pré, led by René and Gabriel. When they first set eyes on the swinging corpse of Thomas Gaudet, they were outraged, then immensely sad that the sickly man had been brutally murdered. He had not known what he was doing, which only increased their rage toward the British. When Pine saw his father, he broke into tears and ran to René's side, asking him to read the sign his father held. René demanded to speak with Winslow and was met with a lash of Turnbull's whip. Undaunted, René and Gabriel continued to lead the men forward. They prayed the rosary aloud in their native French, beginning with the Lord's Prayer.

Winslow was amazed to find that, despite Gaudet's cruel death, the French prisoners exhibited hopefulness in their faces. Winslow wondered what lies Turnbull had told them. For his part he justified his lie that the wives and children would join the men in order to keep the men calm. It would not do to lose his commission in the eleventh hour by a prisoners' attack. But it would soon be none of his concern. He looked forward to washing his hands of this disagreeable business, as he repeatedly wrote in his diary and in his letters to his mother.

Evangeline was awakened from a restless sleep by the sounds of boots marching. She looked out of her bedroom window and screamed. She tried to open the window but it was stuck so she rapped frantically on the window, trying to catch the attention of René and Gabriel walking below.

She ran into Christine's room just as Gabriel and René looked up at the Consulate windows. All the drapes were closed except in Evangeline's room but she was nowhere to be seen. Gabriel kept looking at the window, hoping to catch a glimpse of his love, until he lost sight of it as they marched past the gates of town.

Evangeline woke Christine, who stared dully at two satchels that she had begun to pack when she intercepted the news from Winslow. One was for Evangeline, filled with neatly-packed dresses, her wedding gown on top, with the canvas painting of her mother protectively placed under the other clothes. The other bag was for Christine, but it was only half-filled. She had lost interest when she learned about the hulk René was to board. He would never survive. They had finally expressed their love only to lose each other forever. She did not want to live. How could she, without the only man she had loved in her entire life?

Evangeline said, "They are sending the men away without us."

They ran back into Evangeline's room because of the better vantage point but the two men were long gone. All that could be seen were the tracks in the mud where proud Acadians and their spiteful English captors had marched.

Evangeline told her, "I have a plan."

"What plan? What can I do to help?"

"We must hurry if it is to work. Follow me and bring the bags. Quickly."

Christine threw a few more items into her bag then shut it and carried it, handing the other satchel to Evangeline. They slung the bags across their shoulders, grabbed their cloaks and ran out of the building.

"You take that side of the street and I shall take this one. Tell the women we are marching to the beach to meet our men. They must move quickly, even if it means leaving possessions behind. Hurry!"

Evangeline pounded on the front door of a nearby home. A sleepy Béatrice opened it. "Spread the word. We are going to meet our men. They are already on the shore."

Béatrice nodded, then sat her drooling mother Anne on the stoop outside and asked Francis to watch over her. He enjoyed playing the protector though he was but a child himself. Béatrice ran to the houses on the street behind and called out as loudly as she could. "We are going to the beach! The men are already at the ships. Hurry and join us."

Christine called out to Madame Dupont, emptying chamber pots outside. "The transports are here! Come with us and tell the other women you see."

Evangeline, Christine and Béatrice knocked on doors, announcing the march. Soon the street came alive with women and children following their pied pipers, Evangeline and Christine, singing Acadian songs as they marched down Main Street.

From every house they passed poured out more women and children, and old folks who could walk or ride in carts.

Evangeline passed the word. "Hurry. The transports are nearly loaded. Go faster. Leave your carts and bags if necessary, for we must meet up with the men. Hurry."

While Christine continued to lead them down through the trees, Evangeline ran up and down the line of people whom she considered her charges now. She needed to encourage them, help them, and pray with them. Some of the grandmothers and grandfathers had stopped to rest. She tried to help them up but one of them expressed the sentiment of all.

"We have lived our entire life here. We do not wish to leave. If they shoot us, then so be it. At least we shall die together. But we cannot delay the younger ones from being with their men. Help them, not us, dear child."

Evangeline could not dissuade the little group, as their minds had been made up. She did as she was bid and assisted the young women, many of them pregnant, having a difficult time maneuvering the pathway on the steep slope. She carried a newborn in her arms and carried the satchel of a pregnant woman, helping them farther down until another woman could help them descend the muddy slope. Then Evangeline ran back up the hill to help more of the disadvantaged. It was there that she found Béatrice trying to move her mother from a stump. Anne blabbered nonsensical phrases and, when Evangeline started making sounds with no sense, Anne stood up and started to run down the hill, gleefully followed by Francis. Evangeline and Béatrice had a time catching up with Anne who was the last straggler.

Within an hour, they had notified everyone in town. A few of the single women, including Evangeline's best friend, Jeanne Lambert, had ridden out to the farms to notify the women and children there. Evangeline knew Jeanne had been seeing Gabriel's closest friend, Marc de la Tour Landry, but that they had not yet announced a betrothal. She hoped Jeanne would return in time to find Marc amidst what would surely be chaos on the beach.

After hearing the call, the women sprung into action. Cases and bags were packed with essentials for the trip, and each child was bundled in as many layers as he could walk in to allow for carrying something else -- a loaf of bread, a pot or pan, a family quilt.

The women and children and their old folk who had not been in the Church were packed and assembled on Main Street, awaiting Evangeline's word. She and Christine led the delegation, beginning with spirited religious songs full of hope and prayer.

As they sang, they gathered momentum and at each street more Acadians joined in their procession. When they filed past the Church and saw it empty, then saw Gaudet's body still swinging from the tree, each Acadian made the sign of the cross but kept marching and singing, singing and marching.

Winslow came out of the presbytery to see what the fuss was about when he caught sight of Christine's flaming red hair. He rubbed his double chin. He would miss that one, he thought. But, after all, she was a heathen and her company only a temporary amusement. I shall be content to be out of this unholy place, he thought as he re-entered the presbytery and took up his quill to write in his journal.

On the beach, Turnbull on one end and Adams on the other had issued separate but identical orders for three lines for the men and boys.

"Married men on the right, unmarrieds older than fourteen on the left, boys ages ten to fourteen go in the middle line."

Ten year old Claude Bourg spoke up loudly. "I shall not go without my Papa. I want to go with my Papa."He reached out for his father, Charles Bourg, who had moved up in the line to be next to him. He pleaded, "Papa. Please do not leave me."

Charles had tears in his eyes. His heart was breaking, but he could not jeopardize his son's life so he whispered to him. "You must be brave. You will have an adventure on the big ship, and when you arrive in the port I will be there waiting for you."

That seemed to calm the little boy and he retook his place in line. But the other young boys were frightened. They cried out, "I shall not go without my Papa. I shall not go without my Papa." The boys' fathers were tearful as they tried to maneuver themselves to be next to their sons.

Turnbull cracked his whip and Wicker and Bancroft fired their muskets into the air. Wicker pulled the Bourgs apart and put the father towards the back of the line. Claude kept looking back at him, but his father motioned that he stay where he was. Meanwhile, Charles surreptitiously kept moving up in the line without causing attention until he was nearly back in his old place. He whispered to his son, "Be quiet. We may be going in the same boat. Pretend that you do not know me."

Claude's eyes brightened as he nodded.

Turnbull spit his words loudly. "'Not' is a word I do not understand. The King's command is absolute and shall be absolutely obeyed. You know I do not love to use harsh means but time does not admit of delays."

He looked to his officers and the troops and yelled out, "Troops, fix bayonets and advance!"

The soldiers brandished their bayonets towards the boys. Pandemonium! Fathers lost hold of their sons, who cowered behind them. Boys cried out for their fathers and older brothers. Men and boys alike moved toward the beach to keep away from the bayonets, which kept advancing without mercy. An older man of about sixty years moved forward quickly to escape the pick of the bayonet but he tripped and hit his head on a rock in the sand. Wicker was at the back of the line and motioned to a soldier to lift the head.

Wicker asked, "Is he alive?"

The soldiers knelt to the man's face and lifted the bloody head. "He is still breathing, sir."

Wicker walked over and speared him several times with his bayonet. "Not any longer. Clear this path and toss him away."

The soldier grabbed the body and dragged it into the water as several boys in one boat moaned, "Papa" and "Grandpapa." Adams saw the two and ordered a nearby soldier, "Take the younger boy out and put him in another rowboat."

When the soldier accomplished the task, the two relatives covered their weeping eyes with their hands, then looked across the boats to each other and whispered, "I shall pray for you."

Soldiers fired muskets into the air when the lines started to become indistinguishable.

Turnbull cried out, "Straight lines, you heathen animals."

Turnbull rode his horse between the lines and cracked his whip hard whenever he saw a father holding the hand of his son in the other line. Soldiers then separated them and pushed each into a different launch to make certain they would not be on the same transport. The English troops took pleasure in their sadistic punishment, particularly of the young boys, by separating relatives from one another.

After that, the men dropped the hands of their sons or nephews or brothers so the English would not know who was related to whom.

René called out to Turnbull who rode past him. "When will the women and other children join us?"

Gabriel offered, "We can help you identify families to keep them together. Surely that was the King's order?"

Turnbull turned to him and sneered coldly. "You shall do nothing, traitor. As for your women, once you are on board, my troops will bring them to the beach." He noted Adams shaking his head and remembered Winslow's admonition not to tell them the truth so he let it go and rode off.

Gabriel and René called out, "When will they bring them here?"

A tussle ensued in one of the rowboats farther down the beach. Wicker was trying to pry Claude Bourg away from his father, Charles. Somehow, despite their being torn apart earlier, they had ended up in the same rowboat.

Charles pleaded, "Please, sir, he is a sickly boy and lost his mother early on."

Wicker retorted, "And he is a man now and shall do things that all men do." He grabbed the boy and stuck him in another rowboat.

Claude cried out, "Papa, Papa. Please help me." The boy started choking, as if he could not breathe. One of the older men in the rowboat laid him down and pressed on his chest but that did not help. Another tried to blow air into his mouth but Claude started to turn blue.

Charles dove out of his rowboat, swam to his son's boat and held his son's hand. "My son, you know what to do. Breathe slowly and deeply. Again. Slow and deep." Claude did as his father told him and he regained his breathing. He lay down in the lap of one of the men in the boat. Charles patted his son's head and said, "I am proud of you. I love you, son. Be strong and we will meet again in the colonies."

The boy was exhausted but he looked at Charles and said, "I love you, too, Papa. But please go back to your boat. I want you safe so we can live together again."

Turnbull had taken special interest in making certain no family members were put into the same rowboats. This was no small task as the large Catholic families often had fifteen or twenty children. Of course, many of those were under the age of ten but he watched closely as the males looked at each other. Whenever he saw one hug another in the same rowboat he pulled the younger one off and plopped him, crying his eyes out, into another boat.

By brandishing muskets with fixed bayonets, English soldiers had loaded one rowboat after another with men and boys, careful to separate those who clung to each other. The few fathers who tried to grab sons from the middle or left lines were stabbed with multiple bayonets. Those same weapons were then dipped in the water turning the waves lapping onto the beach red with Acadian martyrs' blood.

Younger boys did not realize what was happening until older men cautioned them not to call out to their fathers. By the time the Acadians understood what was happening, most of the families had been torn apart but warnings in French were shouted quickly that they not show affection to anyone in the family so that they could travel together. In this way, a few relatives ended up on the same boat, though not very many.

Turnbull saw a head bobbing in the water between two rowboats. He recognized Charles swimming near his son's boat. He was livid. He aimed his musket and fired at Charles. The men in the nearby boat shrank toward the bottom of the vessel. At the same moment, Charles either dove under the boat or was shot and sank. Turnbull grabbed a loaded musket from one of his troops and watched to see if the man came up again.   Satisfied, Turnbull rode to the other end of the beach.

Old Man Langlinais, as he was known by all, was the oldest man in town. At eighty-nine years old, Alphonse could still shoe a horse quicker than anyone. He had sold his stables to Henri d'Entremont, wishing to work at his leisure but then bought them back again from Gabriel at his father's death. He had found that he was bored if he was not working. He was often quoted as saying, "Retirement is for old folks and I am not yet old enough." Alphonse was being loaded onto an old hull where René had been deposited. But Alphonse slipped and fell from the top of the hull into the icy water below.

Soldiers in the rowboats thought he was trying to escape and shot him. Turnbull's orders were to shoot first and not worry about any questions later. Alphonse's body was never seen again.

On the day of boarding, Francis Hébert assisted twenty-two men, mostly married and some fathers and sons, to escape from their transport before it set sail. His knowledge as a boat builder enabled him to cut some of the lines and tie others incorrectly so that most of the hands on deck were needed on one end of the ship to prepare for sailing. He then knotted the ropes and helped the men over the side of the boat to safety before they were detected.

Because of the hardships that would have to be endured in the forest and in the mountains for the entire winter before a trip could be made safely through British Nova Scotia to New France, he urged them to swim to the rocks and then hide in the woods. He hoped the Mi'Kmaqs would find them and lead them to safety.

Turnbull saw a young boy of ten run out of line and try to get in the same rowboat as his father. He ordered a soldier to place the boy into a separate boat. Minutes later, as the launches were being rowed out to the transports, the son slipped out of the rowboat and tried to swim to his father. The father knew the boy could not swim very well so he held out his hands encouragingly. One of the soldiers rowing the boat hit the father with an oar and then pushed him overboard. Now both of them flailed in the icy water, moving towards each other.

Turnbull looked to the sea, content that these were the last rowboats to go out. No other men were on the shore. But he saw the waves in the sea. He saw the boy and the father in the water, holding on to each other. The father looked injured but he was carrying the boy as he swam towards one of the rowboats. In his paranoia or anger at having orders disobeyed, Turnbull called his faithful Lieutenant Wicker.

He pointed to the water. "Choose father or son. Or both."

Wicker hesitated. Turnbull pointed his own handgun at Wicker's head. "Their heads or yours."

Wicker closed his eyes and fired off a shot, hoping that he missed the boy. But he was not the best shot in the troops for no reason. He had shot both of them. All that remained was a small pool of blood, quickly washed away in a rowboat's wake.

Within hours after the daring escape, Turnbull appeared on deck and called out, "Francis Hébert. Where are you, you traitor?" When Francis stepped forward, he chained him to the deck and said, "Watch the trees." Francis could not move and all he could do was look ahead of him, through the trees to the town. He had a sense of foreboding. How had the men been captured already? He hoped they had quick deaths rather than the torture that Turnbull was reputed to enjoy.

Then Turnbull took to the rowboat returning to shore.

Evangeline and Christine had led the group of women, children, infants and the aged past the town gates down the road where they had first entered Grand Pré seventeen years ago and down the bluff through the beautiful trees. Looking beyond the woods, they saw soldiers loading their Acadian men onto rowboats. None of the Acadians were left on the beach.

Evangeline cried out, "Hurry, they have loaded all the men. Leave your goods here and run if you can."

She and Christine led the way, followed by Béatrice and a number of the younger girls. The women who were pregnant or with infants or small children scurried but could not run. The old people took their time because they did not believe they could survive the sea journey and preferred to die amidst the most beautiful trees in the world, in their Acadian paradise stolen from them by the English without any legal justification.

Turnbull was about to congratulate his troops when he heard loud singing and crying out coming from the trees. He looked and saw that blasted Consul's daughter and red-headed housekeeper leading all the women and children from town onto the beach.

Many women carried children in their arms and others carried decrepit parents in carts. With all the people carrying goods and sacks and bags, it was a state of utter confusion. When the women saw there were no men on the shore, their anticipation turned to great woe and distress. Bags and boxes were strewn about as women ran to the beach, only to be blocked by a row of soldiers preventing them from getting into rowboats or swimming out to sea to meet their men.

René was pulled off the old hull and rowed back to shore, where Turnbull awaited him on the beach. René was not allowed out of the boat, and kept under the watchful eye and musket of Wicker.

Turnbull called out to him. "Do you want to save the lives of twenty-four families here?"

René was perplexed. "Of course, Captain. What can I do to help?"

"That blasted boat builder, Francis Hébert. He arranged the escape of twenty-four men from his boat."

"But Captain, how can that be? Your guards have put everyone below deck."

"That transport was unusually crowded and they had to fill three levels of holds…never mind that. Can you do something?"

"Do you have a list of those on board?"

"Of course. We documented every man on every ship."

"And have you matched that list with those who supposedly left?"

"That is being done as we speak."

René waited in the launch, looking through the crowd. He spied Evangeline and asked Turnbull, "Sir, may I speak with my daughter and Christine? They are just over there."

He stood up in the boat and waved his arms, catching the attention of Evangeline who, with Christine, were comforting young and old, alike. René was so proud of them.

When they saw him they both cried out his name simultaneously, "René!" "Papa!"

They ran to the beach. Turnbull looked down at them and looked over at Adams, who was just climbing into the boat.

Turnbull relented; the first kind gesture he had ever done for the Acadians. Evangeline *had* given him what must have been the best of their imported wines. "Just this once and not for long. But do not leave the boat."

René nodded and held out his arms to the two women. They made their way to the soldiers barricading the beach from the water. Turnbull waved them through and they danced into the cold water. They both hugged him tenderly and he showered them with kisses.

He looked at them with tears in his eyes. "The loves of my life."

They nodded tearfully. Evangeline spoke first in French. "Have you seen the old hull? They have drilled holes in it and plan to sink it at sea."

Christine added, careful that they only spoke French and not within earshot of any offices who understood some of the language, "If you can manage to get onto another transport now, please do, René. Your hulk will not make the journey and I cannot bear the thought of losing you. Please whatever you must do, please get off the old hulk."

He shook his head and looked at the vessel sitting in the water. It looked like it had already taken on water and sat lower in the tides. "I shall try, of course, but I feel it my duty to try to save the others who do not have this news."

"Father you must not, we need you," Evangeline pleaded with him.

He kissed her on both cheeks. "I saw Gabriel on the full-rigged ship there, nearest the cliffs. Do you see it?"

Evangeline nodded. "Yes, yes I see. I shall try to find him. Thank you, Papa. I love you. You know how much I do."

"There is something I need to tell you, my child. About your father."

Evangeline smiled at him. "But you are my father."

"No, my darling. But you should know now who he is. In the event we are never to meet again."

At that point Adams had made his way back to shore with the list of escapees. Turnbull yelled out, "Enough. You two women back to the beach." He grabbed Evangeline and pulled her away before René could explain.

Evangeline stumbled deliberately to give Christine and her father more time. "Papa, we shall see each other, and soon. Then you can tell me your secret."

René grabbed Christine's hands. "I love you, my dearest. I shall find you and we shall be married. "

Christine kissed him tenderly, then passionately, under the hated gaze of Turnbull. "My love. Did you ever learn where you are to be sent?"

"Winslow refused to tell me. Just remember our plan. Put no faith in the English, no matter what they tell you. I shall meet you in the Louisiana territory port city of New Orleans."

Christine nodded through her tears and kissed him again. "Yes, my love, we shall begin our new lives in Louisiana. I shall wait for you there, no matter how long it takes."

"We shall be reunited and married. We must. God will save us."

Turnbull yelled out, "Enough, I said. Move out of the water."

Wicker leaned over to knock Christine away but René held him back, pleading with his eyes. Christine returned quickly to the beach and Wicker grunted with approval.

Adams handed Turnbull the list of the missing men. He reviewed it, then passed it to Wicker. He gave it to René and dictated to him, demanding he write in French. René balked but he looked at Turnbull, who pointed to Evangeline and Christine. René relented. He took the quill and ink and wrote quickly.

Turnbull grabbed the letter. "Put the English translation below and it had better be exact, Consul, or it is your family at risk. I know where they are, you see."

René did as he was ordered.

"Read it to the Frenchies."

René stood in the boat and picked up the letter. The soldiers broke their line so all the women could hear him speak to them.

"My dear French friends. It seems twenty-four of our men who will be named hereinafter have escaped from one of the transports."

At this the many women cheered and praised God.
René shook his head motioning that they be silent.

"These men must return today or the English have orders to seize all members of their family here in Grand Pré and...."

He looked at Adams then at Turnbull who motioned that he continue. René returned to the letter.

"...and hang them in front of the Church."

With this, many women swooned. One old grandmother fell off the box where she sat and died instantly of a heart attack.

René tried to calm them with his hands. "Friends. If you know where these men are, please convince them to turn themselves in. The English will wait for several hours more. Please go back to your homes and urge them to return to the shore. May God be with you all. Captain Turnbull shall read the names of the missing men."

Turnbull read the twenty-four names, and then nodded to Wicker, who manned the rowboat with René.

Winslow was slowly riding down the beach, beating his breast and speaking to himself. "What have I done? Please forgive me."

He happened to look up and see René in the rowboat. He gave René a blank stare.

René called out, "Why, in God's name, John? During peacetime? Why?"

"You can blame no one but yourself. You should have convinced them to sign our Oath."

"The Bible says forgive...."

"Forgive your enemies? Yes, I do. But we have failed to save your souls. Farewell, Monsieur le Consul." Then Winslow rode off, the last René would ever see of him.

Wicker tightened the chains until René winced. Wicker said, "I gots me orders and I follows them to the letter. You gots a complaint, you takes it up with the Captain."

René looked back to Christine and signaled his love to her. He looked for Evangeline but she was nowhere to be found. No doubt she was helping some poor woman on the beach or aiding a grandparent to walk. She was a generous, loving young woman and he wished he had been able to tell her of her heritage. He hoped she would, in time, learn of it and not think harshly of him for withholding the secret of her father from her. During their sea voyage when Eugenie had disclosed the name of Evangeline's father, he had considered himself fortunate. He did not wish ill on the father, for the incident brought him the love of his life: no, the first love of his life. Christine was his second and he would make certain that he reunited with her, married her and raised a loving family of children with her. That was his fervent prayer.

There was a great commotion on the shore as a search party of soldiers returned with two dead men tied to a horse. Riding down through the trees they reached the beach and cut the bodies loose. The women crowded around to see who the men were.

Turnbull demanded that they be identified. "Who knows these men? Speak now and save their families."

When a woman with four small children approached, the other women cast their eyes downward respectfully. She cried out, "No, no, not mine."

Denying it as she walked closer, when she saw their faces, she screamed. "My husband and my oldest son! No! Please God no." She fell upon their bodies and her other children cried with her.

Christine walked up to Adams and said dully, "They are the Antoine Tulliers, father and son. You killed two of the men you seek."

Adams rode up to Turnbull and the two had a quite conversation. Turnbull nodded then turned and shouted, "Where is the family of Francis Hébert?"

The women were shocked. What did they want of the Hébert family? Francis was not one of the missing men. Francis' wife Evelyn, visibly seven months pregnant, waddled slowly toward Turnbull.

"I am Francis Hébert's wife. How may I be of assistance?"

"You and your entire family shall get in the cart," was the rude reply by Turnbull.

Evelyn's two oldest daughters, ten-year old Anne and nine-year old Marie, and five younger children, aged three to seven, were all lifted into the cart by soldiers who drove the horse-drawn cart up the hill to town. Evelyn gave directions to their house, a large, freshly-painted wooden structure on the other end of Grand Pré. The front yard was pleasing, with late-blooming flowers in a garden and a statue of the Blessed Virgin Mary. The outbuildings consisted of henhouses and a blacksmith's shop, and beyond that were rows of plants and vines, still heavy with fruit.

From his horse, Turnbull looked down at Madame Hébert. "You are banished from this house forever."

"What is to become of us? Shall we take our possessions with us?"

"If you wish, but we cannot be responsible for the consequences if you insist on doing so."

She nodded to Turnbull, "I will be but a minute."

Turnbull gave the order to soldiers, who carried lit torches. "Start with the boats in the outbuildings." Soldiers set fire to the building, which burned quickly. The gardens were next, then the henhouses where the live chickens remained locked in their coops. Such a din was raised that quite possibly it was heard on the beach.

Inside the house, Madame Hébert rushed to gather a sack of coins hidden under the bed. The flames engulfed all buildings surrounding the house. But Madame Hébert still did not appear. The soldiers looked to Turnbull, who nodded to the children.

"The wages of sin is death, but we have spared your lives to take your house and all your possessions. And, it appears, your mother. This is what your father has wrought."

Anne cried out, "What did Papa do?"

"He helped two dozen prisoners escape from his boat and disobeyed my orders. It is only because he did not escape himself that you are all spared."

The soldiers set their torches to the roof of the wooden house. It cracked and burst into flames quickly. Marie screamed, "Maman!" and ran back into the house, barely missing a beam which fell at the front door. Soon the little children all cried out for Evelyn.

"Maman!"

Anne cried out for her sister. "Marie, come back!"

Inside the house, through the smoke Marie saw her mother, who was pinned under the bed. Flames were everywhere. Madame Hébert yelled, "Go back, Marie, go back."

"Not without you, Maman."

Marie wrapped a log in the bedspread and flung it through the window, then dropped to the ground as flames whooshed past her. She pulled her mother out and, with unforeseen strength, was able to lift her through the window. When she turned to climb through the window, flames caught her dress.

Evelyn pulled Marie through the window, and ran with her to a spot in the grass away from the smoke and flames. She rolled the girl in the grass but it was too late.

Marie raised her eyes to her mother and said, "Thanks be to God you and my baby brother are saved. Take care of him. I love you."

With that, she died in Evelyn's arms as the house came crashing down a few yards from where they were. Madame Hébert lay in a crumpled heap on the ground, praying through her tears for her daughter and begging forgiveness. While trying to protect the family's future, she had lost something far more precious than gold. "Please, God, bring back my girl and take me instead. Please. And I know not how she knew I am carrying a boy child but praise be to God."

Fortunately, the wind died down so that the flames did not carry to the neighboring houses, which were situated farther down the road. The Héberts had been a wealthy family with a large tract of land and did not live on a crowded street but Evelyn felt destitute.

When Madame Hébert hobbled to the front of the house carrying Marie's body in her arms, all the children wept.

Turnbull directed his soldiers to move back to the beach. They left the Hébert family the cart, which would be their new home. Of course, Turnbull thought, they had no idea of what was to befall them next.

Turnbull looked at Wicker and snickered. "The only good Acadians are dead ones, in my book. That just made more place for the others."

Wicker saluted. "Yes, sir, Captain. Yes, sir."

By the time Turnbull and his contingent arrived back at the beach, the other twenty-two men had presented themselves. Adams had seen to it that they were divided and put onto different boats from Francis Hébert.

Turnbull looked at the beach. Women sat despondent on their bags and old people cried in their carts. Children, not knowing any better, played with rocks in the sand. Some young boys pretended to be French soldiers killing English ones. Turnbull wondered whose children they were as there had not been any French military here for years.

On the other end of the beach, Evangeline stopped briefly to catch her breath. Through the trees she saw a heavy fog was rolling in. The last rowboats with the escapees were moving quickly away from shore.

Her heart was pierced as with an arrow. She was too late! All of this for naught. How would she ever find Gabriel? Then she decided she would use Turnbull's attraction for her to help her find Gabriel.

Evangeline saw Turnbull galloping down the beach in her direction. She waved her arms to get his attention. "Captain Turnbull, might I ask you where my fiancé, Gabriel d'Entremont, is being sent?"

Turnbull slowed his horse and sneered at her. "Traitors of his ilk are going to eternal damnation."

Evangeline shivered suddenly, not from the biting cold winds but from fear. "But surely you must know. Please tell me."

"Somewhere you shall never see your beloved fiancé again. Westminster Gatehouse, where no prisoner has ever left alive."

Evangeline was distraught but desperate for more details. She tried to confirm what Winslow had told René. "And my father, the Consul? What is his destination?"

Turnbull waved her away. "You shall have much time to wonder about that, missy." He galloped off again without revealing anything more to her.

On the other end of the beach, a group of women had slipped through a lax soldier's barricade and put a launch in the water. They rowed toward the transports. At that point, Captain Adams ordered his troops to take action.

"Bayonets!"

Adams issued an order to the women. "Remove yourselves from the rowboats or suffer the consequences."

Evangeline saw Béatrice and Anne Gaudet in the rowboat. Béatrice was able to convince all the women to get out, except her mother. Anne sat like a stone in the launch. Francis sat next to her but jumped out when he saw the soldiers advancing toward the boat.

As troops readied their bayonets and moved forward, Béatrice screamed, "Sir, please do not. My mother is touched and does not understand normal talk – English or French. There is but one person who can speak to her." At that point she saw Evangeline and called out, "Evangeline, please come and help us."

Evangeline was torn -- she was desperate to find Gabriel and looked over at the large ship near the bluff. She saw René waving to Christine from the hulk which was close to the beach. With a visual sight on their locations, she rushed to help Béatrice.

Evangeline asked the soldier, "Please give me a moment. I believe I can help." She called out to Anne, "Drxbuli klibwi." Anne had a faint glimmer of recognition and she immediately jumped out of the rowboat and followed Béatrice to the beach, where she found a stone and sat on it without moving. Francis planted a rock in the sand next to her and sat on it watching Anne.

"Thank you, sir." Evangeline nodded to the soldier who returned to the line of troops.

Then Evangeline passed a young woman had just given birth in the sand. A midwife was trying to cut the umbilical cord with a stone, but the baby was choking. Evangeline begged for a knife from a solider but he refused.

"No way is I gonna give you my knife. I was told you was gonna cut my throat."

"Sir, it will save the baby's life. Please…please. If you do not wish to give it to me, then would you simply cut it yourself?"

The soldier refused. "I ain't no midwife. No cutting baby cords for me. I cannot bear the sight of blood." He walked away, shaking his head.

Evangeline ran up to Captain Adams and begged for a knife to save the baby's life. Adams was as cold as the icy waters in their view.

"No Acadian shall ever be given a knife. Further, I suggest you not ask again or it shall be given to you and not in a way that you will live afterwards."

Evangeline brushed tears away and ran back to the woman. All her efforts were in vain. The mother had already died of the loss of blood and that the child was as cold as the air. Evangeline had lost them both. She motioned to Béatrice, who helped her bury the mother and infant under the trees. "My mother was first buried here before her remains were moved to the Churchyard. It will bring them peace." She hugged Béatrice and asked, "Have you seen any others who need our help?"

Béatrice nodded sadly. "They are all in need of our help but we can do nothing for them."

Evangeline hugged her and ran back to the other side of the beach. Turnbull galloped to and fro, watching the line of soldiers but in the middle of the beach, a group of women argued with the troops.

A fog began to roll in over the water. Some of the women screamed in anguish and pointed out to sea. "They are sailing away."

Others cried out to the troops, "You promised we would go with them." Women suddenly rushed up to the soldiers and broke through the line, plunging into the freezing waves.

Taken by surprise, the soldiers did not fathom the situation until several women were halfway to a boat. Several troops jumped into a launch and rowed after them. While the other soldiers were trying to make order out of chaos, Evangeline disappeared into the trees and made her way to the far end of the beach, undetected by any troops.

The troops in the launch rowed out to bring the women back, dead or alive. But they had nothing to shoot as the women could not swim and were already floating corpses, blue from the icy water. The soldiers used their bayonets to bring the bodies into the boats. Back on shore, they dumped the women's corpses unceremoniously on the beach. Immediately other women carried them off for burial and to keep the soldiers from desecrating or abusing the bodies of their relatives and neighbors.

Some of the Acadian women had built a series of bonfires on the beach, as much for warmth as to shine a beacon of hope to their men. From the transports, the men caught sight of the fires and waved their hands. The women began to sing songs and wave back to the men. Soon there was singing back and forth in the eerie fog, which continued to creep towards the shore, every now and again revealing the gray outline of a vessel with the motions of hands waving on deck.

Turnbull whipped a path among the women to Winslow. He saluted, then unfurled a parchment. "All Acadian males present and accounted for, sir. And the women and remaining children are now under control.

Acadian males, ten thousand two hundred twelve, less those who died today, of course. Of animals confiscated, horned cattle, forty-three thousand five hundred. Sheep, forty-eight thousand five hundred. Pigs, twenty-three thousand five hundred. Horses, two thousand eight hundred. That leaves another eight thousand or so of women, children and the aged and infirmed, to wait for more transports."

Winslow saluted wearily, then turned to look at the chaos on the beach. He raised an eyebrow as he turned to Turnbull. "Perhaps I should reconsider the promotion you were granted."

Turnbull bowed to him with a wide grin, thinking this was a rare example of Winslow's humor. "And why might that be, pray tell?"

"Because of your intense distrust of the Acadians, the Lieutenant-Governor approved my suggestion that you go with the prisoners as assistant warden at Westminster Gatehouse."

Turnbull sputtered angrily. "But, sir, you assured me of your post."

"That, sir, is your own mind's invention. When you reflect on it, you shall recall we made a promise only of an unnamed commission, which this is. Be forewarned that the traitors must arrive in London with the breath still in them and able to walk unassisted, or you shall be first on the gallows."

With that Winslow turned his horse and trotted back to town, shaking his head and musing to himself. "What have I done? These Acadians are heathens, to be sure, but not exactly animals. I surely have their blood on my hands for what I have done today, King's orders or no King's orders. It is I who shall have to answer for it to my Maker, along with King George."

Turnbull was furious but he was required to follow orders. No jumping ship, so to speak, for him. Drat that Winslow. Blast that Charles Lawrence. They both had lied to him. Lied! To *him*, their most trusted officer. And now he had to make the dreadful winter journey over the high seas with nothing but Gabriel d'Entremont and his traitors to occupy his mind. He kicked the sides of his horse so hard that it whinnied loudly. He rode it up the hill, anxious to stock up on some good French wine and food for the journey, easily enough found in the Acadian stores in town. With their proprietors gone he would fill a bag with all the foodstuffs he could find which he had to admit were delicious, even if they were French.

Back on the beach, confusion and panic occurred as several more women tried to jump into the water after their men but were stopped by troops and thrust back onto the beach. Clearly, they were distraught, possibly even mad, at the thought of not ever seeing their men again. The soldiers formed a tighter human barricade, shooting muskets above the heads of the women on the beach to push them back from the shore.

One woman broke through the line and jumped in the water. Instinctively, Wicker ordered his men to shoot until the woman's body disappeared under the water, far from five of the transports which were moving out to sea.

The other two, the old hulk, and the one closest to the bluffs with the prisoners destined for England, did not move. They were anchored, as if planning to remain there for a while. Adams turned to Bancroft and Wicker.

"Know of any reason why those two transports do not move?"

"No, sir," they said simultaneously.

"Hmm, we shall have to see about that. Where is Captain Turnbull?"

Wicker said, "He said he needed something in town and would be back without delay."

Soon Turnbull returned, trotting his horse past groups of women eyeing him with suspicion. He passed Christine, then spied Evangeline. He leaned down to her and toyed with her bodice ribbons. She slapped him. He grabbed her hand and whispered curtly.

"You should be kinder to the man responsible for your fiancé's destiny."

"Gabriel? Are you going on the ship with him?

Turnbull sneered. "Any last words? He shall not be getting out alive if I have anything to say about it."

Then he rode to the edge of the beach where troops unloaded his belongings from his horse into a launch. Turnbull climbed in, surveying the scene on the beach. He grunted with satisfaction and sat in the middle of the rowboat, directing the soldiers to take him out to the transport at the far end of the shore by the bluffs.

Evangeline followed him with her eyes. Oh no, she thought. He is boarding the transport where René said my Gabriel is and he is going to hurt him, or maybe even kill him. She rushed over to Christine and handed her cape and satchel to her.

"I must see Gabriel one more time. They are sending him to Westminster Gatehouse!"

Christine tried to dissuade her. "He loves you too much for you to risk your life. The soldiers will shoot if they see you."

"Well, we must assure they do not. You would do the same if you had not seen Papa. I am willing to take any risk for my love. I must."

Christine said, "Yes, true love knows no bounds. I shall do what I can. God be with you and keep you safe, my darling girl."

They hugged trusting they would meet again in New Orleans. Christine rushed to a group of women and told them her plan to create a diversion. Evangeline meandered along the beach toward the treeline. Within moments the women started shouting and creating such a clamor that soldiers soon surrounded them. Momentarily the woods were unguarded and Evangeline ran into the trees unseen. When Christine looked for Evangeline, she was nowhere to be found.

Undetected, Evangeline then ran from the trees and slipped into the frigid waters. She had a powerful stroke and swam underwater until her lungs nearly burst. She cautiously lifted her head and found herself enveloped in a misty fog. She continued swimming toward Gabriel's transport, which was a mere gray ghost in the murkiness.

Evangeline spied Turnbull being lifted from a launch onto the ship's deck. Her heart leapt with joy, even in the dangerous situation, for her father was right. Gabriel was on this ship. She watched the soldiers begin to row back to the far side of the shore. She saw crew men rushing to and fro on the deck above. And now Turnbull was on the ship. But where was Gabriel?

On the beach, with all hopes dashed of leaving with their men, the women again joined together in song. They sang lilting Acadian melodies intended to lift the spirits of their men.

At the refrain the women heard the voices of their men joining in with them, but in the thick fog could not see them. The din of song mixed with tears and cries became louder as they all sang together. With the gravity of the situation fixed on everyone's minds, the women began to sing haunting French religious songs and chants, and the men followed suit.

On board the large ship, Gabriel secreted himself in a corner of the deck behind ropes and stores. Turnbull marched up and down the deck looking for him.

"Where is that Gabriel d'Entremont? Bring him to me."

The trembling crew knew of Turnbull's reputation and they scurried like ants all over the ship.

The fog lifted slightly and Gabriel thought he saw Evangeline in the water. It was either a hallucination or a mermaid. She looked all around and thought she saw his waistcoat behind some boxes.

She called out softly, "Gabriel? Gabriel is that you?"

Just then, Turnbull passed. Evangeline slipped under the ship to hide from the cruel Captain's sight. He returned to the other end of the deck.

Evangeline waited a few moments, then surfaced again. The fog lifted slightly and Gabriel came out of his hiding place to look over the deck. She looked up to see him.

They smiled the secret smile that only true love knows. He reached out his arm to her. She stretched up one arm as if they could touch each other.

Her love.

His heart.

Gabriel called out, "My only love. I shall find you, if I must travel to the ends of the earth. God shall guide me."

She responded, "Gabriel my love, I am yours always."

The fog rolled in and he was suddenly taken from behind. Evangeline heard Turnbull's cruel laugh.

"So are you wishing on stars now, are you?"

Gabriel cried out but the wind drowned his voice. "Evangeline, I shall find you...."

Turnbull gasped. "Evangeline? Where is she?" He looked over the ship's railing and saw a woman flailing in the waters below.

He screamed out orders. "Muskets! Load your muskets and fire at the madwoman in the sea. Extra grog to the one who shoots her. And chain this man below."

Even as Gabriel was being dragged into the hold he cried out once more, "Evangeline I love you...."

"Gabriel, my love...I shall not rest until we are together again."

Evangeline swam around to the other side as Gabriel was able to give one last look before being put into the hold.

Turnbull saw Evangeline below. She looked up to see Turnbull grab a musket from a soldier.

Evangeline cried out, "Gabriel my love!"

She stretched her arm out of the water as if to caress his face. As she did, she suddenly felt cold and began to shiver. She started to swim away, but felt frozen in place. Then she kicked her heels and gathered momentum to swim to shore. She took a huge breath and prepared to submerge herself.

Turnbull fired a shot down into the waves where she was.

Evangeline vanished into a red pool of water.

Just before Turnbull pushed him down the stairs into the hold Gabriel shouted with all his might until he felt his lungs would burst.

"Evangeline!"

FIN.

*

"We are now upon a great and noble Scheme of sending the neutral French out of this Province, who have always been secret Enemies, and have encouraged our Savages to cut our throats. If we effect their Expulsion, it will be one of the greatest Things that ever the English did in America; for by all Accounts, that part of the Country they possess, is as good Land as anywhere in the World: In case therefor we could get some good English Farmers in their Room this Province would abound with all Kinds of Provisions."

- Pennsylvania Gazette, September 4, 1755,
founded by Benjamin Franklin in 1728

*

Excerpt from:

Evangeline: *In Love and War*

Volume II of the series *Evangeline, The True Story of the Cajuns*

CHAPTER 1
Burning

October, 1755 – GRAND PRÉ, NOVA SCOTIA

he shrieks of a soaring eagle reverberated from the cliff to the beach of Grand Pré. Other birds screeched in response and the cacophony pierced the fog settling on four ships in the harbor below. But the British troops in the Bay ignored the birds' cries. The soldiers were too occupied with their mission of deporting French Acadian men and boys from their homeland forever.

Three months earlier, in July 1755, British King George II had issued orders to Nova Scotia Lieutenant-Governor Charles Lawrence to exile in the cruelest manner possible all the French neutrals whose families had lived in the territory since 1603. It had been named Acadia in 1524 by Giovanni da Verrazzano for the beautiful trees reminiscent of those in the idyllic province of Ancient Greece described in Jacopo Sannazaro's poem *Arcadia*.

But in 1713 by the Treaty of Utrecht England gained control of the territory from France and renamed it Nova Scotia. The Treaty obligated England to treat the French Acadians as neutrals, allowing them to practice their Catholic religion freely and exempting them from bearing arms against France and their allies the Mi'Kmaq Indians. After the Acadian's unwavering adherence to the Treaty for forty-two years, the King's deportation order directly violated the terms of the Treaty. Although the Acadians had done nothing to justify such an order, George II nevertheless commanded that the French neutrals be banished and their lands and property forfeited to the Crown.

But even worse than being exiled and losing everything they owned was that the Acadian families were ordered to be divided and put on separate ships. British soldiers tore wives from husbands, children from parents, and betrothed from each other. This order was given because of English paranoia that the "large heathen Catholic families" would regroup in exile and return to Nova Scotia to fight and regain possession of their lands.

King George's order to expel the Acadian neutrals from their homes in Nova Scotia breached the Treaty of Utrecht and contravened British law, yet those fine legal points did not deter the British. Their unlawful act was the beginning of yet another war with France. Even more importantly, the exile of the French Catholic Acadians among numerous territories was genocide, as leaves scattered to the winds.

Snow flurries had begun early in Grand Pré in October, signaling the onset of an especially harsh winter. Prince Kitok Mius, the only son of Mi'Kmaq First Nation Chief Mahtok, surveyed the devastating scene from a tree high above the beach. British soldiers had marched Acadian men and boys from the town to the beach. There under the watchful eyes of Lieutenant-Colonel John Winslow and his trusted Captains Turnbull and Adams, troops had loaded the prisoners at bayonet-point into rowboats. Kitok could only imagine the grief and helplessness the Acadian men felt as they waited in vain for their families to join them. The English officers through subterfuge had assured the women they would be called to the ships to join their husbands. But no one was called.

Winslow who had arrived in Grand Pré not two months earlier to implement King George's brutal order to exile the Acadians. Shortly after his arrival in Grand Pré, Winslow imprisoned the parish priest Père Rivière and sent him to the white slave markets of Bostontown without a trial. Then the Lieutenant-Colonel conveniently moved into the priest's lodgings at the St. Charles Catholic rectory to keep an eye on the men who had been imprisoned in the Church and to maintain the women's false hopes that they, too, would be boarded on the same ships. Yet today after months of planning, Winslow found the deportation activities disagreeable to his temperament and had returned to town once the men and boys were loaded onto rowboats to be brought to the deportation ships.

Winslow's deportation plan was cruel and brutal. He would exile the Acadians in animal cargo vessels whose holds had been rebuilt to accommodate three times the number of people as animals. This was required due to the larger Acadian population than originally calculated by the British and the shortage of transports to complete the mission as quickly as possible. Winslow approved the redesign of the vessels' holds to contain three four-foot high windowless cells into which the human cargo would be loaded. The number of Acadians had been underestimated so rations were reduced. Food and water had been purchased for deportation in September, and they rotted and contaminated due to delays in the arrival of the transports. Death and disease aboard the transports would be epic, assuring that the surviving Acadians, if any, would be too weak to retaliate against the British and return to fight for their homes.

Winslow was not partial to the status of the men which he unlawfully made his prisoners. No courtesy had been shown to the French Consul of King Louis XV, Lord René Le Blanc de Verdure. He had been thrown in chains then rowed to an old hulk which did not appear in the least to be seaworthy.

Soon Kitok's long-time Acadian allies against the British would be sent hither and yon. Kitok had overheard Captain Turnbull boast about sending his enemy Gabriel Mius d'Entremont, leader of the Acadian resistance, to the most notorious prison in England -- London's Westminster Gatehouse. Kitok feared he would never again see Gabriel, his closest friend. The Mi'Kmaq Prince knew nothing of English prisons but he had witnessed the cruelty of the English military leaders in Grand Pré and he could not bear to see Gabriel sent there.

Kitok had devised several plans with Gabriel to help the Acadians escape their fate -- being deported from their lands forever. He and Gabriel had made the secret arrangements and had spread the word throughout the secret Acadian militia that anyone who could escape from the transports would be taken to safety by the Mi'Kmaq Indians, their longtime allies. But Gabriel and the other Acadians had been imprisoned in the Church when they presented themselves to the commanding officer, Lieutenant-Colonel John Winslow, for the reading of King George's Edict a month prior, on September fifth.

Kitok carried out the plan himself and stationed Mi'Kmaq braves in the woods near the cliff with dry clothes, blankets, food and horses. They were ready to help the Acadians escape the deportation transports and reach safety in the mountains beyond Grand Pré or in New France. Kitok also sent two braves from the trees to the British garrison at Grand Pré to take all official documents they could find, hoping to learn the destinations of the animal cargo transports. Kitok wanted to track their whereabouts and send aid or rescue them to return home.

Turnbull and Adams had been ordered to give the Acadian women false assurances they would embark once the men had boarded. They carried out their plan well because the men were already being loaded onto the vessels before the women learned of the ruse and marched to the beach themselves.

The men and boys over the age of ten who had been imprisoned in the Church since the reading of the King's edict had been loaded into the rowboats by soldiers carrying muskets and bayonets. Kitok had watched helplessly as British soldiers led by Captain Turnbull pulled Acadian fathers away from sons and loaded them onto separate boats at bayonet point. A young boy scampered from one rowboat into the adjacent launch and into his father's arms. When the father refused to let go of his son, one of Turnbull's soldiers tore the screaming boy from his crying father. He thrust a bayonet into the little boy's body and tossed him into the water, his blood pooling near the launch. The father kept his hand in the water touching his son's blood as long as he could as the rowboat moved forward.

Soon Turnbull ordered all the troops to the side of the beach farthest from Kitok's cliff to avoid any problems when he saw pouring forth from the woods onto the beach thousands of women, children, aging parents, and pregnant women. The march was led by the Consul's daughter, Gabriel's fiancée, Evangeline Le Blanc de Verdure, and René's fiancée Christine de Castille, the French royal midwife and nurse who raised Evangeline upon her mother's death in childbirth on the same beach seventeen years earlier.

When the women saw the transports, they shouted and cried as they rushed toward the water. But it was too late. The British carried out their evil plan without allowing a final word between husbands and wives, parents and children, and fiancées and their betrothed.

Panic and chaos ensued as the women rushed toward the rowboats seeking their husbands, sons, brothers and fathers. Many had already been crammed onto small deportation vessels. The soldiers diligently pulled women back onto the shore but so many eluded them that Turnbull organized a long line of British soldiers armed with bayonets and muskets at the water's edge. He issued the order to use bayonets and muskets if necessary to control the women from entering the water to be with their men.

Wives, daughters, sisters, parents and young boys cried out in agony at the thought of losing their husbands, fathers, brothers, sons and grandfathers, and never seeing them again. Some women dared to challenge the young soldiers believing they would not kill a wife and mother simply for trying to join her husband and children. They could not have been more wrong.

Several women who preferred death to living without their men disobeyed the order and broke through the line of soldiers. Within minutes they felt the weight of the bayonets through their being and died at the water's edge. A pregnant woman lost her child and bled to death because troops refused to provide a knife to cut the infant's cord. Kitok saw a woman break through the troops and wade into the water only to be dropped by a soldier's musket.

Kitok watched sadly as his good friend Gabriel and the members of his secret Acadian resistance were forced aboard the largest ship in the harbor. Kitok signaled the other braves hidden in the trees surrounding the beach and on the cliffs above to ready their plan. Never before had his soaring eagle call been so powerful. But this time his friend's life was at stake. He and his Mi'Kmaq brothers would rescue Gabriel and the other Acadians on that ship before they were sent to a London prison.

But before they could move, the British learned of the escape of twenty-four Acadian men from one of other transport ships. They had slid down ropes and swam to shore at the opposite end of the beach from the soldiers. There, they escaped into the trees where Kitok's braves furnished them with clothes and food for the trek to safety in the mountains beyond Grand Pré. The British threatened to kill the escapees' entire families unless they returned to the ship.

The French Consul was brought back to shore to entreat the families of the escaped men to find them and, thus, avoid their own certain death. He was allowed to say his final goodbyes to his daughter Evangeline and his fiancée Christine. Before he could reveal his long-kept secret of Evangeline's birth and the name of her true father to her, he was put back in chains and taken back to the old hulk. But he and Christine made a pact to reunite in the French territory of Louisiana no matter their deportation destination or how long it took.

After René's entreaties, the men changed back into their wet clothes so as to not reveal the Mi'Kmaq assistance. Each returned to the beach but Lieutenant Turnbull waited with his troops to set an example for any future escapees. As soon as the men were visible, the British shot the first two arrivals, father and son, then beat the other men until their backs bled. They were rowed to the ship bound for the London prison with Gabriel and others believed to be in the Acadian resistance. There, they were dumped unceremoniously onto the deck, tied together with rope as a remembrance of their escape mechanism, then pushed down into the hold.

Turnbull learned the organizer of the escape was the Grand Pré boat builder Francis Hébert who used his knowledge to assist the men. Hébert was badly beaten and his family was dragged to his house and workshop which were burned to the ground. In the fire his eldest daughter Marie died trying to save her mother, Francis' wife, who survived though she nearly died of grief.

The British cruelty did not deter Kitok from his plan to assist any other escapees but none appeared. The message had been spread throughout the transports of Turnbull's threat to kill the family of any escaped prisoner. None of the Acadians made any further escape attempts, believing it better to endure their unknown punishment than subject their families to Turnbull's cruelty.

At that point Kitok realized the futility of his plan to help his friend escape. Gabriel had no living relatives in Grand Pré, his mother Diane having died before the trip to Acadia and his father Henri having died at the hands of the British in the Halifax Harbor Massacre while on a peace mission that summer. Still, Gabriel would refuse to escape because of his honor and his love for his fiancée, Evangeline, her father the French Consul, and Christine.

By the time five large animal transports had set sail, appearing ghostly in the fog, thousands of men had been crammed on board. Kitok could not fathom the unspeakable horrors that awaited the Acadian women without husbands and older sons to protect them. He and his tribe would determine a plan to protect those still in Grand Pré and to prevent more tragedy.

Watching their men sail out of the harbor the women on the beach, through their tears, sang Catholic hymns of hope and prayer. Their voices carried across the water and they were soon joined in song by their beloved men. As transports disappeared into the fog, the voices became fainter, their last connection with family they would never see again.

Kitok returned his gaze to the water below and the ship Gabriel had boarded. He thought he saw a woman's head bobbing in the nearby waves. He looked again, more closely this time, and saw no one. That might mean a drowning woman. He was about to signal his braves when he saw the woman lift her head above the water for a moment before it disappeared again. The woman, who had to be Evangeline, was safe and unseen by the British troops on the far side of the beach, at least for the time being.

Then Kitok saw a British officer being lifted up onto the deck of the same ship. It was none other than the cruel Captain Turnbull. Clearly it was Turnbull's intent to punish Gabriel and his militia even before they arrived at their destination in London. Kitok looked at the troops on the opposite side of the beach. They were too busy to notice Evangeline in their attempts to organize the women into lines to return back to town. There was no reason to give any thought to the last transport setting sail at any moment.

Kitok wanted to take no chances that Turnbull could see Evangeline. He shrieked his eagle cry again and one by one he heard the responses of the ringed owl, the crow, the blackbird and many more from braves strategically hidden along the edge of the forest near the beach, and behind rocks and in trees on the bluffs.

When Sitting Fox heard Kitok's call, he quickly climbed down the tree and set their pre-arranged plan in motion to take the British Fort, which would be lightly guarded at that time. The other braves did the same. Fog began to roll in and their movements were not visible to the soldiers. Meanwhile, Kitok descended from his tree and neared the edge of the cliff. He turned his attention back to the ship where he saw Evangeline raise her arms out of the water to Gabriel who was at the side of the ship. Suddenly, Kitok heard the crack of a shot. He felt his heart stop and as if in slow motion he saw Evangeline disappear under the water, a red pool appearing where her head had been, and he heard Gabriel's painful cry as piercing as an eagle shriek.

"Evangeline!"

Through the mist, Kitok saw Turnbull grab Gabriel at the side of the ship where Evangeline had been. Soldiers dragged Gabriel across the deck and pushed him down into the hold. Kitok knew what he had to do. He shrieked his final eagle cry, not waiting for responses from his braves. He then dove straight down from the cliff into the icy water near the spot where he had last seen her. The two braves closest to him followed, diving from the cliffs through the fog into the waves below. Each swam to the top to fill his lungs before diving again.

Kitok could only pray that they could find her. Perhaps she swam under the water to shore and found refuge in the rocks of the cliff. Kitok's powerful strokes under the water brought him nearer and nearer the ship. Then the ship began to move away. Raising his head again, he gasped for air through the bobbing waves. The ship was taking Gabriel across the Atlantic, no doubt. The other braves swam to the surface as they drank in the foggy air and shook their heads. Then the three of them dove underneath the icy water again.

Kitok prayed as he had been taught by his parents Chief Matok and Princess Snowbird and by Père Rivière at the Masses he performed in their Mi'Kmaq Village. "Please God, please keep Evangeline alive and show me where to find her." He lifted his head again for air and scoured the beach from one end to the other. Evangeline could not have swam fast enough to rejoin the women. And soldiers had blocked the trees which led up the hill to the road, so she could not have taken that route. Was she still alive, or had she died at Turnbull's hand? He could not fail at his mission. He had promised Gabriel to protect her if anything happened to his friend. *But where was she?*

The other two braves surfaced again empty-handed. They submerged themselves again. Evangeline's body was not visible anywhere but Kitok had faith that God would protect her. She was the most loving, generous person he knew, Acadian or Mi'Kmaq. She had always put others before herself, risking her life to help Gabriel and Kitok with their resistance movement. She was a devout spiritual young woman and God would not have taken the life of such an innately good person. He believed he could save her, if he could find her.

Just then he saw a body in the murky water just ahead of him. He compelled himself to swim faster, faster until he was there. The other two braves joined him and helped him propel the body to the surface of the waves. Evangeline's eyes were closed, her face contorted and ashen. While the two braves held her head above the waves, Kitok tried to breathe life into her. They repeated the process again. Then with powerful strokes they carried Evangeline to shore as the ship carrying Gabriel sailed into the fog and away from his love.

TO BE CONTINUED....
In Volume II, EVANGELINE: In Love and War